MAESTRO

BOOKS BY JOHN GARDNER

JAMES BOND NOVELS

License Renewed
For Special Services
Icebreaker
Role of Honor
Nobody Lives Forever
No Deals, Mr. Bond
Scorpius
Win Lose or Die
Brokenclaw
The Man from Barbarossa
Death if Forever
Never Send Flowers
License to Kill
(Based on the 1989 film written by Michael G. Wilson and Richard Maibaum)

THE BOYSIE OAKES BOOKS

The Liquidator
Understrike
Amber Nice
Madrigal
Founder Member
Traitor's Exit
Air Apparent
A Killer for a Song

DEREK TORRY NOVELS

A Complete State of Death
The Corner Men

THE MORIARTY JOURNALS

The Return of Moriarty
The Revenge of Moriarty

THE KRUGER TRILOGY

The Nostradamus Traitor
The Garden of Weapons
The Quiet Dogs

NOVELS
The Censor
Every Night's A Festival
To Run A Little Faster
The Werewolf Trace
The Dancing Dodo
The Last Trump
Flamingo

THE GENERATIONS TRILOGY
The Secret Generations
The Secret Houses
The Secret Families

AUTOBIOGRAPHY
Spin the Bottle

COLLECTION OF SHORT STORIES
Hideaway
The Assassination File

Maestro

JOHN GARDNER

OTTO
PENZLER
BOOKS

NEW YORK

First American Edition

Otto Penzler Books
129 W. 56th Street
New York, NY 10019
(Editorial Offices Only)

Maxwell Macmillan Canada, Inc.
1200 Eglinton Avenue East
Suite 200
Don Mills, Ontario M3C 3N1

Macmillan Publishing Company
866 Third Avenue
New York, NY 10022

Macmillan Publishing Company is part of the Maxwell Communication Group of Companies

Library of Congress Cataloging-in-Publication Data
Gardner, John, E.
    Maestro/John Gardner.
        p.   cm.
    ISBN 1-883402-24-7
    1.Kruger, Herbie (Fictitious character)—Fiction.   I.Title.
PR6057.A63M3   1993   93-19364   CIP
823'.914—dc20

Grateful acknowledgment is made to the following for permission to reprint previously published material from the following:

From *Selected Poems* by Langston Hughes. Copyright 1948 by Alfred A. Knopf, Inc. Reprinted by permission of the publisher.
Translation from "Die Moritat von Mackie Messer" by Bertolt Brecht. Reproduced by permission of Universal Edition.
Extracts from "Gerontion," "La Figlia Che Plange," and "The Waste Land" appeared in *Collected Poems 1909–1962* by T. S. Eliot, copyright 1936 Harcourt Brace & Company, copyright © 1964, 1963 by T. S. Eliot, reprinted by permission of the publisher.
Tiny Dancer by Elton John /Bernie Taupin. Copyright © 1971 Dick James Music, Ltd.
Extract from *Babi-Yar* by Yevgeny Yevtushenko. Reproduced by kind permission of The Decca Record Company, Ltd.
Otto Penzler Books are available at special discounts for bulk purchases for sales promotions, premiums, fund-raising, or educational use. For details, contact:

Special Sales Director
Macmillan Publishing Company
866 Third Avenue
New York, NY 10022

10 9 8 7 6 5 4 3 2

Printed in the United States of America

For Jan St. John
who helped to make a dream come true

Author's Comments

Many people have to be thanked, not least Desmond Elliott, who has managed my professional affairs for over twelve years, who has always been right, and remains an inspiration. Here in the U.S.A. special thanks goes to my new publisher, Otto Penzler, and his lovely wife Carolyn. I first met Otto over twenty years ago and we have been insulting each other ever since. We have both longed for the day when we could work together. Now that day has come, and I, for one, am ecstatically happy. My wife, Margaret, must be thanked for the endless hours she has spent checking manuscript, and putting up with my musical snobbery.

Also, I would like to mention Priscilla Ridgway of MWA who opened certain doors for me, and Vince Talamo, head of security for the Lincoln Center, who gave me his time and advice.

Last, but far from least, my dear friend over the past thirty years, Diana de Rosso. Diana's incredible and glamorous life includes singing at La Scala, Milan, and being a spy, so she qualifies as an expert witness. She has set me right on several important musical points. If I have inadvertently made any musical gaffes, it is my fault for not listening to her.

There is one additional note. Chronologically, this book is set in the autumn of 1991, at a time when H.M. Government still refused to admit that there was such a thing as the Secret Intelligence Service. In May of 1992 the Prime Minister pulled the covers off the SIS and also named C—the Chief of the Secret Intelligence Service. The C who appears briefly in the opening chapters of this book is a fictional character, and is in no way connected to, or based upon, the real, and very distinguished, current C.

Finally, this might appear odd, but I wish to thank a fictional character. All authors of fiction are a little mad, for they live mainly with char-

acters who exist only in their minds. I want to thank one of the main protagonists—Big Herbie Kruger. Kruger has traveled with me through six
novels now and, though I know he is a fiction, I feel as though he is an
old and favorite friend. Thank you Herb.

John Gardner

Virginia, 1993

Indeed we should certainly have been (in Vienna) already, had we not been obliged against our will to spend five whole days in Passau. This delay, for which His Grace the Bishop of Passau was responsible, has made me lose eighty gulden. . . .

Letter from Leopold Mozart to Lorenz Hagenaur, 3 October 1762

BOOK 1

(UNITED KINGDOM. NEW YORK. VIRGINIA. AUTUMN 1991)

1

THE FIRST ATTEMPT to kill Louis Passau was made as he was leaving Lincoln Center after his 90th Birthday Concert. Big Herbie Kruger was standing next to him when it happened and, in the turmoil, he found himself sitting beside the venerable Maestro in the back of an unmarked FBI car. In turn this led to Herbie being present during the second attempt and becoming deeply involved in everything that followed.

Eventually, back in England, there were questions in the House—

"There is strong evidence that a former member of the Secret Intelligence Service—Eberhardt Lukas Kruger—was involved in the recent incident, in New York, concerning Louis Passau, the internationally famous orchestral conductor. Can the Prime Minister assure us that Mr. Kruger had no official sanction from the Intelligence Service or the Prime Minister's Office?"

The Prime Minister, as always at that time—though the situation was to change in the following spring—did not confirm that such a thing as the Intelligence Service existed, but assured the House that the P.M.'s office certainly had not sanctioned Mr. Kruger's presence.

In another part of London, many people wondered why Big Herb was there at all. Those who knew no better said he had come back from retirement and was given the Passau job just to make sure he did not go rogue in Europe. Others maintained that Herbie had come up from his Hampshire cottage without saying a word to his wife, Martha. Later, they said, he knocked on the Chief's door, demanding to join in the activity which had been going on since the autumn of 1989, when, according to the history books, the Cold War ended.

There were even people who said they had seen him roaming around the building. Others told of sightings near his old office in the Whitehall

Annex. These encounters, it was said, all took place towards the end of August 1991, or, as the chronologists put it, during the rise of Big Boris, formerly Boris the Boozer, latterly Boris the Brave. In the end, the two things nobody could deny were that Big Boris Yeltsin had been courageous during the attempted August coup in Moscow, and the fact that Big Herbie Kruger stood beside the grand old man of American music when the balloon went up.

A junior officer was heard to say that it could only have happened because Herb was a music lover; another muttered something about the whole business being stupid anyway. "Who'd want to bother with a ninety-year-old guy accused of being one of Hitler's spies during Big Two?" he proclaimed—Big Two being the way younger people sometimes refer to the Second World War these days.

Most of those who walked the secret halls of the British Intelligence community agreed that the entire thing was stupid, wasteful, and could bring no rewards. Particularly at a time when every intelligence agency worth its salt was out and about in the crumbling Soviet empire: holding auditions and setting up new networks; listening to the death rattle of communism; or humming around the Middle East, trying to beef up assets in all the likely flashpoints, of which there were many.

Earlier, at the end of 1989, there had been an instruction, said to have come from the highest possible source, to get out there and recruit. So every able-bodied man and woman got out there and recruited. Now was the hour; now, it was essential; never in the field of human conflict, et cetera, et cetera.

For the first time since the middle of the Cold War everyone was desperate for HUMINT, as they called Human Intelligence. They needed bodies on the ground, and networks in place, just to be certain that intelligence came back on all levels: political, military, economic, even religious. As the Chief of the Secret Intelligence Service was heard to observe, "Like the President of the United States, *we* need a thousand points of light; but we need them in Eastern Europe and at the heart of the Soviet Union. A thousand points of light hidden under the bushels of darkness."

Then came the Kremlin coup of 1991: a strangely inept affair, brought with stunning immediacy into the world's living rooms, leaving behind it a collage of clear, screen-burned images: the nondescript plotters, looking like archetypal gray men; the familiar takeover bulletins—

Mikhail Sergeyevich was ill; his doctors had ordered rest; this was a crisis; the Army would guard the streets and public buildings; there was a curfew. Then, Big Boris Yeltsin climbing up onto one of the tanks to urge the crowd not to be fooled. Later he sat on the balcony of the Russian Federation building—ironically known as the White House—uneasy, holding a portable bulletproof screen and surrounded by Kalashnikov-toting hard men. The reflections remained. The crowd versus the tanks. Flames in the night. Crushed bodies being pulled clear. Angry words spat and shouted between bemused soldiers and civilians. Tank crews looking bewildered. Then the return of Gorbachev, tired and worried. The arrest, or suicides, of the plotters, and the final card: the Communist Party outlawed. The scramble for escape, the shredders, more suicides, the hauling down of Iron Felix Dzerzhinsky's statue from in front of the old KGB headquarters. White faces at the windows of the building which backed onto the Lubyanka. The fall of Lenin's effigies all over the old Soviet Union and the declarations of individual states to secede from the Union. Chaos, and a new—maybe more dangerous—world.

The Soviet people, the pundits proclaimed, had tasted freedom. The coup had failed because the people demanded democracy: a sentiment that was only partly true, leaving the experts in political warfare wondering what would have happened if Big Boris Nikolayevich had not climbed onto that tank; or if the Kremlin plotters had done all the things really necessary to a coup d'état.

Whatever the answers to those questions, it was perfectly reasonable to suspect the Chief of the Secret Intelligence Service of watching his own back by recalling Herbie Kruger and sending him to the United States on a wild-goose chase. Everyone knew that Big Herb would have given his eye teeth to regroup old networks. After all, he was probably the most experienced agent-runner behind the Curtain in the old days. Men who had known him then even suggested he might go on the hunt in Russia itself. Big Herb, they said, would give several teeth for an hour alone, in a locked room, with certain former officers of the old-style KGB.

The truth was stranger than any rumor or fiction. One hot English morning, towards the end of the coup, the telephone rang in the New Forest cottage where Herbie now lived in peace and quiet with his wife Martha (née Adler), formerly one of his agents—part of the famed Telegraph Boys network in East Berlin.

"It's the Office." Martha had answered the call. "For you, Herb," covering the mouthpiece with her palm. "They want to talk with you."

"Ja?" Herbie said loudly into the telephone, reverting to his old and annoying habit of treating telephones as though the distant party could only hear if he shouted.

"Ja? Kruger here."

A calm man at the distant end asked if he recognized the voice. Kruger said, "Ja, of course: know you speaking from the bottom of a well." Then the voice told him that it would be very pleasant if he could meet with the Headmaster as soon as it was convenient.

"Sure, let me know time and place and I'll be there like a shoot, old sheep." Herb knew that Young Worboys, now far from young, and in an exalted position at the Office, would play it straight.

"What's the harm?" he asked Martha later, as though to quiet his own concern about this call from the past.

"The harm is you've gone private for years." Martha was deeply suspicious of the whole business. "Now they can't do without you? Now, when the map's being redrawn and everyone's running around in circles. Now, they need *you*, Herb, but you don't need *them*. Now they want you for the crisis. Don't go."

"Let's wait and see what they really want. Maybe I bring back a piece of the Wall so we can have it on our piano in a little glass case."

"We haven't got a piano."

"Then to hell with it. Maybe I get a bit of Dzerzhinsky's statue instead." All this in German, of course. Herbie and Martha usually spoke in their native language when they were on their own.

At this point, Herbie would have laughed in your face if you had suggested he was about to become one of the leading figures in the drama-sodden theater of the absurd which followed what he had defined as being "more like a coup de ville than a coup d'état."

The next morning, as though the good fairy had worked some magic with the usually torpid British postal service, there was a card. A humorous card with a jet-black front on which was printed "Folkestone Night Life." On the back was a date and nine words. "See you seven thirty Tuesday next at the Odeon."

"Thought they'd given up using that place years ago," Herbie said to himself while other times, long past, flooded through his head. The safe house was a pretty little terraced three-story place in a small cul-de-sac behind the Odeon in Kensington High Street. He figured that it had belonged to the Office for so long somebody had probably lost the deeds.

"Tuesday next" meant the day after tomorrow—a Thursday—and for "seven thirty" read ten in the morning.

He spotted the surveillance car parked in the cul-de-sac on his way in, and Young Worboys actually let him into the house.

"What cheer, Herb? Lovely to see you again."

"I was reliably informed the freeze had gone out of the Cold War, and Mikhail Sergeyevich's trashed the Communist Party, so what's with the cloak and dagger dugskullery?" Herbie laughed and followed him through the minute lobby and into the main living room. There was coffee on the table, and Arthur Railton, and the CSIS—Chief of the Secret Intelligence Service, known to most as C.

"Hallo, Art, how's old Naldo?" Herbie beamed. Naldo was Art Railton's father's nickname, and several lifetimes ago, in the rubble of Berlin, it was Naldo Railton who had employed a tall scrawny teenager to ferret in the D.P. camps. The teenager had been Big Herbie and Naldo was his first link into the world of secrets.

"Pa's having himself a ball, Herb. You haven't met the new Chief, have you?"

"Ah. C as in secret." Herbie grinned at the Chief. In his mind he heard the words, "You don't need this guy, Herbie. *He* needs you."

The Chief had taken over after Herbie's time, so knew him only from the files and copious stories. Herbie knew him from occasional words dropped by old friends. Worboys was his Deputy and Art Railton, having done a lot of time in Ireland and then the Middle East, was now on the European desk.

"Mr. Kruger." The Chief rose, extending a hand. "I've heard a lot about you. Please sit down. Coffee?"

"Bet it wasn't all good. Ja, yes, I'll take coffee. Black with much sugar. Death through the mouth, eh?" Herb poised over an armchair, swayed backwards and then let gravity take over. With his height and bulk he tended to plummet rather than sink into a chair. He looked around, as though savoring the room. "I remember this place from way back, when you were all feeding from the breast. Nobody changed the decor and it still smells just as bad: sour milk, dust, armpits, and illicit sex." Then Herbie looked straight at the Chief and, as he spoke, took in all there was to see of the man—tall, thin, ascetic-looking, with the blazing eyes of a zealot. "So, you want me back now there's real trouble?" He gave his daft smile, which took in nobody but the CSIS, who knew no better.

"Actually, Mr. Kruger, no." The Chief sat opposite him and Art Railton did the honors with the government-issue china. "I want to ask you a question."

"Let me tell you one thing, first off." Herbie was still in the stupid big smile mode. "Europe, I can do without. They changed the scenery; they changed the names; it's confused. The Communist Party's gone—except for the thousands of good members who might, or might not, accept the inevitable, but I doubt it. Civil War, maybe? Who knows? One thing is for sure: they're all bloody paranoid? Right?"

"Yes, we're aware of all the permutations, all the possibilities, now the Kremlin's opened Pandora's box." The Chief remained very cool. He had obviously been well briefed on the idiosyncrasies of Kruger.

"Sure, Pandemonium's box. All the myths and legends gone. Everybody's heroes went for nothing, like always. They're even threatening to send George back." By George, Herbie meant George Blake, the Soviet penetration agent who had done more damage than any other within the SIS. Sentenced to forty-two years imprisonment, he had escaped and returned to Russia after serving only six years. "All heroes grow old and die. Look at William Tell." He did not move a muscle.

Nobody knew how to take the last remark, but Young Worboys, who had probably spent more time with Herbie than anyone else, nodded and muttered, "And Robin Hood."

"All is changed, and I don't want anything to do with it," Herbie declaimed.

"Then we are in agreement." The Chief looked startled. "Now, my question . . ."

Herbie, feeling that he could be expansive, opened his arms and said, "Ask away, Chief, I have nothing to hide."

"What does the name Louis Passau mean to you, Mr. Kruger?"

There was what Art Railton later described as a long, disjointed silence. Then—

"You're pulling my pisser," Herbie laughed, and the Chief gave an annoyed frown. Art Railton and Young Worboys winced. The CSIS was a known Presbyterian and did not hold with coarse language.

"I'm not pulling anything, Mr. Kruger. . . ."

"Call me Herbie, everyone does."

"Then, what *does* the name Louis Passau mean to you, Herbie?"

"Ach!" Big Herb shook his huge head, like a dog ridding itself of rain. "So, you really want to hear? You want Kruger to make a fool of himself. Okay. Passau? He's simply the best. Genius. Better than von Karajan, Furtwangler, any of those. Better than Bernstein—who was also genius; better than Maazel and Previn. Name any, living or dead, and Passau is better. The man exists for music. His baton is like a magic wand. This man has been dedicated to music since a child, and has accomplished more than any other conductor. The last of the great maestros. The greatest orchestra; the perfect opera company; ballet. You name it, Passau is simply the best. Also, amazing stamina and physique. He will soon be ninety years of age. . . ."

"A week tomorrow," the Chief said, quietly.

". . . and last year alone, at age eighty-nine, he was still conducting— major concerts, and recording sessions. As I say, he is the best. Could even make Lloyd-Webber's music sound original, if he bothered; and—" He stopped suddenly, as though something unthinkable had crawled into his mind.

He looked at the Chief, at Art Railton, then at Young Worboys, "You can't mean it? This oaf, what's his name? The schmarotzer history teacher . . . ?"

"John Stretchfield," Art supplied.

"Ja, that's the idiot. Writes a book, *Hitler's Unfound Spies*, says . . ."

"*Hitler's Unknown Spies*," the Chief corrected, "and Mr. Stretchfield is a renowned scholar and historian. A man with a very good track record on matters of security in World War Two."

"Ja. Okay. *Unknown*. So, this Stretchfield has a good track record. What of Maestro Passau's record on the tracks? This historian fingers Louis Passau as a Nazi spy in Second War." He gave a giant shrug. "Who the hell cares, anyway? Even if it were the truth, who the hell cares? He has given more to civilization, so who in hell cares? Look what happened when the Wall came down. He didn't just sit in the middle and play a cello like Maestro Rostropovich, or conduct the Beethoven Ninth in Berlin, like poor Lenny. No, he canceled all his commitments and took that marvelous orchestra of his on a tour of the old Eastern Bloc, giving them everything from Bartók to Shostakovich and then some. In this spring he did it again: you realize that?"

The Chief nodded, "Yes, Budapest, Berlin, Sofia, Prague and Warsaw."

"Then Tel Aviv," softly, from Worboys as though this had been some added sin.

"So?" Herbie made a noise resembling an old steam train gathering itself up for the first chug from a station. "So? He was Jewish, no? You ever read his life story? That amazing thing he did after World War II. The concert at Belsen, the Nazi death camp? That incredible concert? Ach, who the hell cares, anyway?"

"We do, Herb." Arthur Railton's face showed that he was not joking.

"You gone crazy or something? The Service is *really* interested in a very old, and famous, talented man who might—just might—have done a couple of naughties for the Nazis?"

"It's not that simple, Herb." Arthur Railton patted his knee, as though he were petting an animal.

"So tell me why it's not so easy."

They did. They told him in great detail, and Herbie, having been in the business a long time before he put himself out to grass, listened with rising anxiety. When they had finished telling him, he asked what they wanted him to do about it.

"We want you to represent us at the debriefing and interrogations," the Chief told him. "Have to bring you up to date first . . ."

"You mean tell me the things that don't get in the newspapers because everyone's gone nuts, and KGB're the good guys now? Huh! I know all this." He gave a ferocious nod. "And I know how long KGB'll stay good boys."

"You're well informed." The Chief gave him a fatherly smile.

"We all know it's not over till the fat lady sings, Herb." Arthur Railton was a shade too jovial.

"Which fat lady?"

"It's a saying, Herbie," Young Worboys sighed. Then the Chief spoke again—

"Herbie, there *are* other things. We want you back in. Open-ended."

"And if I agree, you want me to look after British interests?"

"You're an expert on the old ways of the once evil empire. . . ."

"What d'you mean *once*? You know what can happen. The various republics can go off down the hill like the Gathering swine, and some idiot can inherit the kingdom of the blind, which is what it is now. And, in the kingdom of the blind the one-eyed man is king. This is saying also, Young Worboys, like your fat lady doing the arias."

It took everyone a moment to translate the Krugerspeak and substitute Gaderine for Gathering.

"You were an expert, Herbie. Now we need your expertise. There are going to be strange alliances; odd bedfellows; dangerous marriages." The Chief was being uncharacteristically gentle. He usually got his way by bullying and shouting. "Possibly even other coups, and countercoups. As you say, who knows?"

"Okay, so you want me to clean up any mess Maestro Passau just might have made?"

"Something like that."

"And I get all expenses paid? Concorde to JFK? Suite at the Algonquin, New York? Reasonable expense account?"

"Whatever you need, Herb."

Kruger drove back to New Forest, packed a bag, told Martha (who was, in many ways, only a temporary wife) all she needed to know and then headed off to the big old house near Warminster where the Office did everything but kill people.

There he sat quietly and listened to what Art Railton and Young Worboys and other cognoscenti had to tell him, which took a day, at the end of which he asked, "You tell all this to the boys at Langley?"

Art gave Worboys a sidelong look.

"Okay, so you didn't tell them. What about the people at the Puzzle Palace?" by which he meant the National Security Agency (NSA), who do not like being referred to as "the people at the Puzzle Palace." Neither are they too elated when you call them the folks at SIGINT City.

Silence.

"And the G-men?"

"Look, Herb," Art began. "Look, the sources are impeccable. We told our relatives across the ocean a little of it. . . ."

"Enough to hook them?"

"More than enough. But we want you to have the full works, just as we heard it, chapter and verse, with all the cross-references."

"Okay." Big Herbie did not seem surprised. He spent another couple of days reading the runes, by which he meant studying the documents, and one more day being taken over the European scene. On Wednesday he boarded the morning Concorde into JFK. There was a car waiting for him. The Guest Relations people at the Algonquin were splendid, and he had an interesting day.

11

So that was why Big Herbie Kruger was standing next to Maestro Louis Passau when they tried to shoot him, after his nintieth birthday concert in Lincoln Center, New York, on Friday, September 6, 1991.

Mind you, there were many who had doubts about the Maestro's true age. Some said he was a changeling boy and not really anywhere near his claimed age. How, they said with winks and nods, could a man be as vigorous and retain all his marbles if he was so heavy with years? But all was resolved many months later, when Big Herbie became the watershed of Louis Passau's life.

2

FOR OVER FIFTY YEARS he had been good copy. Louis Passau was one of those celebrities for whom the media recites litanies, and says its own versions of masses: the wish fulfillment of the print presses, the garbage mongers, the radio pundits and that relatively more recent rare breed, the in-depth TV superhack.

He was great value for the specialist music critics and commentators, and had been since his sudden appearance as a musical enfant terrible way back in the 1930s. More, what made Passau so different was that he also made wonderful pickings for the diarists, the gossip columnists, the feature writers and the horde of experts who reveled in kiss-and-tell, character assassination, and all possible variations in between.

Louis Passau was news: romance, wealth, extravagance, talent, fast cars, faster women, explosions of short-fuse temper, private airplanes, strange, unexplained, and sometimes sinister interludes, speedboats, political slings, arrows and, definitely, outrageous fortunes. All these made the tabloids, the heavy print presses, the magazines and the telecasts, with constant shock-horror fervor, or laughable delight.

Better still, the public loved him. Not just the concert and opera-going cognoscenti and glitterati, but the whole razzmatazz, the wide spectrum: that amorphous mass to whom some of the newshounds and most of the TV shows pandered.

So it was that when the ticket office opened, on May 5, 1991, for the Louis Passau 90th Birthday Concert to be held on Friday, September 6, in Lincoln Center's Avery Fisher Hall, all available tickets, one thousand eight hundred of them, were gone within ninety minutes.

Avery Fisher Hall seats some two thousand eight hundred, and a thousand of these seats had been reserved for a lengthy list of specially invited guests; a list which, one columnist was to write, "precluded any other serious concert on that night anywhere in the western world."

In June, John Stretchfield's scholarly but sensational book, *Hitler's Unknown Spies*, hit the bookshelves. Among other startling revelations it contained chapter, and many verses, on the part Louis Passau had played on Nazi Germany's behalf—not to mince words—as an active spy against his chosen country, the United States of America. By the end of the month, the scalpers were getting more than a thousand dollars a ticket for the concert.

Though Stretchfield's manuscript was above suspicion—cross-referencing hundreds of sources, citing documents that had never been used until now, and generally making a clear case against Passau—nobody really wanted to take any action. The FBI sat on their thumbs, the NSA was silent, and the CI people at Langley ho-hummed.

All this until they received the report from their brother spooks in London. They suspected it was an expurgated version, but knew that, as far as old Louis Passau was concerned, they could not sit idly on the sidelines. Even if the Brits were only a quarter correct, Passau had a lot of explaining to do and, unless they dug the truth out of him soon, some journalist would get a sniff and the proverbial ordure would hit the propeller.

There were top level meetings at the FBI Counter-Intelligence field office on Half Street, S.W., Washington, D.C. On three separate occasions the Assistant Director drove to D.C. from his own fiefdom—the training center at Quantico. In the end they actually came to a gentleman's agreement with Passau. He would surrender himself on the day of the Anniversary Concert and, immediately after the event, six special agents from the Counter-Intelligence department would ferry the old musician to Quantico and the quarters, never pointed out to visitors, used for major debriefings on matters concerning intelligence and treacherous betrayal.

The Maestro was only told of their interest in the Nazi tie-in, and Passau seemed amused by it all, even when they said there would be a Langley crew present, and also one member of the British Secret Intelligence Service.

So Big Herb came rolling into town on Wednesday morning, was met and driven to the Algonquin, installed in one of the luxury suites and, by two in the afternoon—having taken a light lunch from room service—lay sprawled on his bed, earphones clamped across his large head, listening on his portable CD player to the last recording Leonard Bernstein had made of the Mahler First. It had been his least favorite symphony from the composer who dominated his musical interest, but with Bernstein conducting the Amsterdam Concertgebouworkest, the piece had taken on a totally new meaning for him.

The telephone rang about twelve times and his attention was called to it only by the flashing red light.

"Hi!" Herb said brightly into the instrument.

"This is Bruce." The man at the far end had the right words but Herbie did not recognize the voice.

"As in Bruce and the spider?" He purposely pronounced it "schpider."

"The same. I'm in the lobby."

He was there, close to the elevators: a tall, slightly stooping figure in jeans, Nike sneakers, and a T-shirt upon which was printed "Moscow University 1989." Herbie thought the only thing that marked him out as someone who had never before played for real was the rolled copy of yesterday's London *Times*.

He had to make the best of it, for the Embassy's Assistant Resident had only been in Washington for three months. His name was Charlie Laurence and his instructions were to stay in New York until Herbie was on his way. "When you move Sunray, I'll get back to the real world in D.C." He grimaced. Then he suggested a stroll in the park.

"You got mace and everything?" Herbie asked with a big smile as the doorman flagged down a cab.

Charlie Laurence actually smiled back, which made it all worthwhile, Kruger thought.

"London wants you to know that the Feds'll be headed by a chap called Mickey Boomer," Charlie said as they walked into Central Park, avoiding the heroic joggers and the horse droppings from the tourist carriages which clopped past at regular intervals. Behind them, from the cavern of Fifth Avenue, came the wail of a siren. Put a blind man down in the Big Apple and he would know where he was in a moment, Herbie thought. Nowhere else in the world did police and ambulance sirens have that strange locked-in echo produced by the wide streets and high buildings.

"Never heard of him," Kruger observed.

"They said he'd heard of you." Charlie seemed anxious to please. "But then, most people have heard of you."

"You hear of me, Charlie? Before this business, I mean."

"I heard you lecture once, at Warminster. Worth twice the admission fee. You're a legend, Mr. Kruger."

"Herbie."

"Okay. You're a legend, Herbie. Honor to meet you and all that."

"So what else London tell you? Who's coming from Langley?"

"Yes. Otto Khan and Boris Sangster."

"Big time," Herbie said. In his mind he thought it was shrewd. Old Kubla Khan himself, he of the pleasure-domed bald pate and dreadful silences. Khan would deal with the Hitler stuff—"I Spied for the Führer," or whatever it was called—while Boris would smash his way into the more recent problems concerning everyone's new friends around the Soviet Union: this last being the really pressing problem of which only Herbie, among those on this side of the pond, had *all* the details. Well, Boris would not get far without the extra mileage Herbie had brought with him. Passau at age ninety would brush off Boris Sangster like a fly, leaving the real business to Herbie, if they allowed him to work on his own. One of the last things Young Worboys had said was, "Try to force the issue, Herb. Try to get him on his Todd and go through him like shit through a goose."

"On his Todd?" Herbie had feigned innocence. "What's with the Todd? The Sweeney Todd, Demon Alibaba of Fleet Street?"

"Don't piss me about, Herb." Worboys was long wise to Herbie's eccentric ways. "On his Todd Sloan—on his own."

"Ah!" Big Herbie gave the game away with a grin. "The crockery rhyming slang."

"You'll get a call from Boomer, it seems." Charlie was taking long strides, trying the impossible, to match his pace to Big Herbie's shambling walk.

"He give me an invite to the concert, you think?"

"You'll get the run of the place; and you'll go with the Feds to Quantico. Special flight laid on from La Guardia. Champagne and caviar, I shouldn't wonder."

"Then we go chase up and down the Gerbal tubes, yes?"

"The what?"

"You never been to Quantico, Charlie? Damned great brick buildings joined together by Plexiglas walkways. They call them the Gerbal tubes.

Piece of trivia for you. FBI trivia, what are Gerbal tubes? Comes on the puce card marked little-known secrets."

"Thanks, yes. Must wangle a trip to Quantico."

"You'd like it. They got two commissaries and the food's cheap. Not the Savoy Grill, but what is, thank God."

Charlie seemed to think this was very funny and appeared a little put out when Herbie said he would walk back to the hotel by himself.

"They said I had to keep in touch."

"So keep in touch, Charlie. Pander to my every whim, huh?"

"Anything I can do. . . ."

Herbie gave his big daft grin. "New pecker? Million dollars? How about that for openers?"

Once more, Charlie thought it was very funny. He stored up Herbie's sayings so that he could eventually boast about servicing the legend that was Kruger.

As he was leaving, Herbie told him, "I'll call *you*, don't call me." Pause for the big grin and the photograph. "Unless London wants me to know something yesterday, okay?"

Mickey Boomer telephoned the hotel that evening and invited Herbie to a meal and a briefing. Boomer belied his name: a smallish man with a soft voice and deceptively languid manner. The meal was in some chichi French place where the food was New York French with things like seafood gazpacho on the menu. "Good old French delicacy, seafood gazpacho," Herbie muttered, but Boomer did not get the point.

Afterwards they walked silently back to the hotel. In the lobby, Boomer took a package from his briefcase. "You have a permit to carry this, Herb. Sure there've been changes, and Moscow Center don't take chances no more." He chuckled, "Certainly now their old boss is in the slammer." He spoke of Kryuchkov, arrested with the other "coupsters"—one of the U.S. media's more jarring new words with which they slowly poisoned the English language. Boomer gave Herbie a little cocked head, coy, look. "The decision was made by the D.C.I. Everyone associated with Passau has to carry. The Russian connection is so damned sensitive that you just never know."

"Sensitive you don't know." Herb was agreeing with him. In his room he unwrapped the package. A 9mm Smith & Wesson, forty rounds, two spare clips and a holster which fitted snugly against the small of his back.

Even with what little the Brits had given them, the Soviet connection had put someone on edge. Someone, Herbie thought, had seen the needles flick. Back in London they had discussed the possibility of Kruger being clandestinely armed via the Embassy, but it had not come up with Charlie. If you followed through on the logic of Passau's last few years, then there were people who would not want to wait for his death from old age: even a few more months—in spite of the dramatic changes.

The briefing, on Thursday, was interesting and Kruger returned to the Algonquin with all the updates on the life and times of Louis Passau, orchestral director extraordinary—one hundred and two pages in all. They added nothing to the two biographies—one official and fawning, the other unofficial and scandalous—which had been required reading in London, together with a separate précis which filled in huge gaps and had pictures. Herbie had another edge. He had just about every recording Passau had ever made.

On Friday, he was one of the team waiting for the Maestro at Lincoln Center.

IT WAS MORE like an audience with the great man than what amounted to an arrest. His dressing room had no personal touches, except for the many birthday telegrams affixed to the large, light-bulb–scaped mirror. There was one L-shaped sitting unit: old, covered in black with tiny green flowers printed into the faded material. The FBI and CIA men filed in and were introduced to Passau who, seated wearing a silk robe, acknowledged each of them with a nod, only occasionally looking up.

Herbie thought he saw the old man's eyes give a twitch of recognition but could not be sure. After all it was eleven years since he had come face to face with Maestro Passau. Vienna, 1980, and the dressing room in the Grosser Musikvereinsaal was stamped full of Passau character: photographs of the famous and infamous signed to the Maestro. Eleven years is a long time.

If Passau seemed unconcerned, his wife Angela, fifty years his junior, verged on the hysterical, Herb considered. Her eyes were red with weeping and she moved in a little jumpy, puppetlike manner, hands and eyes never still, shooing them from the dressing room like a country girl bringing the cows into the barn. "Cusha, cusha, cusha calling," he thought, wondering where in hell the line came from.

Not that there was anything countrylike about Angela, in her black velvet, the Barnscome pearls at her throat—she had been the Honorable Angela Barnscome before Passau had courted her and whisked her to the altar. It was his third marriage, as far as anyone knew; there was always the possibility of another bride or three lurking unseen if anyone had the motivation to spend fifty years searching the files.

Angela also wore the diamond clutch that had been Passau's wedding present: worth ten million, it was said at the time. She was rich in her own right, British, known for her poise and English phlegm: the usual stiff-upper-lip stuff. Yet, in the corridor outside, Herbie felt that all the tension had come from Angela Passau and not her husband. Angela Passau who smelled of lemons. Herb wondered if that had a significance—the lemons.

He wandered away from the others, along the passage, glancing to his left through the windows, then down the stairs, into the rear of the balcony, flashing the laminated plastic I.D. Boomer had given him the night before.

In the bad old days, Big Herbie Kruger had been considered the most visible of field agents: his size, the shambling gait, his great head with the crapulous features of a peasant; the idiosyncrasies of speech; the dumb, oxlike look; the stupid questions. Herbie had trapped the unwary with his idiot look and the seeming folly of his queries; used his height, weight and Farmer Schmitt attitude to blind his victims. Under all the doltishness, the man was overloaded with street savvy, as astute as the wisest interrogator, and ruthless as a black mamba—that extraordinary snake which will chase its prey for miles. Over the years, they said, he had developed an intuition second to none in the trade.

It was not until he was actually inside Avery Fisher Hall, with its plush beige seats, the great curve of a balcony and the acoustic baffles, that Herbie realized he had come to view the major protagonists.

The scene from the rear of the balcony would, he knew immediately, be overdescribed in the media as "glittering," "international" and "sparkling." His eyes were first drawn to the left side—concert platform right—a portion of which was usually reserved for the conductor's friends. Tonight, they had taken the entire left-hand section.

"If that collapsed, we'd lose just about every great living musician, eh, Herb?" It was Charlie Laurence, standing just behind him.

Herbie looked him up and down. "You rent the penguin suit by the hour, Charlie?"

"Very droll, Herb, but, no. You, on the other hand, obviously hired that one ten years ago and forgot to return it." Inevitably, in the bespoke dark worsted two-piece, Kruger looked as though he wore crumpled sackcloth.

"Ja, a decade. Let me tell you, Charles, this suit has seen many good days. Wore it at my wedding where, you should know, there was much blubbings from the women who failed to entrap me. It is good cover." He smiled his daft smile. Then—"Look," his eyes lifted towards the luminaries to their left. "Here comes Maestro Giulini with a gang of people. He bring a whole symphony orchestra, you think?"

"Possibly." Laurence was feasting on the great—Maazel, Solti, Rostropovich, Tilson Thomas, Ashkenazy, Previn and more.

"So who's here would interest me?" Herbie asked, scanning the curving rows below him.

"Maestro Passau's wife, and his lawyer just came in."

"Her I've already seen. Don't know the lawyer."

"Spinebrucker. Harold Spinebrucker. Spinebrucker, Havlish and Gold. Megabucks legal eagles."

"So? Anyone else?"

"The writer."

"What writer? No, you mean the dumb historian. Him of the I Spied for the Führer?"

Laurence nodded. "Down there; third row, dark curly hair trying to get his mouth into the blonde's earhole."

"Mr. Stretchfield is well-known for getting various things into ladies." A new voice. Herbie turned to see the plump, cheery-faced, almost Pickwickian form of Chuck—one of the FBI Special Agents who had been at the briefing, then, again, in Passau's dressing room. Chuck, they said, was the Bureau's music critic.

"Chuck. Charlie." Herb flapped a hand to and fro as introduction. It was the movement of a fish's tail.

"Oh, I know who Mr. Laurence is, Herb. My job after all." Chuck gave his beaming ruddy-cheeked smile and shook hands with Charlie Laurence.

"You expert on music, literature, both?" Herb asked in his usual tangled way.

"I'm an expert on most of this one." He laid his finger alongside his nose. "You want to see a real celebrity?"

"Shoot."

"Eight rows back, right-hand side, seventh seat in."

"A brunette. Dark hair. Got her." Herbie screwed up his eyes.

"La Tempesta."

"No?"

"Yes. Take a good look, Herbie. It's her, Constanza Traccia. One of the great sopranos of our time."

"Yesu!" Herb craned forward. "I saw her—heard her—sing *Tosca* and *Aida*. Magnificent; the greatest Aida of our time and there's no recording." He paused, and then softened his face into the stupid dumb-ox look. "Also there were rumors, Ja?"

"More than rumors." Chuck gave a lecherous smile. "Passau even had a yacht named for her. *La Tempesta*. They were inseparable. Trust me."

Constanza Traccia, known, for obvious reasons of temperament, as La Tempesta, had been the soprano cornerstone of Passau's opera company for almost a decade. Feted wherever she went, and undoubtedly Passau's beloved mistress.

Nobody would say why it suddenly ended, nor why Signorina Traccia had given up a meteoric career, but it was the start of the mystery period of Passau's life. The affair was suddenly over and, just as suddenly, Passau was missing. Gone. It was three years before even the press tracked him down to Greece. Nobody close to either Passau or Constanza Traccia would even hint at a reason for the breach. It remained one of the great social mysteries.

He watched as La Tempesta turned her head. Even at this distance, and taking her age into consideration, you could sense the wild, animal quality which had drawn audiences and critics alike. Herbie thought there was a bit of a gypsy look to her—raven hair, wide mouth and a slightly hooked nose. In the collective public mind she remained part goddess, part untamed passionate bitch, part whore and wholly professional great diva.

Herbie tore his eyes away, scanning the rest of the audience. It was not his imagination, there was static in the air, that particular electricity that hums through a crowd gathered to see, or hear, some event so spectacular that each person knows they will be able to say for years to come, "I was there that night." It was, he thought, the same feeling which he had experienced earlier in the year, when the Gulf War played live on the world's TV screens. The same response that must have been present when Christians were thrown to the lions, or at public executions.

"Well, lookie-lookie, what have we here?" Chuck seemed to be mumbling to himself. "I know they're all supposed to be great opera lovers, but . . ."

"*Was ist?*" Lord knew why he had suddenly lapsed into German. Even Herb could not explain that. The famous Passau Symphony Orchestra of America was all but assembled on the platform, together with the Marine Corps Band, who were there to add body to the second movement of Charles Ives' *New England Holidays* tone poem—"Decoration Day." Now the audience appeared to be settling, waiting for the arrival of the concertmaster and then the Maestro himself.

Chuck's eyes were glued to a party of men, four of them, and one woman, making their way into the far side of the balcony. One was old, short, and sagging with the weight of his years, but walking with a kind of presence—a man who knew he was a king, desperately trying to straighten his back: silk evening suit magnificently cut, as though the tailor had used some black art to remove a decade or two from the man, who still retained a full head of dark hair. For an instant gold flashed at his wrists. Just by looking at him, anyone would know this man held a key to power. To look into his face was to look into a kind of horror. The left cheek was scarred, livid and pockmarked, as though at some point in his life it had been scoured by thick steel wool.

Holding his arm was a young woman, Italianate, proud, with olive skin and a figure and carriage that was enough to hoist danger signals to a conclave of monks. Behind them came three larger men. All well-tailored and barbered, their eyes moving constantly, as though they were heirs to the old man's power.

"Who?" Herb asked again, and when the answer came Chuck's voice sounded almost shocked—

"Carlo Giarre. *Don* Carlo Giarre. Carlo 'The Squeeze' Giarre."

"As in the Giarre family?" Even Herbie who, they said, lived his life on two planes and would never share either of them with anyone, knew of the Giarre family. Don Carlo, last of the old Mafia Dons.

"A criminal legend," Chuck said. "Goes way back. Learned to love Puccini from his old boss Big Jim Colosimo. Real Mafia history, Herb. That guy knew Capone, Colosimo, all those Chicago people."

"A fan, perhaps?"

"Sure, why not." Chuck was a hundred light years away as the concertmaster came onto the platform, and the orchestra began that atonal fugue which is the prelude to any concert.

Then Louis Passau was striding to the podium. Not the man whom Herbie had seen slumped in the dressing room, but a tall, distinguished figure, walking with no concession to his years, the lion's mane of thick hair swept back, iron-gray, the face composed, and looking, for a moment, only half his true age as the applause rose and swept over him.

In the dressing room, Herbie had marveled, for the face was relatively unlined: tanned and hard as leather, the eyes clear blue—a color never captured by the photographers. Contact lenses, naturally—Herb knew, having read the medical reports. Almost as old as the century: a life which certainly reflected the history of their times, from war to peace and back again, together with all the incredible changes in between—and all the horrors. Passau had seen so much and remained a vessel containing man's progressions and regressions through the twentieth century.

Not in a million years, Herbie Kruger considered, would you have put this erect, arrogant-looking man at ninety years of age. The doctors had spoken of a truly unimaginable physique; the body of a man of sixty in good health. Passau neither smoke nor drank, kept to a strict regimen, still exercised daily. A body which remained prime and full of power, and a mind seemingly untouched by age. Untouched also, Herbie thought, by conscience, but he would make the journey of discovery with this man and, maybe, find the wellspring of his health and vitality.

As was his custom, Passau did not, at first, acknowledge the audience, standing and giving his orchestra three low bows—left, right and center—before he turned to face what he always called "The paying customers."

The applause went on and on until, finally, Passau turned, sweeping the auditorium with his eyes, putting his finger to his lips in good humor, then damping down the ovation with his hands, orchestrating his own reception.

At last, silence. The odd cough and clearing of the throat as Passau, erect, faced his orchestra and raised his baton.

The program had been carefully chosen. Copland's *Fanfare For The Common Man*, followed by the same composer's *El Salón Mexico*; Charles Ives' *New England Holidays*; the Gershwin Piano Concerto (Ashkenazy was to slip away from the audience to perform with the orchestra); while the conclusion would be Louis Passau's own Symphony Number 1—*The Demonic*—the music he had written during his self-imposed exile in the Greek islands. A huge, towering tone poem that spoke of laughter and pain, life and death, with a final movement involving a massed choir, extra brass and a setting of the "Dies Irae." The critics had said it was Mahler crossed with Shostakovich; that this symphony had its roots in Europe and not in the American experience, but Herbie—who owned the spectacular recording with the composer and his own orchestra—felt there was little Mahler and less Shostakovich. This was all Passau: an original, exorcising his private demons in the only way he knew.

"A program to suit all seasons and conditions of men," Passau was reported to have said at the rehearsal for the Birthday Concert, adding, "Fucking patriotic as well." On his doctor's advice, the concert was to play without an intermission. Even though, at ninety, Passau was an ox, it was known that, while he seemed to draw strength from live performances, he had a tendency to flag once he stopped. Everyone wished to avoid the possibility of a slackening of pace during the second half.

Silence came, like sudden nightfall in the tropics. Passau raised his hands, and so it began, with those first clear brass chords of the *Fanfare*, which seemed almost to crack open the roof of Avery Fisher Hall.

Nobody could deny the emotion, the heightening of the senses, the drama and passion of that concert. Later, many said it was as though they were hearing all the music for the first time—which was something Passau had the ability to do in his moments of greatness. "It is always my aim, with an orchestra," he often was quoted as saying, "to bring out that which every great composer intends. For the music to shatter the time barrier; to be classic, which means to have something new to say each time the work is performed. It is a question of love. A four-sided affair between composer, orchestra, conductor and audience."

That was what happened on Friday, September 6, 1991, in Avery Fisher Hall. Even familiar works, like *Fanfare*, *El Salón Mexico*, and the Gershwin Concerto in F came into the senses as though they had been written in that instant, in the second before each note was played. The effect was overwhelming, though Big Herbie Kruger, so easily swayed and shot through by great music, managed, for a time, to remain apart. That area of his being which lived in the professional world of secrets took control and he spent the first two thirds of the performance scanning the audience, putting names to faces seen only in photographs, checking on Passau's past as the music thundered through the hall.

He noted Veronica Passau, the maestro's second wife who had successfully sued for divorce—her lawyers dragging the names of at least a dozen female musical luminaries into the open as well as that of the principal correspondent. Tonight, Veronica still looked handsome, almost a sister to her daughter—Passau's one living child, May Cosima (named for the month of her conception and after Wagner's lover/wife).

He saw others who owed much to the aged Maestro; the cellist Yevgeny Khavenin, defector from the Soviet Union in the late sixties, given succor, and the first boost to his wondrous career in the West, by Passau. Khavenin's name appeared on a number of the classified documents Herb had committed to his prodigious memory; as had the name Lien Yao, the young Chinese pianist who had been linked for a season or so with Passau. Now, she sat in the balcony, near the other great musical figures, her face inscrutable, yet her loveliness, which matched her talent, clear and still, displayed for all to see.

At one moment, as the music slowly started to pull Herbie into its orbit and away from his job, he thought, "this man; this Passau, he is a freak; abnormal; a man of ninety with such poise and vigor, such command." It smacked, Herb considered, of some kind of warp in nature; against all reason. Louis Passau, whom he had idolized as the greatest living man of music, was an aberration.

Then the music washed over him, finally swallowing him alive— Passau's own symphony with its hammer blows of timpani to the almost shouted repetition of the "Dies Irae" of the finale, growing and growing so that the damned spirits which seemed to whirl in the harmonies became almost tangible. It was the first time in his own, not insubstantial life, that Big Herbie Kruger felt he could stretch out a hand and touch music. At the emotionally draining finale, he found himself giving a quick choking sob, for Passau's symphony reflected so many of his own private agonies.

As the applause exploded around him, Herbie felt a touch on his arm. Chuck, inclined his head towards the exit, whispering—in reality shouting against the din—that it was time to go. Herbie blundered out, his senses in turmoil from the battering of the symphony, his brain whirling with the names and faces, many of whom would play a large part in his interrogation of the old man.

IT TOOK ALMOST two hours before they had Passau ready to leave. First, the audience would not let him go; then the celebrities swarmed into his dressing room. They had arranged with Angela Passau that she should plead her husband's fatigue, and get visitors away as quickly as possible. She did her best, and after what seemed an interminable wait, the FBI took over.

Passau himself seemed calm and dignified. He looked tired, hardly spoke, but remained a figure of great power, demanding respect, and walking with an enviable, relaxed ease.

They went with him along the passageway to the elevator which would take them down to the 65th Street parking lot.

The entrance and exit of the official employees' parking lot of Lincoln Center leads off and onto 65th Street. The lot itself is below ground level, but there is a long curving sweep, down to the doors near the elevators, and then up an incline to the exit. Both the entrance and exit are closed off simply by single red-and-white drop poles. There is nothing substantial to keep unwanted visitors or car thieves out—except for the excellent security.

Passau was flanked by two FBI men, while Mickey Boomer, Chuck, one unidentified CIA operative, and Big Herbie walked directly behind the Maestro, who had said farewell to his tearful wife in the privacy of the dressing room. The official car, a large unmarked Lincoln, had already drawn up, its FBI driver at the wheel and a young agent beside him, riding shotgun.

A NYPD black and white led the lineup, then an FBI communications vehicle, parked in front of the Lincoln, and a further car, a dark blue Chevy, bringing up the rear. The arrangements were that Boomer and the CIA man would ride with Passau while others, including Herbie, would follow up in the Chevy.

Everyone seemed to be milling around the cars for a moment, as though there was some indecision. For once, at the start of this operation, the organization appeared to be falling apart.

Swiftly, Mickey Boomer took control, moving forward and taking Passau's arm, smiling and gently pushing him forward. "The Lincoln, here, Mr. Passau. If you would get into the car please."

In the small jostling for position, Herbie found himself almost up against the Lincoln, close to Passau as the Maestro began to stoop and enter the rear of the vehicle.

The roar and crash came from the parking lot entrance. Herbie turned, just in time to see the black Porsche smash savagely through the entrance pole, its tires burning rubber as it hurtled down the incline. The car seemed to have a superstructure, like a small box of metal scaffolding forward of the windshield, and another at the front of the hood.

He heard Boomer yell, "Get down! Get down!," and saw the first flashes of automatic fire before the echoing rapid shots, magnified in the enclosed area, began to deafen him. His pistol was in his right hand, but instinctively he leaped towards Passau who, at the din, had half straightened as though about to reverse matters and exit the Lincoln.

Herbie landed on top of the old man as the car shuddered from four or five bullets, and the Porsche, still burning rubber, hurtled up the ramp and crashed the bar of the exit, squealing as it turned back onto 65th Street.

In Herbie's mind there was great confusion concerning the various noises and events. The first burning squeal from the Porsche seemed to be overlapped by the terrifying thump of bullets finding their mark, while the cries, shouts and return fire were all jumbled into one sustained track of disordered sound.

For a second, he pulled himself back from Passau; was aware of the police car and the FBI communications vehicle taking off in pursuit of the Porsche. He was conscious of at least one man stretched out on the sidewalk, and of blood. Then he heard Boomer again. Shouting this time, "Herbie, get him in! Get Passau in and go with him! Now! Move! Get the fucking Lincoln outta here!"

He heaved Louis Passau into the car which began to roll almost before he could follow the Maestro and close the door. As they hit the street, the agent riding shotgun called back, "Is he okay? Is Passau okay?"

"You okay, Mr. Passau?" Herbie realized that, for some reason he could not quite figure, he was short of breath.

Passau nodded, leaning against the far side of the car, showing no sign of agitation, wearing a gray double-breasted suit, white shirt, with a blue and white polka dot tie—a matching silk handkerchief lolling out of his breast pocket giving him a slightly rakish look. The Lincoln was gathering speed, and Herbie, getting his backside onto the seat at last, glanced around to see the lights of the Chevy behind them.

"What in holy blazes was that all about?" he asked nobody in particular.

Calmly, Passau said that he gathered somebody had tried to kill him. There was a twinkle in his eye, and the corners of his mouth flickered with the makings of a smile. This guy, Herbie thought, has gone right round the pipe. He's a crazy.

Then Passau peered at Herbie. "Haven't we met before? I don't mean in the dressing room tonight. Some time ago? We have met in the past, yes?"

The streets of New York were around them; everywhere seemed a blaze of light and people. Even the traffic was heavy, but they rolled through it all, switching lanes, going quite fast, their driver doing impossible things, cutting off cabs and private vehicles alike. You could feel the wrath of angry drivers in their wake.

Kruger swallowed. "Yes, once we met. Very briefly we met. My name's Kruger. People call me Herbie, or Herb." He realized that he was gesturing with a handful of 9mm pistol.

Passau put out a hand, "People call me Louis, or, more often, Lou. Nice to meet you, Herb."

3

"I'M GOING THROUGH the tunnel. Okay with you?" The driver cocked his head back towards his two passengers.

"Me you're talking to?" Herbie wore his puzzled look. The confusion was reflected in his voice.

The agent riding shotgun snapped, "Just check the guys're still with us." Then, turning to the driver, "Yes, go through the tunnel, there won't be much traffic this time of night."

"Which tunnel? Bloody Channel Tunnel?" Herbie, still holding the pistol, turned to make sure the trail car was with them.

"I think they mean the Queens Midtown Tunnel." Passau reclined in his seat. He had a distinctly middle-European accent. The Maestro would have pronounced it *excent*.

"QMT!" The Shotgun nodded, looking to his front, as if that settled everything.

"The tail's still with us, okay?" Herbie looked into the smiling eyes of Passau again. "Yes. Yes, we met once." At last answering the Maestro's question. "I saw you in Vienna. Eleven years ago. You conducted the Mahler Second. One of the great moments of my life. Came to your dressing room afterwards. You wouldn't remember me."

Passau made a grunting noise, neither confirming nor denying his memory. "You like Mahler?" He sounded surprised, as though he imagined Herbie's musical taste could not possibly rise higher than *Switched-on Classics*.

"Mahler I don't *like*. Mahler I *adore*. Gustav Mahler is God."

The Maestro nodded, looking pleased. "The adoration of old Gus is well placed. Hope you are liking Mozart also. . . ."

"Mozart's a barrel of apples. Wonderful, but too much. I cannot keep up with the K numbers, and some of the symphonies I cannot detect difference. With *Gustav* you know where you stand. Nine and a half symphonies and two big handfuls of assorted diamonds. Mahler is king, president. Mahler is chairman of the board."

"Keep an eye out at the tollbooth." The driver spoke in a monotone. Like a robot, Herbie thought. He transferred thoughts into words—

"Okay, Hal, anything you say."

"The name's Rube. What's with the Hal?"

"Two Thousand and One. Movie. You sound like Hal."

"Horseshit." The driver indeed sounded like the robot from *2001*. Even more so when he did one-worders like "horseshit."

"Remember we've got some class in the back here. Watch the language, Hal." Herbie was fully turned around. "Shit!" he said loudly and with more feeling than the driver.

"I got it," the Shotgun muttered. "Damned great U-Haul's pulled in between us and the trail car."

Indeed it had: a big slab-sided truck with the dark orange U-Haul logos and a couple of long-haired urban cowboys in the cab. Herbie could see the passenger was resting his feet on the dash. He was probably drinking Michelob.

The car radio burst into life with a flash of white noise, followed by a garbled voice which the Shotgun seemed to understand. He turned his head a fraction to speak. "They're telling us they're behind the U-Haul. . . ."

"Einstein you got driving the trail car?" Herbie spoke with a smile in his voice.

"We're to pull over on the exit. There'll be uniforms waiting so Sunray'll get a safe ride to La Guardia."

"Who is this 'Sunray'?" Passau asked.

"Sunray is you, Lou." Herbie turned to look at him. "For things like this they give us names. Me? I'm 'Blue Boy,' like in the painting."

Passau chuckled.

The driver tossed money into the little correct change container at the tollbooth and they moved towards the tunnel, staying in the left lane, obeying the large sign. Traffic seemed to pour past on the right.

"'Sunray,' huh?" Passau grinned and began to hum quietly.

It took Herbie a moment to realize what the musical genius was humming—"Is old Insects song," he said. A little hint of shock.

"Beatles," Passau corrected. "Not Insects! Beatles! So? Here comes the Sun King. Here comes the Sun King," he sang quietly. "Nothing wrong with Beatles. You know what I heard the other day, Herbert?"

"The name's Herbie or Herb! Not Herbert!" Kruger sounded angry. "Herbert is joke, foolish, as in, 'You stupid Herbert.'"

"Excuse me," with mock deference. "Okay, you wanna know what I heard, Herb?"

"Why not?"

"Couple of young guys, all leather, chains and ripped off Judas Priest CDs coming out of their pockets."

"What is Judas Priest?" Herbie's eyes widened.

"Never mind. Cacophonous heavy metal group. Don't ask what is heavy metal. I tell you what I hear. Exact, just as it was said. I passed them on the street, and one of these young guys was saying, 'Of course, if the Beatles were around today they wouldn't make shit.' Funny, huh?"

"Ach!" Big Herbie flapped a hand. "What do they know? They probably say the same about Mahler."

"Maybe they don't even know of Mahler, Herb."

"Then to hell with them. I . . ." Herbie looked to his right, and stopped talking. A large black stretch limo was beginning to pass them. Ahead he could just see the tunnel exit, but long experience alerted Kruger. There was an unaccountable tingling in his mind, and his stomach turned over. Something was just not right about the limo, which was being followed by a little white VW Cabriolet. "Watch it!" he ordered, and the driver's head moved just as Herbie turned to see the U-Haul pull out and nudge the Volks to its right.

One did not have to be a genius to realize that switching lanes in the tunnel meant either a foolhardy or criminal act. Everyone in the Lincoln knew this was not foolhardy, so it had to be the other thing. The driver began to pile on the horses.

"Christ!" The Shotgun pumped the action on his weapon, and started to lower his window. Then everything happened like a slow motion ballet. Herbie saw the U-Haul push the Volks to one side so that it turned hard right and tried to climb the tunnel wall, which was not an option for a Range Rover, let alone a Cabriolet.

At the same moment the limo slewed in front of the Lincoln, broadsiding in a mist of burning rubber, and causing the FBI driver to stick his foot almost through the floor.

There was no crash—except from the Volks and, possibly, the trail car behind the U-Haul, which was successfully turned sideways on, blocking everything behind them. The black stretch walled off their front.

"Get down, Lou! Down on fucking floor!" Herbie yelled as the automatic fire blew away a considerable portion of engine, the windshield, most of the driver's head, and half of the Shotgun's chest. Three long bursts by two weapons.

Herbie scrabbled for the right-hand door latch, swung it open and rolled his large body out onto the filthy oily road. He did all this with an incredible grace and at the speed of light. Later, during the night sweats that followed the incident, he realized the only thing revolving in his head were the opening bars of the Mahler Sixth—the solid beat of the bass strings, and timpani, too loud: probably his heart.

The two men who had emerged from the rear of the limo were taking their time, changing magazines. They were professionals, dressed in black, with short leather jackets, and they probably thought that a dose of two magazines from their Uzis had effectively offed everyone in the car.

On his feet, Big Herbie, arms outstretched, the 9mm an extension of himself, knew he did not have the luxury of time. He put two rounds into the first man, moving his body, but not his legs, to look over the pistol as it came to bear on the second, who took two rounds in the throat. There was a fraction of time when both killers looked surprised, almost out of sorts that this impossible thing could happen. Then they both tipped backwards, one almost vertical for a second, the other scrabbling at the air before he hit the stretch limo's trunk.

A third man came from the front seat like a rocket, but Herbie took him out before he even had a chance to raise the pistol in his hand. Of the three of them, he was the only one who screamed as the top of his head disintegrated.

"Mother of God, can this be the end of Louis?" The Maestro did a passable imitation of Edward G. Robinson.

"No. Just saved your life. But not these, I fear." Herbie looked at the driver and Shotgun, then averted his eyes. He was shaking, and realized he was going to throw up if he did not take a few deep breaths. Inhaling one deep breath in this tunnel was like smoking three packs of cheap French cigarettes, so he ended up spluttering, looking at Maestro Passau in the back of the Lincoln. The old man suddenly seemed to have aged, his face gray with fright.

"You okay, Maestro? Is okay. Danger's over, but who the hell are these people?"

Passau nodded, then spoke, his voice quivering for the first time, even while trying to put on a bold front. "I could make a guess." He breathed heavily for fifteen seconds.

Herbie thought the old man was in shock. There were noises off, from behind. People trying to get through. Two shots, exploding in the tunnel confines like sticks of dynamite, then sirens, coming from the far exit of the tunnel. Once more, in his head, Big Herbie heard Young Worboys— "Try to force the issue, Herb. Try to get him on his Todd and go through him like shit through a goose."

He went over to the stretch limo and hauled the dead driver by the collar of his jacket. He was already half sprawled from the car, and one pull spun the body onto the road. He looked inside. The keys were still in the ignition. As he lumbered back to the Lincoln, he could see *that* car was not going anywhere.

Leaning inside, he stretched out a hand to Passau. "Trust me, Maestro. Just trust me. Come. Out of the car."

"Name is Louis, or Lou, Herbie. Maestro is unfashionable these days." Passau pushed himself towards the outstretched hand, and now it seemed a great effort of will as well as a physical feat. But, when he stood erect outside the Lincoln, he nodded, put back his shoulders, asked what they would do, and if Herbie would kindly bring his topcoat and scarf, plus the luggage from the Lincoln's trunk.

"We take over the stretch, okay?" Herbie patted him reassuringly.

"If you say so, Herb. If you say so."

The cops arrived just as Passau was settled in the front seat. Herbie went over to the two cars and spoke with the uniformed men, some of whom were fanning out, moving further into the tunnel from which sounds of violence were still coming.

The conversation was quick and easy.

"Blue Boy," Herbie said, flourishing his I.D. to the police captain who appeared to be in charge. "I have Sunray, and I've commandeered that car."

"Who took out those guys?" The captain had flinty eyes which looked as though they saw death in many guises every day and most nights.

Herbie waved the 9mm. "This took them out. Now I got to get Sunray to La Guardia. Is essential we move him on quickly. You know the score, Captain."

The cop nodded, looked closely at Kruger's I.D. "I'll give you an escort. Just wait ten minutes and . . ."

"I'm not waiting for nobody. This is second time someone tries to ice Sunray. I don' want to make it three in a row."

The captain pushed his cap back on his head and scratched his scalp, thinking for all of ten seconds. "Okay, I'll radio La Guardia. The plane's waiting."

They were near enough to the limo for Passau to hear the short conversation. "La Guardia," he said to Herbie when the big man shoehorned himself into the driving seat.

"Sure, La Guardia. Why not?" Herbie looked over the controls, working out which stalk activated the indicator lights. "Always with a different car I indicate right, and the windshield washers come on usually."

"I remember that well." Passau gave a heavy sigh. "With me it was only the speed that mattered. I still drive fast cars." Pause. "Sorry, I *used* to drive fast cars. You think I'll ever drive again, Herbie?"

"Depends on what you tell me, Lou. We got much talking to do. Jawing, they say back in London. Jawing and, sometimes, rabbiting." The limo started at the turn of the key. Slowly, Herbie edged it forward, getting the feel of the steering.

"This kind of talk is new to me."

"You talk a lot and is rabbiting. You talk nonsense, is load of old bunny. This I learned long ago when I first go to England." He was confident now, increasing speed. An ambulance and more police cars passed them, heading towards the tunnel.

"Strange talk. This is slang, yes?"

"This is definitely slang." The limo was back into a normal traffic flow now. "Takes a long time to learn." Herbie realized that shock was setting in. His hands trembled on the wheel: it had been years since he had been involved in violence, and even longer since he had killed anyone in the line of duty. Killing people was not part of his work profile back in the Secret Intelligence Service, in the freezing zone of the Cold War, but he had done it on occasions. He always regretted it in the end, and wondered if he would live to lament this.

They reached a dividing point in the road, the big green and white signs shouted from overhead.

"Weren't we going to La Guardia?" Passau asked, almost casually.

Big Herbie nodded. "Originally that was the idea."

"You just took the exit to JFK, Herbie."

"I know it."

"You want to tell me why we're heading for JFK, Herb?"

"In a way I'm engaged in a felony. Maestronapping—which is kidnapping *con brio*."

"Why?"

"Because is better for you, if we get away with it. Better for us to talk alone, instead of having FBI, CIA and that bunch bashing at your ear. With me, you get only the best questions, Lou. I promise."

"Then you give me asylum?"

"Possibly. Who knows. Depends on the answers."

Passau leaned back, smiling. "It's a long story."

"Save it then and we play at Arabian nights. Bet it makes good telling, Lou."

"Depends where you're standing—like a traffic accident."

"Trust me, Lou, you'll get a better deal with me."

"There's nothing to lose."

"Except both our freedoms, Lou. What I'm going to do is something naughty. A big bit of the naughties. To do it I'll have to tell a few large porkies."

"Porkies?" Passau's brow creased and Herbie looked at him. There was plenty of light now from the sodium arcs along the Van Wyck Expressway. "Porkies?" the Maestro repeated.

"Once more the slang. London slang, what they call the rhyming slang. Pork pies equals lies. See, it rhymes. Pies, lies. Thus, porkies. *Verstanden?*"

"Clever, yes. Porky pies, lies. Good."

Herbie gave a big grin. "As the man in the movie says, 'I think this is the beginning of a beautiful friendship.'"

"So what we do now, huh?"

Herbie was taking the car up to the Pan Am terminal, into the overhead parking. Finally he found a slot, on the third level, pulled in and switched off the engine, leaned back and began to explain.

"Lou, we are not invisible men, right? Neither of us can be chameleons. We have little camouflage. You're striking: a face known all over the world, right?"

"Well, maybe. Some people might recognize me."

"And I am large. I blunder, like a blunderbuss, right?"

"I would say that once seen, Herb, you would never be forgotten."

"This I know, and I use it to advantage many times. We must not be seen by certain people. It would also be a bonus if others did not identify us. You understand?"

Passau nodded.

"Okay, then first I put you on parole. You stay here, in this car. You are like three wise monkeys, okay?"

"You have my word. In any case, I'm tired."

"Just wait, and trust me. I must first buy one or two essentials. I did not even bring my toothbrush. My bag was in the trail car, so it's probably shot full of holes by now, and we have not much time, Lou. I'd say about an hour before they alert people that we might be here at JFK. So, I will not be long. Stay." This last as though to a faithful dog.

Herbie trundled off across the parking lot and took the elevator down, into the Pan Am Terminal. Nobody knew that, in a matter of months, Pan Am would cease to exist: a victim of global financial chaos. In the elevator he tried to smarten himself up. He also put on a pair or spectacles made of clear glass. Not much of a disguise, but if he really concentrated on his walk he might just get away with it.

First he scouted for wheelchairs. There are always wheelchairs in airport terminals if you know where to look. People who are sent to assist travelers tend to dump the chairs once they have collected their gratuity. They like to disappear for an hour or so for a smoke or a cold beer. The chairs are often left unattended for some time. It took Herbie four minutes, and, once he had found a chair, he headed straight for the Budget Car Rental desk and explained that he had a sick elderly gentleman who he could not get down to the car rental area. Could they bring a car up for him if he did the paperwork here and now? As he spoke, Herbie felt in his left inside breast pocket, the one containing paperwork, credit cards, passport, everything he'd need, in the name of Buckerbee. In other pockets he had I.D. and all the trimmings in his own name, and the names of a Professor Spinne, and Gordon Lonsdale. This last had been a piece of humor only Kruger would have the nerve to use. Normally you would not put the name of a notorious Cold War Russian spy on extra paper.

The Buckerbee wallet included a Platinum Amex card which, though she would never in a thousand years show it, impressed the girl at Budget. Car rental agents are rarely interested in faces. They look at I.D. and the kind of paper that gets pushed over the desk at them.

Mr. Buckerbee had German paper: Federal Republic paper, naturally, now the D.D.R. was definitely dead.

He filled in the forms; the Amex card was given the thumbs up from the electronic telephone swipe, and the girl said a silver-gray Cutlass Supreme would be outside the arrivals terminal in fifteen minutes.

It was, and so was Herbie, pushing the wheelchair into which he had loaded Passau. People actually helped to get the Maestro into the car. Later, not one of them came forward. Herbie had made Louis Passau put on his coat and wrap his mouth in the silk scarf he had been carrying in the pocket. "Play almost dead, Lou," he had advised.

"I *am* almost dead."

"So you don't need to do one hell of a lot of acting. Good."

They drove back along the expressway and headed south. Hours later, at a little after three in the morning, a touch north of Washington, D.C., they pulled up, for the second time that night, at a twenty-four-hour gas station.

After Herbie had filled the car he used the telephone booth: dialing an 804 number straight out of his memory bank. It rang ten times before a sleepy, slightly disgruntled, voice answered.

"You remember the night they invented champagne?" Herbie asked.

"Jee-ru-sa-lem, Her—"

"Name's Cross, sir. James Cross, as in a church, huh?"

Naldo Railton, now in his sere and yellow years—seventy-four to be exact—felt his memory retreat across the years to the last time he had spoken like this to Herbie. Naldo, which was a nickname for Donald, was the man who took over a young spindly German boy, an OSS asset in Berlin just after World War Two, and helped turn him into a member of the British Secret Intelligence Service. The lanky boy was Eberhardt Lukas Kruger.

Now, long retired and living out placid golden years with his wife, Barbara, in the shadow of Virginia's Blue Ridge Mountains, Naldo's heart leaped at the sound of Big Herbie Kruger's voice, and his mind ran an endless stream of memories.

"Of course, Mr. Cross. I remember you well. What can I do?"

"You heard anything yet?"

"About what?"

"Good, you haven't heard anything yet. I need to meet."

"Come here. You've got the address."

"Not the wisest plan in the world, sir. No."

"Ah." There was a long pause, during which Herbie strained to catch any clicks, hums or power being drawn off the line which might indicate a wiretap—even though he knew it was unlikely he would detect anything. It was equally unlikely that anyone in New York or Washington had figured he was, as they said in old hard-boiled dick novels, on the lam with Lou Passau. He was banking on it.

"How long?" Naldo asked.

"Three hours tops."

"Right. Town called Ruckersville, to our north. I'll be parked in a white Lincoln. Plates are ONE 391. You'll just have to drive through the place to see me. Got it, Mr. Cross?"

"See you," Herb smiled, then, as an afterthought, added, "Don't grow anything from your backside."

Passau slept, and, half an hour later, Kruger pulled in to an all-night diner, taking steaming Styrofoam beakers of coffee out to the Cutlass and gently waking his passenger.

"We arrived somewhere?" Passau stretched, made sucking movements with his mouth, signifying that it felt like a parrot's cage.

"Soon. I wanted you awake. Coffee. Didn't know if you took sugar."

"Sure I take sugar, one of an old man's vices."

Herbie tore the edges off three packets and dumped them into the beaker, stirring it with the little straw they give you in places like that in lieu of a spoon.

"How much longer?" Passau asked.

"Couple of hours before we meet a friend, then heaven knows. I need a place to squirrel you away. Out of sight and mind. So we can talk. Who tried to kill you, Lou?" The final question fired from the lip quickly to catch the old man off guard.

"Kill me? Oh, those people with guns? I have an idea, but it's a long story."

"You're going to be good with me, Lou, aren't you? You'll talk. Tell all . . ."

"With no porkie pies? Maybe. Depends on what you want. I'll give you all the German stuff, but it'll take time. Stretchfield got most of it right in his book, but then he tried to blackmail me. To understand, you have to learn about *me*, Herb. You have to know why it all happened."

Kruger gave a big mock sigh, sipped the scalding coffee, and said, "I'm more interested in the last five years, Lou. More concerned about Mother Russia. Very interested in the last few months, to be honest."

There was a long silence. Passau contemplated his coffee, and, for a moment, Herbie tensed, thinking the old man might hurl it in his face. Instead, Passau spoke very quietly, "If you want all *that*, it might take weeks. You see, Herbie, you would have to travel with me through this whole damned and bloody century, because—I tell you already—you have to understand why."

"I don't mind as long as we reach the end of the journey together."

"My last confession, eh? Give me extreme unction? Cleanse me from my sins? And me a good Jewish boy."

"However you want to think of it, Lou. I'll hold your hand, and go the whole way, if that's what you want. I'll even try and do a deal for you. Get you out and into safety."

"At my age?" A second long pause. "There must be music. I can't do it without being able to at least listen to music."

"I'll fix it." Herbie took another sip. "We have a deal?"

"Maybe."

"We're two old spies, Louis. A couple of dodos left over from the big freeze. Soon we might be extinct. At least we can leave our story. Others could profit, because the people we both used to work for will still go on. They'll go on with it until the end of time, whatever they say—death of communism, death of fascism, death of all isms. You know it, don't you?"

Passau nodded, finished his coffee and handed back the beaker. "Let's get going before my memory gives out altogether." He seemed very still, very calm and, in a way, very young. "I have a tale that'll take the wax out of your ears, Herb. The genuine article. The laughter and tears. The soundless wailing, the silent withering of autumn flowers."

Herbie recognized the last sentence as a quotation, but he could not catch where it came from.

"You think you know from spies, Herb. You know from nothing till you hear what happened to me."

Herbie nodded, then turned on the ignition again, and put the Cutlass in drive.

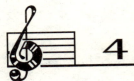

4

SINCE THEIR RETIREMENT to the United States, Naldo and Barbara Railton had made many friends. One of them was an English widow, an American citizen because of her former marriage to a wealthy oilman. Her name was Gwyneth O'Brien and—as she was the first to admit—she lived in what she called "the back of beyond," in a pleasant house built at the head of a small cleft in the foothills of the Blue Ridge Mountains. The nearest hamlet was some nine miles away, and her friends, for whom she threw legendary and lavish dinner parties, always had to travel long distances to reach her. They did not say she lived in "the back of beyond." They said things like, "Gwyneth lives to hell and gone," or "Love Gwyneth's parties, but they should carry health warnings saying, how the heck d'you drive forty miles after soup, fish, roast beef, cheese, fine wines, two helpings of profiteroles and superb cognac."

By a happy coincidence, Naldo always looked after the house when Gwyneth was away, as she was now, on an extended visit to the United Kingdom and her roots. On these occasions she gave Naldo carte blanche with the place. "If you come across a tenant for a short lease, darling, just go ahead," she told Naldo, who, after meeting Herbie in Ruckersville, telephoned Gwyneth in London to say he thought he had the kind of tenant of whom she would approve.

"Go ahead, Naldo darling. Screw as much as you can from them, and make certain they're out by the end of the first week in December. You're in charge."

The meeting with Herbie had been worrying. Naldo sat in his white Lincoln, on Route 29, pulled off the road in the small town of Ruckersville.

He saw no other car stop nearby, and the first he knew of Herbie's presence was the front passenger side door being wrenched open and Herbie's huge face appearing close to his.

"Nice to see you again, Nald, but you're getting careless in your old ageing. Twenty years ago you'd never have sat in a car with the unlocked doors."

"Christ, Herb, you gave me a shock."

"Be bigger shock if it had been some Moscow Center mobster." He settled comfortably beside his old friend and mentor.

"They still exist? Moscow Center mobsters?"

"Come on, Nald, 'course they still bloody exist. Openness, freedom, dissolution of Communist Party, only goes so far. They're going to take a few decades to catch up. You hear any news yet?"

"I listened to the radio on the way over. There seemed to be nothing new that would interest me—apart from the constantly changing situation in the Kremlin."

"They mention a shoot-out in the Queens Midtown Tunnel just after midnight?"

"Why, yes. Yes, they did." Naldo looked at him sharply and with some surprise.

"And what they put it down to? Mob violence? Street gangs? Or some little domestic violences?"

"The mob, as it happens. The cops are saying it was an attempted organized crime killing. Tied up traffic for two hours."

"Fatalities?"

"Yes. The Feds're furious. Three so-called civilians. But five special agents, on a surveillance operation, killed."

"Shit!" There had been the two in the Lincoln; another three meant the men in the trail car. Herbie thought of Mickey Boomer, Chuck, and another agent. Naldo's brow creased. The surprised look had not gone from his eyes. "You involved, Herb? I thought you went private never to return."

"Ja, I was supposed to be gone. Gone and not be forgotten, huh?"

"But you're not?"

"Talked into it by your son, Young Worboys and the new Headmaster," Herbie grinned. "But I have to be like Dad, keep Mum, don't I? You told me that. British wartime shogun, wasn't it?"

"Slogan, Herb." Naldo almost bit his tongue. He had not been with Kruger for more than a minute or so before falling into one of the man's word traps. With Herbie you rarely knew when he was having you on. "What's the score, Herb? How can I help?"

"Time," Herbie said the word as though it was the sole explanation for his presence.

"Time?"

"We ain't got much of it. Could be the FBI guys're already knocking at your front door, and old Barb's saying 'Oh my, he go out, I don' know where.' Then they'll get a bead on your car registration. It won't take long for them to figure out you're my obvious contact. They'll also presume I wouldn't be stupid enough to come riding into your place for all the world to see: like naked man in nunnery, yes?"

"So?"

"Less you know, better will be; so let me tell you what I need. If you can't fix it, I'll take to the road again. I do have another possibility, but it's one hell of a long driving." Without even mentioning Passau, except as "a friend," he quickly told Naldo what he needed.

"Like hunted fox I need a new sit," he finished.

"Set, Herb. Foxes have sets. Foxes and lawyers."

"So that's what I need. A safe set, eh?" He gave a short guffaw.

Naldo thought for a few minutes. "I can take you to a house that's empty, but I'll have to call the owner in London to square it away."

"There's food? The necessities of life? Bottle of brandy, maybe two?"

"No, but I'll bring you everything you need: provided the owner says it's a go. I presume you've got good money?"

"In three different languages, Nald. Good as they give you in London: traveling checks; Visa, Mastercard, Platinum Amex, the works and a bundle of notes. This house? Is safe, yes?"

"Right off the beaten track. They'd have to be mind readers to pick you up, as long as you don't show yourselves." He paused, "This really is necessary, Herb? I mean is it really kosher? You're not playing off-the-cuff games?"

"Kosher as chicken soup."

"Right. I'll lead you to the place, then call the owner from there. I'll be back later in the day with food. . . ."

"Only if the G-men aren't crawling all over your back. If they appear, you should assume they got surveillance—electronic and personal. Don't suppose you hung on to any electronic countermeasurings when you left the Office?"

Naldo shook his head. "If they *are* on to me then I'll find some way of getting food to you. Now, if you follow me, I'll lead you there. Where's your car?"

"Tucked away, back up the road. I got to use a phone booth at some place on our way."

"Any old phone booth?"

"Just your run-of-the-windmill telephone cabinet."

"There's one up the road. You can see it from here. A supermarket. There're phones outside."

"Good, watch for me, Nald. . . . Oh, one other thing . . ."

"Yes?"

"This place we're going. Does it have stereo?"

Naldo nodded, "The owner's a music freak. Knew Benjamin Britten. Big collection of CDs and tapes. That do you?"

"I'll let you know. Happy coincidence, Nald. The nonfiction is always odder than the fiction, yes?" Herbie disappeared from the car and within five minutes headlights flashed behind Railton's Lincoln. Dawn had now broken and the very early morning traffic had started to thicken.

Naldo watched the car pull off at the supermarket. He followed them, checking his mirror all the way, and parked with a good view of the road and of Herbie's Cutlass which was settled into a slot near the bank of three public telephones. Naldo suddenly felt very happy. He was up and running again, doing what he had loved all his working life. It felt good.

He saw Big Herbie plodding to the telephones and had a pretty shrewd idea of what the old agent was about to do. In some measure, Naldo wished he was doing it, but the numbers would have been changed years ago.

At the telephone, Herbie dialed a toll-free 800 number. It was a number that went unlisted, even to the U.S. telephone companies. Possibly the FBI, NSA and CIA knew it, but there was no way they could tap into the secure line at the distant end, which just goes to show that certain clandestine services never change. In London, it was just after eleven in the morning when the Duty Officer's international line rang.

AT THE OFFICE, in London, there was a panic in progress. The D.O. had hauled Worboys in at six in the morning. Cursing, Young Worboys had done his best to contain matters. Now, at ten thirty, there was a gathering in the Chief's office. Worboys, Arthur Railton and a tall, leggy, very desirable but tough silken blonde lady called Pucky Curtiss (Patricia Ursula Curtiss: the initials made into Puc during schooldays, from thence to Puck and onwards to Pucky).

Ms. Curtiss, who was clad in a blue dress that swirled around her body in an overstated sexual manner, was the Office's highly efficient liaison with the U.S. CIA Resident in Grosvenor Square. For Grosvenor Square read U.S. Embassy. Now she was holding forth in the Chief's office, pacing the floor like a prosecuting attorney in an American law court drama.

"I have to tell him something, for Chrissake." She turned her large brown eyes on the Chief, who saw in them the possible germ of murder. "What *do* I tell him? That we have no control over Kruger? That we have no idea how, or why, he's done it? I *do* have to give the man answers." The "man" was Dan Hochella, the current Resident at Grosvenor Square, known, predictably, to all as "Desperate Dan," an apt description, for Mr. Hochella was subject to moments of profound gloom. He also had a way with the ladies, which was one of the reasons Ms. Curtiss had been given the job. Sources had it that Pucky had kneed him in the groin during their first meeting.

"I would suggest"—the Chief did not look her in the eyes—"I would suggest you tell him the truth."

"Which is what, sir?" Her feet were planted apart, almost in a boxer's stance, except that she looked very cool in the blue dress. Art Railton noticed you could see her body moving under the floating material.

"That we are as much in the dark as he is. Kruger was last seen with Passau, and for all we know, they've both been abducted, which is a definite possibility."

"He'll probe."

"So let him probe, Pucky," from Young Worboys. "We've told them all we're going to tell them. That's it. As far as our relatives in the United States are concerned, we've given them everything. Right, Chief?"

"Absolutely," responded the Head of the Secret Intelligence Service without much conviction. "In any case, everyone here's up to their eyes checking on the Kremlin, and the steady trickle of States out of the hole at the bottom of the old Soviet Union. Chaos, my dear. Chaos and the pestilence that walketh in darkness."

44

"He's not going to believe us." Pucky Curtiss bit her pretty lip. "He hasn't believed us from the word go, and you know why."

"Tell us," Arthur Railton said quietly from his chair in the corner. "Tell us why."

"Because we haven't let him have access to Brightwater, which is his right. The agreement was always that we share the take from Brightwater."

"Haven't finished drying him out, Pucky. Don't want strangers loping around Warminster and making him nervous." Worboys was fairly convincing.

"Try it." The Chief put on his commanding tone, which was not quite as convincing as that of Worboys.

"I'll do my best. But please don't blame me if it backfires and we have the heavy mob from Langley breathing down our necks." She stood for a moment, then turned towards the door. "I'd better go before I lose my nerve."

"Good girl," said the Chief in an unfortunately patronizing tone.

Ms. Curtiss' face was storm-tossed as she left.

"You really think he'll bring Langley around our necks?" Neither Worboys nor Art Railton could tell which one of them was being addressed so they both answered.

"Yes!" said Art.

"No!" Worboys volleyed.

A three-click pause, then—

"No!" said Art.

"Yes!" Worboys equally confident; and at that moment the red telephone screeched on the Chief's desk.

He picked it up automatically, then his eyes widened. Placing his hand over the mouthpiece he hissed, "It's Kruger, on the secure international line." He looked quite frightened.

"You want me to talk with him, sir?" Worboys took a pace towards the desk. Arthur Railton did not attempt to move out of his chair.

The Chief passed the telephone over to Young Worboys who muttered, "Deputy Chief, put him on. . . . Herbie? Where in hell are you and what the hell're you up to?"

At the distant end, some three thousand miles away, Herbie wished Worboys a "Good morning," and then added, "What the hell you think I'm doing? Playing the trivial pursuing? I'm looking after our fellow. He's one nice old man."

"I don't care if he's Santa Claus, Herb. Get him back to the Yanks, tout-bloody-suite."

"So he can get himself killed? Worboys, you're a *dummkopf*. This man, twice yesterday, nearly got frozen, and for all I know the Yanks did it."

"He's legally their man, Herb. You nicked him. . . ."

"Ja, in the nick of time I nicked him. This man is Semtex. . . ."

"Dynamite."

"Dynamite, Semtex who cares? He'll make one hell of a bang. Even though Mikhail Sergeyevich has outlawed the Communist Party. Think of all those guys out of work: the thousands who've lived their whole lives for Marx and Lenin. Wasted lives if they stop believing now."

"You give him back, Herb, that's an order. Where are you, by the way?"

"Yes."

"What d'you mean, 'yes'?"

"I'm by the way, and that's where I'm staying. You ask I should go through him like the Montezuma's revenge through a chicken. I'm about to do that. You get the entire product when I've finished. You ask me to do it, then don't beef about it. That right, beef?"

"Yes, Herbie, full marks, a gold star and a green rabbit." By now, Worboys was weary of Herbie's games and his solo activity.

"Good, just wanted to let you know I'm doing what you asked. 'Bye, old sheep."

"Herbie, wait . . . Herb. Oh shit . . . sorry, sir." Worboys quietly replaced the instrument and said Herbie would not tell him a thing, only that he was doing the job they sent him out to do.

"Well, then, we can't really complain." The Chief looked up and smiled benignly.

"All sorts of hell're going to break loose," Worboys began, but Arthur Railton leaned forward in his chair and raised a hand.

"I think I know where Herb would go with his prize," he said, almost in a whisper.

"Where?"

"He'd run to my father. After all, it was my father who inducted him; recruited him from the Americans all those years ago. You want me to call and see?"

There was a good half-minute's silence.

"Not quite yet, I think." The Chief leaned back. "That's a connection the Americans will make. I think we should stay at a distance for the time being."

"If they catch him, they'll lock him up and lose the key. Probably won't even tell us about it. As for Sunray we can kiss him good-bye." Arthur sounded as desperate as Mr. Hochella of Grosvenor Square. Worboys looked at the Chief with some awe. C was rarely as precise as this. Usually he needed propping up and helping across the streets of Whitehall, while he blustered and shouted. The awe fell away quickly.

"Brightwater?" The Chief mulled the crypto over his tongue, as though it was something almost new to him. "Just for the record, would you put the entire Brightwater business into perspective for me."

Both Worboys and Arthur Railton inwardly groaned. "Brightwater" was the kingpin, the hub, the fount of all knowledge, and he had been in the debriefing center at Warminster for some time now.

"But, sir, you've seen all the relevant . . ."

"Oh, yes, Worboys, but you know me. I see my job here as strictly administrative. The cloak and dagger stuff's your department. I don't keep it all up here." He tapped his forehead.

Just for the record, they went through it all again. Last November had been what they all called the Time of Paradox. The time when every available body was out trawling in Eastern Europe and, at the same time, they were hanging out the "Not Hiring" sign in London.

The "Not Hiring" sign was for the influx of would-be walk-ins. They came from all over Eastern Europe. Members of the East German Stasi—the secret police—and the HvA, the external branch of East German Intelligence; from the appalling Zomo goon squads in Poland; the Czech STB; and Bulgaria's Darjavna Sugurnost, the DS.

Low-grade informers and intelligence officers hurled themselves like lemmings into the arms of the British and American Services and, for the most part, were tossed back again.

The thinking was that those who now ran for cover from the Eastern Bloc intelligence and security services would be the least employable. The good people had already slipped off to Moscow to continue work for the KGB which, in spite of some cosmetic surgery, went on in its own sweet way, a fact which had come into clear focus with the August coup. Now, the KGB chairman was under arrest, while others shoveled documents into the shredders as though there would be no tomorrow—as there probably would not be for many of them.

During the early days of that time of change, there were exceptions to the rule. Erik Ring was one. For at least a year, the word had been out that Erik the Red, as he was known, was up for rent, and possibly for sale. Colonel Erik Ring, Head of Liaison between the East German HvA and their masters in Moscow. For fifteen years, Ring had shuttled between Berlin and Moscow; sat in at conferences and briefings; seen the files; and had worked very close to the great Markus Wolf himself—unofficially code-named Karla, because a world-class espionage novelist had used him as a model for one of his major characters, in a trilogy.

In October 1989, Erik Ring truly saw the writing on the wall, and it did not say *"Mene, Mene, Tekel, Upharsin."* Instead it said, "A United Germany is Coming—Possibly with overtones of Democracy." His wavering ceased and he walked, with hundreds of East German day-trippers, across the broken Wall and did not return. Instead he turned himself in to the local SIS Supremo, one Sidney Swinefort. Ring and Swinefort knew each other by reputation and had fought in the *nacht und nebel* of the Cold War. Now they met as brother intelligence men and, within a dozen hours, Ring was in Britain, and on his way to Warminster and a very long debrief. The take from these sessions was to be made available to a Fellow of St. Anthony's College, Oxford, and a long-term KGB defector who were collaborating on what were planned to be the ultimate in Cold War histories. A quartet of books had already been snapped up for undisclosed sums by publishers from all over the place. People in the business already referred to them as "The definitive truth emerging from a huge body of lies."

Even if a written pardon came straight from the Kremlin—with copies to everyone from the President of the U.S.A. to the Prime Minister, downwards, Ring would stay put. His benefactors, also, would under no circumstances admit to having him as their guest. His crypto was, almost obviously, Brightwater, and nobody could deny that the first week's yield from their new asset was spectacular. It was shared, with honesty. All the initial stuff went straight to Langley, via Desperate Dan and the diplomatic pouch, as well as to St. Anthony's, Oxford.

Before John Stretchfield's book, *Hitler's Unknown Spies* was published, the office had advance proofs—it was required reading for all senior officers and departmental heads. Young Worboys devoured his copy in one night and, purely by chance, took it with him to Warminster on his weekly visit to Erik the Red.

That night, they hauled Worboys out of bed at two in the morning. The word was that Erik had gone berserk and was yelling for a senior man from the Office. He would talk with the confessors present, but someone from the Office had to be there: preferably the Chief. The Chief was away on one of his jaunts to Chequers to show off to the P.M., so Worboys was whipped down by car.

Erik was still dressed, sitting in the one easy chair under the framed World War II "Careless Talk Costs Lives" poster, considered to be a little joke by the Warminster confessors. Stretchfield's book was open on his lap and he had a demented look in his eyes.

"What's to do, Erik, getting me out of bed in the wee smalls?" Worboys could see it had to be something more than a normal defector's tantrum. They could usually deal with those at Warminster without bothering the gentlemen from London.

"Look," Erik motioned for him to come close.

The book was open at the twelve pages of photographs, in the middle of which was a glossy of Louis Passau on the box—as they call the podium in the orchestral trade.

Erik stabbed at the picture with his forefinger. He stabbed as though trying to kill it, and he stabbed four times to coincide with his words—

"This man is Kingfisher!" It was as though he had found the Holy Grail.

"You want coffee, Erik, because I do?"

Ring gave Worboys a look which said he was mad to talk about drinking coffee at this juncture. "This is historic moment," he said quietly.

"That's when I usually drink coffee." Worboys asked the confessors to get hold of someone who would make coffee at this hour in the morning. He then squatted down on the floor close to Erik. "So tell me about Kingfisher."

"I once saw a surveillance photograph. In Dzherzhinsky Square. The photograph was of this man, the man . . ." he squinted at the caption, "the man, Passau."

"So?"

"So it was what they call at the Center, buried treasure. Kingfisher was a long-term asset. Untouchable because he was outside the military and the establishment. He was KGB's prime source against the American target, because he had confidence of generals and politicians in United States. He passed on only stellar category information."

Worboys felt his heart turn over. Later, he swore that he stopped breathing. "If he was buried treasure, Erik, how can you finger this guy? He's an orchestra conductor, for chrissake."

Erik the Red nodded with some vigor. "Okay," he croaked. "Okay. I explain. When we did the update briefings in Moscow . . ."

"Who's we?"

"Wolf, Mischa Wolf, and myself. Every six months we did four days, sometimes five. For years we were told that material had come from Kingfisher. Great material. Hearts and minds material, not how many tanks or the morale of U.S. Army. Nothing technical; just tremendous stuff: about the way the military and current establishment were thinking. It was as though Kingfisher was able to climb into people's minds. Proved correct time and time again. Kingfisher was most successful asset against the U.S.A. on the political front. Like KGB had a crystal ball in Washington."

"For how long? How long had they run Kingfisher?"

"They bought him—1959 . . . sixty. Bought him and paid for him. Never did Kingfisher let them down. In eighty-three, when KGB was misreading signals from Reagan, and we were near nuclear catastrophe, it was Kingfisher who shone true light on the situation."

"Okay." The coffee arrived, but Worboys was interested only in what Erik the Red had to say. "Okay, Erik, but how did you put the face to the man, if he was such a buried treasure."

Erik nodded, as though he knew what Worboys was thinking. "Almost accident," he said finally. "Mischa and I, we were with the Chairman. KGB Chairman. It was in Andropov's time. We were in his office. Dzherzhinsky Square office. There were photographs on his desk. Grainy: you could tell they were surveillance because of the quality. There were four of this man." He glanced down at the book again. "Four of Passau. I think Mischa recognized him because, now I remember, he said to Andropov, 'Yuri Vladimirovich, why take pictures of a man who beats time for an orchestra?' Andropov laughed, and said that this man beat in Soviet time. Then he tapped the picture"—Erik the Red touched the photograph in the book to demonstrate. "He tapped the picture and said, 'Kingfisher, Mischa. This is our Kingfisher.'"

"And you didn't recognize Louis Passau, Erik?"

Erik Ring gave a monstrous shrug. "Music I do not know. I was born with a defect. Tone deaf. Music deaf. I couldn't tell a piano from a guitar, my friend. So I've never read about music or listened—except for one time in Moscow they make us go to Bolshoi. For me this is agony." He looked hard at Worboys, and then back at the picture of Passau. "But I do know this is Kingfisher."

From that moment, the confessors at Warminster were put onto dragging all memories of Kingfisher from Brightwater, Colonel Ring, or Erik the Red, whichever you liked to call him. They first went over his story in detail, then, when they were satisfied, they began to bludgeon every trace of Kingfisher's intelligence from their defector. They drew out details of Kingfisher's work, the grades of intelligence he provided, the way in which the job was done. They searched through Brightwater's mind, beckoning out things that their subject had forgotten he knew, for that is the special art of a skilled confessor. Within a month they had a list of close friends and acquaintances with whom Passau lunched, dined, invited to his concerts and spent free time.

Next the list was checked against another, prepared by the Office's Washington Resident. A couple of weeks after that they had just about all the names: generals, senators, men and women—and their wives and husbands—who held great power; people whose thoughts and ideas shaped their country's policies.

Here, in the present, refreshing the Chief's memory, Worboys told him, "If Passau was a Soviet source, he was just the kind of source they needed now, at the bargaining time, at the hour of new birth."

"And we told our American friends exactly what?" The Chief did not look at either of his men.

"Practically everything." Arthur Railton was cagey, and his superior sensed it.

"Let me put it another way." This time he did look at them. "What did we hold back from our American allies?"

There was an uncomfortable silence before Worboys spoke again. "We didn't tell them what we know about Passau's musical tour of the Eastern Bloc, for one thing."

"And what do we know? Remind me; humor me."

"That, under suspicious and clandestine circumstances, earlier this year, he met with former senior officers of the intelligence and security services of East Germany, Bulgaria, Czecho, Poland and Hungary. The hard-line people who appear to have gone underground. The guys who know where all the bodies are buried and who buried them."

The CSIS sucked his teeth. "Anything else?"

"The Mossad, sir. We didn't explain about the two days when he was supposed to be taking rehearsals in Tel Aviv. The couple of days he spent in a safe house. From long range it looks as though he's playing both ends against the middle, if you follow me, sir?"

"That it?" The zealot's eyes bored into Worboys, and the silence stretched to breaking point. Then—

"We didn't tell them about the White House, sir. We didn't tell them how close Passau was to White House sources."

"Well, does that really matter now?"

"Probably does, sir. Yes, it probably does, if only for the history books, and we have people writing the books."

"But our brothers in Virginia must know he has friends in the White House."

"Well, yes. But they certainly don't know about the ones he's meeting privately. The ones he's used as unconscious agents—like Roosevelt's right-hand man, Harry Hopkins, was used by Stalin's people in World War II. KGB're very good at running people who haven't the remotest idea that they're agents. We have names, dates, times. We haven't told them about the unconscious agents at the highest level—and I do mean *highest* level, sir."

5

PUCKY CURTISS HAD recently celebrated her thirtieth birthday, so as she waited for a taxi to take her to Grosvenor Square, she felt an upward surge of delight at the covetous glances thrown her way by passing males. It had been ever thus, but it did the power of good to Ms. Curtiss' morale to know that men found her attractive, and—as one horny member of the Service put it—"rompworthy." Standing there in her stylish, somewhat military cut, business suit, Ms. Curtiss looked all peaches and cream with a soft strawberry center. Indeed, when the time and partner matched up, she could be these things: soft, yielding, passionate and memorable. But Pucky was off men at the moment. A very longstanding relationship had ended in tears and a split which had left her emotions as naked as death itself. As her closest confidante, Bitsy Williams, had told her, early in the relationship, "men who don't leave their wives for you in the first year are unlikely ever to do it." She reminded Pucky of her astute words when the man in question had gone off to Greece for a second honeymoon with his wife, though it helped Pucky not one iota. It was not that she had wanted to marry the bastard. It was essentially a matter of pride. Bitsy worked in what the office called "Guest Relations," which called for the handling of visiting firemen, foreign diplomats, and people who were of interest. In turn, this meant she was wise to the ways of philandering males.

The whole look which Pucky had cultivated throughout her life belied a true picture of herself. Sure, she could be as vulnerable as the next woman, yet beneath it all she was as hard as the proverbial nails, as tough as old boots, and her heart, it often had been said, was made of a small chip from the iceberg that sank the *Titanic*. In affairs of passion, she liked to maintain full control.

Pucky had been brought up in a hard school. Her father was a retired general, highly decorated and a legend from the Second World War. Her mother, who was a match for the general which was saying something, had been the daughter of an exceptionally courageous regiment. In layman's terms, this meant she had been spawned by the regiment's commanding officer.

Pucky was their youngest child, an accident after the almost yearly births of four sons. So she had grown up in a surrounding spirit of heavy competition. Two of her brothers were now army colonels, another was a major in the SAS, and the youngest—Pucky's senior by three years—flew Harriers for the Royal Navy.

"How," she would say to Bitsy, "does a girl follow that?" It was a rhetorical question because Pucky *had* followed it. Brilliantly. An athlete and academic at one of the best private schools in the country, she had gone on to read politics and economics at Oxford. There, someone at St. Anthony's College spotted her, gave her an audition and eased the way into the secret world where she had acquitted herself well and risen to dazzling heights. It was said that she might possibly become the first female CSIS. She was certainly earmarked for Head of Research.

Though, to some extent, she had dreaded this morning's meeting with the CIA's London Resident, Dan Hochella did not, in the event, give Pucky Curtiss a bad time. The meeting was uneasy, but the Resident was too full of his own misery to use any subtlety on the lovely Ms. Curtiss.

"I've been summoned back to Langley," he began when they were seated in the sterile room deep within the embassy.

"Summoned, Dan? What d'you mean, *summoned?*"

"They've told me to get my ass outta London, fast." He shrugged, turned down the corners of his mouth and looked as though he were about to die of anguish. "I go Pan Am tonight."

"Well, that'll be lovely for you. I mean you'll be able to see your people." Pucky opened her eyes as wide as possible, a trick she had learned with men at the age of thirteen. It seldom failed.

"People?" He looked at her blankly.

"Oh, I suppose you'd say your folks." She tossed her head, showing signs of petulance.

"I don't wanna see my damned folks. They're on the edge of a divorce again. You'd think my father would grow up. A banker of, what? He must be at least sixty-two, yet there's always some little bimbo secretary or a favored minion."

"Jesus, Dan, it's not always *that* easy for one's people," She leaned forward, as though about to share some great secret. "My people're always having some drama, but it usually works out. It'll be super for you."

Desperate Dan made a humphing noise. "They're gonna roast me, that's for sure. I'll get posted to some outlandish place and lose seniority."

"Why should they do that?" Pucky knew damned well exactly why they should do that, but she had a sharper mind than Dan Hochella. He was quite good-looking and well-built, she thought, in that particular American football star way: all shoulders and teeth.

"You know why, Pucky. We're all gonna be restructured when the new Russia finally emerges. The politicos are already straining at the leash. Budgets'll be shot to hell. Then there's this business with Sunray, and the crock you people have given us from Brightwater."

"What crock?"

"The crock of shit about Sunray."

"We've given you every last ounce we've got." She allowed her face to go blank, a look of innocence which reached far into the back of her mind yet was visible in her eyes. She even willed herself to think she was a virgin.

"Nuts, Pucky. Nuts and double nuts."

"What's that supposed to mean?"

"It means what it says. Your crew has given us a little rich vein on Sunray, but not the whole nine yards. You've kept something back for yourselves, like bloody agents in place. They always do it—keep back something for insurance—now your Office's doing it. . . ."

"That's just not true. They're still working on him."

"Good. I have an official request here asking for one of our interrogators to be allowed to sit in. It comes flash and most urgent from the D.C.I. himself."

"Put it in writing and I'll take it back to the CSIS myself, but I doubt if it'll do any good. They're damned touchy that lot down at Warminster. . . ."

"It *is* in writing." He all but threw a heavy cream envelope onto the desk. "The point is that *our* intelligentsia are getting ultra touchy. Shit, Puck, have you seen the signals? Bloodshed and mayhem, people killed for Chrissake; and your retired Joe is now wandering around somewhere with the asset. *Our* asset. Langley wants to know what your man's up to."

Pucky put on her serious, slightly angry, face and snapped back, "As it happens, I come with equally purposeful concerns. To put it bluntly, my Chief wants to know what your gang have done with the asset and our man. They're *both* missing, Dan, and we have need-to-know where the hell they've gone. The CSIS is concerned for *our* man's safety. He wants you to let Langley know we're not happy. Blue Boy, as I have to call him, came back into the operation from a happy retirement. There'll be all hell to pay if he's been flushed down the tubes. If something chancy's happened to him, you can forget anything else we learn from Erik the Red. It's *that* serious, Dan."

Hochella began to look even more mournful. He spluttered for a few moments, then said they had better go and talk about it over lunch, which they ate at the Connaught, Ms. Curtiss making sure that Mr. Hochella picked up the tab. They parted amicably, with a vague agreement to keep in touch, and a definite understanding that each would return to their superiors with messages of doom.

It was almost four thirty when Pucky got back to the office to find Shirley, her slightly shop-soiled secretary, in a tizzy. The Chief wanted to see her. He had been calling constantly for two hours.

The meeting was still going on in the Chief's office: Worboys pacing the floor, and Arthur Railton looking calm in one of the more comfortable chairs. They made Pucky go through everything.

"Stalemate, then?" The Chief looked around as though he hoped they would all agree with him.

"So it would seem, sir." Pucky had emphasized that she had given as good as she had got.

"Right, Worboys, get onto Grosvenor Square and tell them their request is denied—the sit-in at Warminster, that is—until they find our man for us."

"You want it laid on with a trowel, or kept cool but firm?"

"Lay it on like a stonemason building a wall."

"Let's hope they don't find him, then," from Arthur Railton. "Knowing Herb he'll be mightily pissed off—sorry, sir—if anyone butts in on his private interrogation."

Worboys departed, and the CSIS gazed upon Ms. Pucky Curtiss as though she were a precious icon. "Ms. Curtiss, please sit down." He gave her one of his rare benign smiles: the one which, Pucky thought, he would give to some heathen he was about to convert to Presbyterian ways. For all her courage, that kind of smile scared the crap out of her. She sat.

"Could you remind me of your field experience?" The CSIS still smiled, and she thought, probably because Art Railton was there, of Shakespeare: Richard of Gloucester in *Henry VI* plotting for the crown that will make him Richard III:

> Why, I can smile, and murder whiles I smile;
> And cry content to that which grieves my heart;
> And wet my cheeks with artificial tears,
> And frame my face to all occasions.

No wonder the Railton family used Shakespeare like the Bible. When it came to the artifice of the secret trade, William S. wrote the book, she thought before she spoke—

"I have no direct field experience, sir." Suddenly aware that Arthur Railton was sitting very still, as though waiting for some huge event to take place, like the parting of the Red Sea, so she added, "And I'm not likely to get any now the main enemy target's changed beyond recognition."

"Oh, I don't know about that. We'll require field officers there for many years to come. Then, of course, there are our friends. Always have to keep an eye on them, my dear." He leaned forward in a more conspiratorial hunch. "But you've done certain things, I know that, Ms. Curtiss. You've couriered, for instance."

"Emptied a couple of letterboxes, yes. I also took a package to the Prague Resident last year. I wouldn't call that field work."

"Maybe," the CSIS clucked. "Maybe, and maybe not. You *have* done the courses though. . . ." It was not really a question, but a kind of statement, left drifting in the air like a wraith.

Pucky nodded. She was getting incredibly dangerous vibes from Art. "Just the usual, sir. Tradecraft One and Two; Evasion; Documents; False Flag One; and the short crypto course."

"Enough. How did she do, Arthur?" The thin face flashed suddenly towards Art Railton, like someone trying to left foot an opponent.

"Alpha Plus on all of them. She's marked as capable of field work and speaks French, German and Spanish like a native."

"Like an Afghan tribesman to be honest." As she said it, Pucky knew she should not be joking.

"The point is, Ms. Curtiss." The Chief looked as though he were standing in front of a Sunday morning congregation and about to deliver a sermon. "The point is that there are two possibilities regarding Kruger and . . ."

"Blue Boy, sir," Art reminded him.

"I think we can dispense with the cryptos, Railton. Two possibilities regarding Kruger and old Passau. Either they're the victims of foul play, or Kruger's got Passau holed up somewhere and is drying him out. Something by which we might just benefit." His pause was studied. "Now, we know that the first option is out. Just after you went off to see our beloved brother in Christ at Grosvenor Square, Kruger telephoned us. We know he's safe, and he's with Passau. However, we would like to feel that our friends in Washington and at Langley really believe the first option is very much on the cards."

"Oh, I think they will, sir." Time to be bright and positive, Pucky considered.

"Yes, well, that's good. Meanwhile we really don't want Kruger to be running around with Passau on his own. If they could be corralled and shipped back here until all the work's done, it might be a good idea, yes?"

"I see the point, sir. Yes."

"Well, Arthur here thinks he knows where Kruger might be."

"He does?"

"Arthur, repeat to the lady what you've said to me."

Herbie, Art Railton told her, had been very close to his father, Naldo Railton. "He was barely fourteen or fifteen when Naldo took him from an OSS officer in Berlin. It was during the interregnum, when the OSS eventually became the CIA. They worked together, on various matters, for years, and Naldo often told me they could almost read one another's handwriting by ESP. They were *that* close."

Now, Naldo lived in Virginia. "I think Herb would make straight for him, and it won't take long for our American brothers to figure the same thing. They have dossiers six inches thick on both Kruger and my father. But they're a pair of wily old players. It's my guess that my old man has already got Herbie stashed away with Maestro Passau. He'll be watching both their backs, and my mother'll be running interference. By tonight, U.S. time, the FBI and CIA'll have my ma and pa under surveillance, but

I don't fancy anyone's chances of getting really near, or thinking that pa'll lead them straight to Herb."

"So, what're you suggesting?" Pucky already had a sinking feeling in her stomach.

"Well, Dan Hochella knows you, and he's heading back to Washington. Apart from that, the American service would think of you merely as a desk agent. Most would probably never even recognize you."

"Let me guess." Pucky did not want it spelled out. "You're going to suggest that I take a few weeks of my leave and visit the States, right?"

"Right."

The CSIS nodded but said nothing.

"And I'm not going in as plain Patricia Ursula Curtiss, Civil Servant, but as Joan Doe, schoolmarm, or some other such, right?"

"Almost dead right. There's a symposium next week at the University of Virginia, in Charlottesville. A get-together, lectures, small study groups of what our American cousins call 'educators.' We thought you could possibly be an 'educator,' Pucky."

"From some red-brick campus? With a special knowledge of"—she held up a hand to stop Arthur from filling in the gaps—"special knowledge of, say, the Napoleonic wars, or some other period of military endeavor."

The CSIS tilted his hand, smiling a murderer's smile, "Not quite but you're almost there."

They suggested that she should be barefaced and fly directly into Washington, then hop down to the Charlottesville–Albemarle County airport. "It's only half an hour's ride, and you needn't go near UVa," Art said. "That's just there as a backup. But I'll fill you in on how to get close to ma or pa, whichever's the easiest."

"You see, my dear." The CSIS even more avuncular now. "We've got a great deal riding on Mr. Kruger's interrogation of Louis Passau—particularly when the old guard at what used to be Moscow Center are doubtless shredding documents like mad. I'm sure he'd welcome help from home."

Pucky got back to her apartment in Dolphin Square at eleven that night. In the meantime she had gone through a long briefing, complete with numerous options should they wish to bring the internationally famous Passau back to the U.K. She had acquired a new persona, money, credit cards and paper in the name of Pauline Una Cummings—and some extra identities—plus a return air ticket, economy class, B.A. In the morning, she would be off to sample the delights of the United States for the first time in her life. That she had never been to the U.S. before was considered a bonus by both Art Railton and the CSIS.

She looked at herself in the mirror and noted the puffy circles under her eyes; she felt fat and ugly, for the Khmer Rouge had just completed their monthly incursion.

"Oh, shit!" she said loudly. Then again, "Shit! I look like a bag lady."

6

"Is the best bloody safe house I ever been in." Herbie gave his huge smile, opened his arms wide and did a strange, uncoordinated, but rather graceful pirouette. "Don't you think so, Lou? The best bloody safe house ever."

"Pleasant, I think. Yes, pleasant." He looked older now, slumped in a large easy chair with his face the color of parchment. Herbie put it down to fatigue. The old boy had not slept properly since the Birthday Concert. Now, his eyes were slightly sunken and red, the skin around his neck sagged, and his hands trembled. It was the first time that Herbie had seen the shaking of his hands. They were large, solid, the hands of a manual worker—not a musician. "Very pleasant," the Maestro said again, dropping his voice as though that was also shot with fatigue.

The house was certainly pleasant. Old, by American standards. Around the latter part of the eighteenth century, Herbie thought. Solid, red brick, nicely weathered, well-maintained with the window frames high-glossed, and one wall covered in Virginia creeper—what else?

To begin with, they sat in the car waiting for Naldo to come out and say all was well. He emerged after fifteen minutes. "She's delighted. Stash the car away around the back, Herb. There's a garage, an old barn really; takes about six cars and a couple of tractors."

When the car was well out of sight, Herbie took Passau's bag and went to the front again, where Naldo waited by the door.

"I'll give you the twenty-five-cent tour." He grinned and the old, boyish look that Herbie remembered so well came into his eyes and face. "The owner spent a fortune on having this place done over."

"A 'she' you say, Nald?"

"Yes, a lady I know and trust. Dependable."

They passed through the front door into a wide hallway, which was more than your average lobby. This was enormous, with high windows and plants positioned to make it look more like a conservatory. It obviously stretched right back through the entire depth of the house, and centered in the far wall were a pair of huge French windows opening onto a formal terrace: very English, with stone urns sprouting flowers, and a spectacular view up the small valley which ended abruptly, about a quarter of a mile away, hard against the foothills, which rose and were swallowed up by the Blue Ridge.

The topographical shape instantly reminded Kruger of the conjunction of a woman's thighs. For a second he thought of Martha and realized he did not even miss her; then he mentally blushed to think that a man of his age, all of fifty-eight years, could still have the thoughts of a randy twenty-two-year-old boy.

He turned to Passau, "Lou?" very serious. "Lou, you do *not* go out of those windows. Never, understand?"

"I can't take a walk in the yard?"

"You don't even go near them, Lou. Look up there, is a perfect place for a sniper. You go outside one morning and—boom!"

"Boom?"

"As in boom, where's the top of my fucking head, okay? No going out there."

Passau nodded. "But how am I to exercise?" he asked. "My daily exercise is important."

"You'll just have to extemporate."

Naldo almost corrected Herbie, but thought better of it.

"You'll have to do your pressings-up and sittings-up inside the house and away from the windows," Herb said with the finality of one of those red statements which threaten legal action if you do not pay up.

Maestro Passau shrugged, and Naldo continued with the grand tour. The owner had gutted the place and started from scratch with much flair and inventiveness.

The left-hand side of the house was given over completely to bedrooms on each of its four levels. A door from the hall/conservatory led to a passage which, in turn, housed a door to the master bedroom, and a flight of smooth pine stairs which seemed to float upwards in a slow spiral. The stairs led to three landings, one above the other, from which passages ran to other bedrooms, equipped with bathrooms, Jacuzzis, "The works," as Naldo said. "The works, like a stylish hotel."

Herbie quietly sang "There's no place like home," slightly off-key.

On the right of the conservatory, a huge, broad, plain, polished staircase, also in pine, rose within a great shaft, the three floors above hemmed in by sturdy balcony rails, and supported by solid, ancient beams. Opposite, large windows were set into the right-hand gable end of the house. The wall, separated by a good twenty feet from the staircase, was dotted with large oil paintings of indisputable age. The owner's ancestors, Naldo said, pointing out each one as they climbed upwards. The uniformed martinet had been at Blenheim; there were two somber-looking politicians from the eighteenth and nineteenth centuries; a cheery little goblin who, according to Naldo, had been the black sheep and dabbled in music: mid-eighteenth century; and a cleric who was once Bishop of Winchester, Naldo thought, or was it York?

To his surprise, Herbie cocked his head and said if it were York he would be an archbishop. "Must have been Winchester, then." Naldo did not think of Herbie as a man who had ecclesiastical knowledge. "Winchester or some such."

The first floor above them was cleverly divided, the largest portion being a dining room with a Jacobean table that would seat around twenty people; a barlike structure separated this from the kitchen, pine again, beautifully made fixtures and fittings, with ovens and hobs on different levels and all the modern means of survival from microwave through dishwasher to a refrigerator in which you could probably keep two cows. Naldo said the conversion had been done by Mennonites. There were many Mennonite communities in this part of Virginia, and their craftsmen had no equal.

The floor directly above the dining room/kitchen was what the owner would call a drawing room, and, above that the library, the shelves stacked with books new and old, many with priceless pedigrees. It seemed that the deceased oil magnate had invested well in rare books. In some ways this was the coziest room in the place, for it contained comfortable chairs, and a complex stereo system with rack upon rack of CDs and records. It was here that Herbie and Passau both knew they would spend the bulk of their time, and now it was in the library that Naldo worked out a shopping list with Kruger. Food, drink, staples, and even clothes and toiletries for Big Herb, for he had, as Naldo laughingly said, using the ancient argot, "got out in his socks."

They also made arrangements for clandestine communication. Telephone rings: three if FBI was on to Naldo; four get out fast; five to say all was safe and Naldo felt happy about coming to the place without leeches on his back; lastly, six followed by a pause to the count of ten, then a further ring at which Herb would pick up.

"You are to give the five rings even if you come straight back with the shopping," Kruger cautioned him, worried because he felt Naldo's age was showing, and had not liked the fact that he had managed to sidle up to his old mentor's car in Ruckersville and take him by surprise. "Please, Nald, behave like in the old days, like in the Cold War, full warning flags. If you can't get to us, use some other method. This is all bloody dangerous. Somebody took serious potshots at Maestro Passau. They were out to kill, and I don't know who is the 'they.'"

Herbie had also taken a good look around the doors and windows. The place was fitted with an expensive alarm system, but Kruger was rarely satisfied with home alarm systems that he had not installed personally. He asked Railton if certain simple electronic things could be purchased, and looked relieved when told that Radio Shack usually carried most of the items which came to mind.

So Naldo drove away, and they waited: Passau sitting dozing in an easy chair, and Herbie wandering from room to room. Though he was a large man, and heavy, Kruger was light on his feet when the need arose. Even awake, Passau would have had problems hearing him: anyone would have had problems.

When he returned to the library, Big Herbie Kruger stood, looking down on the dozing figure, and cursed to himself. He would not be able to start today, that was for certain. Passau was far too tired, and what had to be done quickly was going to take time.

In his head he heard Young Worboys and Naldo's son, Arthur, talking to him only a few days ago.

"Herb, old sport, this man's a time bomb, and you really do have to get to him pretty quickly." This was Worboys, who had cut his teeth on operations with Kruger. Herbie thought of a line from a T. S. Eliot poem, "Here I am, an old man in a dry month, being read to by a boy, waiting for rain." That was how it felt taking instructions from Worboys.

"While the Americans are bound to be a trifle worried, we just haven't told them the real angst. Only *you* know how close this genius is to White House sources; and only you know who talks to him, and I mean talks— very indiscreet. If he's played his cards as we think, then the born-again democratic Soviets'll know exactly how the White House is thinking; what they will do and what they will not do, and that's one hell of a piece of information."

"Advantage U.S.S.R.," Arthur muttered.

"Game, set and match, as Len Deighton would say, ja?" Herbie grinned.

"Shake, rattle and roll," Worboys muttered.

"You like Deighton's books, Herb?" Arthur again.

"Sure, Art. I read them from covert to covert."

In his corner, Tony Worboys smiled. "Don't forget, Herb, that you're the *one* person over there who knows what Passau was up to during his 'Freedom Tour' of the Eastern Bloc. The only person who knows the names of the people he saw, and the only person who knows he was in constant contact with the new underground—the hard-line underground, some of whom just tried the Judas kiss on Mikhail Sergeyevich."

"Ja, sure." Herbie gave a dismissive twist of the hand. " I know it all: dates, times; places and people. I got it up here." He tapped his forehead with his right forefinger and grinned. "Also the American stuff's in same place. Inside thick skull. Can't get out unless they take electric drill to it." He widened the grin and Worboys thought of pumpkins and Halloween.

Now, in the present, the telephone was ringing. Five times, so Naldo was coming in.

"Nobody's called my place, and I've told Barb to go out. I'm meeting her for lunch, but she's been watching my back. It's like old times." Naldo seemed like a child allowed to play his favorite game.

There was enough food to keep them for a week; shirts, underwear, socks, jeans, pajamas and toiletries for Kruger, as well as two boxes of electronic gizmos, batteries, wire, pliers and a small set of screwdrivers.

Herbie paid him with Amex traveler's checks made out to the Buckerbee identity.

"Still playing spies while Eastern Europe finds its democratic legs," Naldo said, with a wry look. "To hear it on this side of the ocean, it's all over bar the shouting."

"On this side of the ocean, is what they want to hear." Herbie did not smile. "Eastern Europe, a new anticommunist democracy? Believe it when it's all done."

"Quite right, Herb. Democracies aren't built in a day."

Kruger gave a caustic laugh. "You know what I worry about, Nald? My own old country. Somewhere, somewhen, a little guy with a Charlie Chaplin mustache is going to come popping out of the woodshed, and it'll be Sieg Heil all over again. My own race still believes themselves masters of Europe. First they'll take the economic market, then they'll want other powers. Give it fifteen years."

"And the ex-Soviets?"

"Come on, Naldo. It's part of thousands of people's life-style, for God's sake. Nip and tuck, a little surgery, maybe. Open frontiers? Good idea. Open market if they ever get the hang of it. Mind you, works both ways. Sure, end of communism, but none of them have experience in openness. Democracy they know from nothing. Going to take a while. Couple of decades, maybe more; and in the very deep water sharks still swim."

Naldo would keep in touch, inform of progress in the outside world, if and when he could. Kruger gave him a great bear hug as he left. "Watch your back, Naldo. We don' know good guys from bad guys no more." Then the large man lumbered upstairs to ask what Passau fancied to eat.

He found the Maestro carefully going through the CD and record collections. "The owner of this place has good music," Passau smiled. "Got most of my recordings, but it's a great collection. No Beethoven symphonies, only the quartets, which shows a serious collector; all Britten; the good Bach; plenty Mozart; all Jandek; some Bruckner; Penderecki, would you believe? A lot of Americans—Virgil Thompson; Barber; Copland; Gershwin—except the Rhapsody, thank God—and Bernstein. Ha, Lenny should be so lucky, he would have loved it, rest in peace: all three symphonies, the *Chichester Psalms*, and the Mass. Ah, and she—it is a she, Herbie?"

"Ja, it's a she."

"She's on your wavelength, all of Mahler and then some. She has five recordings of the Second: mine, naturally, Solti, Bernstein, Inbal and Kaplan." He browsed further, "Oy, and all of Shostakovich, some of it twice. This woman has taste. Strauss, all Verdi and Puccini. My God, and all Wagner, including my *Dutchman*. Now that was a recording session. Five weeks we took, with temperaments flying to all corners of the studio, and the orchestra—*my* orchestra—behaved impeccably, but the singers . . . no, I won't embarrass them by even mentioning it."

"Good." Herbie did not care if the singers had all gone on strike and chanted mantras. Passau glanced at him, a look of alarm crossing his face.

"What's wrong?"

"Lou, who tried to take you out?"

"Who? I have an idea who."

"Soviets?"

Passau laughed, four musical notes repeated. Then again. "You think they'd be that stupid in this day and age? Anyway, why would the Russian democrats want to ice me, Herb?"

"That's for you to tell me. I need to know—and know fast—about the last four, five, years. Maybe more. Urgent I should hear about last two years."

Passau gave a shrug, using his arms as well as his shoulders, the hands turning outwards in an undeniable gesture. "I'll give you all the help I can, Herbie, but it has to move in a straight line. Like impossible to tell you the last two years until we reach them. To help you, I have to explain the whys, and to explain the whys, we have a long journey. I told you already, Herb. You *have* to understand; and you cannot understand without hearing the whole thing. You think I was mixed up—*am* mixed up—with the Russians, in their toil towards a new freedom?"

"I know you are."

"Then you know more than I," Passau snapped, "and, in any case, who's interested?"

"History," Herb gave another of his daft smiles. "History, Lou. The whole truth seldom emerges in history, but this time we should try to get it right. Cut out the myths and legends. There have to be great changes. Reorganization—CIA, SIS, KGB certainly. All of them have to be disbanded and rebuilt."

Passau looked at him as though he were a heretic; as if he, the great musician, was part of the Inquisition, ready to torch Kruger for his apostasy. "Too tired to begin now." He sounded weary. "Too fatigued. Tomorrow, after I've rested, I'll begin, and you won't be disappointed. I promise. But don't forget I am an old man now. I am ninety years on this planet, and I've seen everything. There can't be much time left before I shuffle into oblivion. Can we eat, and can we sleep, my friend?"

"Sure, Lou. You play some music and I'll cook you good, okay." He moved towards the stairs, then, "Lou, you aren't kosher are you? I mean with food."

"Gave it up centuries ago."

Below, in the kitchen, Herbie prepared his great tomato sauce—oil, onions, canned tomatoes, tomato paste. He made meatballs, and boiled a large pan of spaghetti. It was all done to Passau's own recording of the Bruckner Fifth, with that incredible finale—the composer's architectural masterpiece, as everyone always wrote in the record notes.

He went up to the library just as the overwhelmingly magnificent last movement reached its final bars, the drum roll and the hint of the fugue subject leaping out like clusters of diamonds.

Passau was in tears. "Maybe I'm just sentimental, but, to me, it's incredible that one, simple man could produce such glory."

He ate heartily, punctuating mouthfuls of food with traces from the music to which he had just listened. "You know, poor old Bruckner never heard the orchestral version of his Fifth Symphony. . . ."

"No?"

"He heard a version for two pianos—I think it was two pianos—but he was too ill to hear it in a concert hall. Incredible, yes, for a man who wrote ten symphonies—if you count the first one, not numbered—eleven maybe, but he didn't hear the Fifth."

"We start work tomorrow, Lou?" Kruger did not want to get into a lecture on Anton Bruckner now. It was late afternoon, and the old man had begun to slow. Christ, Herbie thought, what if I don't get to him? What if the bugger dies on me?' He went on drinking the good red wine, Virginian—a cabernet sauvignon from Montdomaine—that Naldo had brought, while Passau sipped his Saratoga water. Then Herb assisted the old man to his bedroom, unpacked his clothes for him, and saw him settled.

"You got no medication to take, Lou. Nothing the doctor ordered, no?"

"Nowadays, the doctor tells me what I shouldn't do, Herbie. No women, as if that mattered now, no booze, no smoking, but that all went years ago, when I was quite young. Comparatively young."

Kruger cocked an eyebrow. "Yeah, I know. After Greece. After the islands you gave it up. I read the books."

Passau smiled wearily, "The books lie, Herb."

"How?"

"In the usual manner. You believe all you read? You think I'm an idiot? Herbie, *I* wrote the books—or at least made sure they didn't say everything. You *are* talking about the two biographies, yes?"

"One official and one unofficial. I read them twice. So?"

"So they both lie. You notice anything else about those books? I tell you, they present me as someone fully grown, someone appearing in Hollywood as a full-grown man. Only three paragraphs in one book, and two in other mention my childhood. All they say is that I was the son of a German shoemaker. No detail. Nothing. No education; no news from the old country. Nothing. But I talk too much. Tomorrow I give you the lowdown. Full background, warts, blains, boils and everything, like Book of fucking Job, ja? What time we start?"

"Okay, I wake you around eight, huh? Have a little sleep in, Lou, then breakfast—what you like for breakfast?"

"Three cups of black coffee." Passau gave an impish smile which made him look ageless. "That's been my breakfast for more years than I care to remember. Real coffee, mind you, not the frozen granules. The real thing."

"There's nothing else but the real thing." Herbie left him to sleep, knowing the night was far from over for him. The domestic security seemed okay: all the usual stuff, activated by punching numbers into keypads. Naldo had given him all the codes which were, predictably, years: probably the year of the owner's birth, maybe the birth years of her kids and late husband. Why did they do it? He wondered. Always birth years or an amalgamation of birth dates.

Anyway, Kruger was way ahead of Naldo regarding security. The last thing he wanted was the automatic warning going to a central control along the telephone line. The cops would arrive quickly if that happened. No doubt about it. So he disconnected the wiring and began to build his own little system, covering all the doors and windows, also the stairs on both sides of the house. A job done neatly and with great patience.

As he worked, Kruger thought of old Naldo. It was strange seeing him again after so long. Strange and frightening, age bearing down upon his old friend and mentor. About one in the morning, as he worked on a sensor by the large French windows in the conservatory, he thought he heard the lap of water and the sound of a paddle steamer, then realized that his mind was playing tricks.

Years ago he had set up a system like this in a house on a Swiss lakeside. Naldo was there and someone else, he could not quite remember who. His memory played tricks also: perhaps this was the onset of age for him, and it seemed like only a couple of weeks ago that he had met Naldo in a Berlin house, with the American who had been running him. Other words came into his head, hard on the heels of the mental picture of Berlin's rubble and the days spent in Displaced Persons camps.

"We have heard the chimes of midnight," the voice in his head spoke, and he knew then that the voice, long dead, had belonged to another of Naldo's family, all Shakespeareans to a man and woman, always quoting the Bard, consistently apt.

He did not undress, but stretched on top of the bed, dozing. Once he woke with a start, thinking he was back in that same Swiss villa which could have told so many stories. Then he slept again; dreamed again— this time of Berlin, the city of his childhood, and of much of his dangerous manhood also. His dream flitted in and out of an apartment. There was a Dürer pen-and-ink of an Avenging Angel on the wall, and a set of ruby glasses with fluted stems in a cabinet. Also there was a girl called Ursula. She had been an ever-repeating dream over the years, unexorcized by his marriage. His one true and only love in postwar Berlin. Love among the ruins.

At seven he woke, showered, shaved, dressed and made coffee for Passau. It was ten thirty before he got the old Maestro sitting comfortably in the library, ready to put him to the question. It was Passau who took over from the very beginning.

"There are specific things you require of me, Herbie." He looked rested, and back to his former self, a ninety-year-old with a picture in the attic, for he would have passed for sixty—on the stairs, with the light behind him.

"My name is not Passau, for a beginning." He smiled, a loving look that crept into his eyes and spoke of great nostalgia. "My real name was Louis Packensteiner. Louis *Isaak* Packensteiner to be exact, and even that was not the true family name. The true name was Packenstky. I was born in September 1901, as you already know, but the place of birth no longer exists: a village razed to the ground, depopulated by pogroms and wars.

"The nearest town of any consequence was Passau. In those days we were part of the Austrian Empire—Bavaria. But let me tell you, Herbie, that, though I've had a charmed life, choked with good things, happiness and sadness, the first nine years of my life still remain the most golden time for me. You must understand this, because it underpins *everything* of any importance that has happened to me. *Everything!*" he repeated, leaning forward and almost challenging Kruger to deny the fact.

"You're an intelligent, musical man, Herb, so if you want to think musically about the first nine years of my life, think of all the schmaltzy melodies, think of Peter's tune from *Peter and the Wolf*; think of that major theme in the Third Symphony of Rachmaninov; think of the Sibelius Violin Concerto; think of them all together. I lived, until the age nine, actually, in bliss. I was loved, I had family, a big family and we loved each other as only big Jewish families can. This is the key to everything. I so remember that village. My cousins. My aunts and uncles, the butcher; baker; rabbi. In the village I *was*. You know what I'm saying, Herb. I . . . *was*."

Kruger nodded. He knew well enough what the old man meant. There had been a time in his memory which he sometimes broke from the cage of his dreams. A time when he *Was*. He did not speak. Better to let Maestro Passau talk.

"You know, Herb, last night at the concert," he paused, frowning. "No, that was night before last, yes?"

Again the big nod, like a Buddha.

"Yea, the Charles Ives—the *New England Holidays*—we brought in especially the Marine Corps band for the 'Decoration Day' section. You know, when I was an up-and-coming young musician, I met Charles Ives. He was an old man. Very gritty; shrewd; unimpressed by the success of others. He said, 'Listen to me, son. Nothing but fools and taxes are absolute.' This was his biggest contribution to the conversation. We didn't say a word about music, but he sang, lamentably, at the piano which he played like a drunk in a barroom. Funny, eh?"

"*New England Holidays*, Maestro," Herbie nudged. He liked *New England Holidays*, Charles Ives' tone poem, in four sections: "Washington's Birthday," "Decoration Day," "Thanksgiving" and "The Fourth of July."

"Decoration Day"—Herbie's favorite—looked back to the composer's memories of his own childhood, when it was the custom to decorate the town with flowers which were spring's gift. In particular, Ives depicted, through the music, the solemnity of locals gathering at the cemetery to put flowers on the graves of those who had fallen in the Civil War, the War Between the States; then the brisk march back to town, led by the local brass band. It was for this moment that Passau had contracted the

Marine Corps Band to give the roaring, sudden burst of joyously happy military music—scored as if carried on the air in wonderful, daring dissonance that made you want to dance.

Kruger smiled at the thought. "The brass band. You want to get up and prance around the room, ja?" He almost stood up and demonstrated.

"You know." Passau was laughing, almost giggling. "Herbie, I put in *New England Holidays* for two reasons: first, I love it; and second, I knew my ex-wife, Veronica, would be there, and she would hate it. She loathes Charles Ives' music." He giggled again, like a naughty five-year-old.

"But, when it came, Herbie, something else happened. Something quite incredible. When I brought in the Marine Corps Band, and that huge sound filled the air, I thought of another time. Sadness, for I missed the village where all that love was left behind, yet I relived something else. The band reminded me of my first sight of America. A new period of my life, but one linked to the past, by a sadness for those first happy years of my being. Listen, I'll explain to you. . . ."

7

YOUNG LOUIS PACKENSTEINER was happy for the first time since leaving what he still thought of as home. If truth could be told, he was happy for the first time in over a year. The band was playing great raucous blasts of music, brass blaring, drums beating, making the boy want to dance or march down the gangplank.

The long journey, together with the fear and wretchedness, had begun almost two years before with snatches of conversation and overheard whispers which had brought terror to the little boy's heart. Now, it ended with this gush of music as they walked down from the ship—the Ellis Island ferry. His mother, Gerda Packensteiner, had trouble holding him back and she turned to shout over the crush to her husband, Joseph.

"Thank the good Lord for something," Joseph called back. "He's happy again."

In the now and future time, Louis Passau had yet to make up his mind about the big, bumbling German who was, inexplicably, an Englishman. As they sat in the room of this strange and beautiful Virginia house, with the morning sunshine hot outside the windows, Passau simply had no idea where things would end. Part of him said that he should tell it all, look at it as a final scouring of the soul. But that part of Passau which was so secret and deeply buried at the heart of a plethora of untold facts, was unsure. Aloud, to Herbie he said, "People will tell you that when you become old, so your memory changes. They say you recall things from the distant past with great accuracy and clarity, while yesterday's happenings escape you."

"I've heard." Herbie Kruger sat still and concentrating. He listened to Passau as he had been trained—to hear the music behind the words. Just to be safe he also had a tape running. Part of his night vigil had been to wire the room in the most simple way possible. The tape machine—which had come with him into the United States—was a small "special" provided by the Office: voice activated, with a choice of speeds, which meant that one side of a normal C90 tape would give him three hours.

"Well, it could be true with most people." Passau's eyes were bright and dancing. "But with me it works all ways. Yes, I can bring to mind the distant past as though it were yesterday. Unhappily I can also recall yesterday, last week, last month and last year with equal precision. Perhaps it's something to do with the way musicians train the mind. But, Herb, I can see that gangway, I can hear the music from the band as we got off the Ellis Island ferry. I can even still feel the new happiness, though I also feel the same sadness; the ache, the void which has been with me all my life."

He must have been very young for his age, Passau told Herbie. After all he had lived in a kind of enclosed society: the village, and the immediate proximity of his uncle, cousins, and the local people. In the village everyone knew everybody else.

"When we began the journey, I was terrified. Also, Herb, you must understand that I cannot be accurate about when I learned our family history. Until we began the journey, the one thing that had mattered to me was the village and the family, and I only dimly perceived what lay beyond its borders."

"In this village, what language were you speaking?" Herbie asked quietly.

Passau gave a shrug, "Who knows? A mixture, I think. I know it took some time for all of us to speak even a little English when we arrived in America. I think we possibly spoke a mixture of Hebrew, Russian, German. We certainly spoke German, otherwise I could not have followed what happened a year later. I will come to that, but first let me tell you the family legend as I now know it to be. How we got to the village which became my life."

He told the story briskly, with no frills, only the occasional overheard and remembered fact which was the icing on the cake of the story.

His grandparents—Isaak and Madja Packenstky—originally came from the small town of Kotovsk in the Ukraine. Like a great multitude of Russian Jews, they were confined there, living in what was known as The Pale of Settlement. There were two sons, Chaim and Isaak, the latter named for his father. Also, in those last decades of the nineteenth century, there was fear. Sudden reprisals for something they knew nothing about. The ruling powers of Russia would reach out from St. Petersburg and Moscow, and the Cossacks would ride into a village, or the soldiers would come and drag people away to slaughter, or move them to another location. Those Jews living in The Pale of Settlement were safe in theory only from becoming scapegoats.

"That's what the Jews were, Herb. What they have been at many times in history: scapegoats; a people, a race, who became the sacrificial victims of so many societies; a people who salved collective consciences by suffering. They made the ruling classes, and their serfs, feel that justice had been done if a few hundred Jews were put to the sword, or taken to do hard and necessary work others would not do—the salt mines, the stone quarries, but *you* know all about that."

Herbie nodded; he had known it all at a tender age, because most Germans of his generation knew. Many lied, of course—"We knew nothing of the terrible things that were done to the Jews." But they *did* know. Herb, as a teenager had known: the stories were everywhere. If you lived in Germany during those years it was difficult not to know, unless you were blind, deaf and dumb.

Old Isaak Packenstky was a craftsman. A shoemaker of immense talent. It was a craft that would be passed to his sons and, while they all had strength and health, there was always a living to be made.

When Chaim was three years of age, and little Isaak barely twelve months, Madja became pregnant again, and the great fears seemed worse. There were rumors that even the Ukrainian Jews were not safe anymore. People came to their village with stories of other places, less than a hundred miles distant, being pillaged, the inhabitants tortured, raped and murdered.

Isaak began to hear the warnings and the advice—"When the Cossacks reach the next village it is time to move on."

Isaak made careful plans, for he was not a man to do even urgent things without having some decent plan in mind. Life was like making shoes: if you did not get the right leather and the correct measurements, you might as well not make shoes at all. He knew which way to go, but would wait until the new child arrived, and Madja had recovered. In the event, Madja did not recover.

"My father, like myself, was born in September: at the turning of the year: summer's deathbed—poetic, huh?" Passau did not look at Herbie, but spoke with his eyes set on the wall behind him, as though looking at some spot a couple of generations ago. "My grandmother died giving birth to Joseph Packenstky, my father, and he was brought up by a young girl who wet nursed him and became my grandfather's second wife, though I knew her only as Aunt Nesta. They had hardly buried my grandmother before the final news came. The Cossacks, or whoever they were, had reached the next village. Grandfather and a number of others left, heading west. It was said, in the family, that Isaak, Chaim, Young Isaak, Joseph and Nesta were the only ones to reach comparative safety. They were separated from the others within a week or so, and never seen again."

The family seemed to have an oral tradition concerning grandfather Packenstky's journey. For them it became a kind of legend, a story with many facets, told and retold during long winter nights.

They encountered hardship and great danger, as well as kindness on the long march. In the mountains there was the raw cold, and the baby, Joseph, almost died.

One village, somewhere in what was now Austria, rose against them, refusing shelter, driving them out with stones and setting the dogs on them. But another nearby village took them in, fed and clothed them and, in return, Old Isaak made stout boots for many of the menfolk. Then the family continued their journey, crossing plains and mountains, fresh pastures, lush valleys, bare flatlands, or dark brooding, frightening forests.

Finally they reached the small community where they would settle and make a new family life. The people of this place, which seemed to have no name (or, perhaps, Herbie considered, Passau did not want to name it), gathered around the Packenstky family. Old Isaak returned their kindness by making certain that, each year, the people had first choice of the boots and shoes over which he labored through the heat of the summers and cold of the winters. The years went by and the three boys began to work with leather as soon as they were old enough. The Packenstky family started to prosper. Word got out into surrounding towns and villages that, if you wanted good, strong boots or shoes, you should go to Isaak Packenstky.

Passau said, "I remember my father telling me that, when he was about ten years of age, they had a great outing to the nearby town of Passau, which was some thirty miles away. He described to me that he had been frightened of the noise, the bustle and the crowds of people. They also saw the great cathedral of St. Stephen and, for the first time in *his* life, my father discovered that other folk worshipped God in different ways."

It was about this time—Passau thought—that their name changed. "My father told me that on the first visit to Passau they spent much time waiting in official offices, where people seemed to avoid them as much as possible. In fact, what happened was that they discovered that the law called for people to register their nationality and my grandfather decided they would be Austrian. So, when they got back to the village, the children were told their name had changed. No longer would they have their Russian name, but a new one, allotted to them by the officials in Passau. Now they were Packensteiners, and as Packensteiners they flourished. The years passed quickly."

Chaim scandalized everyone by going against his father's wishes and leaving the village for America, which he had heard was the land, promised to all Jews, flowing with milk and honey. Young Isaak married the butcher's daughter, Elsa Kellerman, a dark-eyed girl sought by all the young men in the village. A few years later, Joseph also took a bride, a Polish baker's daughter, Gerda, whom he had met while traveling to Passau to take samples of the family's shoes.

"When I came on the scene"—Passau still looked at the far of point on the wall—"my grandfather was worn out, dying, and my Uncle Isaak was already the father of three children—David, Rebecca and Rachel. Rachel was my age—born a few days before me—Rebecca a year older, and David just over two years my senior. But they were my closest and most beloved friends, and this, my dear Herbie, is important. You should know that, while I loved my mother and father, I *adored* my three cousins, my Uncle Isaak and Aunt Elsa. They were like a ring of faith and strength around my early happy years. They are with me always. Still, to this day. They are one of the reasons of my life." His eyes came down to meet those of Kruger. He gave a sad smile. "Foolish, eh? The folly of an old man to admit that the truly earth-moving actions of his life were based on the love and proximity of a handful of relatives he knew only for a very few years: a dust mote in the eye of time?"

"No." Herbie gave the impression of thinking hard about the question. Passau laughed—

"Herbie, how could *you* know? How could you possibly tell? You have no idea how my dearest cousins play a part in my life, except that which I will tell you now, at the beginning of our long tramp through the years together."

Herbie's head snapped round. When he spoke it was with a tinge of harshness. "Maestro Passau, you are known as a musical genius; a man of great staying power; a man who has lived and loved life to the full, so I take it that you have emotions, that you are an old man with memories crammed full of feelings, passions, temperament, hatred as well as love. I can believe anything of you. You should know this, Maestro, as we go together, cheek by jowl, through your life. Also, remember, I am not easily fooled."

Passau held up his hand. A sign of peace. It did not escape him that Eberhardt Lukas Kruger could speak excellent, grammatical English when he required it.

Now, Passau began to speak of those few years he had spent in the village, close by his cousins, and it appeared to Herbie that the man's powers of memory were like his genius with an orchestra. He painted a picture of that golden time which seemed to dance before the eyes. You could hear the children at play, and see the village with its rough green-painted wooden houses; its characters, like Herr Kellerman, his Aunt Elsa's father, the butcher; Frau Butterbusch, the schoolteacher; Rabbi Ephrahim, always in a hurry, tripping over his own words; Herr Gottlieb, who smelled of flour, the baker always with a cheery wave to the children; the drunk, Ravisch, whom they teased, and a whole cast of characters who, Herbie thought, could have stepped out of the pages of something written by Shalom Aleichem. He expected that, any moment, Tevye would walk into the picture as though he had come straight from Anatevka, stating that their lives were as shaky as a fiddler on the roof.

Instead, the people were revealed to him through Passau's vivid descriptive powers. In summer the wooden houses sucked in the heat so that everyone roasted and had difficulty sleeping in the air which, according to Passau, "seemed solid, like an invisible wall of sweltering warmth floating around you." In winter, those same houses retained the cold. Rime and ice formed on the inside walls and could not be driven away, even with the heat generated from the big iron potbellied stoves.

His descriptions of the people were, in a way, enchanting. Frau Butterbusch, with skin texture like that of an orange, pitted and reddish. "She walked as though there were a thousand butterflies under her skirt, which she flapped with her hands, as if trying to drive the insects out, and her gait was a kind of skipping motion. We called her—what would it be in English? Frau Butterfly Drawers."

The Rabbi Ephrahim had "a beard which looked as though it had been fashioned from fine wool, and when he was cross or irritated, he had this little habit of shaking his head, first from side to side, then in a nodding motion, his mouth half open, as though he were about to shout—which he never did."

But Passau spoke mainly about his comrade cousins: Rachel, who had hair black as the starless sky. "Many, many years later I gave a performance of William Walton's *Façade*, with two famous actors reading the Sitwell poems. You know them, Herb?"

"Not well, but I have heard."

"There is a line in which Edith Sitwell describes some fantastic being with 'hair black as nightshade, worn as a cockade. . . .' That was my Rachel, hair black as nightshade, and a smooth skin, with great jet eyes which she would open wide when she was excited."

Then, Rebecca—"long dark hair which looked almost brown when next to Rachel. She had the prettiest nose I ever saw, and she would fight like a tiger. Many times she sprang to my defense against other children."

Of David he said, "He was my funnybone. Such a laughtermaker. Still, I remember his japes and jokes. I think of him as a small, bouncing jester. He would have us all in fits of laughter and he could imitate every grown-up in the village. Herbie, if you could have known us children, in those first years of our lives, discovering the world around us, full of bright hopes, and innocent desires."

They played traditional games, like *Himmel und Hölle, Binde Kuh*, and, his best game of all, *Verstck*—hide and seek—and also made up their own adventures, including a forbidden game where David and Little Louis would be Cossacks, and the girls villagers, ripe for plundering.

"We did not understand. How could we? But we acted our fantasies and, I suppose, rid ourselves of demons. Herb, those few years were so happy, and so full of love."

"So when did it all change?" Kruger asked.

Passau shook his head. "I feel I should describe more to you. I cannot tell you how much we were bound together, four children, and I the youngest." His eyes seemed to cloud over, "And the youngest finally let them down. I eventually became their end. That is the terrible thing."

"Words cannot completely describe emotions." Herbie circled a hand in the air. "I take it, I understand it. Your time in the village, with your beloved cousins, was the time of pure gold for you. How did it end?"

"One afternoon." Passau paused, biting his lip. "I was, for some reason, alone. By myself outside the house. I recall it was late on a Friday. The others were inside, preparing for Sabbath. By this time the two families lived together. We had the biggest house in the village, and we shared it, just as we shared everything. I was outside, and I looked over and saw a pair of boots. Then I raised my eyes and there was this stranger standing there: dressed in dark clothes, but with a brown hat, which seemed more fitting for riding than walking. At his feet there were two big leather bags. Good, well-made bags. When he spoke, it was with a loud and cheerful voice. I thought I recognized it. He sounded like my Uncle Isaak. I remember, my mother came out and asked what he wanted. I did not know that he would end my spell of happiness." The old man passed a hand across his forehead. "Herbie, can we eat? Take a break, maybe?"

"Okay, I'll get some food." Herbie sighed inwardly. He needed quick responses and he was not going to get them. He went down to the kitchen and made a couple of omelets. Upstairs he could hear Strauss, the *Alpine Symphony*. He guessed it was Passau's own recording.

They ate listening to more Strauss, the *Symphony Domestica* which had so scandalized people because the music depicted the marital act of sexual intercourse. Passau did not speak as they ate. He cleaned his plate, but took his food in sparing little mouthfuls while his face showed a gluttony for the music. It was as though music was extra nourishment for him: something he soaked up through his senses, giving him stamina and strength.

They drank coffee. Then Herbie firmly turned off the CD player and began again. "So, Louis, there was this stranger."

The tall man smiled down at the boy, and his mother now asked what she could do for him. "You want to see someone?"

"Ah, you must be Joseph's wife. You must be Gerda, so this fellow will be my nephew, Louis."

Behind them, Joseph emerged from the house. "Chaim? My God, it's Chaim."

The brothers embraced and, in a second, everyone was outside, looking at the big man as though he had come from another planet—which, in a way, to them, he had.

"Typical of me," Chaim boomed. "I travel all the way from America, only to arrive back in time for Sabbath."

"Have you returned to us for good?" It was Isaak who asked, and Chaim laughed loudly.

"I have returned in the hope that I can persuade you to join me, in America. It's where your future lies."

Now, in Virginia, Louis Passau looked straight at Herbie. "Those words were like a death knell for me, and from that moment things got worse."

It began with conversations, even arguments, from which the children were barred, but Louis caught parts of the exchanges, certainly enough to realize that, while his Uncle Isaak wanted to stay in the village, his father, Joseph, was swayed by Chaim's arguments.

"Surely, Isaak," he heard his father say, "If Chaim is right, we can expect hard work for a couple of years, then we will have enough money to run our own business."

"What proof has he given us? If it's so good why has he come here to ask us to join him? Let him go back to his grand ways in New York City."

Little Louis thought that was right. He was not sure if he liked his Uncle Chaim who talked of impossible things, huge buildings which touched the sky, wide streets, money by the bushel. Louis clung to his cousins, who reassured him. "Papa is not going, he has put aside Uncle Chaim's offer," Rachel said soberly. "If our Papa has said no, then Uncle Joseph will also say no."

But Rachel did not hear the conversations Louis heard at night, as he lay awake.

"Mr. Chorat'll pay your fares—both on the train and boat," he heard Chaim say. "He has promised me that. There will be work for all, though Isaak seems intent on turning me down. Think of it, Joseph, good schooling for Louis. Eventually partnerships. Together, as a family, we can rule the shoe industry of America. Think of that."

Mr. Chorat, Louis had already learned, was the man who had been so good to his Uncle Chaim. Mr. Chorat gave Chaim a great deal of money to look after his entire shoe-making business for him.

"Herbie, I thought this Chorat man must be very rich. It was the first time I ever thought about rich and poor."

To hear Uncle Chaim talk, there were no real poor in America. Uncle Chaim traveled a great deal for Mr. Chorat, and on the railroads there was great comfort—things called club cars where you could sit at ease, eat and drink.

Even ordinary buildings sounded like palaces, and many people were now riding in the automobiles, which were rapidly taking the place of horses. "Soon, there will be no horses left in New York," Chaim declared. Some of the automobiles were called taxicabs, and you could hire them, together with the driver. He also talked of the omnibuses, in which large numbers of people could travel from one end of the city to the other. But Uncle Chaim was most enthusiastic about what he called the El, which was a railroad built above the city streets, so that people traveled high in the air.

Everything confused the boy—talk about the East Side and the West Side, even a place called the Lower East Side which was, according to Chaim, totally German-Jewish. "Some of the people there do not even try to learn English. How do they expect to get on and thrive in America without learning the language?"

"Herbie, I was totally bewildered. My boundaries had been the village and a couple of trips into Passau, which I did not like. The very thought of this new strange land gave me the shits. I did not sleep, I was worried, I lost weight. It was clear that my parents were seriously thinking of taking Chaim up on his offer."

Herbie nodded sagely, and said nothing, waiting for Passau to continue.

Chaim left one day without warning, and a few weeks later the blow fell. It was his cousin, David, who broke the news.

They were playing at the back of the house, where the ground sloped down to a small copse of fir trees—David, Rachel and Rebecca, all shrieking loudly and romping around in the trees.

Louis ambled from the house, deep in the whirling thoughts which enveloped him, faced with the arguments he had overheard, and the talk of leaving this golden place for some land where people flew on railroads high above cities, and lived on upper and lower parts of unimaginable buildings.

David spotted his cousin, detached himself from his sisters, and came running over.

"Oh, Louis," he panted. "It is terrible news that you are to leave us." At first it did not register, until David explained, "You are to go to America."

Rachel had joined them, her eyes teeming with tears. "Louis, how we shall miss you. I don't know what we shall do. But, maybe, for you it will be a great adventure."

"I'm not going to America." Louis held his ground. Then, unsure of himself, "When? When am I going to America, and who says so?"

"They all say so, Lou. Uncle Joseph, Aunt Gerda and you. Uncle Joseph is to work with Uncle Chaim for Mr. Chorat. We are all to stay here."

"Herbie, I did not want the adventure. But it was to be, and a year later we left. I have no words to tell you what the parting was like. That year, still there in the village, I counted the days, watched the seasons like a condemned man. I could not believe I would not see this place again. Sure, it might sound dramatic—melodramatic—but I can honestly say that, as a little boy, it was as though part of my soul had been ripped away. There is only one other time in my life when I have felt, and been, so miserable. You must see it from a child's viewpoint, Herbie. Everything changed so suddenly, I was physically ill and in mental torment. This is something you have to remember: that the hurt, the scar of parting with my cousins, never completely healed."

He told Kruger that there was no point in recalling the journey. "There have been huge books written about the immigrants, and the bad parts are all true. Yet, a small piece of me became revitalized when I heard that brass band playing, just before we saw Uncle Chaim again."

Passau had taken a long time over the telling of this comparatively small, childhood vignette, having embellished the story in his own style. Herbie found the matter compelling. Nobody had ever been told of Passau's early life, and, being a good listener—part of the interrogator's art—he was inclined to believe that, in Passau's mind at least, those early years, and the trauma of being uprooted, bore heavily on what was to come: on what Herbie wanted to hear.

He went down to the kitchen, as Passau was obviously exhausted from this long session. As Herbie cooked some lamb chops and vegetables he could hear the music from above. The Maestro was playing the Verdi Requiem and, not for the first time, he made a silent prayer for Passau to last long enough for him to complete a quiet, plodding interrogation. He had never seen a man of this advanced age look as fit, and blessed with such a needle-sharp mind, though at his age, Passau could, possibly, go out like a light. It happened to very old people.

They ate together while Passau played Bernstein's third symphony, *Kaddish*. The man, Herb thought, was obsessed by death and, as though tuning in to Passau's wavelength, he took himself to bed, once the Maestro was settled, and listened on his Sony Discman to the Mahler Fifth with its constant references to funereal darkness, gloom, struggle, turmoil and strife.

He freed his mind to think of what he might have learned from the day. Certainly things that nobody else had ever penetrated. Passau had always allowed his nationality to be presented as Austrian, yet today, Big Herb had met the real man, a mingling of Russian and Polish blood.

He thought of the deep wound left in childhood by the ripping from the known safety of the village with no name, into a teeming life. He wondered what a psychiatrist would make of it all. He wondered also what the in-depth confessors at Warminster would have made of it. Passau was a natural narrator. He spoke easily, and painted his pictures as he wanted you to see them. *There is always a danger in a subject who is a good narrator, a storyteller,* they taught interrogators. You could so easily fall under Maestro Passau's spell. I must not hurry him, Herbie thought, yet I must probe when we come to the crux of the matter.

THIRTY OR SO MILES AWAY, the USAir Express Dash-8 whined down onto the runway of the Charlottesville–Albermarle County Airport. Pucky Curtiss—a.k.a. Pauline Una Cummings—had telephoned ahead during her two hours' wait at Washington, Dulles.

The Boar's Head Inn transport awaited her and tomorrow Hertz would be delivering a car to the hotel. She was tired and barely took in the ribbon of car dealerships, malls and fast-food joints that line Route 29, Charlottesville's main artery to Washington and the North. She was in the South now, and knew it by the friendly y'all accent of the driver. She was also in old colonial America and was amused to see they had a Colonial Nissan dealership, picked out in neon.

An hour later she was wondering what century had picked her up as she dined in the main restaurant of The Boar's Head, served by men and women in eigthteenth-century costume. She was also amazed by the charm and politeness that had surrounded her from the moment she had stepped on to the little twin-engined aircraft at Dulles.

Could she have moved back a couple of centuries? She thought not, judging by the neon of Shoney's, Arbie's, Wendy's and Bojangles she had seen on the way in. Tomorrow, she would enter the twentieth century with a vengeance, seeking out an old spy in the person of the legendary Naldo Railton. With luck he might just lead her to bloody Kruger and the symphony conductor.

8

ACCORDING TO PASSAU, Uncle Chaim turned out to be, "A king of shits. To play with a term from the mob, I would call him the 'Tutti crappo di crappy.'" The old man chuckled.

"You certain this is relevant?" Herbie asked. Passau was well refreshed from a good night's rest. "Slept like a baby," he said, "though that is a stupid analogy."

His eyes were bright, he looked twenty years younger, appeared more spry, and ate a huge breakfast—in spite of his claim that he only took three cups of coffee. He was also impeccably turned out in gray slacks, loafers, a mega-expensive leisure shirt, and a loose woolen cardigan which must have cost eight hundred dollars. Unlike Herbie, Maestro Passau could still carry clothes. He had always been known as one of the best-dressed orchestra conductors in the world and, even now, in this hiding place, the creases in his pants looked razor-sharp, and not a hair of his great gray mane was out of place. He looked rich. He also looked formidable.

In answer to Herbie's query he replied, "Relevant? You think it's not relevant? All of it matters. Every major success or blow. Also none of it's been told before. Not the real monster I became: and why I was transformed from a nice, frightened little Jewish kid, who knew from nothing, into a fucking fiend who lived for music, but also lived for what music could do for me: the power it brought. First time, Herbie; first time I tell it all, so unwax your ears. Humor a very old man, Herb. Just listen, huh?"

Herb nodded and leaned back, ready to be transported to immigrant New York in the first decade of this torn century.

Uncle Chaim appeared out of the crowd, his dark face alight with a huge reunion grin. "I came over last night," he said, embracing his broth-

86

er, then his sister-in-law, and finally, with a pinching of cheeks, his nephew. "They said you'd be here tonight, so I went away and came back. Just in time, it seems, eh?" Then he looked at the four bulging valises and the two big parcels tied together with string which they had lugged all the way from the village. "This your luggage? Well, pick it up and let's get going."

Joseph became jaunty and jolly, as though Chaim's appearance vindicated his final decision to make the nightmare trip. "Well, brother, where's your fine automobile?"

Many times, Louis had heard his father say that Uncle Chaim would meet them with a fine automobile, and it was Louis who first detected the sudden change in Chaim's manner. "Just for a second, he looked like a hunted man, Herb. I saw the face alter, and his eyes were the eyes of a snake. This is not hindsight. I can see him like it was yesterday. Clear and in sharp focus."

"Chaim will have his automobile by the time we reach New York," Joseph had told them. "Mr. Chorat is providing one for him."

Now, at the pier, Chaim shrugged. "Not yet. Mr. Chorat says not yet. Any week now, but not yet."

It was Gerda, who had been suspicious from the start. Now she voiced all their concerns. "You *do* have somewhere for us to live, Chaim? You do have the nice apartment you told us about?"

Chaim laughed, but it was a strange snicker. Of course there was an apartment. He would take them to it straight away. The first month's rent was already paid. He had seen to that personally, and Louis' father would meet Mr. Chorat in the morning. In the meantime they would go to the apartment—traveling in a manner little Louis would love. They would ride the El.

"Apart from all the strange happenings of that night, and during the next days, one thing remains absolutely lucid in my head." Passau raised his eyebrows, his face assuming a comical, almost clownish, appearance. "I remember that I hummed constantly. I hummed to keep the devils at bay, for again I felt the awful wrench of parting with the soil and the blood of my cousins. I hummed several tunes, and they were all marches."

It was dark: a mixture of magic and confused anxiety for the child. The smell of smoke and steam; the hubbub of the people around them; the sheer crush, and the lights everywhere. New York, at that time, was an exciting place to be: exhilarating without the edge of violence it was to assume in later years.

Riding the El was like rocketing over the city. Louis sat next to a window, nose pressed hard against the glass. Sometimes they were above buildings; on other occasions, the buildings seemed to be running alongside them. He glimpsed the bustle of the city, and lights—more lights than he had ever seen until now: windows shining, and the streets bright as day, with people walking about in their hundreds. There were more horses than he had expected, but he also saw the automobiles and large high cars that he figured were the omnibuses Uncle Chaim had told him about.

"The place I got for you is a few blocks from mine. Nearer the Lower East Side than I wanted," Chaim said. "Don't worry, though, it's only temporary. We'll soon find somewhere else. There's a few sticks of furniture, and I'm sure Gerda'll have the place fixed up in no time."

Louis felt the tremor of warning go through his mother as the train rocked wildly.

Finally they arrived at the stop Uncle Chaim said was their station. From there they had a long walk. People lounged on corners, and at one point they had to step into the road, to avoid a party of young men emerging unsteadily from stairs that appeared to come up out of the ground. It was a cool night, but men and women sat on steps leading up to bleak, tall and uninviting buildings.

"I shoulda kept my damned mouth closed, Herb. I think what we got is my fault for speaking."

The child Louis said, "I hope we're not going to live in one of these awful places." Of course, they were; and, when they arrived, it smelled—of humanity, and cooking, and staleness. Not as bad as the stink of the ship, but unpleasant.

"On the fourth floor," Chaim said happily. "Apartment forty-one."

Gerda groaned, and the long climb made even the mild-mannered Joseph curse as Louis had never heard before. Eventually, they reached their new home—two rooms and a kitchen. "You share a bathroom with the others, down the hall," Chaim told them.

It was dirty, dingy, and the mentioned few sticks of furniture were just that, a few sticks: a couple of old chairs, a rickety table, two beds—a big one in a small room, and the little one in the room where they were supposed to live. The small room was just large enough to take the bed and very little else.

All hell broke loose. "The linen smells! The blankets are damp! And I've no doubt that there're bugs here," Gerda shouted.

"Chaim!" Joseph turned on his brother. "What have you brought us to? What is this?"

They started shouting at each other, and Louis felt another fear grip him. "I remember it exactly," Passau told Herbie Kruger in the present. "It was like an iron hand clutching at my entrails. A horror."

Yet, something suddenly calmed him. There was a lot of noise in the room, and a great deal of commotion coming up from the street: a rowdy hullabaloo, as though people were fighting all around them, just like his mother, father and Uncle Chaim. But, suddenly, over all the pandemonium came another sound—someone was playing an instrument—a trumpet, he thought.

"There were clear notes, rising and falling in a slow, sad melody and, oddly, that music had a great calming effect on me. Soothing in its sadness. It was as though someone was telling me I was not alone. This is very important moment for you to keep in mind, Herbie."

"My God," Gerda shouted at Chaim. "You cannot do this to us. How could *you*, my husband's brother, have brought us to this?"

"It's a whole heap better than the place I had when I first arrived here." Chaim sounded calm, yet, somehow, unpleasant. "When you have money coming in, and you've managed to save a bit, you'll get something better. You'll have it like home in no time."

Chaim was clever—a man who could usually turn things around by deflecting the truth. They would all come out with him. They would eat at a German restaurant. "I'll also buy groceries for you," he said with an unctuous smile.

"And things for cleaning," Gerda demanded.

"To give the devil his due, the meal was good. The first decent meal we had taken for a long while. We came home—if you could call it home—satisfied, warm and, due to my mother, with a new heart."

"We *will* make the best of this," Gerda proclaimed. They had returned with many paper sacks of groceries; loaded also with various cleaning materials. "Tomorrow, I shall make this dungheap fit to live in. I will not set foot outside of the building until this is a home. Louis will help me."

Chaim had said he would come at seven in the morning, to take Louis' father to meet Mr. Chorat. They were tired and needed rest. Tomorrow was another day, so Joseph said a blessing on their new home before they all sank onto the hard beds with their unpleasant-smelling blankets and sheets. Bugs or not, they slept.

The next weeks were to bring more chaos, but Gerda spent that first full day scrubbing, washing, sweeping and scouring the apartment.

"I don't suppose I helped much," Passau smiled conspiratorially at Kruger. "I have long since learned that it is wise to know very little about drudgery. I have made it a point in life to be sure that someone else cleans things and cooks for one. I always showed, even in those early years, that I had an inability when it came to household chores or being a galley slave over the hot stove."

Kruger nodded, looking curiously wise. "This, my dear Louis, was always my aim. I used to be sure that I did not even know how to lay cutlery on a table. Unhappily, the sexual revolution came upon us. You would find it much more difficult these days."

"Ah," Passau gave a little nod, as if to say, "I was careful not to be young in *these* days."

By seven o'clock on that second night, the tiny set of rooms smelled of polish and disinfectant; the linen was clean, there was one of Gerda's famous kosher meat loaves cooking, together with potatoes and red cabbage, just as her husband liked it, sweetened slightly with apples. When he came into the apartment, however, Joseph Packensteiner looked wild-eyed. He slammed the door and stamped into the little living room, his face a thundercloud and his hands clutching and unclutching like a madman. Louis was even a little afraid of him. Neither Gerda nor the child had ever seen the calm and patient Joseph looking like this.

"Joseph? What is it? Did you bring Chaim back with you? There's a good meal waiting." Gerda's words were hollow, but she tried to appear normal.

There was a long, brooding, silence. When he spoke, Joseph's voice was almost a whisper. "Until he makes amends," he spoke very slowly, "my so-called brother is not welcome in this house. Nor will either of you ever speak with him."

"Frankly, I was very frightened," Louis admitted now. "His hair was all over the place; his eyes seemed to be crimson with anger. My mother was good with him. Gentle, calm—you know, Herbie, the way women are. They're good at that kind of thing."

It all came out while they ate the meal.

"I heard the trumpet again that night. Quite extraordinary, I can hear it now if I put a mind to it. Long clear notes. Infinitely sad, wistful." He grinned at Kruger. "Actually, if you listen hard enough you can hear it in my own symphony. The first movement, the trumpet far off, behind the strings. That's how well I kept it in mind. It was very calming to a little boy with a very troubled heart."

Kruger remained still. Dimly he perceived the form of Passau's confession. It might take a long time but, he thought, any reservations the man might have about not telling me everything will dissipate if I give him his head. He will tell, perhaps, not quite all of it, but there will be enough detail to fill in the gaps by hard questioning.

On that second night in America it all came pouring from Joseph as they ate Gerda's kosher meat loaf—

Chaim was not the great and powerful man he claimed. True, he was employed by Mr. Chorat, who had a small shoe shop, specializing in repairs, but also making shoes to order. The shop was on Catherine Street, quite near to where they now lived, and Chaim was in charge, taking orders and, very occasionally, traveling to places like Chicago where Mr. Chorat had many friends in the Jewish community. The business was good, but there was too much work. Chorat was a fine craftsman, and the little business grew well each year. He helped in the mending and making of shoes, but needed an equally fine craftsman to keep up with the orders. So, it was on the understanding that he would bring back at least one first-class shoemaker, that Chorat had paid for Chaim's trip back to the village. Once Chaim had netted Joseph, Chorat had agreed to finance the trip for his new assistant's family.

"I have to sign an agreement which ties me hand and foot to Elijah Chorat for three years." Joseph spoke the sentence like a curse. "We have given up a peaceful goldmine for a plot of wasteland."

"But Chaim said . . ." Gerda began.

"Chaim has big ideas," Joseph all but snapped at her. The small boy flinched. This was so unlike his kindly papa. "Chaim thinks that, when Mr. Chorat dies—which will be another thirty or forty years by the look of him—he will leave the shop to us. He has no sons, no family of his own. If I had my way we'd all get on the first boat back to Europe."

"Papa, then why don't we?" Louis piped up.

Joseph looked at the boy for a long time, then shook his head sadly, saying it could not be done. The authorities would not allow it. Chaim had vouched for them, signed papers on Joseph's behalf, binding him to Elijah Chorat for a period of three years. "I have no option but to countersign the papers."

"You are sure of this?" Gerda pounced. "You are sure this isn't another of Chaim's tricks?"

Joseph shook his head. "It would appear that it's all true, and we haven't the money to take on an advocate. We're stuck."

Chaim, acting probably out of easy ambition, had gravely misled Joseph. Isaak had been right to withstand Chaim's big talk of a huge market, overflowing with riches. They should, it seemed, have all stayed where they were.

Catherine Street, where Mr. Chorat's store was located, lay on the fringes of the Lower East Side of Manhattan: a sprawling, choked, seething, polyglot area, filled, and overflowing, with immigrants from all over Europe. A large number were from Germany or Austria, and it would have been easy for the Packensteiners to settle for a quiet, if far from luxurious, life among people they could understand.

But Joseph had learned one thing very quickly: Chaim had been right about the central fact in an immigrant's life. "You had to embrace the country and its ways," he was always saying to them. Already men and women were using the term "Americanization." As a start, Joseph told them that very first night, he had enrolled both Gerda and himself in special classes to learn the language. Louis also had much work ahead. Tomorrow he would be starting at Public School No.1, just down the street. It was also required of him, as a good Jewish boy, to attend a Talmud Torah at least four evenings a week. This was so that he could keep up his Hebrew, and be instructed in the Torah, and the ways of his faith. Louis thought life was going to be very full and, maybe, even dangerous. In the next few days and weeks the young boy felt as though he were setting off to climb the highest mountain in the world. There was so much expected of him, and so much to learn.

Public School No.1 stood on the corner of Catherine and Henry Streets, and it was the avowed intention of the school board to make this place a simple, if harsh, seat of learning, in which the mélange of nationalities would be arranged and molded into a whole: an American whole.

So, Louis Isaak Packensteiner, an inoffensive, naive, scrawny, waiflike, stunted boy—"I did not fatten out and sprout upwards until my late teens"—was thrown in at the deep end of learning, and within a year, he grew from a non-English-speaking German Jew into one who could easily converse in the new language, including most of the obscenities—learned after class from his grubby playmates.

The beginning was painful, without his mother's gentle persuasion to guide him. But the end product was an American boy who learned, worked, cursed, fought and swore allegiance to the flag, in his new tongue, each morning—hand on his heart.

His parents took much longer to adjust, though Joseph was speaking a broken, poor sort of English in six months or so. Then, quite fluently—with the aid of his son—within eighteen months. Gerda found it more difficult, and never really spoke perfect English for the rest of her life—continually mixing words and inserting German, or Yiddish, when she became baffled.

For four, sometimes five, nights a week, Louis went down to the basement Talmud Torah on the notorious Hester Street—by day a huge and crowded market, full of mainly Jewish people from a dozen or more countries. Stalls and booths crammed the sidewalks, and out on the street itself—particularly on Fridays, the eve of Sabbath, when most housewives in the area went out to fill their store cupboards.

By night Hester Street was still a lively place to be. Sometimes a shade too lively. Lower classes of women would prowl the sidewalks and rougher men, and even boys, could be seen coming and going from ventures of a dubious nature. Young lads would loiter with girls on the corners. Occasionally there would be fights between rival gangs. Then the predominantly Irish Catholic police would descend and pour out their wrath which fell, in the main, on Jewish locals for whom they had little time.

To start with, Gerda made certain that either Joseph or herself would meet Louis after his study at the Talmud Torah was finished for the evening. More often than not it was Gerda, for Joseph was working all hours and very hard: and not simply at his English, or for Mr. Chorat.

Joseph Packensteiner was planning his future, making many friends among his employer's best, and most respectable, customers. He hated bowing and scraping but was willing to humble himself for his own ends, and also to see his elder brother's nose put out of joint. Within a matter of months the word was out that you could get the best shoes or boots, on the most competitive terms, from Chorat's store. There, they employed a shoemaker who had magic in his hands. This shoemaker, it was also said, was willing to take special orders on the side: work done in his own time.

Joseph, then, would labor late into the night, making the special orders, for which he alone would get credit. That credit would store itself up for future use—once he had completed his term of three years with Elijah Chorat.

Louis knew all this, both from the whispered conversations he overheard between his parents, and from what he felt in his bones. Within six months of their arrival they had moved from the dingy rooms. Not far away, but far enough: uptown Hester Street, where a much larger, four-roomed apartment with its own bathroom, had become available for only a few dollars more each month. There, in one of the rooms, Joseph had set up a workbench, on which he kept his own last and tools.

He also managed to get leather from a source of which he would never speak. "To his dying day, Herb, I don't know where he got the leather. I can only think he did a deal with the some little arch-goniff—which wouldn't surprise me the way my father turned out. But, my friend, I liked things much better once we moved. The ache never left me—cousins, relatives—but, then, it never has. I liked Hester Street. There's nothing like it today. Nowhere. I found it exciting, particularly after I persuaded Mama to let me come home on my own at night. That's when it happened. December 1912. A Thursday. Second Thursday in December. How's that for memory, huh?"

"Memory of what?"

"Herb, I'm talking revelation time here. Like the Christian Paul on the road to Damascus time; like the burning bush; like Moses going into the mountains and coming down with those tablets."

"Okay, so what was special? What happened?" Herbie realized that, in a blink, the old man's eyes were now filled with tears. "Just tell me, Lou. Confession time, eh?"

"Sure." An overtone of bitterness. "Sure, Herbie. If there is a God, then that Thursday in December 1912 was the day he chose to let me know I had a gift. Not just a tiny little talent, but an enormous gift. Maybe I didn't recognize it then and there. Certainly it pissed me off a bit in the early years. But I learned. Even if there's no God; no heaven and no hell, it's all the same. I finally caught hold of that gift and used it. Used it to prise open the world for myself; used it to seduce, murder, steal. I used it like one of those Borgia Popes used the Church. I used it to fuck the world, Herb, and that's what, eventually, made me into a monster. This bit's important, and I have it all here." He tapped his head. "It's here, locked away. Like other things, it's never been told, and people don't even know what I got. What I still got." He glared at Kruger. "What's to eat?"

"I made sandwiches. Nice. Good salt beef that Naldo brought and I put in fridge, Lou. You like salt beef?"

"Do whores screw?"

"I get the sandwiches, then, and you can tell me. I'll . . ." Then the telephone began to ring. Six times followed by a pause. Herbie started counting . . . nine . . . ten . . . Then it started to ring again. Naldo signaling that he needed to talk. Herbie Kruger picked up, but did not speak.

At the distant end Naldo said. "We got three different kinds of company, Herb. None of it good, but I don't think the lines are wired, and the leeches on me are pretty laid back. I can slip them tonight sometime. I'll give you the signal when I'm coming in."

Herbie grunted.

"Ask your friend if he has mob connections, right?"

"Right."

The line went dead.

"Your friend?" Louis Passau's eyes were unreadable.

Herbie nodded. "We got company in town, it seems. Three different kinds he says. He also told me to ask you a question."

"So ask, then we can eat the fuckin' salt beef sandwiches?"

"He'll ask you again, knowing him. He'll visit tonight. He wants to know if you have mob connections?"

"Oh," Passau snorted. "I thought it was important, like the moment of my revelation."

"Have you?"

"Have I what?"

"Got mob connections?"

"Sure, but that comes much later in the story. It's important I tell you about December 1912."

"Second Thursday in December, I know."

"Then fuck you, Kruger. Just get the fuckin' sandwiches, okay."

As he walked away, his feet making the floor spring and judder under his weight, Big Herbie Kruger muttered, "Sure, second Thursday in December, St. Louis Passau, King and Martyr. Okay, you'll like the sandwiches, King Lou. Maybe they'll make a martyr of your guts. Make you crap all day."

9

THE FEDS HAD ARRIVED at Naldo and Barbara's house late on the previous evening. There were two of them, accompanied by an ineffectual-looking, somewhat limp young man from the British Embassy, just to show they were serious and doing things by the book.

"Donald Railton?" one of them asked politely after showing I.D. and when Naldo told him he had got it in one, they courteously asked if they could come in. Naldo ushered them into the large living room, furnished with much of the antique stuff they had brought from the U.K., and gestured to the easy chairs. They sat, and the senior of the two FBI men introduced himself as Bob Singer. The other was called Ross, though nobody seemed to have given him a first name.

The insipid young man from the British Embassy seemed to have no name at all, a fact—Naldo mused—which would probably please the young man's parents, for he was the kind of yuppie marvel his old Office, the Secret Intelligence Service, seemed to be recruiting these days, and good luck to them.

"Okay, let's not be coy," Singer began. "Donald, can I call you Donald?"

"I'd really rather you didn't." Naldo was gritty, using his old Raj voice, which he and Barbara played with a great deal when in company they did not much care for. It usually ensured that they were not invited back.

"Oh. Okay, Mr. Railton, sir. You were formerly a member of the British Secret Intelligence Service? MI6?"

Naldo looked directly at the Embassy man, who coughed and said, "Julian, sir. Julian Wilson."

"Right, Jules," still gritty, but in a manner he hoped the young man from the Embassy would warm to. "Who are *you*, Jules?"

"Assistant Second Secretary, Mr. Railton, sir."

"Assistant to the Resident?"

"Sort of liaison, actually."

"Ah. Well, Jules, I'm a British citizen, living in the United States as a permanent resident alien, which makes me sound like some extraterrestrial blob." He turned to Singer, "You see, old chap, I am not really at liberty to answer your question unless I get it in writing from certain folk. Any ideas, Jules?"

"Actually, sir. Yes." Julian withdrew a long envelope from the inside pocket of his jacket and handed it to Naldo, who slit it open with his thumb and took out the single faxed sheet. There was no address, just a few lines of computer-generated type and a signature.

"Dear Pa," it began—

> This is confirmation from the Chief that you may disclose, to authorized persons (namely members of the FBI Counter-Intelligence Department), your former attachment to the Office. The Chief would also like you to know he will be more than grateful if you give them all possible assistance over the current matter in hand. He does, however, caution you to bear in mind the delicate situation facing us. Further confirmation, should you require it, can be obtained by telephoning the usual number.

The letter was signed "Arthur," which, in itself, was some kind of warning. Naldo's son was, within the family, usually known as Art.

"Have to make a phone call." Naldo nodded to all three men and left the room.

Barbara was waiting in the kitchen and she raised her eyebrows in silent query.

"We have G-men spooks in the drawing room, plus our man from the Embassy—Lord help us," Naldo muttered. "Why don't you go and offer them coffee while I call Art?" He picked up the kitchen extension and dialed the 011-44-71 code for London, followed by a number which would probably get Art Railton from the dinner table.

The number was a call-forwarding line, so Naldo, in fact, got Art's desk at the Office. "What ho, Guv'nor," Art said cheerily on hearing his father's voice, indicating that they should be immensely careful about what they said. Most families have codes of one kind or another, and the

Railtons had been using what they liked to call "one-liners"—mainly Shakespearean—for three or four generations.

"Got your letter, Art. Everything still okay?"

"No change, but do take care, Pa. At your age we don't want to see you take a fall; that last stumble had us worried."

"I'm walking on eggs, old son."

They talked rubbish for five minutes, and Naldo signed off with, "Your letter was loaded with advice, Art. Why?"

"Oh, the isle is full of noises, Pa. But you know that." First the query, to give Art a chance of warning, if there was one. Last, the admonition that Naldo should take care and assume he was under surveillance, both human, and certainly electronic, which meant the phone was tapped. Finally, Art added. "If you get to meet that girl, Robin, do everything you can to help her."

"Naturally." Naldo wondered who in blazes was this girl called Robin?

When he returned to the drawing room, Barbara had served coffee. They passed at the door and Barbara made a face, indicating that she was none too impressed with the company.

"Well?" Singer looked unsmilingly at Naldo. "You gonna talk with us now?"

"Depends." Naldo was uncompromising. "I have no idea what this is about but, yes, I am a retired member of the British SIS."

"You keep up contacts?"

"Some. Mostly letters. Occasionally one of my old colleagues looks me up from Washington."

"An old colleague by the name of Kruger?"

"Herbie?"

"Eberhardt Lukas Kruger. German origin, naturalized British subject 1948. Worked, almost from the cradle, for your old firm."

"Haven't seen Herb in yonks."

"You're aware we're looking for him?"

"No."

"You're aware we're looking for Louis Passau, the orchestra conductor?"

"Yes. Read the *Post* and the *New York Times*. You couldn't miss the story, even though it seems cloaked in the usual secrecy."

"Well, then, you'll recognize the description of Passau's companion?"

"Good grief. Herbie?"

"Give the man a prize." Singer did not have those most necessary attributes, tact and subtlety. He had been brought up in the old school of tough, no messing, straightforward one-on-one interrogation techniques. Truth to tell, his masters had sent him down to visit Naldo Railton simply because they knew he would probably put the Brit's back up, thereby possibly unleashing anger during which Railton might say something he would have cause to regret.

"This big guy, Kruger? He been in touch?"

"I told you. Haven't seen him, or heard from him in—what's the expression I've heard around here?—in a coon's time?"

"Yeah?"

"He's definitely with Passau?" Naldo had been known in his old trade to be blessed with the deviousness of a Tudor courtier. His face was blank, vaguely interested with a small hint of alarm in his eyes.

"Oh, definitely." Singer tried to do a very bad imitation of a plummy British accent, which failed to the extent of absurdity. "We want to know if he's been in touch: called, written, anything?"

"No." Solidly honest in his duplicity. There was a silent count of around ten, then—"You think he's likely to?"

"Get in touch with you? Yeah. Yeah, you're the obvious choice. He's got very few people to turn to. You're top of the list."

"Is he headed this way?"

At long last, Ross—the one who seemed to be a man with no first name—broke his silence. "We have nothing, Mr. Railton. Passau and Kruger just disappeared. As though they left the planet. No leads. Nothing."

"You're sure they're still alive? Could they have been abducted?"

"Unlikely. We think Kruger has Passau holed up someplace and is interrogating the bejasus out of him. But they've vanished." He paused, not for effect but to raise one hand in an attempt to stop Singer from playing the hard man again, an endeavor in which, Naldo was relieved to note, he seemed to be partially successful.

"Sounds like Kruger." Naldo smiled for the first time. "He used to be very good at that. Vanishing, I mean."

"If he *does* make contact . . ." Ross allowed the sentence to remain incomplete. Thin smoke on a breeze.

Naldo sighed, "Give me a number. I'll call."

Singer, looking as aggressive as a roused cobra, passed over a card. "Ask to be patched through to me, or Mr. Ross."

"I'd like to add something." Naldo knew they would take anything he said with a whole drum of table salt, but he liked dragging false trails. "I know Kruger *very* well. As they used to say in my former business, I know his handwriting. . . ."

"Sure." Singer indicated that he would as soon believe a doper just caught with several keys of crack hung about his person.

"He operates very well without outside assistance." Naldo overrode Singer. "Simply because I'm the most likely contact he has in the United States, signifies to me that, if he really is being shifty, I'm the last person to whom he'd come."

"You think we'd believe that?" Singer really was a pain of significant proportions.

"I think you'd be very stupid not to believe it."

"Okay." He was not placated. "But should he make contact, there're two things your old pal Kruger should know. First, in the long run it'll be better if he brings Passau straight to us; second, it seems we're not the only people looking for him."

"Really?"

"Yes, really, sir," from Ross. "And the other people'll give him a much worse time than us. In fact, they'd most certainly kill him, and Passau."

Naldo's mind was suddenly clouded in ice. He felt the old fear come back, shrouding him, as it had so often done during the Cold War. "Perhaps these people, whoever they are, have already done what you say they . . ."

"No." Ross was firm. "They're looking for Passau and Kruger. In fact, they're following us. The local cops, here, spotted them before we did."

"And these people are?"

"Mob guys. Buttons. Wiseguys. Goodfellas, call them what you like. Two of them. Very good, which is surprising for those kind of people. But they're obviously specialists."

"Why?"

"Why is what we'd like to know, Mr. Railton. Our sole interest is a very old orchestra conductor, who is facing certain allegations. . . ."

"Accused of being a Nazi spy? Ninety years old, and you're putting him through an interrogation?" Naldo gave Ross a thin, tight-lipped smile. "I was in the game too long to be taken in by that. I'd put money on you boys having something else on Maestro Passau, but that's none of my business. . . ."

"You're right there, Mr. Railton, so let's just leave it alone, huh?"

"I didn't bring it up. However, you're now telling me that Mafia contract artists are following you to get on Passau's tail. I've read a lot about Passau in the last months: he's been a good filler for most newspapers but this is the first I've heard about Mafia connections."

"It's the first we've heard, as well. It's weird, and I can't say we understand it."

Singer stood, as a signal that it was time to leave. He looked at Naldo with undisguised dislike: not unexpected, for Bob Singer did not like most people. "If you're worried that they've followed us here, leaving Kruger an open target for you, forget it." He motioned to Ross. "The local cops have been running interference for us. They didn't follow us tonight."

Naldo Railton was not so certain about that. As soon as the three men left the house, he unlocked a drawer in his desk, took out his strictly illegal Smith & Wesson 9mm automatic, slammed a magazine into the butt, drew back the slide, putting a round up the spout, as they say. He then activated the safety and stuck the weapon inside his waistband, hard against the right side of his back. He was taking absolutely no chances.

"Neither of them are creatures of habit," Art Railton had told Pucky. "My father was a field man for too long. There's never routine. However, they both haul themselves off to the nearest Giant supermarket once a week, either on Saturday, Sunday or Monday. They do their grocery shopping there, but the times vary, like the days. You just can't tell, so you'll have to stake out the place."

Pucky Curtiss, a.k.a. Pauline Una Cummings, reflected on Art's advice now, as she sat in broiling heat which made the interior of the rented Dodge Colt unbearable. After dinner on the previous night, the jet-lagged Pucky had been given a half-hour map tour of the area by a friendly girl at reception. She had returned to her room, laden with maps and the little guidebook provided by Art Railton in London.

It seemed that Charlottesville, once a thriving, picturesque town with a claim to great fame as the home of Thomas Jefferson's university, the University of Virginia, had, like so many American townships, altered over the years. The old part of Charlottesville had been reduced to one "historic" pedestrian area; then there was Court Square, with its obligatory statue of an unknown Confederate soldier; and the university campus, almost ruined by a new and splendid UVa teaching hospital which had been built with no eye to blending the present with the past historical glories.

Now, the old part of town was struggling for life, while the rest of Charlottesville sprawled outwards, north along Route 29, the road on which Pucky had been brought from the airport. Within the city limits, R29 was replete with fast-food joints, car dealerships and several shopping malls, one of which was located in Seminole Square and sported the Giant supermarket where Naldo and Barbara did their weekly grocery shopping. As promised, the rental car had been delivered to The Boar's Head Inn at seven thirty on that Sunday morning and, by nine, Pucky had Seminole Square staked out as well as possible under the circumstances. The Giant was the largest store in the square, the bulk of which was given over to a parking area. After half an hour, Pucky realized the job was all but impossible. Too many cars moved in and out; there was no central area where she could quietly sit and watch for Naldo's white Lincoln with the registration plates ONE 391.

Though she had never met, nor even seen Naldo and Barbara, Pucky was confident that she would recognize them. During the bulk of the flight from Heathrow to Washington she had studied photographs ranging from head and shoulders, through profiles—left and right—and a pile of surveillance pix which were the usual grainy shots taken at long range. She had also listened, on her personal stereo, to both their voices.

After going through every possible permutation in Seminole Square, she went into the supermarket, marveling at its range and choice of foods which made her own local Sainsbury's look like an old-fashioned corner shop. She bought bottled water and sandwiches, wandered from aisle to aisle, and then along the checkout lines, her eyes raking the people browsing, shopping or standing in line.

She moved the Colt around, taking it from area to area, watching for the

Lincoln, looking at registration plates, making sure she did not get dehydrated by the heat. To her dismay she discovered that the Giant was a twenty-four-hour market which gave her no stop time, though she doubted that the Railtons, because of their age, would drive into town after eight.

She went back into the market again, and stayed there for half an hour, buying items she would probably never use, passing the time and never letting a minute go by without scanning the shoppers.

It was eleven thirty when, as these things so often turn out, she spotted a white Lincoln turning into the area next to where she was sitting. She caught the registration only briefly, so was not one hundred percent sure until she saw, with a lifting of her heart, the tall elderly figure from the photographs uncurl from the driver's seat and head towards the market with his wife in tow. She was in through the main entrance only a couple of minutes behind them.

Naldo and Barbara had their weekly grocery shop down to a fine, organized art. She would initially head for the fruit and vegetables, while he went to the dairy products and then the canned goods.

Naldo was selecting canned soups and only vaguely conscious of the tall blonde girl reaching past him for a can of minestrone. As she apologized, she muttered Puck's last couplet from *The Dream*—

"Give me your hands, if we be friends:
And Robin shall restore amends."

"If you get to meet that girl, Robin, do everything you can to help her." That was what Art had said and Naldo reacted with caution.

"I beg your pardon, did you say something?" He did not even look at her.

"I'm a friend of Art's. He said he would get to you and mention a girl called Robin."

"Yes. Any further proofs?"

"He said you might need another to establish identity. He told me that you would remember the night they invented champagne."

"So we're talking about a large man of German origin?"

"Yes, and I have to talk to you."

He moved further down the aisle. She followed, letting thirty seconds pass.

"It's possible that I'm under FBI surveillance," he said, still not looking at her. "You have transport?"

"A rented Colt. Outside."

"I have a Lincoln. . . ."

"Registration ONE 391."

This time he glanced at her and she smiled.

"Get out to your car when we leave and follow us," he said. "We'll do a little run around the houses to see if they have any mobiles out. It *is* possible that they're only watching the house. If it's all clear, my wife'll move one of our packages so that's it's visible through the rear window. Overtake and fake a breakdown. Okay?"

"Got it." She gave him a dazzling smile and added, "I go, I go. . . . Look how I go. . . ." and so was gone.

Naldo did a full run around to make sure no mobiles were tracking them. He took 29 North, turned into Carrsbrook. Then down, past the neat houses with their manicured lawns, onto Rio Road and into the Fashion Square Mall; then back onto 29 North and over to the Rio Hill Mall; parking and walking into Brendel's where he stayed for ten minutes before driving out and heading south, exiting onto Route 250 and off again, doing the side roads.

Pucky lost all sense of direction, but on a straight and deserted narrow road she saw Barbara lean back and toss a package onto the rear shelf. She accelerated, overtook and went straight on, pulling off the road after about a mile, getting out and opening up the hood, praying nobody else had overtaken Naldo.

The Lincoln pulled up, stationary for just enough time for Naldo to get out and let Barbara take the wheel.

"Shut the damned thing up," he told Pucky. "Shut it and get behind the wheel." Then, for the next fifteen minutes he sat, giving her terse instructions—"Left at the next junction . . . Right at the T. . . ."

Finally, they pulled over into a picnic area a mile or so from Monticello, Jefferson's home, the area's showplace. Pucky spent ten minutes giving Naldo the instructions she had been ordered to pass on. At the time, Naldo did not confirm whether Herbie had been in contact or not.

Barbara pulled up in the Lincoln and Naldo simply said, "I'll be in touch. Stay close to a phone. I'll call you in the next couple of days," which, Pucky thought, was tantamount to admitting he had a direct line to Kruger.

Later, Naldo used a public booth to telephone Herbie, just as Louis Passau was getting interesting about the second Thursday in December, 1912.

10

"I WAS NOT A bright boy, at age eleven." Passau began his story of the events which seemed so important to him. "Skinny looking, underfed, yes. But bright, as in smart, no. Sure, I could read and write. I knew some history dates, yet when it came to genius, I was not. Until the second Thursday in December 1912, that is. I didn't know, Herb. Not the slightest idea.

"I was coming back from the Talmud Torah. Going home at the end of a long and not very rewarding, day. . . ."

Now that his parents allowed him to come and go by himself, Louis Packensteiner really loved the streets of New York. "There was always something to see; a view I didn't notice before; noises unheard. It was excitement, and the clamor—music to my ears. I tell you, I sometimes hear those old noises, like I'm transported right back to the second decade in this lousy century we've lived in, and I can still hear and smell those streets. It was so different then: the lights for one thing and, in Hester Street, among the stalls there were naphtha flares which made shadows. It was wonderful, and I used to drag my heels, take more time, dawdle on the way home."

He was dawdling on that December night. Almost all the stalls and street traders were gone and the darker side of Hester Street had started to encroach on the friendly gusto of daytime.

So, it was with surprise that, on reaching the top end of Hester Street, young Louis found himself almost alone. Then the bigger boys appeared all around him, stepping from the dark pools near the buildings.

"I suppose they were only a handful of years older than me, but at eleven years you think a sixteen-year-old is a man. Funny, isn't it, when

we're kids we wanna be older, when we're older we wanna be kids again?
Anyhow, there were four of them, Herb. A quartet of oafs, brutish, men-
acing, and there was nobody I could turn to. Hell, there was nobody else
around, everyone with any sense was at home. It was a very cold night. I
was stupid, being out at that time with no topcoat. Never, never, Herbie,
never go out in December without a topcoat. Be your death. It was nearly my death that night. A topcoat woulda acted as padding. The sidewalk
was empty one minute, the next it was fulla four guys."

"Well, what we got here?" asked the leader of the pack, who stood an
inch taller than the others.

"We got a little kike," another sneered, from behind Louis. "A little
kike, all on his own at night."

"Past your bedtime, kike."

"Whatcha doin' out this time of night, kike?"

"I'm goin' home." He was not yet really afraid of the boys.

"You got money, kike?"

"All kikes got money." They drew closer, and only now did he feel the
real menace.

"I got no money. You let me pass. I'm goin' home."

"Give us what money you got. I don't believe there's a little kike on the
street with no money."

"Please get outta my way. I got no money, I told yah."

"We'll see 'bout that." The leader spat straight into Packensteiner's
face and, as though it were a prearranged signal, the others piled onto
Louis, dropping him to the ground with the weight of their bodies.

He kicked out, and battered upwards with his hard little fists, but that
only made matters worse. Both his kicks and fists made some mark on the
older boys, who were enraged that he even dared to fight back. One of
them, suffering from a fierce little boot in the groin, reeled away, doubled
up and cursing—"Kill the little Jew bastard. Jesus and Mary, he's dislo-
cated my balls. Kill the little fucker."

They tried to do just that: raining punches on Louis' head, cutting
him over one eye, and splitting his lip. He still struggled and fought, but
now he knew fear and could smell it on himself. They started to rip at his
jacket, and the thin shirt under it. He began to cry, and one of them gave
him a vicious kick in the ribs, which drove the wind from his body. Then
another, and another.

He rolled into a ball, instinctively putting his arms over his head, waiting for the blows which were bound to follow, which might even end his life. He was certain they would kill him.

Then, suddenly it stopped. The hitting ceased and there seemed to be another commotion going on.

He peered through splayed fingers. Two of the boys were running away; another seemed to be hobbling, limping off as fast as he could, while the leader of the group was now a victim. A large hand held him by the collar, while an equally large boot was being applied, with wincing regularity, to his backside.

The person doing the kicking was a giant of a man: very tall, with broad shoulders and a mass of graying hair that flowed out behind him like a horse's mane. He seemed to Louis to be some avenging patriarch, though he was to discover that the man was really only about the same age as his father.

"Now, get the hell outta here, you coward, you *goy schnorrer*." The man placed his heavy boot even more firmly into Louis' tormentor's rear and let go of his collar, sending the boy flying, so that he ended up, face-down, spreadeagled and scrabbling at the sidewalk.

Louis' savior now turned to him. "There, *vingale*, let's see how much damage they done to you."

The hands that lifted him up were strong, like the hands of a man used to doing heavy manual work; yet their touch was soft and gentle, as was the man's voice. "Oy!" he said, "they've bloodied your lip; that'll be a fat one by the morning; and you got a nasty cut over that eye there. Come on. I live only up the stairs, here, in this building." He pointed to a cracked and peeling door almost on the corner.

"This guy had to support me, hold me. You know, I could've sworn that serious damage had been done to my body. I shook, gasped like a drowning man, felt the pain like hot irons applied to my skin. God, I feel it now, it's so vivid. Almost eighty years ago and I still feel it, like I can still see the man."

He had the face of a kindly tyrant; eyes that were a deep dark color— "I never got his eye color right. Sometimes black, others a dark brown"— a great hooked nose, big and curved above thick lips. An extraordinary face. A face that nobody, having seen it once, could ever forget.

"You know, Herb, in a way that man had the face of a caricature Jew; Fagin in Dickens' *Oliver Twist*, or the makeup some actors use when they play Shylock. You remember that Brit actor in the musical *Oliver*, the movie, with over-the-top makeup? This man could have been that Brit actor.

"He cradled me to his shoulder, lifting me up and heading towards the door. You know what I was thinking, all the time, while this kind old man led me towards the door, muttering soothing things? You really know what I was thinking? I tell you. I was thinking of my mother, and I heard her voice screaming in my head. 'Louis, you should never, ever, go with any stranger. Run away if a stranger asks you to go with him, Louis, there are people out there who are bad. You will understand when you get older. But I tell you now, and I mean it. Never let a stranger walk with you, it's the road to things you'd never dream of.'

"She'd say that kind of thing to me at least once a week and the hell of it was that she never told me why. All she'd say was, 'Louis, trust me. You'll understand in time. When you're grown up you'll understand what some strangers can do to a young child.' What good was that, Herb? It was then I needed to be told, not in the future, when I would know everything.

"So there I am, petrified, that this is the stranger who's going to do those unspeakable things to me. This guy is helping me and I am worried out of my head about what my mother'll say."

They went up a bare staircase, then into a room that smelled of tobacco, dust and another odor which he could not identify.

Later he was to discover the smell was that of paper. Piles of paper; mainly music manuscript paper.

"Poor young *bubela*," the man said in German-Yiddish.

"I'm not poor," Louis answered, speaking the same language, a warm and pleasant smile. "So," he said, "a German also. Me, I'm from Austria, from Vienna. And you?"

His lip, eye and ribs were aching and throbbing, but he had stopped crying. "I am from a village thirty miles from Passau, in Bavaria."

"Good. You know Passau well?"

"No, I've only been there three times. I did not like it much. Maybe now, when I've got used to New York, maybe now I'd like it."

"So." He had set Louis in a high, stuffed chair. Then he extended a large hand which seemed to sprout from a tree trunk of an arm. "Me, I'm Aaron Hamovitch. Shalom."

They gravely shook hands. "Shalom," Louis said. "My name is Louis Isaak Packensteiner, and my mother says I should never go off with strange men."

"And your mother is right, Louis. But thank the good Lord that I'm not a strange man." He gave a bellow of a laugh, and muttered the liturgy of all adults, saying that one day Louis would understand. "Now that we are introduced, I shall clean up your cuts and then take you straight home. You know the way, yes?"

Louis said, yes, he knew the way.

"Then make yourself at home, here, while I get hot water and some cloths. I must also use iodine which will sting a little, but you are brave enough to stand iodine."

Aaron Hamovitch disappeared into another room, giving the boy a chance to look around. The furnishings were better than those of his own home, though the apartment was smaller, and more dingy.

A thick carpet covered the floor and there was a profusion of chairs, most of them stuffed with horsehair, like the one on which he was sitting. Small tables, littered with frames containing photographs, were set all over the place, along the walls, and by the chairs. In fact, the walls were just as cluttered, a large gilt-framed mirror almost completely taking up one of them, while every available inch on the others was covered with oil paintings. Louis considered that his benefactor must be very rich.

The centerpiece of the room, indeed, it took up most of the floor, was a large piano, which reinforced Louis' views, for this piano was larger even than the one that Miss Abrahams thumped on at Public School No 1. It was also highly polished, and seemed to be the only item in the whole place that was free of dust.

He was looking hard at the piano when Aaron Hamovitch returned, carrying clean bandages and hot water in a basin. "Ah, you like my piano, yes?"

Louis said it looked very nice.

"Good. Then we have a little tune before I take you home." Hamovitch began to clean up the cuts and bruises.

"You play it?" Louis asked.

This launched his new friend off into a long monologue. Yes, for his sins, he played the piano, and the cello, and the horn. In Vienna he had played with the opera—"Under Mahler; crazy man. I saw him several times when he was here in New York. Just before he left to die. Only last year he died, you know."

Louis politely said he was very sorry, not having the slightest idea who this man Mahler was. It did nothing to stem the tide of Hamovitch's words. He had played with many orchestras. Bless him, Gustav had tried to get him a place with the Met when he was there, but—"they would listen to him about nothing. You know how it is?"

Louis nodded, and wondered how it was.

"So, I stay here. I play and I teach. You play, Louis? If you played, we could do some duets. I have transcriptions of all the great symphonies, made for piano—four hands. We could thunder our way through those. You play?"

Louis sadly said he did not play, wishing he could understand everything that Aaron Hamovitch was talking about. He winced as the man applied iodine to his cut lip, and all he knew was, that in spite of Hamovitch's overpowering manner, the oddity of his face, and the man's size, he liked him as much as he had ever liked anyone, apart from his lost cousins and his father and mother.

"You don't play?" The voice seemed as large as the man. "What d'you mean, you don't play? How old are you? Ten, eleven?"

Louis told him. Eleven. In September he had become eleven. Soon he would be a man.

"It's a little late, but not *too* late, Louis, my friend. Really you should start at five or six, but eleven is not altogether late."

He had finished bathing the wounds. "Right, so now I take you home in a minute. First, I play for you, yes?"

Louis said he would like that and went to stand by the piano.

Aaron flexed his big hands, gave Louis an angelic smile, then began to play.

"Herbie, I don't think I've told anyone the entire truth before. This was a kind of music I had never yet heard in my life. The throbbing stopped in my face and ribs and I was—how can I put it?—I was taken over by a cold, unusually icy feeling. It ran down my spine, then up again to the back of my neck. I thought my hair would stand on end. I can't explain it. It's been my secret all these years. I suppose it was excitement, but hearing Aaron play for the first time made me also feel like a giant. More than that, I had never heard this music before, yet, at that moment, it was as though I had known it since birth. Also, and this I have told nobody but you, I had an erection while he was playing. Odd, huh?"

Aaron Hamovitch came to the last dying note. "There. You liked that?"

"It was . . . it was very pretty." Louis knew this was a lame answer following all he had experienced. "I could not find words to say what I really felt," he told Herbie Kruger.

"Pretty? *Pretty?*" Hamovitch bellowed at the lad in his good-humored way. "You ever hear this before?"

Louis shook his head.

The man gave a huge sigh. "You say it is pretty. I just played for you the first Prelude and Fugue in C Major. *Well-Tempered Clavier*. Bach."

"You want me to bark? Like a dog?"

"Oy!" Hamovitch slapped his forehead with the palm of his hand. "Johann Sebastian Bach."

"Who is Johann Sebastian Bach?"

"God in heaven, eleven years old and he asks who is Bach. You'll be asking who is Mozart next."

"Who *is* Mozart?"

"Who is Mozart? You really ask that?"

Louis was filled with indignation. "I can't be expected to know everybody. But I liked what you played. It was wonderful. Listen . . ."

It was then that Louis suddenly had his revelation. In order to prove the point that he had liked the music, he began to sing. He had a pleasant accurate voice: they had told him that in school and the Rabbi at the Talmud Torah said one day he might even be a cantor, they would see. But now, the voice was bell-like in its clarity.

Aaron Hamovitch sat and stared, his jaw dropping open: for Louis Packensteiner, now repeated, vocally, every note he had just heard played on the piano. He la-la-ed, exactly, the entire Bach Prelude and Fugue No.1 in C Major from Book One of the *Well-Tempered Clavier*.

"There!" the boy said, defiantly, as he finished.

Hamovitch put a hand around Louis' right upper arm. "And you never heard this before?"

"Never."

"Listen." Hamovitch turned back to the piano and played a few bars of something more complicated. "Sing that," he commanded.

Louis shrugged. It was easy. He la-la-la-ed and da-da-da-ed, correct to every note, pitch, space, rhythm, melody—even managing to sound as though he could produce harmonies.

"Now sing the first piece again," Hamovitch demanded.

Louis repeated the first Prelude exactly as before. Not a note wrong.

"And you've never played the piano or had training?"

"Only singing at school, and at the Talmud Torah."

"You read music?" Hamovitch seemed very excited.

"No; what is there to read? I should be going." Louis was suddenly afraid of what his mother would say.

"And, if I tell you the truth, my friend Herbie, I was also a little afraid of what I had found out about myself."

Hamovitch was very gentle. "In one moment, Louis. I promise, in a moment I will take you home. First, just sit at the piano for a second. Just touch the keys. Don't bother what it sounds like, just touch them. Make a noise."

As he sat at the keyboard, Louis felt he had known about pianos forever. Gently he tested the keys. Then, a few moments later, hesitatingly he picked out the first notes of the Bach C Major Prelude. Only with one hand, slow and stumbling, but he found the right notes. When he looked up, it was into a face wreathed in a great smile. There was also—though he could not see it then—a hint of awe in those dark pools that were Aaron Hamovitch's eyes.

"Later, Herbie, Aaron told me that, at this moment, he knew he was in the presence of a musical genius."

Kruger grunted. "This man, Hamovitch, he really knew Gustav Mahler?"

"Oh yes, but you know there was little call for Mahler's work for many, many years. His time has only come again since the 1960s. I, personally, did not really discover Mahler until the late fifties."

This made little difference to Big Herbie Kruger. He was sitting opposite a man who had touched a man who had known Mahler. It was, to Kruger, something akin to the Apostolic Succession. But he put it away in the back of his mind to concentrate on the real work at hand, as Passau talked on.

On the way home, Aaron tried to explain, in simple terms, who Bach was. "The father of modern music," he called him. "Born and dead many years ago, but his light still guides all musicians."

He also told Louis that there were many people gifted in music from their earliest days. Many never discovered their secret, but those who did climbed to great heights.

"There was a man called Berlioz who became a great composer. I do not personally like his music very much, but he was a great man. From being a baby he knew it all. Instinct, I suppose they call it."

Then he went on to tell of a man who was still alive. A man with a funny name that sounded, to Louis, like Sam Sonce, who could play the piano when he was not yet three years of age; and composed music when he *was* three years. Another man, still alive and in Berlin: Busoni—"He writes very learned books and articles about musical theory, and composes a little, but not very good. Now he had no training whatsoever. Nobody taught him a thing.

"Then, of course there was Mozart. His father taught him, but he required little instruction, and he was strange. Did everything: played the piano and violin; composed, almost from the cradle. They say he could write a musical score, with all the parts, while in his head he was composing something else. But he died, burned out, before forty years."

Forty seemed a great age to Louis and he said so. Hamovitch's big paw clasped the boy's hand tightly. "Listen my young one. Would you like to play the piano?"

There was no hesitation. "Yes." In the present, Passau told Herbie he felt, at that instant, he would need no teaching. "I felt I already knew it. Arrogant, yes, but I wonder if you understand?"

Kruger nodded, saying he understood perfectly. "I, myself, came to music late—in my late teens. I play nothing, but I discovered what real music can do for a man, and *to* a man. I could not live without it. It's earth, air, fire and water to me."

"And you're not a professional musician, so think what it must have become to me."

"Oh, I know what it is to you, Maestro."

Passau gave a little sound of disgust. "Wait till you hear my whole confession, Kruger. Then you will know how I sold my eternal soul to the devil for the sake of music, and how I used the great talent, discovered in Aaron Hamovitch's dingy little room on Hester Street." With that he returned to the past.

It had started to snow. The great flakes were whipped down between the buildings, making little Louis' face sting even more, almost blinding him with their force.

"Good. You'd like to play the piano," Hamovitch shouted over the wind and cold. "I teach piano to a lot of people. Some very rich. So rich that I have to put on my best suit and go to their big houses to teach uninspired little girls who only want to show off. Others, not so rich, come to me. I do my best with them, though, as yet, I have found nobody who has that divine inspiration for either music or the piano. I listen to them playing their scales, and the prim girls just able to pick their way through *Für Elise*. This is how I make my living. Teaching the piano."

Louis' heart sank. He wanted to ask what *Für Elise* was but, instead, he came straight to the point. His mother and father would not have the money to pay for lessons.

"No! No! No!" Hamovitch shouted, causing two passersby, heads down against the wind and snow, to stop for a moment and stare.

"No! You don't understand, Louis. You, I teach for nothing."

Finally they reached the shelter of the building in which the Packensteiners had their apartment. Hamovitch looked steadily at the boy, his huge hands heavy on the lad's shoulders.

"It is too early to tell." He spoke quietly but in a way which made Louis attend to everything he said. "Too early yet. But I think you just might have a very great gift. Some call it perfect pitch, which means that your ears can tell when a musical note is accurate and when it is not. It just might be, Louis, that you are a natural musician. I don't promise, mind. But I must find out."

Again, Louis felt the same strange stirrings. The icy feeling rising and falling on his spine, the wink in his loins, and a tickling in his scalp.

His mother was beside herself with worry when Louis arrived at the door with the large, imposing man. His father had returned earlier, set out to find him and was still searching. Frau Packensteiner was on the verge of going to the police department and the hospitals, for there was a story going around that a boy had been attacked on Hester Street. She wept and wailed when she saw her son safe.

"My mother, Herbie. My mother was, shall we say, a tad overdramatic." He sighed, and then again, with feeling. "Embarrassing, my mother.

That night I thought I would die with embarrassment. But there you are, that is mothers for you."

Aaron Hamovitch calmed her. He had a way that would have tranquilized wild beasts and, within minutes, all the agitation and anxiety had left Louis' mother, though she seemed suspicious of the man.

When his father returned, Louis watched while his new friend performed the same soothing trick on him—for Herr Packensteiner was angry and looked stern, unforgiving, when he saw Louis.

Even though Hamovitch worked his charm on the Packensteiners, they were obviously apprehensive. Both of them questioned the man, and Louis, as though there might be some hidden crime which had passed between them.

Joseph Packensteiner swore he would seek out the young thugs and have them imprisoned, but Hamovitch only laughed, praising the way in which Louis had stood up to the bullies. The lad had near crippled one of them, while he, personally, had made sure the ringleader would remember the kicking his backside had suffered. "*Goyim,*" he spat. "They won't come back to Hester Street in a long time. It was lucky I heard the commotion from my window. I was pleased to be of help." Then he added, "Especially to a boy as gifted as your Louis."

A little later he said he would like to talk to the parents alone. So Louis left, to wash and eat his evening meal, which he took to his bedroom.

Later, his father came to him and sat on the bed, looking very serious. "Is this true?" he asked. "Is it true you wish to study the piano with the man Hamovitch?"

Louis said it was the one thing he now wanted in the entire world. "Please, Papa, when can I begin?"

"Not so fast," his father warned. Then, after more talking, he said it might just be possible for him to have a few lessons, starting next week. "I have to look into Mr. Hamovitch's background, though, Louis. We know nothing of the man, and no purpose is served by rushing into things."

"But I want to learn. I want to learn so much."

His mother came into the room at that moment. "Phoof! Musicians?" she scoffed. "What good is it to be a musician? My father's brother, he was a musician, back in Poland, and where did it get him? Study! Study! Study! The violin. A great violin player, they said he would be. Your uncle, Louis; if you had known him, your Uncle Csaba; and how did it turn out? Playing the fiddle, yes. Playing the fiddle for coppers on the street corner. A beggar; a *klezmer*; a Gypsy. Musicians, they're all poor. You get from nowhere in life as a musician. Look, even, at this nice Mr. Hamovitch. . . ." There, she had said he was nice, "Look at him. Living on Hester Street and teaching piano. A great musician, he says you might be. A great musician—your grandfather would turn. In his grave he would turn. Be a musician and be a pauper, that's what your grandfather would have said. Now, a doctor . . ."

Joseph calmed her and said it would do the boy no harm to have some lessons. It would broaden his horizons. They would talk.

In the days that followed, his mother continued her diatribe against musicians, conjuring up, it seemed, a whole army of relations who had failed in an attempt to make their livings from music. It was the first Louis had ever heard of most of these kinfolk and he very much doubted their existence. But he had sharp ears and, ever alert, listened to snatches of conversation between his mother and father. The first sign of hope actually came on the next day when Joseph announced, thinking Louis was out of earshot, that Hamovitch taught the piano to many of Mr. Chorat's richest customers. The very customers he was trying to lure away from Chorat by making special deals and offers.

Then, two nights later, Louis heard his father pass on some newly discovered facts. He said that Aaron Hamovitch had, indeed, been a very famous musician in his time. His wife had died, suddenly, and tragically, in Vienna, and Hamovitch had been very ill. Eventually it had been because he could not bear to live in the city in which his wife had died that Aaron had come to America.

"He has money to last a lifetime," Joseph told Gerda. "People who know of these things tell me he could be a great musician again. That there are offers for him to play with many of the best symphony orchestras, but his friendship with some famous musician has not helped in New York—this famous man, who was his friend, is not liked here, even though he is now dead. Anyway, Aaron Hamovitch lives in the manner he does by choice."

"So they say," Gerda sneered. "Me? I don't believe a word of it unless I see it written down in a language I can understand. Learning to play the piano will go to the boy's head. An honest shoemaker like yourself he should be. A good honest trade." As her father always said—she constantly quoted her father—"Undertakers and shoemakers are people always in demand."

"A shoemaker he'll have to become, Joseph. Though, of course, I would rather he was allowed to study something that will make him really famous and a boon to us in old age. But he does not seem to be blessed with many brains, so, should this music thing get into his blood. . . ." There she stopped, leaving the thought hanging in the air, like a sinister question mark, black and foreboding.

Sadly, Louis thought that was the end of it, so it was to his huge pleasure and surprise that, a week later, Joseph told his son that he would be allowed to study the piano with Aaron Hamovitch, for one hour, three times a week, after the Talmud Torah. He had even arranged for Hamovitch to accompany the boy home after each lesson. Nobody was going to risk a repetition of what had happened on that December night. Eleven years he may be, yes, but the streets were no place, even for an eleven-year-old, late at night.

The arrangement carried one proviso, that, when he was thirteen, and a man, his father would begin instructing him in the art of shoemaking. That was his mother's wish, and she was right to demand it.

The following Tuesday, after the lessons at the Talmud Torah, Aaron Hamovitch was waiting outside, on the sidewalk. Together they walked back to his apartment, Aaron talking all the time—

"This one hour, three times a week, is of course nonsense. But we shall see. In time I shall persuade your father and mother to let you come more often. Then there will be practice. We shall see; we shall see if you're worth it or not."

They mounted the stairs to the Hamovitch apartment, and so Louis Packensteiner passed into a new life, a new world, exciting, stimulating, enchanting, but more demanding and exacting than he ever could have imagined.

Big Herb had been so caught up in Passau's tale that time had passed unnoticed. They were sitting now, almost in the dark when the telephone rang. Five times, Herbie counted. Naldo was on his way and felt safe to come to the house.

He scurried around, pulling the heavy drapes, putting on lights in readiness, while Maestro Passau listened, unemotionally, to Eliahu Inbal's recording of the Bruckner Sixth. Hearing the majesty of its opening, and the progression of its grandiose musical structure, Herbie wondered at the fact that someone so single-minded and direct as Bruckner had been persecuted throughout his entire life. Man's reaction to other men's musical genius was, Herb decided, one of God's huge and complex conundrums.

The symphony filled the air as Kruger began to prepare their evening meal, but it was hardly into the second movement when he heard the car pulling up behind the house, and, seconds later, faced a grim-looking Naldo Railton who demanded a sitdown with both Herbie and the Maestro.

11

MAESTRO PASSAU SHOWED no interest in Naldo's arrival. Herbie had to go over to the CD player and hit the stop button, sending Bruckner into oblivion. Even then, Passau simply said, "You know, that young Inbal could turn into a pretty good professional conductor if he works at it."

"Did you get an answer from him?" Naldo sat looking towards Herbie.

"The question about the mob?"

"What else, Herb, the price of melons? Yes, the mob. Yes, of course the mob; the Cosa Nostra, Our Thing, the Mafia, the Company. Call it what you like, did you get an answer? Has he got mob connections?"

"The answer is yes, but that's all I know." Herbie now faced Louis Passau. "You remember, I asked you if you had mob connections?"

"Sure I remember. You remember what I told *you*?"

"You said, yes. You also said we haven't come to it yet."

"Okay, then what's the problem?"

"The problem, Mr. Passau." Naldo crunched at the words, as though they were rationed and he was counting each one. "The problem is that I have the FBI on my tail. In turn, they have a couple of mob hit men on their tails trying to get to you. I've put my ass on the line, as they so quaintly say around these parts. I need answers."

Passau looked up at him with his blindingly clear blue eyes, enhanced by the contact lenses. For the first time, Herbie saw the true autocrat in the man and for a second or so there was anger as he spoke. "Mr. Railton, I don't know where the fuck you come into this, but I'm pleased that, by the course of events, I am making a full confession of my life to Mr. Kruger, here. I am doing it of my own free will, and I assure you that I will tell him more than I would ever tell some half-assed set of interrogators from Langley."

He shifted his body in the chair. The movement seemed, from where Herbie stood, to be a kind of seated boxer's stance. Aggressive. Then—

"Listen, Mr. Railton, and listen well because I only say it once. If I am to go on this journey through my life with my friend Kruger, then I must do it in *my* way, or not at all. If you want to fuck around with stuff out of context, then so be it: you won't get half of the real juice. I would suggest you leave now, before I get angry and have my final heart attack, which will leave big holes in history."

Naldo swallowed. Only Big Herbie saw his hands clench and could hear the temper being controlled as he spoke again. "Very well, Maestro Passau. I think I understand. But there's one thing you must know. In a strange way we are all trying to protect people, and that means we're trying to protect you. Will you answer one question about this mob connection?"

"One, and one only. Okay?"

"Right, sir. The two attempts on your life back in New York. Do you think that was the mob, or some other link with your past?"

Passau changed, one second the fierce glaring fury, now a soft chuckle. "Of course it was the mob, Mr. Railton. It was always the mob. This is not the first time. They've tried before, and I know who is really pulling the trigger. Maybe they'll get me, maybe not. It matters little, for any day now my health, which has been so good to me, will pack it in; my body will stop functioning, and I will die. It's only a question of time, whether God—if He exists—gets to me first, or whether it's my old Mafia friends, who at least know one reason why I should die, in some agony."

Naldo nodded his thanks, then asked Herbie if they could talk on their own. Bruckner came back to life almost before they were out of the room.

In the conservatory, Naldo motioned Kruger towards a chair, set well back from the windows. There he told him about the FBI coming in like gangbusters with the ineffectual fellow from the Embassy.

"They're still watching my place," he said, "and, this morning, I had another visitor. Very clandestine. I had to think on the fly."

"They're not all the time on your back ?"

"The phone's wired now, I'm pretty sure of that, but they're not following me all the time."

Kruger nodded. "Makes sense. Probably have a manpower problem, so that could change. Who's the new light in your life, Naldo?"

Railton said this was serious. "You know a girl called Pucky Curtiss?"

"After my time, and yours. Never met her, but she's a desk spook at the Office. Liaison with Grosvenor Square, I think."

"Well she's in the field now, Herb. She's here."

Kruger shook his head, "I don't believe the idiots we got these days. Liaison with the resident spook at Grosvenor Square one minute, then here, where they must have a dossier on her. Is crazy, Nald."

"She came with a particular message. The Office thinking was the same as the FBI Counter-Intelligence boys. That you would come hustling to me."

"Then they were thinking dead right, huh? Where else would I go? You tell her?"

Naldo shrugged. "She more or less told me. Says she needs a word." He paused. Then—"Dinosaurs, Herb. We're bloody dinosaurs. You know two-thirds of the American population really believes it's all over . . . forever and a day."

"Say a day without the ever," Herbie quoted, then thought for a moment. "At home as well. Most of the opposition party talk about disbanding the Office. Different tune if they were in power, no doubt. Sure, the Wall comes down. Peace breaks out. A hard-line coup. Mikhail Sergeyevich on the ropes. Big Boris to the rescue. End of communism. Suddenly we're chums with Moscow. They *really* believe it's over. Is like the Pope saying, 'Catholic Church is ended. Finished. Go home and pray no more.' You believe it? A magic wand is waved and all disappear like magic trick. It should be so easy. So what does this Pucky person want to say?"

"She tells me that, if the Office decrees it, they'll get you, and that rather nasty old genius, out: back to England, home and beauty."

"You believe her, this Pucky?"

"She's persuasive and, I suspect, frightened."

"You tell her anything?"

"Not a word."

"But she knows, ja?"

"Possibly."

Kruger's brow wrinkled again. "Look Nald, I'm sorry to be mixing you up in this. But is important. How they laid it out to me in London, is important. Not Passau's old Nazi friends, but things more recent. Things of the present and future. I seize the moment, is correct, seize the moment?"

"You bloody know it is, Herb. Stop playing games. It's me, Naldo who helped you cut your teeth."

"Sure, Naldo. Okay. So events put Passau in my hands: is really just what London wanted in first place. In an odd way he trusts me, but he has to do his own thing. Unload himself to me. Might take months. Could be only a week or so. The guy's ninety and he gets tired, but he enjoys talking with me and I'm all the Office's got over here. I talk with this Pucky girl and she has the dogs on me fast, I think. Then we'd lose any chance of getting to the real heart of the matter. The Office wants names; they want who's really with Mikhail Sergeyevich and Big Boris Nikolayevich. The battle order for peace in the new republic—there's still a battle order, Nald, in spite of it all."

"Wouldn't surprise me in the least, even though today's paper says KGB is being dismantled."

"Sure, they'll change its name. Look, Nald, this old man knows a lot. Sure, maybe the mob tries to knock him off, but I think also that there are people in Moscow—or Kiev, or Petersburg, who also wish he was missing."

"What d'you want me to do, then, Herb?"

"Is she settled in—the Pucky person?"

"At the best hotel in town. Boar's Head Inn."

"No, I mean is she a stayer?"

"I think she's been told to find you before the natives get your scent, yes. Art says to trust her."

"Keep her on the dangle for a few days. See if the G-men are moving in; try to find out what her real instructions are." Herbie gave a little smile which deepened the wrinkles in his leathery face. "See, I don't believe, necessarily, that a girl from London who's worked the Grosvenor Square beat is here automatically to take us back to London. Maybe the Office wants to give her an hour of glory with Langley. I don't know how that works anymore, Naldo."

"I'll hold her off as long as I can. If you need to talk with her, she's at the Boar's Head under the name Cummings. Pauline Cummings."

"As in Cummings and goings, ja?"

Naldo ignored the pun. "If we don't give any of them cause, maybe they'll start looking elsewhere. Herb, where else could you run?"

Kruger grinned, "Cummings and goings, ha! Think about it Nald. Only one other person this side of pond I'd go to, and he's about as old as you. Older possibly. We all worked with him a million years ago."

"Not Marty Forman?"

"Who else?"

"Didn't know he was still alive."

Back in the years immediately following World War II, they had worked close to Marty Forman, a tough street fighter who would have turned to the dark side of the law if it had not been for the Office of Strategic Services: OSS, America's contribution to things secret during the struggle against the Nazis. Marty was one of those men who took to the arcane vale of tears like a good monk to his vocation. When the CIA grew out of the remains of the OSS, Marty was there, a natural: active, astute, intuitive and very tough.

"Alive, well and living in Florida. We talk now and again. We write letters. . . ."

"And, unless Marty's changed a great deal, he'd hand you over without giving it a thought."

"No, Marty would want a piece of the action. Possibly, Naldo old sheep, we could get them to believe I've gone native elsewhere?"

"Maybe, who knows? If I left town in a hurry: fast with minimum baggage. Might work. Stick around, Herb. I'll keep the lady happy if I can. Should it become a problem, I'll be in touch."

"For Chrissake watch your back, Nald. You're not as young as you were."

"Are any of us?" Naldo gave him a rueful smile and let himself out of the door to the rear of the house.

He drove back the way he had come, towards Charlottesville, and then into the area immediately adjacent to the UVa campus. He took a turn which led him into a small cul-de-sac behind several affluent houses and parked in the space he had vacated an hour before, among other cars belonging to guests at a cocktail party given by one of the faculty members. He had parked this, their second car—a little Subaru—earlier in the afternoon. It had been pure luck that the Subaru was in for a service when the Feds hit town. Since then he had come and gone in the Lincoln, Barbara waiting for him when he stashed the second car after picking it up from the dealership. They had arrived at the party together, though Naldo had made his excuses and said he would leave Barbara and be along later. If the Feds were behind them they would see the Lincoln in front of the house, as they would see Naldo and Barbara leave together. The Subaru could be moved around as secondary transport.

Barbara was having a fine time at the party. Naldo had a few drinks, ate the obligatory chicken wings, and they left around eleven.

The Feds had a couple of the local cops, in plainclothes, working shifts at keeping an eye on the Railtons' house. Naldo spotted the car, parked in plain sight. Inside, the elderly cop logged their return. Out at seven P.M., back in with the lights on at eleven thirty. He thanked whoever was the patron saint of surveillance operations that a trained team was being brought in from Washington the next morning. Singer, rightly, felt there should now be a tight watch on Donald Railton and his wife. It would begin before dawn. From then on, the couple would have the dogs on them twenty-four hours a day.

DAWN, AND BIG HERBIE Kruger's eyes snapped open. He was sweating and had been dreaming the old dream about Berlin before the thaw; a girl called Ursula, ruby glasses with fluted stems, and a Dürer pen-and-ink of an Avenging Angel. He recognized the old favorite, the ghost from his past. At the same time, he thought this was the third day of interrogation and he had better get a move on: push Passau.

As he shaved, he knew that the old man would not be pushed. Just as Maestro Passau had proceeded through life at his own pace, so he would manipulate any interrogator. Herb would have to march to the beat of Passau's drum and hope that the nuggets, when and if they came, would lead to a rich vein. He was doing what all the good interrogators did.

To save time, he worked in the kitchen, preparing meals that could go in the freezer and then be cooked in the microwave—lasagna; his own version of the English North Country Lancashire Hotpot, which he left simmering for lunch; and his own sensational stuffed onions, ready, with the lasagna, for the freezer. In the midst of the cooking he took Louis Passau his breakfast, appearing in the bedroom and singing his own, highly original version of "Nessun dorma" slightly off-key, so that Passau shouted at him, "Puccini's raising a dust storm in his grave, buffoon!" Then, almost playfully, he hurled a pillow at Kruger's retreating bulk.

By nine thirty they were at it again, sitting opposite each other, with Kruger ready to hear what happened once the boy Passau began his lessons with Aaron Hamovitch.

IF YOUNG LOUIS Packensteiner expected the first lesson with Hamovitch to start with practical work on the piano, he was sadly mistaken.

"You know from nothing," Hamovitch began, shaking his shock of gray-white hair, then running a hand through it, like a pitchfork through hay. "Of music, you know from nothing at all. So, we must probe, Louis. We must tinker and delve until we discover the seat of talent. When we find it, we unleash it. So, to work."

Hamovitch moved across the cluttered room, twisting and turning like a dancer to avoid the chairs and the little tables with their photograph frames, until he reached a bookcase. From this he took down his own, beautifully bound copy of the Torah, opening it at the Book of Genesis.

"First, Louis, you read." The heavy book was passed to the boy.

"I've just come from the Talmud Torah. I thought I was here to learn about music."

"So you shall. Read, and you might just learn something about music. Read from here." A finger like a leather prong darted out to the page. "Read, Louis. The first lesson of music is discipline. The Maestro you must obey always. For you, now, I am the Maestro, so read."

Thus the lesson began, with Louis reading aloud, about God creating heaven and earth; the darkness; the light; the division of water and dry land; the growth of grass and herb; seed and fruit.

Hamovitch stopped him before they reached the part about the creation of fowls, creatures and fish. Leaning forward, the large teacher began to question—

"Now, Louis, while God was creating this wonderful universe, placing the earth on its axis, the sun and moon to rule by day and night, dividing the waters—while He was doing all this, would there be a great many eruptions, yes?"

Louis agreed. There must certainly have been such things.

Hamovitch nodded his great head. "There would be volcanoes, I should think, and earthquakes, rending the rock and earth asunder, the sudden rushing of mighty waters. Tell me, now, Louis, was there sound to these great shakings of the earth?"

In the here and now, Passau looked at Kruger, nodded and said, "Herb, I recall that first lesson as though it took place yesterday. I know what was going on in my head. In my head there was this picture of great ferment: of the gush and geyser of hot lava from volcanoes; the bubble of boiling mud; the terrifying crash and crumble of earthquakes, making way for the huge mass of waters. To place the earth on its axis, I thought, would be to disturb many things. Hamovitch was so clever, he reached into the mind and drew out pictures. I answered in the only possible way."

"Of course," young Louis replied. "Of course. There would be a great deal of noise."

"Really?" Aaron Hamovitch raised his bushy eyebrows.

"It's obvious."

"Wrong. The first mistake!" In spite of the cutting edge to his voice, the older man was smiling. "This is your first lesson. There are no sounds, and no noise, unless there is someone to hear the sounds. God is spirit, and so would not necessarily hear the noises. If He did not hear, there was nobody else, nothing else. Waves of sound, yes, but nobody to receive it. A madness in silence. You see, Louis, to make music you must have two things: the sound, and someone to hear the sound. Someone to be moved by it, to weep at it, or laugh, dance, or feel his imprisoned soul soar to the heights; or be comforted, frightened, delighted, even, possibly, revolted by it."

"Herbie, my friend, this was the most incredible man. There were times when I thought Aaron Hamovitch was possessed by some kind of devil. He was intense, yet wholly dedicated. Music was his life, for the sheer joy of it. Not like me, where music became a means to an end. You follow me?"

Herbie Kruger, keeping his identity as an interrogator, inclined his head and raised one large hand, a slight movement, as though indicating that Passau should continue.

In that moment, years before in the room above Hester Street, Hamovitch looked surprised, as though the thought he had revealed had only just occurred to him. "Louis," he continued, "*All* sound is a kind of music. The newsboy shouting, 'Extray! Extray!', the dogs barking, people screaming at each other, fighting, the automobiles in the street, or the horses. Even the rattle of the El. Even this"—he brought his hand down onto the table with a sudden loud thump which made Louis flinch. "That is a sound. All sounds are basic music. Sound only needs marshaling a little, then you have something any fool would recognize as music. From this moment, I want you to live listening to the music of life, because it is everywhere."

The teacher went on to explain what he meant by marshaling sounds to make them into recognizable music. He taught the boy the three elements of the organization—rhythm, melody and harmony. "Engrave those words on your heart," he told him.

"But he was good, and clever, Herbie." Passau's face lit up in a smile. "He taught me the rules of music, but he also taught that the essential thing to remember in music is that you could break the rules."

From this simple start, Louis began to learn. In the weeks and months ahead, the lad was to spend increasingly more time with Hamovitch, who had been right about one thing. Louis Packensteiner was a natural musician, who learned almost intuitively. "This boy," Hamovitch said to himself—"I know this, Herbie, because he told me so later"—"is the true gold from which great musicians are made."

A few months after their first meeting, Aaron decided that Louis should be exposed to the full richness of music: the orchestra. A treat was devised and Hamovitch obtained two tickets for a very special symphony concert.

At that time, the great, and equally temperamental, Arturo Toscanini was in charge of the Metropolitan Opera in New York, emerging only occasionally to conduct concerts. This was one of his rare appearances in the concert hall and Louis was quite unprepared for the shattering impact of hearing a full symphony orchestra.

The boy sat, overwhelmed and bewitched by the surge and texture of the desks of violins, violas and cellos, the woodwind, the brass and timpani, all of them working in unison, producing a combination of great sound—wonderful, organized music.

This was his baptism of fire, his introduction to symphonic music on a large scale, relatively late in his young life, at almost twelve years of age.

The featured work that night was the Beethoven Ninth Symphony, and when the soloists and choir came in with the vast setting of Schiller's "Ode to Joy" in the final movement, the boy wet himself: oblivious, in his concentration, amazement and awe.

"I tell you, Herbie, I had difficulty in sleeping, that night. I had made the first decision of my life. During the concert I did not take my eyes off Maestro Toscanini. His power over the music was to me awesome. This man, in front of the orchestra, had complete control, and this was now my first and foremost goal. I told nobody, but it was that night I knew I would one day become as great a conductor as Toscanini and, by Christ, I did it.

"We worked, my God how we worked. In those years, even when I began to help my father and learn his trade, I sucked up music like a sponge. For the next years, I hardly thought of anything but music, though great changes were taking place around me, and in the world outside. The first of those changes, Herbie, was to bring a clash between what was honest toil, to my father and mother, and what was the real value in life as far as I was concerned.

"The business of learning my father's trade came upon me suddenly, almost without warning. It was very dramatic. One day I was a boy going to school, and spending most of my spare time studying with Aaron Hamovitch. The next, I was learning my father's trade. To me it came in the wink of an eye. A truly unnatural wink. It happened like this. . . ."

12

THEY DID NOT EVEN STOP for a morning break. Herbie had found Passau liked coffee, usually halfway through the morning session. Today, the old man seemed to have made the journey back to his boyhood so completely that very little stood between the reality of the past and the truth of the present. He continued to talk, slowly and carefully, occasionally using his hands in a gesture, or to paint invisible signs or scenes on the canvas of the air. His voice would also alter, as though he were an actor playing all the parts in the drama.

Passau was engrossed in the narrative of his life, though Kruger could not tell how much of it was true and how much a fiction which had taken the place of truth down all the Maestro's days. At the moment it did not matter greatly but the time would come when every nuance would be important. He remembered an old confessor, at Warminster, telling him, "Always remember that all autobiographies are selective."

"Beside what happened to me, in those first years in this country," Passau continued, "the other events were already taking over, though I was not always truly aware of them."

Domestically, important things *were* taking place. As soon as he could read and write English with moderate accuracy, Joseph Packensteiner made application for full American citizenship. He passed the simple tests and, a little over two years after their arrival, appeared before a judge to answer the final questions.

Packensteiner senior emerged from the courtroom as an American, and the judge, after hearing evidence, waived the sections in the so-called New Law of 1906 and allowed Joseph's wife and son automatic citizenship with him.

This, in a way, seemed to give the little family a new identity, and a sense of pride. Chaim had misled them on many things but he had constantly said that, once in America, it was necessary to make the country your own. Forget the ties of the past.

One tie that Louis could not forget was the bond with his three cousins, for whom he pined even in the midst of discovering his dormant talents as a musician. His thoughts of the three children, his greatest loves, were as strong as ever. In fact, music seemed to bring them closer as it worked its magic on his emotional life. He would labor, he pledged, so that one day they would be proud of him, and he could go back for them. His vision of the future was of great success, followed by a triumphal march back to a huge, tearful reunion, after which he would bring his beloved Rachel, Rebecca and David to America and share his life with them.

"It was a sort of obsession, just as music became a total preoccupation," he said with a half smile at Herbie.

"From the very beginning there were letters. At the start, family letters, which made my father and mother weep, for Uncle Isaak was doing very well back in the village. Then, later, so well that he actually moved to the town of Passau itself. He flourished and became rich—about the same time as my father really commenced to make money—I'll tell you about this in a moment, Herb.

"Then, when I was in my teens, I began to get letters from David and the girls. Oy, Herbie, you should have seen some of David's letters when he became interested in girls. So explicit I had to hide them under a loose floorboard. David was certainly a boy for the girls. What would your average shrink say about the fact that my first sexual fantasies were lived vicariously through my cousin? You know, he also described how his sisters were growing, and once he saw Rachel naked. David would have made a writer. He described this time he saw Rachel; depicted it so accurately that I fantasized doing it with her. I almost could hear her voice saying, 'Lou, oh Lou.' You imagine what guilt I had over that? The onus of ages, Herb. Guilt, I know about guilt. . . ." He was sidetracking, off into tributaries of his life that probably had nothing to do with what Kruger was really after, but there was no way of stopping him. "I know from guilt, okay, Herbie." Again he fixed his eyes on that point, behind Herbie Kruger's head, which seemed to have become the gateway to his past. "Ah, but I tell you what happened—"

The next big change took place on the day Joseph completed his servitude with Mr. Chorat. Those three long years into which he had been duped by his brother Chaim.

While he worked out his time, Joseph took on more and more in the way of private commissions which he fulfilled in the apartment late into the night. Sometimes he would sit until after midnight, bent over his cobbler's last, shaping, cutting, stitching and nailing special orders.

This extra backbreaking work paid off handsomely. Most of his private customers were people of influence whom he had stolen from his boss. As soon as he obtained citizenship and was within six months of his release date from the binding contract, Joseph began making subtle approaches to these men and women, who were all more than satisfied with both his work and prices.

He asked advice about starting his own business. Then he found suitable premises, uptown, fashionable and a good half-hour's journey, on the El, from the family apartment.

Next, with the help of a banker's wife—who came down into the shabby end of the city because she was so satisfied with Joseph's work—he obtained a loan and made arrangements to purchase and refurbish the little shop premises on the day after his release from Chorat became legal.

To his wife and son he said nothing of these plans.

"Herb, believe me, I knew nothing until after it happened, and what I know of his final break from his odious master I learned much later, from listening to my father talk to my mother when they thought I was asleep."

"Earwigging," Herbie commented.

"What? What is earwigging?"

"We English," Herbie knew people smiled when he said this kind of thing with pride. "We English use this expression when someone listens in to conversations. In my business we do much earwigging. Some in my trade talk about electroplating when they're bugging the telephone calls."

"Earwigging? Electroplating? All English are mad." Passau shook his head, as though clearing it from some daze.

At the completion of work on that last legal day of his commitment to Chorat, Joseph gathered together his own tools, as he did every night, and made his way to the man's small office. It was on the dot of closing time, and he left a pile of unfinished work on the bench.

Elijah Chorat, although a master craftsman and no fool, was an unpleasant man of whom Joseph rarely spoke, except when he wanted to let off steam to his wife. He was short with a bony face and greasy hair which he wore combed back from the hint of a widow's peak. His eyes, Joseph was to say, were the eyes of a small rodent and his teeth were equally tiny, making the likeness to a rat complete.

He had, of course, completely lost time of the days, let alone the years, when Joseph Packensteiner came into his office on that Thursday night. He glanced up from his paperwork and snappily asked what his employee wanted.

"My wages to date. I leave now," Joseph told him bluntly.

"Wages? What you talk about, wages? Back to work, Packensteiner. It's late working tonight."

Joseph leaned across the desk. He could smell the man's bad breath, laced with garlic, as he waved his copy of the legal commitment within an inch of the shoemaker's face. "The day, Chorat. You don't remember the day? Or the date? No?"

"Oh, get on with it. I ain't got time . . ."

"Today, my contract with you is finish. Kaput! End!" Joseph stubbed his finger down onto the paper. "There, in white and black ink. All legal. Today is all completed. I go now, with my money, please."

It took a minute for Chorat to realize that he was in trouble. "I give you a raise." He tried to smile, fighting for time.

"Raise go up your ass."

"A partnership, then. I give you partnership."

"Partnership go up your ass."

"Look, Packen . . . Joseph, jobs ain't easy to find. You'll live to regret . . ."

"I got a job to go to. All I want is my money."

To give the devil his due, Chorat knew when he was beaten. He shrugged, counted out Joseph's wages and nodded.

Joseph Packensteiner walked out of the shop, without another word, not even pausing to say good-bye to his brother Chaim.

On the following morning he left the apartment, at the same time he always did, without even mentioning the change of circumstances to Gerda. That day he signed the papers for the bank loan and purchase of the shop, then started to make arrangements for the refitting of the place. He even hired a boy apprentice. With his son, and this other boy, he could manage very well. That night, when Louis returned from his lesson with Hamovitch, his father smiled and said he had news.

"I tell you, Herb, I was dumbstruck." Passau's face mirrored the face of the boy he had been. "I came in, full of Tchaikovsky's Fifth Symphony which Aaron had been going over with me, and my father said, 'Tomorrow, I'm pulling you out of school. Tomorrow, you begin to work with me.' I didn't even know if I would go on with the music. It was like an avalanche on my head."

His mother had danced around the room and insisted on being allowed to see the shop her husband had bought.

"The next morning we went to the place. It was well situated and my father seemed to be doing all the right things. The other boy he had hired was a tall, pimply youth. Sheldon, his name was, Sheldon Pamensky. He spoke English very well—a boy about my age, I suppose.

"The worst thing was standing in the middle of that shop, where workmen were fitting up a counter and signpainters were busy outside, my father put his arm around my shoulders and told me that I would be an asset to him. He would teach me the whole business of shoemaking. 'Together,' he said, 'we shall make other shops. If you learn the trade as well as Mr. Hamovitch tells me you learn music, then the name of Packensteiner will soon be all over America. Together we shall expand, Louis. We shall expand and become rich.'

"I was terrified, Herbie. I knew that my future would be in music. But my father thought this was merely a good way to keep me out of trouble. I remember my mother saying, 'It seems a good hobby for a boy, but it can't be serious. Nobody makes real money from playing the piano or a fiddle, still, it keeps him from mixing with the wrong types.' Ha! Herbie. How she was wrong."

Joseph Packensteiner was a fair man, and though he felt the music was a waste of time, he rarely kept his son working late at night. He allowed him to go on with the lessons and gave Louis generous time off, but he would not countenance slacking on the job.

"The two of us, Sheldon and I. This was our first job. We would have to take the measurements of people who my father knew well, or friends they brought to the shop. I tell you, Herbie, I was amazed at the number of customers. My father was a cunning bastard. He had really plundered

Chorat's clientele. Later we began to work with leather and I came to loathe leather. My hands went hard and callused. I worried that this would affect my playing, but I had no options. I went on working for my father and laboring even harder with my music."

Louis went to many concerts and opera performances with Hamovitch, and toiled happily over the piano. With all his contacts in the world of music, Aaron Hamovitch was always able to get his hands on tickets. In all, Louis learned the main classical repertoire by hearing it, following with a score, and playing four-handed transcriptions with his teacher at the piano. In this way he polished his technique, and also learned every nuance of all the great symphonies and concertos.

By the time Louis was fourteen, Aaron Hamovitch knew he was ready to be launched as a concert pianist. He had great plans for his pupil. First it would be one-night solo performances of works by Chopin and Liszt. Then, he knew, as sure as night followed day, that the boy would be invited to play with one of the orchestras. Louis already knew the major, and even some of the relatively modern concertos, by heart—the Beethovens, some of the Mozart, Schumann, the Grieg, and the more recent Rachmaninov Second which, at the time, was considered almost avant-garde.

When he thought all things were ready, Hamovitch approached Louis' parents for their permission to thrust his protégé onto the concert platform.

"Herbie, I only discovered this much later, because Aaron did not even hint of it at the time. He went to my parents and they laughed at him. 'The boy will make a good cobbler,' my father said. 'Yes, Mr. Hamovitch, go on teaching him. Let him play. Take him to these concerts and the opera. I think he benefits from them. But, please, please do not encourage him to think he can make money playing the piano. Madness will come, he will not see life in a proper perspective and he'll end up neither a good cobbler nor a good piano player.'

"My mother said, 'If God had wanted our Louis to be a musician, He would have given him a dowry.' That was her way.

"I recall that I never told Aaron that my real desire was to become an orchestra conductor, though he showed me the rudiments and, as you know, made me follow concerts with the score. I viewed the future with dread, but Aaron never once talked of the shape of life to come. Yet he knew, just as I knew, that I was destined to live a life in music, by music and because of music.

"When I talked to Aaron about my fears, he said, 'Wait and be patient. Life is a strange thing, Louis. Your time will come, I am sure. Eventually you will go to music not shoemaking, but wait. Work hard and wait.' So I did just that. Worked and waited. The shop was closed for entire weekends. We had the Sabbath on Saturdays, and the Christian Sunday was free. Aaron would give me lessons and take me to concerts at night during the week, and he would teach me for half a day on Sundays. He would make me practice for hours, and at home I would work, memorizing scores late into the night."

"Ja, you were like blotting paper." Kruger sounded diffident.

"Like a sponge."

"Okay, like a sponge, Lou. I have this picture of you with a score, working by the light of a candle." In his own way, Herbie was pushing quietly. "So what next, Lou?"

"The war was going on in Europe, the one we called the Great War. We heard very occasionally now from Uncle Isaak and Aunt Elsa. I would get letters from my cousins about four times a year. They were not doing so well with the war. Then, suddenly, they were doing very well because Uncle Isaak landed a contract to make boots for the military. But we didn't hear so often, and my mother was getting to be a little dissatisfied with life."

The area where the Packensteiners lived was becoming more and more dangerous. Gerda nagged at her husband to make money so they could move out. The Lower East Side was a breeding ground for young gangs, each with their own territory. "Today, the street gangs, people think it's a phenomenon of our time. They forget the street gangs of the past. Why, in some areas, Herb, near where we lived, you just did not go through certain streets. You knew your place and there were fourteen- and fifteen-year-olds who thought very little of murder. Death by violence has always been a fact of city life, and it was a fact that I soon became familiar with. Anyway, it was just after my sixteenth birthday, fall 1917, that I made a friend. Well, really I came across an old friend. A friend who would, in many ways, change my life."

It was a Sunday, and the teenager had spent the morning with Aaron Hamovitch. The weather was good so, in the afternoon, Louis decided to take a walk around the area. On a street corner he was addressed by a familiar voice—"Hey, Jewboy Pianist, howya doin'?"

"This was a boy I had known in school. For the time being, I'll call him Charlie—or, as we pronounced it then, on the Lower East Side, Cholly."

"I'm doin' okay, Cholly. How's by you?"

The boy was swarthy, bright-eyed, sharp, muscular and quick with his fists. In school it was rumored that his father was prominent in the Black Handers, well-known for their methods of extortion and violence in the Little Italy area of the East Side. Even at age eleven Charlie was thought to be a member of the Little Five Pointers, a junior group attached to the most ancient and violent of the old feudal East Side gangs, the Five Pointers, named after an intersection in the Sixth Ward. The Five Pointers had almost a century of brutal history behind it. Other boys had kept away from Charlie in school, though he had always been very friendly towards Louis, who had permission to use the school piano during recess and for an hour in the afternoon—a favor bought for him by Aaron Hamovitch.

There had been a time, just before his father had hauled him from school to learn the trade of shoemaking, that Charlie asked him if he could play any Italian music—"Like from operas?"

Louis had invited him to stay in the assembly room one recess, while he played some overtures to operas by Verdi, Rossini and Puccini. "Yea, my fadduh and his friends, they're crazy about that music." Charlie had nodded pleasantly. "They listen a lot to the Grand Opera on phonograph records. Nice music. I'm gonna call you da 'Pianist.' How about that, kid? Louis 'da Pianist' Packensteiner."

Now, on that Sunday afternoon, Charlie asked if he wanted to take a walk.

"Sure, why not? Got nothin' else to do except go home and get lectures on bein' a good shoemaker. My old man makes me work in his store now."

"Yeah, I heard. Big shoemaker now you're outta school."

"Big shoemaker, my ass. Big pianist more like."

Ten minutes later they bumped into a pair of Charlie's friends. "Meet my friend. He's a good fellah. Louis da Pianist."

"Looks like a kike ta me, Cholly," one of the lads said.

"Okay, he's Jewish. But he has the right attitude, and he's my friend, just remember that."

As they walked on, Charlie asked, "You don' belong to no racket, do ya?"

"Racket? No."

"I mean, like ya ain't a member of any of the gangs. Ya ain't connected with the Havemeyer Street crowd or anything like that?" The Havemeyer Streeters were the most aggressive of all the Jewish street gangs.

"I don' have nothin' to do with any of them, Cholly." He even began to adopt his friend's manner of speech. "I like a quiet life. I got things of my own goin', like music. Sure, I know some of them to speak with, but I keep away."

"Well, I'll tell ya, Pianist, if ya ever want to pass through any of the Italian territories, ya make sure ya're wid me, okay? I mean I know a lot of guys. I got connections, right? Any trouble, ya get holda me fast."

Over the next months and years, the unlikely pair became good friends and Charlie often took Louis through the toughest, most disreputable neighborhoods, vouching for him if they were stopped by young Italian hoods.

One evening, Charlie did three things for Louis Packensteiner. He opened his eyes to a different kind of music, gave him a peek at sexual initiation, and saved his life. All in one night.

"Tell ya what we should do," Charlie said. "We should take a ride over ta Harlem. Good things over there. I heard a friend of my fadduh's say there's good stuff to do in that area."

Louis, under Charlie's tutelage, had become very streetwise, though he sometimes wondered where Charlie got his money. He always seemed to have money for anything, from omnibus rides to cigarettes. "Yeah, so let's go to Harlem," he agreed. He had never been into that district before, but had heard it was lively in more senses than one. He was growing up very fast.

At the time, Harlem was a sprawling, ill-defined sector, once fashionable but now showing signs of seediness. There was a predominance of black people, but they lived peaceably with the white folk, though the whole area was a spawning ground for crime. It was certainly a district where sharp operators, of both races, could entice clients to the colorful night spots mushrooming along "The Main Stem," as the major artery— 125th Street—was dubbed.

On that night, Charlie and Louis gave the more garish of these places a wide berth, eventually stopping outside a small night spot, reached by going down a short flight of narrow stairs from the sidewalk, once used exclusively for tradesmen and deliveries. The door to what had originally been the servants' quarters was now slicked up with bright paint, and a shabby little awning was fixed above it so that the entrance appeared to be capped by an old-style poke bonnet.

The door was open, the glow of dim lights from the inside enticing, beckoning the boys like a pretty girl with her skirts. More than this, music filtered up onto the street—a kind of music Louis had never heard before.

"Ya wanna go in?" Charlie asked.

By instinct they knew this was really forbidden ground for a couple of youngsters, but the music was so different, and so attractive to Louis, that he was forced to nod agreement.

They crept down the steps and loitered, uneasily, by the door. Inside, the room was packed; smoke hung in the air and the conversation was at a low level, as though everyone was intent on listening to the music.

Nobody stopped them as they slipped inside. Most of the people had glasses in their hands, and there seemed to be a large number of gaudily dressed young women in the place. The clientele was mainly black, with a sprinkling of whites.

On a platform at the far end of the cellarlike room, a man sat at a piano and thumped out a slow, heady rhythm, while a fat black woman sang a sad wail of a song.

"Come on," Louis whispered, and they edged through the crowd until they stood just below the platform.

> "I thought I heard Buddy Bolden shout,
> Open up that window, let the bad air out,"
> the black woman sang.
> "Oh, I thought I heard Buddy Bolden shout,
> Open up that damned window, let the bad air out,
> Just open the window, let the bad air out.
> I thought I heard him shout."

Louis was more interested in the new-sounding chords of the pianist than the words of the song, which seemed to be treated with great respect by the people who listened.

"I thought I heard Judge Fogarty say,
Thirty days in the workhouse, take him away . . ."

At the end of the song, there was immediate applause and cheers from the crowd. The singer left the platform, but the pianist continued to play. The music was very different from that which he had played while accompanying the singer. In this man's hands the piano seemed to develop from one instrument into a whole group. First, Louis distinguished a constant and heavily rhythmic beat in the left hand. This was good, he thought. It made you want to tap your foot. Aaron was always quoting the great Mozart at him—"Mozart said that rhythm is the most important aspect of music." Well, this guy certainly thought the thumping rhythm was all-important, but Louis marveled at what the man's right hand was doing. There were chords, and mixed melodic lines that would have been very difficult to repeat, or even follow, on any other instrument. It was an entire small band playing there at the fingertips of one man.

Someone reached up and put a glass of beer on the piano. The pianist stopped to take a short break and drink his beer. As he did so, he caught Louis' eye and gave him a big smile. Almost at the same moment, both Charlie and Louis felt large hands grasp their collars.

"What in hell you two kids think you're doing here, huh? You got no business here."

Twisting their necks, they saw the hands belonged to a massive black man who did not look at all happy. "C'mon, you both outta here." Their captor started to pull at the boys, almost lifting them off their feet.

"Hey, whacha doin'?" Charlie shouted. "I'm fuckin' seventeen years old."

Loudly, and steadily, Louis lied, "I'm seventeen. We came to listen to the music. I'm a musician. Let me go."

Hearing this, the man at the piano gave a huge laugh. "The gentleman's a musician, Joey. Send him up here. Don' spoil the fun."

Louis felt himself being hoisted up onto the platform, while the man who had been holding them reluctantly released Charlie.

"So, you a musician, kid?" The man at the piano smiled, showing brilliant white teeth. He smelled of booze and was, Louis thought, not much more than five years older than himself.

"Yeah, I'm a musician, but I never heard music like you play."

"That so?"

"Is it ragtime?" He had heard Aaron muttering things about ragtime being the music of the devil.

"Hell, no kid. This ain't ragtime. This jass."

"Play some more."

The pianist grinned, and Louis watched carefully, noting rhythms, melodies and chords, as the magic fingers ran over the keys. "Boy, this is jass," the player repeated.

"It's not like the music I play."

"You know about music, kid?"

"Quite a lot, yes."

"Okay, this music is known as stride. Stride piano ain't difficult. Ten-note chords, right? Watch. Ten-note chords; steady heavy rhythm, and give 'em a good mixture. If you can play two notes at once, you give 'em melody and harmony at the same time, got it?"

Louis nodded and watched. He certainly did get it.

Suddenly the pianist stopped. "Okay? You got it, kid. Your turn. You a musician. You play."

He was trying to have a joke at Louis' expense, the boy knew that, but, stubbornly, he decided he could beat the man at his own game. "Okay." He tried to sound diffident, rearranging the piano stool, then concentrating.

Louis' natural gift of musical memory and mimicry surfaced. His head was accurately full of the melodies, harmonies and rhythms he had just heard. Placing his hands on the keyboard, he began.

After a few stumbling attempts he suddenly discovered that, just like learning to swim, this kind of music came naturally to his fingers and brain, already so used to the mathematical intricacies of Bach.

In fact, after playing a few bars of the pianist's own music, settled firmly into his memory, Louis began to put in his own melodies—only they were not his, but originally those of the master, Johann Sebastian Bach. The result, he thought, was not bad for a first attempt. Was this, perhaps, the freedom in music about which Aaron was always talking?—"There is no logic. No real rules. In music you are free."

The boy lost all sense of time. He also felt the crowd fall into a feet-tapping silence, punctuated by the occasional call of, "Play, kid, play!" or "Go, man, go! Git on out there!"

He finished to a roar of applause, and had a feeling he often experienced these days on waking in the morning. Light-headed, and stiff between the thighs.

"Hey, kid," the pianist beamed beside him. "You right. You a real musician, okay. What's you name?"

"Louis. Louis Packensteiner."

"Well, Louis. Well, I reckon we'll be hearing more from you. Shake some skin, boy." He extended a hand. "Just call me Jim. Name's Johnson. James P. Johnson, and you're welcome to play here any time you want."

"Thanks, Mr. Johnson, but I guess we better be gettin' home now."

"Your ma and pa know you're out?"

"Yea, but I reckon we're kinda late."

"Well, you take care goin' home. See ya, kid."

Charlie looked amazed, awed even, as Louis climbed down from the platform. His feet touched the floor and a very pretty, slim black girl smiled at him. "My, my, you're sure a neat piano player, shugah," she said, leaning forward and kissing Louis on the mouth.

This was another new experience. The girl filled his mouth with her tongue, and at the same time cupped a hand to the stiffness between his thighs. "Why," she giggled. "Well, you sure got something that should be taken care of. That where you do your piano practice?" She kissed him again, her tongue reaching to the back of his throat, and her hand kneading him between his legs so that he exploded, panting, his seed pulsing into his underdrawers.

When he finally left with Charlie, Louis was hobbling. He felt that he had been drained and his testicles ached. In the back of his head, he knew that he would soon have to do the real thing. Maybe he could come back here and find the girl again. She would do it with him, he knew she would.

But even this wonderful, though fast, semi-initiation, went from his mind when he realized it was getting close to eleven o'clock. They managed to get an omnibus, but it only went so far. Their final route, after the bus dropped them off, led through dangerous ground. They discussed it during the ride.

"Nothing else for it," Louis said, "we have to walk."

They both knew it meant going through a predominantly Jewish area. At this time of night the ardent young Jewish hoodlums would be around—Havemeyer Streeters or one of their off-shoots. "That's okay for you, Pianist. You're Jewish. Not the kinda place for a good Italian boy like me."

"You seen me through Italian turf, Cholly. I'll take you through Jewish turf. It's easy."

"Thought you had nothing to do with the gangs around here." Charlie sounded surly.

"I don't, Cholly, but think of it as me returning a favor. I'll see you're okay. I promise."

Charlie was unhappy, but Louis felt full of confidence after the night's experience. They took to the streets and walked rapidly, keeping to the more crowded thoroughfares and better-lit areas.

At last, though, they could not avoid taking a cut through a dark alley which would lead them close to their own home ground. They hesitated, then turned the corner. A gas lamp burned, throwing flickering shadows against the brickwork. Then, both boys pulled up like startled horses. The shadows parted to reveal three youngsters, lounging, as though waiting for them.

The three boys were a good deal older than both Louis and Charlie, who whispered, "Here we go."

"Don' worry," Louis said, feeling his stomach turn over.

"Who we got on our territory, then?" The trio stepped directly in front of them. Louis thought, immediately, of the day Aaron had saved him. But this was different, uglier.

"Goyim," one of the boys said, spitting.

"*Shalom*," Louis said loudly. "I'm not a goy. Louis Packensteiner, taking a friend home. No fuss, okay?"

The largest boy peered into his face. "You look kosher, but who's your pal?"

One of the others had gone up to Charlie. "Lousy wop, we got. Lousy fuckin' wop." He turned on Louis. "What's a Jewish boy doin' with a stinking wop bastard, then?"

"He's okay."

"Okay my ass. Nor're you okay, bein' with him."

Charlie spoke for the first time. "Ya want trouble, yid, then ya got it."

"Let's deal with the goyim-lover first, eh?" The leader took another step towards Louis.

All three of them must have seen the glint of Charlie's knife. It was the first time Louis even knew his friend carried one, but there it was: a sudden click and gleam in his hand, the long blade pointing outwards, and Charlie's body assuming a crouch.

The next few seconds confused Louis. He heard the leader shout something about getting the Jewish traitor first, and he saw the boy's long coat open up to reveal a heavy, metal shape rising towards his face. A shotgun, the barrel pointing full between his eyes.

Then Charlie gave him a push to one side, sending him sprawling, shouting, "Run, Lou! Just run! Get outta da way!"

But Charlie had fallen sideways right into the blast. The explosion filled the alley as the shotgun was fired. Charlie screamed as a whole charge of rock salt hit him. Rock salt was a favorite weapon for street hoodlums. Real shot was difficult to come by, and expensive, so they made their own cartridges from black powder and rock salt. It rarely killed, which was another plus.

He caught the charge full on the left side of his face: a spray which lacerated his cheek, making long, deep, pockmarked wounds: marks he would bear for the rest of his life.

"Charlie was lucky not to lose an eye. But he believed in a scar for a scar, Herbie. He was Sicilian, you see. He made the boy pay."

Already Kruger began to see a dark shadow over the story, a shadow cast right into the present.

Charlie was back on his feet, and saw that the leader was the only one properly armed. The others just had blackjacks, or socks packed with nails.

Again, he shouted at Louis, telling him to run. But Louis stood transfixed. Then Charlie sprang towards the boy who had put a couple of barrels of rock salt into his face. His hand came up, flicking the shotgun away like a piece of matchwood, his wrist performing a swift up and down movement. "It was like some tennis player's best shot: the wrist and the hand working with the entire strength of his arm behind it, Herb. Never will I forget that."

The one with the shotgun gave a scream of agony. Even in the half light Louis saw that the boy's face had been slit. Blood poured from his cheek and the shotgun fell to the ground with a clatter.

Charlie whirled around, as another of the boys came at him, flailing a sock full of heavy nails. He was inside the boy's guard with a duck and a weave. There was a second cry, louder than the first, as Charlie meted out the same treatment—the slit from ear to jaw: and all of this happening before the sound of the shotgun blast had died away. "Herbie, those guys could've poked their tongues right through their cheeks. The knife had really opened them up."

The third Jewish boy was not taking chances. He turned and ran as his two pals groped around, moaning and clutching their faces with hands dyed in their own blood.

Louis Passau paused and, during that pause, Big Herbie Kruger saw Charlie today, as clearly as he had seen him only a few nights ago at Lincoln Center.

A very old man who knew he was a king, desperately trying to straighten his back, bent by years. His silk evening suit magnificently cut, as though the tailor had used a black art to take years off the man, who still retained a full head of dark hair. Gold flashed at his wrists. Somehow anyone would know this man held a key to power, though the left side of his face seemed horribly scarred and pockmarked.

"Don Carlo Giarre," Herbie said in a whisper.

"Of course, Carlo Giarre," Passau laughed. "Sometimes, for fun, I'd call him Cholly." The old man imitated the accent he must have used in those far-off years. "When it happened, Carlo again told me to run. We both ran and, some years later, he taught me the trick with the knife. It's a very old form of Sicilian punishment. In America during those years it became a trademark. Sometimes other gangs would copy it, to shift the blame."

As they ran, Louis shouted, asking if Carlo was okay. "Does it hurt bad, Cholly?" He could see that the cheek looked like a steak ready for the broiler.

"Stings like fuck. It's gone in deep, and I'll be marked, but not such a mark as those kike bastards'll carry to their graves. No offense, Louis."

"How could I have taken offense, Herb? I knew that Carlo had saved my life that night. I was forever in his debt. I owed the man a life."

"And did you ever pay him, Lou?"

"Pay him? No, I foolishly increased the debt, to the point where Carlo's honor had to be satisfied. He's waited a long time, as you'll see. We were friends for many, many years, and did much together. But now . . ." He raised his hands, in a plaintive gesture.

Herbie thought he looked like one of the saints you saw in a stained glass window, depicting the Holy Ghost's arrival on the heads of the Apostles.

13

"BY THE TIME I was seventeen, Herbie, you know what I could do?"

"Surprise me, Lou."

They had lunched on Herbie's Lancashire Hotpot, which the old Maestro had pronounced, "Wonderful! Excellent! The best I ever tasted. What was it?" Now, Passau continued his narrative.

"I could play most of the repertoire's concertos without music; also things like the *Goldberg Variations* without music—though not on a harpsichord because we didn't have a harpsichord. I could sight-read any score: hear the whole orchestra in my head. Also, Aaron, after a lot of hints from me, arranged for me to have a few hours instruction with a famous conductor—at least he was famous, you will never have heard of him. . . ."

Herbie bristled, "Who? What was his name?"

Passau gave him a superior smirk. "Believe me, Herbie, this was a great coup. Aaron Hamovitch had the most incredible contacts. He got me three hours with Karl Muck. There, you ever hear of Karl Muck? I doubt it."

"We're talking about the Karl Muck who would be with the Boston Symphony Orchestra about that time?" Herbie gave a self-satisfied, semiautomatic smile. He could feel the invisible bullets catching Louis Passau right in the hauteur.

"So?" He was trying to sound enigmatic. "Not many people know of Karl Muck these days."

"If it's the Karl Muck who was an absolute bastard with other musicians; the Karl Muck who carried dueling scars from Heidelberg with pride, and dressed in Edwardian fashion until his death, I think sometime in the thirties; the one there was all the trouble about when it was

146

said he refused to play 'The Star-Spangled Banner,' and whose last concert was for Hitler? If it was *that* Karl Muck, then I know him."

"It was all lies about him refusing to play 'The Star-Spangled Banner.' People made that up, and said he was anti-American. But, if you know of him, Herb, then you'll realize it was a tremendous coup for Aaron Hamovitch. You know something about music, Herb?"

"Why you think I was put on this in the first place, Louis? Because I knew about the cubists? Muck was an autocrat. Did not like some musicians. Was very rigid. Would never tinker with scores like some conductors."

"Your blessed Mahler for one, Herbie. You know, in Vienna, Gustav Mahler would never change a note. When he came to New York he would cut great chunks from scores. He thought Americans knew nothing about music: thought they were Indians and cowboys. Once he even reduced Mozart—*Don Giovanni*—from three and a half hours, which is about right, to two and three quarters hours. Your precious Mahler was a genius with his music, but not a very agreeable man. You know that?"

"I know all there is to know about Gustav Mahler, and a good bit about all the others. Yes, as you say, quite a coup for your friend Hamovitch. Karl Muck, I recall, once refused to bother with a new composer because they told him, 'this is a self-made man.' He said . . ."

"'Really, all the composers I know have mothers and fathers,' yes. He *was* terrifying, but my three hours with him lasted for six hours, and I learned more than I would have done in a year with Toscanini. He taught me that the conductor was the servant of music and the servant of the score. By the age of seventeen, I was almost complete in my musical education. I also knew that, if I were to become a conductor, then my job was to illuminate."

Herbie nodded, as though this did not surprise him. "Also by the time you were sixteen, Louis, the war that had engulfed Europe had also pulled the United States into its furnace."

Passau shrugged. "Oh, yes. Yes, indeed. Uncle Sam needed me on every street corner so I went and offered my services. I recall that I had dreams of glory which always ended up with me conducting a fantastic concert with two military bands playing Beethoven's *Wellington's Victory*, with massed cannon and riflemen. I also thought there would be airplanes flying overhead. In the end, they would not have me."

"Because you had German origins?"

"Because I had flat feet. Oh, indeed some completely German communities were faced with terrible attacks, windows broken, homes set on fire, beatings in the streets. Some were taken off and arrested as spies."

"Including your six-hour teacher, Karl Muck."

Passau's face lit up. "Yes, it is ironic, Herb, that I should find myself in this position, when the man who gave me my first lesson in the art of directing an orchestra was thrown from America as a spy for the Kaiser."

"Hilarious." Herbie closed his eyes. "Tell me the next hundred pages of your history, Louis. I'm all ears."

"Well, my father was prospering, and he was by now thought of as wholly American. Nobody bothered us, and when the Johnnies came marching home again I was almost eighteen years old, filled out, tall, the blue eyes. Hey, my curly hair drove the girls wild. But I was too cowardly to do anything about it. Aaron taught me, I still went around with Carlo, worked for my father and lived pretty well."

At weekends Louis and Carlo continued to make trips to Harlem, and Louis learned more kinds of piano playing, including ragtime—bouncy, syncopated sound, played against a regular two-four, or four-four, beat.

"I think I knew, even then, that one day this kind of sound would emerge, in one form or another, and be enfolded into the classical repertoire. I even thought I could detect it in works written long ago. If you've read the books about me, then you'll know I was to get great criticism in the fifties for my recordings of Monteverdi's *Orfeo* and *Poppea*. People said I had modernized them. I hadn't, of course, it's all there if you look."

There were moments, Herbie Kruger thought, when he really disliked Passau. The man was a genius, everyone knew that, but a genius does not have to tell everybody how wonderful he has been. Big Herbie controlled his desire to inform Louis Passau, once and for all, that he was a pompous, overblown prick. Instead, he even actively encouraged him, because the kind of information he was getting from the old man was detail that had never surfaced, in interview, article or book. All of it was new so, being a spymaster with immense experience in all aspects of the trade, Herbie lusted after any item dropped by the Maestro.

These thoughts slid through his mind now, though he had no idea that, during this particular session, it would be lust, in the usual sense, that would play a predominant part.

"What I did, consciously, during the days working for my father, was to appear ham-fisted, with ten thumbs. I botched work with leather. I could never shape things exactly as my father wished. I became a numskull on the subject of shoemaking, though, alas, proved to be adept at dealing with the customers in the front of the shop. You see, Herb, I could never resist the chance, or the urge, to be charming. That in itself almost robbed music of a leading figure."

Joseph cajoled, bullied and constantly railed at his son, who could not even cut a piece of expensive leather with any accuracy. Yet Joseph was a worried man, his business went well, he was making both money and a reputation, but Gerda was showing signs of failing health. In her late thirties and early forties she had the look of a woman well over sixty years of age. Her hair went prematurely gray and she had arthritis which, on some days, made walking impossible.

Aaron talked again to his pupil about the future, for he had made several further advances to the Packensteiners, pleading with them to give Louis the chance he deserved.

"I should not speak with you like this, Louis, but it might be that you will have to make some painful decision in the next year or so. You are either going to be tethered to your father's business, like some scapegoat, or you will have to leave and meet your own destiny. That will, I know, cause great pain, huge anguish, particularly to your mother. But it is possible that it's the only way you will do what you were born to do."

Young Packensteiner nodded, miserable at the thought of bringing further heartbreak to his sick mother.

"Truly," Hamovitch told him, "you have to gather up immense courage. When the time comes, you will have to leave, like a thief in the night. It'll be of no benefit for you to stay and face it out with your parents, however much you love them. If you disclose your plans, they will only cling harder, and you will find it more difficult to escape."

"Herbie, my friend," for once Passau did not look smug. "Herbie, Aaron could not know how prophetic he was. Leave like a thief in the night, he said. I left like a thief. No doubt about that."

In the autumn of 1919, Louis made up his mind. He would carry on for three years only. If his father had not changed his mind by 1922—when he was twenty-one years of age—he would leave. During that time he would find some way of getting money together, to fund his escape into the world outside his parents' home and Joseph Packensteiner's business. Three years, then it would be a rift, maybe for all time.

But, first, there was to be another parting of the ways. Carlo regularly joined Louis on Sundays for sprees in Harlem where Louis watched, with unashamed envy, as the rich folk came to visit the area, going slumming in their glad rags. He began to drink a little, became well-known in some of the clubs and night spots, even sitting in with bands for fun and a few bucks.

Around the middle of October, the young men set out, one evening, for their old haunts and, on the omnibus, Carlo broke the news. "This'll be our last trip, Lou."

"Our last trip?"

Carlo did not look at him. "I'm goin' outta town, Lou. I gotta job away from New York. Lotsa money. A good life. My old man fixed me up with a buddy of his who's a real bigshot in Chicago. Guy by the name of Big Jim Colosimo."

For a couple of seconds, Louis was shocked. "Diamond Jim Colosimo?" Then the shock turned into envy. "He's a gangster, Carlo. I read about him in the papers."

"Sure, maybe he's into a few rackets; but you shouldn't believe all the newspapers say. Point is he's rich, kid; and he runs the biggest place in Chicago. Everyone goes there. All the famous people, even opera stars. Everybody. So I'm goin'. Some day I'll come back rich."

That night, for old times' sake, they went back to their favorite haunt, the first one they had ever visited. They were greeted by people who knew them as regulars in the area, men and women who had heard Louis play. The barman set up drinks for them and Carlo excused himself. He was away for a long time. In fact, Louis was not to see him until much later in the evening. As he sipped his beer at the bar, he became aware of a short, pretty black girl, who could not have been more than sixteen or seventeen years old, standing next to him, smiling. He could smell the scent she was using, and she pressed the side of her body close to him.

He had seen her around the place before; even made remarks to Carlo, for she was a slinky, sensual girl who moved in a way which made any real man begin to walk with a slight stoop.

"Hi, Lou." She came even closer to him, then whispered, "You wanna come upstairs?"

"What?"—"Herbie, I never had a feeling like it, not even when the young girl squeezed my cock after I'd played piano with Jim Johnson. This one? She woulda made a stud mouse feel like a stallion."

"I'm a present," she said. "Carlo's paid for me. We can take as long as we like, Lou. I'll make it real nice for you."

"Carlo's paid?"

"Sure, he's paid. Says it's a farewell present. I'm young, clean and here just for you, Lou. Or, maybe you don't like me."

"Herbie, old friend." The ageing Maestro's eyes seemed glazed over. "They say you always remember the first time, and the first girl you ever had. Well, I'll tell you they're right. If I could still get it up, I'd fantasize about her."

"I'm sure, Lou. Can we take it as read that you had a great time, eh?"

"*Great! Great*, you say? Herbie, for a young man I doubt if anyone on this planet had such a first time. . . ."

"It's what we all think, Lou." In spite of himself, Herbie recalled a dilapidated room in Berlin, just after the Russians had won the battle. He even saw, and smelled, the girl, maybe a couple of years older than himself. He remembered her name was Lotte, and she took his virginity from him with a longing, loving tenderness which made both of them forget their precarious situation. He thought often of Lotte, and wondered what had happened to her.

"Herbie, I tell you, this girl, her name was Melodie with an 'ie'—leastways, that's what she said it was, and it could have been right. She played it like an instrument, Herb. You ever had a woman like that? Like an instrument on which you play the most wonderful music? Melodie was like an entire orchestra. I still think of her when I conduct *Sacre*"—by which he meant Stravinsky's *Rite of Spring*. "All those throbbing and pounding strings. She was amazing. She was my first for quite a long time. I went back to her, and we were lovers: which meant I didn't pay her anything. But she was an inspiration, that little black Melodie."

Herbie was surprised. Passau seemed genuinely moved. But, as ever, he spoiled it.

"I tell you, Herb, that girl coulda sucked the paint off a Rolls-Royce."

"You have quite a reputation, Lou. With women, I mean."

"They became necessary to me. Like a drug, and I could never be satisfied with just one. I think all my life, after Melodie, I needed women. After concerts, after I had poured out myself on the box with a great orchestra and a great performance, I always needed a woman. You know what the Italians say?"

"Apart from 'Mama mia'?"

"They say that screwing is the poor man's opera, though I think opera is the rich man's aphrodisiac."

"You could be right, Lou. What was the final outcome?"

"On that first time I had six outcomes, Herb, and I'm not boasting."

"I believe you. There's a story that you once fired your leading tenor—a very famous man—because he caught you with your prima donna."

"Not me. That was Toscanini, but it's told about any conductor who gets a reputation. They all get caught by the tenor when they're with the diva, yes. And they all fire the tenor. It's not true, of course, but that's how they tell it." He gave a thin smile, which was not a true smile in that it did not go near his eyes.

"So what happened next, Lou?"

Carlo Giarre left a Chicago address and telephone number with young Packensteiner. "Don' forget, Lou," he said at their parting. "Anything you need—a job even—just write, or arrive. I'll be there, and I'll keep in touch."

He was as good as his word. The following year, when the newspapers were full of the story of Big Jim Colosimo's gangland murder in his own famous Colosimo's Cafe, Louis received a short note with a new address, telephone number and a scrawled message—*You can get me here most of the time, or leave a number for me to call you back. Plenty of work here for a guy like you. Plenty of dough as well.*

The address was still Chicago: a place called The Four Deuces.

By this time, the Volstead Act had become law, under the full title the National Prohibition Act. America was officially dry of liquor, and this spawned every evil in the book. New addresses and telephone numbers arrived from Carlo, and his notes begged young Packensteiner to join him. "Get rich the easy way," one of them said. Another was scribbled from a bed in the Jackson Park Hospital: "Be out in about a week. They don't use rock salt here." It was inevitable that this strange strong mixture of friendship would survive. In the end one of them would come running for the other.

There were different letters, of course—from Isaak and Elsa. They now told a tale of success turned to fear. With the war over, the need for army boots had ceased to exist. Business dropped, and there was trouble everywhere. In Russia, with the revolution, in Austria, Romania and Hungary. Things did not look so good now but, even though Joseph wrote impassioned letters, his brother and sister-in-law could not be persuaded to come to America.

Louis also had more letters from his beloved cousins, who told the same tale, though the girls wrote of flirtations with officers—they were always officers—and a genuine love match between David and a local girl. He would be married within the year. Like his father, Louis tried to tempt them with stories of life and money in America. When they wrote back, not one of his cousins ever responded to the inducements.

"I constantly fumbled work with leather and shoes," Passau sounded smug. "I drove my father to despair. But, in the spring of 1920, he managed to get the better of me."

Joseph purchased a second set of premises, a new shop and workroom, in the very fashionable area near St. Patrick's Cathedral. It was to be the showplace of what he saw as a whole chain of stores. By this time the boy, Sheldon Pamensky, had proved to be a natural craftsman. He also had a cousin, Benny Pamensky, who was already a shoemaker of some skill but little brain.

To begin with, Louis expected his father would take charge and move into the new shop. But, to his surprise, he found that Joseph had stolen a march on him.

"I've given up any idea of you ever being able to make shoes," his father told him one morning. "The new place will open next Monday. Benny will be the shoemaker, I'll visit once in a while, we'll get another apprentice. You, my fine son, will be the manager. Up on Fifth Avenue, they expect to see some style in their stores. You have that kind of smartness, so you can run the place."

The following Monday saw Louis, in a new black suit, take charge of Packensteiner & Son, Fifth Avenue. Benny had the workshop in the back, and a boy, Abe Schilling, with him.

By late in 1920, Louis had settled into the new position. He had also found a way of obtaining the cash he needed to squirrel away if he was ever going to escape from New York and his parents.

It was simple once he had organized it. What was more, because his father paid him a pittance, he had no conscience about stealing from the business—filching from the till, falsifying accounts. He even pocketed cash when someone came in to settle an account, which he, naturally, left in the ledger as still unpaid, taking care to see that no further bill was sent to the customer.

Towards the end of 1921, Joseph announced that the Fifth Avenue store was to have another employee, Benny's young sister, Ruth, barely seventeen years of age, to assist in fitting the many ladies who came to the shop. She would also run the stockroom, so she worked under the lascivious eye of Louis, who—as the old man now put it—"Found that I had an erection every time I looked at her. I had saved just over one hundred dollars, by stealing from my father and to be truthful, Herbie, I would gladly have thrown this at the Pamensky girl, just to cop a feel."

She was slim, dark-haired, and wore the usual long skirts of shopgirls, but somehow her skirt was tight, almost as tight as her blouse which looked as though it could never restrain her growing, swelling breasts.

"Herb, I lusted after her, and it was almost my complete downfall. It should have taught me a lesson. The lesson of that old proverb, 'a standing cock knows no conscience.' I lusted. Oh boy, did I lust."

It started on a Wednesday evening in early December. Joseph Packensteiner had taken to visiting the store every other day and he had made his visit earlier in the afternoon. Benny—and the boy, Abe—had gone home, as they usually did around six, leaving Louis to close the place up and settle the till.

Just after six o'clock he told Ruth that she could also leave while he cashed up. He was particularly interested in dealing with the cash that evening because, after his father had left, two large accounts had been settled in ready money. He planned to let one of them, a sum of over twenty-five dollars, remain on the books, while he would let the other—thirty dollars—show as being paid.

The day's takings, minus the twenty-five he planned to pocket, could be handed over to his father with pride. Better for the girl to be out of the way when he cashed up and falsified the till ledger.

But Ruth had other ideas. She looked as though ice would not melt between her lips. "She had a smile I have never seen on a girl before or since," Passau commented. "I never want to see a smile like it, either. It was tantalizing, as though her lips beckoned you, yet, somehow, it was the smile of a snow queen."

"Frosty?" Big Herbie asked.

"No. A smile of sugar icing."

She was a girl of high intelligence, the kind who was determined to get to the top in any way she could. She was not going to be like her mother, who scrubbed and polished office floors from three in the morning until seven. The Packensteiner business was going places. One day it would be worth a lot of money. True, she nursed a secret desire for the blue-eyed, curly-haired Louis, but that simply made her long-term plan easier. She would have her share of the Packensteiner future, which she saw as the Packensteiner fortune.

On that particular evening she said there were still some shoes to be put away, and some to be made ready for delivery first thing in the morning. She had promised Benny that she would leave them, boxed and parceled, so that Abe could get them out first thing.

Louis told her not to be long about it. Then, making sure she was safely in the small stockroom, he began to enter the amounts in the ledger: placing one pile of money in the canvas bag he would take home to his father, while the twenty-five dollars in crisp notes were left to one side, ready for his pocket.

He completed the task, and had just slipped the notes into his jacket when he turned to see Ruth standing in the stockroom door.

"I'm finished now, Mr. Louis." She stood about three paces from him, smiling her sugar-icing smile. "Looks like you've done your own bit of business as well. Your papa know that you take your wages straight out of the till?"

Louis automatically turned on his smile. "Ruth, Ruth," he shook his head. "You think I would steal from my father?"

She did not bat an eyelid. "I guess you would, Louis. You're quite a man and, if you'll pardon me saying so, your papa's a shade stingy. I wouldn't blame you if you had sticky fingers."

"And if that was the case—*if*, mind you—I suppose you wouldn't think of telling my pa?"

She came towards him. "That depends, Lou." She was within touching distance.

Carefully, Louis took the wad from his pocket and peeled off two dollar bills. Swiftly, her hand came out, pushing the money away.

"You don't want it?"

"Maybe. But not that way."

"How, then?" The back of his throat had gone dry, while the familiar beat had come into his loins.

"A little night out, maybe. A visit to the theater. *Sally* is still running at the New Amsterdam and I'm told it's a real good show. Then, afterwards, we could have a little supper, and . . . well, who knows."

He did not even have to think about it. He said he would get the tickets tomorrow—"In my lunch break, I'll go right down and fix it. If that's really what you want."

She cocked her head on one side. "Hadn't you better come and check I done everything right in the storeroom, Mr. Louis?" It seemed to be an open invitation. Yes, he said. Yes, he had better come and check.

The street door was locked and, as they got into the dimly lit stockroom, the girl quietly closed the door behind her.

"You'll really take me to see *Sally*, and out to supper at some swell joint later?" She was standing very close to him.

"Sure I will, Ruth." His arms slid around her tiny waist. "Why not?" He could feel her flesh under his hands.

"That would be really great. . . ."

He did not let her finish, drawing her to him; feeling her arms slide around his neck and her mouth close on his, lips open, tongue jabbing down his throat. She pushed herself against him, and he knew she must be aware of his hardness through her skirt.

"I tell you, Herbie, this was like one of those stories they have for women. What they call them?"

"Body rippers?"

"No. Bodice rippers, Herb. If I describe what happened, it would be like one of those bodice rippers."

"Do you have to?"

"If you don't mind. I like to think about it once in a while. It's all I *can* do, now. Think about it."

She went wild, kissing him back, pulling him down among the shoeboxes on the floor, her tongue working like the piston on a railroad engine. He felt for her breasts, but they seemed to be encased in some kind of starchy plating, so he let his hand drift down to her knee, pulling her dress up so that he could feel her stockings above the knee. There, he found, she had not yet discovered the convenience of short drawers. She still wore the old-fashioned, longer bloomers, rucked and lacy in the leg, and against her thigh, so that he could not get his hand inside and had to be satisfied with the feel of her through the cotton.

At the same moment, her hand fell upon his crotch, gripping and rubbing, driving him on.

"Let's get these damned things off," he croaked, and broke the spell, for she pulled away from him.

"Oh, Louis! Oh! No! No, we mustn't. Not yet. Not yet, my dear Louis." She straightened her skirt, and began to tidy her hair. He saw that her cheeks were scarlet.

"I'm sorry," she said. "It's too fast for me. We have to get to know one another." Suddenly she whirled around. "This is so forward of me, but I love you, Louis. I love you so much."

"Of course," the old Maestro said, now in the present, "her timing was perfect. I had been playing around with little Melodie in Harlem, but here was a good, white Jewish girl. I wanted her like a dipso wants a drink, or a starving man needs food. I think at that moment I'd have promised her anything in the world, I'd have cut off my cock for one time with her. But I knew I could have her if I dipped into some of my capital and played a waiting game. Boy, that Ruth was something. Anyway . . ."

The telephone rang. Six. A count of ten. Then it began to ring again and Herbie picked up listening for Naldo's voice.

But it was not Naldo Railton at the distant end.

"Pauline Cummings, for Mr. Buckerbee," Pucky Curtiss said, from her room at The Boar's Head Inn.

14

OLD SPIES OFTEN become terminal cases to their tradecraft. After living many lives within one mind and body, suspicion becomes enshrined within the person. Well into retirement, men who have spent years in the field will still automatically take precautions which, in normal life, are fussy and unnecessary. Some will continue to use old tradecraft, built up like the layers of an onion, so that it becomes habitual, and dangerous in the real world which is free of such fictions. There is also a further problem: the heightened intuition, fine-tuned by constant apprehension.

Naldo Railton had, until Big Herbie returned to his life, managed to adjust. Living several miles south of Charlottesville, in a loosely shackled community called Esmont, his house was screened by trees on the road frontage and around the sides. The rear looked out on open country, reaching far off to the panorama of the Blue Ridge Mountains.

His nearest neighbors were half a mile away, on either side of the property, their homes only visible in the winter when the trees were bare. Until now, the watch on his home had been in plain sight, the local police unconcerned at keeping a car or van just off the road, and visible to their subject. Fall had yet to turn the trees and set them on fire, with golds and reds and yellows. Fall is Virginia's most beautiful season.

The car was gone when Naldo looked out first thing in the morning. He thought nothing of it until he walked onto the deck which ran around the rear of the house. Only then did his intuitive senses begin to pick up the old vibes. He knew he was being watched, and common sense told him they probably had high-powered directional mikes aimed at the house, from at least two hiding places.

He could see nobody, but all the arcane experience he had soaked up in World War II and the long deep freeze of the Cold War came rushing into his mind and body. He scribbled a note to Barbara, putting it on the table in front of her when she came downstairs. He had never wanted any of this to happen again. He had left both the Secret Intelligence Service and his country a bitter man, weighed down with the folly that had become the norm in Europe. Now the folly was here again.

After breakfast, they both went out onto the deck. It was a warm morning, almost a summer heat, with no breeze. Hard to imagine that in a month or two the leaves would be shredded from the trees.

The previous morning's mail had brought his copy of the British magazine *The Gramophone*, so he called a record store to ask if they had a new recording of the Scriabin piano concerto, picked almost at random from the advertisements. They had, and he asked them to hold it for him. "I'll be over in an hour or so," he told the cheerful man on the line, knowing that the watchers and listeners would be ready for him.

They were very good, which made him think they had probably been brought in from Washington: almost certainly FBI Counter Intelligence people with the necessary equipment. He picked them up on the outskirts of the city, a beige, nondescript car with an extra aerial and two men up front. They stayed back, two cars behind him, so, to be certain, Naldo turned off the main drag and did a long loop that would eventually bring him out on 29 North.

They were not there for the entire loop but, when he finally got back onto 29, the beige car appeared again, as if by magic. But Naldo knew it was no illusionist's trick. The detour could have only taken him to the point where they waited. For a minute or so he wondered if they had planted a homer and he made a mental note to check the car out in the garage back home.

He got onto 29 South, pulled off at the Seminole Square Mall, and collected his CD. As he drove home, the car disappeared but, two cars behind, he picked up a battered van. This one had two antennae, one of them high and whipping around in the slipstream, a man and woman up front. Funny, he thought, across the miles, in the old U.S.S.R. they were dismantling communism, tearing down the statues of Lenin and yesterday's men, hiding the icons of the past as though this would somehow alter what had been. While here, in free and lovely Virginia, men and women moved through clandestine routines because of an old man, almost the age of the century itself.

It was time to cash it in, Naldo decided. He had done his time. The

Curtiss girl was in town. Let her take over. After all, nobody knew she was there; her phone, like the one at Herbie's makeshift safe house, would be untapped. She also had a car which the Feds would never suspect.

He wrote her a quick note in spook speak, giving her everything she would need, addressed it to Ms. Pauline Cummings at The Boar's Head Inn, and told Barb that they should treat themselves to lunch out. "Maybe you can buy yourself a dress or something as well."

It was the van that followed them this time. Naldo had been careful not to mention where they were going, so that no stakeout would be in place. The trick would be to get the envelope across the reception desk and safely into Pucky's pigeonhole, before anyone followed them inside, as he was certain they would.

He dropped Barbara, with the note, at the main door, then went off and parked the car. As he locked it, he saw the couple from the van loitering, taking their time getting out of the vehicle. He suspected they had possibly called for backup, which was just the way they played it.

Barbara ran a finger lazily tracing the line of her jaw as they waited for the menu: her body language said that she had made the drop at reception, and they settled down to a pleasant meal, conscious that the FBI couple were only three tables away, having placed themselves strategically so that they could view all entrances, exits and the Railtons' table.

When Naldo and Barbara left, almost two hours later, the couple did not move, and Barbara glanced towards the row of boxes and keys behind reception. The note had gone, and there was a different girl on duty. Safe, clear and home, except for the beige car which had once more taken over.

Back at the Boar's Head, Pucky read Naldo's letter three times, committed everything to memory, and waited until just before dinner to go through the coded ringing sequence to get Herbie.

"Pauline Cummings, for Mr. Buckerbee," she said into the silent telephone.

"You got Buckerbee." She knew Herbie's voice because they had played a couple of old tapes to her in London.

"Your friend, D Major. He's out of it." Naldo had directed her to use something that only Herbie would remember. Just after World War II, they had both been part of an ultrasecure operation dubbed Symphony. Naldo's crypto then had been D Major and he felt that both Symphony and his old code name, though just about as insecure as you could get in the present circumstances, would do the trick. Herbie would listen.

Herbie listened.

"He has the dogs on him. I need to see you. I know all the tradecraft, and he's spelled out exactly where you are. I'm coming over tonight."

"No," Herbie spoke very quietly. "How much field work you done?"

"Enough."

"There's never enough. You sure the line's safe?"

"One hundred percent."

"Okay, we'll soon know if it is loused up. Meantime, what you do is run the back doubles tomorrow. All day."

"Back doubles?" Pucky, for once in her life, was lost.

"Shit. You not done enough in the field. Me, I'm unhappy about you, but you're all I got. Okay, back doubles is avoidance and surveillance check. You dance through all the local roads. You double back—is probably why it's called back doubles, but I don't think so. You watch for cars, antennae, or vans. Then on foot you watch for same people. Look at shoes. If my friend's gone cold, it means they've a good team he cannot throw. This also means probably a fair number of people involving . . ."

"Involving?"

"Involved, what's the difference? Watch hands, watch shoes. Teams don't have time to change shoes. Christ, you can read that in John le Carré. Is elementary, my dear Watson. Call me again, same time tomorrow. Same procedure. If you're clean, and only if you're clean, I'll see you, okay?"

"I want to see you tonight."

"Use your French stick, girl. . . ."

"French . . . ?" They had told her about Kruger's word games, and she guessed, in time, that he meant loaf of bread—head.

"You're not safe on the streets yet, so I can't risk you exploding this place. Start checking now. Okay?"

"You're sure?"

"Seven hundred percent sure, old sheep. Go to."

Pucky sighed. She did not like any of it. Reluctantly she replied, "Very well."

"Good." Herbie then cryptically added, "The play's the thing, wherein I'll catch the constipation of the king. 'Bye."

The line closed.

"Problems, you got?" Passau seemed relaxed, but Herbie thought he detected a nervousness in the eyes. He was also flushed from talking about the long ago abortive moment in the stockroom with the nubile Ruth.

"No." Herbie looked at him and smiled. "No, I haven't a problem, Lou. *We've* got a problem. Possibly. Don't know yet. I'll let you into the secret if things get tricky. You want to tell me more about Ruth before we break for dinner?"

"Why not?" He leaned back in the chair and closed his eyes, as though savoring the memory. "Oh boy, she was some cookie that Ruth. Never gave up. And I was such a dumb kid, Herb. So dumb you'd never believe."

"Tell me about it."

The day following the fumble in the stockroom, Packensteiner made plans for the outing. He got tickets to *Sally* for the following Wednesday and was excited almost every waking hour. He was sure he would get his way after the show and a good supper. As they left the store that night, Ruth whispered to him—"After we've eaten, shall we come back here for a while?"

Again he was disappointed. The passion was intense, and he even managed to drag her drawers down to her ankles, while she got her hand in through his fly.

Then it all went down as before—Ruth pulling away, and saying, "No, Lou! Not yet!"

They would have to wait, she told him. Just for a little longer. She was a virgin and had always promised she would save herself for the right man, and then only in the marriage bed.

"This girl almost drove me crazy, Herb. I wanted the bitch so much that I couldn't even see straight. My God, I took her out, used all my savings that I'd stolen from my father. I even put off my final date for leaving because of the bitch. Lord, I nearly offered to marry her, but at least I had the sense to keep that option at bay. She would've done me properly if I'd offered. As it was she almost did for me. Jesu, what a terrible thing it is to be a satyr."

"Lou, with your reputation, you could be classed as one of the Satyr Day Saints." Herbie thought this very funny, but Passau showed not even the flicker of a smile.

It went on for months. September 1922 came, his birthday; still Ruth did not give in. He saw her regularly and, eventually, realized what she was truly after, for no woman, he considered, could ever hold out against him this long unless she had an ulterior motive.

It was now October. He would have to make one big killing from the store, then show Ruth that he meant business. After that? Who knew?

He was concerned about the money he had already stolen and knew it could not go on forever. This year, he thought, echoing it to Aaron Hamovitch, "This year I'm going for sure."

"You said September, originally, Louis." The big man shook his unruly head of hair so that it made a moving halo around him. "You go on like this, and you'll never leave."

Louis' main worry now slid from the chase after Ruth's virginity to the concern of money. Already, if his father was to make a thorough examination, he could prove nearly two hundred dollars had been purloined.

Then, in November, the opportunity came to make one large, quick killing. A wealthy woman, the wife of the banker who had made Joseph the original loan for the business, came into the store with her three children. The total order was in the region of three hundred dollars.

Louis presented the order to the workshop—which meant, in effect, to his father—as three entirely separate transactions, carefully making them out to people he knew were slow at settling their accounts. Mrs. Meyerberg, the banker's wife, settled promptly, on the nail, and on the first of the month.

On that first day of December, Louis' eyes seldom strayed from the shop door—anxious lest he either miss Mrs. Meyerberg or, worse, if his father came in unexpectedly while she was there to settle her account.

The banker's wife came in just before lunch. She was a fussy dumpling of a woman who paid all her accounts by check, in person, as though this brought about a great saving in mailing costs. Louis greeted her with his usual show of charm.

As she was about to write her check, she asked if she had the correct amount, "Three hundred dollars?"

"Three hundred dollars exactly, ma'am." Louis paused. Then—"Mrs. Meyerberg, I wonder if you could possibly make this check out to cash. Payable to the bearer. We have a number of tradespeople coming in to-day—suppliers' representatives, you will understand. It's always easier for us to pay them in cash."

"Of course, Mr. Packensteiner." Mrs. Meyerberg gave her dimpled pudding-faced smile, as though she were doing him a very great favor.

"Anything, Mr. Packensteiner." She wagged a finger at him and there was a small glint of humor in her eye. "Anything, as long as I get my usual receipt."

Louis wrote out the receipt, and the check changed hands. After the lunch break, Louis was a little late back into the shop. In his pocket, three hundred dollars almost burned through the lining. In his mind, the plans were already made.

He lost no time: first getting Ruth on her own. How about a night out on Thursday? The usual—dinner in a fancy place to which he often took her, just off Times Square; then back to the store. She smiled and nodded energetically.

This was his last chance, Louis thought. It had to happen to Ruth on Thursday, whether she liked it or not.

That evening, he stopped in at a hotel and asked to use the telephone. The call he made was long distance, to Chicago. He spoke for around five minutes. Then, on the following night, he made a trip over to Grand Central Station to purchase a one-way ticket, first class to Chicago, for Sunday.

On Thursday, he took Ruth out for what would be the last time. They ate well, and he made sure the young girl had more than usual to drink. As they stepped out onto the sidewalk she clung to him and giggled. "Louis, dear, I feel quite giddy. My, all that wine. I know what you're after."

"Let's go back to the store and talk about it," he said. He did not suppose that she noticed he was not smiling.

For the first time, Ruth seemed more pliable. There was no talking once they got to the store. Louis would never know if she had finally decided to surrender herself to him or if the drink, or even his charm, was the main cause.

Hardly were they inside, before the girl coiled herself around him, like a python, her hands moving everywhere. They half groped and half shuffled their way to the stockroom. There, in the pitch black, Louis quickly undressed her, not hearing any of the usual expressions of doubt.

As he pinched her breasts, and cupped them, Ruth seemed to be tearing at his pants, opening his loins to the air, so that his manhood sprang from his clothes—"Like a jack-in-the-box, Herb." She grasped at him. "Exquisite agony, Herbie. Oh, I can feel her now. Times gone. Feelings gone. But I can feel her."

He could not remember how they got to the floor, yet, forever after, he recalled her voice, quiet and a little frightened, as she whispered, "Louis! Have care, but don't worry about hurting me. Go on, even if I scream."

She did not scream, except in a kind of ecstasy, clasping him hard and locking her legs against him.

On the second occasion, some thirty minutes later, she even took most of the initiative. On their reluctant parting, she clung to him and muttered that she had been a fool to wait for so long. Then, as an afterthought—"Louis, if you've . . . if I'm . . . if there's a child. . . ."

Louis grinned. "Then we get married damned quick," he said, knowing he would not be around if the piper had to be paid.

On Saturday night, he packed the cardboard suitcase before going to bed. He did not need to worry about waking early. His train did not leave until four in the afternoon—a time when his father and mother habitually went for a stroll together.

However, there was no lying in, or sleeping late on the following morning.

He came out of some erotic dream very slowly, conscious of raised voices in the main room of the apartment. As his eyes opened, to his horror, Louis heard the sound of violent sobbing. It was a noise he knew well enough, for it came from Ruth.

He lay there, frozen with fear, then, with no warning, the bedroom door burst open and Joseph Packensteiner stood on the threshold, fury on his face.

"Get dressed, and come out here at once!" He commanded.

"What's wrong, for heaven's sake?"

"Get out here and explain yourself," his father shouted, slamming the door.

Louis dressed quickly; did not stop to shave, but ran a comb through his hair. When he emerged, he had decided on the only course of action. He felt completely in command, looking calm, and vaguely interested.

Ruth sat, still weeping, in a chair. Behind her stood a powerfully built man, dark and approaching middle age. From his looks alone, Louis recognized him as Ruth's father.

His mother was hunched, rocking, in an attitude of both pain and grief. She glanced up, red-eyed and reproachful, at Louis, who smiled pleasantly, bowed to Ruth's father, and said, "Shalom."

"My son, Louis," Joseph Packensteiner said, in an unnaturally clipped manner.

"Ruth?" Louis creased his brow, and looked around him, as if lost and uncertain. "What's the matter? What is it?"

It was Ruth's father who answered, "I think you know very well what the matter is, Louis Packensteiner."

"I . . ." he began.

"Oh, Louis. I didn't mean to tell them," Ruth wailed. "Mama found blood on my clothes. My father beat me, and they made me tell them who had done it."

"Done what?" Louis was pleased that he could sound so amazed. "Blood? I don't understand."

Ruth's father took a step forward. "You have defiled my daughter. You have raped her and defiled her."

Louis shook his head in bewilderment. "Defiled her? I have . . . What nonsense is this?"

Ruth's sharp intake of breath was audible to everyone in the room.

"Come on," Louis was shouting now, his voice full of indignation. "What do you mean? You're accusing me of something . . . something foul. Accuse, then, so I can give my answer."

Ruth's voice lifted an octave, in horror. "Louis, after all we've been . . . after all you promised. . . ."

Louis shook his head, and spoke gently to her, "Ruth, what are you talking about?"

The girl let out a long moan.

Joseph Packensteiner appeared to relax a little, the heat going out of his voice. "Ruth has accused you of taking her by force, as a man will take a woman. She says you have been alone together on many occasions; that you have given her meals in fancy restaurants; and that you have now raped her. To her credit she says it was her own fault. That she led you on."

"Ruth?" Louis laughed. "I've raped . . . ? Papa, that's nonsense. Would I go out with somebody who merely worked for us? If you ask me, she's got herself into trouble with some young boy and wants to blame it on a family who can provide . . . Oh, yes. Now it makes sense. Benny made a joke at the store the other day. He said she was sweet on me because I was my father's son. It's the business she's after, Papa. The business and the money. Get rid of them now."

Ruth began to scream, near hysteria, so that her father had to restrain her with his hand on her shoulder. "Louis Packensteiner, you're a liar. A liar and a thief. Mr. Packensteiner, go and check your receipts, and the money from the store. Your precious son's been bleeding you."

Louis appealed to his father. "Papa, she's crazy. Would I steal from my own flesh and blood?"

"I would hope not." The iron had returned to Joseph's voice.

Ruth continued to shout abuse and accusations. Then, her father spoke up. "You have an easy way to find out, Packensteiner. If your accounts are in order, then your son might be trusted. If not, then he is a thief, as my daughter says; and if a thief, then what else?"

The silence now seemed to swell within the room. At last, Joseph nodded. "You speak sense. I shall go today, and collect the books from both stores. I shall go through them tonight. First thing tomorrow I shall visit the bank. It will not take long to find out if Louis is a liar. I agree with you. If he lies over one thing, then he could lie over another. Tomorrow we shall see."

"Indeed, tomorrow we *shall* see," Louis echoed, with confidence. "There must be some law in our country against people who make false accusations."

At the door now, one arm around the sobbing Ruth, her father replied, with some menace, "There *is* such a law among our people."

"Good. Then tomorrow it will all be settled." Louis turned his back on the pair as they left the apartment.

At three o'clock that afternoon, Joseph and Gerda Packensteiner left for their usual Sunday walk. Only today, they were to call at both the stores to collect the books.

Though he barely had time to make the train, Louis paused long enough to scribble a farewell note, saying good-bye to his parents, promising the money he had stolen would be repaid, and that he was not running away from consequences, but to make a life for himself in music. "Aaron Hamovitch does not know where I am going," he finished. "He will tell you, though, that I have been planning it for a long time. The girl Ruth is the liar. At least believe that."

He made Grand Central with only a few minutes to spare and, as the train pulled out, heading for Chicago, he lit a Chesterfield cigarette and leaned back in the comfortable first-class compartment. Tomorrow he would be with his old friend, Carlo Giarre, who now worked for a new boss. A man called Alphonse Capone. Capone, Carlo said, ruled Chicago better than the police ever could. He had a job waiting for Louis.

By tomorrow night, he thought, I shall be playing piano in one of Mr. Capone's clubs. I shall be paid for it as well.

Louis Packensteiner also decided, at that moment, to change his name. From now on he would be called Packer. Carlo's boss would get that legalized pretty quickly.

Big Herbie Kruger had hardly looked at Louis Passau as he told his story. Now, he lifted his eyes. The great Maestro was weeping.

HERBIE KRUGER LEANED forward and placed one big hand on the old man's left shoulder, which heaved under the sobs.

Herbie was a man of infinite compassion.

"Maestro," he said quietly. "This is like being in analysis: like talking it out with a shrink. It's bound to hurt, reliving some of this stuff. There *has* to be pain. What the hell, so you were a pretty bad boy, huh?"

The shoulders stopped shaking and the old man wiped his eyes with the back of his hand. "Shit, Herbie, I don't cry over bad things. Listen to me. Don't let people ever tell you that, when you get older, it's a relief, that you feel happy when there is no point to the chase anymore. Me? I'm upset because nothing like any of those times will ever come again. It's a shitty reflection on life, Herb. God's little joke. He gives us so much to use and misuse, then he takes the whole fucking lot away."

Kruger withdrew his hand, as though he had touched a hot stove. Standing up, he went silently to the door. It was bad enough, he considered with some fury, to be forced to listen to a blow by blow account of this vile old man's youthful peccadilloes. But to show some sympathy, because he thought Passau was in a glut of guilt over past crimes, only to discover he was wallowing in self-pity. . . . Well, fuck him, he thought.

This was a man who had interpreted the greatest music ever written; a man whom he had revered, who had the ability to make people laugh, cry, think, broaden their horizons, and now—"This idol has feet of funny putty," he whispered.

Passau called out from behind him, "Herb, do me a favor, huh?"

"Whatcherwant? Copy of *Playboy* magazine?"

"Don't be like that, Herb. I only wondered, has the lady of this house got a good recording of *Sacre*?"

Muttering to himself, Big Herbie went over to the tall CD holders near the player. "Sure, she has von Karajan, Maazel and Dorati. Take your pick." Behind his reply, Herbie thought, "You want to pester your brain with images of what you could not now do to that poor Ruth girl, and the thousands of others in your life?"

"She hasn't got mine?"

"The lady has taste."

"What do you mean, taste? Stravinsky himself sat in on my 1956 recording—now available on CD."

He talks like a TV commercial, Herbie thought. "Well, is not available here."

"So. Stravinsky was a funny devil. I visited his workroom once, in L.A. If it wasn't for the piano, you'd think he was some graphic artist. He had bottles of ink, graded by different colors; pens, erasers, scissors, paste. Incredible. Pity he missed the computer age. Igor would've been at home with computerized music."

"Which one you want?" Herbie tapped his foot.

"He talked only of his own music, you know. Hadn't time for other people. You know what Aaron Copland said about him? He said that Stravinsky was the Henry James of modern music. I couldn't understand that. Incredible."

"Which one, Louis?"

"Karajan was a precision instrument, an accurate mechanic. *Sacre* is primitive, but there is soul. I'll take Maazel. Would you put it on for me?"

"Sure, Maestro. You want me to wipe your ass while I'm about it?"

"What?"

"Never mind. There you go. Igor Stravinsky in all his glory. *Le Sacre de Printemps*, or *The Rite of Spring* as us lesser mortals call it."

As he pottered around in the kitchen, Herbie heard the heaving, pulsating menace of the strings. The old bastard must love that piece, he thought. The rhythms were very good for copulation. Then, with a sense of loathing, Herbie realized he had actually done just that, many times; and to the second movement of the Mahler First, the old Frère Jacques march; and, he clearly recalled with some horror, in a safe house—very drunk—to a recording of the Berlioz Requiem.

All men were equal in sin, though some were more equal than others. Aloud, he said, "Let him who is without sin cast the first stein," then laughed to himself. Passau was such an evil old man: Herbie almost dreaded what would come out next. He was also very concerned about the girl, Pucky Curtiss.

He put the lasagna in the microwave, thinking about Pucky. He had never met her, but his old friends in the trade brought him reports. A yuppie, they said. A college-educated yuppie who thought she had all the answers from behind a desk.

No, that was not fair—he set the timer on the microwave—they said she was good. Smart, very clever, learned quickly and was close to the top brass. This in itself made her dangerous. If the top brass were soft on the Americans, the Pucky woman would come charging in, ready to hand both Passau and himself to Langley without a qualm. The trick would be to make her see what they could gain through keeping a tight hold on the reprobate musician.

So, he could do one of two things. Run now, tonight, taking Passau with him. Florida. Marty Forman would front for them. But, in the end, Marty would want a large slice of the pie, which would go straight to Langley. Marty was a hood but, he suspected, Langley would toss him a few thousand dollars for being an extra good boy.

Should he risk it and deal with the Pucky female? If she did not play ball, there were always things he could do. Like what? Herbie asked himself. Like restraining her? Holding her against her will? Big deal. Big time spook stuff. Anyhow, what was the point now? The Cold War had come to an end, and the old Marxist-Leninist—Stalinist also—doctrines were being given the last rites. Over. Finished. The days of the old-style spooks were numbered. But, Pucky Curtiss? Well . . . ?

He worried half the night about Pucky Curtiss, but the fact that he did not subject the old man to a long drive, through the darkness into the never-never land of Florida, meant he had made a subconscious decision to take Pucky Curtiss head-on. Lock horns with her, he thought, wondering what kind of complexion she had.

Maestro Passau, if truth be told, had a bad night. Herbie was right. Any interrogation that meant bringing the darkness and pleasures of the past into the light of the present had a disturbing effect. Louis Passau wondered if, in his dotage, he was starting to develop a conscience. Why should he? After all, his conscience had never bothered him before. His pride had made him deny it was guilt which had made him sob. The denial was yet another falsehood in his long list of deceits. Sure, he was telling Kruger the truth—well, one version of the truth—but his pride stood between the image he presented of himself and the honest workings of his emotions. As he dropped into troubled sleep, he knew that his conscience was being shattered into a million shards by just thinking about his past. In sleep, the demons prowled around his subconscious.

He dreamed of a hot Mediterranean morning, the sea deep blue and the buildings dazzling in their whiteness. He stood on the beach, his feet feeling the heat lapping around his toes, and the woman came running towards him, the sand spurting from her heels like bullets slamming into the beach. Her dark hair fanned around her head as she ran calling him by name—"Lou . . . Louis . . . darling Louis."

He woke, suddenly, at dawn, shouting in his sleep, "Stanza . . . Stanza . . . Stanza . . ." When he realized it was a dream, he wept again, in secret and not for himself. Not out of any self-pity, but because of that shattered illusion which was Louis Passau's guilt; because so much misery had been visited on so many people.

"SO, LOUIS, YOU went to Chicago and you worked for the infamous Al Capone."

Passau nodded, showing no pleasure.

"Well, talk to me. Tell me about it. Orchestrate it for me, Lou. Make your strings, woodwinds, brass and timpani tell me what happened to you in Chicago."

He began to talk, but it was a false start. He sidetracked, then backtracked about the final hours with Ruth, her father and his parents in New York.

Herbie thought, "If I were a psychiatrist, heaven forbid, I might think this man had some very unpleasant memory rooted in that Chicago period. Could be: after all, I was the first person to hear that Maestro Passau had even been in Chicago in the twenties, let alone worked for Capone." Aloud he said, "Lou, you know someone once said, 'Autobiography is a vehicle for telling the truth about other people.' Tell the truth about the Capone years, eh?"

Finally, after fumbling for the words, the Maestro began to tell the story, and was soon back in his stride, painting pictures which moved and lived on the screens of both their minds.

Capone looked forty years of age: big, heavy-bodied, though the muscletone was hard as rock beneath. He had bull-like shoulders upon which the large round head sat as though grafted between them.

He licked his thick, sensual lips and, under the light-brown hair and shaggy eyebrows, bright gray eyes appraised the boy, as though he were trying to put a price on him.

Even though it was almost eleven in the morning, the man was not yet dressed. He lounged back in a chair, clad in a royal blue silk robe over pajamas of a similar color, but with gold piping around collar and cuffs.

Louis, who had spent much time in New York window shopping at the high-class stores on Fifth and Park Avenues, knew the pajamas were French models, made by Sulka at almost twenty-five dollars a pair. A fortune. He had seen similar ones in Sulka's window, and in the glossy magazines. Louis already had a taste for good clothes. He wanted to make enough money to buy only the best. Sometimes he even got a hard-on looking at the men's fashion magazines. Music, women, money and good clothes often gave him an erection.

Capone smiled, and Louis saw that his lips had a purplish tint to them. He raised one hand, and a diamond flashed on the middle finger as he ran his palm around his dark jowls. In a few years, the face would become fleshy as he put on weight.

Somewhere behind him, a man in a barber's apron moved, whipping up a lather in the shaving mug. There were other men in the room. Louis Packer was aware that a lot of eyes were on him.

"The kid I told ya about, Mr. Capone." It was the second time Carlo had said it.

Capone nodded slowly, reaching for a cigar. One of the men sprang forward to flick a lighter and Capone pushed it away with his hand. "How many times I gotta tell ya. Ya don't light cigars with cigarette lighters. Ya light them with a match. Got it?" The match flickered at the end of Carlo's fingers, and as Capone rolled the cigar in the flame he looked up at Louis. "Yeah, the Jew kid. You told me, Carlo."

Louis had arrived at Chicago's La Salle Street train station around eight that morning. As promised, Carlo Giarre was there to meet him, with another man, whom he introduced as Frankie Rio. Both of them looked tired, as though they had been up all night, and Carlo explained that they would not be able to see Mr. Capone until later in the morning. "He ain't inclined to getting up early," Carlo grinned.

"None of us is that way inclined." Frankie Rio did not grin. His expression seemed to be permanently sullen.

Carlo explained that they *had* been up all night. "We did a little job, see? Then, after that . . . Well, the boss likes the night life. He always takes some of the boys out with him. We got him home at five this morning: good to see ya, Pianist; glad ya took me up on the offer."

There was a black automobile outside the train station and they drove to a diner that served breakfast. A sign outside read, "The Best Breakfast in Town. All you can eat for $1.00."

The owner served them personally, and appeared very anxious to please the three young men. Carlo called him "Jimmy," like he knew him well, and introduced Louis as, "My friend, Louis the Pianist. Ya won't forget him next time he drops by, will ya, Jimmy?"

"No, sir." Jimmy smiled nervously at Louis. "You're welcome to eat here any time you want."

Louis noticed there was no charge for the breakfast, which was the best he had eaten in a long time. Though his mother was a good cook, her food was plain, and breakfast had never been much of a meal in the Packensteiner household. Now he had coffee, and flapjacks with honey, scrambled eggs, toast, jelly. "Anything you want, you just ask," Jimmy said, and they did not even leave him a tip.

Around ten thirty they drove to a building that looked run-down and decrepit by daylight. Along the front wall, above a small door, there was a sign, laced with unlit neon. The Four Deuces, it said, and there was a large hand showing four deuces fanned from a deck of cards.

Carlo tapped lightly on the door—three double knocks—and a voice from inside asked who he was. Carlo spoke softly, and there was a clicking of locks and the sound of bolts being withdrawn.

A small lobby led to another door and so into a large room, dark and unattractive in the light from four small windows set high up, and the couple of overhead bulbs that were switched on. Two elderly black women swept around a landscape of tables which had their chairs piled onto them, upside down, so that they looked like strange four-legged skeletal animals.

The man who had opened up to them was small, like a ferret, but sharply dressed in a pearl gray double-breasted pinstripe, which Louis regarded with some envy. In fact, almost the first thing he had noticed about Carlo and Frankie Rio was their clothes.

Carlo had grown: filled out, his face tougher, his eyes showing a new, wary knowledge, and the splattered pockmarked left cheek seemed more noticeable, giving him a sinister edge, particularly when he hardened his eyes—a new trick which proved frightening. He had obviously learned a great deal since their last meeting: more confident and better, if flashily, dressed: a brown double-breasted, beautifully tailored suit, silk shirt and tie with a matching fedora, cocked jauntily on his head.

The man who had let them in tilted his head towards a stairway, muttering, "He's up, but I don' know if he's seein' anyone yet."

Louis felt uncomfortable, dowdy, clutching his cardboard suitcase and wearing the cheap suit his father had bought for him when he started to manage the Fifth Avenue store.

As though sensing his old friend's discomfort, Carlo gave him an easy smile. "Don' worry, Pianist. Mr. Capone likes music. Just act natural."

Now, standing in front of Capone, Louis felt even more of an interloper. He looked down at his shoes, which were also cheap and needed polishing. Capone wore very expensive brown leather bedroom slippers, polished and well cared for. He recognized the design as French; he had seen them, either in a smart store window or a magazine. He thought that if Capone placed a foot on the floor between a girl's legs he could have seen right up her skirt in the mirror shine of those slippers. Louis' mind, he had discovered, rarely strayed from girls these days. Anything he saw seemed to have a connection with sex. He presumed it was something to do with growing into a man.

Capone's hand paused for a second as it traversed his left cheek, then flattened, as if to hide the scar that ran, livid, from ear to jaw. Louis remembered the night with Carlo and the Havemeyer Street boys. He thought of what Carlo had told him about the knife cuts, like the one on Capone's cheek. A Sicilian punishment. There were at least two New York Jewish boys going around permanently marked by Carlo's knife, and he wondered about Capone. Why did he bear the mark of a Sicilian punishment?

Capone turned his large head away, again as though to hide the scar. "Carlo tells me good things about ya, Jew kid. Calls you The Pianist. . . ."

"Louis, 'The Pianist,' Packer, yea."

He should not have spoken. Anger flared in Capone's eyes. "Don' interrupt me when I'm talkin', Jew kid." For a few seconds everyone seemed to stand, frozen and still. Then Capone laughed. "Ya gotta learn things quick here in Chicago, kid. So, ya like to play piano?"

"It's what I do best."

Capone grunted, saying something about that being the right way to live your life: doing what you did best.

"We do some things pretty good, eh, boss?" one of the attendant men said.

Capone turned his eyes towards the voice. "Yes, Harry, *some* of us do: and don't ya ever forget that we do it under the guidance of Mr. Torrio."

"That's right, Al." "You said it, boss." "Always under Mr. Torrio, Al," various men replied.

Capone said that he bet his sweet ass they did, then turned back to Louis. "Come," he said softly. "Come play piano for me downstairs, eh?" He rose in one quick movement and, with a wave of his hand towards the door, he motioned Louis to follow him. There were initials, a monogram, on the silk Sulka robe—AC. Louis swore, as he saw the monogram, that one day he would have that. Everything he wore, from underwear to shirts, would be monogrammed *LP*. The day would come, maybe sooner than he expected.

They went down into the club and the two cleaning women scurried away like frightened rabbits as soon as they saw Capone. The gangster lifted a chair from one of the tables, straddling it the wrong way round, cradling his arms on the chair back. Some of the other men followed his example, while others just leaned, bored, against the wall. Then Capone motioned towards a piano, set on a small band dais in the corner.

Louis went over and sat down at the instrument, hitting middle C, then trying a few chords. The piano had been used a great deal. "This is in need of tuning," he said, glancing back at Capone.

"Oh, so it's in need a tuning," Capone mimicked. "What d'ya expect, a Steinway Grand?"

"All instruments need tuning from time to time, Mr. Capone."

"This mean ya can't play, right? 'Cuz it ain't tuned?"

"No, I can play this."

"Okay, then play."

"What do you want me to play, Mr. Capone?"

Someone out of sight tried to mimic his voice, like Capone had done, "What you want me to play, Mr. Capone?"

There was some laughter, and Capone turned, his eyes spreading fear around the room. There was a deathly silence, then the big man threw back his bull head and guffawed. "How about ya give me the prelude to Verdi's *Aida*, Jew kid."

Everyone laughed, except Carlo, who knew better.

Louis simply nodded, then, arrogantly, looked around, his hands resting on the keyboard.

"Waddya waitin' for, Jew kid?" somebody shouted.

"For everyone to shut their mouths and be quiet." Louis tried to make the anger flare in his own eyes, as he had seen Capone do it.

Nobody moved, or replied, so Louis turned back to the keyboard.

He could transpose most of the great operatic scores straight onto the piano keyboard. It was what he had done with the entire orchestral repertoire, in duets, and alone, under Aaron Hamovitch's guidance. So the short introduction to Verdi's opera was not difficult for him. First, the soft and beautiful theme associated with Aida herself, in the higher register; followed by the stronger, descending notes of the melody connected, in the opera, with the priests.

An overused, out of tune, bar piano is no complete orchestra but, as Louis began, so Capone stiffened, sitting very still as Louis took the brief introduction to its conclusion.

When he had finished, he looked at the gangster and saw that the light gray eyes seemed to be filled with tears. The large head nodded. "So ya know opera? Okay, so ya like opera. Well, so do I, kid. Bel canto, huh? Ya like that?" He shifted his cigar from one corner of his mouth to the other. "So that's okay for cultured people like myself, but what about the dumb fucks who know nothing? What about the broads and the Johns we get in places like this, The Four Deuces, every night of the week. What ya play for them, huh? I'm askin' ya."

Louis turned back to the piano. He did a couple of Joplin rags—"Maple Leaf" and "Stomptime"—then slid into a classic blues, thinking mainly of the words he had first heard with Carlo so long ago now—

I thought I heard Buddy Bolden shout,
Open up that window, let the bad air out.

He knew who Buddy Bolden was: more than he had known when he first heard the name. Bolden, the father of New Orleans jazz: now, at this very moment, in an insane asylum, mourned as already dead by those who knew him in his early years. Knew him when he could blow a horn so loud that, on a still night, you could hear him two miles away—from the Mississippi River to Lake Pontchartrain.

Louis did not even think about Capone and his hoods as he slid from the classic blues into a hard boogie, using the strong repetitive, key-changing, left-hand beat, that was known as Pinetops boogie, from its originator, Pinetops Smith.

Finally, he brought his audition—for he knew that all this was some kind of test—to a close with an upbeat version of "The Sheik of Araby," the great popular song of the time, whistled by butcher boys and hummed by respectable matrons in the privacy of their boudoirs.

Nobody spoke, or applauded, when Louis stopped playing. He saw they were all looking towards Capone, as though waiting for his approval. Slowly, Capone nodded, his mouth again shifting the cigar from one corner to the other. "Guess the piano playin' is okay, kid. Tell ya what we're gonna do." The hand moved to his cheek again, diamond ring flashing. "Yer buddy, Carlo, brought ya here, and he's doin' an important piece of work at the moment. Ya see, we got a place called The Barn, over in Burnham. Carlo's runnin' muscle there. Ya know, kid, makin' sure nobody gets outta line. We got a little band, comes in every night, just to keep everybody happy. Well, ya can fill in on piano when the band takes a break. Ya can help Carlo as well." He paused again, as though thinking, then he smiled. "If ya can prove y're okay. Right?"

Louis had no clear idea of what he meant, but he was not about to turn down the possibility of a job. He nodded and said he appreciated it.

"Oh, ya will. I'm sure ya will," Capone laughed, then motioned to Carlo. He had some errand he wanted Louis' friend to run; in the meantime, Frankie Rio and the man called Harry—a fat, lumpy man, with a thick foreign accent—would, as Capone put it with another smile, "Take care of him."

The two men were not overly friendly, as though keeping their distance, withholding any form of camaraderie until Capone had made some final judgment. They led Louis to the back of the building where there was a room the size of the entire Packensteiner apartment in New York. The room had been turned into a gym, with all the latest equipment, including showers for use when you had sweated off excess fat. He wondered if Capone ever used it. It was doubtful.

Frankie Rio told Louis to strip to his shorts, then the two men leaned back against the wall, lighting cigarettes, as they put him through a series of exercises—making him skip rope for fifteen minutes; then row hard on the machine, for another quarter hour. They ended up by getting him to lift progressively heavier weights.

While working at the store, Louis had kept himself in reasonable shape. He knew the dangers of the streets and, once in a while, he would go up to a gymnasium off Times Square, run by one of the Packensteiner clients. This man was a wealthy prize-fight promoter, with a string of fighters in his own stable. He allowed Louis to exercise, and even got one of his heavyweights to give the young man some lessons. Louis, the fighter said, was a quick learner. "Could be a good boxer if you gave it some time."

Louis had told him he had neither the time nor staying power to be a fighter.

"Oh, you got the staying power," the boxer told him.

Even so, he was breathing hard, and sweating a good deal by the time Frankie and Harry had finished telling him what to do in Capone's private gymnasium. They were still a little hostile, so Louis was not altogether surprised when, as he put down the last of the weights, Frankie Rio moved in close to him, bringing back his right fist to deliver a rabbit punch.

Louis sidestepped and the fist went past him. He saw a flicker of annoyance cross Frankie's face, then the expression turned to one of amazement as Louis landed a left and right, in a one and two, to the man's stomach, and finally a straight left to the jaw, sending Rio reeling against the wall.

He immediately stepped back and assumed a boxing stance but, either Rio had learned fast, or Harry had warned him off.

Harry—Louis later discovered his name was Guzik—indicated a door. "Take a shower, Pianist," he grunted.

Frankie Rio shook his head, then felt his jaw. Harry was smiling, so Rio had lost face. "Ya did good, kid," Rio said, trying to make the best of it. "When ya've showered, dry off and get dressed, okay?"

Louis nodded. "No hard feelings?"

Frankie looked at him as though he would kill him if he could, but thought better of it. "No hard feelings, kid." There was little conviction in his voice, and Louis knew he had probably made an enemy he might have to watch.

179

Oddly, Louis, who had been very tired after the long trip from New York, now felt fresh and invigorated. Sure, his muscles ached a little, but it was as though fresh blood was pumping through his body. In all, he felt good and alert. Ready for anything.

When he came out, dressed, from the showers, only Harry Guzik was waiting for him. "He wants ta see ya now." Harry smiled, though his eyes remained cold and aloof.

Capone was dressed, surrounded by the same group of men, when Louis was shown into another room, his office, a few minutes later. He was told to sit down and wait while Capone issued instructions and checked papers. Frankie Rio was not there, and he noticed one or two of the other men nodded and smiled at him, trying to be friendly.

At last Capone sent everyone out of the room except for Louis, to whom he did not speak for some minutes while he sat, looking him in the eyes and occasionally nodding. Finally—

"Well, kid, I gotta good report on ya. Two things. First, my boys always gotta keep in good shape. Everyone takes regular exercise. I need people around me who are ready for action anytime and anywhere. I hear ya almost sent Frankie to sleep. Harry says yer fast, so ya might find yerself doin' other jobs for me as well as playin' the piano.

"Okay. Second, I got another saying as well. When a guy can't do the business with a broad anymore, then he's finished. Ya remember that, Pianist. Carlo swears to me on his mother's eyes, that yer okay in that department, so I accept his word. If I ever hear different, ya got trouble, okay?"

Louis said okay.

"Right, ya start work out at Burnham today, with yer buddy, Carlo. So ya won't feel lonely. Like I said before, yu'll play piano when the band takes a break, and yu'll assist Carlo when he needs ya. There'll be other work as well. In good time. In this outfit we all of us have to do other kinds of work. And this outfit's big, Pianist. Very big, and it's gonna get bigger. Ya hear me straight?"

"You're the boss, Mr. Capone." Louis grinned.

Capone's smile faded for a second, then he put his head back and roared with laughter. "Ya think so, kid? Ya think I'm the boss, huh? Well, let me tell ya, I am in a manner of speakin'. But I do the donkey work round here. Now listen good. If anyone comes snoopin' around and asks ya what I do, ya tell 'em. I'm the bouncer. That surprise ya?" He laughed again. "I'm the hired help. But with a lotta responsibility. Also, if any strangers ask ya, my name's Al Brown. Okay?"

"Okay."

The laugh still echoed in Louis' head when he left the room. Carlo was waiting for him, together with a short, dark man. The latter was to drive them over to Burnham, an area just on the southern city limits.

He hefted his cardboard suitcase in his hand, following Carlo and the driver down the stairs into the still empty main lounge of the club. He had no doubts as to what The Four Deuces really was. A speakeasy, where people came to get illegal booze and, probably, a girl for a couple of hours. He, Louis Packer, who had been Louis Packensteiner, was now mixing with men who broke the law daily. He was certain of that: they would be bringing in bootleg liquor; selling it, making it, even stealing it.

The same men with whom he now associated probably did much more than just supply booze and women. He knew enough about the crime gangs in New York. These people would be into all the rackets—extracting revenue from shopkeepers, running gambling games, and all the other things. They were the kind of men who paid off old scores with heavy baseball bats and guns. His eyes were open.

They were halfway towards the door that led to the entrance of the club when the noise of voices came from the lobby: the outside door opening and several people talking. Three men came in, brisk and businesslike, walking as though they knew where they were going and what they were there to do.

Carlo touched Louis' arm, as if warning him. Two of the men were tall, burly, and dressed in smart dark coats and black fedoras. Each had his right hand firmly stuffed into a pocket. The third man walked slightly ahead of the other two—bouncy, determined, a short man wearing a double-breasted gray street coat, with a hat to match. He was neat, looked very sharp, energetic, and had small piercing eyes which seemed to look everywhere at once.

Carlo gently drew Louis back as the trio approached. The shorter man could have been a banker, or a real-estate agent. He had the look of a successful businessman about him. A man who was used to giving orders and getting his own way. He was a leader.

"Carlo," the short man nodded a greeting.

"Afternoon, Mr. Torrio." There was great respect in Carlo's voice.

"Al in?" the man asked. The accent was harsh East Side New York. He did not raise his voice which, to Louis, made him different. Men he knew who spoke with an East Side accent usually talked loudly, shouting, drawing attention to themselves.

"He's upstairs, Mr. Torrio."

Torrio nodded, then looked at Louis. "What we got here?"

"Friend of mine," Carlo explained. "Louis Packer from New York. He's a pianist; gonna work with me over at The Barn. Mr. Capone checked him out."

Torrio looked at Louis, who could sense danger in the man's eyes. "Keep ya nose clean, kid. Do as yer told, and we'll see ya okay." Torrio hardly paused in his stride during this exchange, and the two men with him did not even look at Louis.

Outside, the wind blew gustily from the lakeside. The Four Deuces was situated on South Wabash Avenue, almost in sight of the lake, and a couple of blocks from the Loop district—the gin and sin area in this part of the city.

"Herbie, I have to tell you that I was a little frightened. I did not really know what would happen next."

"So, what did happen?" Herbie wanted things to move along at a good pace, and the old man looked tired.

"First, Carlo gave me money. Then he took me to get my hair cut." He shrugged and gave a sad little smile.

In the car, Carlo passed over a couple of twenty-dollar bills. "Al says I have to give ya this."

Louis pushed his friend's hand away. "I got money, Carlo. I don't need it. I got money of my own."

Carlo rested his hand gently on Louis' lapel. "Ya got money?" His eyebrows raised. "Yeah, what ya got? A few hundred lousy bucks?"

A few hundred, yes, Louis told his friend.

"Listen, Pianist." Carlo leaned back waving the two bills under Louis' nose. "Yer gonna need every cent of what ya got: and if ya play things right, yu'll make a goldmine. Save the little money ya got. Al sees his boys okay. Yu'll double what ya got within the week."

Louis frowned and took the bills. "Mr. Capone told me that he was only the bouncer for The Four Deuces." He said it quizzically, as though questioning his friend.

Carlo laughed. "Sure. Any trouble and that's what Al is, the bouncer. He's Johnny Torrio's right-hand man. Johnny works out the deals and does the talking. Al sees that everything's run neat and tidy. Both of them were Five Pointers in New York. They say that's why Torrio took Al into his outfit." He seemed about to continue, but the car pulled up outside a little barber shop with a sign that said, "Amato Gasperri. Prop."

They were greeted by the same man Louis had seen earlier in the day, wearing the barber's apron in Capone's quarters. It was a small shop, with a long rack of shaving mugs above the mirrors fronting the barber chair. A lot of the mugs had names neatly painted onto them in gilt.

"Hey, come on in, Carlo, and you, gentleman." Amato ushered them in with a broad welcoming smile. "Some of the boys were here, but they gone now. They come in. Take shave. Play some pinochle. They gone now."

"Mr. Capone says to shave my friend here. Ya keep him in mind, Amato. He is Louis, The Pianist. Ya know how Mr. Capone likes the hair done. Neat, okay?"

"Sure, sure." The little balding man bustled around, showing Louis to the chair, draping the sheet over him, making certain he was comfortable. Louis had never been treated like this at a barber shop in New York.

"I see you okay. Nice a boys. All a Mr. Capone boys nice a boys. All come here once in a while, eh, Carlo."

Louis watched the mirror, seeing Carlo sit down and light a cigarette. Then his eyes strayed to the rack of shaving mugs. The first one on the rack bore the name "Jim Colosimo." Under the name a cross had been painted in black.

"I was sorry to hear about Mr. Colosimo." Louis aimed the remark at Carlo, and immediately felt the atmosphere change: a tension in the barber's manner. The little man was poised with his comb and scissors over Louis' head. He seemed to be waiting for Carlo's reaction.

"Yeah. Yeah, it was a bad thing." Carlo spoke as though Louis had mentioned someone he did not know. It was an indifference he had not expected.

The barber relaxed. "I closa da shop for the funeral. You didn't a come to the funeral?"

"I was in New York." He was aware that he had made some kind of terrible error.

"Soma funeral, I tella you. Everyone there. Alla people from Mr. Capone and a Mr. Torrio there also."

Carlo shifted. "Just do the hair, Amato. Do the hair, give him a shave, make him look a million dollars. We got shopping to do."

"Then, my dear Herbie, Carlo took me out and bought me clothes like I had never seen before. Three suits off the peg; three more I was measured for, and the material was chosen. He bought me shoes, shirts, ties, socks, overcoat, raincoat. The works. Mr. Capone was paying for it all, he said. Hundreds of bucks in an hour or so. All down to Alphonse Capone. I felt like a king. Then"—the old Maestro leaned over and clutched Herbie's wrist—"then, Herb, in the car going out to The Barn, he gave me the real score. He told me what had happened, what *was* happening, and what he thought was going to happen. It was horrific. I had landed myself in the middle of a pit of vipers."

"But you didn't take the first train out, did you, Louis?"

Passau shook his head. "I'm maybe a little crazy. But in those days I wasn't that crazy. Capone had already made some kind of investment in me. I had to stay. At that moment, there was no option. But, I tell you, Herb, I was there with some of the most dangerous men who ever walked the earth."

"Tell me about it, Lou. Just go on and talk."

"Lunch," said old Louis Passau. "Lunch, and then I'll tell you what I was told, and what happened. Jesus, I feel the fear from it even now."

16

"YOU EVER SEE that movie, *The Godfather,* Herbie?"

"Yes. Saw all parts. One, Two and Three. Read the book also. Couldn't put it down, like the ads say. Very graphic."

"Let me tell you, Herb." Passau was into his stride again, after eating the rest of the Lancashire Hotpot, which Herbie had frozen overnight then nuked in the microwave. There had been two good-sized portions left. Passau took one and a half of them, without even asking if Herbie had enough. Herbie was unfulfilled in the lunch stakes. But, as with most things, Passau appeared to have no conscience.

"Let me tell you," he continued, "I worked with those mob guys in Chicago for six years, and *The Godfather* doesn't tell it right. It's like the comedian says about Robin Hood. He didn't steal from the rich to give to the poor. He stole from everyone and kept everything. You ever hear that?"

"Never heard it."

"Well, this is just like those mob guys. In *The Godfather* they talk about the honored society, respect and the rule of *omerta.* . . ."

"Explain *omerta,* Lou." Herbie knew exactly what *omerta* was, but he felt pretty pissed about Lou Passau eating all the Hotpot. He could really have done with a whole plateful for himself. It was also good interrogation technique. Let the client prattle on: paddle up tributaries away from the main stream, then yank him back to the things that really mattered. Big Herbie was sure that something very important in Passau's life had happened during the Chicago days, and he was going to be the first to hear of it.

"Okay. *Omerta* is the law of silence. In plain talk, you don't snitch on your fellow gangsters."

"You don't grass."

"What's with grass, Herb? Grass is like pot, isn't it? Dope? They weren't into dope."

"Not in England, Lou. In England they call a snitch a 'grass.' They even had a guy did a police program on TV. He showed all the stuff the cops had recovered from robberies, and did reenactments of crimes so that witnesses might remember things. The crooks called this guy 'Whispering Grass.'"

"The English are crazy. But so were the guys in Chicago, and those guys were *evil*. The evil empires are all the same: if they're religious, criminal or political—and I know political, Herb. As you will hear, I know political in depth—or shallows, whichever way you want to put it. These people, they'd be funny if they weren't so deadly—like Hitler and Stalin would've been funny. Cruel clowns, bumping into each other; barbarous buffoons, murderous madmen. There was no honor, no respect—except through fear—and no courage. Look, I am saying this even though I left the city before things got *really* bad. These Chicago guys were a mess. A really ridiculous mess, and I first knew that when we finished buying up the clothes stores and got back in the car to drive out to The Barn in Burnham. Carlo gave me the lowdown that very first day."

In the rear of the automobile, Carlo brought his face close to Louis and talked, almost in a whisper, as though he did not want the driver to hear everything.

"Listen, Lou. Between them, Johnny Torrio and Capone got this city sewn up." He went on to explain that, like New York in their boyhood days, Chicago was divided into various territories. The South Side was run by the Genna family; the North Side—between the lake and the Chicago River—was the preserve of an Irishman called Dion O'Banion, who had a partner, Hymie Weiss. "Far South Side is the O'Donnell brothers," Carlo told him. "The eldest, Spike, pulled a five stretch in Joliet; his brothers were at The Four Deuces this morning. They saw ya, Pianist. Steve, Walter and Tommy. Me, I don't trust them. I guess Johnny Torrio was set for a sitdown with them today."

He went on to say that another O'Donnell family—"No relation to the O'Donnells I tol' ya about already"—ran part of the West Side.

"Herbie, by the time we got to The Barn out in Burnham, my head was reeling with names. There was Saltis, Touhy, Druggan, the Lake Gang, Ralph Sheldon, Bugs Moran—he worked with Dion O'Banion. Deany we called him. I hadn't even got the geography of the place worked out, so how was I to figure the various territories?"

When they arrived at The Barn—which was a huge converted warehouse—Carlo opened up a side door, and the driver, who acted like a deaf mute, helped Louis in with the suitcase and the packages of clothes. There was a very large main room, with a bar at the far end, flanked by two doors. Carlo led the way to the one on the right, motioning to the door on the left, which he said was the way to the kitchens and the rear of the place. "We've got a big loading bay and storeroom back there. We live up here." They entered a long room, dim and dark, though Louis made out the shape of a piano near the stairs. At the top of the stairs there was a wide landing with two door-studded corridors leading back towards the front of the building. Louis heard girls talking, and some laughter.

Directly facing the stairs was the door to Carlo's domain: an office, with an apartment behind it. "We open at ten. Ten at night, that is," Carlo said, as though this was a perfectly normal time to open a business. "Ya share with me for the time being. Now, ya probably know, I'm the head bouncer here. This is my preserve, but ya share it with me, Pianist. I have to show ya the ropes, because we're old buddies. That's what Mr. Capone tol' me. But, listen good, when the action starts, ya do exactly what I tell ya, right?"

Louis said that was fine by him.

The Packensteiner place in New York was an outdoor privy compared to Carlo's apartment.

There were good rugs on the floors, and the bedroom contained two beds: a huge double bed, and a small cot under the window. "If I'm busy, ya can drag the cot into the other room," Carlo grinned. "Or go and bunk in with one of the girls, maybe. But there's rules about the girls."

In the living room a large ornate mirror decorated one wall, and a sunburst clock glittered on another. There were nice pictures and the furnishings were mainly mahogany, with stuffed armchairs and a Chesterfield which looked very cozy. Under the mirror stood a large and flashy cocktail cabinet.

"You do yourself well, Carlo." Louis again felt like a country cousin. He was just not used to this kind of opulence.

"Ah, it belongs to the outfit." Carlo shrugged. "Play things right, Pianist, and yu'll get the same. Drink?"

Louis said he would have a lemon soda and Carlo laughed, "Look, kid, this isn't hooch I keep here. It's not the spiked stuff. I got the real McCoy, not the rotgut we serve to the Joes downstairs."

Louis said he would stick with the lemon soda.

"Ya gotta lot to learn, Pianist."

"I know I do, and I'm looking for you to teach me, Carlo." He thought of the moment of tension in the barber shop when he had mentioned Big Jim Colosimo's death. "I guess I put my foot in my mouth talking about Colosimo out loud at the barber shop."

"Nah, don't think about it. It's just we don't talk much, not about what happened."

"What *did* happen?"

"It was inevitable, Everyone liked Big Jim. He was good to me, like to everyone else. Christ, it was Big Jim who brought Torrio out from New York. You knew Torrio was his nephew some way?"

Louis shook his head.

"Well, Big Jim had the place buttoned up. Ya know, City Hall, the cops, everyone. He ran all the places down on the Levee—the joints, cathouses, everything, and he had his café. Most famous place in town. Everyone who was anyone went to Big Jim's. Actors, politicians, opera singers, he liked opera singers a lot, like Al. Liked listening to music on the phonograph: Verdi and Puccini mostly. Hell, that's why Al had ya play that *Aida* thing. That's Al's favorite, just like Big Jim. But Uncle Jim just didn't move with the times. Now, Johnny Torrio had a real eye to the future. He saw the dough that could be made when prohibition came in. He used to say, 'No laws're gonna keep this city dry. The suckers'll need someone to supply the booze, and they'll need somewhere to drink it.' He called it the law of supply and demand. Far-seeing man, Mr. Torrio. But Big Jim was getting old. Set in his ways. He went along with things when the Volstead Act came in, but his heart wasn't in it. Sure, he helped organize the liquor business and, with his connections, it was easy. But, as the boss out here, he lacked imagination. Torrio said he didn't have the flair for it. Torrio saw there would be trouble among the various setups if Big Jim remained boss. So Johnny did the only thing . . ."

"You mean, Johnny Torrio had him . . . ?" Louis looked aghast.

"Never say it out loud, kid. Don't even think it. But I guess that's what happened. The cops couldn't make it stick, but the word is that Torrio had Frankie Yale come down from New York to do the job. The

Sicilians're very thick here. Ya gotta remember that, and it was only good business. There was nothing personal in it. There wasn't no other way."

Louis felt a little sick. "So, Torrio took over?"

"Oh, he did more'n that. Johnny Torrio expanded. He got all the boys together. Shrewd, Pianist, very shrewd. He saw what was happening, like truckloads of booze being hijacked, shootings, smashing up other people's joints. So he had them all together, a big sitdown, and they worked out a deal—like not operating in other people's backyards, and making sure trucks could pass through each other's areas without getting hijacked. He made sure all the joints were supplied regular, and by the right people. It makes for a quiet life, I'll tell ya. For a while there was a regular war going on here. Johnny Torrio was the peacemaker. He's the big man around town. People respect him."

"I tell you, Herbie, that straightaway there, in The Barn, I wondered if I'd got myself into a situation over my head. Stealing a few hundred bucks from my old man's store; screwing Ruth in the stockroom; even the dangers of crossing some gang turf on my way to see Aaron, this all paled next to what Carlo was talking about.

"It seemed pretty terrible that a nephew should arrange to have his uncle gunned down, simply because he had too much power and didn't know how to use it. The whole business was like some of the violent plots in grand opera. Perhaps the opera helped in the way those imbeciles operated. I remember, at the time, my head was ringing and I thought it rang like the bells in the coronation scene from *Boris Godunov*. Aaron had taken me to see it, first time ever, at the Met, with Toscanini conducting. I was very impressed by the spectacle of the coronation scene. Mind you, it was like vaudeville if you put it next to my 1949 production."

"Of course it was, Maestro," Herbie said, raising his eyes to heaven and trying to keep himself from making a truly stupendously deflating remark.

"Herbie, these guys did not hesitate to pull the trigger if they thought it was right for business. I could see that running liquor and women, for those who wanted them, was very big business indeed. Helluva bigger business than shoe shops. And I also realized that the higher the financial reward, then the more risks these people were willing to take."

Back in 1922, Carlo must have seen the look on Louis' face as he thought about these things. "Don't worry, Pianist. Like I tell ya, everything's taken care of: from the Police Department to City Hall, and yer in Torrio's showplace. Wait till ya see the kind of people we get in here tonight. Now, get outta those clothes and into one of them sharp suits we bought. In a few hours yu'll be earning your living here."

So Louis shampooed his hair with the fancy stuff Carlo had bought him, shaved, for the second time that day, and slapped cologne over his body—"The first time I ever used cologne, Herb. I thought it was kind of sissy, but Carlo did it, and I smelled it on Capone; so I thought when in Rome . . ."

He chose a light blue suit, with a cream silk shirt and a cream tie with some blue pattern in it which picked up the color of the suit. On his feet he had handmade leather shoes, better quality than those his father made. "I thought to myself, Herb, if I stick with it, I'll fart through silk for the rest of my life. It was there, in Chicago, I really got my taste for clothes. Later, I saw the stuff I wore there was a little flashy. I learned dress sense, but that was later, in Hollywood, where the biographies begin. As far as anyone else is concerned, I arrived, fully grown, out of a star trap on Sunset Boulevard. You ever heard Chicago mentioned in my public past?"

Herbie shook his head.

"You ever hear of me conducting the Chicago Symphony?"

Again the shake of the head.

"Damned right you haven't. I never dared even to visit Chicago for a very long time. Anyway . . ."

When Louis emerged from the bathroom, Carlo let out a long whistle, "Hey, Pianist, ya look sharp. Ya look like ya just broke outta the egg."

Louis' job was easy enough, and it took him only one night to get the measure of what went on at The Barn. He figured it was the same setup as all the other Torrio and Capone joints. Come to that, the same setup as all the joints owned and run by any of the other gang families in Chicago.

There were two large, burly men in tuxedos—Jo-Jo and Mouse—who spent all their time in the small entrance which was walled off from the main room, called the Lounge. There they checked out the customers, made sure they had the right connections and, apart from those allowed, that they were not carrying weapons. This they did efficiently, by creating a kind of aura of thuggery around them. People rarely argued with Jo-Jo and Mouse.

The Lounge was dotted with tables, and the staff of six waiters went through the crowds with trays of drinks and quick food, like sandwiches and the kind of things, Louis learned, served at smart cocktail parties in the old days. The small band, made up of white boys, played a much tighter kind of jazz than that which Louis had heard in New York, with the bass instruments sometimes playing two beats to the bar, while the solo breaks seemed more expansive, but almost orchestrated. These musicians rarely extemporized, so it was by no means jazz in the true sense of the word.

No customers were allowed to drink at the bar, and Louis spent a lot of his time in a more austere backroom, into which particular clients came through the door to the right of the bar.

The room at the back was oblong: narrow, with a staircase at the far end, and padded benches down each of the longer walls. On the walls there were old prints of voluptuous half-naked ladies draped over stone benches or beside broken pillars, and some indoor plants to give the place a homely feel to it. The clients came through from the lounge, and sat on the padded benches, and Louis played piano near the staircase, between sitting in when the band took a break.

In that backroom he soon got used to seeing the girls—twenty of them on a good evening—come down the stairs in a strict order, based on some kind of secret superiority. They were usually scantily dressed in diaphanous negligees, teddies or more exotic underwear which, Carlo said, was imported direct from Paris, France. Each of the girls would parade slowly around the room, and the client seated nearest the staircase got the first choice. If he went upstairs with a girl, everyone moved up a place, though he was free to wait around for any girl for whom he had a special liking.

Louis played slow blues and, sometimes, ragtime. He got to know the girls at The Barn pretty well: the dark-haired Linda, who was only just twenty; the tall and lovely Betty Anne, who claimed her parents were wealthy Bostonians; Carol, who had been in burlesque—small and neat, but with eye-catching outsize breasts which made her look all out of proportion, though this did not seem to worry the clients. He had a particular fancy for Liz, who, he was certain, had some Negro blood in her because of the thick lips and flared nostrils. There were others— Kate, Jane, Beverly, Chris, Harriet, and, of course, Dianne who was in charge.

Dianne, a little older than the others, was sharp-featured and hard in manner. She rarely took a client upstairs herself, but her job paid very well and she kept the girls in order, stopped fights, imposed fines and looked after the cash side of the business.

There were plenty of chances for Louis to have any of the girls whenever he wanted, but Carlo had said they had rules about that. Later he explained, "If ya want one of them, Pianist, ya ask me first. We can't always keep a check on these broads. I guess there's a lot of the clap around, and worse than that. Ya ask me, though, because I keep an eye out, and so does Dianne. We know when the girls get to see the doc. So, always ask."

When the band in the Lounge took their break, Louis would leave the cathouse area and use the band piano. He only had to play background music: a bit of blues, but mainly the popular ballads and songs of the day, jazzed up a little. He often wondered if it was necessary because the men and women who came to sample the alcohol in the lounge talked a lot and were a noisy bunch.

On Louis' third night at The Barn, Torrio came over with Capone and Harry Guzik's brother, Jake. They brought a couple of hoods with them—Frank Nitti and Steve O'Donnell. Like Carlo, Louis did not take to O'Donnell. The man appeared to be faraway in his mind all night, as though thinking of something else. He did not seem to listen to what Torrio and Capone had to say, as if he harbored some kind of grudge. Resentful was the word that popped into Louis' head.

Capone came over to the piano, while Louis played in the Lounge, and asked how he was getting on. The man was like a big, dangerous animal, but there was no denying the charm he could bring out whenever it was needed. Torrio came over as well, but Louis found him cold and unfeeling, like he imagined a banker would be if he walked in off the street and asked for a loan.

Jake Guzik hovered in the background.

Later, Louis would discover that the Guziks originally hailed from Moscow and there was another brother besides Harry and Jake.

Jake Guzik had worked in diners, serving tables, when he first arrived in New York, and most of the mob spoke of him as "Greasy Thumb" because he had acquired the habit of getting his thumbs into the plates of soup he carried as a waiter. The nickname was to become more sinister in later years, when he displayed an amazing mind for figures, and became Capone's treasurer and financial adviser. He was an amiable fat man, unlike Frank Nitti, who Louis put down as a natural killer; sadistic, unemotional and a man who enjoyed his work.

Louis was surprised to find that he was given one free night a week and, at the end of his first seven days, Carlo came to him with an envelope. Inside were two one-hundred-dollar bills.

"Yer pay," Carlo explained.

A couple of C notes for playing piano. "I get two Cs every week?"

"Maybe a couple a high Cs, sometimes, if yer good." Carlo grinned, his pocked and scarred face taking on a wolfish look. Louis laughed. Carlo would have difficulty telling a high C from a B natural, even with his love of opera.

Though Carlo gave Louis his money each week, it came directly from Torrio, via Jake Guzik. It took a couple of weeks for Louis to catch on to the fact that Jake came around in the wee smalls, when the club closed, every night of the week. He came to check on the takings. Torrio was clever, and very careful. There was no way in which either Carlo, or the men who kept bar, could tamper with the profits, because each bottle, and every barrel, had to be accounted for, and each bottle and barrel had a set profit.

The situation with the girls was equally, if not more, complicated. Dianne ruled the roost upstairs, together with a couple of older women who were big-boned and very hard; bull dykes, as you could imagine wardresses in the Women's House of Correction. When a john went upstairs with a girl, one of these women handed the guy a towel. The girl also got a towel from the woman, but the john paid two dollars for his. The standard rate was two bucks for five minutes, and the two wardresses made it clear when the five minutes were up by banging on the door and demanding further cash, which meant that most of the guys parted with ten bucks for five towels to start with. The girls negotiated the real price, and each girl was paid half of what she made in one night, minus a ten percent "towel charge," but plus a commission on any booze she got her customer to have brought up to the room.

Some of the younger, and stronger, girls would make upwards of one hundred dollars clear profit a night. They had a big party one night when Liz, the one Louis fancied, made a record of two hundred and fifty clear. On that night Carlo gave Louis the thumbs up to make out with Liz.

"She was a good teacher, Herb," the old man said. "I learned some great bedroom gymnastics at her knee, and other places."

For three or four weeks, Louis was asked to do nothing else but play piano. He met some of the other musicians, who had been standoffish for the first couple of nights, and he got on especially well with a young Chicago boy called Milton Mezzrow. Mezzrow's friends called him "Mezz," and he played as sweet a clarinet as you would ever want to hear.

He warned Louis, "You do as you're told, Pianist, unless it's a real matter of principle with you—like music or relatives. Even then, only stand your ground with Capone. Some of these guys would blow your head off for sneezing while they're speaking. Capone, though, he's usually fair and, nine times out of ten, the guy'll respect someone who stands up to him. But you've got to watch for his moods and never, never cross him when Torrio's around."

"And that, Herbie, turned out to be very good advice." Passau paused, not looking at Kruger. "Herbie, I think I'd like a little music now."

Big Herbie stretched and rose, pacing to a point where he could stand back, yet see clearly out of the window. It was late afternoon, with the promise of a lovely September evening. The trees had yet to turn and burn the fire of autumn. They were still the faded green of summer dust and some still carried other colors.

So, he thought, Maestro Passau is uncomfortable in Chicago. Herbie had some of it figured out. Not completely, but there had been hints. He thought he knew where the World War II stuff fitted but could not yet even make a guess at what had followed, leading to the more important, recent events.

His experience told him that Passau was gibing, holding back, not wanting to get to the heart of things. There was, undoubtedly, something particular during the Chicago period that had possibly affected him for the rest of his life.

"Herb, some music. Yes?"

All Herbie's instincts told him that he should refuse, play the inflexible son of a bitch and make Passau go on talking. But instinct also said that Passau was so mercurial that he could easily clam up, refuse to go on, even decline to cooperate completely. Then where shall we be? Herbie shook his head, marveling at the beauty of the view.

"You can choose, Herb. You choose something." There was almost a hint of desperation, as though he wanted to run away and hide in some music. God knew, Herbie thought, he, of all people, should appreciate that need.

He nodded at Passau. "I choose the Mahler Sixth"—he went over to the CDs—"and not *your* recording, Maestro. Bernstein, the most recent one. She has it here, Bernstein with the Vienna." He opened the jewel case and took out the first CD. "Amazing that it should be a Jewish American who brought the Vienna Philharmonic back to *their* composer, eh?"

"He did an incredible job." Passau did not sound impressed.

"To have not played Mahler for so long, then for them to resist Bernstein until he made them play again."

"Lenny was always persuasive, Herb—if that story's true, which I doubt. Lenny had a good propaganda machine."

The thud-thud of that gawky march and the first great theme of the Sixth came sweeping down from the speakers. It was the lead-in to Mahler's passionate musical description of his wife. Herbie knew that, but, whenever he heard the strings go marching off, his imagination took hold and he thought of huge, skeletal, Giacometti-like figures striding down from a mountain, crashing through trees in the foothills, laying waste to everything.

He also thought of a time long gone when he had listened, in his head, to Mahler's Sixth, to hide from demons who chased him. To shelter in order that he could better deal with the people who had him, back in the frozen days when the Wall was still a killing field. Herbie, so often in those days, had used the symphonies of Gustav Mahler as tradecraft: his own cerebral hiding places during the dangerous and dark nights of his own soul. For a long time, Mahler had been cover for him. Sanctuary. Who was he to pass judgment on another great musician who obviously wanted to find his own deliverance in a similar way?

Mahler's work thundered on, into the quiet, almost pastoral moments, with cowbell cloppings, leading to the doom-laden haunting themes.

The wonderful soaring tune, which all but overpowers in the lilting moments of the third movement, was always difficult for Herbie Kruger to handle. All men have a trigger to the emotions, with some it is a fragment of song, or a long-forgotten line of poetry, others feel it in a view seen again, unexpectedly. With Herbie, who could be a sentimental dolt, he admitted, many of Mahler's more spectacular themes dropped the hammer on him.

They were both listening intently and, when the final dark melody began to build, signifying the sudden ending, Herbie felt, more than saw, that Louis Passau was weeping, just as *he* so often wept.

Herbie looked up, his own eyes moist from personal memories—the fluted ruby glasses, the Dürer woodcut, and the treachery of Ursula—and caught Passau's damp eyes in his.

It was a bonding. An exchange of vows. The interrogator and the subject becoming allies. He hoped that Louis Passau would now be able to go on and reveal the dark secrets lurking in the cavern of his soul.

They ate early—the stuffed onions—listened to more music, the Bruckner Ninth and Bartok's Third Piano Concerto. "I remember when people said this sounded like a freight yard," Passau laughed. "You couldn't get anything more melodic, with those great complex themes. I often worry about music critics. They never seem to keep up with the times. They're always praising the past, just as they praise mediocrity."

Herbie put on the Shostakovich Thirteenth, with its brooding and powerful settings of Yevtushenko's poems: beginning with "Babi Yar" reflecting the horror of the Jewish massacre in Kiev.

> There is no memorial above Babi Yar.
> The steep ravine is like a coarse tombstone.
> I'm frightened,
> I feel as old today
> as the Jewish race itself.
> I feel now that I am a Jew.

"The critic of the *New York Times*—what was his name? Schonberg? He called *this* 'an example of poster-propaganda music.' How soulless these professional listeners can become." Louis Passau looked miserable, and they sat in silence for a while.

Just before nine, the telephone rang. Five times, to say all was safe and Naldo felt happy about coming to the house without leeches on his back. Only it would not be Naldo, Herbie thought. It would be the Pucky person.

PUCKY CURTISS HAD suffered a strange and nerve-grating day.

At eleven that morning she asked for her suitcase to be taken down to the car. She paid her bill and then took lunch, served once more by the boys and wenches in their eighteenth-century costumes. She really did find this part of America difficult to understand. There were moments, as yesterday looking at the university's rotunda, when she felt she was in a time warp, yet at other times she was bemused. She had done the audio version of a double take when she had heard the TV weatherman refer to Virginia as "The Old Dominion"; and again when she saw a bumper sticker which boldly announced "Hang On To Your Confederate Money. The South Will Rise Again!" It was difficult for her to reconcile the recent history—old for Americans—and the current values. Everything about this place was a paradox to her, from the intense lushness of the Blue Ridge to the ugliness of buildings which did not even try to merge with the older architectural styles. Also, as one who lived mainly in London, there was the culture shock of amazement at the friendly and eager politeness of everyone she met.

"Y'all leavin' us, Mz Cummings?" the girl at reception had asked when she paid her bill, and the manner of asking barely hid an unfeigned dismay. "You've only been here a couple of days." As though the girl were genuinely sorry to see her leave.

Pucky had said she had to get back—"I must be in Washington tonight," she had lied, against the unlikely possibility of anyone questioning hotel staff about her movements. In the ultimate paranoia of all field agents she had the mental vision of hard-faced men showing her photograph to frightened reception girls.

After lunch, she overtipped and then wondered why. It was something Pucky Curtiss would never have done in England.

She stood for a moment in the doorway of The Boar's Head Inn, looking out across the parking lot with its colorful backdrop of flowers and grassy banks. She turned her head slightly at the sound of a car door closing and saw, to her great consternation, two men standing by a white Chevy. The driver had his back to her as he bent to lock the door, but his passenger's face was clear at fifty yards.

With mounting anxiety, and a fair proportion of disbelief, Pucky saw Desperate Dan Hochella, late of Grosvenor Square, talking across the car roof to whoever it was who had brought him to The Boar's Head Inn, Charlottesville, just in time to see her, and, presumably, start every alarm bell ringing from here to Washington and back to London.

He was the last person she needed, and about the only person she knew who could blow her cover in the U.S.A.

17

IN SITUATIONS SUCH as this, never move quickly or erratically, they had taught during those endless fieldcraft and tradecraft sessions at Warminster. When she had listened, learned and played the little secret war games, Pucky had thought of this kind of thing possibly coming up in Eastern Europe, if at all. Now, with the collapse of communism, all that appeared to have gone. What had occurred in the last few days seemed to have removed the rug under everyone's feet. So why had she come? Why was everyone making such a fuss over one old man who might, and again might not, have been a World War II agent, and a Moscow Center asset during the big freeze. It made no sense.

Pucky, a high achiever since kindergarten, thought she would always remain on the administrative level. She even fantasized about becoming the first female CSIS, after many years of running people from desks. Rarely had Ms. Curtiss seen herself as a modern-day Mata Hari in the field. Not that Mata Hari was historically acceptable as a role model.

Do not panic, she told herself, turning lazily, lifting her right hand to brush some of her glorious blonde hair out of her eyes—a gesture, she realized too late, which was characteristic and might just alert Desperate Dan to her presence.

She kept her strides long, but languid, back into the main lobby. Take a left and head for the ladies' room, the instructor's voice in her head had a nervous edge. At least he cannot follow you in there. Want to bet?

She stopped at the thought. Already she was assuming that Dan Hochella was actually looking for *her*. If he was, then she had hit big trouble.

She locked the cubicle door, then gave herself five minutes by the Cartier watch Mummy and Daddy—the general and his lady—had given her last Christmas. For a second she wondered where she would be this Christmas. If Dan was in the lobby when she came out, which she figured was unlikely, she would have to play it by ear. Brazen it out, get a message to Kruger telling him the jig was up, run for it. Jesus, the game's afoot, Watson. This was the kind of rubbish you were supposed to cut your teeth on.

She walked out exactly on the five-minute mark. No Dan Hochella in the reception area, or outside. Willing herself to abide by the rules they had taught, she went to her car, which started at the first twist of the ignition. Ten minutes later, she was on 29 North, heading towards Washington.

She went through all the precautions, watching for a tail, sweeping the rear mirror regularly. No odd traffic patterns appeared, so she reckoned that they were not on to her. Never assume anything. She had seen that on a bumper as she left Charlottesville, and knew it to be true. Art Railton had gone through all the emergency procedures with her before she left London, and he had also said it—"Pucky, old love, it's the first golden rule. Never assume anything." So, she acted as if they were on to her, even though she picked up nothing in the sensors of her eyes, ears and brain.

The drive to Dulles International should have taken two hours. Pucky made it in three, negotiating wild and erratic detours because of road work. Within six miles of the airport the traffic was backed up solidly, and that helped to slow her down, allowing her to sweep the cars behind her with more caution. Surely Dan Hochella could not have been looking for her? It did not make sense. Nobody knew. Her papers were Grade A, untraceable back to the Office. They could never make her in a thousand years.

But they had, and she knew it as she stood at the Hertz counter, returning the car. Two of them. A man and a woman, both strategically placed so there was no way out. Shit, Pucky thought. Shit on toast. Think, girl; you're supposed to be wonder woman. You had it all nicely planned. Do something now. Who are these guys? Why?

She lugged her case up to the B.A. check-in desk, flashed her ticket and asked if they had a seat on tonight's London flight. It did not leave until eight fifty-five and that meant nobody would start yelling until seven thirty at the earliest. She watched her case slide away through the conveyor belt's rubber flaps and thought now I don't even have a spare pair of drawers to my name. She was left with what she stood up in. Stone-washed Levi's, a crisp favorite shirt, bought at Fenwicks, underwear from Marks & Spencer, loafers and her big shoulder bag which held three sets of I.D., her tickets, credit cards in two names, travelers' checks for five hundred dollars, around two hundred dollars in cash, and an assortment of junk which included two ticket stubs from last November when she had seen *Les Miz* for the third time with her old chum, Bitsy Williams. Fat lot of good *that* had done her.

The surveillance was still on her, the woman in a smart tailored suit, the man in jeans and a T-shirt with flowers and grass on the front and the legend "Compost Happens." They had her boxed nicely; bracketed, according to all the good handbooks. "We're not playing this game according to Mr. Hoyle, we're playing it according to *me*." Now where the hell had that come from? Was it her last lover but one who had an incredible collection of comedy on record? Yes. The Poker Game, but for the hell of it she could not remember who had done it. Phil Harris? Was it Phil Harris? And what other twenty-nine-year-old would even have heard of Phil Harris and The Poker Game? How in hell had they ferreted her out? And how in hell, Pucky, had you suddenly lost a year? She now did the only thing possible: went to a phone booth and dialed the magic number that would take her, straight and secure, to Art Railton and advice, possibly a little help as well.

THE MARKING OF Pucky Curtiss had been one of those things that happen in novels. You read it and say, "No! This guy's playing with coincidence. That could never happen." The problem is that even the most unlikely things happen at night and in the real world. Coincidence is always the exception that proves the rule. Take a book called *Tinker, Tailor, Soldier, Spy*, written by John le Carré in 1974. This fiction deals with a Russian mole, code named Gerald. Gerald's Russian case officer turns out to be a fellow called Polyakov. Fiction. In 1989 the Soviets announced that they had arrested a long-term penetration agent—a mole, as they have been saying in the trade since Francis Bacon first mentioned moles in the seventeenth century. This 1989 mole was code named Top Hat and, guess what? His name turned out to be Polyakov. There is coincidence.

Desperate Dan Hochella had arrived back at that big complex which is so well signposted—CIA—at Langley, though the row was still going on as to whether it was really in Langley or McLean.

The Deputy Director Ops Europe had carpeted Hochella over his handling of matters in London: matters regarding the tip the SIS had received from Erik the Red, a.k.a. Erik Ring and Brightwater. "We *know* this whole thing stinks, Dan. The Brits're playing games and now we've lost their guy with *our* asset, Sunray—oh, what the hell, Louis Passau. You haven't had your eye on the ball, you haven't kept on the SIS's case. The whole mess is slipping through our fingers." He went on for some time, in the same vein, then told a truly desperate Dan Hochella that he would just have to study the stuff here, in the complex, then go back and try harder. "Every hour we're out of touch with Passau is a year lost. That's how I see it."

"Even now, when everything's changed?" Hochella asked, weakly.

"Believe me, especially now. This isn't straightforward, Dan, there's more than the file. Stuff even you should not know. Stuff, I suspect, that's going to be locked away until Gabriel blows his horn, and then some. But at least you should be aware of what's on file."

He then told Dan to get down to records and use the password, Filigree, to get the up-to-date file. "Read, mark, learn and digest, Dan. London hasn't been pulling hard enough."

Dan was at the door when he asked, "Who's your liaison at Century House?"

"Curtiss." Even Dan's voice sounded faraway, plunged in the slough of despond, as John Bunyan would have said. "Pat Curtiss."

"What's he like? Sharp?"

"He's a she. Pucky Curtiss."

"Okay, I'll pull her file as well. Maybe we should see if she has any pressure points. Leave that one to me."

Now, came the coincidence. When Hochella had been through the printout of Filigree, committed it to memory, and thought he had a real handle on it, he returned to the office of the Deputy Director Ops, Europe.

It so happened that the DDOE, as he was known to his friends, was closeted with one of their people from Berlin, but when he was told of Dan's presence, he said, "What the hell, send him in."

The guy from Berlin was a Covert Action type, a singleton, as the argot had it. Singletons rarely even checked in with embassies, though quite often Embassy Residents were hauled from their beds to service them. Love was not lost between run-of-the-mill Residents and CA people. All that would change now that "The Main Target," as they used to call the U.S.S.R. was all but neutralized. The introductions were made and the DDOE apologized to the CA man for the break in their meeting.

"I have this woman Curtiss' file here, and she *has* one small pressure point. A married guy. Usual. Affair. He broke it off and went back to his wife, normal shitty treatment, but she might just be vulnerable." He slung the file down on the desk and it flipped open at a series of surveillance photographs of Pucky. The CA type did a double take, reached for the file and said loudly, "I *know* her. You can't miss her. A stunner," or words to that effect. In fact he went on for quite a while describing Ms. Curtiss' charms, then ended with, "I came in via London a couple of days ago. That woman was on the same flight. Know her in a Chinese whorehouse at midnight."

They put Dan on it with an officer experienced in the art of tracing foreign agents who have slipped into the U.S. of A. in a quiet, even silent, manner. A couple of days later, they picked up the trail left by Pauline Una Cummings, and set off to scour central Virginia.

FBI Counter-Intelligence, the CIA's uneasy bedfellows, led them to Charlottesville. That morning, they had done the Sheraton and the Omni. Dan was hungry when they got to The Boar's Head Inn, so they left showing Pucky's photograph to reception until after they had eaten; bad fieldcraft, sloppy work on the part of his companion. But they finally got around to doing it, just as Pucky, in her wild imaginings, had foreseen. The photograph, the shake of the head, then the closer look and the nod. They even had the registration of the car the lady was driving. "She told Mary she was going to Washington. Said she *had* to be there," one of the girls volunteered. Hence the double act who picked her up at Dulles.

IT WAS PAST ELEVEN o'clock at night in London, when Pucky's call was patched through, on the ultrasecure line, to Arthur Railton. It took Pucky two minutes of fast talk to give him at least a glance at the topography, if not a good thorough look at the landscape, and Art lost no time at all telling her to get the hell out, shake the leeches and call him later. He closed down on her. Lord knew what kind of monitoring devices the American Service provided for their footpads.

Pucky replaced the receiver and went down to the arrivals area, the most crowded part of the already bulging and outdated Dulles airport. She had moved very quickly, taking the stairs and not the escalator. The two watchers were, at least temporarily, left-footed.

She plunged into one of the tunnels that lead from the internal flights luggage carousels out to the parking lots and pick-up areas. God knew what she would do when she got to the other side, but the pair were not with her when she came out into the late afternoon sunshine. A yellow shuttle bus stood, half full, to her left, its destination showing above the windshield. It read "National Airport." So be it, she thought, climbing aboard and taking a seat at the back. Three other people followed her, and the driver started his engine almost before the last passenger was seated.

As the bus pulled away, Pucky saw the male member of the team come out of another of the tunnel entrances, behind her. She dropped her shoulder bag, spilling some of the contents, and forcing her to scrabble around on the floor out of sight, which was just as well because, though she did not know it at the time, the female watcher had come out of another tunnel and walked the length of the shuttle, making no bones about looking for her. Full of the knowledge that their "person of interest" was not aboard the National shuttle, the female watcher gave her partner the clear sign, indicating their quarry was still in the airport complex.

Pucky felt pleased with herself, and an hour later, she was renting a sporty little Honda from the Avis desk at National, using her panic I.D. of Patty Crawford.

So Pucky drove all the way back south to Charlottesville, incidentally passing Dan Hochella and his colleague on the way, and stopping off twice: once to make a more secure call to Art, on the magic line; and once, in Charlottesville's Fashion Square Mall where she used Office credit cards to buy another suitcase and fill it with two changes of clothes, a froth of underwear, a whole new range of cosmetics, a Sony Walkman and a half-dozen tapes from Sam Goody, plus two overpraised paperbacks to ensure sleep.

Art had given her some fair and decisive instructions, once she had told him her side of the story. So, when she called the number Naldo had given her, using the five rings signal, Pucky was quite clear about the message she had to bring to Blue Boy, a.k.a. Big Herbie Kruger.

She observed the correct procedure on arriving at the house, driving round to the back, parking the Honda next to Herbie's rented silver gray Cutlass Supreme.

As soon as Herbie opened the door and saw the tall, slim girl with the world-class figure and all that shiny blond hair, he knew that, should he ever be tempted to commit adultery, it would be with her, or someone quite like her.

"You are the Pucky lady?" It was not really a question, but a kind of statement.

"Pucky Curtiss. I'm traveling under a new I.D." She gave him a run-down of what she had learned in the harsh world of secret reality that day. This made Herbie begin to fuss around her, offering food, cups of tea, strong drink, aspirin, vitamin pills, anything that came into his head. A long, gentle massage was one of the things that came into his head, though he did not mention this aloud.

She would kill for a bowl of chicken soup. Nothing easier, Herbie told her, knowing he had several tins left from the store Naldo had provided. He even had French bread in the freezer and could crisp that up in the microwave in no time. Meanwhile, he would introduce her to their guest of honor. "A tried and tested category one son of a bitch, but he's the only one we got." Herbie smiled, choosing his idiot incapable child version, which usually went down well with young women.

Louis Passau was, of course, full of real charm. "She's what we need, eh, Herb? A woman about the place. Keep us cheerful. On our toes. Make us stop farting in public, huh?"

"Oh, merciful heavens," Pucky thought.

"I swear, Maestro, I shall kill you," thought Herbie.

Yet, when Herb returned with a tray containing a large bowl of Campbell's chicken soup, and the best part of a French stick, there she was, having her pants charmed off by the nasty old reprobate.

". . . So there she is, and you are too young, but she was a very fat prima donna. And, as you know, in the closing moments of *Tosca*, the diva is hysterical: with a cry of '*Scarpia, davanti a Dio,*' she hurls herself from the battlements of the Castel Sant'Angelo. In fact, what happens is the lady falls four feet onto a padded mattress. Well, as I told you, the stage staff were really very angry. There had been scenes, rages, demands all through the rehearsals. So, in this opening performance, very prestigious, they replace the mattress with a trampoline, and she hurls herself off, then bounces back, and again, and again, and again. I thought I would collapse there and then, right in front of everybody. She was still bouncing when the curtain came down."

Pucky had her head thrown back in a silvery laugh, and Herbie would have given a year of his pension to kiss that throat.

"You tell the porkies again, Lou." He stood very still.

"What are porkies, Herb?"

"I told you already, Lou. When we started our little adventure I told you the cockney rhyming slang. Porky pies equals lies."

"When did I tell lies?"

"What happened with the trampoline in a production of *Tosca*. This is an old story, and it was *not* you conducting. This happened at New York City Center, 1960."

"So, I am allowed some dramatic license."

"Dramatic bullshit. Excuse me, Pucky."

She took the tray and began to attack the food as though she had a really bad addiction problem with chicken soup.

"Your bedtime, Lou." Herbie sounded pretty stern, like a male nurse in a mental hospital.

"I am not so tired tonight."

"Then why couldn't we work? You were tired. You wanted to listen to music instead of working like the trouper you've been."

"You want to work now? I'm ready for more work."

"No!" Herbie was tempted to say that the great Maestro really wanted to show off in front of the pretty lady, but that would not have been good psychology. Passau knew what *he* wanted. "Well, now it is I who am tired," Herbie said sharply. "Tomorrow, bright and early, we work, okay?"

Passau shrugged. "Then I'll have one little drink before bed. A Perrier. No, make that a Saratoga water. With a slice of lime."

"Okay, Lou. One Saratoga, then you must rest. We also have to let this young lady rest. It has not been an easy day for her."

"The soup's absolutely smashing, Mr. Kruger. Golly, I needed it."

"Please, I am Herbie, or Herb, to my friends."

"What's this absolutely smashing and golly? What kind of talk is that?" Passau was on the verge of becoming belligerent.

"This is how very nicely brought-up English girls talk, Lou. Stick around, you could learn to speak proper, okay?"

The Maestro swallowed the last of his Saratoga water and eased himself from the chair, very slowly, as though he found it exceptionally difficult.

"You all right?" Pucky put her tray down. "Here, let me help. . . ."

"He's fine. Let him do it himself. He's perfectly capable."

"A fine way to treat an old man in need of TLC," Passau grumbled as he made his way to the door.

"TLC?" Herbie grinned. "You want tomato, lettuce and cucumber, Lou?"

Passau grunted an obscenity.

"I come and tuck you up."

"Send the well-brought-up young lady."

"No way."

"Is he really okay?" Pucky asked when Louis was out of earshot.

"Maestro Passau will outlive all of us. He's fine." There was an uncomfortable silence. "You come to give me the bullet?"

"Bullet?"

"Bullet; the sack, and a bag to put it in. You come to fire me, Pucky?"

"No, it's not one of the options."

"Near the top of the list?"

"No. The future depends . . ."

"On what?"

"Your side of the story. London *is* a little frantic, but they said I should base my decision on how things're going. I either stay, or try to get us all out. London, it appears, wants the whole of Passau's story."

"Okay, I tell you the story so far."

He did just that, asking constantly what else he could have done. "London wants the entire thing. I have a sincere conviction that, faced with a firing squad of ham-fisted interrogators, he would have clammed up. We got something going here, Pucky. He's making me his confessor. I already got stuff that would make me thousands on the autobiography market."

"We're not talking autobiography, Herbie."

"Oh, yes we are." Herbie told her of Passau's stipulation.

"All or nothing at all?" Pucky asked, tilting her head back.

"Good song title. Yes." He went into the reasons. How Passau said everything had to be told, in order to make sense of what happened in the end.

"And he *is* going to tell you what happened?"

"Unless he dies on me, which is unlikely, yes. Yes, I believe we'll get the full strength, as they say."

"How long?"

Big Herbie shrugged. "Couple of weeks. Couple of months. Don't know, Pucky. Impossible to tell. We get through a lot in a day, but he's had a long and evil life, this one. Why not listen to the tapes. There's a personal stereo around here, I've seen it. I can fix it so it runs at the speed I'm using."

"I've got a Walkman. . . ."

"No, let me doctor the one here. Keep yours for listening to music. If I fix it, you can start straight away. Listen tonight and in the morning. Tomorrow night I give you tomorrow's tape. Then you can decide."

"London really needs to know what happened: the war, then the Cold War, then in Eastern Europe during that bloody tour."

"Eastern Europe *and* Israel. *I* am desperate to know also, but a team of interrogators wouldn't get it now. Listen to the tapes. If, by tomorrow night, you think it's all wrong, that we have no chance, then get us out, but I wouldn't advise it."

"Don't do anything in a hurry," Art had said. "Herb's first rate. Herb knows what he's doing as a rule. Hear him out before you make any decisions."

"Okay," she said. "You've got a deal. I'll listen to the tapes."

"Hope you got a strong stomach. This old man is rich in sin."

"I'll take my chances." Pucky smiled. She had heard so many stories about Kruger, and now, against all odds, she liked him.

"Herb?" she asked, as he started on the tape machine. "Herb, you know a lot of the answers. What're they all playing at?"

"Who?"

"The Office. CIA. FBI. The changes in Russia are so heady, yet we're playing old cold games. Why?"

"Search me. Obeying orders."

"There's something not quite right about it. Someone's tried to kill the old man. . . ."

"Twice . . ."

"Twice. Yet we're all skulking around. Art sounded as though this was a big deal. It's really us against the rest of the world. We should be able to run to CIA and say, here he is. But it doesn't look as if the Office is inclined to do that. What is it about Passau? Why now?"

"As I said, obeying orders. Ours not to reason why."

"Well, something smells."

"Always did, Pucky. Always smells in the field. You get used to it. Sometimes stinks to high hell, then, years later you find out why. Something nasty in the woodpile, yes?"

"Maybe."

"No maybes, Pucky. How long you been in the business?"

"Long enough."

Kruger gave a laugh. One note, pitched high. "Let me tell you, is never long enough. Me? I was out. Retired, gone private as they say. There's one thing I know, let me tell you, you nice Pucky person. In this business nothing is ever what it seems. Rule of life in this second oldest profession. If we ain't got the commies to spy on, we'll find someone else. Even spy on each other. Nothing is ever what it seems. You remember that when we get to the big finish, and I hope we're both around for the applause. Okay?"

Pucky Curtiss did not have the first idea of what he meant. She shook her head, not looking at him; not knowing what was going on in that large pumpkin on Kruger's shoulders.

Herbie worked for twenty minutes, using the small screwdrivers Naldo had brought from Radio Shack. He had done jobs like this many times in the past, and it was relatively easy to slow down the mechanism of the Panasonic personal stereo he had found on the owner's bedside table. The tricky bit would be making it run normally again when they finally left.

Pucky listened partway through the night, was brought breakfast in bed by the doting Kruger, and carried on listening while he went downstairs to start another day with Passau.

"Okay, Maestro. You fit?"

"As a flea, Herb."

"We left you playing at Mr. Torrio's Barn. So what next, Lou?"

18

LOUIS "THE PIANIST" Packer soon settled into a routine, playing at The Barn six nights out of seven, getting to know the regular customers and making himself useful. But, within a couple of months, either Torrio or Capone began to send messages to him, late at night. The messages were delivered by a battered-looking tough who usually had a car waiting outside. The car was there to drive Louis to play at another cathouse, or speakeasy: like the nearby Burnham Inn, The Speedway or The Coney Island Cafe.

Sometimes it was even further away—out to the Roamer Inn, or the Burr Inn at Blue Island—managed by one of Torrio's henchmen, Mike Heitler, known to most people as Mike de Pike. On one evening, Louis was taken over to Chicago Heights to play at the Moonlight Cafe; on another, to Stickney—an area crammed with his bosses' cathouses—and to the Shadow Inn, where, on more than one occasion, he glimpsed two leading Chicago aldermen who wielded great political power on Johnny Torrio's behalf. These two men were Michael Kenna and John Coughlin, known to the newspapers as "Hinky Dink" and "Bathhouse John." The nicknames, Lou had already discovered, were shortened by Torrio-Capone initiates to the diminutive titles of the "Dink" and the "Bath."

"Herbie, even if you've read all the books, you have no idea of the power of these people, or how popular Torrio and Capone were in those days. Sure, you've seen Rod Steiger play Capone in the movies, and that other actor, what's his name? de Niro, in the movie they made, *The Untouchables*. But you've no idea how people really liked these guys. They were kings. They ruled Chicago, and the people loved them because they were doing a public service by breaking the law."

"Weren't people frightened of them?"

"Only if they had reason to be frightened. Torrio, Capone and all the other mobsters only went after their own kind, or people who crossed them. Chicago was a wild, wild city in those days. People led normal, everyday lives, but there was this strata at the top, and people like Torrio and Capone were like pop stars are today.

"Sure, they were ruthless criminals and I'm not trying to defend them, or make heroes out of them. But, in some ways, they *were* heroes to people. These days, with the inner city street gangs and the drug problem, it's real nasty, and the authorities only skim the surface. In those days, these people, who eventually turned into quite terrible, obscene monsters, had a period when they were bigger than the establishment."

The men around the Torrio empire were now all calling Louis either "Jew-kid" or "The Pianist."

"It meant I was accepted by them—not that I'm proud of that, Herb. As I told you already, there was no true honor among these people. But, when you were given a nickname, you had arrived. God help me, I felt quite proud when someone told me that Capone had boasted about Louis 'the Pianist.' He'd said, 'That guy's some kinda genius. Plays ragtime and Rossini, both.' I had become a personality, Herbie. Years later, I even read one of the books about the Capone era and there I was, in print, twice. Two mentions of Louis 'the Pianist' Packer, and only a couple of people ever knew it was me."

One evening, some three months after he had started to play at The Barn, Louis met the man who was, eventually, to change the course of his life.

The meeting took place at a special function which Louis heard about only at the last moment. On this particular night, Carlo came down into the club just after it had opened, sought out Louis, and told him that he was required urgently. "This is a command performance, buddy. The boss just called." He did not say whether it was Torrio or Capone. "They're sending a car over for ya at eleven, and he wants ya all slicked up. Taking ya to the Hawthorn Hotel. They're all out at the opera and they're bringing back this big star—what they call 'em? a prima donna—who's promised to sing for them. Pianist, yer gonna provide the music for the star."

The prima donna turned out to be the internationally famous soprano Amelita Galli-Curci, praised and revered in every opera house in the world.

A large private room in the Hawthorn Hotel had been set up for the reception. Tables were loaded with food; waiters stood at the ready, and there was champagne—"The real stuff, from France"—and Louis recognized the great lady immediately when she arrived: a dark and very attractive woman personally escorted by both Torrio and Capone, together with ten or eleven of their lieutenants surrounding them.

"I'd never seen these people looking so smart and prosperous, Herb. Sure, Capone and Torrio were always well turned out, but that night it was special. Even people like Jake Guzik and Frank Nitti wore tuxedos, and Capone looked slim and really elegant. Boy, they were so proud to have the diva there."

Capone was at his most charming when he brought the soprano over to introduce her to Louis.

"My first impression was that she treated me as a musician of equality. Herbie, that truly popped my socks. I never forgot her."

She had smiled at Louis and said, "Mr. Torrio and Mr. Capone tell me that you're a fine pianist and know the major opera scores by heart. Is this true?"

Capone left her alone with Louis who somehow managed to remain calm, though the very name of Galli-Curci would send some accompanists into utter panic. His old teacher, he told her, used to say he had a perfect ear. "I seem to be able to get through the essentials once I've heard a piece played."

"*Rigoletto?*" she asked.

He nodded, "Of course."

"Gilda's aria in the first act?—'*Caro nome che il mio cor*'?"

"Oh, yes," Louis nodded again. It was that aria which made Verdi's opera such a great attraction for a soprano.

"Good," she smiled. "*Bene*. We do that last. You know, the role of Gilda has brought me great success: my first triumph in Rome, Milan, and here, in Chicago. Gilda is very lucky for me."

"Are you in Chicago to repeat the triumph?"

With a laugh she told him, no, this would be her only performance. "I am here only to do some negotiations. I leave in two days." She was on her way to New York to start rehearsals at the Met.

Quickly she shifted the conversation, returning to matters in hand. What else would they perform? She settled on "The Last Rose of

Summer"—"I often use it, accompanying myself, in the lesson scene for *Il Barbiere*"—and "Home Sweet Home."

Louis thought these were odd choices for a prima donna of such standing, and the idea crossed his mind that she might have selected the songs to make it easier for him. But she quickly disillusioned him, saying that these were airs she liked to sing. "Also"—she gave a sly smile—"these people really want to hear me sing an Italian aria. Doing the two popular songs in English, first, will whet their appetites. So, there will be great applause for the *Rigoletto*." Louis would have sworn that she winked at him.

Very professional, he thought. Being Italian herself, but with great knowledge of American ways, she had hit on a perfect combination which would be the most successful with the small gathering. He wondered if she would dare try the same trio of songs in concert back in Italy. He guessed she probably would, and for the same reasons: effect and climax.

When their performance began, Madame Galli-Curci led, rather than allowing Louis to accompany her, during "The Last Rose"; but she let him set the pace for "Home Sweet Home." By the time they reached "*Caro nome,*" she put complete trust in him and, in a strange way, Louis' playing could have been that of a whole orchestra, not just a piano. He went into the introduction before the beautiful, clear soprano voice cut through the thick tense air in the room—"*Gualtier Maldé,*" she sang, then on into the fully developed melody, "*Caro nome che il mio cor.*" The room seemed to contain a great charge of static electricity. "*Walter Maldé . . .* Dear name, my heart enshrines."

Louis could almost see the scene from the opera—Rigoletto's daughter, Gilda, lighting her candle, gracefully ascending the steps from the courtyard to her room; believing she had a lover called Walter Maldé; deceived by the lecherous Duke of Mantua, a deception that would eventually bring about her own death: a sacrifice to save her imagined lover from the hands of her father. Galli-Curci's voice soared into the high notes, seemed to poise, hanging in the air, then moved easily up and down the scale to the end of the aria.

The ruthless, tough, murderous men—her audience—were visibly moved, emotionally affected, by the performance, and why not? Louis thought. Grand opera was really an extension of their own life-styles—

Rigoletto planning the murder of his daughter's suitor, employing a hired killer, just as Carlo had intimated Torrio had engaged Frankie Yale to kill his uncle. Power, murder, revenge: these were the overlying themes of grand opera, and the themes by which these men lived.

After basking in the lengthy applause and cheers, Madame Galli-Curci leaned towards him. Louis, completely in her spell, thought she did not look anywhere near her forty years.

"You work for these people?" she asked.

He nodded.

"You play the piano in their . . . their establishments?"

"Yes. It's nothing to be ashamed of. Brahms did it. Brahms played in . . ." Louis searched for an inoffensive word. "He played in houses of ill repute."

She gave a little laugh. "Oh, yes, and he was never married. He used prostitutes all his life." She suddenly became very grave. "You, my friend, have a great talent. Please, please use it as it should be used. Do not squander it."

"To squander it I have to make something of it first."

She smiled again, then nodded, before allowing herself to be led away by Torrio. Capone was left by the piano for a moment. "Ya did okay, Jew-kid. Now play something while we eat, huh? Something classy, okay?"

Louis began to play his own transcriptions from the works of great Italian operatic composers: Rossini, Puccini, Verdi.

"I tell you, Herbie, that night I surprised even myself. It was like waking up to the fact that my years with Aaron Hamovitch had taught me so much."

Presently a waiter came over with a small bottle of champagne and some sandwiches. The man said Mr. Capone wanted him to eat. "Ya can knock off the music for a few minutes." His tone was that of the hired help talking to the hired help.

Louis poured himself some of the champagne, and took a bite at one of the sandwiches. He did not even stop to think about what it contained. Since leaving his family in New York he had ceased to worry about his inherited religion. It occasionally gave him small twinges of guilt, but his first object now was survival, and in this place, with these people, he could not afford to be a slave to the Sabbath, or the old food laws of his people. As it happened, the sandwiches were filled with smoked salmon—"Herb, I think it was during this time that I acquired not only a taste for good clothes, but also a desire for only the best in food. Whenever I hear 'Caro nome che il mio cor,' my taste buds explode and I get a craving for smoked salmon. Unbelievable! When my opera company was only rehearsing *Rigoletto*, the staff knew they should have smoked salmon to hand."

Most of the men circled around Galli-Curci, paying court and homage, vying with one another to talk with her. Then, one of them slowly detached himself from the herd and came over to the piano. He was slim, young, very dark and good-looking, obviously Italian. His whole manner was elegant. He wore tinted eyeglasses and his smile appeared friendly, though Louis had already learned never to trust a man by his smile.

"You play very well," the young man said. Behind the tinted glasses his eyes seemed to be judging Louis' intelligence. This one did not seem to be like the other mobsters in the room. "Genna," he introduced himself. "Tony Genna."

So, Louis thought, this is the one they called Tony the Gentleman, or Tony the Aristocrat. Anthony Genna, the only member of that feared Sicilian family with any education or culture.

"Killers," Carlo had said. "Never cross the Gennas, Pianist. They're a breed: plain and fancy two-handed killers. It's in the blood from way back in Sicily. Mind, Tony's a little different because he's been educated."

Louis rose, knowing this was a sign of respect, offering his hand as Tony Genna asked what he did in Torrio's organization, nodding and smiling as Louis told him.

"But, Louis, you're a real musician. You love music, yes?"

Louis admitted this was so.

"Okay," Genna said. "I got a regular box at the opera. I also like music: opera, concerts. One night soon we'll go together. I'll bring a couple of broads who have brains as well as the other equipment. We'll make a night of it, okay?"

Louis said he would like that very much. His night off was usually in the middle of the week, when business was quiet. Wednesday as a rule.

Genna told him that sounded fine. He took out a hand-tooled leather wallet, extracted a card and wrote down a telephone number. "Just call me there anytime. Whenever you feel like it. I have a good box we can use any night of the week. Just let me know, okay?"

Louis said it was very kind of him. "You know music, and I like that in a person," Genna said. "It'll be a pleasure to share the enjoyment." Then he lowered his voice, "With most of them," he inclined his head slightly towards the other men, "it's just emotion. Bel canto emotion. Sure, it has to come from the heart, but it also comes from here." A finger tapped his temple.

Louis just smiled. He did not want to nod or even indicate that he was agreeing to anything in public with Genna.

Later, Capone came over and said he had done very well. He hoped Louis realized what a privilege it was to be allowed to accompany Madame Galli-Curci. Nevertheless, he patted Louis on the shoulder and slipped two hundred-dollar bills into his handkerchief pocket.

As it turned out, it was a couple of weeks before he even had a chance to call Tony Genna. On the Monday after the reception Carlo told him that he would be needed at The Barn on this Wednesday night.

"There's a load coming in, and we gotta spike it," he said. "I'll see ya get extra pay. I'm doing ya a favor, right?"

Louis had no idea of what to expect. He certainly did not know what spiking entailed. But it did not worry him, he had a favor to ask Carlo anyhow. He was saving money quickly, and was now determined to return what he owed to his parents, but he did not want to send it himself, or give away his new name or any address where they might come looking for him.

Already he worried about the outcome of his night in the stockroom with Ruth. For all he knew she could be trying to bring charges against him for rape—though he also knew that, in New York, it would be very difficult for a girl like Ruth to make anything stick. Also there was always the possibility that she was pregnant. He did not worry permanently, or even lose sleep over these possibilities. But occasionally they nagged at him.

He found that nowadays he felt little for his father, and wondered if he was becoming callous. Naturally, he was sorry for his mother, but could feel no real pity. Was this peculiar? Was it normal? Who could tell? Later in his life he knew he would probably regret this shell, which seemed to be building around his heart like a thick hide, there to protect him from the emotions and pain of human relationships. Now, all he wanted to do was make some kind of reparation. Already he had enough to return two hundred dollars without putting himself at financial risk should some offer come up that would allow him to quit working for the mobsters.

"You still got plenty of contacts in New York?" he asked Carlo, who said that New York was no problem.

"I just want an envelope delivered to my folks. It's got to be done by someone who doesn't know me, and who isn't going to lead them back here. Just deliver the envelope and wait for a reply, in case one of them's sick or something."

"Five bucks, it'll cost ya," Carlo said, without even looking at him.

"Only five bucks. Look, Carlo, I don't want them to know anything about me. Only five bucks?"

"Let me tell ya, Lou, there are people in this world who'd kill for five bucks, if ya know the right places to look. Ya can buy an awful lot of silence for five bucks. Just for the price of a meal and a drink. Okay?"

Louis wrote to his parents that night, at least in the early hours of the morning, after The Barn had closed—

Dear Father and Mother,

Just a word to let you know I am okay, but still sorry about the money. I told you that I would repay you, and the enclosed is the beginning of this. Please do not try to find me. The person who brings this letter does not even know it is from me, or who I am, so it is no good questioning him. If you do not want to write, just send a message, I will understand, but I do want to know if you are both okay. Be well and happy.

He signed it *Louis*, sealed it, together with the two hundred-dollar bills Capone had given him, and entrusted the letter to Carlo.

The answer came back within a week. A plain envelope. Inside, was Louis' original envelope, opened. His letter was intact, but scrawled across it in red pencil were the words, "I no nobody name off Louis." It was signed "J. Packensteiner." The two hundred-dollar bills were also inside. They had been neatly torn in half.

"Y'okay, Pianist?" Carlo asked, noticing that Louis had gone white, and was almost shaking with anger.

"Yeah. Yeah. I'm fine." To himself he vowed, "I now know nobody by the names Joseph and Gerda Packensteiner." As far as he was concerned, his mother and father were dead. It took only twenty-four hours for him to expel them from his heart and mind.

"This was not so with my dear cousins back in Bavaria, Herbie. This you have to understand. Even after I left New York I would write to them every month. Every fucking month I wrote them. Letters to all three of them. To David, Rebecca and Rachel."

The letters were clandestine, in that Louis swore his cousins to secrecy: writing as though from the old New York address, wagering that his father and mother would not tell his aunt and uncle, in Bavaria, of the shame he had brought on the family. In the first letters from Chicago he said very little, but enclosed a small slip of paper, giving David his new name and address. He judged David would keep his mouth shut.

"There were other strategies I used also, Herb." The old Maestro gave a grunting laugh. "You see, I was already using subterfuge; I had already started training as a spy, yes?"

Kruger did not reply. He just gave a special nod of the head, turning his face slightly sideways. It was a mannerism he had been using for a couple of days now, whenever he wanted Passau to get on with his narrative. It was gradually beginning to work, the strange turning of the big head and the nod: Pavlovian signals. If he went on using it, Passau would, he hoped, psychologically reflex and just go on talking. It worked now.

It was during the same week Louis sent the letter to his father that he found out about "spiking." He already knew that the main gangs operating in Chicago had their methods of either making or obtaining alcohol—both the real thing and the cooked-up rotgut. Also Torrio had shares in several breweries which still operated illegally.

On at least three nights each week, trucks would move through other gangs' territories, delivering barreled beer to the Torrio-operated bars and clubs, and to the privately owned speakeasies which Torrio supplied by pressuring their owners to buy only from him. If these joints held out from buying, Torrio's people would go there when they were crowded, late at night, and break the place up using baseball bats. Heads were split open, and some innocent people suffered. If the owner still did not comply, his joint would be bombed or, worse, a couple of hoodlums with tommy guns would blast their way in during opening hours and teach them a more severe lesson. It was only business, they said. Nothing personal.

Carlo explained what was to happen on this particular Wednesday night. The customers were screaming for booze that had a kick to it, and Capone had come up with a way of supplying their needs. Torrio liked the idea, so the plan went into action.

Every available pair of hands was needed, including those of the musicians, though the waiters, barmen and the girls were exempted. "If we pull them out, we lose money," Carlo explained.

At two thirty in the morning Carlo called his hand-picked men out into the yard at the rear of The Barn.

Three truckloads of barreled beer had arrived, and several Capone soldiers—as they liked to call themselves—were unloading the barrels and setting them out in rows. One of the Capone people, known simply as Jack, appeared to be in charge, and it was Jack who put them through their paces. First he handed out braces and bits, galvanized buckets, and handfuls of short wooden sticks. They had to drill a hole in each barrel plug, allowing exactly three-quarters of a bucket of beer to drain out of every barrel. Then they were to plug the hole with two or three of the short sticks.

In one corner of the yard there were two more men with a portable icebox. As each barrel was emptied of its specified amount they would bring over a second pail and a small hand pump. This new pail held a mixture of ginger ale and raw alcohol, equivalent to the amount of beer removed from the barrel. The mixture was pumped into the barrel, plus a small amount of air. When this was done, Jack would move from keg to keg with a new plug which he would drive through the temporary bung of sticks. He did this with great precision, using a sledgehammer. One swipe at each barrel and nobody would know that the original plug had been tampered with.

The resultant mixture of spiked beer was known, in the trade, as "suds." It had a kick like a mule, and brought the Torrio-Capone mob seventy-five dollars a barrel: a profit of almost seventy percent. Later, Louis learned that this lethal mixture was, in fact, one of the more innocuous forms of strong bootleg booze. Other kinds of spiked beer caused severe problems to drinkers—problems which ranged from kidney failure to blindness.

The week following Louis' introduction to the mysteries of spiking he made arrangements to go to the opera with Tony Genna. Almost as an aside, he mentioned it to Carlo, whose brow darkened as he looked hard at Louis. "Be very careful, Pianist. Them Gennas. *Siciliani*. They run the toughest operation in town, and there's no sentiment; not like old Big Jim Colosimo."

"Colosimo was sentimental?" Louis raised his eyebrows.

"Ya'd be surprised. He was a regular guy, Big Jim. He really cared about the people who worked for him. Biggest-hearted guy I ever met. Did ya know he had a farmhouse? Fixed the place up real nice. He used it as a rest home for broken-down whores. They got good food and regular hours. He put those girls back into good shape. Yeah, Big Jim had a long gold streak of sentiment about him. The Gennas, they just push a girl out if she gets sick or too tired. They just let 'em die. But not Jim Colosimo."

"I didn't know any of that. Who runs the place now? Who ran it after Big Jim was . . . died?"

Carlo scratched his head. "Oh, he sold it before they iced him. Some of the girls ran away, and wouldn't go back to work. He got real mad and closed the operation down. Then he sold it."

"That was sentimental old Big Jim?" Louis thought with a private smile. Carlo went on talking, telling him that the Gennas ran the whole of what was then known as Chicago's Little Italy: a well-defined area, not far from the Loop. According to Carlo, all those who were connected with the rackets had already organized trading in liquor, long before the Volstead Act became law in 1920.

Even crooked politicians, like the "Dink" and the "Bath," had stockpiled vast amounts of booze, which they hid away in warehouses and cellars all over the city. The Gennas had got a jump on a lot of people by obtaining a license to handle industrial alcohol, some of which they distributed to legitimate users, keeping the bulk of their stock for themselves.

Carlo laughed a lot. "See, they got this warehouse over on West Taylor Street, almost next door to the Maxwell Street precinct house—well, maybe the cops were a hundred yards away, but they was close. They had all the Maxwell Street cops on their payroll. Got them to turn a blind eye, and *blind* is right: those guys use fusil oil for flavor, and distill the alcohol in vats over big stoves. They got half the homes in Little Italy distilling the stuff. Just cooking raw mash over their kitchen fires. Ya can smell it in the streets over there, and I can tell ya, Louis, it's poison. People go blind and mad from drinking that mixture, but those Gennas just can't keep up with the demand. And, apart from that, they're real killers, like I told ya before.

"That's why they call them the Terrible Gennas. Ya take that Angelo. Bloody Angelo, they call him; and *Il Diavolo*—that's Mike Genna. Tony's okay, but the others, *terribile*, and once ya get mixed up with one of them, even Tony, it's just a matter of time before they try to use ya."

The Gennas, it seemed, had one of the wildest men in Chicago on their payroll. "The Scourge," Carlo called him: Orazio Tropea, who was thought to possess *il malocchio*—the evil eye.

"The guy says he's a sorcerer, and I guess people believe him. They even got one of your kind on their payroll—Samoots Amatuna, big member of the Musicians' Union. Tried to knock over his manager by hiding a pistol in his violin case. Y'ever hear of such a thing? Tony's okay," he repeated. "But ya watch out for the others."

Louis promised he would, and Carlo told him to have a good time on his night off. "Me, I have to see the boss tonight. I gotta favor to ask Capone. Important favor."

"Herbie," Passau's voice seemed to falter. "If I had only known then the full consequences of my meeting with Tony Genna, and the nature of Carlo's favor from Capone, I would have packed my bags that night and taken the first train out of there. We will get to it in time, but the truly awful things that happened much later in my life are traced right back to that time. I wouldn't wish on a dog any of the anguish that came out of that." He paused. Then, "Lunch?" he asked.

So, Herbie thought, as he headed for the kitchen. So I was right, there is something dreadful buried deep in the Chicago years. During the previous evening, he had made a large pan of Bolognese sauce, out of ground beef, tomatoes, carrots, celery and garlic. He now began to simmer the dish again, and dropped several handfuls of spaghetti into boiling salted water. While this was cooking he went up to the bedroom where he knew Pucky Curtiss had been listening to the tapes on the doctored machine.

She was still in bed, propped up on pillows, making notes as she listened through the Walkman headphones.

"Fascinating, Herbie." She switched off the tape. "Fascinating stuff. He's certainly a gold-plated bastard."

"You heard enough to get any clues? Like the Shylock Holmes?"

She did not laugh or even bat an eyelid.

"Yes," she said. "Yes, I've picked up on the obvious things, but what we need, as you well know, Herb, is the most recent stuff. We must know if we're going to get what happened last year—the visits to East Germany, Bulgaria, Czecho, Poland and Hungary, and what he's done since. That's the bottom line."

"How else we going to get it? Stick matches under his fingernails? Give him the Chinese burn?"

She frowned, pushing her reading glasses down her nose a fraction and shifting under the thin sheets. Herbie could see she was naked, and felt like a thirteen-year-old with his first really aching boner. He sat down, thinking, "my God, I got a hard here that a cat could use as a scratching pole." He did not mean to think coarsely, but his body was well out of control.

"I see no other way," Pucky said. Her lips spread into a slow, somewhat sensual, smile, as though she detected Herbie's embarrassment. "No other way at all. You're quite right, an entire query of interrogators would fail now. They'd still be working on the old reprobate when the angel of death arrived for him. The only problem, as I see it, concerns time and remaining undetected."

Herbie shrugged. "Well, we're going to run out of food in a day or so. But you have a car that nobody can trace. They're not going to tie you to the one you rented at National Airport."

"But they're probably still watching for me."

"So, let them watch. Naldo told me the big supermarket in town, the one where you made contact with him, is open twenty-four hours."

"You're suggesting I go there and stock up?"

"I got money. You got money. We're going to need foodstuffs. Foodstuffs and booze, both."

"If they're really looking, they might easily recognize me. They're not idiots. If they suspect I'm still around that's just the kind of place they'd watch."

"Amazing what dark glasses and maybe a wig can do."

"And where in hell do I get a wig?"

"Here. The lady who owns this place, I been in her bedroom. . . ."

"You've rummaged through her things?"

"Sure. It's always necessary to find out what assets we have to hand. This lady has three very good wigs. All dark. Black as a badger's . . . I mean jet black. They'd do the trick."

"Herbie," her voice had a teasing little edge. "I do believe you're a transvestite. You've been trying on her clothes."

"Transvestite your bum," Herbie said with a big grin. "Anyway, her stuff'd never fit me, even if I was your common or garden freak." He gave her a wicked look, his eyes dancing. "Tell you one thing, Pucky Curtiss, this lady gets a lot of stuff from Victoria's Secret."

"Victoria's Secret, Herb? And how would you know?"

"I seen the catalogue. Very rousing stuff. Very *you*, Pucky. You should get a nightdress or something. This is disconsolating for a red-blood-ed male."

"I think you mean disconcerting, Herb." She did not even blush.

After a moment, she said she would go on listening to the tapes. "I'll join you for dinner tonight." She gave him what her mother would have called an old-fashioned look. "Then, maybe, I can see the wigs. See if it's safe for me to go out alone."

When he had gone she stretched back on the pillows. Everyone had talked about this large ugly man's charm. He certainly had a cheeky way with him, and he was not as ugly as some people claimed. She smiled to herself and then thought, "Pucky Curtiss, grow up. Kruger's old enough to be your father. Well, almost old enough."

After lunch, and Aaron Copland's *Appalachian Spring*, Louis carried on with his story. Within minutes, Herbie was transported back to Chicago in the mid-1920s.

19

CARLO'S PROBLEM, Louis discovered much later, concerned his cousin: his father's brother's daughter. The brothers had quarreled many years before, otherwise approaches would have been made directly through Carlo's family. This was far from advisable, and Lucio Giarre, the uncle, had made a neat and timely detour, having written straight to his nephew, Carlo. In any case, he knew that Carlo was nearer than anyone else in the family to the real seat of power in Chicago.

The girl was around nineteen or twenty years of age, and showed no sign of wanting to marry any of the young men who were always hanging around her parents' apartment. Terrible interfamily fights had ensued, particularly when the girl's parents had attempted to force her to marry one particular man. As Carlo's uncle had written—

> He was a nice boy, and it would have been a good match, but she is a willful child and does not listen to nobody. I have told her many times that she should take heed of her elders, and that tradition demands she marry the man we pick for her. She is now of the age. But girls today seem to disregard the old ways. She fights us all the time, and, for the peace of the family, I feel it would be better for her to get away from home for a season or two. Could you possibly ask Mr. Torrio or Mr. Capone, for whom we have great respect, if they could find any decent work for her? You know what I mean. I do not wish for my little Sophie to get mixed up with bad women, and I am sure you would say the same. I know you like and respect her, Carlo. Even you might think of taking her in marriage. This would keep it in the family. In spite

of the differences between your father and myself, I ask humbly
if you can help?

Carlo's uncle knew his nephew was a soft touch. He had always liked
Sophia—they all called her Sophie—and the pair had played together as
children, before the rift had come between their two fathers.

But what to do with a bright young Italian girl, almost twenty years of
age, and very attractive, here in Chicago? There was really only one kind
of work Torrio or Capone could put her to, and if Carlo knew his cousin,
she would not care for that. Besides, his uncle would flay him alive if he
discovered his Sophie was whoring.

Yet Carlo was conscious of his obligations; after all he was a Sicilian
and his family, large and strong back home, was growing in the United
States. Already four more cousins and his aunt and uncle—from the village which bore their name, on the island's eastern coast, in the shadow
of Mount Etna—were on their way to New York, via Ellis Island. Soon the
Giarre family, in America, would be very strong in numbers. Yet, now, this
moment, he had to do something. Capone had no Sicilian blood in him,
but at least he was Italian, a Neapolitan, so he would understand about
family matters.

On the night Louis went off to the opera with Tony "The Gentleman"
Genna, Carlo saw Capone in private. Capone listened without inter-
rupting, then sat for a while, sucking on his big Havana cigar.

"Carlo," he said at last. "Ya puttin' me in a difficult position. I don'
have to tell ya the kinda work we got for broads here. There ain't really no
other way a broad can make a living in our operation. Not if she wants to
live good." He paused, taking another suck on his cigar. "Mind, I appreciate ya point. She's family, and ya know what I thinka family. *You're* family far as I'm concerned, so I'll tell ya what I'll do. If ya can make a place
for her at The Barn, a job where she's not turning tricks for johns, ya got
her. Ya have full responsibility. Ya put her to work. *Ya* keep her virgin
white, if that's the deal ya got with yer uncle. Me? I take no responsibility, except I pay the salary. I can't be fairer than that, huh?"

Capone was fair, Carlo admitted that to himself. But he saw problems
ahead. Sophie was terrific looking and the last time he had set eyes on
her, when she was around sixteen, even he had thought she would make
a great lay. She had a ripe and perfect figure, huge black eyes, thick jet-

black hair. At that age, Sophie had a way of walking and moving that would arouse any man. If she came to The Barn, he would have to watch over her like a guardian angel. As for him marrying his own cousin, Carlo fancied her sexually, of course, but he would never tie himself to a family member. He had other fish to fry. If and when he married, it would be to someone way outside his own clan. For him to marry Sophie, or even touch her in the wrong way, would be disaster.

Then, suddenly, he had another idea. The more he thought about it, the more he liked it. Louis was an old buddy, and Louis would do as he was told. Exactly as he was told. No doubt about it. Louis could be the answer to the whole thing.

Back at The Barn, Carlo called his uncle in New York. Sophie could come to Chicago next week. By the time she arrived, he would have a good, honest, clean job all staked out for her.

His uncle's gratitude was almost embarrassing.

It was late when Louis got back to The Barn that night, so Carlo did not even bother him with the plan. He merely asked if Louis had enjoyed his evening.

They had been to see a lavish production of *Aida*—Tony Genna, Louis and two girls that Genna had brought along as their dates. After the performance, Tony took them all to one of the Genna-controlled restaurants. Louis had enjoyed a fine night. The opera had been magnificent, and the restaurant was one of the better places, and did not sell any of the Genna poison, only the best Italian wines brought in illicitly by boat. The food was excellent, and his date proved to be pleasant and pliable. She shared a large apartment with Genna's girl, and they all ended up at her place.

Before going in, Tony had whispered that it would not be a good idea for them to stay all night. In any case, he had to get home to the family—"I must check on one or two things."

Louis caught on quickly, and considered that the real truth was the girls were probably high-class Genna-operated whores. Tony would be penalized for keeping them from work.

Louis' date was called Anna-Louise and she had a distinct New York accent, long golden hair, which proved to be unnatural when she stripped, and breasts fashionably like those of a young boy.

She was very experienced, though she treated Louis correctly, as though he were doing the seducing. It was on this night that Louis got his first taste of oral sex. Or, to put it another way, as he later thought, Anna-Louise got her first taste of Louis. She certainly appeared to take as much pleasure in its giving as he did in the receiving. She had a wide and generous mouth and Louis experienced the most exquisite sensations as she went down on him, seeming to take him almost to the back of her throat.

Louis still did not associate sex with the emotion of loving. In his own way he had loved his father and mother before that had turned sour; certainly he loved his cousins with a sense of pride and longing passion. This thing you did with girls was for pleasure and relief; it had little to do with emotion.

"Later, Herbie, I discovered the true horror and anguish when you mixed the two together, love and sexual passion. That deepest of human feelings, when I finally discovered it, real love brought me nothing but pain, as you will see."

When they left the girls' apartment there was a car waiting, together with a pair of hoods: one to drive and the other to act as a bodyguard. None of the Gennas traveled without some kind of guard. Like Torrio and Capone, they were big wheels and, therefore, at constant risk, particularly if the uneasy truce—manufactured by Johnny Torrio—ever broke down.

"Ya meet any of the other Gennas?" Carlo asked. Louis had indeed met them over an early morning drink at the Genna residence. Carlo was very interested to hear what Louis thought of them.

"Kinda scary." He did not really want to talk about it, for he had felt like an interloper, under constant scrutiny while in the Genna home. There was also something else that worried him: a sense of pent-up violence. Not that they were unpleasant. In fact they treated him with careful consideration; yet, the whole time he was there, Louis had this strange feeling that the Gennas were working out angles, sizing him up, testing him out. He was glad Tony had been with him, for the rest of the Gennas appeared vulgar and uncouth beside their educated brother.

In particular, Angelo and Mike seemed dangerous. Over drinks, in the early hours, they spoke almost casually about what they had done that very afternoon to a saloon keeper who had been caught cheating on the family.

"Right in duh balls," "Bloody" Angelo said with glee. "I shot him right in duh balls."

Mike—"Little Mike," or "Mike the Devil"—laughed, throwing his head back. "Jesus, he scream, that one. I never heard anyone scream so good. We left him for a good five minutes, to know his balls was gone before I finish him off."

As he was leaving, Tony patted Louis on the shoulder. "We'll have another night out soon," he smiled. "We didn't even get a chance to discuss the opera." Then, his face took on a masklike quality, showing neither pleasure, pain, nor sadness: just a deadpan look. "Don't take too much notice of the talk in there." He spoke quietly. "The boys are high-spirited, that's all. Sometimes I have to use my influence to stop them going over the edge. You see, they've found out what power can do, and if you allow power to run away with you . . . well, who knows how you end up. So, take no notice, let me worry about them."

But Louis did take notice, to the extent of repeating most of Angelo's and Mike's conversation to Carlo.

Carlo did not seem perturbed. "I tol' ya, Pianist. Killers. They'd snuff ya out like a fly. Look, we got our share of that breed right here, working for Johnny and Al. They scare the shit outta me, but those Gennas, they're real bad news. Some guy tell me a joke, a riddle, the other day. What's the difference between a gorilla with a machine gun and the Gennas? Ya want to know the answer? Well, ya can reason with the gorilla, right?"

It was lunchtime the following day when Carlo asked Louis to come out and eat with him. They went to a nearby delicatessen, where everyone seemed to know Carlo, and bought sandwiches and coffee which they took into a booth at the far end of the place. As usual, Carlo sat where he had a good view of the door.

"I got something to ask ya, Pianist," he began, then launched quickly into the story about his cousin, Sophia. Louis chewed on his pastrami on rye, nibbled a dill pickle, and sipped his coffee, nodding all the time and wondering what was coming next.

"Now, she ain't no whore, I'll tell ya that." Carlo stabbed his finger across the table. "Nobody touches her, and any funny stuff is out, *capisce?*"

Louis nodded, still waiting for the punch line. Somehow he felt that Carlo had a really important favor to ask of him.

"Ya see, I got complete control of her. She's my total responsibility. I gotta see she comes to no harm, right?"

"Right," said Louis.

"I'm father and mother to her. Father, mother, guardian angel, everything; and that's where ya come in, Pianist." He continued to explain that Sophia Giarre had what he termed, "A fair voice, like for singing. She used to sing at the church back home, and I heard her sing around the house. My uncle thinks she's blessed with the greatest voice ever, okay?"

The thought filled Louis with dread. Already he was wise enough, in musical knowledge, to perceive in others that perverse and rose-tinted distortion regarding the musical talents of relations, or people emotionally near to them.

"What I figure," Carlo continued, "is that ya work with her. See if ya can lick her into shape—for singing, that is. See what I mean? Ya can teach her a few numbers. Y'play piano and she sings for the customers. Y'also make sure that the johns know she's forbidden fruit—and that applies to yerself, Louis, as well as the other rams around here." The seriousness of this last remark was underlined by the use of Louis' real name. Seldom did Carlo call him anything but Pianist.

Louis Packer was appalled. He knew what dangers and nightmares could lie ahead. He had a vision of some ugly girl with legs like tree trunks, an off-key voice, and a figure already plump on a diet of spaghetti and meatballs. A real chromo.

"Lou, ya'll do it for me, won't ya? After all, I fixed things for ya. Just do this one thing: be kind to her, help her, keep the johns away—and those fucking bull dykes we got in the cathouse—and yerself. Be a brother and a helper to her. Do that for me and I'll see ya set okay for life." He sounded so desperate that Louis could not refuse him.

"There's nothing easier, Carlo. 'Course I'll see she's okay. You know you can trust me. When she get here?"

Sometime next week, Carlo said, but Louis was not listening anymore. He knew the difficulties about family commitments, and at least he was being true to his family by maintaining contact with his beloved cousins.

He was already getting mail from them, full of their own news: David now married; Rachel and Rebecca well on the way to becoming betrothed. To Louis, working as he did among whores, illicit drinkers and gamblers, under the control of the mob, his cousins' stories of life in the town of Passau, and their simple, immature, emotional loves seemed far removed, even unreal. More than anything he wanted to bring David, Rachel and Rebecca to America, so they could see a different sort of life, even make new kinds of lives for themselves. His cousins were, after all, his only real family, for he had put his father and mother out of mind.

On the following Wednesday, Sophia Giarre arrived and life changed drastically for Louis Packer.

"But, Herbie, on the night before she came into town, something happened which made me more aware of the ruthlessness of the people I was working with. I suppose I'd been playing around and not thinking straight," Louis told Kruger in the present. "What happened had a profound effect on me, by which I mean it scared the shit out of me on a permanent basis. It also gave me a taste of things to come: the great terror that Capone finally released."

On that particular night, trade at The Barn was not brisk. It was around ten thirty. The band was playing in the lounge and Louis, after running through a couple of numbers on the piano in the cathouse reception room, wandered out to the bar. Carlo was standing at a table talking to a couple of clients, sipping a glass of wine from the good supply they kept for special customers.

The two old friends went over to the bar, and were there for about five minutes, talking about arrangements for Sophia. Carlo had turned one of the girls' rooms into a very respectable bedroom for her, complete with a crucifix over the bed. Louis was about to return to the cathouse waiting room, having promised to go to La Salle Street train station with Carlo in the morning, when three men he had never seen before came through the doors from the lobby. The guardians, Jo-Jo and Mouse, followed them, indicating these men were trouble.

"Stay loose, Pianist, I think we gotta little problem," Carlo spoke out of the corner of his mouth.

"Cops?" Louis asked.

"Don't figure. Never seen 'em before, 'cept maybe the tall one. I think I seen him a few years back, in the nineteenth ward." Louis had heard many stories about the bloody battles and murders during the struggle for mob control of the old nineteenth ward of Chicago.

The trio looked like mobsters. They even dressed in that flashy way Louis associated with the men who were always around Torrio and Capone. One was tall and slim, shifty-eyed and a little preoccupied with his own importance. The two, flanking him, were squat and heavy. Thugs, both of them, Louis thought.

Carlo turned back to the bar, telling the bartender to get a couple of the boys out front fast. Capone and Torrio had recently insisted that their major speakeasies should have at least three guards, "soldiers," on duty during opening hours. It was as though they were expecting trouble, for these were picked men, loyal to Torrio and Capone, who had proved themselves in the past, and knew how to handle fists, brickbats and weapons.

They were always armed, as was Carlo these days. Louis often found himself fascinated by the shoulder holster with its deadly little snub-nosed pistol. He got a good look at it every time Carlo wandered around his quarters without a jacket.

The three newcomers came to the center of the bar and Carlo motioned Louis to stand behind him. It was as though he was protecting his friend, just like in the old New York days. The tallest of the three asked if they could see the manager.

The bartender said he would see if the boss was in. He also wanted to know who was asking for him.

"Never mind about that. Just tell him there's some people here ready to do him a favor."

"Yeah," said one of the smaller thugs. "Yeah, tell him we've come to do business."

As he spoke, the door to the cathouse waiting area opened and two of Torrio's guards came into the lounge: Mario and Luigi. Carlo signaled for them to stay back, then he turned towards the three men. "Ya want the manager, gentlemen?"

"What's it to you, buddy?" They had obviously taken Carlo for just another patron.

"I *am* the manager. So, can I help you?"

The tall fellow smiled, shaking his head. "No, Mr. Manager. But I think we can help you."

"How would ya do that?"

"We're in the liquor supply business," the stranger said smoothly. "We figured on supplying you with good quality liquor."

It was Carlo's turn to smile. "Who sent y'guys here?"

"We're in this on our own. We gotta good supply source in New York. We figured there'd be a ready market for booze here in Chicago."

"It's what we heard," said one of the other men.

"We already got suppliers." Carlo remained impeccably polite.

"Fuck 'em," the tall man said pleasantly.

"Yeah, fuck 'em," the talkative hood parroted.

"The guys we deal with ain't fuckable." Carlo's smile did not change.

"Then you'll have to find a way, buddy." The taller man leaned forward, very close to Carlo. "I'm tellin' you we're takin' over in a big way, friend. In future you'll be buying from us."

"Ya got samples?" Carlo's eyes flicked towards Louis, who had moved from behind him to the left.

"We certainly didn't come with empty hands."

Carlo shrugged. "I'll see these gentlemen in my office, I think." Then, loudly with an eye on Louis, "They seem to hold the aces, and I've only got four deuces."

Louis decided it was safer to use the telephone in the kitchen area. There was another in the cathouse waiting room, but Carlo would have to take the men through there to get to his office. He had walked three paces when the tall one asked where the hell did he think he was going?

"I only play piano around here." Louis kept on walking, changing direction and moving towards the dais where the band sat motionless. "I'm going to work."

As he reached the band he turned and saw the three men being ushered through the door to the right of the bar. He did not wait any longer, hurrying straight to the kitchen area.

Frank Diamond, as he liked to call himself, answered the phone at The Four Deuces, and Louis gabbled out the story of what seemed to be going on. Diamond asked two fast questions—How many were there? What did they look like? When Louis told him, Diamond said there would be someone over within the half hour. Then he hung up.

The third Torrio man on duty that night was in the cathouse waiting room. He was known as Mike the Mush, because his false teeth did not fit, so he never wore them, which meant he mushed his food with his gums. "Something wrong, Lou?" he asked, nodding towards the stairs, up which Carlo had taken the three men, followed by the other two guards.

"Could be, Mush. You carrying?"

"Sure, Pianist. I always carry. You want for me to deal with the guys upstairs? The other boys are outside Carlo's office."

"I think Carlo's got trouble. Give me that gat of yours."

The Mush shook his head. "No, I'll come with you, Pianist. I never let this outta my sight," tapping the weapon under his jacket.

Louis surprised himself by his own tone of authority. "Give it to me,

Mush. Your job is here, right? You can handle the girls without a pistol. There's a problem and I'm involved. They're sending people over from The Four Deuces. Now, gimme that pistol."

It worked. With a token show of reluctance, the Mush handed over his small, snub-nosed revolver. "Mind you bring it back in good condition," he said, lamely. In his head he must have told himself that, if Louis the Pianist could give orders like that, then the command could only have come from Capone himself.

Louis stuffed the weapon into the waistband of his pants and went up the stairs two at a time. Mario and Luigi were both outside the office door, guns in their hands. The mutter of voices could be heard coming from the other side of the door.

Mario shook his head, indicating to Louis that he should not go in. So, he put his ear to the door. The voices were raised slightly, and he got the impression that Carlo was talking about some kind of deal with the three men. There was the clink of glasses, then the sound of Carlo's voice, carrying on a long monologue. Obviously spinning them along. But, as the voices on the other side of the door became more and more relaxed and friendly, so Louis was aware of more tension within him.

Ten minutes passed. Fifteen. Twenty. Then there were noises from below and Capone, followed by Frank Diamond and Frank Nitti, came up the stairs.

Capone spoke softly—

"Carlo keepin' them happy?"

Mario nodded. Capone gave a little twist of his rubbery lips. "Okay, stand back. I try a little gentle persuasion." He opened the door, his large frame almost filling the space between the jambs. "I'm told ya guys wanted to see me," his voice was level, calm and controlled. "Carlo here is my manager. I am the owner of this joint, and some people know me as Al Brown. Mean anything to ya people?"

Louis just managed to get a glimpse of the taller man. He had been sitting near Carlo's desk. Now his face showed a mixture of surprise and fear. Capone went on talking, as though nothing was out of the ordinary. "Guess ya fellas're new in town, huh? Don't know the ropes. Fact I heard about ya already, I think."

The taller man regained a little composure. "We came from New York. Got good contacts. We figured on making some supply arrangements here in Chicago." He was obviously not going to be intimidated.

"Look, I give ya some good advice, eh?" Capone was almost soothing. "Ya get on a train, and ya go straight back to New York. That'd be best, I think."

"Well, I don't think! My people wouldn't like that very much. Next time they'd send real heavy guys down."

"Okay," Capone's big head nodded. "Okay, ya give us names and addresses of yer people, then we'll ship ya back to them. In a refrigerated van, we ship ya back, huh?"

"In a meat van." Frank Nitti drew his pistol and went in behind Capone. The scuffle that followed lasted only a few seconds. Frankie Diamond had followed, and Luigi and Mario were behind him.

By the time Louis got into Carlo's office, the three strangers were backed, in a line, against the wall. There were some guns on Carlo's desk, so Louis reckoned they had been disarmed. All three men looked nervous. Louis himself felt frightened.

"Ya came to the wrong city." Capone was not smiling anymore. "Just tell us who sent ya, and we'll call it quits. I'll put ya on the road back to them with a personal message."

The tall one, who had done most of the talking, seemed to wilt. Now his voice shook, "Look, we didn't mean no harm. I'll tell ya the truth. We just got into the business for ourselves. We heisted a load of liquor off the docks in New York. It was too hot to pass on there, so we reckoned we could supply other places. We heard Chicago was good. We was trying to do ya a favor."

"We don' need no favors," Capone said pleasantly. "Ya bring the stuff wit ya?"

"Sure. We got the whole truck load just round the corner."

"Okay, no hard feelings. We'll take the booze off ya hands. Then we'll get ya outta town, nice and quiet." Capone motioned to Frank Nitti and Diamond. "Get some of the boys downstairs to unload the hooch. Then see these guys off as far as the city limits. No hard feelings. Life's too short for bad feelings, okay?"

The three strangers left with Nitti and Diamond. They looked white, shaken and concerned. Louis saw Frank Nitti take up the pistols from Carlo's desk.

When the group had gone, Capone turned to Carlo, "Fix me up to be driven back to The Four Deuces," he snapped. "We've had enough of these free-lance bastards trying to muscle in on us. Ya did good, Carlo. I'll see that Johnny hears about it. It's getting like any two-bit hood thinks he can come here and force their lousy liquor onto us. Johnny's worked hard to keep the peace here. We got it all nicely set up, running smooth, so we gotta keep it that way. Any more bums come in here, Carlo, don't even ask my permission. Get rid of them. Get rid of them fast." His eye caught Louis, standing in the doorway with Mush's revolver sticking in his waistband.

Capone rubbed his blue jawline. "Look, ya even got the Jew-kid pianist here packin' a piece." He gave an unpleasant little laugh. "Ya play on that thing as well as you play piano, Jew-kid?"

"Never tried, Mr. Capone."

"Let me give ya a tip, Pianist. Never just stick a piece in yer waistband like that. Ya could shoot yer pecker off." As the laughter subsided, he said, "Get some practice in. Ya might have to learn how to use one o' them things before we're through."

It was not until he saw the front page of the Chicago *Daily News*, as they waited at the train station the next morning, that Louis realized how serious the previous night's events had been.

The headlines blared from the front page—

NEW YORK MOBSTERS FOUND GUNNED DOWN OUTSIDE CITY LIMITS.

It was a cold, damp morning, but the weather was not the only cause of the shiver that passed through Louis Packer. The story—which was on the front pages of all the major eastern papers—told of how a night worker, returning home in the early hours of the morning, had come across the bodies and called the police. All three had been shot at close range through the back of the neck. Clutched in the hand of one victim was a playing card—the ace of spades. Scrawled on the card were the words "New York liquor traders not welcome here."

The bodies had been quickly identified as those of three small-time racketeers, well known in New York for their interest in club and restaurant protection. Louis had no doubt who the three men had been.

Carlo nodded agreement when Louis drew his attention to the story.

"I guess Al's just trying to teach some people a simple lesson," Carlo said, with no emotion in his voice.

Louis Packer was still shivering as the train from New York drew into the platform.

"No wonder I was shaking, Herbie. No wonder. That train," Passau said, his voice cracked and suddenly old. "That train brought me, one way and another, the greatest happiness of my life. It also carried the grief of ages, and I didn't even know it then. Not for years did I know it." He looked up at Kruger. "I can do no more today, Herb. Tomorrow, I go on. But not anymore today."

This time, Herbie thought, the old Maestro really meant it. This was no excuse. Passau's hands trembled and he looked paper white. He muttered something else, but Herbie could not hear him properly and had to ask him to repeat what he had said.

"*Domani*, Herb. *Domani*."

Why in heaven did the old Jewish musician suddenly tell him tomorrow in Italian?

"Okay, tomorrow, Lou. Tomorrow." Herbie left him, alone with a Delius CD playing. *Brigg Fair*.

Pucky Curtiss was up, dressed, a shade provocatively, Herbie thought, and clattering around in *his* kitchen.

20

THEY BICKERED. There was no other word for it, except those you would find in any thesaurus. Pucky Curtiss got in Big Herbie Kruger's way, within the confines of the kitchen, and he got in her way. In the morning, Herb had taken a chicken out of the freezer and set it to defrost. He had planned on doing his renowned chicken casserole, but Pucky wanted to make a chicken curry and was doing a square search of every cupboard in the place. Eventually she discovered rice and a jar of biryani paste.

"I don't even know if the Maestro is able to eat curry," Herbie spluttered. "Anyway, there's no chutney. Curry is no good without chutney. Is like kissing your sister."

"We're an expert, are we, Herb?" Her tongue, he thought, was a shade caustic.

"I am pretty good cook."

"Well, it'll make a change." Pucky had her heart set on cooking. "Go and ask that evil old man if he likes Indian."

Herbie slunk away, to find Passau lying back in his chair listening to the Rostropovich recording of Prokofiev's *War and Peace*.

"Delius get you down, Lou?"

"Poor old Fred," Passau grinned, showing the perfect teeth which must have cost a fortune and a half. "What a way to go."

"Well, I have news for you. The delectable Ms. Curtiss plans to cook curry for us."

"Then I shall die happy."

"You like curry?"

"Thrive on it."

"Jesus." Herbie stumped back to the kitchen. "He likes bloody curry."

"Good, then he's in for a treat."

Two hours, and a good deal of cursing, later, the three of them sat around the table eating what Herbie grudgingly admitted was a biryani of class. "Even though it's better with lamb," he added.

"Poor old Fred," Passau muttered again.

"You what?" Pucky asked.

"Delius he was listening to, before the Prokofiev," Herbie supplied.

"But why 'poor old Fred'?" She looked out of her depth.

"Fred Delius. Died of syphilis."

"Really? I didn't know that, but then I know precious little about composers."

There was a long pause, after which Louis Passau said he had often thought of writing a little monograph on the deaths of composers. "So many of them died in bizarre ways," he expanded. "Delius, with all that voluptuous, rhapsodic music. I think he was one of the truly unique composers of our time. And to die of syphilis, which he caught as a young man—well, there's hope for all of us."

"What about these bizarre deaths of composers?" Pucky sounded genuinely interested.

"Well," Passau seemed lost in his own thoughts. "Well, poor young Schubert also. Another syphilitic, though he died of typhoid fever; Chausson fell off his bicycle and fractured his skull; Scriabin went by a carbuncle on his lip; we'll never know if Tchaikovsky drank that glass of unboiled water on purpose, or if his cholera was accidental. . . ."

"And Mozart, murdered by Salieri." Pucky's eyes widened. "I saw the movie, *Amadeus.*"

"Is rubbish," Herbie snapped.

"True, true. As Herbie says, 'is rubbish.'"

"No? That was a great story."

"A good story but a pack of garbage. Very well written, great drama, but Wolfgang's death was a shade more prosaic. Almost certainly a form of rheumatic fever; though Salieri, who died a crazy man, became so obsessed that he might have believed he murdered his bête noire."

"I want Mozart to have been murdered by Salieri." Pucky sounded disillusioned.

"Nobody's stopping you believing it, if it makes you happy. It certainly made Peter Shaffer rich." Passau yawned. "Take your pick, Ms. Pucky. Poison, rheumatic fever, a streptococcal infection, bronchopneumonia."

He stretched and pulled himself up from his chair. "I must go to my bed. Oh, and Mozart didn't go to a pauper's grave either. He simply had a third-class funeral, and the grave was unmarked. St. Marx's cemetery. Cost three gulden. Good night to you both."

As he reached the door, Herbie said, "Capone died of syphilis, Maestro."

"Not if I'd had *my* way," one hand on the door. "I still have much to tell about that bastard."

"I'd stick my pension on it," Herbie said once Louis was out of earshot.

"And I'd better make a huge shopping list and get over to the market." Pucky stood. "I'll need this wig you've ferreted out."

Herbie shook his head. "Not at this time of night, Pucky."

"What?"

"You don't go to this Giant place at night."

"Why not?"

"Think about it. If they have surveillance out, you'll be easier to spot—with or without a wig—when there're few people around. You go tomorrow, and you go late afternoon, when lots of people're standing in line and bumping shopping trolleys into each other, and the kids are playing merry hell with their mothers 'cause they're bored stiff. But I show you the wig, okay? Also there are other clothes you should wear. You enjoy my talks with Maestro Passau?"

"Evil old bastard. I just hope they bring in the goods."

"They will."

She looked hard at Herbie. He had suddenly become very confident. "I tell you, Pucky, and I know. This guy today gave me a signal. He is telling the truth. He'll tell it *all*—almost all, anyway—because he has to get many sins from his chest. I have a betting with you. When we get down to the real gritty-nitty, he'll give me everything. Everything but the one important piece of information."

"Everything but . . ."

"Ja, listen. They all do it. This old guy has seen all things. Christ, he's been all things. He is great musician. Nobody deny that. I am also thinking he has been very good agent. Possibly excellent agent. Maybe better for KGB than Blake or Philby. Now, all good agents give up stuff a piece at a time, until it's all out in the open. Yet they all do the same thing. Hold one piece back; keep it for the insurance. When we get to it, I shall have to extract the last piece. Mark me well."

On the following morning, Louis Passau took up the story where he had left off, at La Salle Street train station, with Carlo, waiting for Sophie's arrival.

"As I told you, Herb, I was expecting a real dog. I had this picture in my head: Sophia Giarre, a plump little dumpling of a girl. An unsophisticated Italian woman with bad teeth."

"Before you start on that, think about last night, Lou." Herbie looked him straight in the eyes. "Last night you spoke Italian. '*Domani*,' you said. 'Tomorrow.' Why the Italian? You were wrought up, stretched out like a rubber band."

Passau gave a deep sigh. "I remember. I sometimes speak Italian when I recall the whole stretch of things. Sophie taught me Italian; or at least she taught me *some* Italian. Then . . . well, there's another thing. It's connected, and it's real desolation. We'll get to that, but it's quite a way down the road." He seemed to be pushing something from him, his hands making a strange movement, palms outwards and the wrists moving in small circles. "Let me get back to Sophie, and her arrival in Chicago."

Louis was totally unprepared for this tall, slender girl with an oval face and eyes the like of which he never before had seen.

"My cousin, Sophia Giarre." Carlo made it an almost formal introduction. "My friend, Louis. Usually called the Pianist."

She was dressed both fashionably and at no mean cost, from the smart little cloche hat to her dainty black shoes, matching a long fur coat, the collar turned up so that her face seemed to be framed against the black fur. Her eyes looked steadily into Louis' face with a kind of amused expression. She extended a gloved hand, without saying anything. When she did speak, it was in the tone of one dealing with an inferior.

"My luggage," she said, indicating the two leather suitcases which the train conductor had deposited on the platform.

Carlo quickly saved the situation and waved in a porter, telling him where they had parked the car. Then he turned to his cousin, "So, ya finally made it to Chicago."

"What the hell's it look like, Carlo? It was either marry the *imbecille* Mama and Papa had picked out for me, or come to Chicago. As soon as I'm famous, I'll change my name."

"Ya think that would be good?" Carlo's manner had become indulgent. "The Giarres are gonna be very well known in a few years."

"Yes. Well, so am I."

At that moment, on the platform of La Salle Street station, Louis' breath was taken away by this girl. He realized that he was standing there like a clod, his mouth and eyes wide with wonder.

She had long dark hair, fastened up under the cloche, but drifting down, very thick, over her ears. The olive complexion, generous mouth, small nose with perfectly circular nostrils were things he took in, as one would examine a famous painting. Never before had he even looked twice at a girl's nostrils and marveled at God's handiwork; but the eyes knocked him out—black as night and, as he was later to learn, usually smiling as though from some hidden, plumbless depths. When those eyes were not smiling, you could almost touch the danger signals that sparked from them.

When they got back to The Barn, and Sophie had freshened up, Louis saw that the fur coat had simply hidden more perfection: a slender figure, tiny waist and breasts which showed small and beautiful under the blouse she wore. Her skin and figure appeared to have been untouched by the pasta and fatty foods which must have been the staple family fare of her New York Italian household.

For the first time in his life, Louis was looking at a woman with more than simple lust in his heart. This was an experience he could hardly understand. Certainly he wanted her; what man would not? But there was more than mere desire of the flesh. Something else had taken light in his mind and heart.

"What ya think, Lou?" Carlo had asked, while Sophie was in her room.

He stood, stumbling with words, for once lost and unable to express himself. What *is* wrong with me? he thought, then pulled himself together. "Carlo, as for looks and presence, no problem. But we have to see if there's any possibility that she has a singing voice."

"I tol' ya, Pianist. She been singing since she was a kid."

Louis had half admitted to himself there was a chance she could sing. In the car coming from the train station, his hopes had risen as he talked to the girl.

Somewhere along the line, he thought, Sophia Giarre had extracted herself from her roots. Her voice had no trace of that harsh and nasal New York Italian twang, usually so easily detectable. Instead, there was a well-modulated musical pitch: a correctness which probably meant at some point she had gone to a voice coach. It looked and sounded good.

They walked over to Carlo's favorite delicatessen and, when they finished eating and Carlo had explained the situation, Louis suggested they should try out some numbers at the piano, back at The Barn.

It was early afternoon, the girls were still sleeping, and there would be very few people on duty.

Sitting at the piano, Louis ran his fingers over the keys. "Carlo tells me you've a good voice, so let's try something. What's your favorite?"

The eyes smiled and she leaned across the piano so that her breasts strained against the thin material of her blouse. "My favorite what, Pianist?" She gave a little pout. "I shall call you Pianist, like Carlo does."

This was teasing, he knew it and had seen it in other girls. She was being blatantly sexy with him. He had not bargained for the possibility that she was a little teasing sex bomb. Bomb would be the right word. A bomb ready to explode in his face, bringing Carlo's wrath down on him like a thunderclap.

He spoke sharply, "Quit playing dumb, Sophie. You're here to work, and the sooner we know what you can do, the better it'll be for all of us. Now, your favorite song?"

She flushed. "Can you play 'I'm Just Wild About Harry'?"

"Why not. What key d'you want?"

"Oh, just follow me. On three. One . . . two . . ." and, without pausing for a breath, she launched into a sparkling, loud and upbeat version of the popular song. All doubts flew out of the window. She had an extraordinarily true voice. It was so clear, almost innocent, but with such a potential range that Louis immediately felt he would be prostituting this girl by even attempting to turn her into a saloon singer.

As she belted through "I'm Just Wild About Harry," you could hear humor in her voice—humor, dash, verve, even sexual candor. But hearing it for the first time made Louis pause and think about what he was doing to his own talent.

Before Sophie's arrival, he had often spent whole afternoons in The Barn, with a pile of music, to work alone and uninterrupted, at the piano. From his first month in Chicago, he had regularly bought piano scores of the great classical repertoire. It was not the relatively easy swinging jazz, stride, or Chicago style that really mattered to him. He could sit down and play that kind of music for hours on end without repeating a single number. Deep inside, he knew his only real fulfillment lay in the great classical works. So he was aware that playing the music forced on him by circumstances was merely a phase: a way, he constantly told himself, would be found.

Eventually he would break out from the brothel-speakeasy existence, just as he would escape from the mob. If he taught this girl the tricks of saloon singing, the techniques of the blues, and the raucous songs the patrons wanted to hear, she would never really know the great, inspiring joy of what he thought of as "real music."

"Don't get me wrong, Herbie. I was not a musical snob. I saw that a lot of the popular music had a place in the scheme of things. I knew the two had to coexist and, in the near future, some of the good popular music would become part of the serious music of the day. It was already happening. But, with Sophie, well, I felt maybe I was depriving her of a greatness. In the end, I just let it ride."

In the couple of weeks that followed, Louis felt distinct, though diminishing, guilt about spoiling a potential opera star. Sophie, he knew, would have made a great soprano.

But there was money involved. On the day of Sophie's arrival, Carlo had promised that he would negotiate a raise, with either Torrio or Capone, of thirty dollars a week, going up to fifty once Sophie began to work properly.

So, with the conviction that, soon, he would find a way out of Chicago, Louis set to work. He knew that to make things happen for him he had to generate a great effort now, for his own survival. Pride and guilt were easily swallowed and he began the long daily workouts with Sophie.

She was not the easiest person to train but, after a few days, she appeared to find the motivation and enthusiasm. Sparks flew between them; there were violent rows, shouting matches, as Louis pushed her harder and harder, teaching her how to change key in midline, giving her exercises that would improve the strength of her voice: working and working until she caught on to a style of her own. It finally came out halfway between the great blues and jazz singers and the melodic popular songbirds of the time: the female balladeers.

She complained bitterly to Carlo. "Says yer working the shit outta her, Pianist." He gave his old cheeky grin that so charmed women. "Tells me I gotta warn ya off. Tells me ya gotta let up on her."

"What you tell her?" Louis played three descending chords.

"Told her she had one chance and one fucking choice. If she don't like hard work, then she should go back to New York and marry this guy her mama and papa picked out for her."

Louis told Carlo that neither Torrio nor Capone knew what kind of investment they had. "Italian, she certainly is, but with style, great personality and, probably, originality. She could bring in more clients here, Carlo. I'm talking hundreds of clients. Also you got to make sure she doesn't just appear in the cathouse waiting room with me. You have to get her out in the main lounge."

Carlo cocked his head and grinned again. "You with her, I suppose. Star billing out front to draw the crowds."

"You should think about that, Carlo. I can't run your business for you. I can't tell you what you should do. But I can tell you to think about it."

"When do I get to hear her? Properly, I mean, like an audition."

Originally Carlo had given them two weeks to work things out. The two weeks were now almost over. "Give me one more week, Carlo, and I'll show you something that'll knock you sideways." Louis did not plead. He had learned that was not the way. To plead was to operate from a position of weakness. He was in a position of strength now, and Carlo easily granted the extra week.

"But the end product gotta be worth it, Pianist. If it ain't, then I got my ass in a sling from Johnny and Al both."

Now, Louis thought, was the time to bet, to go heavily out on a limb. "Then put Sophie on, with me, in the lounge, one week from tonight. Invite our bosses over to see the show. They won't be disappointed, I promise you that, Carlo."

When Sophie arrived for their next lesson, Louis bluntly told her they were on—"One week from tonight. Half an hour minimum, and that means more like an hour what with the encores you're gonna get. Oh, and by the way, Mr. Torrio and Mr. Capone'll be there, so we'd better get a real good program mapped out."

She became almost hysterical at the thought, convinced she was going to be a failure, blaming Louis for not having taught her enough or prepared her properly for a debut like this. "I thought it would only be for the jerks who come in to drink the booze, or the animals who go upstairs to fuck."

It was the first time Louis had heard her using language like this, and, oddly, it shocked him. He thought of her all the time, awake and drifting off to sleep. She was his first thought in the morning. She haunted his mind, troubled him and, whenever he saw her, his heart leaped at the sight. This was something he still could not understand, for it had never happened to him before. He could not get a handle on what it was: obsession, fascination, or what?

"The word 'love' wasn't in my vocabulary, Herbie. Never realized that it had me on the ropes. It hurt, but the pain was exquisite."

They worked hard during that last week. Louis even turned down an offer from Tony Genna to attend a prestigious production of *Tosca* that was passing through Chicago on its way to New York.

In the end, they put together what he thought was a well-balanced spot: "Melancholy Baby," sung in a sexy, come-on manner, with some really fancy high notes and descending, sliding scales, which Louis built into his version. She was to follow this with the old standard jazz favorite, "Careless Love," then straight into a highly provocative, blatantly sexual number which began—

I got an all-night trick again,
So keep a-knocking but you can't come in.

Louis accompanied this with a broken-octave walking bass, which would set people in the right mood for the next number, which he had composed himself, and titled "The Barn Door." Like so many off-the-cuff jazz pieces written in Chicago—such as "Sunset Café Stomp," and "The Royal Garden Blues"—"The Barn Door" was a celebration of the speakeasy-brothel in which they worked. Louis had written the whole thing in an hour.

"And I tell you, Herb, that's what it must've sounded like. Like it was written in half an hour. If we had a piano, I could still play the thing, but the words, oh my God! So bloody banal, I can never remember them now. I know it ended, very fast, in an almost Mozartian patter-song style. A popular aria for The Barn, and how many words can you rhyme barn with, huh? Harm, qualm, darn, arm, farm, and so on. I used them all and it worked. God, they were terrible, the lyrics."

The show would end on a similar belting note with Fred Fisher's popular hit, "Chicago."

It would be the big finish. "You'll leave them breathless if you work it properly," Louis told her. Sophie was not convinced, but after they had run through the whole thing about fifty times, she seemed moderately happy. He gave her hell during those last rehearsals: shouting at her, bawling her out, cursing at her, making her go back and do it from the top, pointing out her weak moments, so that she would be aware of them, and not fall into old bad habits.

When Louis was completely satisfied, he sent her off, with Carlo, to buy a dress for the big night. "Nothing vulgar, Carlo," he counseled. "I want her looking real classy. Take advice from the best people only."

"I know a woman in the trade. She'll see Sophie okay. She brings in dresses for all the real smart celebrities: the cultured crowd. Don' worry."

Sophie returned, bubbling over with excitement. Carlo had been wonderful; she had tried on thirty gowns, real evening gowns that cost a fortune. The lady who had helped was wonderful, again and again, Carlo was wonderful, Louis was wonderful, the dress was wonderful. She insisted Louis should see it right away—"Oh, my God, Lou. Carlo was so generous. I can't believe my cousin can be so generous."

Louis did not say that Carlo could afford to be generous, he was using Torrio's and Capone's money. Carlo shrugged it off, "If the dress is wrong, blame her. She finally chose the damned thing. Women! I tell ya, Pianist, I pity the man who marries her."

"Herbie, that was like a key in a lock. 'Marries her.' That was it. Like a damned great bolt of lightning, I knew. I loved her. I was in love, and it wasn't a comfortable feeling, I tell you."

Sophia Giarre proved she had style and dress sense. The gown was just right. A very simple black sheath. With her jet hair piled up, Sophie would look older than her twenty years. Older and more sophisticated. The moment she appeared wearing the gown, modeling it for him, Louis also saw, and felt, that it did a great deal for her sexuality. Sensual at the best of times, this black gown gave her an almost tangible eroticism. It was enough to make Louis feel embarrassed and squirm in his chair. He kept his eyes firmly on the girl, and did not even dare look at Carlo, for it was Carlo who had unlocked the door to his emotions.

The long hours spent working with Sophie, being very close to her, were suddenly crystallized when he saw her appear in the new gown—a ripe and fully grown woman. He wanted her at that moment, wanted her physically, and also wanted to tell her he loved her, to talk with her, learn about her past and share his own ambitions with her. He thought he detected a glint in her eyes, also, as she looked at him, and he wondered, with a sinking heart, if Carlo had noticed.

There was one last run-through; then, before they knew it, the evening was upon them. The evening of Sophie's triumph, or failure. It would be his triumph or failure also.

They had decided she would go on at midnight. Until then, Louis went about his normal duties. He thought, maybe, it was his imagination, but it seemed as though more people than usual were in The Barn that night.

Torrio and Capone, with their women and bodyguards, came in around eleven thirty. While Carlo was getting them settled at a good table, Louis went to Sophie's room, where he found her ready, but in a state of agitation and nerves.

Carlo had given Louis a bottle of real French champagne a week or so before. "I picked up a couple of bottles from the boss," he said. "Ya might as well have one of them. I prefer straight whisky anytime of day." Now, Louis thought, this was as good a time as any to open the bottle. At least it would be put to good use: calming Sophie's nerves.

She paced the room, her hands clenching and unclenching, and her dark eyes showing recognizably genuine fear. "I'm going to be terrible," she kept repeating. "You've done all you can, Louis. But I know, I just know, those bums out there're going to tear me apart."

"They'll do nothing of the kind." He poured each of them a glass of champagne. "Drink it quickly." She obeyed, and he poured another glass. Then a little more. Sophie was not used to alcohol and he wanted to avoid getting her anywhere near drunk. If he could just bring her to a relaxed high, give her initial confidence, then, he was sure, the first song, and the audience reaction, would do the rest.

She giggled on the second glass, saying the usual thing about the bubbles tickling her nose. He told her just to sip the last half glass. She began to relax, but the deep fear showed, vital, in her eyes. In the most natural of actions, Louis put an arm around her waist. Then all the feeling between them exploded. Her arms slid around his neck, and she pressed herself close to him so that he could feel her body through the thin material of her dress. She kissed his ear, then bit into it with her teeth, muttering, "Caro mia! Oh, Lou, caro mia!"

Then, she whispered, "I want to kiss you, but we're on in a minute. Louis, why didn't you hold me like this before? I've so wanted you to."

She pushed her thighs close to his, wriggled, and pressed the whole of her body against him as though, by some magic, she could pass flesh and bones through their garments and get her whole self inside him.

He pulled away, gently. He did not say what he knew he should—that she was forbidden fruit; that Carlo would kill him if he ever caught them, even like this. He had known fear before, but this apprehension spread through him like a delicious scent of danger. When he spoke, his voice seemed to be jammed into the back of his throat and he hardly recognized himself—

"I love you, Sophie. God help me, I really love you."

She threw her head back and, for one terrible second, he thought she would laugh at him. Then she smiled, her eyes fixed on his, lips parted in a look of commingled love and lust. "I love you, my darling, Louis. I truly love you."

Footsteps on the stairs. They leaped apart, and Sophie was putting the finishing touches to her hair when Carlo knocked at the door. When he entered, he paused for a second, looking first at Louis, and then at his cousin.

"I just came in to get the nightingale and bring her down." Louis looked steadily at his old friend and thought he saw the tiny hint of suspicion vanish from Carlo's face.

"They're ready." Carlo wished them both good luck. "The joint is crowded and they're pretty quiet. The word's out that Johnny and Al are there to see ya, so people will take notice."

The three of them went downstairs and headed for the lounge.

"She was a smash, Herb. I tell you I never heard 'Melancholy Baby' sung so provocatively. It was as if she was reaching out, giving a personal invitation to every lonely man in the whole room. God, you could feel the drinkers at those tables, all drowning their fantasies in her. Incredible. Truly, I never heard any ballad singer do as well, not even Sinatra. She was *Fabelhaft*."

"But Lou, you were, what is the word? Based? No, biased. Yes, you were biased."

Louis Passau simply nodded. "Then, yes. Then I was biased. Later things became more difficult."

The remainder of their performance that night was just as electrifying. Nothing, Louis thought, could have been bettered and, by the time they got to "Chicago," everyone in the place was captured by Sophie's dynamism, her enthusiasm and emotion.

At the end, the place went mad, with people stamping, banging on tables and yelling for more. Carlo hurried up, whispering to Louis as Sophie took her moment of glory—"Get her out, Pianist. Get her outta here. Some of those guys've been drinking for quite a time. It'll only take one to go for her and we'll have a riot on our hands." Later he said, "Christ, I didn't know that cousin of mine could turn on the sex like that. Every man in the place had one thought. Fucking—Sophie for preference."

He had hustled her out as soon as Carlo warned him. Once back in her room, which had been enlarged, by taking out a wall, to make a dressing room area for her, Sophie threw her arms around him, trying to drag him towards the bed.

"For Chrissake, honey," he muttered. "We're not gonna be alone for long. The big boys'll be coming up to see you. They'll want to congratulate you."

"And you as well, Lou. Without you . . ." Her eyes were misty and spoke whole libraries of love.

"With or without me, you were magnificent. . . ." But before he could continue, there was a knocking at the door. Torrio, Capone and Carlo, with several of their men, were in the room, shaking her hand and nodding with pleasure. Even the grim little Johnny Torrio was smiling. "You gotta triumph here." He looked at Carlo, his eyes sensing big money at The Barn.

Capone fawned over her, then he saw Louis and began pumping his arm. "She's gonna bring in business like we've never seen." His rubbery lips curved up in a wide smile. "Ya'll accompany her, Jew-kid. Mainly here, at The Barn. But I want her doin' spots in all our bigger places. I'll get the papers to run some pieces on her. Ya know, gossip columns, that kinda thing; and we'll take advertisement space. Ya been a great help, Pianist. We won't forget ya."

Louis excused himself. He had to get on with his job and he did not want Carlo, or anyone, accusing him of spending more time than necessary with Sophie.

He went down and played for about half an hour, and he could not recall ever seeing the place so full. They had men waiting outside, tipping the waiters to jump the line. After a while, Carlo came down to say he was going over to The Four Deuces with Torrio and Capone. "Ya've done wonderful things for my cousin, Pianist, and I'll see ya get yer piece of the action. But ya've done enough for tonight. The Mush is here, and Mario and Luigi. They'll take care of the place till morning. I'm putting the band pianist in here and paying him double time. Y'relax. Get some food. Big Al's sending stuff over from The Metropole. Eat with Sophie, huh? Help her unwind." He grinned, resting a hand on his friend's shoulder. "Watch it though, Pianist. Remember what I told ya. No funny business, or I'll see ya in the river, okay?" He gave a big laugh, as though even the thought of Louis and his cousin was funny and impossible.

"There'll be big things come outta this, Lou," he continued. "Big things and big money. They're real pleased about Sophie. Real pleased." He took two steps away, and then came back. "Ya notice anything tonight?"

"Such as?"

"Such as Steve and Tommy O'Donnell."

"I saw them out there, hanging around the big noises like always."

"Look out for them, Pianist. They're with our people all the time these days but they don't show no respect. Every time I see 'em sucking up to Al and Johnny, at The Four Deuces, I get uneasy. I get a feeling that makes me sick to my stomach. They're puttin' on some kinda act. I hear things. I hear like those O'Donnells hate Italians. They been seen with the other O'Donnell boys, ya know, the ones who run that section out on the West Side: "Klondike," Myles and Bernie O'Donnell.

"They're seeing Deany O'Banion all the time as well. I mentioned this to ya before, Lou. If Johnny Torrio's peace ever breaks down, it'll be because of them. None of those bastards like us Italians. . . ."

"I'm not Italian, Carlo."

"Nah, but yer family. I tell ya, I wouldn't put it past the O'Donnells and Deany O'Banion to try and split us against the Gennas, the Gennas being Sicilian. So just watch out for them, and keep your ears open. I don't like the O'Donnells bein' so close to Johnny and Big Al." He shrugged, "But then, I don't like ya spending time with Tony Genna either. That could have its uses, though. Just keep listening out, Pianist, okay?"

Louis thought he was exaggerating the importance of the O'Donnell brothers, and his own friendship with Tony Genna. Everyone got jumpy from time to time. He had seen and heard, after the trio from New York had been murdered on the city limits, that a lot of people had become trigger happy. There had been some killings and woundings. Even Capone, they said, was suspected of having gunned down a man in a saloon, but nobody could make it stick. Al had been holed up at The Four Deuces for a few weeks, constantly using his favorite alias, Al Brown.

That night, though, Louis could smell only success. There was not a trace of cordite or gunpowder in the air as he walked up the stairs to Sophie's room. Mingled with that sweet smell of success, was the musky scent of sex, which he knew had to come.

"You ever seen that movie, Herbie, *The Sweet Smell of Success?*"

"I think so, Lou, yes."

"Tony Curtis plays the little guy, Sidney, and Burt Lancaster's this big-time gossip columnist. I love that line, when Lancaster says, 'Match me, Sidney,' so Curtis has to light his cigarette. That had a great score by Elmer Bernstein. I knew Elmer. He was after my time in Hollywood, of course. Great score."

He is wasting time, Big Herbie thought. He does not want to go on. Then Passau took a deep breath and began again.

Capone had arranged for a huge meal to be brought over from The Metropole to Sophie's room. There were salad dishes, chicken, meat pies, cold cuts of every kind, a great chocolate cake and a crate of champagne. A waiter had been driven over, by cab, with the whole thing. He had laid it out on a special portable table, glittering with silver cutlery and crisp with white linen. Louis tipped the man, who was just leaving as he arrived, telling him to come back for the dishes and flatware in the morning. Then he deliberately closed and locked the door behind him.

There was a big Chinese screen in a corner of the room. Carlo had bought it cheaply from some antique dealer who owed him a favor. Now Sophie came out from behind the screen, wearing a thin wraparound over her lace underclothes. She put herself into Louis' arms and seemed to fit there, as though made for him. They did not wait for the food, another hunger had to be satisfied first, and they made their way towards the bed, stripping off each other's clothes, leaving a trail of garments like a ship's wake running into harbor.

Sophia Giarre was a virgin, but she was ready for him. After the first time, she said she had been wanting it from the moment she saw him. "From you, Louis. Only from you. I've never wanted a man before. For me, you are the first and last."

For Louis it was, by turns, like diving into a magic place, drowning in some strange kind of ecstasy, and being driven across whole continents. She was as natural a lover as a singer. Together they performed whole symphonies of sexual music. Louis heard great scores, full of melody in her scream of climax, and he thought this moment to be more satisfying than any experience life had offered to him until now.

When they finally got around to eating, it was almost six in the morning, so they had to gulp down food and wine quickly, lest her cousin should arrive back and catch them. Their scent so pervaded the room that they opened the window, letting the cold morning air blow in to freshen the place.

In the months to come, they spoke often of the chances of making their affair permanent. Yet there were several stumbling blocks, not least of all Carlo. Then there was the whole question of faith. No Catholic could ever think of marrying a Jew. Yet, on one occasion at least, Sophie said, "You know, baby, I'm sure they'd find a way of getting around the mixed-marriage problem if everyone knew how well Jews fuck." They had laughed a lot at that.

So, at least for now, Louis Packer was a happy man.

Most nights he would accompany Sophie, performing not only in the most prestigious of the Torrio-Capone night spots, but also in the big legal hotels that provided entertainment, like The Metropole itself. He was also a regular guest of Tony Genna at the opera and concerts and, while he had reservations about the rest of the Genna family, Louis found Tony a pleasing companion. He was entertaining, witty, educated and with a considerable knowledge of classical music.

"You know, Herb, I look back at those days and often think that, if it hadn't been for Tony Genna's intelligence, I'd have probably turned into a thug or a hoodlum myself. I'd have eventually wound up like all the rest who indulged themselves, bribed cops, politicians, innocent people; killed, robbed, destroyed and tortured, in order to maintain power during those years. Years of folly. But, in some measure, my friend, I possibly did just that anyway."

The only things that marred his wonderful relationship with Sophie were the constant need for secrecy and the fact that she showed no interest at all in classical music. Apart from an obviously deep emotional feeling for Louis, Sophie's other joys came mainly from the money she earned which enabled her to buy clothes, geegaws, jewelry, and live a pampered life.

"But, in some ways," Passau said, in the present, "I was also indulging myself. I was popular, could afford to dress well and go to the best places during my spare time. And I used my position within the mob's machine to give myself a good time. I began to hoard money, opening a bank account outside Chicago, though I did spend a lot on Sophie and buying more musical scores. Then I had a phonograph and started to collect the records which were just coming onto the market in bulk."

Louis probably knew it could not go on forever, but he had no idea of the blood and horror that was to start spilling into the streets and the gin-joints of Chicago and its environs, even before that year was out.

"If I'm truthful, Herb, I must have seen it around the corner. But, like war, you don't really believe it until it's on you." He stopped, as though in midsentence, his eyes screwed up, looking at the figure who had just entered the room behind Herbie.

Kruger slewed around, one hand reaching for his waistband, behind his right hip.

She seemed taller, and the dark hair was long, falling and brushing her shoulders. Even the spectacles made a difference.

"So, how do you like it, darlings?" said Pucky Curtiss. "This is my going to market, sir she said, outfit."

"Pucky, you give me culinary failure creeping in like that. You could have killed us all, including yourself." Big Herbie, possibly roused by Louis Passau's story of illicit love between Catholic and Jew in 1920s Chicago, saw her slim hips, and the set of her breasts. To himself he thought, "Herbie, you old lecher, what you could do with this Pucky girl if you were only a few years younger. No, what you could do with her anyway, you male porker, you."

To his surprise, Pucky beckoned to him, asking if he would step outside for a minute. On the landing she placed a hand on his shoulder and moved close to him. "How's the old bastard doing?" she asked.

"He is getting leg over with nice Catholic singer in Chicago." He smiled, blankly.

She nodded. "Which reminds me, Herb. I wanted to apologize to you. I was bloody rude in the kitchen last night. I'm sorry. Will you please take this on account." She hooked a hand around the large man's neck and drew him to her, pressing her lips hard and quickly against his.

"Jesus, Pucky. You do that again, please."

"Later, Herbie. Later. When I've done the shopping. Forward hussy, aren't I?"

"Forward, yes. Hussy, yes. Do I mind? No." So Herbie Kruger, long-time husband and faithful lover of Martha Adler, knew there was some justice after all, and he went off to make sandwiches for Passau, Pucky and himself.

While making them he sang, off-key—

"Come mitt me mein melancholy baby,
Cuddle up and close your ears."

21

THEY HAD EATEN THE sandwiches, had coffee, and listened to a little Mozart. Now the old man was talking again. It was like turning on a tap, Herbie thought. When you got Passau on a roll, he just spewed out his secret past like a drunk ridding his body of alcoholic poisons.

It came—Passau told him—as these things usually do, unexpectedly and without any fanfares. Carlo had been spending more and more time with his bosses, helping to run what was evolving into a very large organization, particularly with regard to the complex business of shipping in booze by land and water.

"We both continued to live at The Barn, Sophie and I," Louis said, in the present, "but soon found we were only performing there about twice a week. Torrio and Capone caught on pretty quickly, so they moved us around all their better clubs and those thinly disguised brothels. We drew many customers. We put a lot of money in the Torrio and Capone purses."

Passau stopped, his eyes far away on that still, central point behind Herbie's shoulder, the point Kruger thought of as Louis' gateway to the past.

"And things went well with Sophie? I mean the affair." Big Herb quietly touched Passau's withers with the light question.

"Sophie?" He said it like a long-forgotten prayer. "Herbie, except for one other woman in my life, she was everything to me. Sophie Giarre was the morning and evening star; she was music. . . ."

Kruger thought he recognized the phrase, or something like it. Inexplicably, he thought of Burt Lancaster.

"She was . . . she was life itself to me. I loved her with as deep a passion as I have ever loved, except for one other—as I said. The problem with Sophie was her Italian temper, and her lack of ambition. Her voice could have been the glory of the international opera houses, but she had, what do they call it these days? She was not a high-achiever. The saloon singing came easily to her once she'd mastered it. When she developed her own style, she didn't need to work hard. She enjoyed doing it. Like all great creative people, she loved the adulation, but it stopped there.

"That she loved me, I have no doubt. There was never anyone else at that time for her. But the major trouble was her jealousy and her shallowness. She really couldn't even bother to think about the things I needed so much: the great music, wonderful art, the towering works of literature, the timeless, ageless things that are God's reflection in the minds of men."

"And that became a real difficulty?" Herbie, low-key. "Get on with it, Louis. Tell me what happened," he was thinking.

"Eventually it became a very big issue. Sophie was all the wonders a man required, but she was superficial. She was also obsessive. In the end there were long periods in our short time together when she became like a nagging tooth. Then, when it was forgotten, she would transport me to a land I had never fully known. A place of laughter, of intense physical joy. Her body was like living in a poem. But, when you pulled back, the poem became a lewd limerick. You understand?"

"Oh, more than you can imagine." Herbie thought of his wife, Martha, and her little obsessions, the endless prattle about the price of meat, the trivia of life. Pucky sauntered through his head and he saw her, in almost adolescent terms, beckoning to him in tarty underwear. The vision led Big Herbie away for a moment and he had to consciously pull himself back to the real matter in hand.

"Herb, you can love a woman with endless passion, yet you can actively dislike her at the same time."

"I know it." Herbie nodded his big head.

The work, for Louis and Sophie, was hard; the hours were long, the audiences demanding. But the relationship became more ardent, more enclosed. Sometimes, Louis thought of himself as a prisoner. They used every possible chance to make love, and even managed to stay together all night on some occasions, when they were playing dates away from the watchful eyes of Carlo.

It was Carlo who brought the first hint of trouble, towards the end of the summer of 1923.

Louis was taking his regular day off, having accepted an invitation to attend a concert with Tony Genna: just the two of them—the concert, followed by dinner at one of the Genna-owned restaurants. On the previous night, Sophie had made a scene about it. Even in a few months she had become possessive.

"I never get out with you, darling. Apart from those places we play outside town, we can never behave like a normal couple. Louis, why the hell can't I come along?"

He explained, carefully, as he so often had, about the inadvisability of being seen together in public, making their affair obvious. "We just can't socialize together, Soph. If Carlo got even a hint, I doubt you'd ever see me again."

Sometimes, her reaction would be philosophical. She would nod, shrug her shoulders and raise her eyes to heaven. On other occasions she would explode and begin to rant about the situation, particularly against the petty-mindedness of the Italian family system, which would quickly turn into a denunciation of Carlo who, she claimed, had always been frightened of her parents.

"You think I don't know what goes on with Carlo?" she blazed now. "Whores, killings, law-breaking, mob rule. Carlo's all part of that. But, because I'm his cousin—family—I can't do what I like with my own body.

"They're old-fashioned, Louis. They're out of date, my parents and family. Mr. Capone also. It's okay for men to go around doing what they like, but if the beloved daughter, niece, cousin or sister decides to fall in love, it's wrong and they'll be damned in hell."

Then she turned on Louis. "Well, go out and enjoy yourself with that Sicilian murderer, Tony Genna, but don't be surprised if you come back and find I've gone off with one of the clients from this exclusive whorehouse."

Louis calmly went on dressing, while she railed at him and slammed out of the room. She was just in time, for, a minute or two later, Carlo put in an appearance. They were playing at The Barn that night, and Louis, deftly flicking his double-end tie around the starched wing collar, glanced into his mirror to see Carlo with a face like a thundercloud.

"Problems?" Louis asked lightly, hoping the black brow was unconnected with Sophia and himself.

"Looks like it." Carlo slumped into a chair and helped himself to the bottle of good Scotch Louis was allowed in his room. "I been saying it for months. Now, I think it's coming."

"What?"

"The O'Donnells. Ya know, Steve, Walt and Tommy. Al mentioned they hadn't been around the Four Ds in almost a week. Sent me out checking on them, and I hit the jackpot. Their big brother, the real brains—Spike—got outta Joliet last week. They been seeing lotsa guys: the other O'Donnell family, and Deany O'Banion. Word is they're planning to break the pact and start supplying places under pressure."

"They got that kind of muscle?" Louis turned, reaching for his tux.

"Well, I guess they could make things difficult. Not like those three punks who tried it on a while back. Spike's got some good friends in New York." He stopped to light a cigarette, as though giving himself time to think. "Look, Lou, if ya get a chance, tap Tony Genna. See if he's heard anything."

"There's a lot of talk," Genna told Louis over dinner on the following evening. "My family have heard things. But, Lou, I'm full up with Beethoven and Rachmaninov. What a mixture to assault any ear, eh? The ancient and the modern. Or perhaps you like that Rachmaninov concerto?"

They had been listening to the Beethoven Fifth Symphony, and the Third Piano Concerto of Sergey Rachmaninov, a relatively modern work. Louis said, yes, he liked the piano concerto. "It complements his Second Concerto, Tony. You could put both of them together and make one huge piece from them. In a way, the Third is simply an extension of the Second. But you're quite right, the program was wrong. Beethoven and Rachmaninov are like oil and water for a concert."

Tony Genna nodded. "Oil and water, huh? Like both the O'Donnell families and Dion O'Banion sitting next to the Gennas and the likes of Torrio and Capone."

"That would seem to be it." Louis grimaced, and Genna laughed. He knew, from their many conversations, that Louis Packer was not cut out for the rackets.

"Take my advice, Louis, while I can still give it. You're a musician, a serious musician, and you belong to a different world. I cannot join you in that world because I have the family to think about. I have to stay. You can get out anytime you want."

Louis thought about the endless nights, playing piano to hoodlums and their customers; he thought of the places where he performed with Sophie. Most of them were badly decorated, if at all, with brick interior walls and cheap tables. But for his attachment to Sophie, this was a terrible, barren place. Yes, he must find a way out.

But, it was almost three years, and a lot of blood and death, before Louis Packer made it out of Chicago. Reflecting on it later, he wished that he had cut his losses, taken Tony Genna's advice and walked out into the night, taking a train far away from the Windy City, the Toddlin' Town, City of the Big Shoulders.

Instead, he went on playing, doing solo spots, and accompanying Sophia Giarre. To look back on that was to see and hear a lot of jazzy music, played to the crash of revolvers, shotguns and Thompson submachine guns; to step from the piano over the bodies of all those killed in the next few years. But through it all, Sophie sang, wildly, better, and with more and more success. In bed she behaved wildly also, and with greater abandon, as though the events, and the danger through which they lived, gave an edge to the moments of pleasure.

"And there was a great deal of pleasure, Herbie. A huge amount. Not just the sex, for I discovered through Sophie that love is not just good sex."

Kruger nodded, and thought Louis was right. No, he considered, love is not just sex. Any man knows that, but also any man knows that good sex helps one hell of a lot. Take his own wife, Martha, for instance. Please, as the comedians would say. He had shared real dangers with her. She had lived on that razor edge of an agent in place. But now the dangers were over, and so was the sex. Some of the mortar that was love had lost its binding qualities.

Way back in the 1920s, in the city of Chicago, war broke out within two weeks of Louis' talk to Tony Genna.

THERE MUST HAVE BEEN upward of two hundred cars in Seminole Square when Pucky Curtiss found a slot, picked up her long shopping list and strode out in the disguise of black wig, tweedy suit, and dark glasses. She knew, the instant she made the first pass through the square, that there was at least one team watching. She had no idea of how she knew, but she did. Intuition? A slightly higher perception than usual? Maybe. Possibly it was the famed agent-runner from way back in the Cold War, Big Herbie Kruger, who had relayed some invisible wisdom to her, like bishops are supposed to pass on the Apostolic Succession to priests at ordination. Back at the Office they thought like that.

"The SIS is like the church," they would say. "It has similarities with the Church Militant."

During the drive into town she had pondered about her behavior with Kruger. He was well-named "Big" Herbie, with his height and broadness of shoulders, but it was an uncoordinated bulk. He shambled, without a graceful movement in his body. Then she thought of him, sitting with old Louis Passau, and the speed with which he had pulled the automatic pistol. Now *that* was amazing. He was lounging back, a lump of man, splayed in an easy chair, then, in less time than it took to blink, he was completely together, even compact, the pistol in his hands like some magic trick.

It was the same with his speech, full of misplaced and mispronounced words, yet concise and economical when serious matters were on the line. He was all they said about him. In the special classified handbook on agent running, he was thinly disguised as "Harry," whose old cases and operations were set out for study at Warminster. Harry used all his quirks of nature to advantage: the lumbering gait, the bouts of heavy drinking, his long streak of sentiment, and the tears that came easily when listening to the music of Gustav Mahler.

Big Herbie Kruger was a source of power and Pucky Curtiss was aware that simply coming into close proximity with this legend had led her to feel the way she did about him. "I'm not talking love, here," she said to herself behind the wheel of the car, "but I'm going to have Kruger. Eventually, I am going to have him. I am going to steal the Holy Grail of his secret from him and make him feel for me," which was breaking all the rules of tradecraft.

Now, as she approached the crowded entrance to the supermarket, she knew they were watching. Probably a team of two, in a van, though she could not see it. Possibly one, maybe two, agents in the store itself.

As she pushed the cart along the aisles of canned goods, the fabulous fruit displays, the exceptional piles of vegetables, and the other wonders you could not get back home—in the tight-little-bright-little U.K.—she saw another danger. Naldo and Barbara Railton had chosen this moment to do their own weekly grocery stockpiling.

They would not recognize her in the proverbial month of Sundays, but she had to stay clear of them. Whatever kind of surveillance team the local cops, or the Feds, had on Barbara and Naldo they would examine everyone who came close to them. They would scrutinize, photograph, and note the car registration of any strange face seen more than a couple of minutes, loitering near the Railtons. Pucky could not afford that. She was fireproof with the disguise, but dreaded the license number of her car being noted, for it might be their only safe transport out of the area when the time came.

As she thought about it, picking canned goods from the shelves and tossing them into a rapidly piling cart with a mind of its own, she knew that they would have to run soon. Virginia was no place to be if the authorities remained alert, still believing Passau and Kruger to be there.

It took a very long time for Pucky Curtiss to complete her shopping, late that afternoon.

CARLO HAD BEEN RIGHT. Spike O'Donnell, sprung from Joliet, and his hoodlum brothers began to team up with anyone else who had no time for the Italian monopoly. Torrio-Capone houses started to receive visits. Usually it was one of the O'Donnell brothers with a herd of hoods brought in from out of town.

"From now on, we supply you with booze," they said to managers and proprietors. "Or else." The last two words conveyed destruction. "Or else," meant "or else you get your place smashed up, and maybe a few people get rubbed out."

It began to happen often and, naturally, Torrio and Capone fought back. Hardly a day passed without a shooting, or some speak being raided and splintered into matchwood. Innocent people died as well as those connected to the mob.

At the end of the year, things took another turn for the worse. A new mayor, Judge Dever, and a newly elected chief of police, Morgan A. Collins, took office and pledged to drive the gangster element from the city. Whole areas of Torrio-Capone joints were shut down. Even The

Four Deuces and The Barn were served with closing orders and duly padlocked. Louis Packer was moved into a small apartment in Cicero, and Sophie went to stay at a plush hotel, all expenses to Mr. Capone. The authorities had now sealed off the lake and river routes from Canada. and the importation of good liquor was forced to be done overland—more difficult and certainly more dangerous.

Johnny Torrio left the country to settle his old mother in Italy, while Capone took over, using the Hawthorne Inn, on Twenty-second Street, as his headquarters.

"I went there a few times," Louis told Herbie, "but as little as possible. The place was permeated with an atmosphere of danger. Capone even had bulletproof shutters fixed to the ground-floor windows."

It was during this time, with Torrio out of the country, that Capone started to become the real leader. He began to organize the infamous takeover of the suburb of Cicero, a move that would take his money-making properties outside the jurisdiction of Mayor Dever and the police chief, both of whom he failed to corrupt.

Louis found himself regularly playing piano at places in Cicero soon after the spring of 1924, when Capone was virtually the one-man controlling influence. The last elections in Cicero had been rigged, some people actually voting at gunpoint, and Capone soldiers stood near every ballot box. Louis did as he was told but tried to plan his own getaway. It was only because he played a club in Cicero one night, with Sophie, that he even knew Johnny Torrio was back in America.

By then he was getting in over his head. Carlo had been promoted, running one of the biggest clubs in Cicero, and Louis often found himself riding shotgun on consignments of liquor being trucked in from other states or Canada. He complained to Carlo, saying he was a pianist, not a gunman, but Carlo simply looked bleakly at Louis and said, "If ya wanna stay here, and make money, then ya do as yer tol', okay?"

"So I began to make my own plans, Herb. In secret. I told nobody. I moved all my money, except for a few hundred dollars, right out of the State of Illinois. I closed the account I had set up just outside Chicago and I bought a car in an assumed name. I even managed to collect a couple of pieces of I.D. for myself under different names. Nobody knew about the car. I kept it in a small lock-up on the edge of the city, always full of gas. Ready to go at anytime."

The one thing he needed, though, was real money. In the out-of-state account he had salted away almost thirty thousand dollars, earned both legally and illegally. Louis knew this was a fortune to some people, but it would never be enough to stake him in the world he was determined to enter.

"I needed to save at least another fifty K to be safe, Herb. You understand that? Another fifty grand and I could make my real life. But the opportunity was not yet there for me. I was forced to wait."

In a roundabout way, the chance was to come, together with the motivation, through the fast-rising gang boss, Dion O'Banion.

Most of what went on among the warring factions passed by Louis. He kept his eyes and ears open, but did not wish to know too many details. He did what he was paid to do and listened, mainly to Carlo, who was very close to the seat of power.

Then, slowly, Carlo began to change his attitude regarding his cousin Sophie. He began by making obvious, and telling, remarks to Louis about Sophie's future. These comments at first made Louis apprehensive, for they appeared to indicate that Carlo had become, not suspicious, but certain that the pair were guilty of that greatest of family crimes in the Italian unwritten code.

Talking of Sophie one afternoon he said, "Ya know what she needs, Pianist? She needs a husband. A man she can trust. A man she can turn to. Now, if ya wasn't . . ."

"I know, don't even tell me, Carlo. I know what you mean, and I know you're saying I'm not suitable. You need a good Catholic Italian boy."

"Just a good Catholic boy would do," Carlo grinned. "And a chair and a whip, like a lion tamer, eh?" They started to go through this routine about once a week and after the lion tamer bit, Carlo would add, "Know what I'm sayin', Pianist?"

"Let me explain what things were coming to, Herbie." Louis Passau sat erect in his chair. "The entire underworld of Chicago was in a melting pot, and quickly splitting into two distinct factions. Most of the Irish, Poles, and Jews aligned themselves with Dion O'Banion. Now he was a very good-looking guy, and he loved flowers. He doted on flowers. Dion even had a half share in a flower store and spent an awful lot of time there. They specialized in doing what you call floral tributes for gangland funerals. Wreaths, that kind of thing.

"But Deany was a tough, ruthless, leader. He didn't have to think twice about having someone iced, or even doing the job himself. You know, the

O'Banion mob had men like Hymie Weiss on their payroll, and Hymie invented a new technique. When he took people for a ride, he would have them driven to some remote spot where they were shot in the back of the neck, right there in the car. Usually with a twenty-two caliber bullet. Sound familiar, Herb? It's still the favored mob-style method of execution."

Big Herbie nodded. "KGB liked it also," he said, dry as a moth wing.

"They also had a couple of other nice guys: "Nails" Norton and "Bugs" Moran. Now Moran's style was killing by motorcade. He'd have four or five cars circle around a victim's house, blasting away, like Indians around a wagon train. Truly, this was happening in Chicago."

"I believe you, Lou. I believe you."

On the other side there was the Torrio-Capone organization, allied to the Gennas; and the small, powerful Druggan bootleggers.

Yet, inside the rival camps there was further dissension. Nobody could be really certain of who would become suspect. Louis felt wary, being one of the only Jews working for the predominantly Catholic Italian-Sicilian mob. It was uncomfortable, particularly as he also found himself caught midway between the Capone-dominated people and those related, or allied, to the Gennas. Already there were sudden, unexpected assassinations, ambushes, threats. Eventually, he was certain, the leaders would come under fire.

After visiting the opera one night, Tony Genna asked Louis if he had heard anything within the Capone hierarchy about relations between the Gennas and Dion O'Banion. The question came out too casually for Louis.

Instead of replying in the negative, which would have been the truth, he asked—

"What should I be hearing, Tony?"

Genna made a gesture, as though brushing a fly away with his right hand. "My brothers, they're hotheads. They worry me. I got a tongue lashing from Johnny Torrio last week because my brothers stepped out of line, forcing one of O'Banion's places to buy our liquor. I told him we can do it cheaper than anyone."

Louis passed it off with a laugh. "Maybe your people're doing it cheaper, but your stuff kills quicker as well." He had not forgotten the production of rotgut liquor the Gennas had organized into a cottage industry within their fiefdom.

Genna shrugged. "Maybe." Any humor had gone from his face and voice. "But O'Banion's getting too big, Louis. It's time he left town, for the good of his health. Did you know he hijacked a couple of convoys of our best stuff? Canadian whiskey. I tell you, in confidence, Louis, that it is our family's feeling that Dion O'Banion's days are numbered."

In November, O'Banion was shot dead in the flower store. The bullets that riddled his corpse were found to have been anointed with garlic, an old Sicilian superstition which held, untruly, that a man wounded with a bullet rubbed in garlic would die of gangrene, if not by the bullet itself.

Torrio left town immediately. There was an attempt on Capone's life. Nobody doubted that O'Banion's murder had been ordered by Johnny Torrio and carried out by the Gennas.

Only a few weeks later, at the wedding of Angelo Genna, where Louis had been asked to play, he heard the remark that finally made up his mind.

"Herbie, I knew that I had to leave, money or no money. I just had to get out quickly. The town was going to burst open, and death would stalk the streets by daylight as well as under cover of darkness."

As he played, Carlo and Capone stayed near the piano, watching the happy newlyweds cavorting with their guests. During a pause between numbers, Louis heard Capone say, "Just wait a short while, Carlo. Hymie Weiss has taken control of O'Banion's mob." He laughed, "They're out looking for Johnny and they won't find him. So, when they get frustrated, they'll go for the Gennas. They'll clean those Sicilian bastards off the streets, then we can pick off Hymie's people, one at a time. Maybe Johnny's getting a little old for this game. Maybe he shouldn't come back. But, if he does . . . well. Soon, my good friend, Carlo, we'll have the whole city to ourselves. Just have a little patience, huh?"

Louis reasoned that nobody could be trusted anymore. During the next few days, he sought desperately for a way to raise the money he needed, but knew he would have to go with what he had. His car was ready.

"I had, for some time, faced the fact that I would have to leave Sophie." Passau gave Kruger a sheepish smile. "Anyway, it was over. Finished. I thought I would never love any woman again." His tone was frighteningly matter-of-fact. But then, it was a long time ago.

So, Herbie thought, Sophie, the morning and evening star, had finally set.

On the night before he planned to make a run for it, Carlo came into the club where he was playing, a newly opened place which doubled as a brothel, out near the Hawthorne race track.

Louis gave his old friend a smile of welcome, and, in the break, asked, "They keeping you busy, Carlo? I haven't seen you in a couple of days."

Carlo gave one of his diffident shrugs. "Well, we look after Johnny. He's decided he wants out. He's fixing to retire. Me? I'm lookin' after number one, Pianist. Eventually Big Al's gonna retire, and I wanna be up there near the top." He paused, and grinned his old grin at Louis. "Hey, we come a long ways together, Pianist, huh? Yeah, they're keepin' me busy enough. I'm even supervisin' the convoys of good liquor we're bringin' in from Canada. Ya know how much dough's invested in all that? A fortune. A fuckin' fortune. Just take the one coming in two nights from now. One hundred thousand clams worth, just bein' brought in by six trucks, along the main highway. By the time we pass it around, we come away with three hundred thousand bucks. The profit's incredible."

Louis' mind lit up. Fireworks on the Fourth of July, he thought. Six trucks. Half a dozen men, driving slowly through the night. For a well-organized team of hijackers they should be easy meat.

"Isn't it dangerous, Carlo? I mean with all that dough involved?"

"Nah." His right hand made a small flourish, and he laughed. "Ya know the way the trucks come in, Lou. On the main highway. I mean we got the cops organized again now; they take care of everything. It's routine. They meet the cops around four thirty in the morning and we have everything stashed away before eight. Everyone gets their share; everyone's happy. I don' even lose much sleep."

"Herb, it was the answer to my prayer, and I decided to wait another couple of days." He smiled, dreamily, as though he was tiring. "As I recall it, Sophie came over that night. I was like an acrobat, Herbie. Like a fucking acrobat. A real flying sophisticate."

Kruger heard Pucky's car pulling around to the back of the house. He looked at Passau and wondered how this old man, with his gigantic knowledge of music and his huge memory for facts and the weight of his sins, could look so good. Already he had been amazed at how Passau arrived downstairs each morning looking so crisp: the pants sharply pressed, and shirt and pullover clean and neat, his face shaved so you could have polished a diamond on it.

He shook his head, "So, you managed to hijack a hundred grand's worth of booze, all by yourself, Lou?"

"Well, not the whole lot. I did have some help, and the help had to be paid. But it got me out. I'll tell you about this tomorrow. I think I'll have a little sleep now, okay?"

"You just sneeze away, Lou."

Passau opened one eye. "I think the word is snooze, Herb."

But Herbie was already making his way down to help Pucky with the food.

She stood in the conservatory, the wig thrown off, and her lovely blond hair dancing in the light.

From above them came the sound of Berlioz. The *Symphonie Fantastique*. It was the fourth movement, "The March to the Scaffold"—"One of the final things in music," people had written, arguing that the composer should have finished there, among the muffled drumbeats and sonorous brass.

As he looked down at Pucky, Herbie could only hear the awful finality of the drums. It gave him a shiver, as though, from the grave, Hector Berlioz was trying to tell him something personal.

22

PASSAU HAD THE STEREO turned up loudly, and the Berlioz continued to intrude into the kitchen—the clanging bells heralding the Witches' Sabbath. Herbie had lugged Pucky's purchases up from the car; now he helped her to stow them away in cupboards, fridge and freezer.

"Enough for an army, eh?" He laughed.

"An army marches on its stomach, Herb," she said. "I should know. My father was a general, God help me."

"God help you," Big Herbie parodied.

"Amen to that." Pause. Count to ten. "We'll have to move out of here, Herb. You know that."

"Move? Why?" Then, with concern. "They spot you? They blow the cover off your car?"

"No, but they're around. Naldo and his wife were doing their shopping; a chance in a million. They've got a team boxing both of them. Cops, Feds, CIA, some bloody outfit."

"So, why we got to leave?"

"You're the expert, Herb."

"Sure."

"Come on, Herbie. *You* know why we have to get away from here. Christ, you practically wrote the book."

"No. I just obeyed orders, like the SS in the war. Name, rank, number. Just obeying orders."

"Herbie, I did the kindergarten at Warminster. They use your old cases as models."

"To show people what not to do, ja!" There was a hint of bitterness under the sentence, like an orchestration that uses the cellos to hint at darkness below a happy melody from the brass.

Pucky stopped putting two bags of sugar onto a shelf, turned and came close to him. "Herbie, whether you like it or not, you're a Cold War secret hero. Maybe, in a few years, they'll tell the story. Someone will write it. . . ."

"And find himself in the law court, with Official Secrets Act. That's about it. They tell my story, and everyone will have damned good laugh. Big fat idiot, Kruger. Some turnip put in a report I was most visible spy in Berlin."

She reached out, her right hand squeezing his shoulder. "You think you were a failure?"

"'Course I was bloody failure."

"No, Herb. They teach it now. Truly, they say you were the greatest. They tell how you used your characteristics to advantage."

"Don't know what you're talking about. Why we got to leave, Pucky?" He twisted from her hand, unscrewed the cap from a bottle of vodka, and began building himself a stiff dose: plenty of vodka, two eyedrops of tonic. No ice. "Come on, if you been trained proper, you know all the answers. Pretend the communists still hold old Russia to ransom. Why we got to leave?"

"You tell me."

"Okay." Herbie took a gulp from his glass and gasped. "Okay. So the Feds, or whoever, are still watching Nald. This means they believe we're here still. In turn the logic is that Nald'll get spooked and try to make contact: dead drop; slip the leash and come running, make a wrong number call. That's *your* logic, Ms. Pucky Curtiss. I *know* Naldo won't get spooked." He gave her a big grin. "So, Pucky, you win. We got to go anyhow. Even though dear old Nald could never be spooked in a hundred-year surveillance op, we still got to go, in case. Just in case. Satisfied? Third rule of Big Herbie Kruger, most visible spy ever. You paint a rock-solid officer into the corner, then you leave him, because he can't leave you. Am I right, or am I right?"

"That's what you taught them, Herb."

"Ja. You know why I taught that?"

"Because you once broke the rule, and the guy you thought impregnable went soft?"

"You a quick study, Puck. Ha," it was a little, one syllable laugh. "Puck. 'Either I mistake your shape and making quite, or else thou art that shrewd and knavish sprite . . .'"

". . . 'called Robin Goodfellow.' Jesus, Herb, I wish bloody Shakespeare had never written *Midsummer Night's Dream*. You don't know what hell I went through in school." She stopped and frowned. "How is it you're so good at poetry and Shakespeare, yet you can murder the English language?"

"Old secret. Naldo Railton and his family dinned it into me. Codes and ciphers." He gave her an enormous wink.

That evening, they both cooked, laughing a lot and disregarding Louis Passau's constant shouts, nagging that he wanted company. Later, over dinner, the old man dominated the conversation, sprinkling it with anecdotes and name-dropping that would have shamed a Hollywood gossip columnist.

Finally, he yawned, "I must rest. Tomorrow, good Herbie, we come to the end of one phase in my life and enter another."

Kruger simply nodded, gravely. Pucky smiled and wished the Maestro a good night. Then they went together and loaded up the dishwasher.

"I'm off." Pucky evaded Herbie's outstretched arm. "I need my beauty sleep."

"You had your beauty sleep," Kruger called after her, kicking the dishwasher. Then he set the alarms, taking extra care that night, and not knowing why.

When Louis Passau and Eberhardt Lukas Kruger met the following morning, Passau again looked like a men's fashion ad. Not a hair out of place, the razor crease in his pants, and the top button of his shirt casually undone for effect.

Big Herbie figured that it came from all those years of living out of suitcases: London, conducting *Tannhäuser* one night, the next in New York on the podium doing Brahms, Liszt and Shostakovich, and three days later in Melbourne for an American night of Ives, Gershwin, Copland and Hanson.

Worse than working for the Office, Herbie thought, but it was the only explanation for Passau's immaculate turnout. Why did he not smell like an old man? A man of ninety should carry a fragrance of age, but Passau smelled of lemons, just like his wife smelled of lemons. What is with the lemons? Big Herb wondered. He also wondered about Sophie. Why, he asked himself, do I think I have seen her in the flesh? Passau's descriptions were more than word pictures. He made the young girl become fully dimensional: a creature of flesh and blood stood in the room between them when he spoke of her. Surely she must be dead or, like Passau, very old. So, why? Herb thought. Why was he so sure he had actually seen her? Yet he was convinced he had set eyes on her. Not quite as Passau described, but certainly her. A little older but . . . where? How?

Pucky, they had decided, would listen in on headphones through the recorder. "I think he will be doing too much of the off-showing, Puck, if you sit in." She agreed.

"So, Lou," he began now. "So there you were, with all hell breaking out, and your boyhood friend, Carlo Giarre, tells you about a load of whiskey coming in. Tell me about it, eh?"

LOUIS WOKE AT TEN the next morning. "I wrestled with my conscience, Herb. Truly, I wrestled with it."

But not for long, Big Herbie thought.

At eleven he went to a telephone booth and called Tony Genna. They arranged to meet for lunch at a small out-of-the-way place never used by any of the Torrio-Capone people.

Tucked into a booth at the back of the room, where they could both see the main entrance, they ordered coffee and tuna sandwiches. Neither of them spoke until the talkative waitress was out of earshot.

"Herbie, to this day I remember she was called Millie. She had her name on one of those little badges on her uniform, and she talked like she was on the Olympic chattering team. I can see her quite clearly, even today."

"She play a part in what happened?"

"No."

"Okay, Lou, keep to the story then, huh?"

"Just adding some color, Herb. I amaze myself sometimes. To think I can even remember her name."

"What happened, Lou?"

Tony Genna asked what was on Louis Packer's mind. "Sounded important on the horn, Pianist."

Louis took a deep breath. "I'm going to put my neck on the line, Tony."

"Shoot, It's safe with me. You know that."

"Would you be interested in a booze convoy? Six trucks, coming in tomorrow night? One hundred grand's worth of regular booze, shipped in by road from Canada. It's being trucked down here now."

Tony Genna, the undoubted counselor of the Genna family, went straight to the important facts. How many men? What other kind of protection was there? What was the bottom line on the deal?

Louis told him all he knew. The convoy would have to be taken on the state highway, not less than ten miles out of town. He figured there would be one driver and one guard in each truck, with two men in a car scouting ahead. Corrupt police officers, paid for the job, were set to pick up the convoy and escort it into Cicero. The meet with the cops was fixed about five miles out of town—outside city limits. It should be easy to take the trucks, then turn off and follow back roads into town, leaving the police waiting for a cargo that would never arrive.

As for the deal, Lou put it to Tony Genna that he knew how much could be made out of one hundred thousand dollars' worth of good Canadian liquor. He was prepared to be personally present when the convoy was hijacked, and would not take a penny until the dirty work was done. "Not a penny, Tony. That should prove I'm not screwing around. I'm risking everything on this."

"Yeah, but how many pennies, Louis? What kind of money are we talking here?"

"Half the bulk value. Fifty grand, as soon as it's done. You're going to make over four times that much."

Genna nodded. The deal was fair. Louis was putting it on the line. If the Gennas double-crossed him, he was dead. If the shippers found out, he was also dead. "Who owns the consignment?" Genna asked.

It was the moment of truth. "Capone." Louis looked him in the eye. "It's Big Al's shipment."

The Sicilian did not even blink. "You're prepared to sell out Capone? So why didn't you go to someone like Hymie Weiss, now he's taken over O'Banion's slot? God rest Deany's soul." Tony Genna crossed himself.

"Because you've always shown friendship. You've always told me to get out and follow my real talent. Also, I think you must know what's going on. Big Al will be taking over soon. He'll wait, and maybe let you fight it out with the old O'Banion crew. Then he'll probably kill off the winners. Capone wants to own Chicago."

Genna gave a brisk nod. "I could go to Capone now, and talk fast. You'd be dead before the sun goes down, Louis."

"I know. But I want out, Tony. If you turn me down, or if I think you'll go to Capone behind my back, I'll be a hundred miles away before the sun sets. It's simply more convenient for me to leave with a good stake in my pocket. Anyhow, Capone can afford one consignment. He brings them in every week. The reason he hasn't been hit before is that nobody knows where, or when. I found out about this last night. Someone close to Capone trusts me."

Genna thought for a while. "We've still got one or two Irish boys on the payroll. I'll have to use them, make it look like the Micks've had a hand in it." He looked hard and unsmilingly at Louis. "I wouldn't like Al to think *we* were involved. Now, you *are* leveling with me Louis? No tricks?"

"You think I'd take a risk like that?"

"I think you've taken one hell of a risk already. If I didn't know you better, I'd think you were setting me up. Or setting up the whole of my family."

"If I were doing that, I know I'd be a dead man. I want to live."

Genna did not smile. "Oh, if it's a setup, you *will* be a dead man. No doubt about that. And if you're on the level, the word'll get out and some day Capone'll kill you."

"Not the way I have it figured, Tony. As long as you play fair and I get the dough on delivery. Now, let me get it straight." He went over the proposed route, the protection, the money and all the details, for the last time.

Genna finally nodded. "I'll meet you here at noon tomorrow. Then I'll tell you what we've decided. If it's on, then we'll talk through the plan."

That night, Sophie came home with him after the show. They did not get to sleep until dawn. At eleven thirty they were both scuttling around the apartment.

"Sophie said she had an appointment with someone." Passau smiled bleakly at Herbie. "She seemed very excited. Hyper, they'd say nowadays. Eventually I found out what it was all about. But that's another story."

He told her he had promised to meet an old buddy. "Might be seeing Carlo as well," he added for luck.

Each of them had their own reasons for not speaking the truth, and Louis did not get to his meeting until twelve fifteen. Genna looked very anxious when he arrived.

Louis was petrified. Across the road from their meeting place, he had spotted a long black car. In it there were three men and a driver. It was the first thing he asked about after shaking hands with Genna.

"It's okay, Pianist. They're my people. Just taking care, that's all. Now, you *are* certain about tonight?"

"Absolutely."

"You're one hundred percent sure they're not setting *you* up?"

"Certain." Indeed, he was. A couple of bantering exchanges with Carlo the night before had convinced him that the consignment was coming in, with police protection for the last five miles only.

"All right." Tony Genna took out a small, carefully drawn map of the main state highway leading into Chicago. They had arranged everything. A point some eight miles up the state highway, outside the city limits, was marked with a cross. "See, the road narrows here." Genna stabbed the paper with his forefinger. "Also there are bands of trees on either side, and a slip road about a hundred yards off, here . . ." Again the well-manicured finger prodded at the map. "I've arranged our own little police force. Not regular cops, mind you. But we've got a couple of real cop cars at our disposal. With any luck, they'll think it's their regular protection. We pull the cars across the road, and the convoy stops: right?"

Louis nodded.

"And I have men in the trees, along here, on both sides of the road. I would like to do it without bloodshed, if possible. Just get them down from their cabs and truss 'em up. Leave 'em in the trees, here, while my guys drive the whole shebang off up the slip road. They'll split up when they've gone. Each driver will have a separate destination, and we'll move the load onto our turf over the next few days."

"And me?"

"You got transportation?"

"I have a car, yes."

"Then you'll go wherever you like. I, Tony Genna, guarantee payment to you in full. Fifty Gs, as soon as we've checked the loads—and we'll do that before my boys leave. We do it on the spot. Then you can take off to wherever you please, and no questions asked. But you never heard about tonight if Capone's men catch up with you. You just decided to skip town. Leave a note if you have to, though I wouldn't advise it, and I tell you now, I am not going to see my family take the rap for this."

He had rehearsed some of the men. They were to speak in front of the hijacked drivers, and the guards riding shotgun. Most would have Irish accents, and Hymie Weiss' name, and the names of two of his cohorts, would be mentioned aloud. "It should be foolproof," were Genna's last words on the subject.

They would meet, at the appointed spot, just before three in the morning. "Or as near to three as possible. Three thirty, latest. If you aren't there, Louis, I'll call it off, and my brothers'll come looking for you. Understand?"

Louis understood.

He went back to his apartment and spent the afternoon getting the last of his things together: a few clothes, and the great pile of musical scores and recordings. A phonograph could always be bought somewhere else. There were also some books on music, and he took along the little snub-nosed revolver Carlo had given him a few months back, together with packages of ammunition. Just in case.

He had cleaned out the few hundred dollars in his one local bank account. In a few days he would do the same from the out-of-state account. "It was in St. Louis," he volunteered to Herbie for the first time. "I thought the name was appropriate."

Now all that remained was for him to bring the car over and find some good excuse to get away from Sophie that night. Already he had decided that he would leave no note for her. "Better a clean break," he said to Herbie, in the present; and Kruger's face hardened as he thought, clean break my ass. If Sophie did not know, she would be left hanging; wondering for the rest of her life. He marveled at the coldness of the man.

That night, they were playing the Hawthorne Smoke Stack, and he figured Carlo would be away, engrossed in other matters. With luck he could be out of there by two, or two thirty at the latest. As long as he hit the rendezvous before three thirty he would be home and dry. Hiding the packed valise and the other items stacked in cardboard boxes in a closet, Louis set out to cross town and pick up his car: a black Model T in very good condition.

That night, business was brisk in all departments: drinking, gambling and the trade upstairs with the girls. Sophie was to do three spots, the last one ending around one thirty, which suited Louis just fine.

The problem was that Sophie was in an unusually clinging mood. She had a lot to talk about after they left, she said. So, quite early in the evening, Louis began to set his way of escape by complaining of a bad head. He had been feeling beat up all day, he told her. "Maybe I should get home right after your last show. Go to bed with hot lemon, whiskey and, maybe, aspirin. I feel shivery. Need a long sleep."

"Oh, Lou, baby, Sophie'll come back and see you're okay. I'll settle you, all warm and cozy." She appeared to be most concerned about him, and Louis had to pile it on. "Tell you the truth, Sophie, I feel wretched. Think I've picked up a bug." He advised her not to come by his apartment. "If it's catching, I don't want you to get it. Anyway, Carlo might drop around. I know he's in town tonight."

"I don't care about Carlo anymore." She looked at him with bright eyes. "I have things to tell Carlo." In all, she took an awful lot of persuading, but eventually agreed, saying she would fix things. She would bring Carlo round to his place in the morning. She wanted to talk to both of them at the same time. Feeling uneasy, Louis arranged for one of Carlo's men to drive her home. He eventually got away from the Smoke Stack at around a quarter after two.

He had parked the Model T a couple of blocks from the club, and drove carefully back to his building, taking another twenty minutes to load the baggage into the car. By three he was speeding out of town, towards the meeting place with Tony Genna, who flagged him down as he slowed, looking for the exact spot.

"The slip road's back there," Genna pointed. "Get your heap off the road and out of sight. Don't forget to turn the lights out, then come down here on foot."

He could see the patrol cars, pulled up, one on each side of the road, manned by Genna hoods in police uniforms, and he kept his face turned away from them during the walk back to where Tony stood waiting.

"You and I're going to stay out of sight, in the trees, and watch the fun." Louis could not see his face, but the tone of his voice was like cracked ice, making him shiver. He could tell that Tony Genna was not smiling and, for a moment, there was panic. Would the Genna family really let him go with the money? Their ruthlessness was legendary and he saw, maybe for the first time, that his life was doubly in jeopardy.

There was a slight chill in the air, and Louis was glad of his topcoat as he crouched, silently, with Genna among the trees. He could not see the other men but an occasional cough or mutter, the flare of a match, or the scrape of a foot, betrayed their presence.

He tried not to squint at the dial of his wristwatch but judged that it was around three thirty before the rakish little roadster that was the scout car came roaring down the highway, flashing its lights, turning off and pulling onto the side of the road behind the squad cars.

The police flivvers started their engines, put on lights and eased across the road, the occupants climbing out, leaving only the drivers in place.

When the engines were idling quietly again, the whole stretch of road lit by the headlamps of the cars, Louis could hear the steady rumble of the trucks. "Should've blocked them off at the other end as well," he muttered to Tony Genna, who cut him off. "Shut your mouth, Lou. They're big trucks. Nobody's going to have time to back up or turn around."

At that moment, the lights of the convoy started to glimmer in the distance, the line of vehicles plodding closer to the ambush.

They slowed as the patrol cars were lighted in their beams. The lead truck stopped. A figure climbed down from the cab and walked towards the police cars. From where he crouched, Louis could hear his voice. He even recognized it. The man was Mush, who had so often acted as muscle in The Barn's cathouse. "You expecting us?" He spoke loudly, but was relaxed, even though the remaining five trucks had come to a halt at least a hundred yards away from the roadblock.

"Sure, we're expecting you," shouted one of the men dressed as a cop. "Bring the other trucks on down."

"Then get your cars out of the way. We gotta make up time. You never did this with the cars before." There was an edge of suspicion in the man's voice.

"Hold it a minute," the fake cop called out, starting to walk towards the figure.

"We're going to blow it," Louis said softly and, at the same moment, Tony Genna shouted, "Now!"

Men rose from the trees and began to converge onto the trucks.

The lone man from the convoy now knew something was very wrong. He turned, his head thrown back to shout towards the other trucks, but a burst of pistol shots from the Genna "cops" stopped him in his tracks. His boots struck sparks from the road metal as he seemed to skid on his heels, like an ice skater, body arched backwards, before he hit the ground, twitching.

The cops began to run forward, but already the night was torn apart by gunfire.

The shooting lasted only around thirty seconds, but to Louis it seemed like an hour. The men in the cabs did not stand a chance in the hailstorm of bullets and shotgun loads that ploughed into the cabs. In the far corner of his mind, Louis realized that Genna's men were totally professional, aiming carefully at the cabs, and not firing stray rounds that might damage the trucks' cargoes.

Tony Genna murmured a heartfelt, "Shit! That was the last thing I wanted to happen." Yet there was something about his voice that gave Louis the impression that this was exactly how it had all been planned.

Someone called, "They're all out," and the two men rose from the trees to view the carnage. All twelve of Capone's drivers and shotgun men lay dead, some in the road, others cut to pieces in the cabs. Blood streaked the road surface, looking like oil, black in the lights from both police cars and the trucks.

Tony Genna gave quick orders for the bodies to be hauled out of sight and dumped in the ditches or pushed behind the trees. "I want those trucks on the slip road as fast as you can do it," he shouted.

Louis stood and watched. He could not take his eyes from the terrible, ghoulish work. Then the police cars began to turn, fully manned, driving up the slip road.

Slowly he walked back towards his car. The trucks were rolling in the same direction, new drivers at their wheels. By the time he reached the last truck, the tarpaulins had been drawn back, and Tony Genna was moving from vehicle to vehicle, with two other men, checking the cargo. He seemed to take his time, but at last he came over to Louis, as the trucks started to move away, their headlights switched off.

"Okay, Pianist." Genna slid a hand into his pocket, removing a bulky manila envelope. "You want to count it?"

"I trust you, Tony."

"Trust and respect. They're the two things that matter. They are also the two things we most often destroy. I'd count it if I were you."

Louis smiled, in spite of the nausea that rolled around his stomach. He ripped the envelope open and saw a heavy wad of bills inside. "I trust you," he said again. "Good-bye, Tony, and thanks. You'll understand if I say I hope I'll never see you again."

Genna nodded. "We had some good times at concerts and the opera,

Louis. Tonight, the killing I didn't like. But, thank *you*, Pianist. Now, I never heard of you. Okay?"

Louis climbed into his Model T, started the engine and backed down to the highway. It was a long drive, first to the St. Louis bank where he cleared his account and took the money in cash, then detouring to the outskirts of New York itself. Apart from the bank, he only stopped to replenish gas and water, or to have a meal.

He left the Model T in a parking lot in Paterson, New Jersey, with all his belongings—apart from money—inside, and walked to the nearest car dealer where he bought a smart little car with a large and very solid trunk. "Red, as I recall: crimson, an early Stutz." Passau said, as though testing his own memory.

He drove the car back to the lot, piled his things into it from the Model T, and took off towards Washington, D.C.

In Virginia, a couple of days later, after buying new clothes and one or two other items, Louis Packer mentally changed his name for the last time.

"I had decided on this when I got the fake I.D. in Chicago. I was particularly clever, I think. All the usual stuff on one of the sets had no names filled in. I did it, Herbie, in a small hotel. Funny," he gave a humorless laugh, "the place was not far from where we are now. A little farther south, but quite close. History runs in circles, don't you think?"

"I always believe that." Herbie held the Maestro in his eyes, which were hard and unforgiving. "So, you became Louis Passau, huh?"

Louis Passau was born in that small Virginia hotel. Locked in his room, he took Tony Genna's envelope and spread the money on the bed. Tens, twenties, fifties and hundreds. A lot of hundreds.

As the cash lay fanned out on the coverlet, he saw something strange. One piece of paper, the size of a bill. He drew it out. Neatly typed on the paper were the words, "Never trust anyone. You are five dollars short."

"So Louis Passau was on his way," Herbie said, clearing his throat. "Where next?"

"Next? Oh, we're coming up to the beginning of my life. To the point where it all starts in the biographies and interviews. That moment I seemed to appear, fully grown, out of the womb of Wilshire Boulevard in Los Angeles. Where I came into being in a puff of smoke, and took over, at the last moment, from Maestro Androv to conduct the visiting Manhattan Symphony Orchestra. Poor Androv. He was taken very ill, with gastric trouble. But you know that story, Herbie. It's in all the official accounts."

"So is your first marriage and other stuff. But it's a few years away, Lou. What did you do directly after Chicago?"

"What do you think I did, Herb? Shout my mouth off all over America saying I ripped off the mob? That I was free for conducting engagements? I had never conducted an orchestra in my life. No, Herbie. I went like a fox. I went to earth, and I stayed in my earth for quite a long time. Remember, I was terrified. There was certainly a price on my head. I holed up, Herbie. I holed up where nobody could find me and, during that time, apart from myself, only three people in the entire world knew my new name, and knew where I was."

"Let me guess . . ." Herbie began.

"No guesses. For the next few years, only Rachel, Rebecca and David, in Bavaria, knew where I was and how to stay in touch. We exchanged letters the whole time, and that, in a way, eventually led to another disaster."

It was like closing a book. Ending a chapter in his life that had never yet been told to any other human being.

"He's not going to take me any further for at least another day," Herbie told Pucky Curtiss as they prepared a light lunch.

"Isn't it better to press him? Make him go on, now that you've reached a weigh-point in his life?"

"Normally, yes. But, however willing old Lou seems to be, it's taking a great deal out of him. I think he's pleased to have been able to share this much with another human. I said it before, Pucky, is like making his confession to a priest. Always is with defectors. They get a load off their minds. Going to take him a day at least to come to terms with it."

Pucky, peeling tomatoes spooned out of boiling water, gave him a pained look. "What did he look like in there, when he was talking about the ambush?"

"What he look like? Like Louis Passau. What you mean, Puck?"

"On the tape he sounded cold, as though he also pulled the trigger that night."

Very quietly, Herbie said, "It's my guess that he did. If you want the real truth, you'd have to put his story under a microscope, and we haven't any time for that. Is my guess that he started the shooting. My guess that, if he could've got away with it, he would've killed Genna that night. He wanted no witnesses left alive. There was really only Genna in the end, because, as he was telling it, he made movements to show how he kept his face away from all the Genna hoods. Yes, Maestro Passau is the epitome of unscrupulous corruption. His soul must be riddled with cancer. Like a Gruyère cheese, his soul, Pucky. Shot through."

During the rest of the afternoon, they left the tape running and Herbie merely chatted with Passau. He went back over the Chicago days again, occasionally asking questions which linked that time to the present. Towards the end of the afternoon, he asked, "What's it like to conduct an orchestra, Lou?"

"Great power, Herb. Very great power. Real power. Better than anything a mortal man can experience."

"Yes, but what is it really? What is it technically?"

Passau thought for a few moments. "Well, it's certainly not like that great British Maestro, Tommy Beecham, said, 'It's easy. All you have to do is waggle a stick.'"

"I don't want to know about Sir Thomas Beecham. I even saw him conduct once, Maestro. I want to know what you believe symphonic conducting is. Could it be what some Russian once said, 'a black art'?"

Passau thought for a moment, and then talked at length.

Later, Big Herbie said to Pucky Curtiss, "This man you can't trust. This is obvious, I know. But we have to be extra careful, for he's a thief. He steals people's ideas and uses them like some composers plagiarize the music of others, or novelists plunder plots and characters from fellow authors. You hear what he said about conducting?" He did not wait for an answer. "He said, 'When you are conducting a great work—opera, ballet, a symphony, rhapsody or concerto—you have to *be* the composer: This is *my* music, you must say. This is part of *my* body—it belongs to *me*.' Now, Puck, you know who he was making a quotation from? He quoted from another Maestro. Carlo Maria Giulini. Maestro Giulini said that. I read the book. Was edited by a man called Jacobson. Excellent book."

"That's why they put you on this job, Herb. Art Railton told me you knew music like the back of your hand."

"Back of my hand, my ass. I know enough music to play three instruments, Pucky."

"Really?"

"Ja, the turntable, the tape deck and the CD player."

But Pucky Curtiss was faraway, and very concerned about what was happening to her.

After dinner—a meal punctuated by short silences between Louis Passau's reminiscences—Herbie had dealt with the dishwasher, put on the alarms, then taken Pucky by the hand and made her sit down across the kitchen table from him while he talked.

"I tell you my own history, eh, Puck. Make *my* confession to you, so you know what an idiot you deal with."

He stayed only with the essentials. There were no details of operations or agents, except Naldo Railton.

She listened to him, like someone listening to a holy book being read, as he told her of his childhood in Berlin; how his father had died, a Luftwaffe pilot, during the Battle of Britain; how he had grown up hating the Nazis and all they stood for; then, how, after the Fall of Berlin, he had acted as a ferret for the American OSS, going into the Displaced Persons Camps and sniffing out sheltering Nazi officers; and, lastly, how his case officer handed him over to the British Secret Intelligence Service in general, and Naldo Railton in particular. He was fourteen when they began to train him, and the work had been his entire life.

Later, they talked once more of the shadow that hung over both of them: Maestro Louis Passau.

"He hid for how long?" she asked.

"Three, four years, maybe more. All the books make him show up in L.A. sometime around either 1930 or thirty-one, the dates are fuzzy round the edges. But from there on we have a skeleton to work with: Hollywood, the first marriage, the Manhattan Symphony Orchestra, the tragedy, and so on, through the forming of his own symphony orchestra and the vast wealth. We can track him down the years."

"I wonder what happened to poor Sophie. I think she loved him very much."

"I wouldn't feel too sorry for Sophie. She was well out of it. Anyway, she would be looked after. Diamonds and sapphires, anything she wanted. Mafia Princess, Puck. In the mid-1930s the Giarre family came into its own. One of the famous five families, the Giarres, and Don Carlo still lives, a year older than the Maestro. You see, I do my homeworkings."

"So do I, Herbie, and my instinct tells me we should move on soon."

"When?"

"I need to talk to Art in London."

"Not from here. Maybe a telephone booth but not from this house 'cuz that might leave a trace. Bloody American phone companies detail every call. The owner would spot it, and it could land old Naldo in the *merde*. If Art gives the okay, you know where we can go?"

"Yes. I'll check with Art tomorrow." Light was beginning to seep through the drapes, they had talked through the night.

On the following morning, when Pucky had left in her disguise to telephone Arthur Railton, Herbie sat down again with Passau.

"So, you went to ground. Whereabouts, Lou? I need it for the record."

"Oh, it's on the record if you know where to look. But I'll tell you anyway. It was unplanned, but it went like this. . . ."

He started to talk again, unburdening his soul of the countless sins that would have killed any decent man.

BOOK 2

(CAPTIVA ISLAND. AUTUMN 1991)

1

THE LITTLE HOUSE WAS made of irregular stone blocks, whitewashed so that the building seemed to levitate over the red rocky outcrop. Three rooms and a kitchen. Quite small, but it stood alone at the edge of a valley, above the small town which looked Mexican, with its adobe buildings and pink roofs, a church with a campanile, a small square with a fountain at the center. Round. Water springing from the mouths of four dull green fish, their heads raised to heaven. When there was a drought and no water, they looked like weird saints at prayer. In jest the local people called them the "holy mackerel."

To reach the house, one had to climb for the best part of a mile along a narrow dirt track overlooked, all the way, from the windows. It was perfect. It even had its own water supply, from a well that some settler had managed to drill years before. Apart from the town, there was desert as far as the craggy skyline. One narrow ribbon of road shimmered like a mirage, and a dozen or so huge clusters of brick-colored spiky rock dotted the area: great stalagmitic fairy-tale, or nightmare, buildings. When there was a night wind these graphs of stone seemed to whine as though haunted.

It was perfect for the man they called the Hermit. He had come in a creaky old truck. He bought building materials, and the vehicle wheezed and spluttered towards the house. They said that Pinto had cheated him by asking so much for the broken-down cottage. It took a year for the Hermit to fix the place. Then he went away again, returning in the truck with furniture, books, and then the piano.

The townspeople thought he was loco, but it did not stop them cocking their heads and listening, on a still quiet evening, to the sound of the instrument as it filtered down into the square. They all remembered the day he brought the piano and drove up the hill with the instrument roped to the back of the little truck. Halfway up, the truck had lurched and started to slide backwards. It stopped altogether, then seemed to gather strength before inching upwards again. People laid bets on whether the piano would get to its destination.

The Hermit had come into town that night, and he paid two strong men five dollars each to help carry the piano into the house. After that, he came into town once a week to buy food and other essentials. Occasionally he would drive down at night on a different kind of errand. Nobody ever asked for him, and the mailman brought letters every six weeks or so. The letters were interesting for they had foreign stamps on them. Germany some said, but only old Mrs. Brajos, the postmistress, and Frank Duse, the mailman, ever saw them. "Every man is entitled to privacy," Duse would say. Sometimes, the Hermit would receive packages from New York. Duse would nod. "More books or phonograph records."

It had taken him over a year to find this place—near the Arizona–New Mexico state line—and another year to fix it up. Once he was settled he thought he was safe. When he was looking for the right place he crossed and recrossed many state lines. Later, he admitted that the first year was a nightmare. Twice, he knew they were following him. These were the occasions when he saw two thugs he recognized as Capone hoods inquiring at hotel desks, just as he drove up. Eventually they seemed to give up, but he saw the newspapers and their headlines reminded him of the precarious life he was leading:

Bloody Angelo Genna shot to death at the wheel of his car after a chase.

Mike "The Devil" Genna taken for a ride, as they used to say.

Tony Genna shot five times, in daylight, on Grand Avenue. Died in the county hospital.

He knew why this had happened and knew he was not safe. Five bucks short. A life short.

He had got rid of the Stutz and bought the truck shortly before finding the house.

"What kind of time scale we talking here, Lou?" Herbie asked.

"Time scale? How can I remember time scale? Mid-twenties. That's all I remember."

"You remember all the other details, why not the dates, Lou? Uncharacteristic of you. Bet you can remember the color of Sophie's shoes the last time you saw her. Maybe even color of her underwear, yet you . . ."

"Don't ever talk about that kind of thing to me. Don't ever say things about Sophie like that. Got me?" His hands trembled, and he went a kind of pale gray. Herbie thought he was going to have a heart attack there and then.

"I'm sorry, Lou. Didn't mean to . . ."

"I don't care what you mean to . . . just don't be frivolous about Sophie. She's no person to be frivolous about." Very loud, rising to a shout.

"She still alive, then, Lou?"

"No, she . . . what you asking this for?"

"You said, 'She's no person to be frivolous about.' Like she was still alive." A raw nerve there, Herb considered. Raw and still hurting. He had been right. Something else had happened in the Windy City. Something else concerning Sophie.

"She's probably dead by now. How should I know?"

"You're the fount of all wisdom, Maestro."

"Pcha! Fount my ass."

"So, what dates we talking?"

"I told you, time meant nothing to me. I can't recall what dates. Next date I can recall is . . . hum! Well, 1930, or possibly 1931. When I went to Hollywood."

"And you're not really certain of that? If you can't recall the dates, how can I believe anything else you say?"

"Because you have my word on it."

"Word of a killer?"

"I killed nobody. Genna, and his people, they killed. I killed nobody." Then a silence like a long and horrible scream. "I killed nobody. Not then."

"Later?"

"Hear me out, Herbie. Listen to the story. Maybe you'll learn something."

"You killed later."

"I told you, wait. Every man has his little foibles. . . ."

"His armadillos, ja?"

"Peccadilloes, Herbie. Then, with age, the guilt comes."

I knew it, Kruger thought. Knew it. The old devil's a murderer on top of everything else. He wondered if the victim had been Sophie. Aloud, he said, "Okay, well, what happened? I mean, what happened during the time you stayed in this house. Any callers?"

"Nobody knew where I was. Nobody except my cousins. This was a period of preparation, Herbie. Like a monk. You understand? I lived and worked like a monk. I had money, but I lived a life of abstinence. A simple life."

Kruger grunted. He made a mental note to get Pucky to find out the dates of the Gennas' deaths. Put it in perspective. "So you were like a monk. It was lonely, yes?"

"Sure it was lonely, but that was the point. I had to be self-sufficient. I did not want to go out into the world again until I had truly mastered my calling."

"And you didn't want to go until you knew it was safe, yes?"

The Maestro made a putt-putting sound with his lips. "You say I was a coward?"

"No, I say you had a very strong instinct for self-preservation."

"This is true. Sure, I wanted my skin intact, so I withdrew from the world, as it were."

"And the letters were from your cousins?"

"They were the only people in the world who I had outside contact with, yes."

"And you wrote regularly to each other?"

"Of course. It was . . . well, there were difficulties. Things happened."

"Tell me, Lou." The old man had more than hinted that the strong bond between him and his cousins had been the cause of something serious in his life. "Tell me. The truth. It's no good, Lou, unless you tell the truth."

"Okay, when I got settled, at first I yearned for some human contact. I thought of David, Rachel and Rebecca in Germany. They were on my mind a great deal, particularly when I was cut off and alone, working. So I wrote to them. Long letters, I wrote. Very long. Why not? They were the only real family I had now. Mind you, I enclosed shorter letters they could show to their parents. Funny, I still thought of them as children. Vulnerable children. But I told them more or less the truth."

"What was the truth, Maestro?"

"That I'd had problems."

"You didn't tell them about Chicago?"

"Don't be foolish, Herb. No, of course I didn't tell them. But their letters made me even more stubborn. Made me work harder. Made me miss them even more. Never has a day gone by that I have not missed them. . . ." He trailed off, as though some sudden emotion had him by the throat.

"You said that before."

"Yea, I know, and I'll go on saying it. Part of my life, Herb, was catastrophe because I missed them. The letters they sent all brought bad news."

"Such as?"

"Such as my Uncle Isaak had died. Such as David had married and his wife had died, in childbirth. Now Rachel was looking after the infant, and her ailing mother—come to that an ailing business."

Things were bad back in Passau, from which Louis had taken his new name. He desperately wanted to reach a point where he could bring his cousins over to America.

"It was not to be, Herb. I was still working on fixing the house, when I got another shock. David wrote to me. I can even remember the words he used—

"'Lou,' he wrote, 'this is a hard task. For a long time we have all suspected that you have been out of touch with your mama and papa. So it is possible you do not know the heavy truth. Your mama, our dear aunt, died last winter in New York.'

"That hit me, Herb. I became filled with guilt. Could I have made peace with my father? Should I have tried? Should I have visited them? For many weeks I thought and dreamed about my mother. In my dreams I heard her laugh. I tell you about her laugh, Herb? She had a musical laugh, even though she did not like music. It was a little burst of sound, beginning with a C chord, and rising, then dropping. Distinctive." He demonstrated, and Kruger heard the opening bars of Passau's symphony. The Demonic. "I was now saturated in guilt. Even blamed myself for my mother's death. I was cloaked in sadness."

"Very poetic, Lou, but you didn't go to New York? You didn't go see how your pop was doing?"

"What would've been the use? I mourned my mother's passing in my own way. Then I worked, like I have never worked."

So, in his midtwenties, the newborn Louis Passau settled down to study his craft. To continue and refine the labor begun with old Aaron Hamovitch in New York.

He said he was alone, often lonely: working a day of strict discipline. Beginning again at the beginning and moving forward. His investments were the house, the piano, the phonograph with its clockwork motor and the big horn, the recordings, the scores and books on music and technique. The little house was his cell and his studio, and there was money left over for the moment.

"What moment?" Kruger asked.

"Wait. For the moment when my career began. Thought you'd read the books. If you've read the books, then you know when my career began."

"You said the books lied."

"Only in some things. The essentials of my career are recorded fact. What you're hearing is what went on behind the facts. What nobody else ever heard. So just shut up and listen."

The days were almost religiously marked. It was as though by strict discipline and hard work he could atone for the evils of Chicago. He rose early—six, six thirty—and performed some brisk physical exercise while the coffee heated on the stove. By seven thirty, breakfast was over and he began to work—either studying the books and scores, or at the piano—until one o'clock. From one to two thirty he broke for a meal and then more physical exercise, even on the hottest desert days. Then, work again until seven. Another meal. More exercise, and at least two more hours at the piano.

"This was my life, Herb. I learned. I read scores—the major repertoire—as someone else might read novels. I learned them completely. You could have put me in a concert hall and said, conduct the Brahms Fifth, Tchaikovsky Fourth, Beethoven Second, I could have done it. Without the score." He tapped his forehead. "It was all there. Every note of the repertoire. Operas, symphonies, concertos. Everything."

"Mahler Second?"

"Probably, but maybe not. Mahler wasn't in the repertoire in the twenties and thirties. Not really. I grew a beard: neat, trim, not like some shaggy mountain man, and I worked. For years, I worked. Like a monk."

"Like a real monk, Lou? None of the ladies? You were inviolent?"

"*Inviolate*, Herb. No, but I was in Violet, and Patsy, also in a little Mexican girl whose name I forget."

"Like the dates, yes? The girls came up from the town with no name?"

"What do you mean? It had a name."

"You didn't give me any name, Lou. You're a clever guy, you sin by omission."

"How?"

"You leave things out, Lou."

"Okay, yes, the girls came up from the town. Maybe once a month I used to go down to the local cathouse and one of them would come back with me. Stay for two or three days. You never done that? Go to a girl from a cathouse?"

"Not in a long time, Lou. How did all the work affect you? You got good at the job?"

"I told you. In a couple of years I knew a great deal. I was also very fit. Work and exercise. I made the access road safe, and built steps down the side of the rockface on which I lived. When they were built—right down to the desert floor—I would run up and down them. Winter and summer. The piano was difficult. Had to tune it constantly. The weather was not good. But the time passed by, and suddenly all things changed."

"You remember the date, when all things changed?"

"Sure," casual, like sipping wine. "'Course I remember that. I'd never forget it. October."

"That's a month, not a date. You said you weren't sure of the date. 1930 or thirty-one, you said, only a few minutes ago."

Passau gave a little smile, lips pursed. He nodded. "See, keep you on your toes, Herb. The photographs of me begin in 1931, Hollywood. What led me there started in October 1930. It's ambivalent in the books."

"So you would be twenty-nine, thirty years old."

"Age? What is age, my friend? Who said age only matters if you're a cheese?"

"You look younger in the pictures, Lou, You look twenty years old, not nearly thirty."

"I have a good bone structure. I always looked younger. Would you take me for ninety years now?"

"Ninety-five," Kruger gave a chuckle. This was not getting anywhere. They jogged along. Jaunty, jolly, parry, riposte. Push him. Get him on the ropes. "So tell me about it? Was it like St. Paul on the road to Damascus? A voice saying, Lou, come to Hollywood."

The old man lifted a hand, then let it fall on his knee. "No, Herbie. It was the Trout."

"The Trout?"

"*Die Forelle*. Quintet. Piano and four strings going like crazy. Schubert. Da-da-dada-da-dum-dum; da-da-dadadada-pomp. *Die Forelle*, fourth movement."

"Oh, *that* Trout. Ja, know it well. This takes you to Hollywood and a life of luxury?"

"In a way, yes. One morning I wake up. Someone is murdering the Trout below my house. Slowly garroting Franz Schubert's bubbling piano quintet in A."

HE CAME OUT of a deep sleep, dreaming the same nightmare that he would share with nobody for many years—even when it changed and became worse. At first he thought someone was in the room with him and had put on the phonograph. Or that cats were being tortured somewhere nearby. The noise jarred and sounded like a cry for help—which in some ways it was.

Passau threw on his pants, stuck his feet into soft moccasins, then went out the door. Below him, five hundred yards down on the valley floor, there were people and strange pieces of equipment: large cameras, portable lights, and a generator, and little trailers. Also a fake wooden hut. If that were not enough, there was an awning by one of the trailers, and under it a quintet: a portable piano, and four elderly men with the strings: two violins, a viola and a cello. At the piano, a large man—

"Hunched like a deformed wildebeest, Herb. The truth."

The strings and piano had obviously been hired as a job lot, for they could not keep time, and were throttling Franz Schubert's piece. Even at a distance, Louis Passau's ears—his whole being—were offended.

"These so-called musicians had never before played together. This was obvious." He set off down the steps running and shouting so that the people below stopped what they were doing and stood looking up at him.

They watched the long-haired, bare-chested, shouting man descending upon them. Later, Stefan Greif, the movie director, would tell people that Louis seemed like some kind of avenging angel. They had not noticed the steps cut in the rockface and the Maestro, sure-footed, came running down them with such agility that some of those below could have sworn that he was floating down the incline.

"What in hell is going on here?" he asked loudly, and of anyone, when he reached the valley floor, the red sand hard under his feet.

People were turning to one man—short, stocky, in boots and riding breeches and a crisp white shirt. He looked like a very angry man: his face crimson, and forehead in a deep frown. He came right up close to Louis, as though trying to stare him down. His eyes were black and aggressive—"Bottomless, like dark, unattractive pools, like you could get somehow drowned, or out of your depth in them, Herb. Also there were his eyebrows. Thick and arching, like a V over the eyes." The man's nose looked as though it had been stuck on with putty, an afterthought. His hair bristled like porcupine quills, and when he spoke, his voice was thick with a middle-European accent.

"What the hell you want?" he shouted so that spittle sprayed over Passau's chest. "We're trying to make a picture here. A movie. Get off my set. Off-off-off-off!!" Like a barking dog.

"This land belongs to nobody, so it belongs to everybody." Passau looked straight into the man's eyes. There were a lot of people gathered around them and the sun was already hot. "If it belongs to everybody, then this screeching should stop." Lou gestured towards the now-silent musicians. "Nobody should be allowed to mangle Schubert in a public place like this. Even in the desert it is an insult to the composer."

For a moment, he thought the man in the breeches and boots was going to strike him, but he suddenly threw back his head and laughed. "At least you could tell what they were playing." He flapped his hand and the crowd began to disperse, drifting back to their cameras and the lights. "Stefan Greif," he thrust a hand forward. "You have heard of me, no doubt."

Passau took the hand and said, no, he had not heard of him.

"Well, good for you. I am known throughout the country. You haven't got a movie theater here?"

"There is one in the town, sure. But they hold no interest for me. If you're making a movie, Mr. Greif, why this insult to music? I hear you have talking pictures, singing pictures, pictures with music in them. But . . . but this. . . !"

Greif dropped his voice. "I agree with you," he all but muttered. "This . . . it is a travesty. It also makes my life very difficult."

"Well, why?"

"Because of our star. Because of the great and famous Miss Rita Crest. You've heard of her, I presume?"

"No. I have no interest in movie stars. I know they exist, but they can exist without me. I am a musician. Musicians can get along okay without movie stars. Why, though, is she responsible for this discord?"

"Ah," Greif fiddled with the top button of his shirt. "You're a musician. Could you get these five apes to play the thing properly?"

"Why let them play at all?"

Greif sighed, took Louis by the elbow and led him a few paces away, as though the handful of strides would ensure they would not be overheard. "You know nothing about movies, I take it?"

"Nothing. I know as much about movies as I know about necromancy."

"Well, that's practically the same thing. You see . . . I don't know your name. . . ."

Louis Passau told him.

"You see, Mr. Passau, the movie business has taken a great leap forward. A few years ago everything was silent. Just pictures that moved and told a story. Now we have sound. We have music. Sometimes even we have laughter. But Miss Crest . . . well, she became a big star when everything was still silent. Let me tell you, she is still great. One of the few really talented people in our business, but she has difficulty believing this. She has a kind of stage fright."

"Actors get stage fright; she's only a movie star."

Greif did not seem to have heard him. "In the days of shooting a silent movie we employed a small orchestra, or some such, to give the actors and actresses mood. To prepare them. They got used to this, and Rita—well, Rita still wants the mood music. And she *is* an actress, Mr. Passau. The music thing is in her contract. So we usually have four or five musicians along to get her in the mood. These apes, though, they could only prepare you for murder. So Rita . . . Rita is in hysterics . . . in that little trailer there, which is her dressing room. In hysterics because of the terrible music. She wants Franz Schubert, what she's getting is scrambled Schubert." He made a gesture signifying hopelessness. Then—

"I've shouted at them. They've tried—six times they've tried; and six times they've produced a caterwauling. You're a musician, Mr. Passau. Could you do any better?"

"I might."

"How?"

"First by finding out if these are really musicians. If they are . . . maybe, yes."

"If Rita had real music she would calm down. We could shoot the scene. . . ."

"And you would be away from here."

"Quite."

"Then I'll try."

In the present, Herbie said that it all sounded implausible.

"Of course it's fucking implausible, Herb. You ever been near movie people? Still, after all these years, they're implausible. But this happened. I promise. Movie people, even then in the early days, were good at heart. They had this wonderful dream of making great movies. Of conquering audiences. They lived this dream. . . ."

"And people who live dreams . . ."

"Are not as other people, yes. But Rita really did require this soothing before shooting a scene. It went on until the end of her life. She needed sounds to calm her and prepare her."

"Greif doesn't tell this story in his book."

"You read Stefan's book?"

"'Course I read it. *Through the Lens*. He mentioned you, but he doesn't tell this story."

The old man nodded. "I asked him not to tell it. It put Rita in a bad light and, of course, I wanted Rita's name. . . . I wanted her to be seen as a star, without these strange quirks. Stefan wrote about her without the warts."

Herbie nodded. "You're going to tell me you got these people to play the Schubert, and Rita Crest comes out of her trailer and does the scene. Then you go off with her to Hollywood and all lived happy ever after, eh, Lou?"

"Something like that. Sure."

"How?"

"How what?"

"How d'you make the monkeys play proper?"

"Through my knowledge. Through my command. They were my first little orchestra, and they weren't bad once someone led them."

"How?"

"I talked to them a little. They were all able musicians, but they didn't know one another. They couldn't decide who was to lead them, so they were all going off in different ways, different tempi. . . . They squabbled."

"So explain."

"What's to explain?"

"How you did it."

"I told you. I talked with them. Took over the piano. Took about an hour, but finally we played the Trout and you could see the fish leaping through the water, you could hear the water sizzling over the rocks. They were beautiful."

"You did it in an hour?"

"Sure. Look, Herb, it was technical. You want me to go through it note by note? That would waste my time and your time. Herb, you know music. I realize that. But you don't know from technical. You know from listening. I'd bet you don't know a crotchet from a quaver. It would muddle you. Worse, it would muddle your bosses when they get to read the transcriptions."

"What transcriptions?"

"Of the tapes you're making."

"Who said I was making tapes?"

"Nobody, but you're a fool if you're not making tapes. Jesus, Herbie, we've got a long way to go and I'm not gonna louse up my life story by going into the technique of making music. If you expect me to sit here and say, 'Next I said to the orchestra, okay we try it from twenty-four, and this time I want . . .' whatever. It's like sex in a thriller. Gets in the way."

"Not in the kind of thriller I read."

"There's no accounting for taste. Just believe me. I made these guys play, and, yes, Rita came out of her dressing room, and I clapped eyes on her for the first time. So begins another episode in my life."

Far off downstairs, Herbie heard the door slam. Pucky was back. He told Passau they would break. "We go on later, Maestro. Let me get food."

"Okay, but nothing technical. I'm not going to explain the complexities of the art, because it's a different language, only understood by musicians. Now, I'll listen to music."

He did. Turned up at full volume. Bartók this time. The third piano concerto. Herbie had never realized Bartók could be so full of melody, though perhaps that was Pucky's influence.

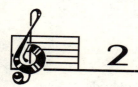

2

PUCKY HAD TAKEN off the dark wig and was shaking out her golden hair, standing in what they called the conservatory, well back from the windows.

"You talk to Art? You speak to him, secure?" Herbie realized that he had been concerned all morning, in the back of his mind, about the contact with London.

"Three times. All very safe."

She had driven from place to place, on the outskirts of town, choosing public telephones located in the open. None of them could be overlooked, or easily targeted by directional mikes. At first, she had dialed the ultrasafe 800 number and alerted Arthur Railton, who was ready when she called again—from a phone outside a general store in Batesville—half an hour later. The first thing he said was, "Only stay on for ten minutes. Then find a new place."

"Already doing that, Fred." He was Fred while she used Heidi. She carried the list in her head. Different cryptos for the days of the week. Monday was Gil and Beryl; Tuesday, Tony and Sue; and so and so, on to Sunday, when it was John and Pam, then start again.

The conversations were detailed, and between the calls Art Railton had sought further instructions, and cleared other devices which they might use.

"So, what's the verdict?" Herbie's voice had lost the teasing, mangled quality which had persisted while interrogating Passau. Now he was all business, very correct. *"Alles in Ordnung,"* Pucky thought. No games, no playful dyslexic language.

She told him exactly what Art had instructed. "Five days. A week tops, then we move out. We go to Florida. . . ."

"Wrong time of the year. Out of season. Very wet. Thunder. Hurricanes maybe."

"There's an island off the Gulf Coast. Connecting bridges. Name of Captiva, did I mention it before?" She did not wait for a reply. "There's a place called the South Seas Plantation. Wonderful apartments: three or four bedrooms. Do your own cooking. I've already called them. Said Sunday or Monday, that would mean leaving here on Friday." She took a brochure from her shoulder bag and passed it to Kruger. Unfolded, it showed an aerial view of palm trees and sand. Connecting roads ran between a series of delightful-looking clapboard buildings, hexagonal, with sun decks jutting from the seaward sides.

"There are two or three apartments to each house." She sounded bubbly, like a young girl planning a vacation. "They're beautifully furnished, with the latest in kitchens and bathrooms. . . . I saw photographs, and I've booked two—one whole building—so that nobody can get near."

"They got Jacuzzis?" Herbie grunted. "I become quite fond of Jacuzzis since we been here. I feel like a warlock who's fallen into his own caldron, but most relaxing."

"I don't know. I expect some have Jacuzzis."

"This is very private?"

"No, but you can make it private. If I can get myself other clothes and another wig, I can keep contact with London, buy the food, see the people who run the place. Nobody need see you and the Maestro. If we arrive late, you can stay in the car and I'll do the external stuff. Same if we stay in motels on the way down. Unless we drive four on and four off. Do the trip in one long hop."

"Maybe. If we get there in one piece, with Passau alive at the end of a trip like that. What then?"

"You go on sweating him, while Art and his people work out a route back to London. I gather London has this complex on Captiva pretty well sewn up."

"Which only means they'll have a couple of heavies staking us out."

"Probably. On no account—he said this six or seven times—on no account are we to turn Passau over to the Agency. That is cast in stone. Fishy, eh?"

"So? Yes, bloody fishy. Like week-old herrings." A lifting of the eyebrows, and a cocking of the head as Bartok floated downstairs. "What's going on, Puck?"

"I don't really know. But Art sounded twitchy. When they sent me out, before I left . . . well, going to the Agency was always a possibility. Now it's a no-no."

"Wonder why? Like you say, fishy." He turned and looked out of the windows at the long, tapering garden that ran up towards the Blue Ridge. One man could get a clean shot from up there. He stepped back, further into the shadows. "We get lunch for the old reprobate?"

"Okay." She wore jeans and a white shirt, the jeans belted tightly. Herbie thought the view from the rear was sensational, and almost said so. His hand hovered, then he coughed. "You ever get insatiable desire to pinch someone's bum?" He could not believe he had said it.

"Not really, but I understand." She looked over her shoulder. Grinned. "Feel free, if it gives you pleasure, Herb."

This reduced the urge. "Funny how you can turn me off, Puck. How you going to get fresh disguise?"

"I've thought about that. They're probably still watching Naldo, and taking trips around the immediate vicinity: keeping their eyes open. So I'll drive to Richmond. It's only a couple of hours. I can get two, maybe even three, new wigs and some clothes, without causing alarms and excursions. Chicken noodle soup and scrambled eggs do you?"

"Do me. Maestro Passau will eat what he's given. I say so. Richmond sounds good. I got a shopping list also." He followed her up to the kitchen.

"Clothes?"

"Maybe. I think later. Possibly buy them on the way to Florida. You any good with computers, Puck?"

"Not the industry standard stuff. Not the IBMs. Very good with the Apple Macintosh."

"Good. Then you buy one. Use one of the credit cards they gave you. You buy a Mackle Appletosh. You get a modem and some good software. Word processing. Communications—oh, yes, also we should have an IBM emulator: there's something called Soft PC, or PC Soft. Something's soft anyhow." He gave a big grin to show he was playing the fool. "There's a nice little portable laser printer you can also buy—don't grab a portable Mac. We want the real thing. Try an LC, it's got color which makes it pretty. But we need the communications software. You any good at hacking on the fly?"

"I get by."

He nodded. She was simmering the soup and getting trays ready, briskly slicing a French stick.

"I think you're probably very good at it. You do all this tomorrow, and your disguises. Disguise no good for me and Passau. A blind imbecile would pick us out at two miles. This afternoon you catch up on this morning's take; you can do the rest of today's before you sleep, after dinner. There are things you'll need to find out—that's partly why the computer. Get a package of stuff that'll take us into Compuserve or any of the other on-line facilities. There are things we have to know. Then, later, I might get you to hack into a couple of places for me. You might even have to make another trip to Washington before we leave. There are a few inconsistencies in the old man's story. How's that for English? Inconsistencies?"

"You're getting word perfect."

"I prefer Microsoft Word 4. Very good WP program, okay? WordPerfect I don't like so much. Matter of taste."

She laughed. "I've a feeling you're not exactly computer illiterate, Herb."

"I know my RAM from my ROM. Get plenty RAM, by the way."

"Chance would be a fine thing," she said, and Herbie almost believed her. He thought she looked dazzling standing at the stove, stirring the soup. Very domesticated. Make someone a good wife. Then Martha flitted into his head.

The Bartók finished as they arrived upstairs with the soup.

"Rotten performance," Passau sneered. "The pianist won by a head. We got chicken soup? Smells delicious. You make it, fair damsel?"

"I opened the tins." The fair damsel put a tray on his lap.

"We got serious things to talk about, Lou." Herbie lowered himself into a chair, balancing his tray. He took a spoonful of steaming soup and slurped noisily.

"So what's new?" Passau sipped, in a very sophisticated manner.

"We're going on a trip."

"You taking me to London, Herb? Pucky going to sit and hold my hand all the way? Bet London's got a whole team waiting to whisk me off to that place you got near Warminster."

"How d'you know about Warminster, Lou?" Casual, understated.

"Lots of things I know. When you're as old as me, you pick up lots of things."

"Leprosy?"

"I am a leper now?"

"To some people, it seems."

"Ah."

"Why would London get worried about Langley moving in on you, Lou? Does Langley know something we don't?"

"Maybe. Who knows? A long life and you carry secrets like a snail carries his home. It's possible Langley wants to bury me. We really go to London, Herbie?"

"Eventually, maybe. But first we're off to Florida."

"Florida? Why in the hell Florida? It's full of old people and doctors' offices. Biggest concentration of doctors in the world, Florida. They keep old people alive so they can eat the oranges." His voice went up, heading towards the angry zone.

"And go to see Mickey Mouse. Disneyland, Lou."

"That's where you should head for, Herbie. Fucking Disneyland is right up your alley—you should pardon my French, Pucky."

"We're going to a very nice part of Florida, Lou. Gulf Coast," she said brightly.

"Wrong time of the year. Why Florida? Why can't we stay here? I like it here, and what about music? There's plenty of music here. Will there be music in Florida?"

"Will there, Puck?"

"Not unless we take our own."

"We need a container truck to take all the music I shall need. No, I'm not going to fucking Florida, pardon me again, Pucky. It's not fair."

"You'll go where we take you or we'll feed you to the wolves, Lou. I'll do what I can about the music, okay?"

The Maestro sulked. They finished their soup in silence, and Herbie went to the kitchen and stood next to Pucky while she scrambled the eggs.

"What else did Art have to say? Anything about the goings-on in what used to be the evil empire?"

"Yes. He said to take care. It's going to be a long haul, and not easy. The Russian service is still active—here and in Europe, the U.K. of course. He reckons there're not going to be any sudden revelations from the archives. Guess what? Half the archives seem to be missing. He says nothing's changed in the field."

"No surprise. Ten years. Maybe twenty to get it all straightened out. More pepper in the eggs, Pucky. I bet the Russian Service have buried all the interesting files. They talk about the truth coming out. A sharing of old secrets. But most of the secrets've already been put out of harm's way, I think."

Maestro Passau sat looking at his feet when they returned with the trays. He ate more or less in silence, though they tried to jolly him along.

After lunch, Herbie stayed with him and tried to push him back to the first meeting with Stefan Greif—and, more important, with the actress, Rita Crest—in that odd desert place in which he had been hiding.

It took an hour to kick-start Passau. Even then it was clear that he was not going to say much.

"Look, Lou, you promised. I mean we had a deal. You tell me your life story, uncensored, and I try to make sure you're safe."

"For how long, Herbie? Time must be short anyway—for me, I mean."

"Self-pity'll get you nowhere. You enjoyed your life, yes? Well, tell me. Take it from the top, Lou. You got the five old guys playing. Then Rita comes out and does her scene for Greif, yes?"

"Yes. Eventually she came out."

"What did you think?"

"Of her scene?"

"No. Your first impression. First impression of the lovely Rita Crest."

Passau stared at his feet for a while. Then—

"Her name was really Creskowitz. Polish, I think. You know she never came clean to me about her ancestors. Maybe she had started to believe the publicity by then, but it sounds Polish, yes?"

"Just a lot."

"Bella Creskowitz. Tall. Five-eight, five-nine, with an amazing body. Slim, like a boy. Slim and supple, with small tits—good but small. Also great legs and a face that could light up the day—and the night, of course—but that was a bit later." He stared over Herbie's shoulder again.

"That was then, of course. The face went in a few years. Faces reflect the inner workings of the mind, Herb, so her face frayed at the edges a lot. But then, when she came out of her dressing room to do the scene, she looked like a million bucks."

"And she was worth more than that."

"Sure she was." He looked up and locked eyes with Kruger. Then, hurriedly, "I didn't know that then. I had no idea how much money she had until much later."

"Okay."

"She came out complete with body and face, and the long red hair. Striking. A natural. She worked on the scene for two hours. In hot sun. I stayed down there until they had finished."

"What she have to do?"

"Ride like the wind, with these Indians chasing her. Fake Indians, like the hut. White guys dressed in buckskin and feathers. Get off the horse at the fake hut. Larry Stube—romantic interest—dashes out of the hut, starts to pull her in, then gets zapped by an arrow. She shouts at the Indians—'You devils! You murderers! Savages!' Drags Larry to the doorway and gets zapped herself. They have this long bit of dialogue while they're dying—about three minutes. How they love each other and will go on until the end of time. I couldn't figure why the Indians didn't come and zap 'em again. It was the end of the picture— *West with the Wind* it was called. Very sad ending. Old-fashioned movie. Nowadays the Native Americans would have shown mercy. What did we know then, eh?"

"Weren't they a long way from home? A long way from the studios? Greif and his unit, the actors, I mean."

"That was Greif. He had this thing about getting all the action shots done far from L.A. Nobody else did it. They had begun to do shooting on location, but it was usually nearer home. Stefan Greif was way before his time. He wanted his actors to feel the land. The desert. The sun. The dust in your throat. On the studio backlot they all went in for a shower and a change of clothes between takes. He said actors had to feel the dirt and hardness of the old west. I don' know, Herb. First of the Method directors he could have been."

"So when you get to talk with her for the first time?"

"Not that day."

"I would have thought you'd have made a move on her if she was so gorgeous, or was this guy, the actor, Larry Stube . . ."

"Larry was a screaming queen, Herb. He played all these tough guy parts, but he was what nowadays they call gay, right?"

"Okay. Nothing wrong with that."

Passau made a derogatory sound at the back of his throat. "In those days it was against the law." As if that said everything.

"Pagan." Herbie looked suitably solemn, thinking what a hypocritical old fart Passau really was. "So when you get to talk with her?"

"A week. Ten days later. In Hollywood."

"You went that soon?"

"Sure. Why not? That night, Greif comes up to my place and we talk. He was experimenting with putting music on the track. Rita had to have the mood music before she played a scene. Let me tell you, Rita was a pain in the ass about her damned mood music. But Stefan had an idea that there should be special music to cover the action. He wasn't the only one doing it, but he took it further than anyone else. I gave him dinner that night. Corned beef hash, up in my cabin, and we talked about music. He was knowledgeable. Said movies should have tone poems playing along. That's the expression he used—tone poems. Most of the directors used any old stuff. He asked me what I would suggest for the Indians riding after Rita. I sat down at the piano. Didn't even think. Did half an hour of straight rum-ti-tum. Heard war drums and horses hooves and savages. He said it was brilliant. Said he could use it. Asked if I'd come back to Hollywood and write it all down. Work on the thing with him."

"And you did. . . ."

"I said no. Then he told me they'd pay me." For the first time that afternoon, Louis Passau looked up and smiled. "After that he told me *what* they would pay me. Then I said yes."

"And that was your first movie score, Lou? *West with the Wind?*"

"I wrote an hour of music after I got to Hollywood. Like he asked: a tone poem. Love theme, cowboys and Indians theme, chase. They used less than ten minutes of it. But they paid well."

"And you got to meet Rita." Herbie sounded arch.

"Yea, I got to meet Rita Crest."

STEFAN GREIF HAD A small, pleasant house in the hills above Sunset. The studios were beginning to take control of the business, vying with each other for the best pictures, the best actors, technicians and directors. Greif, who was to become a very great movie director, had signed up with Metrobius, an emerging studio with an impressive financial power base. The guiding force of Metrobius was the forty-year-old Maxim Ebius.

Ebius had been in the garment business in New York, and sounded like it. But he turned out to be one of the naturals in movie production. He knew money: knew how to make it, invest it and use it to his advantage. Like all the really effective studio heads of the early days, he was a dreamer, but his dreams were anchored to the ground, to his instinct and to what was available. Maxim was one of those Hollywood gamblers who hedged his bets and knew when to pledge more and when to be ruthless about withdrawing. He gambled on Greif, and won handsomely.

"Stefan had this quite small house until the late thirties when he built on," Passau said. "Very correct. A lot of old furniture. Real stuff from Europe. Even then, I remember, there was this nice little Monet on his dining room wall. I think later he had a huge collection, valued at millions, but in those days he was careful. A lot of them were careful, even actors. Some of the great actors didn't even buy houses at first. They didn't think talkies were going to last."

Before *West with the Wind*, Stefan Greif had made five pictures: four silent and *The Angel*, which was his first talking picture. "You ever see *The Angel*, Herbie?"

Kruger shook his big head, but said nothing.

"He had done that with Rita. Very powerful. Successful as well. It was a war movie, of course. Rita was a nurse—First War; what we called the *Great* War. What did we know then?

"There had been already one war movie that did good business—*Wings*, directed by William Wellman. First good aerial photography and sound effects. Then *The Angel* grabbed everyone's imagination. Obvious story. American nurse in France meets up with old boyfriend, now wounded and like to die. The usual mush, but Greif made the thing damned realistic."

"Overnight success," Herbie commented.

"You might say that. Very bright man, Stefan. In one night he talked me into following them back to Hollywood."

Passau remained cautious. He paid a man to keep an eye on the cabin and set out two days after Greif and his unit returned to Los Angeles. "I owned that cabin for another three years. I always had a bolt hole. It was like a safety net."

He drove to the nearest train stop. "One of those little halts they used to have. Like a bus stop. I left the truck there, in the fucking desert, and bought a car when I got to L.A. Inexpensive; secondhand. I remember Greif made me buy something more decent, brand new, when he saw that car. Even in those days the inner circle took note of what you drove and what you wore. I was shunted around tailors. Got a new suit made in twenty-four hours for fifty bucks."

Greif kept his word. There was an office available—with a piano—at Metrobius Studios. "I was like some of the actors, Herb. This was too good to last. I stayed in a hotel. It was nice in those days. No smog, no freeways. Good weather, and a lot of people making movies."

Two days after his arrival, Stefan Greif invited Passau to a dinner party, where he first saw the small Monet in the dining room. It was also his first real meeting with Rita Crest.

"Nice little painting you got here, Stefan. Pretty. You get someone to do it for you? He has talent. The trees are good. Look at the trees in this picture, Ailsa." Max Ebius flapped a hand at his wife, gesturing for her to come over and look at the painting which had so obviously taken his fancy. He was a little man, birdlike, who walked in short steps with his head thrust forward. His beaky nose gave him a predatory look. His bullying tactics were well-known and he would stand with his aquiline face thrust two inches from the faces of his victims. His wife, Ailsa, was tall, well-fed and cosseted by her husband's money. "A very stupid, spoiled woman," Passau said.

"They had no style, Herb. Once I seen him blow his nose with his fingers. Outside on the backlot. Then he wiped his fingers on the grass. A rough diamond, they called him. But what they meant was not couth."

Stefan came and stood between Max and his wife. "It's a Monet, Max." He pronounced it properly—'Monay' all one word—not like other Americans who said 'Mon-Ay,' with the accent on the second syllable, all wrong.

"Hey, Money," Max laughed—his laugh was a kind of donkey bray. "That's what makes the world go round, Stefan. Give you a grand for it."

"Not for sale, Max. Come and meet Louis Passau."

Passau had just arrived. "I don't remember if he had hired the guy who looked after the house by then, Herb. Guy by the name of Gates. British, small-part actor. Did butlers very well, but he became Stefan's butler for real and never got another acting job. Not ever. I think that night Stefan had a girl in to take the wraps and things. A long time ago, Herb. I guess Gates was later; funny what you forget."

"Funny what you remember," Herbie thought.

Max Ebius craned forward to look at Passau. The handshake was weak, but his eyes seemed to be clocking up what this man could be worth. "Oh, yea, you're the pianist Stefan's made me put on the payroll. Hope you're worth it, Passau."

"Composer," Greif corrected.

"So? Composer. Pianist. What's the difference?"

"You going to play for us tonight, Mr. Passau?" Ailsa asked. "There's such a nice little tune going around. Now what's it called, honey?" She had a nervous habit, lifting her right hand and quickly rubbing all her fingertips across her thumb. People said Max made her count the weekly take in cash. It was not true.

"No good asking me. I can't tell one tune from another." Ebius still looked at the picture, as though taking in every detail.

"I know." Ailsa was dressed in a long black creation which, Passau thought, made her look like a giraffe in mourning. "I know—

'Even when the darkest clouds are in the sky,
   You mustn't sigh, and you mustn't cry;
   Just spread a little happiness as you go by.'

She sang in a high, off-key soprano, but it was obvious that Ebius thought his wife could have appeared at the Met.

"You play that one for us, Mr. Passau?" she asked, coy and gushing.

"I'm afraid I'm not sure of the key. I haven't heard it before."

"What kind of pianist are you, Passau? Not to hear a song everyone is singing?" Ebius looked as though he was going to peck him to death.

"I am not a follower of popular songs."

"Why we hiring him, Stefan? The guy doesn't know from popular songs. In the movies we have to have popular . . ."

"Max," Greif said quietly. "He doesn't have to know popular songs. He *composes* his own music. He's not just a pianist. He writes music."

"And we pay people for that? Ain't there enough free music around that people have already written and died?"

"Do you wear old clothes, Max?"

"Whatchermean?"

"Louis tailors music for the picture, like you used to make suits for individual customers."

"That was a long time ago, Stefan." He was eager to change the subject. But, at that moment, the two other guests arrived—

"Stefan, who is this wake for? You didn't say when you sent that darling invitation. Hallo, Ailsa. God, how can you stand to let Max out of your sight for a minute. Aren't you afraid some quite unscrupulous woman will just gobble him up and ride off with him into the night."

Crystabelle Challis, the fluffy little blonde who had already made her name as a movie comedienne, stood in the archway leading into the dining room. Behind her, as though playing second fiddle, Passau saw the more statuesque Rita Crest.

Greif went over and gave Crystabelle a hug. "It's turning out to be Louis Passau's wake, I think," he chuckled.

She settled her gray laughing eyes on Louis. "Oh, you're the divine man who made organ grinders out of the monkeys. Yes, Stefan told me you're brilliant." She walked over and kissed the air by his cheeks, then did the same to Ailsa and, last, to Max who had no idea that she had been joking at his expense.

"Challis was not, of course, her real name, Herbie." Passau smiled, as though the memory warmed and nurtured him. "She really was what you would nowadays call a sex kitten. She was only around five-two, but she was a woman who was all curves, from legs, to waist, to tits to cheeks, to her smile and even her hair, an explosion of blond curls. She was funny, cheeky, saucy, you might say, and I instantly wanted her. So, I should imagine, did everyone else in the room—apart from Max, of course. He was not allowed to want any other woman except that long streak of black water, Ailsa. Ailsa Ebius kept him on a dog chain. Everyone joked about it, because no woman alive would ever invite him into her living room, let alone her bed. Except his secretary Myrtle, of course. Myrtle was quite a girl, in her own doglike way.

"I tell you, Herb, I can see that room now. Elegant. Silver on the table, beautiful china, candelabra, very romantic. He was clever for he had low sofas around a low table. You ate like a king with Stefan, and you ate in comfort. It always reminded me of what ancient Rome must've been like. And there was La Challis making everyone laugh. I recall she had just finished a movie called *The Blonde in the Window* and even Max congratulated her on the performance. She played a waitress who bets a week's wages that she will sit in the restaurant window and pose as a wax dummy for one hour. Sounds corny now, but it was very funny."

Crystabelle Challis monopolized the conversation during dinner and everyone, with the possible exception of Ailsa, seemed to be charmed by her. Certainly, Passau thought that the elegant Rita Crest paled beside this slightly vulgar but animated blonde.

"Stefan loved to cook," Passau said, in the present. "If I recall, we had an incredible meal that night. Exceptional, but then dinner with Stefan was always something to remember.

"Rita hardly said a dozen words to me, though I was seated next to her. She thanked me for saving her performance by getting the five old musicians to play properly, but I got the impression that Stefan had reminded her to do this. She seemed faraway. Wrapped up in some other thought. I know I suspected that she had a lover who had been left at home.

"Anyway—and this is strange—when dinner was over, Stefan suggested that we should go out on the terrace for coffee. She lagged behind—Rita, I mean. Everyone else got up and the men were being polite and ushering Ailsa and Crystabelle from the room. Rita just sat there."

"Shall we join the others?" Passau asked her.

She moved very slowly, as though she really had to think hard about what she should be doing. Then, as she rose, she turned and spoke very quietly, "In about ten minutes I am going to plead faintness and ask you to drive me home. Is that all right? You have got a car, haven't you? Stefan said you had." She smiled, and for the first time that evening she seemed to light up. Mischief played around her smile and in her eyes.

"Sure I have a car. You really want me to drive you home?"

She nodded. "We have to give him the excuse to break it up and say he will drive Crys home. You know about Stefan and Crys, of course?"

"Herb, what could I say? I said, of course. I had no idea about Stefan and Crys. But I had to go along with it. I tell you that thing between Stefan and Crys was a big secret in Hollywood for years. Eventually it got blown, and part of that was my fault, but, Herbie, my goodness, I remember I really had the hots for Crys that night. Rita, lovely as she was, seemed somehow out of reach. I didn't even think of making a pass. You know she had bad skin? It doesn't show in her movies, and I hadn't noticed it when she was doing the scene below my cabin, but she had actor's skin. It's the makeup. Or, rather, it used to be the makeup. They do it better now, but in those days they didn't really know how to feed the skin."

On the terrace, Max was now holding forth. Crys had silenced him throughout dinner. Now he was determined to have his say. Passau could only vaguely remember what the studio head talked about—"He was very good at manipulation, and running the studio, but, my God, Herb, he was a bore."

Crys Challis was making little muttered asides as Max spoke—

"What I am really looking for now," he droned, "Is a first-rate story about the War Between the States. Something which will appeal to patriots . . ."

"Which patriots?" murmured Crys. "You'll have to make two movies, one for the South and one for the North. The South doesn't realize it's over yet. They still keep Confederate flags in their attics."

"I see us shooting the battle scenes on the actual sites," Max continued.

"And we'll start another fucking war," from Crys.

"I want look-alikes for Lee, Grant, Jackson."

"Would that be Hyme Lee, Israel Grant and Moysha Jackson?"

"Shhhh." Greif patted her hand, and Passau felt a little twinge of jealousy.

"Would you look for the right story, Stefan? I see this as a perfect picture for you."

"We've already had *Birth of a Nation*, Max. It's too soon to play with that theme."

"*Birth of a Nation* had no voices and effects. I want to hear the great speeches and smell the powder, get my eardrums pounded by the guns."

"I'll pound your eardrums for nothing," chirped Crys. "Yesterday I met a man who claimed he had a leading role in *Birth of a Nation*. Said he was the little boy who ran for the doctor."

"Oh, Lord," from Rita who had hardly spoken all evening.

Passau looked at her and she had gone very pale. Her eyes were glazed. She looked really ill.

"You okay, Rita?" Stefan was on his feet and feeling her forehead. "You're hot."

"A little faint. I think I have a migraine coming on."

There were expressions of sympathy.

"A cotton sack with an ounce of cumin," Ailsa said. "You should hang it around your neck always next to your skin. My mother swore by that remedy."

Crys, sotto voce, replied that most witches prescribed an ounce of cumin next to the skin. Especially for migraine.

"Lie down and drink some cold herbal tea, Rita. That's what my mother always did," Max, the ever tactful.

"I think I shall have to go home. No, I don't want to break up the party, Crys. Could . . . ?"

"I'll drive her home," Passau heard himself saying. "Just tell me where she lives. I'll drive her."

"Herb, I must have been convincing. She muttered something about Laurel Canyon. Next thing I knew we were out in the car."

Passau drove out onto the road. Rita lolled next to him in the front seat, then, quite suddenly she sat upright and laughed. "How was I?"

"Jesus!" He braked violently. "You really okay?"

"Of course. I asked how was I?"

"I believed you. I thought you had really become sick."

"That's acting, Lou. I may call you Lou?"

"Sure. Sure, why not."

"Good. I'll give you directions. I want you to stay for a while. I have a nice piano and some of the Liszt transcriptions for four hands. We could play a little."

"Herbie, I was thunderstruck. She stopped there and then being a mouse. Totally in command. And her house was lovely. She also had taste and, my God, she could play. We played all the Liszt transcriptions of Wagner. She knew music, and we played. How we played."

"You not feel strange, Lou?" Herbie spoke very softly, as though he was not really addressing the Maestro.

"Strange?"

"You'd spent so much time on your own, in that cabin. Now you were out in the big wild world and talking to people."

"No. No, not strange. I tell you though, Herb, I felt different. I felt fully grown. An adult, as though I was now truly a sophisticated adult."

Herbie gave a little nod of understanding.

"She really was a very good pianist. We played the Paganini improvisations also."

"Liszt didn't write any variations for *four* hands, Lou."

"No, but there are many arrangements of his transcriptions. Arrangements for duets. Ask anyone. That's what we played. Then we talked and she gave me a drink."

"And you enjoyed that?"

"The drink?"

"No, talking to the lovely Rita Crest."

"I tell you what I enjoyed most, Herb."

"What?"

"I enjoyed most when she took hold of me and rammed her tongue down my throat. That was the best part on the night we met."

Silence, then Lou humming softly to himself. Herbie recognized the tune. Lou Passau was humming Liszt's *Liebesträume* No. 3. The most famous one, known by every piano teacher and pupil in the world. The *Dream of Love*.

"I HEARD THE LAST few minutes of your afternoon session." Pucky was peeling potatoes. She planned to use the frozen cod she had bought. "Cod, fries and beans," she said. "Fish and chips."

Herbie nodded. He was not a great fish-lover, but that did not mean he was a hero. Already he had learned that you had to be a great hero if you disagreed with Pucky, particularly if she had made up her mind about something.

"So, you heard of the little frivol going on between Stefan Greif and the Challis actress?"

"Mmm-hu."

"I see her once. Challis, I mean. She was very old lady. Retired to London, you know. This would be early fifties, I suppose. In a restaurant. After I saw her I watched all her movies, late night on the television. She was quite funny."

"Dated."

"Aren't we all, Pucky? Aren't we all?"

"Not you, Herb. You'll never date." She turned towards him. "You know what I liked best in the latest chapter of the Confessions of St. Lou Passau, Musician and Lecher?"

"What?"

"This bit." She stepped towards him, snaked an arm around his neck, pulled him to her so that he thought he would come out the other side, and kissed him, long on the mouth, her tongue penetrating his lips and moving in and out like a piston. He was so stunned he did not even kiss her back.

"Now," she said. "Go talk to the Maestro again."

Slowly, he walked, slightly stooping, from the kitchen, his brain in a whirl and his neglected body humming more than the *Liebesträume*.

Passau enjoyed his fish and chips, particularly when Pucky gave him the malt vinegar with which he covered his plate, so that the food floated in a quarter of an inch of the stuff.

"You'll *do* for him. The man'll get ulcers with all the vinegar," Herbie chided in the kitchen as they washed up and he gave her the final instructions for tomorrow—getting the Macintosh computer, the software and her wigs and things in Richmond.

Since she had kissed him, Herbie could not look her in the face. As she was turning to go to bed, he coughed. Then—

"Why you do it, Pucky?"

"Do what?"

"Stick your tongue down my throat and make me lose my mind?"

"Because you're exactly who you are. Hang around: there's more where that came from."

Herbie returned to setting the alarms, muttering, "My mistress with a monster is in love."

BIG HERBIE DID NOT sleep well. Part of his mind strayed first to Pucky Curtiss, while the remainder did some serious thinking about Lou Passau's story. The facts, following his arrival in Hollywood, were already well recorded in the two Passau biographies, with some odd paragraphs and footnotes in Stefan Greif's autobiography, and in the well-researched book on the actress, Rita Crest, *Crest of the Wave*. In the event, none of these books provided the unvarnished truth—mainly, it was suggested, in fear of litigation by Louis Passau.* Herbie did not have to be told that the descriptions had been well sanitized. There had always been some kind of mystery surrounding the couple, though the books all agreed that it was one of the famous love affairs of the Hollywood thirties and, like all truly heartrending love stories, it had the makings of tragedy.

His mind toppled back towards Pucky Curtiss. He saw that delicious bottom encased in jeans; then her little pink tongue. After that it was not much of a leap to the tongue probing his mouth and, from there, Herbie dropped into the realms of fantasy.

Pucky seemed terribly young to Herbie. Young, and in a way fragile. This did not stop his thoughts conjuring up pictures of Ms. Curtiss in various states of undress, and in a good many situations which kept sleep at bay for a considerable time.

Finally he dropped into a shallow sleep and dreamed. He dreamed that he was in the house in Berlin, with the Dürer Avenging Angel, and the red glasses. Lou was there with Rita Crest, and he was with Pucky. It became a *ménage quatre* and the four of them seemed constantly on the

* *Crest of the Wave*. Carlton S. Greenbriar (Phantom Books, 1940. Rev. Ed. 1956).

brink of performing some highly dangerous acrobatics. Then Rita walked through a door, and her face had turned into a skull, and finally into another face he recognized only too easily. Herbie woke, sweating, hearing the steady rhythm of a bolero which he quickly realized was his heart. Thankfully he fell back into a dreamless sleep.

While he slept, things were happening in England which would have a profound effect on Kruger's future—and not just Kruger's, but Pucky's and, not least, the world of Maestro Louis Passau.

In London, the CSIS had been off on a goodwill tour, meeting his opposite numbers from several European countries. He went with a full retinue, including Young Worboys, so, for all reasonable purposes, Art Railton had been left minding the store. When the balloon had gone up, forty-eight hours before—and twenty-four in advance of Pucky Curtiss' telephone calls—Art had worked on the hoof. But the day before that? Well, it was unexpected and required a lot of digging, for what happened was in some ways a fall into darkness, back to the bleakest days of the Cold War.

They got Art Railton out of bed at four thirty, London time. There was little he could do but wait for the Chief to return, and warn Pucky, when she called, that on no account were they to let Sunray, a.k.a. Louis Passau, anywhere near the lads from Langley.

On the Chief's return, Art Railton was closeted with him and Young Worboys for half a day. The encapsulated gist of the business was that the British Embassy in Bonn had received a walk-in. Years before, walk-in defectors were not uncommon, though they were always treated with wary suspicion and kid gloves. Since the recent official demise of communism they had expected a few, but nobody was hanging by their fingernails. Defectors, as everyone was told, were unlikely until the situation in Moscow became more clear.

This particular walk-in was described as a lady in her late forties who claimed to have worked for many years with the KGB units operating out of the Karlshorst headquarters in the old East Berlin. More, she claimed that she knew where some bodies were buried—for "bodies" read deep dark secrets which, even now, would make interesting analysis.

One thing had hit Arthur Railton straight between the eyes. The lady claimed that, up until last year—even after the infamous Berlin Wall fell—she had been responsible for assisting in debriefs of a Russian penetration known to Moscow as Kingfisher. She also did more than hint at a CIA knowledge and involvement in some of the aforesaid Kingfisher's dealings—an involvement the relatively new hierarchy at Langley would be happier without.

Only after he had ordered Bonn to get the lady into the UK quietly and with haste, did Art Railton check the highest classified category database and type in her name—

Ursula Zunder.

It was like hitting a mother lode. The computer asked for his name, twice, then his clearance code. Once these had been typed in, the screen filled with the equivalent of thirty or forty pages of amber typescript.

Ursula Zunder, one-time asset under network Schnitzer. Crypto: Electra. Then came the horrors, and Art recalled hearing the story—during some briefing—about Ursula Zunder and Herbie Kruger, who had, among other things, run the Schnitzer Group.

Scales fell from Art's eyes. This was *the* Ursula Zunder. The love of Big Herbie's life. The love and his undoing. Ursula had been Kruger's Judas, the cause of that incident they had all tried to forget—the time when Big Herbie had been in KGB custody for longer than anyone liked to admit.

"So, here she is again, eh?" from the Chief who sounded bored, as though the vast changes in the former U.S.S.R. had taken some of the urgency out of living. Nothing, of course, could have been further from the truth.

"She was taken down to Warminster last night, sir. Yes." Art gave Worboys a sideways glance which said that Ms. Zunder was probably going to become a lot of trouble.

"You've seen her, Arthur?"

"Very briefly, sir."

"And what did she say to you?"

"She asked where Herbie was—asked after him. She suggested that, should he still be in the field, he would be a marked man."

"Really? Now isn't *that* interesting? And Ms. Curtiss gave you a friendly call, I see."

Art told him what advice had been given to Pucky, and that cheered him up. "You want to deal with the Zunder woman, or go off to the colonies and see what can be done for our large friend and his elderly subject?"

"Really I'd like to do both, sir. But I don't see how . . ."

It was like talking to a plaster effigy. The Chief was faraway, his mind taking a short vacation on its own.

Nobody, of course, at that moment knew of Herbie's recurring dream. How, indeed, would they know that, years before, Ursula Zunder's apartment in old East Berlin had contained the ruby glasses and the Dürer? Herbie had thought her dead from the early 1980s. Was she here now to perform some kind of penance? To atone for the chaos she had caused all those years ago?

"So, MAESTRO, you had a jolly night with the movie star. Then what did you do, move into her nice house?"

They were at it again. Pucky had left for Richmond to do her shopping and Herbie was alone with Passau, sitting opposite him in the large library at the top of the house.

Passau looked at him. Quizzical was the word that sprang into Herbie's mind.

"She was very straight about it," Passau said.

"About what? The sex?"

"No, me moving in with her. She said no."

"That surprise you?"

"Not really. In any case, she was some lady, and I felt . . . well, I felt I should really try and make the money to keep *her*. What did I know? The house was pretty nice. Luxurious even, but I thought . . . Anyway, when I left that morning she said she loved me."

"I'm frightened," she said, standing in the large hallway. She wore a sheer silk robe with nothing under it. Louis Passau knew, because he had seen her put it on. It was four thirty in the morning. Chilly, and no sign of dawn. "It's never happened to me quite like this," she continued.

"What?" Louis did not really understand what she was saying. His mind had strayed on to his surroundings. The house was very impressive, so he was torn between taking in the decor and feasting his eyes and mind on Rita.

"Louis. Look . . ." she began. "I don't know how to say this, it's crazy . . ." Her right hand clasped at his left upper arm as though she did not want him to leave. Yet she had said he would have to go. "I must be at the studio by six thirty," she whispered to him after the last time. Neither of them had enjoyed much sleep.

"You see," she went on, drawing closer to him, "I don't usually do this."

"I understand."

"No, I don't think you do, Louis. Sure, I've never been a saint. I'm not trying to claim that I was a virgin, or . . ."

"I understand," he repeated, almost whispering: pulling her very close and thinking, "What have I ever done to deserve a night with such a woman?"

"I usually have to know somebody really well. I only met you properly last night, and . . . this sounds stupid . . . I feel I've known you forever."

"Like we grew up together?"

"Yes, Lou. Yes, like we grew up together. Do you believe in reincarnation?"

"I don't know. Never thought much about it."

"I feel that I've known you from some other time. Don't get me wrong. I'm not a nut. I've never believed I had any past life before, it's only . . . Oh, heck, Lou, I know you so damned well. It's as though I was in love with you."

"It can happen that quick."

"You think so?"

"I know so."

"I love you, Louis."

"Rita, I think I . . ."

She stopped his mouth with a kiss. Then—

"Go now, Lou. Call me tomorrow. I have a free day tomorrow."

In the present, old Lou Passau raked his fingers through his hair. "It was strange, suddenly being loved by such a celebrity. I remember I said I had to work the next day. I called her though."

"And it all blossomed . . ."

"Sort of. I mean we were both busy. I finished scoring *West with the Wind*. You have to remember that the companies just forming themselves into studios were going through a great transition. Before talkies, they'd shoot a picture in a couple of weeks. Now, it took longer. Six, seven weeks. And we worked. My God, we worked. It was three months before either of us got a proper rest. Rita shot *Autumn Glory* and *The Running of the Deer*. I scored both of them. It was a great challenge. I was well paid and—better still—I got to work with musicians. I had an orchestra. I was conducting."

"And you were seeing Rita?"

"Oh, sure. Three, four times a week I saw her. We'd sneak back to her place. I tell you, within two weeks I *was* in love with her." For once, Passau's smile seemed genuine. Then he laughed. "You know, we thought we'd been so damned clever. We thought nobody knew. Also, it was as though we had invented sex. Personally."

Herbie thought he knew the feeling, but it was not recent.

Louis was sitting having lunch in the commissary. Alone, working on the manuscript score for *The Running of the Deer*, oblivious to the costumed stars and extras chattering around him. A hand squeezed his shoulder. "You old dog, Louis Passau. Who'd have thought it?"

Crys Challis was grinning down at him. "Can I sit with you?"

"Sure. Why am I a dog?"

She leaned across the table and spoke very low. " Woof-Woof, Lou, I've never seen Rita like this. She denied there was anything between you, but *I* know better. You were seen leaving her place at some incredibly unlikely hour."

"I was? Who by?"

"By whom, Lou. You don't fool me."

"By whom, then; and why don't I fool you?"

"Because you both go around with that look. Cat-who-got-the-cream look."

"How's Stefan, Crys?"

"He's fine. We just do it, Lou. We don't care anymore. We just act naturally." She pulled a face, like a child pretending to be an ogre on Halloween. "Like beasts in the jungle, Mr. Passau. We deny nothing, and we deny ourselves nothing. Loved the music for *Autumn Glory*. People're saying you might get the first award ever for music."

"Really."

"And I think Rita's already given you an award for other services."

"Gee, Crys, I love it when you talk dirty."

"You shouldn't hide your light under Rita's bush . . . el. Give some of the other girls a whirl."

"Come on, Crys. Don't get foolish."

Suddenly, Crystabelle Challis' face became serious. It was a first for Lou. "I mean it," she said. "Truly I mean it, Lou. Rita can only bring you trouble. Don't hang around too long."

"What d'you mean?"

"Ask around. Ask about Mike Morrisey."

"What about Mike . . . who?"

"Had a real future as an actor. I mean *real*. He was always up with the crowd at Pickfair. This town's aristocracy, Mr. and Mrs. Fairbanks, and all the hangers-on."

"If he was so good, why haven't I heard of him?"

"Because Rita sucked him dry, my dear. She's a lovely, talented girl, but . . . well, ask around."

"And you asked around?" In the comfortable room, with the books, CDs and stereo equipment, Kruger leaned forward, as though vastly interested in the answer. "You asked around about this actor, this Mike Morrisey?"

"Sure, I asked. Casual. Not aggressive. People who knew the business."

"You got answers?" Herb really wanted to press on. The bottom line was thirty, forty, fifty years away, and he would like to get there before the old boy died.

"Not really. People said, what a shame. Yes, it was sad about Mike Morrisey. A great talent wasted. But I got no real truth."

One of the publicity people let him know that, as far as Metrobius Studios was concerned, it was not a good idea to ask about Michael Morrisey. So, in the end, he asked Rita.

They were in bed. Sunday afternoon. Her lovely Spanish house near Laurel Canyon.

"Someone mentioned an actor called Michael Morrisey," he began, turning his head on the pillow and finding himself looking into the big gray eyes, which opened wide, fear leaping from its hiding place behind the irises.

"Jesus Christ, Lou? What've they been telling you?"

Louis Passau had been around long enough to recognize real fear.

"What have the bastards been saying?"

"Nobody's told me anything, honey." He had also been around long enough to recognize the rising scale of her voice. The pitch of fear. "Someone mentioned this actor, Morrisey. Told me he was brilliant. Asked if I'd seen any movies he was in. Then another guy, one of the musicians, said you'd known him. Also the same person said he had great talent, and his story was a tragedy."

"And that's all? That's all they said?"

"Everything. You're upset, Rita. What's wrong?" He slid an arm around her shoulders and pulled her close under the sheet which covered them.

"It's unpleasant, Lou." Her eyes flicked away from his, and then back, and away again. Wary, uncertain. "He was my lover—oh, what? Two years before I even met you." The eyes sliding away from him again. "A brilliant actor. That was obvious to everybody. He had a presence which lit up the screen. If he had been around when talkies came in, he'd have made every other man in this business look like a midget. Mike's voice . . . he had, how can I describe it? A distinctive voice, and he knew how to use it."

"So what happened, hon?"

"He wanted to marry me. I said no. I really didn't want to make that commitment." She bit her lip and stared at the ceiling. The rest of it came out in a rush. "He asked me over and over again. Eventually I had to end the relationship. He had started drinking. Then, one night, he turned up here. Drunk, shouting at me. I was heartless. I had led him on. He couldn't live without me. I tried to reason with him, but it did no good. He shot himself. In the bathroom." She nodded towards the door.

"Herbie." Maestro Passau's face had assumed the nearest Herb had yet seen to grief. "Herb, I asked her, there and then, if she would marry *me*."

"Oh, Lou. Lou, do you mean it? Really mean it?"

"Of course I mean it. I love you with everything I have. I'm not much of a catch, Rita, but I'd give anything, what little talent I have, to make you my wife. You'll marry *me*?"

"Of course, darling Lou. Of course, I'll marry you."

Louis Passau shifted in his chair. "Herb, I didn't ask her what was so different about me? Why would she marry me and not this actor, Mike Morrisey? Many times I've thought why didn't I ask? If she had been honest, and answered truthfully . . . well, it was only after we married that I found out, that I discovered the real Rita Crest." He stopped speaking, as though he had dried up and there was no more to say.

"You wish me to get lunch, Lou?"

"Why not? It's twelve noon." A long silence. Then, as Herbie reached the door, "I'll tell you about the wedding this afternoon. The wedding and my memories of some of the famous I knew and loathed in Hollywood."

"Whenever you feel like it, Lou." Herbie went down to the kitchen. He glanced at his watch. Passau was a good timekeeper. It was one minute past noon.

IN ENGLAND IT was one minute past five in the afternoon, and Arthur Railton was just wheeling his Rover through the gates and up the drive to the house the Office kept near Warminster.

They were waiting for him: the confessors as they liked to call themselves. The inquisitors as others called them. Two of them, contented-looking men in slacks and sports coats. One had a pipe clamped between his teeth.

"Hallo, Gus," Art greeted the pipe-smoker. Gus Keene was the Lord High Inquisitor. A fellow of infinite jest, if you liked his kind of humor which tended to be on the grave side. "How is she?"

"Difficult to tell, Art. Maybe I'm losing my touch. Getting long in the tooth."

"You, Gus? With that pretty young wife? Never." Keene said nothing as they walked across the scrunching gravel. "Like to see her on my own first, if I may."

"Of course. We haven't started anything. Go right ahead. She's in the guest wing."

Art went down to the elaborate area called the guest wing. It was pleasant and relaxing, like a first-class hotel suite. Only it was below ground and there were security locks on the doors and round-the-clock surveillance cameras and mikes.

She was sitting in an easy chair, and the first thing Art noticed was her hair. Snow white and she really couldn't be much more than forty-nine years old.

"Electra," he said. "I bring greetings from an old friend. Schnitzer himself asked me to say hallo."

Her face seemed to become instantly younger. The eyes, in particular, began to sparkle.

"What a helluva way to make a living," Art Railton thought. "You lie until you believe it yourself."

"He did?" Her English was very good. Almost too perfect. "Herbie's forgiven me?"

"Everything's changing, Fraulein Zunder. What happened between you and Herbie's in the past. It's time to forgive and forget. Reconstruction, it's called."

4

"SO YOU GOT MARRIED, and lived unhappily ever after, eh?"

They had lunched on shepherds' pie, which Pucky had made and left to be finished off in the oven. Passau covered his with tomato ketchup—"I got all the worst American vices, and I hate that revolting pseudo haute cuisine."

It was after the shepherds' pie that Herbie had to kick-start Passau again.

"So you got married, and lived unhappily ever after, eh?"

The Maestro's head whipped up, and there was a brief flare of fire in his eyes. But he did not shout. "No, we did *not* live unhappily. For the first year—almost our whole time together—it was good and very happy. I *mean* happy. I tell you, Herbie, we were in love, and doing nicely, thank you very much. But you know this really, don't you? All the books tell it as it was."

"Not quite, Lou. They say that Rita became difficult to live with, and that led to tragedy."

"To begin with, it wasn't difficult. Yes, *I* was difficult and so was she. Herb, we were artists, what do you expect? Yet our combined artistic temperaments canceled each other out. We were difficult people, but that didn't make our lives together much of a problem. We were each other's morning and evening stars. Know what I mean?"

Kruger nodded. Ah, yes, he knew exactly what Louis Passau meant, because spies are like artists—artists and priests. "A clash of touchy egos that brought harmony? That right?."

"You got it. We managed because we enjoyed each other's work. We were never in competition. Not for the first year anyway."

The first time they tried to get married "It didn't take," as Passau put it, with a gruff laugh.

They had driven off one weekend, heading towards San Diego, but they could not find a judge.

They waited for another couple of months. Already, since their first meeting, Rita had made *Autumn Glory*, and had almost wrapped *The Running of the Deer*. Now, they were both starting on what Stefan called the studio's answer to *The Birth of a Nation*.

Max Ebius had found what he said was the right story: a book called *The Hollow Heart*, by an unknown author, Peggy Reed. He put his two best scriptwriters on it, and changed the title to *Blood of a Nation*—"Max was never one to worry about plagiarism," Passau said. He then sent for Stefan who read the book and declared it was unfilmable, which meant nothing to Ebius who showed him the script a couple of weeks later. There was a part tailor-made for Rita, though you could never have found it in the book. Stefan agreed, Rita agreed, and Passau began to research music of the War Between the States.

"We had two weeks off when we were supposed to be working on pre-production stuff—or, at least Rita, Stefan and the others were supposed to be hard at it. I gave it out that I was researching the score. One Saturday afternoon, I went over to Rita's place and found Stefan there. He was going on and on about the movie. . . ."

"It's never going to work." Stefan sounded at the end of his rope. "Max is all enthusiasm, but *he* doesn't have to make the picture—not with the budget he's given me." He paced up and down in the big front hall of Rita's Spanish house, which he always, rather scathingly, called "Old Mother Crest's Hacienda." One look at Rita and Louis knew Stefan was making her nervous. She sat in the window seat, at the far end of the hall, with her legs twisted up and her arms wrapped around her.

"Stefan used to do that kind of thing, Herbie. He didn't mean it, but it used to happen. He'd get in a state about a movie and pour it all out. Naturally, he made other people concerned with the project very edgy."

Passau saw the signs of tension, so he stepped in—

"Hey, Stefan. You got your problems, we got ours, let's not share until you start shooting, huh?"

"Rita's my *star*, Lou. She's got to know how I feel."

"Then you tell her when we get to first rehearsal which, with you, means first day of shooting, right? You spoke like this to your leading man?"

"Danton Buck? You're kidding. Danton only sees the problems when he tries to do his first scene."

Danton Buck had a short career in Hollywood. Short, but full of drama. Nobody had any idea that *Blood of a Nation* would be his last film.

"You know about Danton, Herbie?"

"Only what I read in books."

"Well, it was worse in real life. He was the precursor of guys like Errol Flynn. He was a lousy actor, but a pretty face and very athletic, in all senses. Drank like there was no tomorrow, and quite often there wasn't with Danton. He was also into drugs, but I didn't know about that until later. That was what really killed him."

And others, Herbie thought.

In the past, standing in the hall of Old Mother Crest's Hacienda, Louis Passau knew he had to change the subject, fast, or Old Mother Crest was going to throw a tantrum.

So, Lou Passau moved in to divert the approaching squall. "Hey, Stefan, you want to do us a real favor?"

"How real? You know, in this business reality isn't the name of the game."

"Very real. Come and be a witness for Rita and me."

Rita gave a little squeal of delight, and her mouth went back to normal.

"Witness? Witness what? I wouldn't mind being a witness at Max Ebius' murder trial."

"Witness for our wedding."

"Wedding?"

"As in marriage, nuptials, taking of oaths, tying the knot, Stefan."

"You and Rita?"

"Male and female. It's usual in a marriage."

"You're getting married?"

"That *was* the idea, Stefan."

"But the picture . . ."

"Marriage will not stop us doing the picture."

"Marriage is time-consuming—as in consuming the time when we're working on the picture."

Rita had disappeared, so Louis reckoned he had done the right thing.

"And where are you getting married, Lou?"

"We thought we'd just drive out, say to Santa Barbara or somewhere and find a judge to marry us. That's why we need you as a witness."

Stefan then began to argue about something else. Lou had got him off the picture, and onto another problem. "You think it's wise, with Rita's history of . . . well, the outbursts?"

"She rarely bursts out with me, Stefan."

"Maybe you're right. Perhaps it'll do her a lot of good. She does seem very happy around you." He went on and on, still pacing the floor, but the spring in him unwound without causing any dramas. By the time Rita came back, Stefan Greif had almost convinced himself that the whole thing had been his idea in the first place.

"We tried a few weeks ago." Rita stood in the doorway leading to the rest of the house. When Lou arrived she had been wearing an old skirt and some kind of checked shirt. Now she stood in all her glory, a crisp white dress—almost certainly an original, and probably a steal at a thousand bucks.

Rita, as everyone in the business knew, was a slow dresser, but that afternoon she had done the equivalent of the four-minute mile, complete with matching shoes, a wide-brimmed hat and long, very fashionable gloves. "I bought the *tout ensemble* after our abortive attempt, Lou. I've had it ready for the last month." She was all glow and excitement. Passau noticed and remembered all his life that the big gray eyes sparkled as though filled with diamond dust.

All Louis Passau could do was let out a low sigh. His knees seemed to be intent on buckling, and his stomach dropped into his shoes.

"You mean it!" Stefan sounded brighter now. "You really mean it! I couldn't be happier for you."

"Then come and be our witness, Stefan," Rita said, in the low sexy voice she had used for Stella French in *Autumn Glory.*

"Why not? I get to kiss the bride?"

"You even get to kiss the bridegroom if you're unlucky." Rita gave him a cheeky grin. They drove out to Santa Barbara, and found a justice who was very willing to perform the ceremony—"A kind of Frank Morgan guy. His wife would've been Binnie Barnes."

By this time Stefan was becoming obsessed with the concern that they might have planned a long honeymoon and would not be available for preproduction on *Blood of a Nation.*

"Strictly a couple of days, Mr. Greif," Louis kept telling him, but he still wound himself up, so they took him back to the house and fed him champagne until he felt no more pain. In the end they called a cab to drive him home, tucking a note into his pocket to remind him of what had taken place. The note also asked him to leave them alone for three days.

On that warm evening of their wedding day, they drove out along the coast, eventually reaching a hotel which looked suitably plush.

As the bellboy took the cases and they walked towards the front desk, Rita whispered, "Just you wait and see what I'm not wearing under this dress."

They remained in their suite for three days, seeing only the room-service waiters and shooing the maids away whenever they attempted to make up the room.

"Three days, Herb. Never did I have a honeymoon like it. No, that's not quite true. There was another occasion. When my memory gets fouled up with the bad things about that marriage, I always try to think of the good times."

Kruger nodded his large head. "Is the best way, Lou. I have a similar problem. Is what *I* do also."

"You want to talk about it?"

"No, I want to talk about you, and what happened with Rita."

"On the three-day honeymoon?"

"No, that I can guess at. I want to hear about when it fell apart. That's if it really has got anything to do with what we're chasing here. What the books only hint at. Great love story, leading to great tragedy. That true, Lou? Is it—what's the word?—pertinent?"

"Yes, it's pertinent, and it was certainly a great and tragic love story. Definitely. What can I say? The first months were unimaginable. Like a fucking poem. How best can I describe it to you? We shared so much, Herb. So bloody much. And there was always laughter."

He paused and looked up, again not into Kruger's eyes, but towards that point on the wall behind Herbie's head. Kruger had the strange, but distinct, impression that Passau was making some of it up as he went on; busking it; vamping until ready. That he would not tell the complete truth, because it would hurt him: like the stories he told about Sophia Giarre and their last days in Chicago. Passau had been deeply emotional about Sophie, and there was more to come, of that Herbie was certain. Now, talking of Rita Crest, his wife, there seemed to be no depth of feeling in what he said. No reality, yet there was truth.

So, Herbie thought, you do not really mourn Rita. She gave you a push, if the books come anywhere near to telling the truth. She gave you a push into the stratosphere, yet you have no truly fond, emotional memories. Rita, Maestro Passau, was a means to an end. There might not even have been love. Then, Louis almost changed Kruger's mind—

"Possibly, Herbie, because you love Gustav Mahler so much, something simple might convey it to you. You know the Rückert poems he set to music?"

"*The Rückert Lieder*, ja, of course."

Passau began to quote. His voice was thick, and the poem sounded almost banal. Behind the words, Herbie heard Mahler's music:

"*Ich atmet' einen linden Duft,*" Passau began.
  "I breathed a gentle fragrance.
  In the room there was
  a branch of a lime tree,
  a gift
  of a dear hand.
  How lovely was the lime fragrance."

"You see, it means nothing without the music. *Verstanden?*"

Herbie sniffed. Of course he understood. It was not the poem and its mawkishness, but Mahler's setting that gave it the twist and the depth.

"For lime, read lemon, Lou? I am right, yes?"

"Don't know what you're talking about." The old man turned his face away so that Kruger could not see his eyes. Herbie remembered the scent of lemons in the dressing room at Lincoln Center, and again on Passau's wife, Angela.

He tried to break the mood. "To begin with it was all light, fire, and air, yes?"

"Of course."

"She made movies. You personally scored them. You met the famous names now legends."

"We lived life up to the hilt. Sure, we met everybody. From the old silent days as well as that present when anything seemed possible."

"Tell me about the people, Lou."

This launched him into a festival of anecdotes, some of which Herbie already knew, others he had never heard. It was impossible to gauge whether the Maestro was repeating things he had heard from the people involved, or if he were simply embellishing the tales, told second- or thirdhand.

It was strange, back then, Passau told him. Everyone was conscious that they were at the beginning of a new era. They still thought of the silent films as being the greatest.

"Thalberg, the great Irving Thalberg, actually said 'Talking pictures are just a fad.' And Harry Warner, who laughed at himself later, remarked, 'Who wants to hear actors talk?'" "There was one story about how Clara Bow came dashing out of an office when a fire alarm went off, at Paramount. She was yelling, 'Pray God it's the sound stages.' They were full of stories like that."

"So, Lou, you had a great time, but when did it start to go wrong?"

"In a minute," Passau seemed to be dismissing Kruger's question. "First, I have to tell you about how I made a little further progress. When we got back from that three-day honeymoon there was a letter for me. On headed notepaper: the Los Angeles Philharmonic Orchestra. From the resident conductor, Artur Rodzinski—he was followed by the great Klemperer, you know. They had tried to get Rachmaninov as their principal conductor but he wouldn't do it, so they ended up with dear Maestro Rodzinski." He paused, savoring some memory. Then, with a smile, "The letter was to ask me if I would have time to be deputy conductor."

"And you jumped at that?"

"Of course I jumped at it. Rodzinski was an exciting young man— around thirty at the time, I think. Went on to do wonderful things. A great Wagnerian. Artur was a good friend. You know, when it happened for me with the Manhattan Symphony Orchestra—when some people were against what occurred—Artur stood by me."

"What *did* happen, Lou?"

Passau waved his hand in front of his face, as though trying to get rid of an insect. "That is later. After . . ."

"After Rita's death?"

Silence, with Passau biting his upper lip. He seemed in no way moved. Then he nodded. "Yes. Yes, after Rita died."

"But you took on the job as assistant conductor? You had the time?"

"I *made* the time. Max Ebius didn't like it much, but he couldn't do anything about it. I suppose I conducted concerts about once a month, and sometime deputized if there was a problem."

"Like the problem with Maestro Androv?"

"What problem?"

"Lou, there was talk. Just like there was talk about Rita."

"Boris Androv was a pompous old fart."

"He was also very famous."

Passau's head made a quick, jerky movement. "Who's telling this story, Herb? You or me?"

"As long as you tell the truth."

"You think I don't tell you the truth?"

"There would be no point in you lying, Lou." Kruger gave a silent chuckle, and in his thickest accent mouthed, "Ve haf vays of making you tell the truth."

Passau did not laugh. Instead, he sat cloaked in his own silence, staring over Herbie's head to the door to his past.

"What about the movie, Lou? What about *Blood of a Nation?*"

"Oh, God. One of my best scores, and some lovely work by Rita, but it was a disaster. Too long, too many confusions."

They were on location for weeks. Greener areas of southern California became the battlefields, with extras sweating under Confederate and Union uniforms. "There were six deaths when we shot Bull Run One, Herbie. Explosives went off accidentally. Six bodies spread over a square half mile. A shambles and chaos. There was huge waste. Five hundred thousand dollars for a southern plantation house on the backlot. I tell you, it looked just like Tara from *Gone with the Wind.* Later people, I heard, said when they did *Gone with the Wind* some of the designs were stolen from *Blood of a Nation.* But Rita was wonderful. She spent hours on a southern accent. I know. I worked with her on it. Me. *I* did that." He thumped his chest in rhythm.

"And after?"

"After? Oh, a couple of nice, quiet comedies. *Dulcimer*—Max didn't like the title and I don't blame him. Then . . ."

"*Nights of Lightning?*" It was the picture Rita was working on when she died, and Herbie knew it.

"Yes. Yes, of course. It was *Nights.* They never finished it." He took a huge breath, then sagged. "What you want me to say, Kruger? You want a written confession?"

"Just the truth."

"Okay. Okay." Passau became edgy, voice rising, fingers picking at his trousers. Then a deep breath. "You want to hear about Rita's death? You want all the details. The details people have only speculated about?"

"I think I have to know, Lou." Kruger looked directly into the old man's eyes. "You said that I had to know everything if I was to understand." He waited. From faraway, above them, came the sound of a jet aircraft. "You'd rather be on that plane, Lou?"

Slowly Passau shook his head. "I loved her, Herb—truly I loved her—my first sin was being so tied up in my work that I noticed nothing . . . even after a hard day at the studios she seemed bright and active—always full of life, and fun. . . . We'd spend days together, when we were both off. . . . She came to a couple of my concerts, she took an interest in my music, and I would coach her with her lines. . . . There was always . . . fun. . . . Her energy seemed—well—it seemed boundless." The words did not come out in one long steady flow. He hesitated, as though his speech was somehow punctuated by a defect in his memory. There were no tears or sobs; no self-indulgence. Just an old man trying to find the right words. "Truly, Herbie, I had no idea, but they say the husband or wife is the last to know. . . . We seemed close . . . read each other like open books."

"So when did you find out?"

"A party. We were at Pickfair. Lots of people there. A house full of stars, you might say. I remember it particularly. The one and only time I met John Wayne. In his youth he looked wonderful. A powerhouse. When he walked into a room he owned it, so full of confidence he was. Everyone was there. Cooper, Wayne, Astor, Harlow . . .

"Crystabelle Challis came up. I was talking to Chaplin. Yes, the great clown himself. He told me some story about turning down a screen test where he would have to speak. He refused and turned down a fortune. I remember he said, 'At least my integrity has stayed intact.' Then Crys came up, and Chaplin snubbed her.

"What was that all about, Crys?"

"Charlie? Oh, Charlie and I didn't see eye to eye about something."

"Money?"

"No, Lou, not money. Legs. We didn't agree about whether I should have my legs open or closed. I wanted them closed; he wanted them open. I won, so we don't speak anymore."

"I'm sorry."

"I'm not. Where's the millionaire playgirl?"

"Who?"

"Rita."

Louis laughed, "Crys, you have the funniest sayings. Why call her that?"

"Call her what?"

"The millionaire playgirl."

"Why not, Lou? That's what she is, or hadn't you noticed?"

"What're you talking about?"

"Oh, Christ!" She put a hand to her cheek, then covered her eyes. "You really don't know, do you?"

"Know what?"

She gave a long sigh. "My big mouth. Of course you don't know. I guess that's why she married you. Because you were obviously in love with her and knew nothing. Look, Lou, don't ever let her even suspect I told you. A couple of years back, just before you two met, her old man died. Left her twenty million. Oil. A cool twenty million."

"Dollars?"

"Well, I'm not talking about china dogs, honey. Of course dollars. Her salary from the studios just about keeps her in the booze and . . ."

Lou went suddenly cold. "And what?" Freezing.

"Heroin, honey. Don't say you haven't noticed that she's smashed half the time?"

"No, Crys. No, I hadn't noticed, and what's this about heroin? Surely, Rita doesn't . . ."

To Big Herbie, he said, "The kids today think they discovered drugs, and in a way they did—or their fathers did, in the sixties. But back then it happened. I knew some people used heroin, or coke a little, but I'd never seen it. Not openly. People talked about 'drug fiends' then. They were depicted as depraved, deranged people, lower scum than the winos on skid row. I never thought for a minute that Rita. . . . I don't think I want to talk anymore today."

"Lou, if you don't do it now. . . ."

"Sure, yes. I know. If I don't do it now, I'll never do it. Okay. Rita was on heroin and booze. I couldn't see it. Just could not see where all the energy and fun came from. How she was able to do a day's work, come home, and go to a party yet still be ready to make love, and laugh. Even after Crys told me, I didn't believe it. You understand that? I didn't really believe."

He had never asked her about the money, and he said nothing about the drugs and the drink. Over the next few weeks, all Louis Passau did was watch and try to make up his mind. Part of him said that Crystabelle Challis was simply stirring up trouble; slandering her friend. But the other half of him started to notice little things. How Rita looked tired and seemed down when she arrived back from work. He now tried to make a point of being at home when she got back. The fatigue appeared to dissipate within a short time of her going to "freshen up" on her return.

Once, he wakened in the night and found her, lying beside him, freezing cold and shivering. "Must have a chill," she said. Yet the shivering stopped after a short visit to the bathroom.

Lou Passau began to search for other clues. He was still not completely convinced that Crys Challis was telling the truth. He sought her out and pummeled her with questions.

"Lou, sweetheart, you're looking at her through tinted glasses. Everyone knows she has problems. She's cheating on you. Doesn't deserve you. She's cheating, not with other men, but with booze and the white powder. I think only you can save her. Confront her with it because, if you don't, she'll kill herself."

So Passau looked again. He searched the house while she was out. "Herb, I started to feel betrayed, you know what I mean?"

"Oh, yes, Lou. Yes, I know exactly. Betrayal is a part of life that never goes away." He thought again of the little, neat apartment in what used to be East Berlin. The Dürer and the ruby glasses, and Ursula, slim and adorable, making dinner, humming a tune. She liked Weill and Brecht. Used to go to the Berliner Ensemble. Towards the end she was always humming "Mac the Knife" from *The Threepenny Opera*—"Oh, the shark has pretty teeth, dear. And he keeps them pearly white." He could hear her clear sweet voice from over the years, and could feel her warmth, smell her smell.

"I love you, Herbie. To the end of time, I love you. Promise you'll never leave." When the Office pulled on his string, it cracked his heart to leave. So much that he broke all the rules to go back, and she caught him. Snap! The trap baited all those years. Baited with stories of love, and promises.

For some reason he heard the voice of Shakespeare's Lear howling. Why should he think of that?

"Okay, I tell you what happened." Passau looked at him, as though he had been talking all the time while Herbie had ridden his mind back to the act of his betrayal.

"First, I confronted her. I suppose it was the dumbest thing I ever did, and it certainly was the first cause of her death."

Below them a door slammed, and faraway Pucky's voice called out.

"Shit!" Herbie said loudly, realizing that the room was turning red and dark with the sunset. Shit and double shit, he thought. He had brought Passau to a difficult point. For, love her or not, the death of Rita Crest had to have been traumatic for him. Now, the moment was all but gone. "Lou, you listen to music, eh? I go down and see Pucky. We all had a hard day. What you want to hear?"

Passau let out a sigh, knowing that he had been let off the hook, at least for today.

"Give me Lenny's last recording of Mahler Six. It has great drive."

Also great emotion, Kruger thought, as the rattling march began to rip from the speakers. He went out on the landing and realized that he also had been let off the hook, for his head spun with thoughts of those days and nights with Ursula Zunder, his lover-spy-betrayer from years ago. His head was a whirlpool and his heart was an icemaker full of mixed emotions.

Down in the conservatory, Pucky had drawn the drapes and the lights were on. Once more she was shaking out her golden hair, and Herbie Kruger faltered on the turning of the stair.

"Is not sunlight, Pucky," he said. "But seeing you there, it reminds me of a poem."

"Poems yet, Herbie?"

"Ja, and I get it right. Old Naldo taught me a long time ago, and I always wanted to say it to a beautiful woman."

"Then say away, Herb."

He quoted—

"Stand on the highest pavement of the stair—
Lean on a garden urn—
Weave, weave the sunlight in your hair—"

"Herb," she said, her eyes genuinely misting up, because big old, clumsy old, clever old Herbie Kruger had spoken with such passion, and sorrow. She went over and took his bulk in her arms, and was not to know that Kruger was thinking of a German girl and a shit of a KGB officer and, years ago, King Lear howling in his head because she had betrayed him and his adopted country, and the pair of them had been—like Louis and Rita—each other's morning and evening stars.

"Herbie?" she said after a while, then realized he was weeping, and she had no way of knowing why.

5

ON THE FOLLOWING MORNING, Pucky was up and out of the house by the dawn's early light. The previous evening, after the cuddles and a few expert kisses ("Kissing's a lost art, Herbie," she said. "I never lost it," he whispered), she showed him her purchases. Three wigs, two dark, one auburn, in different lengths and cuts, plus some clothes which, in her real life, she would not be seen dead in. There was also the Macintosh LC computer, complete with internal modem and a pile of software.

She modeled the wigs and the clothes while, upstairs, Passau played music: Bruckner, the Fourth Symphony, *The Romantic*, which made Herbie think of medieval knights and maidens as depicted in illuminated manuscripts. It was certainly not what the composer intended, but that is what it did to Herbie.

As for the clothes, Kruger went for the Spandex silver though Pucky said it made her look like the Michelin Man. They cooked dinner and ate it upstairs with the Maestro, who insisted they all listen to Strauss— Richard, naturally—the Alpine Symphony which Pucky did not care for, though Herb sang along which irritated Passau enormously.

"This is only for orchestra, not for singing," Lou cautioned.

"Who says is not for singing?"

"Richard Strauss wrote it for orchestra."

"So? Actually he probably wrote it because his wife made him. Never was there a composer so henpecked. You ever read Alma Mahler's letters?"

"Didn't need too. I met Paula Strauss, and you're right. The devil of a woman. Had a tongue on her would put a hornet to shame."

After dinner, Herb went down into the kitchen with Pucky. There was a little more fooling around, but nothing serious. Then he sat her down at the table and told her what he wanted doing in Washington tomorrow. . . .

"You should be able to ferret this out in the National Archives. Federal Triangle. You can't miss it," he said, sounding very English. He made Pucky repeat the entire shopping list.

"Get lunch at the Old Post Office building. Food is okay. And while you're at it, might be a good idea for you to return your car, then go somewhere else and get a Lincoln town car under different identity. Lincoln town car is good. Bit flashy, which nobody will expect. How many you got?"

"Identities?"

"I'm not talking noses."

"Two and a bit."

"Okay, use the bit."

He gave her another kiss as they said good night, and this time things went a little further. Pucky lay in bed with her whole body wreathed in a large, happy smile, wondering if she really could hook Kruger, or whether he was simply going through a midlife crisis. As she fell asleep she realized that she was getting more and more serious about Herbie. Why else would she have visited Victoria's Secret? More, why else had she bought alluring undergarments there? When lovely woman stoops to folly, she buys herself sexy underwear, she knew, even if T. S. Eliot had said something different. What was it?

> When lovely woman stoops to folly and
> Paces about her room again, alone,
> She smooths her hair with automatic hand,
> And puts a record on the gramophone.

Something like that. So Ms. Pucky Curtiss of the Secret Intelligence Service dropped into sleep and dreamed of a woman approaching her in the street and saying things like, "Isn't the world so adorably Jewish? Isn't it wonderful?" When she woke, only the face of the woman stayed with her, and she could not get it from her mind for a couple of days.

Herbie slept like a troubled teenager, and did not understand why, for his dream was the eternal one of Berlin in the days of the Dürer print, only now the girl was a teenager, like himself, and they sported on the grass and drank beer, laced with raspberry juice, at Grunewald.

Meanwhile Lou Passau spent the night tormented by dreams of Rita Crest and the reality of her death, which he could recall vividly. When he woke, Passau knew he had buried some secrets so deep that he had not thought of them for years, in case they slammed him into guilty madness.

While they all slept, back in England Art Railton left the so-called guest suite at Warminster. He was very tired, and also—having done a mammoth session with Ursula Zunder—utterly bewildered and concerned.

When he had heard her entire story, he asked why she had run for cover. "Things have changed so drastically"—he looked at her using his best innocent face—"so why leap over now, when it's all over?"

"That's exactly why." Her voice still had the lilt of youth. "For heaven's sake, they're arresting people like me. They're after Mischa Wolf, they've put Grepos on trial for killing wall-crossers. In England they're howling for old John Cairncross to be publicly humiliated, and the Russians still talk of sending George Blake back to serve the rest of his sentence. With what I've got on my conscience, they'd eat me like a bowl of Zwiebelsuppe."

Art reflected that he could go for a bowl of spicy onion soup himself.

"You might be selling Herbie down the river for the second time. You *have* done it before. After what you've told me, it would seem that the Americans would put him in a shredder—with Maestro Passau for company."

The conversation continued, with Art using every trick he knew. "Then what?" became the two most important words in his vocabulary.

Before he drove back to London he saw Gus Keene, and his wife Carole, with whom Gus had been carrying on for years before he made an honest woman of her—not that female confessors could ever be called completely honest. Towards the latter part of the Cold War they had made a wonderful team. Between them they knew all the questions and most of the answers.

"Got it all on tape, have we, Gus?" Art was standing by his Rover, parked in the turning circle in front of the crumbling old house. There was a predawn chill in the air and he wanted to get going. Art found Warminster particularly depressing these days. Its ghosts were sad figures, like the lost souls of men and women who had died in an unnecessary war. The whole place felt seedy. Sad, but it would probably be sold off in the reorganization that now seemed inevitable.

"Would I do a thing like that, Art?"

"You've probably got video as well."

Gus Keene raised his eyebrows, and gave Art a friendly punch on the shoulder as he got into the car. They watched as he drove away.

"You really got it all on tape? I hope." Carole Keene looked up at him, her eyebrows arched.

"If the machines're working properly. Lord knows how we've managed all these years. The equipment's straight out of the ark."

As they turned to walk back into the house, with the first streaks of dawn coming up behind them, Carole said she would like a peek at Herbie Kruger's ex. "Quite a catch really."

Her husband clamped his pipe between his teeth. "Yes, she's a catch all right." He looked grim for a second. "I also think Art's playing some profound game linked with dear old Herbie. And as for Herb, I believe he would kill the Zunder women if he got within a mile."

"SO, LOU, YOU confronted Rita, yes?"

They sat once more in the same room at the top of the pretty house in Virginia. Pucky had left at dawn, without saying hail or farewell to anyone.

"In a manner of speaking, yes. I *had* to."

"Sure you had to. How did she take it?"

"It wasn't good, and I guess I didn't handle it well. I told you what a beautiful woman she was?"

"Many times, Lou. Statuesque, you said, but she had bad skin from the makeup."

"I think it was also the drugs. I found nothing in the house, you know. Addicts, alcoholics, whatever, are cunning about their supplies."

"I've heard that. So, what did you do?"

"Funny, she was from Texas, but you wouldn't have known it. She was third-generation Polish. Didn't really find out until it was all over. Father struck lucky. She wanted to be an actress, left home to join summer stock at nineteen. The old man cut her from his will. Later, Crys told me she was amazed when she found he'd put her back in."

"What then?" Herbie knew Passau was making detours.

341

"I figured she always kept the heroin in her case—what did they call those things, like damned great leather lunch pails. . . ?"

"Vanity . . ."

". . . cases, yes. Vanity cases. She carried one everywhere, and kept it locked. That's where she stashed the stuff."

"So tell me, Lou. Get it out of your head."

"I never told anyone before. Not a soul. It's difficult."

"This is confession time, Lou."

"I never felt real bad about it before. What happened at the time was almost an accident. Damn, it *was* an accident. Why do I find it difficult now? It's been over sixty years. . . ."

"Few love to hear the sins they love to act. This is Shakespeare, Lou. He knew which was which."

"I don't even know what was a sin."

"Come on, Lou. Then what?"

Passau did not look at him. He did not fix his eyes on that point behind Kruger which had seemed to be his gateway to the past. He looked down at his soft slippers as though somewhere in the doeskin there was an answer to his dilemma.

"Okay, when I finally got around to asking her, I made her drunk first. Didn't mean to. She just got drunk on top of the drugs."

They were both working on the new picture, *Nights of Lightning*. By this time Passau was paying most of the house expenses, and they had done up one of the rooms as a studio for him, complete with a Steinway Grand and a plain deal worktable.

The movie had been taken from a popular novel and Rita played a shiftless girl drifting from job to job in the Deep South. She was arrested and wrongly charged with murder in a small Louisiana town. The courtroom scenes were going to be the best anyone had yet put on film, and Stefan Greif had already done wonders to clothe the protagonists in the hot steamy heat of a southern summer. He would damp down hair and clothes with water before a take and have heaters going so that the cameraman and technicians worked bare-chested.

Louis had seen some of the rushes, and Rita's work was more than wonderful. She was turning in a performance which approached greatness, while he sat at his piano, at home, composing a score based on folk tunes from the Old South. He used spirituals such as "Lay This Body Down," "We Will March Through the Valley," and "I Know Moon-rise, I

Know Star-rise," entwined and plaited with melodies reminiscent of "Forked Deer" and "Mississippi Sawyer." Years later, Passau had adapted the whole for a ballet titled *Southern Storm*. In all, things were going well until the night when he screwed up enough courage to confront his wife with the truth about her addiction.

She got back at seven o'clock. Louis heard the door slam and her usual shout, letting him know she was home. He came out of his studio and caught a glimpse of her, looking tired and drawn.

"I got some champagne on ice, hon," he called. "And I've told Consuella to take the night off."

She called out at the bathroom door, "Give me fifteen, sweetheart. I've gotta shower and freshen up." The voice now seemed less bright and chirpy. "It was as if she had a problem with her larynx, Herb. I remember I wondered if she always sounded like that when she came in. Had I never noticed?"

She was out in less than fifteen minutes, in a terry-cloth robe, her eyes bright—too bright; her manner sparkling. It was as though her whole body was giving off energy. "You gave Consuella the night off? Why, for Chrissakes?"

"Because she has to see her brother. He has a problem," he lied. "Anyway, I thought it would be nice to have the evening to ourselves. Just the two of us, huh?"

"Why not? I've had a bitch of a day." She took the proffered glass of champagne, and drank it in three fast swallows. "Lou, I'm going to ask you a favor." She sat next to him on the long leather settee. She felt clammy to the touch, and he saw that when she moved her hands they seemed to jerk, in spasms. "I'm going to have to ask you to go to bat for me with Stefan." She was all movement, as though her entire body was being devoured by a nervous tic.

"With Stefan? But . . ."

"Oh, yea, I know, Lou. He's a nice guy and a brilliant director—could you fill that up again?—but he really has been riding me hard on this movie. I don't seem to be able to do anything right for him."

This was news to Louis. Stefan was never done telling him how well Rita was working. "What's the problem?" He put up his hand to her face, gently pulling her head around, forcing her to look at him. "What's the real problem, Rita?"

"Please, Lou. Give me another drink. The *real* problem is that Stefan wants too much. I'm giving him everything I've got. He wants more all the time. I can only do my best."

He refilled her glass, and she again drank it quickly, almost faster than the first glass.

"Give me specifics, honey."

She gave no hint, no warning. The change was in both voice and manner. "You doubting me, Lou? You think I'm making this up?" Her voice began to rise.

"Not at all, hon." He felt his stomach roll over. This was not the Rita he knew. He never had spoken with her like this. "No, if I'm to talk with Stefan, I have to know some details. With Stefan you can't . . ."

"Just go in with guns blazing? Why the hell not? You're my husband, Lou. I don't ask much of you." She thrust the glass forward to be refilled. Passau had only taken one sip from his first glass.

"You sure?"

"Sure of what?"

"Sure you want another drink?"

"Of course I'm fucking sure, Lou. What the hell's gotten into you? It isn't as if I'm asking something difficult. Just give me another damned drink."

He tried to make his smile look reassuring. "Hey, it's me you're talking to, not Stefan." He poured her third glass.

"So, I give Stefan a hard time?"

"Rita, honey, I didn't say that."

"Well, it sounds like it. Just talk to him for me, would you? Tell him to lay off." She turned away, then stretched over for the bottle. Louis grabbed her by the wrist.

"No, Rita, you've had three glasses of that stuff while I'm still on one. . . ."

"Well, that's your fault, Lou. You deny me a drink now?"

"I never deny you anything. It's just that you're getting through the stuff very quickly."

"Jesus, Lou Passau, it's only champagne for Chrissakes. Babies could drink this. It's not as though it was hard liquor."

Reluctantly he let go of her wrist and she poured herself another glass, putting the bottle on the floor beside her. Then she turned, drank half the glass and looked him straight in the eyes.

"So, you gonna tell Stefan to stop making waves? Or are you gonna go back in your studio and write more tinkly little tunes they can play while I'm giving my fuckin' all?"

It was as though the pupils of her eyes had turned to pinpoint lances. Their light was turned onto Passau, burning into his face like white blow-torches. "It seemed she was looking right through me, as if she couldn't see me, Herb. I was really frightened, because Rita was obviously off somewhere else. Not with me, and not even on this planet."

"Where d'you keep the heroin, honey?" There, he had said it, and for a second he thought she had not taken in what he was saying.

Then the explosion. "The what? The WHAT?" Indignant and shaken at the same time. "What you fucking talking about Passau, you jig-maker. . . . You fucking tunesmith. . . . What're you talking about?"

"You know what I'm talking about, Rita. The booze is one problem, the heroin habit's another."

She pulled herself upright, but her legs were out of control, buckling and making her stagger sideways. She grabbed hold of the settee and swayed, eyes unfocused with whatever cocktail of heroin and booze she had now topped up with fast-swilled champagne.

"Just what the shit're you talking about, Passau? You tell me. Heroin? You think I'm dumb enough to take that muck. . . ."

"Rita, I *know* you are. I want to help you."

She made a huge effort to pull herself up straight and stand without holding on to the settee.

"Never . . . never . . . never ever . . . insult me like that again. If you want to help me, call Stefan and tell him to stop fucking with me. Right, Louis Passau?"

She walked, her legs slewing left and right as she tried to told a true course from the room.

"That was it, Herbie. That was all it took—well, there may have been some more talk. Yes, there was more than that; she flung insults at me. She went on for ten, maybe fifteen, minutes, but that was the basic line. I accused her, and she walked out—well, staggered out—and locked the bedroom door."

"So, what then?" Herbie was not to know that Art Railton had been using the same words all through the English night.

"So, nothing. In the morning she was as though it hadn't happened. She didn't mention it again for a week. Things just went on as before."

"She stonewalled you?"

"If that means she didn't talk about it, yes."

"No making up. No, 'Lou, I'm sorry I was pissed last night? Sorry and all that.'?"

"Nothing. Not for a week."

"Not even about Stefan?"

"I called Stefan."

"Then what?"

"Well, you know Stefan . . . no, you didn't know Stefan. . . ."

"Hardly."

"For a minute I was back there. You ever do that? Think you're back in some other place?"

"Only when I want to be. Or when I dream." Herbie frowned, "And I don't ask to dream."

"Funny, since we been doing this, Herb, sometimes I've almost regressed, gone back to live it again. Only in the emotions, of course. . . ."

"Of course. But that's what it's coming to these days—our old trade. Now is changed. A lot of the work will be just old men sitting in a room doing time-traveling. Going back to find out why."

Passau grunted. "What trade?"

"You'll get to it. What then, Lou?"

"What when?"

"When you spoke to Stefan."

They met at Stefan's house in the Hollywood hills.

"Louis, we all thought you knew," he said, eyes open wide showing innocence. The place had been redecorated, and workmen were outside. Stefan told him he was enlarging the house. Said it was getting too small.

"What d'you mean, you thought I knew?"

The director touched his cheek with a forefinger. Then he touched the tip of his nose. It was as though he was going through some kind of arcane signaling. Finally—

"You are the only person I've ever known with whom Rita seemed natural. Crys said she'd warned you."

It puzzled Passau. "Maybe that's what she meant. She didn't spell it out. Am I very stupid, Stefan?"

"Louis, you're not stupid at all, but I thought you realized. Everyone in the business knows. Rita can only function as an actress when she is hopped up with booze and heroin. She's a brilliant actress with the help of these things. Hell to work with, but brilliant." He sat back and took a deep breath. "The problems are really very serious. She can only work for a certain amount of time every day, and that time is getting shorter and shorter. It's running out for her. She has to have music on the set. She also has to have a certain dosage of heroin, which she tops up with alcohol to keep on a high. As it starts to break down, she goes to pieces. A little too much booze on top of the drugs and she's incapable. She does a maximum of three hours work a day—that is three hours *good* work. Lou, I don't think she'll be able to do that much longer."

"But she always seems . . ." "Of course," he thought. "Of course she always seems fine in the evenings. Another quick shot, maybe a glass of something to get her charged up, and she *would* be fine for the five or six hours spent most nights with her husband, or out at dinner, maybe a party."

"They're cunning, Louis. Addicts are cunning, and she's been very clever to keep the truth away from you for so long."

"Either that or I'm naive."

"Or you didn't *want* to see it."

Passau, now in the present, lifted his head and locked eyes with Kruger. "You know, I think Stefan had the final answer. I didn't *want* to see it. Story of my life."

"It happens, like shit happens. They call it self-delusion."

Passau nodded. "I certainly deluded myself, because, after that night, everything fell into place—that's an old cliché, I know, but it did. I saw she was distanced from life when she came back in the evenings, and I realized the things I thought so wonderful about her were simply the removal of all her self-respect, a breaching of her moral scruples."

He had marveled at Rita's eroticism, then wondered at her modesty at other times. Now he saw these were the two sides of the whole woman, and one aspect was being eroded by the crutch of drugs and drink.

Stefan Greif had said, "She's going to die, Lou, if someone doesn't do something."

"So you did something, Lou?" Herbie asked some sixty years later.

"Oh, sure. Sure, Herb. I did something for her. I killed her."

Herbie nodded. "You going to tell me about it?"

"Why not? I haven't told anybody before."

Rita behaved naturally in the days that followed her outburst. It seemed to Louis that she had also given up any pretense. She came in from the studios each night, disappeared for a while and emerged as her bright self. Twice she initiated Olympic bouts of sex, during which she floated away from him and spoke obscenities. "It was like devil possession, Herb. You think that's what possession really was? Drugs?"

Once she even made a joke, saying she had to retire to the bathroom so she could get herself back to normal.

Max Ebius had invited them to a party two weeks after the original showdown and, on the night before, Rita finally broke down and told him the truth.

He woke, suddenly, in the middle of the night, knowing something was wrong. It was not just her absence from the bed, but a sense of danger that appeared to filter from the darkness. For a second or two, as he came from sleep, Passau thought maybe there was a fire, or intruders.

She was in the bathroom, naked, leaning over the washbasin, dry heaving, her whole body running with sweat, urine coursing down her legs, wild-eyed and barely able to stand.

He helped her. Made her drink coffee, washed her down and got her back into the bedroom. She seemed to go off to sleep immediately but, after a couple of minutes, her eyes popped open wide and she began to cry, great racking sobs shaking her body. It obviously hurt her each time she shook. "Lou," she sobbed, "I've tried to be good, Louis. Haven't you noticed? I've cut down on the drink. I know I've got to change. Something's got to happen. You were right. . . ."

After the scene when he had first confronted her, he had made some inquiries and found a doctor with a private clinic, up near Arrowhead. He told her that he would do all he possibly could and she should spend time in the clinic.

"As soon as the movie's over. As soon as we wrap it, I'll go in, but only if you promise to stay with me, Louis darling. I can't do it alone. I don't know if I can do it at all, but I'll have a better chance if you're with me."

He promised her, there in the bedroom, reeking of her sweat and urine. He said he would be with her for every moment, each step of the way. There he made a pact with her. A pact he should not have made.

That was the problem. There were two weeks left to run on the picture, and exactly two weeks before Louis had promised to stand in for Maestro Rodzinski. The great Boris Androv, arguably the most famous and flamboyant conductor in the world, was to visit Los Angeles with his privately funded Manhattan Symphony Orchestra. Rodzinski had been ordered to take a rest. Though he did not want to be out of town when the famous Androv would be performing, he felt if he did not get away now, he would not find another space until next season. Against his better judgment, Rodzinski had asked Louis to oversee Androv's visit, to deputize if need be.

"Naturally I jumped at it. Who wouldn't? As it turned out . . ."

"I know how it turned out, Lou. Keep telling me about Rita."

Max had arranged for the studio set dressers to erect a marquee on the lawns in front of his huge showplace house. "This was a dream house, Herb. You ever seen pictures of it? No? Incredible. Like a fairy-tale palace. But Max had it designed by the people at the studio and built by them as well. That way he didn't pay any extra for the construction. The party was really to celebrate his move to the new place. The only problem was that Max had no taste, and the studio people were doing a castle one week and a museum the next—sets on the sound stages. Max's place came out half castle, quarter deluxe New York apartment, and quarter English country house."

Rita had taken a shot before they left, but had promised to stay off the drink, except maybe a glass of wine. They had been at the party for only an hour when he realized Rodzinski was there. Rita stuck to Louis as if they were welded at the hip, and he tried to avoid the Maestro. All the arrangements had been made by letter and over the telephone. Boris Androv was set to arrive on September 14, the day after shooting of *Nights of Lightning* was due to finish. Rita was booked into the Arrowhead clinic on September 14.

Inevitably, Rodzinski caught up with them.

"Artur, how lovely to see you." Rita had seen him bearing down on them.

They exchanged pleasantries, then Rodzinski said he would have to be going. "I don't like these functions much, and I am very tired." He gave each of them a smile. Then—

"Mrs. Passau, you'll never know how indebted I am to your husband. Standing in for me during Androv's visit is a lifesaver."

"Really? Oh, I'm so glad." She turned to Louis, happy, not yet having grasped the significance. "You didn't mention it, darling. You're going to look after the great man?"

"Oh, it'll be a privilege."

"Will I get to meet him?"

"Of course," from Rodzinski. "I presume you're going to be hostess when Louis greets him on the fourteenth."

There was a pause, long and full of noise, a background of chatter. Far off across the lawns, on a specially constructed stand, a band played "What Is This Thing Called Love?"

"The fourteenth?" she said. Her voice was jagged ice. "The fourteenth of what?"

"We can talk later, Rita," Louis tried.

"No we fucking cannot talk later." Her voice rose and, sensing the obvious, Rodzinski backed off into the crowd.

"I'm still coming with you, Rita." Passau knew his voice held no conviction.

"You're going to be in two places at once?" Tears started at her eyes. "Don't play games with me, Lou. I thought you meant it." She turned and walked off into the crowd.

It was fifteen minutes before Louis found her, but in that short space of time Rita had managed to get the best part of half a bottle of Scotch down her.

"This was the start of the famous 'scene.' You know about that, Herb?"

Big Herbie nodded. "Sure, but let me hear it from you."

"If you read the books, they got it right. Practically every word. I had to allow my biographers to print it. After all, half Hollywood heard it that night. It was given word for word in evidence at the inquest. Greenbriar has it all in his book about Rita. She screamed at me. Told me exactly what I was, in front of every big name in the business. Then she said she was going home. Said she was leaving me.

"I followed, and it's all true about her insisting that she was capable of driving. Saying she wouldn't be driven by me. What she actually said was, 'I won't be driven by you, or ridden by you, or anything more by you, you bastard.'

"It was Coop—Gary Cooper—who calmed her down and said she should let me drive her home. I told her she'd got it wrong. That I would be with her on the fourteenth."

"You lied to her, Lou."

"Sure I lied to her. I was trying to gain time. I had every intention of taking her to Arrowhead. All I had to do was make her see that I was putting it off for a couple of days."

"Which is not the best of things with an obsessive addict, Lou. In fact it's criminal."

"I know that now. I tried to reason with her in the car. . . ."

"I'm taking you to Arrowhead, honey," he said as the car rolled out of Max Ebius' driveway.

"You think you're going to take me there and dump me. I know what you're going to do . . . you . . . you . . ." She was very drunk.

"No. Just listen to me, Rita."

The bend ahead was long and tight. The car settled nicely into the turn; white wooden palings defined the edge of the road. With a shriek of exasperation she reached over and jerked the wheel out of his hands.

("She was so quick. It was unexpected. I could do nothing to save us," he told Kruger as the afternoon began to bleed away outside.)

They hit the white posts. Seven of them, ripped away as the car went broadside into them, then tipped and swayed over fifty yards of steep incline.

After they hit, Passau had heard a terrible crack and, from the corner of his eye, saw Rita become a rag doll, flung against the windshield. Gingerly he opened the door and the interior light snapped on.

"She was looking up at me. Glazed, staring. I'm certain she was dead, Herb, certain."

A thousand pieces of blind panic shot through his head. He had a bruised arm, that was all. Yes, he had been drinking, but it was Rita who had caused this. There would be people who would believe him, and others—maybe the police, almost certainly the studio—who would not.

He leaned into the car, and dragged her over, so that she draped across the steering wheel. ("I hardly stopped to think, Herb. I just knew I had to make people believe she did it. I remember her skirt was all rucked up. I pulled it down out of modesty.")

Passau went to the back of the car. It only took a light push to send it over. It rolled three times, hitting the rocks with a trio of crunching bangs. When all was still again, Louis Passau hurled himself over the edge and rolled down. He got up, bruised and cut, six or seven paces from the wreck. Then he began to scream for help.

Rita Crest had gone straight through the windshield, on the driver's side, and was half decapitated. Lou Passau walked away. That was what people failed to understand. The car looked like a truck had hit it so, by all the rules, Lou Passau should also have been dead.

"A freak, Herb. A freak. I should have died there with her."

"Is the truth, Lou?"

"I swear it's the truth."

"She was dead after the first impact?"

"She was dead."

"You're one hundred and two percent certain."

"I'm . . . I'm pretty certain. Live people move when they have their eyes open."

"You checked her pulse?"

"She was dead, Herb. Dead like a doornail after we hit the palings. Stupid bitch."

"People said you'd rigged it. *You* said to me that you killed her."

"'Course I killed her. I should've leveled with her. I should have told her from the start that we couldn't go until the sixteenth. The woman was desperate. She had taken that plunge into the unknown by saying she would have treatment. Of course I fucking killed her, Herbie."

In spite of the underlying emotion, Herbie felt that Passau had not allowed him to see Rita Crest with any clarity. He had visualized Sophie Giarre but not the Maestro's first wife. Either Louis Passau was holding back or he had ceased to see her in true focus. Perhaps the years had blurred her edges and made her as two-dimensional as an old snapshot.

Kruger opened his mouth to speak and, as he did so, the telephone rang.

Out of habit, Herbie counted. Five. Five rings and Naldo was coming in. But Naldo had discontinued, and the code no longer applied to Pucky.

"You stay here, Lou. Stay quiet like a mouse. Don' know what to make of this one."

The pistol was in his hand as he went downstairs and waited, out of sight behind the back door.

He heard the car pull into the rear of the house. Footsteps, and the door slowly opened.

"Herb?" Naldo called softly.

"Jesus, you give me fright of my life, Nald. What's up?"

"Sit down, Herb. Sit down and please don't kill the messenger.

Electra's surfaced. Art called and I got back on some secure line they have. Art spent last night with her at Warminster."

For a moment, Big Herbie did not take it in. "Electra? Which Electra? Christ, Nald, she's dead."

Slowly, and a little sadly, Naldo shook his head. "No," he said, and again, "No, Herb. She's alive and reasonably well. She asked after you."

Suddenly, for Herbie, it was as though his whole life was enveloped in pain, groaning and shrieking from an agony he thought would never return. It was like some ghastly war wound, healed and forgotten, now reopened and pumping gouts of sorrow from his system.

"I kill her," he said softly. "If she's alive, I kill her personally. Make her wish she'd never been born."

6

THOUGH ELECTRA SEEMED like someone from another person's life, she had haunted Big Herbie Kruger down the years. It happens with great loves and great treacheries. A snatch of some tune; a laugh, or the sound of footsteps on a dark street; a familiar smell, or taste; the memory of a restaurant, or place, shared with the lover or betrayer, and the entire episode leaps into the mind. In Herbie's case, hardly a day went by without some reminder, even though eleven years had passed since Ursula had revealed herself as his personal traitor. She remained his constant dream, as though she still had him under surveillance.

Electra—Ursula Zunder—had come into his life in the ice age of the Cold War, the early 1960s, before the Berlin Wall cracked that extraordinary city in two. That was the time he ran the network called the Schnitzer Group.

Even now, Herbie could remember, in every last detail, how Ursula had entrapped him, and how he had fallen, "Love, the whole business. Love, the magician. Love and death. Love like I never knew, and have never known since," as he described it later to the hard men at Warminster. He should have known that it was a honey trap but, oaf that he considered himself at the time, he had not spotted it.

"A man led by his dick," one of the confessors had said, and Herbie almost flew at him in rage.

"Not like that, idiot! It wasn't just the sex! Don' you know about anything? You ask me the questions and you don' fucking understand. You don' deserve to be confessor. Jesus, get me Gus, at least Gus Keene knows what it's all about. I don' have to answer the questions of schoolboys, or put up with the adolescent jokes."

As it happened, Herbie was right. That particular inquisitor was just

354

out of training. He disappeared the next day, like so many people in the Service. His colleagues could not even ask where he had gone—on some sensitive op, or booted out, signing the Official Secrets Act again for the insurance? In this case he had been fired. Years later, Herbie spotted him in a Swiss hotel, in charge of a school trip, and thought it was tough luck on the children.

Still, after living so many other lives, he remembered his first sight of her face: the gray-flecked eyes, Italianate nose, and the laugh lines which bracketed her mouth. She was incredibly young but, then, so was he.

They had a meal together after the first meeting and he simply walked her to the door of her apartment and gravely shook hands with her. In the weeks that followed, as he dodged back and forth from the Russian to the British and American zones, with cover as an engineer, he learned to love for the first time—a deep, passionate emotion that went further than anything he had ever known in his life. It was not obsessive; it just *was*. A love that, to use the religious phrase, passes all understanding, and he did not even stop to think about it. She was the woman for whom he had been waiting and, he thought, she felt the same—as though they had been joined in life by some invisible umbilical cord. They appeared to worm their separate ways into each other's minds, meddled with them, and exchanged lives, though it was a long time before he even thought of developing her, as the argot of those secret days had it.

When the moment came, though, she proved a willing pupil. Later, he reflected that she might even have thought she was being set up under the cover of a false love. He came to examine that possibility during the years they spent apart; and again after the great stupidity, the time when the only Mahler he listened to in his head was *Des Knaben Wunderhorn*, those songs which included the *Sentry's Serenade*—

I am not going to the green clover!
The garden of weapons
Full of halberds
Is where I am posted.

She did not run with him when he had to get out, blown to hell and back partly through the idiocy of his own service, in 1965. But the time of the *Sentry's Serenade* was later than that. The days when the secret hierarchy was fiddling around, one hand not knowing what the other was up to. When they allowed him back into Berlin. To monitor, they said. To stay on our side of the Wall and watch, even though they had left his network out there starving, with no contact, only the occasional pick up or dead drop to reassure them. Nobody permanently holding their hands and urging them on as he had done.

Herbie had given his life and all his dedication to the men and women of that network in East Berlin, and he had to stand by and watch as the dolts who were supposed to run the Secret Intelligence Service let the blood slowly drain from the people he loved.

In the end everybody knew the Schnitzer Group had been completely blown. The only question then was who did the blowing?

Big Herbie Kruger, in his blind idealism, finally disobeyed everybody, crossed the Wall and thought he had found the traitor. Too late he discovered that it was himself, for the betrayer was the love of his existence, Ursula Zunder, who led him, like a Siren, into the arms of the KGB. She even wrote to him after they had him locked up and ready to be put to the question, and he still had every word engraved on his memory: a letter which still spoke of love, but a love divided between him and the system to which she was bound. In many ways it was naive—an apologia for communism which had turned love into something monstrous. The letter ended—

> I can never stop believing in communism—though it has assassinated your love for me, and rent us apart. I love you forever. Forgive me—
>
> Ursula

Herbie realized, now, deep in memory, why, when talking of betrayal to Lou Passau on the previous afternoon, he had heard the howl of Shakespeare's King Lear on finding his daughter Cordelia dead. It was the howl he had given, in full voice and grief, when he read Ursula Zunder's letter all those years ago.

"Howl, howl, howl, howl! O! you are men of stones," he repeated now, under his breath, as Naldo stood, silent, watching him as though he was violently dangerous. How old would she be? Nineteen when they had met. Early twenties when he had to go back over the Wall; midthirties when she had uncovered her true self. Now, she would be in her late forties.

"I kill the bitch," he muttered again. "Naldo, tell Art to get me out of here. I want to see her and kill her. Watch her disintegrate."

Naldo Railton shook his head. "You don't mean that, Herb. Really, you don't mean it."

Herbie almost fell into a chair, shaking his large pumpkin head slowly from side to side. "No, I don' mean it, Nald. Yet in a way I do. See, I think of her all the time. Every day I think what it could have been, and know it's useless. I suppose I still love the bitch. Love her and hate her. Life and death. They're the same thing."

"They're two sides of the same coin, Herb, yes."

He raised his eyes and Naldo saw they were watery, large and round, like a child looking at its first Christmas tree, in wonder. "What I do, Nald?"

"You get on with debriefing this old reprobate musician. Art wants to talk to you. He wouldn't say why, except I had to tell you that Ursula is germane to your current work."

"Is not German. Ursula is Russian-born."

"*Germane*, Herb, not German."

"Ah. This means she's relevant, yes?"

"Yes. There's a connection. Art says she knew your old man, your conductor."

"Ah!" As though he understood. In the seething caldron that was his mind he wondered now how Ursula felt about her beloved ideal. How did she see the world, now communism was outlawed? How could she function without the state being God Almighty? How many Ursulas were there in what was the once and future Soviet Union. Did *she* now feel betrayed?

"I telephone Art?"

"No, he says he'll get in touch. You must carry on as planned, which I gather means you're leaving here. . . ."

"Ja. Day after tomorrow we go."

"I don't want to know the details, Herb. Art says he'll know how to talk to you."

"Love of my life," said Big Herbie as he stood and gravely shook Naldo's hand. "Thanks, Nald. Thanks for coming." He seemed to have recovered his senses. "That Pucky girl, she's a real piece, huh? Quite a surprise to be working with a young woman like this."

"She any good?"

"With training she could be the best. But you know how things are, Naldo. The Service is too secret for its own good. Too much paper push-

ing and not enough real field officers. The books of fiction make us all heroes by the last page. We know there aren't any heroes, Nald. Just people
trained in secret then buggered about by men and women who've forgotten what they're there for. Paranoid, yes?"

"Pretty paranoid, Herb. You want me to take a message to Martha?"

Martha, his wife, had also been with the Schnitzer Group, and she
knew the secrets. Herbie had married her to get out of the trade and
Martha Kruger, née Adler, lived quite happily as second, or even third,
best. They both knew it was a convenience that could end at any time.

"Just tell her I'm okay, if you can. Don't compromise yourself, Nald.
Behave proper, like the old days, eh?"

Naldo nodded, then, untypically, embraced his old friend as though he
would never see him again.

When he had left, Herbie climbed the stairs and found Passau sitting
in the darkening room with no lights turned on. He pulled the curtains
and switched on one of the standard lamps. For a terrible moment he
though the Maestro was dead in his chair.

"You want to tell me what happened after Rita died, Lou?"

"They buried her. Forest Lawn. I went to see her tomb last time I was
in L.A."

"Okay, you tell me what happened when you found out she'd left you
a fortune? Or what the real truth was about you taking over as conductor
at the last moment when Boris Androv came rolling in with the
Manhattan Symphony Orchestra. That happened, didn't it?"

"You know it happened. I took over from the great visiting conductor,
Boris Androv. I stood in front of his orchestra, The Manhattan Symphony,
and gave the performance of my life. Next day I was a genius. Overnight
success, but I started a trend, Herb. You know the same thing happened to
Lenny Bernstein and to others. Lots of Maestros took over when another
great conductor was sick. Next day they were living legends."

"Sure, Lou. But you were a little different from Maestro Bernstein and
the others, weren't you?"

Passau raised his head. Herbie could not tell if the eyes were smiling
at him or mocking. "I was the grieving widower, yes. Show must go on.
That kind of thing."

"No, Lou. Tell the truth and shame the devil."

"What the hell you talking about? What devil?"

"Is a saying. Tell the truth and shame the devil. The way you're shlepping along we'll never get to the good parts of your story, Lou. The real reason we're talking at all."

"You want just the spy story, Herb? If that's all, send for le Carré or that other guy. With me you get the whole thing. In-depth profile."

"Okay, so you bury Rita, and there's an inquest, yes?"

"'Course there's an inquest. Herb, you know already the D.A. tries to pin the whole thing on me. They're out for my hide. If it had been the Old West they'd have lynched me."

"But you even got Gary Cooper in court to testify. . . ."

"Sure. A lot of other people as well. Coop stood up for me, and Stefan. Lotsa people. The D.A. didn't have a case."

"And you've now told me the truth?"

"Everything."

"Okay, let's talk about Maestro Androv and his visit. How the grieving young Mr. Passau managed to hold up his head and conduct a great concert."

"Tomorrow, Herb. I want to think about Rita."

"She left you almost twenty million dollars, Lou. What is there to think of?"

"At the time of the concert I didn't even know that. Let me listen to music now, and you get food. I'm tired. Been a long day."

The barriers were up, and Herbie knew when not to push. Passau wanted to hear the Mahler Second. Bernstein.

"I sometimes think, Herb, when you get to the final moments, when you have lived through a brilliant performance of the Second, you can say it's all a man needs from life. One real moment of understanding through music. If you've lived a bit, got sins on your conscience, doubted a lot, all you need is a good Mahler Second. At the end, you *know*, and nothing else matters. You can die a happy man."

Herbie nodded as he slid the first CD into the machine. "I know what you mean, but stay with us a few days longer, Lou. I need the whole story."

"Don't worry. I'll make your hair curl yet. Now, silence."

They sat through the first two movements, and Herbie put on the second CD. They were well into the final moments of the music when he heard Pucky call out from below.

Passau did not move, so Herb went softly out and down the stairs. He had not wanted to leave the glorious sound which kept pulling his heart back to the source of all things.

He stood on the stairs looking down at her, and she must have misinterpreted the expression on his face.

"You were right, Herbie. You were one hundred percent right. He had a brother. Six years his junior, and Louis isn't *his* name either . . . Herbie?"

"Okay, Puck. I come down." He took one step reluctantly, as though it was a physical effort to pull himself away from the sound. Then he came close to her.

Pucky put up a hand, her fingers brushing his face. "What is it?"

"An unpleasant piece of my past came to call this afternoon," he began, and then had to turn his face from her as Barbara Hendricks' crystal voice cut clean through the magical still circle of Mahler's turning world: woodwinds and strings, harbinger to the final breathless wonder of triumph, the climax of the symphony—

O glaube, mein Herz, es geht dir nichts verloren.
Have faith, my heart, for naught is lost to thee.

Pucky felt his discomfort as he took a huge breath to quieten his own heart.

From above them came the sound of the Mahler Second, the music sweeping like a waterfall down the stairs.

DURING THEIR EVENING meal there was, to use the phrase spawned by the Gulf War, the Mother of All Rows. A brace of mothers in fact. First Passau, who remained unusually taciturn, apart from the two outbursts, would not eat the fish: salmon brought back by Pucky from the supermarket on her return from Washington. She had poached it, with a delicious white sauce. The recipe for the sauce, she maintained, was an old family secret and Herbie kept badgering her to reveal the special touch that made it so good. She remained close-lipped and only the Maestro pushed the dish away.

"What's up, Lou? I thought you liked salmon. Good for the brain." Pucky tried to coax him, but the more she enticed the angrier Passau became. He would have a little cheese. He did not want fish. He became so blusteringly adamant that Herbie wondered if fish had a particular meaning to the day's interrogation. He went down and did a couple of large Welsh rabbits, a speciality using a lot of powdered mustard. This Passau ate without a murmur, except to ask what Herbie called the dish. "It's not like the usual toasted cheese."

"No. Welsh rabbit, as in bunny. Sometimes it is wrongly spelled r-a-r-e-b-i-t."

"So." Passau smiled for the one and only time that evening and, under his breath began to sing—

"Be vewy quiet. I'm hunting wabbits."

Herbie looked bemused.

Then they told Passau the move had been fixed. They were definitely leaving the day after tomorrow. He objected, putting up a series of defenses which together Pucky and Herbie demolished one by one. They were going to be more secure; he would like the surroundings; he could look out at the sea; the whole thing would be more relaxed; they would make the journey in easy stages, so that he would not be tired out.

"Music?" he said finally when all other barriers had been demolished.

"What about it?" Pucky leaned over and touched the mottled hand. Once more, Herbie noticed that the fingernails were beautifully manicured: the old man took great care of himself, proud of his personal appearance. The secret of his mien, Herbie had discovered, was that the man carried a whole series of vanity products in his luggage; there was even a superb traveling iron, and Passau used it to put the creases into his trousers. After years of living out of trunks and suitcases, Lou Passau had learned the art of grooming from the many people who must have been around ministering to his needs. It was a kind of pride which probably helped to keep him going.

"What about it? What about the music?" Pucky repeated, for the Maestro had gone into the sulks.

"You know what about it," he said finally, chewing on the last piece of the Welsh rabbit.

"To do anything, he needs music. It soothes the savage beast."

"Don't you mean breast, Herb?"

"No, I mean what I say. With Lou it is the savage beast."

"Okay, it can be arranged, Louis."

"How?"

"Tomorrow I go out and buy a portable CD player, small speakers, and a load of CDs. Make a list."

"You'll never get all the things I need."

"She'll get what she can, Lou. The rest we'll pick up by mail order when we get down to Florida."

Passau made no comment, but when the dishes were cleared away he asked for paper and a pen. They left him, listening to the Mahler Second again, writing a list. "The Mother of All Lists," Herb said as they started to clear up in the kitchen. "You had a good day, Puck?"

"I told you. You were right, and more. There was no Louis Isaak, and there were two brothers. . . ."

"Prove it."

She fished in her shoulder bag and drew out an envelope. It was a copy of the information gleaned from the great mass of files at the National Archives. "It only took a couple of hours. Amazing what they've got in there."

"The date's right." Herb peered at the photocopy—beautiful, faded handwriting that had come down the ages from 1908.

"Their names, and a brother. See, he had a brother." She leaned against him as her finger traced along the lines which told of the Packensteiner family's admittance to America via Ellis Island. Herbie smelled the sweet scent of her hair, and a muskiness which spoke of other things. "Joseph and Gerda, the child, Saul Isaak, aged seven years, and a twelve-month-old baby, Abraham Joseph."

"For Saul read Louis, or for Abraham read Louis. On the other hand, maybe the brother died, but I don' think so, Puck. You're a clever girl. He never even mentioned the brother. Fishy."

"You think it has some real bearing?"

"The brother was six years younger. By Lou's age in Chicago—Saul's age, twenty-five, Abraham Joseph would have been nineteen. By 1930 or thirty-one, he would have been twenty-four, twenty-five, which is what the old reprobate looks in all the early pictures taken in L.A. Makes you think. Makes you wonder."

They got Passau to bed, though it took an unusually long time. The list of music he wanted would have cost a fortune, even if they could get it all.

"I'll do my best," Pucky said. Her voice seemed to have a soothing effect on the old man. It did other things for Herbie whose mind had again become much occupied with memories of Ursula.

In the kitchen, she hung around as Herbie set the alarms. "I'll put everything back, normal, on Friday morning. If we leave around noon, should be plenty of time. You got the Lincoln town car?"

"Of course. The last thing I did in Washington."

"And you didn't have any friends with you?"

"Nobody, Herb. I did everything just as you told me, then more. Nobody was on my back."

"Good, let's keep it that way. Pucky?"

She made an expectant face without saying anything.

"I ask you the other day and you don't give me a proper answer."

"Asked me what?"

"Why you stuck your tongue down my throat."

"You liked that?" Very foxy.

"'Course I liked it, Puck. Why?"

"Because I find you attractive."

"Is against the rules, Puck. In the field is against the rules. They ever teach you that at Warminster?"

"Yes."

"They give you a for instance?"

"A case history?"

"You know what I mean."

She sat at the table, and did not meet his eyes. "They had a case file with the names changed, yes."

"Tell me what it was about."

She went through the entire business. A case officer, in the field. East Berlin. A deep love affair followed by a recruitment. The love affair continued after the recruitment. The network was broken. Years later the case officer went back, under the guise of trying to find out who had blown the network. In reality he went back to see his lover and she turned him in.

Herbie damped down his anger. "What they call this network?"

She gave him a quick, troubled, look. "Just Group A, or something like that."

"Really?"

"Yes, really, Herb."

"And who was the stupid case officer? The control?"

"It's a long time ago. I forget."

"Who'd you think it was?"

She looked up at him. He thought those eyes could swallow a man. "Was it you, Herb?"

"'Course it was me, but they didn't tell the truth. I went back, not to see my former lover. Well, maybe I did, but it was a side issue. I went back to get whoever had been turned."

"And it was the lady?"

"Sure. Just thought you should know." He told her that Naldo had called while she was returning from Washington. That Art Railton would be making contact. That the lady from the past was back. "They got her in Warminster. There's a connection. Her and the Maestro . . ."

"And *you*, Herb."

"Sure, and me."

"And you're out of bounds? That what you're telling me?"

"Out of bounds is always there to be crossed. Rules can be broken."

She stood up and came to him, kissing him deeply and feeling him respond. As with the professional side of his life, Big Herbie suddenly lost his clumsiness, becoming gentle and tender. He stripped her there and then, in the kitchen, and wondered about her provocative gossamer-thin underclothes.

When he took her, Ursula flashed into his mind and he had to open his eyes and look at Pucky's face to banish the ghost. After that he knew it was Pucky, and nobody else but Pucky. She groaned and clung to him: a noisy, and incredibly intuitive lover. Herbie was in control. He said nothing and did not even sigh, though the pleasure was intense. He did not even feel guilty about Martha. The sex was better than he remembered ever, but the total experience added up to more than simply sex—the sacrament of love, the outward and visible sign of the inward and invisible meaning. Ursula Zunder had been exorcised: something that had never happened with Martha, dear lady that she was.

Later, in bed, he spoke for the first time. "You are some amazing woman, Puck." His eyes said more and she, always bad at timing, screwed up her courage and said she thought she loved him. Then, because there was no immediate response, repeated it, "Herbie, I think I'm falling in love with you."

The pause was so long that Pucky felt she had probably ruined what could have been a nice friendship. Then he spoke—

"I love how you are. You smell like a cornfield. Maybe I feel the same.

Don' know how it can happen so quick." He sounded as though he were questioning her conclusions.

"It does for some people. Across a crowded room, and that kind of thing."

"Happened for me like that, once. Long, long time ago. The woman we talked about. The one who led me to the Russians. I never really got her out of my system, not even after I married. Still here, with Passau, I dreamed about her." Another long pause. "I stopped dreaming an hour ago. What you want me to do, Pucky?"

"What d'you mean?"

"You want me to stop this. The lovemakings?"

"No."

"Don' really know how it's going to be, Puck. Maybe I love you also. Who knows? Can't tell yet. What we going to do?"

"Maybe we should see how things go."

"Okay. I know you are my morning and evening star, my music."

"Now who's pinching lines? That evil old man said that about poor Rita."

"Sure, and he stole that first. I remembered later. Burt Lancaster, *Elmer Gantry*. Good movie. I love you, Pucky. Let me count the ways."

So they made love again and, afterwards, in the early hours, "What light from yonder window breaks? God, is disgusting. I could be your father, I'm so old."

"Would that be adding incest to injury."

"Ach! Shut up, woman, and be ready for me."

He took her again, and thought how amazing she was. She seemed to float in his arms, a feather, yet the very essence of womanhood. Their coupling was different, for she urged him on and they laughed a great deal. Yet, in the midst of the laughter, as she twined her long legs around his large hard body, there was the unspoken wonder of each trying to become the other. This was something Big Herbie Kruger had, until then, experienced only once before.

THE NEXT MORNING, after Pucky left, fully disguised and using an identity she had not worked under before, to do the mammoth CD purchase, Herbie again settled down in front of Passau.

"You want to tell me about Maestro Androv?"

"It's all on record. Short, a little fat, bald-headed, a brilliant conductor. Inclined to arrogance. What more you want, Herbie?"

"Everything. You said you started a trend."

"A little joke, my friend. Lenny Bernstein's genius came to him overnight because Bruno Walter went down with the flu and couldn't conduct a Sunday afternoon performance to be broadcast by CBS. Something similar happened to other conductors of our time. But I was the first. Boris Androv was taken ill during the night before his concert in L.A. with the Manhattan Symphony. I took over. Simple as that."

"Really? Come on, Lou, did he fall or was he pushed?"

"Good question. Hard to remember now."

"Try. You have dinner with him the night before?"

"Of course I did. You know, Boris hated eating in public. Always used room service. I thought it would be a treat for him. I had him out to eat with me. In Rita's house—well, mine, really, but I didn't know that until after the concert."

"And who cooked the dinner?"

"Consuella. She was distraught because of Rita's death. Well, she had been the housekeeper since Rita first came to Hollywood. Naturally she was upset; she was Mexican. But she cooked for us."

Herbie took a stab into the dark. "You had fish, Lou?"

"How do you know that? That's not in any of the books."

"What was it?"

"I don't remember."

"Stop pissing me about, Passau. The evil that men do stays with them. You got the whole thing in your head."

"We had soup, I think that cold French stuff. . . ."

"Vichyssoise?"

"I think."

"And then?"

Passau gave a great sigh. "Like last night. We had poached salmon."

"With?"

"New potatoes. French beans, I think. A salad."

"Sauce?"

"There was a sauce Consuella made with the salmon and two kinds of dressing for the salad."

"You eat everything?"

"Sure."

"Absolutely sure." A long pause, then—"We had different salad dressings. I had the oil and vinegar. Maestro Androv preferred the blue cheese."

"You knew this before he even came to the house?"

Passau nodded, not looking at Kruger.

"Say it aloud, Lou. You knew it *before* he came to the house?"

"Sure I knew. I made enquiries. Wanted to give him what he liked. He loved the soup, adored salmon, and liked blue cheese dressing on his salad. It was easy to find out; I just made one call."

"So, you doctored the blue cheese dressing?"

"Sure I did. Herb, I had to make certain I'd be on the box—on the podium—the next night."

"What you put in it, Lou?"

"I don't know. How can I remember a thing like that from all those years ago? I put some powder in it to make him sick."

"So, where did you get the powder?" It was like drawing teeth.

"From the doc who was supplying Rita with drugs."

"You *knew* who was supplying her?"

"Sure, her doctor. He was the first one I went to after I set out to help her. He didn't actually tell me he was the supplier, but he looked so damned shifty that I figured it out. Not difficult, Herb."

"And you just asked him for something to make Androv sick?"

"I said it shouldn't be lethal. He gave me the stuff."

"In return for silence about providing illegal substances for your deceased wife?"

"Something like that. We didn't use that kind of language then. Illegal substances, that sort of thing."

Herbie threw his hands in the air. "You blackmailed him."

"That's an ugly word, Herbie. I just asked him what to use. I said it was a practical joke."

"How sick did he get?"

"He was in the hospital for three days."

"Some practical joke. Three days. What did the doctors say?"

"That he had some kind of stomach ailment. They called it acute gastric enteritis. I sent him flowers and grapes."

"Big of you."

"Boris was grateful. He gave me a job. His associate director."

"And the concert?"

"You know about the concert."

"Refresh my memory."

The telephone had rung at six in the morning. The Manhattan Symphony Orchestra's manager.

"Maestro Androv's been taken very sick." The man sounded out of his head with worry.

"Oh, my God." Louis had been in a deep sleep, but he remembered everything, awake and fully in command as soon as the bell rang. "Not serious, pray God not serious?"

"He's bad. The doctors won't commit themselves."

"Merciful God!"

"The concert, Mr. Passau. We can't cancel. Can you take the Maestro's place?"

Louis counted to fifteen before replying. "I will do my best. Can you have the orchestra together in a couple of hours? No, say nine o'clock?"

"Of course."

"Herbie, he went on thanking me," the Maestro said in the present. "So I got up. Took a shower, called the hospital—by then they said he was in no danger. I went to the rehearsal and we worked until three in the afternoon. That night I did the concert: we did the *Leonora Overture*, then Strauss' *Don Quixote*; for the second half, Tchaikovsky's Fifth Symphony. A hard night, but the orchestra was wonderful. Couldn't have had better, and I showed them who was in charge. They were unhappy about parts of my reading of the Strauss, but they did it my way."

"So the next day you were hailed as a genius?"

"The reviews weren't altogether unfavorable. In fact I got three good things the next day." He ticked them off on his fingers, "One, I was recognized; two, the attorneys told me about Rita's will; three, I visited Boris Androv in the hospital, and he asked if I would become his assistant director. I said no, but I would be his associate director. He agreed. It was a little pitiful to see him, the poor man had really been most unwell."

"You went back to New York with them, and the rest is history, eh, Lou?"

"Some of the rest is history. Some will be new to you." He did not answer any further questions that day. "I must prepare for this journey," he said. "It is a long way to Florida, and I don't know if I'm even going to like it there."

"You'll like it." Herbie sounded threatening.

7

IT WOULD TAKE TWENTY hours of driving. By splitting it up, and stopping early each evening at random motels, they could get to Captiva Island, on the Florida Gulf Coast by Sunday afternoon. So Herbie took out his security system, cleaned up and tried to leave things as he had found them. He began at five thirty in the morning and they left the house just before noon, Pucky wearing her long black wig—"My Morticia Addams look"—and Louis Passau riding comfortably in the back with Herbie. Passau insisted they have the radio on, and it was tuned to a rock and roll, country and western, station which he demanded to hear. The music was strictly for ageing baby boomers, and the young shit-kicking set.

Passau and Pucky sang along with Dr. Hook and the Medicine Show, joining in with the rocking, witty, "Queen of the Silver Dollar."

Herbie was outraged. "What is this garbage, Lou? You, of all people, who can draw huge emotion from an orchestra, and you sing this rubbish."

Passau patted him on the arm. "You're a musical snob, Herb. This is also music. Enjoy . . ."

"But what's it all mean? Four electric guitars and a drum kit."

"It's the modern equivalent of chamber music."

"Is the modern equivalent of chamber pots."

"It's people being happy."

"It's people throwing up bilge. Crap. Bad for the eardrums. Terrible for the nerves."

"They said that about atonal music." Passau wagged a finger. "It's crap if you listen to this stuff alone and nothing else. It's okay for taking in small doses. Makes you feel happy. Nothing wrong in feeling happy and enjoying yourself." He leaned towards his interrogator. "I tell you something else for nothing, friend Kruger. You listen to some of this, then real music sounds more heavenly."

Garth Brooks was at it now, telling tales about men who would leave everything to follow the rodeo.

"When we going to have a bit of Elton John?" Passau asked the air and, as though he had some direct line to the d.j., Elton came on singing "Tiny Dancer."

Again Passau and Pucky sang along—

"Blue jean baby,
  L.A. lady, seamstress for the band . . .
  . . . Tiny Dancer in my hand."

"I had a dresser once called Tiny," Passau mused. "Dresser and body-guard. Stood six-four in bare feet. Strong as an ox."

"I bet you needed a bodyguard." Herbie smiled at him wickedly. "All the things you got up to. The husbands probably came after you wanting to ram your baton where the sun never shines."

"What do *you* know?"

"I know what I know, that's all. You go to New York with Boris Androv. What then?" Herbie pressed record on the tape recorder in his bulging pocket. The tiny microphone was fixed behind the right lapel of his crumpled jacket, only a foot or so from Passau's face. Pucky pointed the car onto Interstate 95, heading south.

"I worked." As though that was all there was to it. "The work is very hard, Herbie. You could never know."

"For a year you were Androv's associate director. So how did you work?"

"I told you, Herbie, it is technical. Technical you don't want to hear."

"Try me."

There was a long pause. "Okay, switch off the radio, Pucky, and listen to me, Mr. Kruger. You say I have a particular magic, that I can weave music from the air, interpret what any particular composer wanted other people's ears to hear so they would sing, laugh, cry, fall in love, or see God's face. True, I can do all these things. *How* it is done is another matter. I can give you the techniques—though you won't understand them—but it is impossible for me to explain the magic, okay?"

"If you say so, Merlin—ah, Maestro."

"Okay, pick a piece of music—not Mahler, that would take too long. Just pick something popular from the repertoire." As Herbie hesitated, so Passau prodded, "Go on. You're the expert listener."

Kruger nodded. "Right. Something from Beethoven okay?"

"Oh, we have to? Beethoven is not my first choice. You know people have strange ideas about Beethoven."

"Different strokes for different folks, Maestro."

Passau grunted. "Go on then, pick something nice and popular."

"Okay, Ravel. *Bolero*. A few of years ago you couldn't go anywhere without hearing the bloody *Bolero*. Some ice skaters used it, and it became number one hit to everyone. Later it was Pavarotti singing 'Nessun dorma'! Top of the pops. Suddenly everyone was an opera-lover, though most only heard 'Nessun dorma.'"

"I told you, Herb. You're a snob. Okay, Ravel. *Bolero*. You got to imagine I have a whole orchestra in front of me here. You can imagine, yes?"

"Sure."

"Okay." So Passau began, addressing the invisible symphony orchestra. "There isn't much you can do with the piece. It's ingrained into people's minds, but we'll try one or two things that'll make it sizzle, right?"

First, he was purely technical, as he had promised. He broke the throbbing rhythms down, took the music by the scruff of the neck and analyzed it. After that, he worked with the mythical brass, the fictitious strings and the imaginary percussion, going through each part separately before bringing them together. He was off in a world of his own. Singing pieces of the score for the brass, divorced from the rest of the orchestra, then doing the same with the woodwinds, followed by the strings, after that the percussion. Herbie could almost hear this fictional orchestra, conjured in the Maestro's imagination.

Passau broke the simple, strident rhythms apart, then put them back together again. He rehearsed the entire orchestra, stopping them to give some detailed note about how he wanted the theme built, or the pauses held a shade longer, or where he wanted the sound to build—"This is heartbeats," he said at one moment. "This is lifeblood being pumped through the arteries. You have to be at one with the entire life force that is in the music. No, I want it more obstreperous, more pagan. I want it as God might hear it as He breathed life into all mankind. It is like constructing with bricks of sound. . . ." And so, and so, until, ". . . The climax is huge, a massive sound, it is orgasmic. Think of it as sex: the outpouring, the organs melding, a huge, world-engulfing orgasm . . . and very, very fortissimo, by which I mean it's got to remove the earwax."

Herbie's mind whirled to the dazzling one-man show. He could have sworn that he heard every note of the piece; that an entire symphony orchestra had been with them in the car. "Never have I had such an experience," he declared later to Pucky. "I've always thought *Bolero* was a surface piece, automatic, no depth. This old man made the thing *live*. It was like the conjuring of some primal spirit. Primal is right, Pucky, yes?"

"Primal is very right, Herb. I nearly went off the road twice."

After his bravura display of wizardry, Passau leaned back and went to sleep. Herbie had not the heart to wake him, and resigned himself to the fact that the Maestro, for all his sins and unpleasantness, had him in thrall—in undisguised wonder.

Herbie leaned back and watched the road, thinking of the many performances of great music that he had heard conducted by this extraordinary man—not so much in person, but in his own collection of recordings. His mind turned to the old man's Mahler cycle, at times more moving and inspirational than even Bernstein or Solti. Inevitably, he drifted back to the days when he had listened to Mahler's music in his head, without a recording to jog his memory. It had been the ultimate in his tradecraft during the Berlin days, when he had used imagined music as a place in which to hide: his secret womb of sound which was his mental priest's hole when the KGB, and God knew who else, searched for him. It had been a place where his mind could scuttle into when he was utterly alone and frightened.

Herbie dozed, and for once did not dream about the apartment with the Dürer and the ruby glasses. Instead, his dreams took him to the side of a lush pasture where all was sunlight and flowers. The woman under him was Pucky Curtiss, and they made deliciously smelling hay while the sun shone down.

She was crying out—

"Herb! Herbie! . . ."

He woke with his body aroused. In the distance great jagged spurs of lightning forked from the bruised sky, and there was the crash and rip of the storm attacking the car, as though they were under mortar fire.

"Herbie, I can hardly see!" The windshield wipers had lost the battle with the drenching rain. "Pull off, Puck! Get onto the shoulder!" he yelled, and the car slewed, jerking to the right and pulling up sharply behind a monster rig forced from the road.

Passau woke, announcing that he was hungry.

"You're lucky to be alive." Pucky had been shaken by the sudden onset and violence of the storm.

"I told you we'd get a lot of rain coming to Florida at this time of year." Passau wagged a mental finger.

"We're miles yet from Florida, Lou. Just shut up and wait for this to clear."

It stopped raining and they drove on, into sunshine, the blacktop sending up drifting clouds of steam as the surface dried from the rain.

Half an hour or so later they got off the Interstate and found a little group of fast-food joints, a gas station and a motel which looked clean and well-kept. It was almost six thirty and they had covered three hundred miles of the thousand that would take them to Captiva Island.

Pucky did all the paperwork and drove them to the three street-level rooms, next to each other within the square U of the motel. There were some eight or nine other cars parked around the lot, one family argued outside a room further up, while two big men unloaded a car directly across from them. Herbie would have preferred to wait until dark when they might have some cover moving the short distance from car to motel room doors.

They got Passau into his room first. It was clean, had a color TV, telephone and fresh sheets. There was also a strip of unbroken sanitized paper across the lavatory telling them it was hygienically sealed, a statement that brought a flow of bizarre humor from Passau, who sank back onto the bed. He looked exhausted, but had enough energy to ask if they were going out to dinner.

Herbie explained that Pucky was going to bring dinner to them from one of the fast-food joints.

"I want to go out to dinner. See a bit of life. Stretch my legs."

"You'll stretch them in here. We stay here with you, Lou, until it gets dark. Then we can move out into our own rooms. Puck'll bring food here and we'll share a meal. It'll be fun."

"Ecstatically exciting!" The Maestro shrugged.

Herbie and Pucky shared the room two down from Passau, leaving an empty room between in case Pucky got noisy again. They had eaten remarkably well, considering: huge shrimp, yucky with hot red sauce, cold chicken and every salad you could name, plus enormous deserts made mainly of chemicals but tasting like fresh strawberries. Passau put away the best part of a bottle of some California white wine which he pronounced only fit for making French dressing.

"Doesn't stop you drinking it," Kruger said, without malice, for he wanted the old man to be well and truly ready for sleep.

They lay together on the big double bed, and everything seemed very stimulating, more illicit in an American motel.

"You really believe he's the younger brother, not the original Louis?" Pucky asked in the afterglow.

"Got to be. Work out the dates between Chicago and Hollywood. They're vague. He tried to fudge them, but there's a lot of time—too much time, or too little, depending on how you look at it. Why he's the brother, I haven't a clue."

"Like the guy's only eighty-four, which is still incredible but makes more sense."

"You going to play it as a trump card?"

"Not yet. Later. I did some sums. He could still have worked in Chicago; could still have had a great time with Sophie; could still have known Don Carlo; still have sold out Capone booze. He's obviously a genius. Did you get that whole rehearsal thing in the car?"

"Get it? I was *there*. I heard the music. I always thought of Ravel's *Bolero* as ten minutes of one tune going nowhere. That was sexy."

"It was sexy, no doubt about it, which reminds me. . . ." Herbie began to lay his hands on Ms. Curtiss again. Ms. Curtiss squealed in delight and responded, hand for hand.

HERBIE DROVE FOR all of the next day, and there wasn't much talking. They tuned the radio to various stations that went in and out of range. Mainly classical, but with occasional lapses: it was incredible that so many radio stations appeared to play nothing but sixties' music, the Beatles and the Stones were predominant. After three hours of it, Herbie became rather fond of Eleanor Rigby with her face by the door in a jar.

On the Saturday night they stayed in a motel just off Interstate 75, north of Ocala and Silver Springs. The air was heavy, full of moisture, and

Passau dozed on and off throughout the day, waking up, full of energy for the evening. The motel had a pool and he threw a small tantrum, wanting to take a swim.

In the end he came round and seemed to understand. They ate together in his room, where he once more demolished a lot of wine. At this place they got real strawberries.

Early on Sunday morning they took to the road again with Pucky, in the redhead wig, at the wheel. She drove slowly, and it was late afternoon, with the sun going down in their faces, by the time they crossed to the beautiful island of Sanibel, and so over a bridge onto Captiva, with its narrow winding roads, junglelike foliage and the sea never far away.

At six forty-five, the Lincoln town car turned into the parking lot in front of the administration building for the South Seas Plantation. Everywhere there were palms and green foliage. Baskets of flowers hung from the building, and people bicycled or walked slowly along the paths which led off towards the sea and the apartment houses. Insects clouded and attacked the lamps around the entrance.

Pucky went off, clutching her shoulder bag, to register them under their trio of assumed names.

"Looks nice. We go out to dinner tonight?" Passau asked.

Herbie was concerned lest he was reverting to childhood. "You know we don' bloody go out, Lou. We're incommunicado."

"Oh, I thought we were in Florida."

"Don' piss me about, Passau. Tomorrow we start remembering the past again."

"I feel like I should have a vacation. Lie on a beach."

"Maybe in ten years time, when we've got you to England, and I've completely dried you out, maybe then you get a vacation. I'll take you to Torquay or Bognor Regis."

"I've been to Bognor Regis. It's piss awful."

"How about the Isle of Man?"

"How *about* the Isle of Man?"

Pucky returned and climbed in behind the wheel. "All set," she announced. "We have two apartments, as they promised. We've taken over one whole unit. It costs a fortune."

"They didn't want to come out and help your senile old father and your incontinent uncle, Puck? Incontinent is . . . ?"

"Correct? Yes, Herb, it's correct; you know it's correct. We've got to get a move on, because I'll have to drive a half a mile or so back to collect provisions after we've moved in."

"Provisions as in steak, eggs and fries?" the Maestro asked.

"You got it, Lou." She negotiated the turn out of the parking lot and headed into the plantation, telling them to look out for 105-slash-106. "And steak, eggs and fries are not good for your cholesterol, Lou."

"Give me a break, Pucky. If you don't have any heart trouble by the time you're sixty forget about the cholesterol."

The unit was almost hexagonal in shape, painted white and gray, with a drive-in area underneath, and daunting wooden stairs leading to the pair of apartments. Herbie all but carried Louis Passau to the top. He said they should use the top apartment and just keep the other one for informality.

The place was charming. Big rooms, a deck which ran around the entire outside, huge picture windows, bathrooms with showers and Jacuzzis, and a well-modeled kitchen.

Herbie lumbered down again to lug the suitcases up the stairs. It took three trips, even with Pucky's help, and by the time she had gone off in the car to do the shopping, Passau was yelling for music. "You promised me. You said Pucky had bought a machine and a pile of CDs." He was worse than a five-year-old.

Herbie took little notice, except to make coffee (a basic stock of essentials had been left for their arrival) and start to unpack, but Passau drove him mad with constant wailing, so he unpacked the Sony Discman, plugged in the battery-powered speakers, and put on the first CD in the pile. It was Shostakovich. The First Piano Concerto. For several minutes the Maestro was silent. Then he began to complain because it wasn't *his* recording with Ashkenazy.

"Hey, I did most of the unpacking," Herbie announced when Pucky returned, looking flushed and carrying large brown paper sacks. "Opened your case, Puck, but didn't touch anything. You've a distinctly feminine taste, haven't you?"

"They are all treats, Herb, darling." She kissed him lovingly on the cheek after making sure Passau could not see them from where he sat, still complaining about the Shostakovich.

They had just started to put the groceries in the cupboards and fridge when the doorbell rang.

"Who the hell . . . ?" Herbie began.

"Probably maintenance. They said at reception that they would call in to make sure everything was working. I'll go."

Kruger had to grab her by the arm, holding her back until he could place himself behind the door with the big pistol in his hand. He felt that the journey and the obviously relaxed atmosphere of this vacation paradise had made everyone go a little crazy. Who knew what was lurking around the place?

"What cheer, Puck, where's Herb and the demon conductor." Art Railton slid into the small hallway and saw Kruger. "Well, Herbie," he grinned. "This is another fine mess you've gotten us into."

8

ARTHUR RAILTON FLASHED a charming smile at Pucky, then turned it into a grin for Herbie. He closed the door behind him and strode across to where Passau sat, now resigned to the fact that the Shostakovich performance was not half bad.

"Louis Passau," Art stretched out a hand. "It's an honor to meet you, sir."

The Maestro looked at him with suspicious eyes, lifting his hand some four inches from his knee, so that Art had to bend slightly to shake it.

"Arthur Reynolds," he lied, still smiling.

Passau's eyes flicked toward Herbie. "He's a friend, this Arthur Reynolds?" The way he spoke the name left no doubt that the Maestro was old in the practice of deception, so did not believe for a moment that Art's name was Reynolds.

"Best friend you ever had, apart from me and the Puck."

"You going to get me back to England?"

Art hesitated a fraction too long and Herbie jumped in. "If anyone can get you back, Arthur can."

"I want you to know," the Maestro was carefully measuring his words. "I want you to know that I am talking to my friend, Herbie. I won't do it with anyone else. I will tell him my life story, warts and all. But him alone. None of your good cop, bad cop people at the place you call Warminster."

"You know about Warminster?" Art raised an eyebrow.

"We been through all that, Art," Herbie pitched in.

"Okay." He slowly sat down, gauging Passau's mood. It was perfectly clear that the great musician was not going to talk with anyone until the Shostakovich was over. Art winked at Herbie, and Pucky said something about food, retreating to the kitchen with a look that maintained she was going to prepare a meal because she wanted to do it, not for any stupid domestic ideas that females were the ones who ground the corn, cooked and sewed, and looked after the welfare of their menfolk.

Herbie sat across from Art, the Maestro between them. What Kruger had said was the absolute truth. After a life dedicated to filching information from other countries, he trusted only three people within the British intelligence community: Young Worboys, Art and himself. Four if you counted Pucky, and he was not yet absolutely certain about her. To his way of thinking, the intelligence communities of the world were now running on fumes. They had never been totally brilliant, any of them, but now, with the Cold War over, an uncertain time ahead, with bleak long-term prospects, he put his trust, not in the princes of secrecy, but in the one true god of his experience. To his mind, few old hands were left, and of those, only a minute number bore scrutiny.

The concerto came to a rousing finish and Passau leaned back with a sigh.

"Is one of the things we enjoy, the Maestro and myself." Herbie gave his daft grin. "We have wonderful musical evenings, Art. Is a pleasure to do business with such a man."

"I'm glad to hear it." He looked across at the old man. "Herbie treating you well, Mr. Passau? Looking after you?"

"Wouldn't be here now if it wasn't for Herb. Saved my life, and he's keeping me going. Moving me along until I've told him what he wants to know."

"You're doing this of your own free will? No one's forced you?"

There was the glimmer of a smile, not so much in the mouth but deep within the extraordinarily clear blue eyes. "Nobody *can* force me, Mr. Reynolds. Nobody."

"But you do have things to say?"

"Yes, I have things that should be said. The earth can't hold me much longer, and I should tell someone. That someone is Herbie. Okay?"

"Why now, Maestro?"

"Why not . . . ?" he began. Then—"You like poetry, Mr. Reynolds?"

"Thrive on it."

"Then let me quote you something very simple. An American poet you might not know, you being a Brit . . ."

"... And also a Brit from Head Office, as it were?"

Passau gave a solemn nod. "I know about all the Head Offices in the world. I quote, and this is the reason I'm talking to friend Kruger:

'The rent man knocked.
He said, Howdy-do?
I said, What
Can I do for you?
He said, You know
Your rent is due.'

"That's a poet of color, as they say. Langston Hughes. My rent is due, Mr. Reynolds, and Herbie Kruger is the rent man. I'll pay him and him only. What he does with the rent afterwards is his business."

"I can understand that."

"Good." The one word came out very tired, and Passau closed his eyes for a moment, as though drifting off to sleep. When he opened them again they fixed on Herbie. "Tiring trip, Herb. I think I'll listen to something else, have a bite to eat, then go to bed and sleep the sleep of the just."

Herbie put on the next CD that came to hand. They still lay in the canvas bag in which Pucky had carried them back to the house in Virginia. It was Shostakovich again. The Eleventh Symphony, full of bravado, courage and revolutionary fervor.

Art Railton did not move a muscle. He wanted to talk with Herbie alone. Kruger knew it by a kind of telepathy, honed with members of Art's family over the long years.

They all sat in silence—Passau with his eyes closed—until Pucky came out and said there was supper if anyone was hungry.

Over cold meats and salad—Pucky promised they would be back on hot meals tomorrow—they talked of deep and wide interests, like their favorite movies, the latest plays and musicals running in London and New York and, most important of all, the correct way to make French dressing.

Louis Passau did not contribute much to the conversation. He pushed cold ham and tongue around his plate, ate a few mouthfuls, drank a couple of glasses of wine, and told them his favorite movie of all time was something called *The Big Knife* with Jack Palance, Ida Lupino and Rod

Steiger. None of the others had heard of it. He also made a telling comment on *Les Miz*—telling for him anyway.

"It is so beautifully directed," he said, the voice now old and drenched with fatigue, "but I have to smile when I see all those good, solid conservative people coming out with damp eyes and their hearts stirred by a revolution which, in the real world, they would despise."

That was the sum total of his conversation, and both Art and Herbie wondered if the comment about conservative people and revolutions was for their benefit, a preamble to his own, almost certain, political involvement after World War II. Pucky finally got up and helped him to his room. Art said they would wait for her before talking, and she came back flushed, but smiling. "The old bugger tried to cop a feel," she said, laughing.

"He'll never give up." Herbie did not laugh. "First question at Pearly Gates—if he gets there, which I doubt—will be, 'Who's that foxy-looking blond angel over there, the one with the good legs?'"

"Angels," said Art, soberly, "have no sex. That's the word according to St. Augustine. Or was it Ignatius Loyola?"

"Talking of angels . . ." Herb began.

Art nodded. "I have some with me. You're as safe as we can make it here. I have five guys. Two watching by day, three by night. We've covered most of the angles, but I don't think anyone else is around."

"Who'd you expect to be around?"

"FBI, the Mob and the Agency. The Mob and the Agency—or at least some inner conclave of it—want Louis Passau under the earth. By definition they probably want you with him, Herbie."

"Any idea why?"

"Not the Mob, no. But I've got a large slice of information on why other people want him silenced."

"And do we take the old boy to England? Is that an option?"

"It depends on what you've got for me."

Herbie's big head bobbed, signifying that he understood. "As far as our trade is concerned, we have very little. He's a born dissembler and he knows his way around. He says we get the whole story and nothing but the whole story. His argument is that we won't understand it until he tells exactly what happened in his life."

"And you believe that?"

"As far as I believe anything. I'm not really certain that I'm talking to the same Maestro Passau all the time. So far, we've reached the 1930s and the old bastard has faked himself into being an overnight conducting success. I think it is starting to become interesting to people in our line of business." He paused, looking at Art. "Back in London, when you sent me out here, I was told there were true reasons for drying out this rock of ages once and for all. In spite of the events in Eastern Europe. In spite of his age. In spite of everyone being friends and burying the hatchet.

"Okay, now I ask you is it really still so vital to clean out this old guy? I mean *really* vital?"

Art nodded. "Even more so, now."

"Ah! So we're coming to my long-lost love. To Ursula."

Art felt, more than saw, Pucky Curtiss stiffen. "So," he thought. "Good for Herbie. He's melted the ice queen." Then he said, "I spent an entire night going over the immediate concerns of Ursula Zunder."

"What next?"

"Go back a snake, Herb. I have to say that after you left on this assignment some of us became concerned. You hadn't been gone for more than twelve hours when there were serious doubts. It was even suggested that we should recall you."

"Nobody told me," Pucky sounded a mite huffy.

"Need-to-know, Puck. By the time you came in we were all intent on placating Desperate Dan at Grosvenor Square. The balloon had gone up. Well and truly gone up. Shooting. The magic disappearance of the Maestro and Herb."

"Why?" Herbie asked. He sat still, his face blank.

"Nothing specific. Sources over here tipped us that some people were anxious to render Maestro Passau terminally unconscious. It was even suggested that he would never get to Quantico. Also we had this feeling that the Agency might finally cut you out of the deal."

"They couldn't have been nicer in New York, Art."

"I know, but most of those guys ended up dead in the Queens Midtown Tunnel, right?"

In his head, Herbie heard the sound of crunching metal, and the gunshots, hugely magnified in the tunnel. Again he caught the last scream of the third man he had killed, and saw the blood.

"So, I presume all the stuff you gave me at Warminster is still pertinent? Is right . . ."

"Pertinent, yes, Herb, and yes, it still stands. However, someone else has come into the equation."

"The someone else being Fraulein Zunder, ja?"

Art nodded and slid his eyes towards Pucky, then back again to Herb. "How much does the Puck know?"

"Almost everything. I told her my past and my present. Only left out the bits about cutting up people with axes and keeping them in the fridge."

"You've become quite chummy." Art left the remark hanging between them.

"Not much to do in Virginia during the long evenings, once the Maestro's gone bye-byes."

"Mmmm."

Nobody spoke for a full minute.

"You want to tell us, or you keep us in suspense for the rest of our lives?"

"I'll tell you. Right from page one. Okay? First off, Ursula's been a busy girl over the years, Herb. Someone must've taught her very well indeed." He went on to give them a full rundown on his long night's journey into day with Ursula in the guest suite at Warminster.

"YOUR NAME, for the record—true name, that is?" he began, as though filling in some official form.

"Ursula Anna Zunder. You know my name already, Mr. Railton."

"Yes, but this is very official. I'm starting the debrief." He paused and looked at her. "I don't mean to be personal, Fraulein Zunder, but you should have your hair fixed. Dyed. You're not old enough to have white hair."

She gave an infectious little laugh. "It *is* dyed. I'll let it grow out while I'm here—if you're going to keep me here."

"I think, for the time being, we should."

"I hope," she looked grave again. "I hope my hair does grow out. It has changed color many times in the past few years. Like my name has changed, and my nationality. I have been kept very busy since . . ."

"Since you bagged Herbie and had him shut up for longer than any of us liked."

She gave a nod, not meeting his eyes.

"Who were you working for, Ursula? I know, but I have to hear it all again."

"Since my late teens I've worked exclusively for KGB." She sounded like someone filling out her C.V., as though it was the most natural thing in the world to spend her life working for the former Russian Intelligence Service.

"And that is why you've run to us now?"

"Because the new Germany is being a little tough with people like me. Because there have been some drastic, dramatic changes, and because I have information which I believe will still be very valuable to you."

"Why shouldn't we just throw you back and let them put you on trial? Maybe they wouldn't even do that. I gather they're being selective. Not everyone is going to stand trial."

"Oh, I think they'd want *me*. My name appears on some very sensitive documents. Some have probably been destroyed, but KGB are now talking about opening the files. Some of these are almost certainly already doctored. They'd be given to you, or worse, to the Americans. I've a feeling I would not even get to trial. There'd be an accident. You see, I'm a liability to everyone—to KGB and CIA. To put it melodramatically, I know too much."

"You're not a liability to us as well?"

"Perhaps. I don't know. I do know I can solve some problems for you."

"Such as?"

"Kingfisher. You know about Kingfisher?"

"Some."

"I realize, from when I saw you the other day, you're already aware of a great deal I have to tell you, but I doubt if you have it all. You know who he was—is? Kingfisher?"

"Yes. In a way we have him. At least your former lover has him."

"Here?"

"Not quite yet, no. But . . ."

"Louis Passau is with Herbie?"

"Something like that. Just tell me what your connection is, your affiliation with Louis Passau."

She asked for more coffee, and if he minded her smoking. When she was settled, Ursula Zunder began.

Though she was Russian born, she had lived most of her life in East

Germany, her father having been a senior KGB officer, confidant of many legendary figures of the old Soviet hierarchy. "There are not many active KGB who are women. The old Service was backward about that. Women were used mainly for what you call honey traps. I did that, of course. But I was trained for other things."

In 1985 she had been given what she called a new "legend," which meant a complete identity, with a past, present and foreseeable future. "In fact I had two main legends. You must pay close attention to this as it is very, very important, so you will understand."

On one hand she had been Franziska Bauer, with an apartment in what was then West Berlin, and papers which, if examined and checked on, led a false trail to Stuttgart, Munich, Wiesbaden and back again. "It was so complicated," she told Art, "that only the most tenacious would get past Munich."

There were other, minor, identities, for fallbacks, but her second main legend was as Anna Brüke, whose address was the same apartment as Bauer's in West Berlin. This was her travel name. "If anyone checked on me they would find that I was a senior editor working for *Stern* magazine. I was, as it were, a double. Anna Brüke was a real person."

This was a risky way to do things, but it helped mightily with the immigration authorities when she went in and out of the United States, which was often.

"They had some kind of a line on the real Fraulein Brüke. It was very good. Only once I recall a panic, when I had to leave the United States very quickly. What Herbie would have said, I had to get out in my knickers." She blushed appropriately but a sexual fusion filled the air, not directed at Art. She still had the hots for Herb, he thought. That's what she was telling him.

"On that occasion, the real Anna Brüke made a sudden decision to fly to New York. They knew about it the day it happened and I was out within four hours. The Russian Service could be very good on agent handling."

Art nodded. She was not telling him anything he did not already know. "And you were handling Kingfisher?"

"Of course. There were two of us. A German-born musician, name of Willy Oscar, who was his control in Europe. I did crash meetings when Willy was not around, but mainly I handled him on his home territory. In the U.S.A. Kingfisher was very special for us. He gave some incredible material. Told us almost what the President of the United States was thinking before even the President knew." She added a nice amused smile, to show this was a joke.

"Then what?"

"I felt honored." She lit another cigarette. "I *was* honored. The information he provided was specialist by nature: financial things, the mood of the American military, the latest stuff from the Pentagon, even White House memos. It was different, but very good material."

"What were the nuts and bolts?"

"You mean meetings? Pick ups? This kind of thing?"

He nodded, and she described in detail how she ran Passau in America. The dead drops, and general tradecraft. Then the meetings—sitdowns in an apartment on Lexington Avenue. "Very smart. A beautiful place. It had a kitchen the size of my whole Berlin apartment. It was a dream place. I think the staff—the concierge and service people—considered that I was his mistress."

"And were you?"

Her head went back as though she had been shot, and her eyes flared with anger for a second. She had nice eyes, Art thought. She opened her mouth to speak, then thought better of it.

"Well, were you?" he asked again.

She looked away, then murmured "Yes, on a few occasions."

"So they were right."

"He had many mistresses, and I think he used the Lexington Avenue apartment to entertain them. You're not a woman, Mr. Railton. The man had—has—a singular attraction to women. He radiates power, and that turns people on. I resisted him for a long while, but he expected any woman who would meet with him alone to lie down with him."

"We're talking about a very old man."

"We're talking about a very extraordinary man."

"And he was a good lover?"

She seemed to have recovered some of her humor, giving him a shy smile as she said—"I've known better."

"You met with him, on a regular basis, at the Lexington Avenue apartment?"

"It would be considered regular, yes. About once every three or four months I would fly in. I always stayed at the same hotel—one that the real Fraulein Brüke did not use—the Intercontinental. It was the normal place, though there were at least seven crash meetings when he had something critical to give us. That is seven extra times between eighty and ninety-one."

"The years you handled him, yes?"

"I handled him right up to just before his nintieth birthday, Mr. Railton. Right up to after the August coup. KGB did not shut down overnight you know."

"So, you actually ran him in the U.S.A. from eighty?"

"Correct. But these extra meetings were lumped together, between eighty-seven and eighty-eight."

"And the crash meetings were all at the New York apartment?"

"No. Three of them were. Four took place outside New York. One in Los Angeles, another in San Diego, the third in San Francisco and the fourth in Chicago. He was touring at the time—with his orchestra, or the opera company. We met in hotels."

"You can recall the reasons for these meetings being urgent?"

"As I said, they all took place in eighty-seven and eighty-eight. They were bad years for me. I spent much time running around after him."

"Why the urgency?" Art pressed.

"At the time they appeared to be very important. In retrospect, when we began to reexamine his work, at the end of 1989 and in early ninety, they turned out not to be so important at all. In fact he seemed to be trying to impress us; trying to enhance his importance. This is the real problem with Kingfisher, Mr. Railton. In the final analysis we thought he might be working both sides of the street. That is correct? That is the way you say it, the same as KGB?"

Art frowned, wondering if she was doing a Herbie on him. After all, Herbie had trained her. He gave a curt nod. "Working both sides of the street, yes."

"We knew at the end. I can give you a lot of details. It would take days, weeks even. But we knew. Kingfisher was being run also by CIA and . . ."

"They'd doubled him?"

"I never figured out. I was never given the chance to figure it out—whether it was from the very beginning or only the last few years." She gave a brief smile and stubbed out the cigarette. "No, he wasn't an official double. We knew that. It was something more. He was being run by a small cadre of officers inside CIA. That is what is so strange. Moscow told us they already knew he was under the control of CIA officers. My

colleagues, those who analyzed the information, Willy Oscar and myself
. . . we were told to forget about the CIA involvement."

"Just like that?"

"Exactly like that. Mr. Railton, we were left in no doubt at all that
Louis Passau was some kind of a conduit between a group of high-level
Agency officers and members of KGB."

"For what reason?"

"That's the most interesting part. Senior officers of KGB were talking
to a group of senior officers of CIA right up to the August coup in Moscow
this year. They talked through the direct channel that is Louis Passau: sent
him messages while he sent stuff back to them, directly from the Agency.
I know. I carried the messages. Perhaps you can understand why I am a little afraid, and why Louis Passau should also be frightened now. You want
to hear all the details? It will take a very long time, for it has the ingredi-
ents of a wonderfully complex conspiracy and throws a lot of doubt on
what is happening in my poor split and shattered country now."

In the present, inside the large room of the Captiva Island apartment,
Art Railton stopped talking and leaned back in his chair, while Kruger
and Ms. Curtiss sat, mouths open, incredulous. What Art was telling
them was the kind of intelligence link of which global nightmares are
made, and they knew it.

9

"SO, YOU SEE WE have a tinderbox here." Arthur Railton looked from Herbie to Pucky and back again.

"Towering bloody inferno." Pucky's eyes hinted at battle fatigue.

"Bomb, with the fuse already on injury time. She telling the truth, Ursula?" Herbie sounded as though few people ever told the truth.

"I suspect there's more in heaven and earth than dreamed of in your philosophy, Herb."

"Shakespeare," Herbie informed Pucky, unnecessarily. "Is hard," he frowned, the great forehead almost growling with its deep furrows. "This is writing history: forbidden fruit; poisoned tree."

"If it really is so, then we have a huge conspiracy on our hands; that's the general opinion. And you're right, Herb. It's true secret history and it changes recent events in Eastern Europe." Art shifted uncomfortably. Herbie's interrogation skills told him that Art was unhappy about everything he had told them. It showed in his body language, one arm thrown defensively across his chest, his legs drawn up, face tense.

"They putting Ursula through the mill? Warminster?"

Art nodded. "The mill, mangle and spin dryer. Gus is doing the full business. I spoke with him before coming out here. He's inclined to believe most of it. You catch any of this yet, Herb? From the old man, I mean."

Kruger gave a grunt. "Art, this is like Arabian Nights. I almost signed him up for the book rights. I told you, he's giving me his life, bit by bit. We got to the mid, late 1930s. You read the biographies, so you know that's only the start. He's just gone to New York with Androv and the Manhattan Symphony. Also collected twenty million bucks and passed

Go. Did Not Go To Jail, so probably collected a further two hundred dollars."

"Tomorrow morning I'm going to Monopoly Passau."

"Monopolize, Herb."

"Sure."

RAIN SLASHED AND stippled the long windows of the apartment. Outside, the sky was the color of pewter and the wind lashed at the palm trees, sending sand leaping around the beach.

"Beautiful view. Might as well have gone to Bognor Regis." Passau had been allowed near the window. Herbie would pull him back if any boat came within rifle distance, otherwise it was safe. There was nowhere to hide out there.

"At least it's warm, Lou. This kind of weather bloody perishing in Bognor."

"Bugger Bognor."

"What's next, Lou? You going to tell me some more? You went off to New York with a cool twenty million—and profits from the booze heist— in your bank account. You were Androv's associate director for one year, almost exactly one year. Reading between the lines, you also made a bee-line for the Friends of the Manhattan Symphony, particularly Veronica Duncan. . . ."

"Howells-Duncan, she was double-barreled."

"Howells-Duncan, then. Double-barreled. Mother was chairwoman of Friends of Manhattan Symphony, right? One year, almost exact."

"You know it all, you tell it."

"Come on, Lou. I've figured out how dangerous this is. Start talking."

After a long pause, during which Maestro Passau continued to look out at the view, he began to speak of that time during the fourth decade of the century.

"I got myself a nice little apartment in a service building on Lexington. Nothing showy . . ."

"Not what I heard."

"Later it was showy. Later I bought the apartment next door and had the place redesigned. Knocked down walls. To start with it was simple. Right and proper for associate director."

"So what did you really do during that year? It ended with fireworks. Spectacular."

"I worked. I learned the business."

"Thought you already taught yourself the business."

"Herb, being a good conductor doesn't teach you how to run an orchestra. There's more to it. The organization alone boggles the mind. Very difficult stuff. That I learned."

New York in the thirties was a good place to be. There were still many people, cushioned by creative wealth—as Louis later put it—and these people wanted entertainment. Hollywood thrived and, strangely, so did both classical and popular music. Songs like "We're in the Money," and "Pennies from Heaven" cheered people up on the radio. Great orchestras, like the Manhattan, were in demand. Yet Louis Passau was not as happy as he should have been.

He came into New York like a lion and was, naturally, lionized. In the first six weeks he conducted seven of the ten concerts.

The reviews were outstanding. Passau was the great future hope of American symphony orchestras. He was invited to parties, got his name in the papers.

In particular, members of the management committee of the Friends of the Manhattan Symphony had him to dinner, or cocktails. Louis did not miss the significance of this, for the FMS was the driving force of Boris Androv's orchestra: a cabal of very wealthy people who knew, enjoyed and loved great music enough to pay for it in handsome, tax-deductible, donations. Without the Friends the orchestra could not function, and Louis made an impact on the most influential—for the first six weeks.

In the Captiva apartment he gave a long sigh. "Funny, Herb, it was exactly six weeks. Boris knew what he was doing. Gave me my head, left me to sink or swim, then pulled the rug on me. Six weeks to the day. He was clever, Boris. Had class, a good safe background. A very acceptable man. Happily he didn't know I had money."

Boris Androv sat at his wide desk. On the wall behind him hung a single page from an original Mozart score, mounted and framed in gilt. A gift, two years previously, from the FMS, it was the only decoration in the room, if you did not count the conductor's baton, fashioned in gold, and mounted on an ebony stand which stood on the desk next to a pair of telephones. Maestro Androv did not like clutter.

"Please sit down, Louis. We need to talk."

In his still relative innocence, Louis imagined he was there to discuss the major concerts of the season. He understood how to deal with gangsters, yet somehow he thought of Maestro Androv as a pushover. Instead, he discovered a shark.

"You weren't at the Howells-Duncans' cocktail last night, Boris. You missed a great party."

"So I understand, Louis. Mrs. Howells-Duncan was on the telephone this morning at the crack of dawn. You were apparently paying a great deal of attention to her daughter, Veronica. Louis . . ."

"A lovely girl . . ."

("Herb, she was spectacular. Tiny waist, a figure you'd die for. Tits just right. Willowy, they called her in the gossip columns. Willowy blonde. Gossip columnists haven't changed; they still use clichés.")

"Louis, you're going to have to understand these people," Androv said, very cold, as precise as a Bach concerto. "Veronica Howells-Duncan is only eighteen years of age. . . ."

"Funny, I could have sworn she was much older. She has quite a head on her shoulders."

"I don't think it's her head Mrs. Howells-Duncan's concerned about." Androv said it straight, no hint of amusement.

"Concerned?"

"Louis, she called me to express concern. Grave concern." For the first time, Louis noticed the way Androv moved his body when he spoke. He also managed to express petulance with a little pout of the lips. He had already discovered that Maestro Androv had no sense of humor.

"Why would she . . . ?"

"Express concern, Louis? Wouldn't you express concern if you had a daughter of eighteen who was monopolized at a party by a man almost twice her age? A man whose background is not known. . . ."

"What d'you mean?" Passau had started to get a little testy.

"I mean, Louis, that you're an unknown commodity. Especially to an old family like the Howells-Duncans. There was a small problem, I understand, with Harriet Markus-Cohen."

"Harriet's a grown woman."

"Unfortunately, Miss Markus-Cohen *is* a grown woman, Louis. Grown women talk. Mrs. Howells-Duncan told me she was not going to let her daughter be put at risk, like Harriet."

"I don't know what you're getting at, Boris."

"Well, the story is that you and Harriet Markus-Cohen had started a . . . how can I put it? . . . a relationship."

"Boris, I'm a full-grown man also."

"Then, as a full-grown man you're going to have to learn some social graces, Louis. The people who support the Manhattan are what the newspapers rather commonly call 'old money.' They have breeding and lineage. You have to understand that I am a third-generation Androv. I would be quite acceptable—I *am* quite acceptable—to these people. I would be welcomed into their families as a son-in-law. My father was a banker of considerable reputation."

"And my father was . . ." Passau blurted in anger.

"Your father was exactly what, Louis?" Androv had assumed his most chilling, ruthless, persona. "Nobody knows what your father was. *You*, on the other hand, are a gifted orchestra conductor. But that's all. These people—people like the Howells-Duncans, the Lowells, Bridges, the Markus-Cohens—they are a different matter. They will admire you. Pay money to hear the orchestra under your baton but, never, never, will you be one of them. They'd as soon welcome a Hollywood producer into their midst as yourself. You have to understand that they would never allow you to cross that great social divide and become part of the family."

"Who said anything about becoming part of any family, Boris?"

"That's another facet of the same problem. It appears that you suggested some kind of liaison with Veronica Howells-Duncan. Her parents have absolutely forbidden her to see you on her own. It's left a nasty taste in the mouths of some of our most important benefactors. You're going to work, Louis. Work, and keep your head down. As director of this orchestra—which I built with my own acumen and hard work—I am telling you that you will now refuse all invitations to parties. You'll be too busy, in any case. You'll be rehearsing the orchestra night and day. You'll also be spending time on the organizational side. You'll get to know everybody in the Manhattan, from the juniors who handle scores, to the drivers. I'll see to it. And, if you don't like it, you can give me your resignation—now."

In fact there were no invitations for some time after the first six weeks. No public invitations, anyway. In private it was a different matter. That very same night, after the meeting with Androv, Louis returned to his apartment and found a note, left with the porter. It was from Veronica Howells-Duncan who wrote—

My Dear Mr. Passau,

I am afraid my parents do not consider me a grown woman at the age of almost nineteen. For some ridiculous reason they have forbidden me to see you in private, as we arranged last night. I simply think you should know this, before I come to your apartment, as we discussed. I am taking no notice of their restrictions. You are a talented and brilliant man, and I would like to see more of you.

"And she did see more of me, Herb. She saw just about every inch of me."

Herbie nodded him on, which meant he was urging him back to the second half of the 1930s. It was "What then?" time again.

Louis Passau was not going to take the obvious snub lying down. Well, some of it he took lying down, because two days after Androv had outlined his future, Veronica Howells-Duncan became his willing lover, just as Harriet Markus-Cohen had done—and continued to do—together with the wife of one of the younger members of the FMS and a red-headed waitress who worked at a deli just down the street.

For several months, Passau juggled his full and agile sex life. It took some juggling, because Androv, true to his word, made sure that every hour of every day, and often well into the night, his associate director was occupied. Louis, to be fair, had never been afraid of hard work. He had learned many tricks on the streets of New York and in the clubs of Chicago. In reality, the upper crust of New York society, plus the pretensions of Boris Androv, were nothing to him. He decided to fight in a more subtle manner for he realized that he *had* made a grave social gaffe.

The likes of Veronica Howells-Duncan, Harriet Markus-Cohen and the FMS wife—the dark and nubile Sue Lee Howard, whose husband was a Texan, in oil—could teach Passau many things, and he was, as they said in theatrical circles, a quick study.

"You know, Herb, the best way to learn a foreign language is to learn from a lover," he said in the present, with the rain teeming down on the Gulf Coast. "This is what I learned from those kind and generous ladies. I learned about things other than music. Silly things, but things that appeared to matter. You ever notice how some Americans are more class-conscious than the Brits? It was the same, in Russia, believe it or not. But, then, people had more to lose in Russia."

The silly things included such banalities as food, wine, the way to dress, the books to read, the artistic events to attend. In those early days, Passau had thrown invitations to private viewings and theatrical first nights into the wastepaper basket. Now, he attended the more prestigious of these. Usually he went alone, and his clothes gradually altered from the flashy and somewhat vulgar to those of impeccable taste.

He would see his lovers at many of these events. He would acknowledge them, but never speak with them, or show any close friendship to any one person.

Passau knew how to take hints. Though he was rarely seen in public with a woman, he did lunch and dine at the best places, always tipping handsomely. Maître d's, waiters and doormen remembered him and greeted him by name, and it was duly noted that he dined with big names in the world of music. He met people like the Gershwins, Maestro Koussevitzky and, on one occasion only, Toscanini himself.

Passau told other stories of those meetings. Oscar Levant, pianist and wit, close friend of the Gershwins, had once commented, in answer to Louis excusing himself from a lunch date because of the pressures of work—"So little time, and so little to do."

He would often see Androv at private viewings and, when there was no concert to conduct, at first nights, or across a crowded restaurant. The Director of the Manhattan Symphony Orchestra treated him with an almost off-hand disdain at first, but, as the months went by, he was forced to acknowledge his associate director, if not as an equal, at least as a colleague. After six months, Androv actually allowed Passau one concert to himself.

They performed the *Tannhäuser* overture, Chopin's *Fantasia on Polish Airs*, and Sibelius' First Symphony, which was relatively unknown to New York audiences. The press was ecstatic. The *New York Times* actually asked why Maestro Androv was keeping his treasure off the podium. Others were later to follow suit. There had been over fifteen minutes of applause after the Sibelius which, one writer claimed, was the musical feast of the year.

Androv remained cool—if anything a shade cooler—and with reason. Passau had not watched and learned from those hard Chicago gangsters in vain. He saw through Androv's facade towards the end of the summer, but he was also concerned about one aspect of his own love life. Veronica Howells-Duncan was not only getting careless regarding their secret, but also began to suggest they come out into the open. "Please, Louis, I'm sure my parents will treat you differently. They were so enthusiastic after the concert," she told him one evening as they lay in bed after the main event, smoking cigarettes. "In fact, I think they've guessed we're still seeing one another."

The line, thrown away lightly, started the alarms buzzing in Passau's head. "Why would you think that?" He did not look at her. It was six in the evening, his one afternoon off. In two hours he was due to oversee a rehearsal.

"Oh, I don't know. Something my father said."

"And?"

"Oh, after the concert he asked me outright if I had ever seen you again. . . . Well, Louis, after the row and all that stupidity . . . you know, when they said I was never to see you alone."

Louis grunted, blew a stream of smoke towards the ceiling, and turned his face towards her. "You didn't tell him, did you?"

She smiled at him in the dim light of the room. "I was absolutely non-committal, darling. But I really do think you should see them. I mean there's no reason why we shouldn't marry next spring."

He had not planned on marrying next spring, or even the spring after that, and the conversation had taken what he considered to be an ominous turn. Certainly, Veronica would be a catch for him and, of all his lovers, she, undoubtedly, had become the best. After all, had he not trained her himself? Marriage to her could even push his career along, but another wife. . . ? The thought almost appalled him. In any case, he was certain that the powerful Mr. and Mrs. Douglas C. Howells-Duncan would fight to the last drop of their blood to remove him from their daughter's life.

"Louis, you're faraway. Penny for your thoughts."

"Nothing. Nothing important, my darling. Nothing at all."

"Then pay attention to me." Her hand closed around him and she began the lovemaking all over again.

After she left, swearing her undying love, as ever, Louis dressed for the rehearsal. Androv was going to be there, and it was Androv who had become his real target. He had some definite ideas about the Director of the Manhattan Symphony Orchestra. No firm proof, but sound theories that, should he get his hands on proof, would put the fear of God into Maestro Androv. It would only be a matter of time before he set things in motion. Perhaps, he thought, it would be wise to begin soon.

As things turned out that evening, the ball was about to land in his court. Quite unwittingly, Boris Androv was playing into his hands.

"I'd watched Boris," he told Kruger. "Watched him for months. He was clever, a born man of intrigue. . . ."

"Machiavellian," Herbie said.

"That also. A brilliant musician, but I had a pretty good idea what else he was. I was not quite sure how he got away with it, but past experience told me he was involved in some pretty strange things."

"Strange things?" Herbie asked.

"Well, not strange these days. Simple, Herb. I thought he was gay— not the best sexual preference in the 1930s." He gave a little laugh, laced with irony. "I was wrong. It was worse for him than just being gay."

In those days, the headquarters of the Manhattan Symphony Orchestra was in a big old concert hall in the East Fifties. Originally it had been built as a theater, but the investment corporation had run out of money before completing the project. Androv and his supporters had taken over the debt, finished the building, and made the first headquarters for the MSO.

That night they were rehearsing the Beethoven Ninth. Androv was to conduct it on the following Saturday—this was a Thursday in early September—and the great man sat in at the rehearsal. He had taken to doing this, and Louis knew exactly why. If he, Passau, rehearsed a piece first, with Androv on the sidelines, Maestro Androv would get the full value of Maestro Passau's originality.

As they came to the exultant "Ode To Joy," at the close of the piece, Louis remembered the first time he had heard it, with his teacher, the huge, boisterous Hamovitch, in New York all those years ago.

He glanced towards Androv and caught a glint in the man's eyes. He could not say what it was, but he knew that the Director of the Manhattan Symphony Orchestra was looking at him in the same way some of the worst hitmen from the Chicago days looked at an unsuspecting victim. It was a cross between jealousy, hate and a secret knowledge that something catastrophically bad was about to happen. It was a look that chilled the blood.

He missed a beat, the orchestra and choir went slightly ragged, then recovered, but Louis Passau was holding one hand across his eyes, feigning illness. He swayed, and clung to the desk in front of him.

"You all right, Louis?" Androv was beside him, one of his pudgy hands wrapped around his associate's left forearm.

"I feel faint, Boris. Maybe something has disagreed with me. I shall have to rest."

"I'll take over. Don't worry about a thing, Louis. I'll finish the rehearsal. Just go up to my office and rest. I'll drive you home."

"Maybe I should go home now."

"No! No, don't do that. I'll take you. Another hour should see this finished. Just go to my office and lie down."

He was too quick, too instant. There was even an undercurrent of anxiety in his voice. Passau felt fine, of course, but thoughts flashed through his mind. Had Androv planned some revenge, similar to the food poisoning in Los Angeles? Why was he so concerned that Louis should wait for him to finish? Boris Androv was behaving in a strange and unusual manner, repeating that Louis should lie down and wait for him. He virtually told Louis that he must not even attempt to go home by himself.

Passau pretended to stagger from the rehearsal hall, but the moment he was outside, he ran. Down the stairs, into the street, hailing a cab, even telling the driver that there was an extra five bucks in it if he could get back to Lexington Avenue in record time.

There was nobody on duty in the lobby of the apartment building when he arrived back. He took the elevator to his floor, and was somehow not surprised when he saw the door to his apartment was slightly open.

Gently he pushed at the door.

In the darkness, he saw the beam of a flashlight, and the shape of a bulky figure bent over the small bureau—which stood in the large vestibule—where Passau kept important papers and correspondence. He switched on the lights and spoke, before the man had a chance to turn around.

"I'll blow you apart if you even twitch," Louis whispered, using the threatening, calm voice he had heard from some of the Gennas' most dangerous men.

"Just put your hands on your head and don't try anything stupid or you'll be spending the night in the morgue." Louis was convincing enough. He even felt a slight frisson of fear within himself.

The figure straightened up and Louis moved forward, standing just behind the intruder, a finger jabbed into the man's back as his left hand expertly frisked him. He had a Colt revolver in a shoulder holster, and a billfold containing a private investigator's I.D. The name on the I.D. showed as Robert D. Flynn.

"Okay, Robert—or do you prefer Bob . . . ?"

"Bob, my friends call me Bob." The accent was New York. Fast, excited and afraid New York. You could smell the sudden gust of fear as though it had almost voided the man's bowels.

"Okay, Bob. Move very slowly into my living room. Keep your hands on top of your head and walk towards the easy chair over there. Please don't try for a medal. The man who taught me to shoot could take the eyes out of a snake at fifty paces."

He kicked the door closed, and seconds later had Robert D. Flynn sitting quietly, hands on head. Mr. Flynn did not look happy with life. He had ex-cop written all over him: pugnacious jaw, blue-veined nose, big heavy-lidded melancholy eyes which were, somehow, alert, moving slowly but constantly, as though searching for a way out. Flynn was also overweight, with a heavy beer gut popping over the belt of his trousers; his shoes were scuffed and worn, and the cheap gray suit deserved a long-service citation.

"Private Investigations Unlimited," Passau read from the I.D. "There a lot of you working for this outfit, or just you, Bob?"

It was not all that warm, but Bob Flynn was sweating a lot. His eyes still moved constantly, and he licked his lips, but said nothing. His thin hairline was positively soggy.

"Want me to call the cops, Bob?"

"I've got a P.I. license there. The cops know who I am." He sounded dry in the throat.

"So they'll tell me I've shot a shamus. Tough. I caught you in here going through my desk." Passau cocked the Colt revolver.

"Look . . ." Bob Flynn's eyes began to dance around again, not really settling anywhere, certainly not on Louis Passau.

"I'm sure the cops love you, Bob. Though they might not take too kindly to you breaking into my apartment. You give me one good reason why I shouldn't shoot you, then call the local precinct?"

"Look, Mr. Passau, I . . ."

"You know my name. That's a good start, Bob. Maybe we can do business."

"I didn't mean no harm. Give me a break. I'm just doing my job, Mr. Passau . . ." He did not sound sincere enough to Louis.

"And what is your job, Bob? As a private dick, what're you looking for?"

"He said you wouldn't be back until much later."

"No, Bob, that isn't the answer. I asked what you were looking for."

Flynn hung his head and refused to meet Passau's eyes.

"Okay, Bob, you're not going to tell me, so I'll call the cops now, and when they arrive I'll tell them you tried to make a break for it so I shot you." He thought he could detect the tiny beginnings of a smirk on Flynn's lips. "Bob, you don't believe me. Now that's not a smart move. Let me show you." He moved the revolver slightly to the right and fired one shot, praying that nobody in the other apartments would report the noise. The bullet clipped Flynn's left shoulder. He gave a fat squeak of pain, dropped his hands from his head and clutched at where a small trickle of blood showed against the ripped cloth.

"Hands on your head, Bob." Passau really had not even meant to graze him. "You stupid bastard!" Flynn mouthed. "I oughta . . ."

"The next one'll take your head off." He lifted the gun, closing his left eye.

"No! No, Mr. Passau! No, look I'll tell you."

"Let me tell *you*, Mr. Flynn. My guess is that you're employed either by Mr. and Mrs. Howells-Duncan, or Mr. Boris Androv. If I were a betting man, I'd probably go for Androv. You were told to get some solid information—letters, or some such—which proved an involvement between me and Miss Veronica Howells-Duncan. . . ."

"No! Yes! Something like that. Can I look at my shoulder, it's burning like hell?"

"Keep your hands on your head. And what do you mean, no-yes? Which is it?"

"I'm employed by an attorney, not by the people you said." Flynn was certainly very frightened now. He thought he had come up against a crazy man—which, to some extent he had. "And, yes, I was told to look for letters, photographs. You and the Howells-Duncan girl. They showed me a picture of her."

"And you didn't find any."

"No."

"So what happens now? No proof, so what are you to do next?"

"I had to watch you. See if I could put you and the girl together. That's all. There wasn't anything more than that. Christ, you can't kill a guy for . . ."

"Oh, but I can, Bob. Who's the attorney?"

"Guy called Gold. Big law firm. Spinebrucker, Havlish and Gold. Very big. Asher Gold. He's a junior partner. . . ."

"And how did he choose a one-man operation like you, Bob? Big law firms employ uptown investigators. . . ."

Flynn hesitated, then, as he continued to look into the barrel of the revolver, he relented. "Asher Gold owed me a favor. It was my turn to collect."

"And this Asher Gold was working for whom, Bob?"

Another pause, then a change of heart. Passau kept the gun leveled straight at his head. "He mentioned this guy Androv. Just him, I don't know about the others."

Passau nodded. "So you calmly broke in here and went through my desk. What was he paying you?"

"Twenty a day, plus expenses."

Louis laughed out loud. "Twenty a day? You must be crazy, Bob. *Twenty* a day?"

"I was broke."

"Even so. I'd pay you far more than that but, unhappily, I can't trust you, can I?" What a shame. I'd pay you twenty grand for information on friend Androv. Twenty Gs *plus* expenses. What a pity."

"You would?" The pain in his shoulder must have eased. Passau had his complete attention now.

"I *would* have. How can I possibly trust you, after this?"

"I'd take this guy Androv to pieces for twenty grand, Mr. Passau. Take him to pieces like a car engine. Put him together again for the same price. Everything included."

"But how can I trust you, Mr. Flynn?"

In the here and now, on Captiva Island, old Louis Passau gave a long chuckle. "This idiot, Herb, was so frightened. I played with him for an hour. When we finally came to terms and worked out a deal, I knew it was a risk. He could have walked straight out of my apartment and gone to Gold. He could even have reported to the police. Said I'd shot him. There were a dozen things he could have done, but I figured the man was greedy."

"So you just let him walk out?"

Passau chuckled again. The sound came from deep within his memory. "Do I look like I was born yesterday, Herb? No, he signed a document. I don't know if it was legal or not, but he signed it. He also spent the night in my apartment, and I stood over him when he called this lawyer, Gold. I got to know Asher Gold quite well later on. Anyway, I locked Bob Flynn in my guest room for the night, brought him out to make the call, then locked him up again while I went to the bank. I bought him, like Mephistopheles. I bought his soul and his silence. He was mine until the day he died.

"He was even there when Boris came to make sure I was okay. That was the real test. About two hours after I clipped Flynn's shoulder, Boris turned up, looking anxious. My man, Flynn, could have yelled and caused one hell of a stink, but he stayed quietly in the guest room. Like a mouse. Boris looked relieved as well. He'd obviously told this shmuck Gold that I'd be out until late. He must've really been frightened when I walked out of the rehearsal. He went away happy."

"And you, Maestro, put this dumb private eye onto Androv? You took that risk?"

"Calculated risk, Herbie. By the time Flynn left my apartment I *knew* that I owned him. The only doubt was whether he could do the job or not. That worried me some. But, in the end . . ."

"In the end, Boris Androv resigned."

"Right, Herb."

"Why?"

"Underage girls, Herb. The dirty little bastard wasn't gay, he had a taste for very young girls. You see, one thing, he wasn't very well built, if you understand what I mean. That didn't excuse him. He was a real mess."

"Tell me about it. Then what, Lou?"

"Then Flynn turned out to be quite good. He had information in less than a month, proof—nice big blown-up glossy photographs—in two months."

"Then what, Lou?"

"Then I took the bugger apart, Herb. To the cleaners I took him."

"And he gave you the Manhattan Symphony Orchestra on a plate. I read the books, Lou. Boris Androv shakes music world by retiring. Shock! Horror! Gives up in favor of Maestro Louis Passau. You were really on your way, Lou."

"It wasn't as easy as the books make out." Passau's head came up. He was not smiling. "I'll tell you what happened, yes?"

"Please."

"First, I bought a Rolls-Royce and hired a chauffeur. How about that? The Friends of the Manhattan Symphony Orchestra sat up. Eyes popped out all over the place."

"What next, Lou?"

10

"AND I ALWAYS THOUGHT of musicians—great musicians—as having temperaments but being basically nice people." Pucky turned her head towards Herbie, on the pillow.

"I believe most of them are. Passau's an aberration, but I think he almost met his match in Boris Androv. Musicians and actors, they're not like ordinary people but, like ordinary people, they carry their own devils with them through life."

They had agreed, before arrival on Captiva Island, that Pucky should continue to listen from another room as Herbie did the interrogations. Passau would be inclined to slow down, show off, and embellish if she was physically present, so she had spent the day with their makeshift recording apparatus in the third bedroom, listening through headphones.

Kruger had also brought his bits and pieces of electronics from Virginia. On the first night, he spent three hours connecting a personal alarm system to cover the main door and the two windows that were relatively accessible from the ground. While he knew Art Railton's team was probably as good as they came, he still relied on belt and braces.

After they had eaten and got Passau to bed, Art arrived at the front door. Within minutes Herbie knew that the gentlemen from London had almost certainly wired the apartment before Pucky and he had arrived with the Maestro. They probably had the other apartment electronically covered as well.

Sod 'em, Kruger thought. They would certainly have wired the bedrooms. That would give them fun listening when he went at it with Pucky so, before they finally retired for the night, he had made a visual sweep and, sure enough, there was a tiny radio bug neatly inserted into a picture frame near the bed.

He removed it and flushed it down the nearest lavatory. It took a lot of paper and five flushes to get rid of the little electronic ear.

Art had seated himself in the main room, almost calling a meeting of three to order. Herbie considered that young Railton was becoming a slight pain, the man from Head Office letting them know he was in charge.

"Herb," he began, his face friendly but tone firm, leaving no doubt that he was the boss. "Herb, we're going to have to move the old boy on. Cut through the dross. Leapfrog to the things that matter."

That was the clincher that Art was listening in. There was little Herbie could do about it. He shrugged, "You want to try, Art? The Maestro says *everything* matters; that we'll only understand if he confesses his whole life." He scratched his big head. "Actually it's a question of *me* understanding. He just won't give it to anyone else."

"Then you'll have to find a way. We've got about three more days here."

"Three days?"

"We're trying to set up a quiet exit."

"England, home and beauty?"

"That is the safest bet, under the circumstances. London's approved it, so it's really only a matter of time—like it's only a matter of time before they'll be on to us."

"Who? The rogue Agency people or the Mob?"

"Both, I should imagine, and I want you to be further up the road with Passau before we're forced to break off the work again."

"I hope, sincerely, that London isn't up to trickery." Herbie gave his famous growling scowl. "Put Passau in Warminster with Gus Keene's crew and he'll clam up."

"They *are* aware." Art sounded an inch or two off-hand.

"They better be bloody aware. I wouldn't put it past the old reprobate to turn his face to the wall and die, just to spite everyone. In any case, Art, *how* important is all this?"

"You've asked before, old chum. And we've told you. There are several reasons for knowing the truth—a link between the August coup and the Agency—the long and winding secret road of history. That, and more. If we prove there's been any funny business, we have a mighty strong lever, and we need a damned great lever if we're to keep our end up in the nineties."

Herb gave another growl. "This is still all Cold War tradecraft and sheninigans. . . ."

"Shenanigans, Herb."

"Whatever. We're behaving like the generals at the start of World War II—when they thought it would be like the trench warfare of 1914 to eighteen. Why can't we just talk to the Agency?"

"You know why we can't do that, Herb."

"Okay, just playing the devil's advocate."

They talked a little more before Art left, with another instruction for Herbie to get a move on.

Pucky fell asleep quite quickly, but Kruger lay there in the dark, smoking, his mind turning over the final part of Passau's duel with Boris Androv. The Passau version.

Androv's sexual tastes turned out to be quite revolting, even to Louis Passau in his old age—and the old Louis was not normally squeamish. Androv liked girls of around twelve or thirteen years of age, and there were plenty of people—even Louis was amazed—who would supply them.

It seemed that the concert hall–struck mother, or choirmistress, would do almost anything to further a talented child's career. Androv had a steady stream of girls who came directly from choirs or music societies, even schools which had earmarked a budding prodigy. Sometimes their mothers condoned, in an attempt to curry favor and see their daughters set on the road to success. Embryo singers and instrumentalists passed through Androv's Riverside Drive apartment where he would hear them sing or play, give advice and instruction, and then suggest further, and very different kinds, of instruction, which took place in his bedroom.

"He liked to do rather unpleasant things with these kids, Herb. I tell you, even I was revolted." Passau showed no emotion on his face as he talked about the dubious nature of Androv's trips to the bedroom with girls on the verge of puberty.

"Can't understand how he got away with it, except people didn't talk so much about child abuse in those days—didn't *know* so much. I often wonder what scars he left. If some of those kids suffered permanent psychological damage."

Herbie wondered how many scars Passau, himself, had left during his journey through the world's bedrooms. "The private dick, this Flynn, he got all you wanted, Lou?" he asked.

Passau nodded. "He turned out to be quite good, if you gave him enough money. It was, I think, the profit incentive. He watched, and he managed to get pictures. I never asked how he did that. Better I shouldn't know, 'cuz it was probably by some illegal act. But when I knew we really had the goods on Androv, I made another move."

What Passau talked about was a visit to the law office of Spinebrucker, Havlish and Gold. "I went straight to the top, not to Asher Gold. That wouldn't have been a good move. I spent a few hours with Martin Spinebrucker, the senior partner. I'm still with them. Martin's son, Harold, looks after my business now. But that first visit put the cat among the pigeons."

"Let me guess. You told them you had money?"

Passau gave a smile of satisfaction and threw a sly look in Herbie's direction.

BEFORE THAT FIRST visit to the tall, patrician-looking Martin Spinebrucker, Louis Passau had bought the car and hired his first servant. The car was a Rolls-Royce—a Sedanca de Ville, gray, large and luxurious. The servant was a chauffeur-bodyguard, Thomas "Tiny" Dyson. Recommended by Bob Flynn, Dyson had tried his hand at being a professional boxer, but had scruples about falling down when told to by his manager. He stayed with Passau for a decade, and his very first outing in the Rolls was to drive his new employer to the law offices of Spinebrucker, Havlish and Gold, situated near Wall Street.

Passau's arrival had obviously been noted, for Martin Spinebrucker seemed to be in an almost fawning mood. A Rolls spoke of money and, if Spinebrucker had one true love in life, it was money. He fawned even more when Passau left the building. Louis described him as "A stiff conservative prick. Like he had a broomstick rammed up his ass. This guy, Herb, he was all good looks, gray hair. What the Brits call old school. A royal pain, but good at his job. The whole firm is good still."

"He also had links with the Manhattan Symphony . . ."

Passau ignored that, riding over Herbie's comment, as if it was not appropriate yet. "You see, Herb, I had been very careful. Moved the money around a good deal: split it up, opened several accounts, spread it thinly."

During the week before his meeting with Spinebrucker, Passau had closed most of his accounts, softened up a banker who was on the Friends of the Manhattan Symphony board, and presented to him a picture of great wealth.

"I didn't say any of it was Capone money, naturally." Passau bounced on his chair, having fun. "Nor did I let anyone know any of it had come from Rita. The papers in Hollywood had been muzzled about Rita's will, and her wealth." He shook his head. "You know, her father thought it was not really gentlemanly to have money. An odd throwback. Anyway, as far as the bank was concerned, it was a personal fortune: a family fortune." He gave a toothy grin that spoke of dental work costing thousands of dollars. "Confidentiality," he laughed aloud. "Confidentiality means nothing. I imagine by the time I walked into Martin's office he knew what was in the bank—down to the last cent. I left the lawyers' office that day as a valued—very valued—customer."

Passau put everything in Spinebrucker's hands. By the evening he was certain that practically the entire upper echelon of the Friends of the Manhattan Symphony knew he was a multimillionaire. Better still, that his money was old money, which made him respectable. He went straight back to the Lexington Avenue apartment and called Androv. He wanted a meeting with his boss. That very day. As quickly as possible.

"You would have been beside yourself, Herb. He must've already got the news that I was not the struggling movie composer he imagined me to be. He was full of that nauseating camaraderie you get from people who think they're on to a good thing. I had an envelope containing forty big glossy pictures of him with the little girls. I took it with me, of course. Went round to his place like the speed of light."

Androv greeted him like a long-lost friend: an old and valued intimate. There was even champagne on ice. The tubby little man, with his too-perfect head of curly hair, assumed Passau wanted to talk about the winter season of concerts. He even began ticking off details, saying they would share the podium. Fifty-fifty. He also mentioned that the Markus-Cohens had been in touch that morning. They were holding a private dance the following week, in honor of their daughter Harriet's twenty-fourth birthday, and they wanted to be sure that Androv brought the nice Mr. Passau with him.

Louis sat there, among the antiques and paintings which were Androv's pride. When the Maestro began to run out of words Louis calmly opened his briefcase, took out the envelope and began to place the photographs, one at a time face upwards on the floor.

To begin with, Androv did not take in what he was seeing. His brain refused to process the information, and his eyes just did not believe what they saw. He looked down at the photographs, looked away, gave a nervous laugh, looked down for a second time.

He became very still. The silence grew, like a great thunderhead of wrath which would blow the room to fragments.

When Androv spoke, it was an anticlimax. "Where did you . . . ? Why . . . ?" Then the full realization, "How much do you want, you shit. . . ! You snake . . . ! You . . . ! How much?" His head was thrown back, and what he lacked in height was made up for by the pose of total arrogance.

"How much?" Passau asked smoothly. "How *much*, Boris? I don't want money."

It took a few seconds for it to sink in. Then the full force of his situation exploded in his head. First, he began to shout—"Damned if I'll let you . . . ! Do what you like with the damned pictures. . . ! Nobody's going to believe you. . . ! Do what you like. . . !"

Passau slowly began to pick the photographs from the floor. "Okay, Boris. If you want a really hard time . . ."

Androv had turned, striding across the room, his shoulders set square. He seemed to be taking paces unnaturally long for his short legs.

For a moment, Passau thought his bluff had been called. That Androv was mad enough to risk exposure. His eyes were still on the photographs when Androv launched himself back across the room. This time there was a long knife in his right hand, the blade flashing as he raised his arm over his head.

Louis moved, motivated by the fear that Boris had gone crazy. He managed to block the sweeping arm with his own forearm. He twisted aside, rolling out of the enraged conductor's reach, hearing the knife thud onto the floor.

Androv was fighting for his life. Passau reached out and grabbed for both of the man's wrists, but his hands were shrugged aside. He twisted away and was half onto his feet when his adversary came in close, grappling with him on the floor.

This time he managed to grasp the right wrist. Androv had the knife again, struggling to free his hand and bring the blade down into Passau's throat. As he fought, Louis began to cringe away, the point of the knife only inches from his windpipe as they rolled, locked together, across the carpet.

Finally, panting and straining, Passau threw Androv's body from him, brought his knee into the man's groin and wrenched the wrist so that the knife fell from his hand. He slammed his knee up again, catching Androv below the jaw. This time, the conductor stayed down, winded, groaning and whimpering.

"The photographs . . ." Passau towered above him, the pictures in one hand and the knife in the other. He was also gasping for breath. It had been a short confrontation, but he was trembling from head to foot. His limbs seemed somehow to be divorced from the rest of his body. In many ways none of it was real to him. "The photographs go to the newspapers, together with a report, at noon tomorrow," he said between gulps for air. "At the same time, copies will be delivered to each and every member of the FMS." Another gasp. "Boris, this is about the fitness to be in charge. You are a pervert and not fit to clean streets, let alone head the wonderful organization which you have built. Well, you built it, now you've destroyed it. Name me as your successor and nothing will happen. The photographs and negatives will be returned to you. You have until noon tomorrow." He walked slowly from the room, half expecting Androv to jump him again.

"You know the rest, Herbie. Need I say more?"

"For the record, Lou. Just for the record."

Boris Androv called a press conference that same night. He pleaded ill health and his doctor's advice. The whole thing hit the papers the next morning. The man who had built the undisputedly best symphony orchestra in the United States had resigned his directorship and handed over all rights to his Associate Director, Louis Passau.

"I never saw him again, Herb. Never."

"He died, Lou. One month later according to the biographies."

"Sure." Like swatting a fly. "There was irony. He actually was sick. Fatally sick. Cancer." Passau gave a little smile. "If I had waited, what then? Certainly little Boris Androv would never have allowed me to take over. If I had waited . . . ?"

"But you didn't wait, Lou. It all happened. You had control of the Manhattan. Then there was the great row."

"Row?"

"In the books it was a row."

"What row?"

"Firing over thirty members of the orchestra. Firing them, changing the orchestra's name, and starting work on the rebuilding of what became the Passau Center."

"That was no row, Herb. It was a small disagreement. The people I fired were all Androv's musicians. Men and women I'd had trouble with already. Their contracts had run out, so I didn't renew them. I simply hired new people, better people. My people."

He also went to the zoning and building authorities, with plans to restructure the old theater which was the Manhattan's headquarters. By 1938 it was completed: a great four-tiered edifice; very modern, looking like the superstructure of an ocean liner, with rehearsal facilities, concert hall, an opera house and offices. It was the most modern concert complex in New York. Possibly in the world. People still went to just look around it. The views from the huge long curving windows were incredibly beautiful. If you stood in one of the sweeping, half-moon shaped spaces outside the concert hall or the opera house, you had the impression of being on some majestic airship, or futuristic aircraft, for you seemed to be floating over the city. It was a trompe l'oeil conceived by Passau himself, and, naturally, the building was renamed The Passau Center for the Performance of Musical Arts. At the time, people wrote that this was an ugly, tautologous name for such an amazing building. Most called it simply the Passau Center.

While the building was being erected and refurbished, the orchestra toured the United States and Europe. Within a year, it had a new name—The Passau Symphony Orchestra of America. Louis Passau had arrived, and was hailed from that moment as America's greatest asset in serious music.

He was invited to the White House on several occasions. The orchestra gave a charity concert in Washington, D.C., and the President and Mrs. Roosevelt were the Maestro's greatest fans. In London, there was a Royal Command performance: Louis was presented to the king and queen; he traveled to France, Italy, Spain, Portugal, Denmark, Finland and Sweden. He met every living composer and symphonic conductor of note. He was invited, though not asked to perform, by the rising Nazi regime in Germany, and did not cross into Russia, though he was invited—by Stalin, no less.

"Hitler's people," Passau spat at Herbie. "They gave me permission to come in, but barred me from conducting. My orchestra could give a concert, but I could not be on the podium. So I didn't even go home. Didn't even see what was left of my family."

After Europe, there were other concerts in the United States: special benefits, dedications to charities. The dazzling, never-ending firework that was Louis Passau began to throw splashes of color into the air. A legend had been born and had also come of age in a few short years.

"You also married Veronica Howells-Duncan, Lou."

"Sure. Yes. We married. I made an honest woman of her. She was very happy. Doted on me, Herb."

"You weren't happy?"

"I was like a pig in shit, Herb. I had Veronica, a new apartment on Fifth Avenue, and the refurbished place on Lexington. I used to see Harriet Markus-Cohen there every Thursday afternoon when I was in New York. But we traveled a lot in those first years. Veronica stuck to me like a leech. Couldn't get rid of her." He beamed across at Herbie. "Until I bought Woodstoke Hall. That was a masterstroke. Kept her busy for a long time."

That was also in 1938, Herbie recalled. The same year as the Passau Center was opened with a gala concert. Woodstoke Hall was a ten-acre estate near Rhinebeck, looking out onto the Hudson Valley. A wonderful house that some tycoon had brought from England in 1901: transporting it brick by brick, stone by stone, and timber by timber, each numbered and marked so that it could be rebuilt in a spectacular location. It was a fifteenth-century manor house. Even the windows were original, though the tycoon had improved the heating system and put in electricity before he was wiped out in the Wall Street crash.

Passau gave his young wife a free hand and she made it into the ultimate showplace. Louis talked about it now, on Captiva Island, with a certain fondness, though Veronica had kept it in the divorce settlement.

Then he seemed to dry up, looking moodily out to sea until Herbie asked, "What then, Lou?"

"I don't want to talk no more, Herb. Let's listen to some music and have lunch."

It was barely noon. Passau was either being lazy or stalling. Herb plumped for the latter for the Maestro had a brooding look, the kind he now recognized as the prelude to a moment of truth.

"We go on a little longer, Lou. Hardly been at it for two hours. So you were a busy man, a famous man with a wife and a mistress. . . ."

"Several mistresses. You think I just played around with Harriet?"

"Okay, several mistresses. You were king of the castle, Lou, so what next?"

"Not much. I was launched. I became a different person. You change when it all happens, you know. That's what they mean by the secret of success. The secret is that you change. Worked hard, played hard. It's in the two books. You read it, you know it."

Kruger suddenly pounced with a question from the past, and scored a goal, hit the bull's-eye, won more than a Kewpie doll. What was it, Passau had said? "I didn't even go home. Didn't even see what was left of my family."

"You haven't mentioned your cousins lately, Lou. Your long-lost cousins. Remember? David, Rebecca and Rachel. You think about them, get in touch with them again?"

There was an extraordinarily long pause.

"You a fucking mind reader?" Passau did not even glance in his direction.

"What next, Lou? What about your beloved cousins?"

"I wrote when I had time." He seemed to have recovered his equilibrium. "David wrote now and again. I pleaded with them to let me bring them over. We like it here, they wrote back. Everything is fine. Sure it's fine, I wrote them. With Hitler in power it must be great. Laugh every minute."

"So you were concerned about your cousins?"

"Concerned? What's concerned, Herbie? Went out of my mind with worry. I threatened, tried to seduce. Everything to get them out. I even wrote to people I knew had pull in Germany. Why did I even bother?" He still would not meet Kruger's eye.

"And, Lou?"

"Okay." A long, shuddering sigh.

Here we go, Herbie thought. Jackpot.

"It was a Thursday." Long pause. For a moment Herbie thought he would not continue. Then—

"I remember it was a Thursday. . . ."

"The day you used to meet Harriet in the Lexington Avenue apartment. Thursday afternoon."

"That's right. I remember also, I was working on the schedules for the winter concerts. It was late September. Thirty-nine. Hitler had invaded Poland. Britain and France had declared war. In Europe the balloon was going up. . . ."

"And?"

"My God, I'd completely forgotten Sylvia. . . ."

"Sylvia," Herbie repeated. "Who is Sylvia, what is she, Lou?"

"I had this secretary called Sylvia. Redhead. Spectacular legs . . ."

"Lou! Don't digress."

"Who's digressing. I'm reminiscing. Sylvia Lebwitz. Oh, Herb, Sylvia was something else. . . . We'd do it in my office, door locked and I'd bend her back over the desk. Oh, she nearly cut me in half that Sylvia. . . ."

"Lou! Get on with it."

More silence. "Thursday morning. Late September. Sylvia comes in. Says two guys've come in to see me. No appointment. Want to talk about some charity concert. I even remember their names. Mr. Bukholtz and Mr. Haaven. Just two ordinary guys. You couldn't tell, Herb. They didn't even look sinister, like in the movies. Open-faced. Bukholtz was running a bit to fat maybe. Haaven was fit, younger than Bukholtz."

"What can I do for you, gentlemen?" Passau stood behind his desk, arms open, welcoming them in, gesturing to chairs.

They sat, unsmiling, but looking somehow expectant. Sylvia, her of the legs and sexual squeeze, closed the door.

"You didn't return to your home country, Mr. Passau," Bukholtz said.

"When you were in Europe, you didn't come to Passau, Mr. Passau, or should I call you Mr. Packensteiner?" from Haaven.

"I don't follow you."

Both men smiled: open and frank smiles, but smiles which sent a spike of ice into Passau's neck.

"You still have relatives in Passau?" Bukholtz again.

"I . . ."

"These relatives." Haaven came towards the desk and, like a magician with a deck of cards, flipped three photographs onto the blotter. The pictures were of David, Rachel and Rebecca.

"Things are not so rosy for your relatives in Passau these days." Just a bare, freezing statement.

"No, I . . ."

"Things can be made a little easier, if you decide to cooperate, Herr Packensteiner. Things can become rosy again."

He stopped speaking, a gout of emotion welling to his face and eyes. For a moment he looked all of his ninety years: old, defeated, sick.

"Come on, Lou. It's hard, I think, but come on. Tell me. What next?"

"They wanted me to serve the Führer and the Fatherland. If I did as they asked, things would be made easier for my cousins."

Outside it had started to rain again.

11

"JUST LIKE THAT? As easy as that?" Herbie sat to one side so he could see Passau's face, and keep an eye on the windows at the same time. Not that he could see anything now, for the rain was monsoonlike.

"Yes, just like that. . . ." Passau began. "No! No, of course not just like that. What d'you think I am? No, before the pictures came out there was a lot of talk."

Bukholtz and Haaven did an entire double act before going into the main spiel. "I put it in a capsule for you, Herb. Made it easy."

"Well, take it out of the capsule. Tell me what you remember."

When they first came in they actually announced that they were "from the old country." They talked about times past and times present. There was nothing sinister.

"That was what threw me, Herb. Looking back on it, people got stereotypes fixed in their minds. Nazis, the SS, Gestapo, whatever, were presented as unyielding, tough guys. Mostly sadists. Unpleasant characters. These two were nice, quiet fellows, like they lived in the suburbs, in neat little houses with neat little wives: one dinner party a month, and fuck the wife Friday nights, regular as clockwork. They seemed ineffectual."

It was the key to all operations like this. Herbie knew because he had a great deal of experience. You come on as the mark's friend—understanding, on the same wavelength. Or, in Kruger's case, a bit muddled: a dumb ox who was jolly and harmless. Worked like a charm. Rarely failed.

They were with Passau for a good half hour before the burn, gradually leading up to the point where the plight of Jews in Germany, Austria, and now Poland, became clear.

"It's not good for Jewish people, now. Under the new regime," Bukholtz said, almost out of the blue. "You know this, Maestro?"

"Of course."

"So the future is not good for the Packensteiners you left behind in the town from which you took your name." This was Haaven. "Well, they're not all Packensteiners now, are they? David's still the same, but Rachel and Rebecca, they're married. You know all that. The letters you've written show us that you really want them to come out. To come here, to America, land of opportunity."

"In my innocence, Herb, I thought these two had contact with my cousins. That they were talking about helping to get them out."

To the two Germans, in September 1939, Passau said, "You've seen my letters. They showed them to you? You can help?"

"We've seen the letters, yes," Bukholtz said.

"They didn't show them to us, but we saw them," from Haaven.

"Yes, we can help," Bukholtz continued.

"They didn't show . . . ?"

"We had a peep at them. Before they were delivered. No mail from overseas, for known Jews, is left unopened before it's delivered." Bukholtz gave Passau a weary smile. "We get to see the letters first. This is how we know about you and your desire to make certain your three cousins—and their families, of course—stay safe."

"We can help." Haaven did not smile. "We can help if you will help, Mr. Passau."

"I'll do anything. You can get them out? Get them to me?"

"Not quite yet. There they are." This was the moment they dealt the photographs onto the desk. "And, I'm afraid, there they stay. If you do not agree to what we suggest, then they will stay there permanently. I doubt if you'll even find their graves if and when you come back to your Fatherland."

"What d'you mean, if and when I . . . ?"

"Do as we ask, and they will be safe. You have assurances. From us."

"What is it I can do? How can I do anything?"

They explained that, in the event of America coming into the war, on the side of Britain and France, Louis Passau could do a great deal.

"You can be a secret ambassador for us."

"You can give us information. Information vital to the Third Reich."

"But America's not going to come into the war. The majority of people, and the majority in Congress, favor an isolationist policy." ("See, Herb, what an innocent I was?")

That could change, they said. In fact, they were ninety-nine percent certain it would change. "Your President isn't exactly sitting on his hands at the moment. Give it a year. Maybe two years. America will be forced to enter the war. After that, you can be the greatest help to us."

"If I agreed to this, you'd let them come out?"

"Not for a while. Regard them as hostages. They'll be well taken care of."

"Let them out and you have a deal."

Bukholtz stood up, walked to the desk and tore up each of the photographs, sprinkling the confettilike pieces back onto the desk. Haaven rose. "A great mistake, Mr. Passau. You could have saved their lives. You won't hear from us again."

Bukholtz nodded, "And you won't hear from your cousins either."

"Wait! Stop!" They were at the door, pausing, turning their heads to look at him. "What assurances would I have, should I agree?"

They came back into the room and told him that he would get at least one letter a month. "From each of them." Bukholtz smiled. "They will be postmarked and dated. You will know they are alive. The war shouldn't last very long in any case. Germany is more prepared than you can imagine."

"We don't ask a great deal." Bukholtz shrugged.

"Just the occasional favor." Haaven smiled.

"But what could I *do*?"

They sat down again and told him. Should America go to war, he would be part of the war effort, that his orchestra would be in demand, that he would be asked to give concerts, tour bases, meet people. Already he had an entrée to President Roosevelt and other important people. If war came, he would have friends and acquaintances in very high places; he would hear things—not just about troop movements and such like, but about morale, about how people were thinking, how the generals were thinking.

"Also how the private soldiers are thinking." Bukholtz had become very friendly. "This is also important in war: to know how the soldier in the ranks is thinking. You would be of inestimable value to the Third Reich. Your own Jewish descent would get lost in the files. When it's all over, you will be a friend. Germany will rule Europe. That is the destiny of the German people. You will be a German again, with no restrictions. We will see to it."

Passau did not even hesitate. "I'll do what you ask."

Fifty-two years ahead, he sat staring into the rain. Herbie thought that the Maestro's face showed no sign of remorse. "So, you did just that?" he asked.

"Sure I did it. They had me tied in knots." He stopped, choked a little. If Herbie did not know him better he would have believed the old Maestro was really touching private emotion, showing some kind of contrition, but he had plenty of cause to be cynical about Passau's motivations. Music, he had decided, was the only source of passion and genuine feeling in the man's complex makeup.

"I . . ." Passau began again, as though he had trouble with his larynx. "I really thought that agreeing was in my best interests, and would save my family back in Germany—Austria, wherever. Already, Jews coming out of Germany were telling tales so horrible people thought they were exaggerating.

"At the time I believed it would come to nothing—what I promised. That America could never be involved in what was going on in Europe. Most Americans really did believe that we wouldn't get into the war, that isolation was the answer. I never thought that . . ." He trailed off. Perhaps, Herbie thought, the memory of his first betrayal of his country really had got to him.

"But it did . . ." Kruger began.

"Almost straightaway, they gave me work, gave me things to do."

"They give you a comic name and all that stuff?" Herb asked.

Passau nodded, then smiled. "I was Unternehmen—a business concern. That, the writer who blew the whistle—Stretchfield . . . ?"

"John Stretchfield, yes."

". . . That he got wrong. Said I was code named 'Dorn'—in English a thorn."

"I'm German by birth, Lou. I know what it means."

"Sure you do. About the only thing Stretchfield did get wrong."

"I read the book. Pretty convincing."

"Yes, well, I got things to tell you about him, also. But that comes later."

Herbie nodded. Passau would only take one step at a time. Nobody could budge him from giving the events in his own exact chronology. "Okay, so you were Unternehmen. What then, Lou?"

"They said all would be explained to me. I would get a call. There were trigger words—I even forget now what they were." He turned towards Kruger, a smile spreading over his face, hands extended. "So there I was, the only Jewish Nazi spy in the business."

"We all have to start somewhere in this trade." Kruger tried to match the old man's attempt at levity. "They left you, then soon got in touch again."

"Sure, they left the office. Me? I was in a state. I called Sylvia in and banged her there and then on the carpet."

"And kept your tryst with Harriet? Tryst, that is right, yes?"

Passau was not up to the word games. "I spent the afternoon with Harriet. Did I tell you she was also married by then? Big guy in real estate. Forget his name now. Anyhow, I drove up to Woodstoke Hall—Rhinebeck—that night. Spent the weekend with Veronica. Remember all that as clear as yesterday. Funny, huh? Remember that, but can't remember the code words. She was very loving, my wife, that weekend. I needed love. Didn't want to be alone. Monday I went back to New York. We had a heavy schedule; many rehearsals, lot of concerts. In thirty-nine I was also trying to get the opera company off the ground. What later was known as Opera at the Center. Dropped into work. Two weeks later I'd just about forgotten the whole thing. I was working and living a very—what would they say today?—a very high-profile life. Parties, dinners, mixing with people who were big names. As I say, two weeks later I pretended it had gone away, and what could I do for them anyway?"

"Then the telephone rang, Lou?"

"Sure. Then the telephone rang. Call to arms. For the Third Reich, to keep my cousins safe."

"How'd they run you, Lou? How'd they train you—they had to train you; I know the business too well."

"Yeah." Big sigh. Off-loading his conscience. "Two women. In his book—the *Hitler's Unknown Spies* thing—Stretchfield only mentions a guy called Loddermann. I met him, maybe twice, and I guess his name was on the file Stretchfield came across. In fact, I *know* it was. The women didn't figure in any of the reports. Two of them, Flora and Irene. Never knew their real names, except I saw Flora one time after the war. At some reception, on the arm of a tycoon. Boy, she went white as a sheet, as they say. Like she'd seen a ghost. I think she figured I was going to blow the whistle on her." He began to ramble, and Herbie whipped him back into line.

"Come on, Lou. 1939. What then?"

"There were codes. Telephone codes, to set up meetings, like I said. I got quite good at it. Used the Lexington Avenue apartment. Good cover. See, Herb, I learned the words: good cover, me meeting girls at the place on Lexington."

"Sure, great cover." Herbie thought of what Art had told them. Years later, Passau was to meet Ursula at the place on Lexington. Very good cover, down the years, working for two opposite ideologies. Jesus, Louis Passau, Master Spy.

They—the girls—had taken Passau through what amounted to some elementary tradecraft. "I didn't have the time for that shit, Herb. I wanted my cousins and their families safe. I just said I would do my best."

"And they wanted, what?"

"Straightaway they wanted anything I could get from my so-called friends in the administration, about how America might he helping the British. What could I give them? I made stuff up. Herbie, through the entire war I only saw the President twice. That is twice to speak to. My power was on the podium and with my orchestra. Sure, I met people. Later I was at military bases. I met generals and privates. I met folk who had their fingers on the pulse of the nation. Of all the allied nations."

He threw his head back and laughed, loudly for a change, and there was genuine humor there. Herbie heard it, and in a way rejoiced.

"To read the chapter on me in Stretchfield's book, you'd imagine it was all cloak and dagger, glamour. It wasn't *like* that, Herb."

"I know it."

"My war was mainly fought from the podium. I conducted music, for money and for the joy. Also for the American people. The other was a sideline, as though it didn't really matter. I don't think I gave them anything they couldn't have discovered from other places. Yet, when Stretchfield unveiled the information he had on me, it looks like I betrayed America big time."

"What *did* you give them, Lou?"

Instead of answering, Passau gave a thumbnail sketch of his view of World War II. After the terrible day in December 1941, when the Japanese attacked Pearl Harbor, he wrote to the President asking how he could help in the war effort. Back came a terse note—

My Dear Passau,

Just keep playing wonderful music. Music is an international currency and this is where you can be of most help. I have sent your note on to the appropriate channels and you might be able to assist in keeping up the morale of our youngmen.

The appropriate channels had eventually come through to him. Would he consider a series of concerts on military bases at home? Later they might even ask him to travel overseas. In the spring of 1942 the Passau Orchestra of America undertook their first tour of bases within the continental United States.

"I tell you, Herb, I was scared. These were boys, young men, cannon fodder mostly. They danced to Glenn Miller. I wondered how serious music would go down in camps and on bases. I thought—I remember—that I might have to turn to the audiences and say, 'Now, me and the boys would like to play a number by that popular composer Pyotr Tchaikovsky.'" He laughed again, the same humor bubbling across the room.

"To my surprise, the audiences were good. They listened, were appreciative. Some came to see me after and told me how much the concert had meant to them. They were good times and always, in the Officers' Club, there was talk."

"Some of which you took back to Flora and Irene?"

"Yes." Curt, the humor flushed down the tubes. Did he possess a conscience after all? Herbie wondered. So he asked what kind of information?

"Oh, it's so long ago. It's difficult to remember."

"Come on, Lou. This is your confession. What kind of information?"

A sigh. Silence. Mouth open then closed again.

"Lou?"

"Okay. Okay. Yes, I gave them the names of outfits training. What kind of thing they were doing. I gave them the names and numbers of American units going to the Pacific and then to Europe. Number of airplanes. All that kind of stuff. They probably knew already. . . ."

"Not necessarily, Lou. You must take some responsibility. You gave them sensitive information."

"It didn't seem like it at the time."

For three years—1942 to 1944—Passau spent about four months of the year touring United States' bases. He routinely gave concerts all over the country, and also took the orchestra to the Pacific theater of operations. In 1943, he visited England. The rest of the time was spent working very hard at the Center in New York. Organizing, rehearsing, performing concerts and, from 1943, opera. He had three assistants, a designer and a stage director for the opera company.

"What did you bring back from the Pacific, Lou?"

"Same kind of stuff. Names, numbers, airplane types, morale, readiness, ships."

"And you passed on all that to the girls."

"Sure, most of it."

"Busy life, Lou."

"I tell you, Herbie, you know you're in the right job when the drudgery is also fun. Yes, sure, busy life."

"Must've been hell on your second favorite occupation."

"My what . . . ?"

"Your sex life."

Passau gave a tight little smile. "Sylvia went off to work in a factory. Harriet became a WAVE. My sex life was my wife. We got very close in those years."

"Your wife and the girls: Irene and Flora."

"Sure. From time to time. Tell you the honest truth, Herbie, I couldn't get involved with them. Not on the same level like with Harriet, or even Sylvia."

"And you felt no conscience in selling out your country?"

"Nothing I gave the Nazis was of great importance."

"How could you tell?"

"I could tell, okay?"

"And what about the trip to Europe?"

"The first one? England?"

"The second one's public record. Gave yourself brownie points with the second one, Lou."

"Okay, the first one. 1943?"

"That's it. What'd you give them from the 1943 tour?"

"Same kind of stuff. Met Eisenhower, Bradley, Patton. Even Churchill. Asked me to play "Land of Hope and Glory." Also Elgar's *Enigma Variations*. Give me dinner out at that country place. Churchill got a little drunk at dinner and started spouting Shakespeare at me. 'If music be the food of love, play on.' I was part of the warp and weft of history, right?"

"So it would seem. Stretchfield says you had contact with the man Loddermann."

"Before we left, yes. Only times I saw him. Once before going. Once after I came back."

"Tell me about the first time."

"Sure, yes. I went to meet Irene. Instead of Irene there was Flora with this guy she introduces as a friend. Loddermann. No first name. Nothing."

"This was in the place on Lexington?"

"Yes."

"And what did Loddermann want to talk about?"

"Buildup. Allied buildup in England. For the invasion."

"Stretchfield says you gave vital information. Told the Germans of all those fake armies. All the stuff to make them think the landings would be in the Calais area. In *Hitler's Unknown Spies*, he says you provided detailed intelligence on the diversionary stuff."

"If I did, they took no notice, right? After D-Day they paused; they still believed the main assault would be in the Calais area, not Normandy. I told them nothing of that, but they didn't listen if I did tell them."

"You're confusing me, Lou."

The Allied forces in the United Kingdom had built up a huge feint in late 1943, right up to June 1944. Using radio signals, dummies, scraps of other information, they misled the Germans, making them believe that vast invasion forces were being built up in the southeast of England, signaling an attack by the obvious, shortest, route across the English Channel—the area around Calais. Many still claimed the German army in continental Europe knew it was a ruse, yet in the days that followed the invasion—Operation Overlord—the Germans failed to commit their best armor to the battle raging in Normandy, fearing a second assault along the Pas de Calais.

"What's to confuse? It's straightforward."

"You're saying you gave them nothing on the real buildup?"

"I knew nothing of the buildup. Stretchfield's got his nose in the wrong place. I'll tell you later. Okay?"

"So what did you bring back? What did you give to Flora and Irene?"

"Nothing significant."

"And to Loddermann?"

"Ah."

"Lou! Come! On!" Broken up into single words. Shouted.

"Okay. Right, Loddermann met me when I got back to New York. I gave him observations. Same old stuff. People I'd seen, places I'd been. Bomber squadrons, weapons; okay, I gave some stuff about landing craft they were testing at one place. But nothing significant."

"Name, rank and serial number, Lou, right?"

"You got it." Count of ten. "Herb, can we eat now? Please. I get hungry."

Herbie looked at his watch. "Doesn't time fly when you're having fun," he said.

In the bedroom, Pucky was taking off the headphones and changing the tape. Kruger had gone over the room again and regarded it as safe from Art's listeners.

"I'm pushing him fast." He gave her the big grin, the one for the cameras. "We don't need much detail, only what he learned about how to operate. Experience which he brought with him to the Russians. This afternoon, I probably push him harder. Maybe we even get to the Russian involvement, I don' know."

Pucky nodded, gave him a peck on the cheek and said she would get them lunch. "Tuna fish salad do you?"

"Why you got to say 'fish,' Puck? If it's tuna it's fish, right?"

"Right."

He took her arm, holding her back from the door, looking at her with not a little lust. "Tonight . . ." he began.

"Oh, goody . . ."

"No, tonight we got some work to do with the computer, Puck. Tonight I want us to do some hacking. I got numbers. So we find a little more about who is really who. If Lou Passau is Saul Isaak or Abraham Joseph Packensteiner."

As they reached the door, the Maestro was calling for Kruger to put on some music for him. "I don't hear music for hours on end, Herb."

"What you want? You looked through the collection we bought?"

"Anything. Give me anything. You choose."

Herbie put on Prokofiev: *Romeo and Juliet*. "Star-crossed lovers," he said cryptically, and old Louis Passau's eyes filled with genuine tears.

We are getting near to the riddle of La Tempesta, Herbie thought. He went into the kitchen to help Pucky with the tomatoes, muttering under his breath—

"Yet she must die, else she'll betray more men."

"That's not *Romeo and Juliet!*" Pucky smiled.

"No. But it's Shakespeare, baby." Once more the big smile. Then, "The isle is full of noises, Pucky. All we have to do is listen to the music."

12

"OKAY, LOU. These people—Flora, Irene, Loddermann. You never saw them again when it was all over?"

"Only that one brush with Flora."

"And you never ran into the two guys who first set you up—Bukholtz and Haaven?"

"Never."

"They ever give you any clue how they got the raw intelligence back to Germany?"

Lunch had been a quiet business, the music still weaving a spell around the apartment. Serge Prokofiev's ballet had a way of concentrating the mind: throbbing, luxurious melodies, clashing harmonies. Dramatic. Passau seemed locked into the sounds. Living in a different world. Herbie thought that maybe he had retreated to happier days. When he started to question again, he went in tough and hard: the master cracking the whip. "So tell me, Lou, what did you know of their methods?"

"I didn't ask. Didn't know. Didn't want to know." Passau shut his mouth like a trap.

"And all the time, they kept their side of the bargain?"

He nodded.

"An answer, please, Lou. Nods don't count."

"Yes, you know. You fucking know what the bastards did."

"I figured it out. It's not in your biographies, Lou. But you don't have to be a genius to know what happened."

"Okay. Yes. Yes, and yes. I received letters. Regularly. Sometimes handed to me by the girls. Sometimes to my office, in the regular mail."

"The regular mail? You remember the postmarks?"

"All over. All over the country—New Hampshire, Arizona, California. Who cares? They came and they were good."

"How good?"

"Good enough."

"Details, Lou. I know it hurts, but details I want."

"The letters were, at the beginning, reassuring. They were under some kind of restraint, they said, but it was comfortable. They were not ill-treated. The food was sufficient. This was a word they always used—'sufficient.'"

"They were together?"

Passau nodded again. Paused. Nodded a second time, then whispered, "Yes." At last, Herbie saw that the Maestro was genuinely in difficulty; unfeigned emotion, sorrow was written across his face, and moved deep in his eyes. His breathing was heavy, as though he had some kind of constriction.

"You okay, Lou?" He leaned forward, one hand on the old man's shoulder.

Passau nodded. "Give me a minute. There are two memories in my life which still have the power to hurt me. Nothing else." His voice had dropped to a whisper, and he was still having difficulty with his breathing.

Herbie thought, "Don't die on me, Lou. There's something in your life which still has a bearing on the present, and I've got to know. Don't die on me, Lou." For a moment he had one of those terrible fugues, where he was uncertain whether he had said his thoughts aloud or not. Passau's eyes were closed and, for a second, Herb wondered if he should shout for help.

Then the spell broke. The old man opened his eyes, taking a huge gulp of air, as though by some necromancy life had returned. "I'm okay, Herb. Fine. Just a little faint. We finish for today, please?"

Herbie shook his head. "Sorry, Lou. Face it head-on. You'll only have to tell this once." It was a lie, he knew, but what do you do?

Passau's head drooped onto his chest for a count of ten, then he raised it again and gave a tiny nod. He looked like a man near death, so Kruger waited another minute. Very slowly the color came back. "What was the question?" Louis Passau asked.

"Your cousins: were they together?"

"Yes. All of them. David, his wife and three children. Rachel had married a man called Krevitch. She had two little girls—well, they were not so little by then. Rebecca was also married. Joseph Fine was her husband. Worked precious metals in Passau. I have a gold pendant on a chain. Sometimes wear it. Made by him. They had one child. A son. Yes, twelve members of my family. All together. Well treated. Food sufficient."

"You ever find if this was true?"

The nod once more, then the single affirmative. A lag between nod and word, as though it took time for his brain to signal to his voice. Another thirty seconds. "Yes, later we knew they were together. It was some old castle, or big house. A mile or two from Celle, Lower Saxony, northern Germany. There were several families there. Not all Jewish. The place was a short distance from where they finally built the camp: Bergen-Belsen."

"You didn't find this out until later?"

"Their movements were traced when it was all over. But the letters kept coming. Definitely written by my cousins. I don't think they were forced to write good things, not until matters became irrevocable."

"And when was that, Lou?"

"I guess early in forty-four. January 1944."

"What happened?"

"A letter. Bright. Happy. From Rachel. She and Rebecca had told me, in almost every letter, that they were allowed to practice regularly." He stopped, as though that explained everything.

"Practice?"

"The violin. They were both good." He gave a little toss of the head. "Not concert standard, of course."

"Of course not, Lou." Quietly, but appalled inside. Nobody in Passau's family was allowed to be concert standard except the Maestro.

"They told me what they were playing. How they practiced every day."
"And?"

"In January 1944 the letter from Rachel was to tell me that she, with her family, and Rebecca with hers, were being moved. They were to play in an orchestra, she said. She was happy, delighted. The only thing that made her sad was that David would stay behind. She told me openly, in this letter, that they were going to be in an orchestra, in a place called Auschwitz, and I nearly went mad.

"Jewish people in America knew about Auschwitz by then. We all knew about the death camps. Auschwitz was on everyone's lips. We had pleaded with the authorities. Asked them to selectively bomb the place—the gas chambers, the crematoria, the wire. It was only later that I learned about the orchestra of Auschwitz. You know about that, Herb? The musicians of Auschwitz?"

"A little." In fact he knew quite a lot. A group of musicians in the terrible camp had been banded together under the protection of one of the senior female officers, a woman called Maria Mandel—Lagerführerin Mandel. She was the female SS officer in charge of the so-called Orchestra Block at Auschwitz. Beautiful, slender, golden-haired. A fanatical Nazi. Some said that she had once taken a Jewish lover, so spent the rest of her life atoning for it. So she was a women who obeyed orders, fought to keep her orchestra together, showed sympathy on one hand and ruthless, near bizarre, sadism on the other.

One story had touched Herbie, and stayed with him since he first heard of the woman and the orchestra of Auschwitz. One day, during what they all knew as the Selektion, when families were separated; when husbands, wives and children were put into different groups—some destined for immediate death, others sent to labor which would eventually kill them—a beautiful child detached himself from his mother and toddled, arms outstretched towards Mandel. She had picked him up and taken him away. For a time the child was always with her, well-dressed in a sailor suit or other nice clothes, always blue, taken from the piles left by children on their way to the gas chambers.

Those who had seen Mandel and the child, recorded how she played with him—Mummy and Baby games—how she gave him chocolate, and how, in the end, she took him, herself, to the gas chambers.

This was the woman who decided the fate of the individuals in the orchestra: the orchestra which played to soothe the troubled minds of those arriving at the death camp; the orchestra which gave special concerts for prisoners and staff; the orchestra—the last thing so many heard as they were marched towards the showers: those terrible chambers of death, where lethal Zyclon-B gas, not water, gushed from the sprays.

Herbie pulled himself from his own small knowledge of the musicians of Auschwitz. "They were in the orchestra, Lou? That dreadful orchestra?" This time he did not press for an audible "Yes."

Then, he asked, "Didn't many of those people survive?"

Once more, the long and trembling sigh. "I talked to some of them in later years. Some of the Auschwitz musicians. Yes, many survived. Not

Rachel and Rebecca, though. Not their families. When the final panic began, at the end of forty-four, they returned, with the other survivors, to Bergen-Belsen. But they did not live to see the British troops overtake the camp."

Passau suddenly doubled back on his narrative. "1944," he began. "A happy and sad year. In May, almost exactly a month to the day before the Allied invasion of Hitler's Europe, Veronica, at long last, gave birth to a little girl. She had already lost two children: one when she was three months' pregnant, the other at five months.

"We had almost given up any idea of having children. She went through so much pain and suffering. Then, almost a miracle: a perfect little girl."

May Cosima Passau, born May 6, 1944. The apple of her father's eye. She had been at the Passau 90th Birthday Concert.

Herbie gently drew him back to the matters uppermost in his mind. This was the greatest emotion he had yet seen in the old man. "January, the letter from Rachel, which so upset you; May, the birth of your daughter; June the invasion—Operation Overlord. What then, Lou? What further intelligence did you give to the girls?"

"Little. Meetings were set up. They came with lists of questions, trying to grab stuff from my memory. Things learned when I had been in England."

"You answer any of those?"

Passau shook his head. "Made some up. I couldn't remember anything. Not really. They said I should try because Hitler had the wonder weapons. The invasion would fail."

"You had other letters? From David, Rebecca and Rachel?"

"When I heard they were being sent to Auschwitz, I knew it was the end. Since forty-three they had been moved from the castle into the new camp at Bergen-Belsen. You know about that—about that camp?"

"Yes. I know *all* about Bergen-Belsen, Lou." It was like asking a doctor if he knew about death. In the days following the collapse of the Third Reich, the Americans—mainly the OSS—had recruited the young Herbie Kruger. At that time he was stick-thin and gangling. He also hated the Nazis and all they stood for. The Americans decided to use Herbie as a ferret. They would put him into the camps set up for DPs— Displaced Persons—and his job was to ferret out the many confirmed Nazis who had sought sanctuary in the DP camps.

The Americans were not overly scrupulous about the jurisdiction held over DP camps. By then—the early summer of 1945—Bergen-Belsen had become the largest of many camps being converted by the Allies. It was under British command, with the Royal Army Medical Corps trying to nurse the survivors—and the many others who ended up in that part of Germany—back to health. Herbie Kruger's first assignment was to be insinuated into Bergen-Belsen by the Americans, without British knowledge. They told him that their security could be maintained if they did not have to go through the American authorities. They could hoodwink the British, and then come out smelling like roses by bagging Nazis from under the noses of the Brits. So much for Allied cooperation.

Herbie had mixed with, talked to, helped and comforted many of the inmates who had been on the death marches, or had suffered in other camps. He felt he knew the history of Bergen-Belsen by heart, for when you had seen the place you knew all about it. He talked to the walking half-clothed skeletons who were, unbelievably, human beings, left destitute of hope, health and dignity. To him, it was the whirlpool of the Holocaust. After all these years he still suffered the occasional nightmare about the place where no birds sang and the sights were not meant for human eyes. All this cascaded through his mind as he said, "Yes. I know *all* about Bergen-Belsen, Lou." This, and more: the history of the place, as he heard it in 1945—

Originally it had been a prisoner-of-war camp, but in 1943 things had changed. It became an Aufenthaltslager—a detention camp: a place where they held people supposedly designated for exchange for German nationals in Allied countries. As he remembered it, there were five satellite camps: one atrocious place for prisoners brought in to do the building; another was a "special camp" for those Jews who had papers showing that they had been accepted by other countries. Many groups passed through the Sonderlager, the special camp. Several thousand of these wretched people simply paused there, on their way to Auschwitz and the gas chambers.

There were also the "neutral camp," the "star camp" and the "Hungarian camp." In the neutral camp conditions were better, less cruel. Herbie thought that would be where Passau's cousins had been kept.

In 1944 everything changed again. Bergen-Belsen became the place that marked the end of the Death Marches from other concentration and death camps. For thousands it was the beginning and the end of horror. The crematoria belched out their pungent smoke, but there were no gas chambers. People in Bergen-Belsen, in the final days of the Third Reich, died from brutality, lack of food, typhus, phenol injections into the heart. There was also a firing range.

When the British Army arrived, in mid-April 1945, corpses were strewn everywhere, and the awful walking bones shuffled about in a daze. The British went into shock. They had not expected to discover such a place, and in the first five days a further fourteen thousand people died. In the weeks following, another fourteen thousand died of malnutrition and disease.

"Yes. I know *all* about Bergen-Belsen, Lou." In the seconds it took to say the words, Herbie Kruger recalled all this, and his own days there in late June 1945. The bodies had gone, the ragged camp pajamas had been replaced, but the air was still sweet with death, and the walking corpses still shuffled about, refusing to move outside the perimeter.

With a sudden jolt, Herbie remembered sitting at the door of one of the huts, talking to an old man, who was probably under thirty years of age. His bones protruded from parchment, translucent, tight skin, and his eyes were sunk, like deep gouges into his face.

"Were you here last week?" he asked of young Kruger, in a reedy voice.

"No. I only just arrived."

"Last week there was a concert. A big orchestra came. They had a choir also. They played and it was wonderful. The most wonderful thing of my life." The man staggered to his feet and tried to caper around, trying to relive this moment of joy, until he collapsed with stomach cramps and was taken away by two medical orderlies.

Herbie's mind grasped at the dreadful coincidence, for he was a believer in coincidences. A bolt of shock went through him. He had missed seeing Louis Passau, with his orchestra and chorus, by a week. Now, he sat with the old man reliving personal truths about that terrible place where the rows of huts, and the very earth gave off a sense of brutality and mindless, cruel, unnecessary death. Kruger knew he had probably stood near the graves of Passau's cousins. He also knew that he had netted four SS officers at Bergen-Belsen in the last days of June 1945.

"Yes. I know *all* about Bergen-Belsen, Lou."

Passau grunted. "David and all his family perished in the typhoid epidemic. Rebecca's husband and son died in Auschwitz. In the 'showers.'

Rachel's man, Kevitch, and her three little girls were separated from her during the journey back. She was crazy with grief. I had all this from one of the musicians of Auschwitz. Rachel and Rebecca died back in Bergen-Belsen. Most of the orchestra was saved, but Rebecca was clubbed to death by a Polish kapo—the Nazis appointed some of the more brutalized prisoners as kapos, but you know that."

"I know it, Lou. And Rachel . . . ?"

"Was shot, in some hideous error. I heard this also from one of the musicians. She was walking back to her hut and got mixed up with a handful of women, herded together by the SS. She was taken to the firing range and shot." Tears streamed from his eyes. "You know, Herb? You know how it all ended? Everyone left in that orchestra was to be shot, with others also. They knew it. Three o'clock in the afternoon, April 15, 1945. The British arrived at eleven in the morning, but that was too late to save any of my relatives. All gone, for nothing, and I had become a traitor for twelve unmarked graves. . . . I never saw them, Herb."

"Really?" Kruger thought. Aloud, he said, "Lou, you hadn't seen them since you were a small child. . . ."

"It made no difference, Herbie. No difference. I never saw them, flesh of my flesh, blood of my blood. You're not Jewish; maybe you don't understand. They were my link with my past. All that was left of true family. No day passes without me remembering them. Who they were. They were always children. I never saw them."

"You gave a concert at Bergen-Belsen, Lou?" In his head, Herb clung to Louis' words "I never saw them."

Passau nodded, but said nothing.

"It's a famous concert. It's been written about."

"Yes. You can read of the concert in Bergen-Belsen but you can never live through it, Herb. Never. You can never know what it was like."

Kruger told him of his own visit to the place, one week after the concert, but the old man took no notice. "It was in June," he said. "I asked the authorities if we could go and play music in the American and British zones. Strange, things moved so slowly at that time, yet permission came through overnight. Within three days of asking, we were on our way. We played at a lot of places, yet I remember only one concert. We played for the dead as well as the living. I can still hear it: we played Berlioz. *Symphonie Funèbre et Triomphale*, because that music transcends religious beliefs, a celebration of triumph over death. Herb, Mahler was not yet in vogue, otherwise it would have been the Second Symphony. We also did the English composer, Gustav Holst's *The Planets*. That seemed right, and we finished, the wrong way round, with the overture to *The Barber of Seville*—Rossini, because it is light and full of fun. You know, Herb, that the military, at funerals, always march away from the graveside playing something happy, buoyant? That was our happy music. But with the Berlioz I think we touched the dead. I held hands with my cousins for the last time."

He gave another heavy sigh, expelling every ounce of breath from his lungs, then swallowing new air. Outside, the pelting rain had stopped and a thin sun had broken through, staining the wet sand and the water, over which two pelicans struggled to maintain height.

"Why the Berlioz, Lou? Why not the Verdi Requiem? That also goes far above religion and beliefs?"

"The Berlioz? It has military aspects. Written in memory of dead heroes. The victims of the Holocaust are heroes. I think it was right." Suddenly he was plunged into deep thought, worrying, Herbie felt, about possibly having made the wrong choice of music all those years ago. Then the old man's amazing powers of memory linked past and present. "You know, there was something else that made me choose the Berlioz. When Berlioz was a young man in Paris, his father sent him to train as a doctor. The first time he went to a class on dissection he was so revolted that he ran away. It's all in his autobiography. I can still quote the passage by heart. I think I had been reading it at the time."

"You can still quote from it?"

"I think I was reading the book at the time," he mused. "Yes, it was the book that made up my mind. Some find the passage funny. I found it prophetic in a way."

"Quote." Herbie did not believe Passau still had the power to recall a whole passage from Hector Berlioz's memoirs.

The aged Maestro looked at him, seeing the challenge full in his eyes. Slowly, as if in a trance, he spoke—

"'When I entered that fearful human charnel house, littered with fragments of limbs, and saw the ghastly faces and cloven heads, the bloody cesspool in which we stood, with its reeking atmosphere, the swarms of sparrows fighting for scraps, and the rats in corners, gnawing bleeding vertebrae, such a feeling of horror possessed me that I leaped out of the window and fled home as though Death and all his hideous crew were at my heels.'" He gave a thin smile, which matched the sun outside. "It went something like that. Fitting. Could be even a description of Bergen-Belsen. When we played the Rossini some of them tried to dance, can you believe that?"

Herbie remembered the emaciated figure, with its death head, capering and falling to the ground. "I believe it."

They both looked out onto the now more pleasant view, and Herbie gave a sharp intake of breath, grabbing Passau and dragging his chair back from the window as a sleek motor launch moved across the water, leaving its plume of foam behind. Then he relaxed. String-bikini–clad girls waved, and one clung to the pilot's arm, blonde hair, like a scarf flying behind her, the young man at the wheel smiling. They were all tan and teeth, health and fitness. He thought of their innocence. Of the obscenity Germany had become under Hitler, the crimes and sheer horror of the Holocaust. For a moment it was all boiled down to this one old man, weeping for his ancestors. He had been right. The words of the choir in Berlioz's work came, halting into his mind—

> Glory! Glory and triumph
> for these heroes!
> Glory and triumph!
> Come, elect of the other life!
> Exchange, brave warriors,
> your laurel wreaths
> for palms of immortality! . . .
> Glory and triumph for the heroes.

"Is enough for today, Lou. What you got next? Big wheel concerts, recordings and triumph?"

Passau shook his head, and the tears welled up again. "I got the worst," he said. "The very best and the very worst of my life. I got the *Magnificat* and the *De profundis*.

"YOU MOVED HIM on quite a way, Herb." Art had come over, late, after they had eaten. He did not even try to hide the fact that he had people listening. "Keep him going and you'll eventually hit pay dirt. Really push tomorrow, eh?"

"Sure." Herbie gave him the daft smile. "I knock his socks off, Art. Make him bleed a little, huh?"

Oddly, Herbie's bitterness did not sink in. Art Railton gave a little gesture, cocking his head. "Thus is the poor agent despised. O traitors and bawds, how earnestly are you set a-work, and how ill requited!"

"Shakespeare," Kruger explained to Pucky, or anyone else who might be listening.

"All things, to all men, through all time. William had the last word, eh, Herb?"

"He did good exit lines, Art. You going so soon?" Art had risen, striding towards the door. "Good night," he called happily, "Good night, sweet Prince."

Kruger took a pace towards him and quoted back—

"So shall thou feed on Death, that feeds on man,
And Death once dead, there's no more dying then."

They went into the bedroom where Pucky had set up the computer and connected the modem. They worked until two in the morning, hacking into files within one of the State Department's mainframes in D.C. It was a good night's work, and they had printout results to show for it. After everything was tidied away, they went to bed and gave each other pleasure, so that Herbie thought his heart would break with happiness.

The old order of the camps, the terror and brute bestiality of that time, slid away in the gentle massage of love, though it returned to him in dreams. A skeleton dressed in ragged concentration-camp pajamas danced the tango across a room where ruby glasses stood on a shelf, and the Avenging Angel detached itself from the Dürer, leaping into the arms of the prancing specter. Off they went, down a long corridor at the end of which a fire burned and black smoke reeked from the ovens.

He woke in a cold sweat—the night terrors—clung to Pucky for comfort, and wondered what awful dreams beset old Passau.

13

THE SUN SHONE, as though there was no such thing as rain, and as if clouds could never again threaten or spoil a day. Small craft skittered back and forth, half a mile off the beach; occasionally a wannabe water-skier clung desperately in the wake of a speedboat. In the apartment, they turned the air-conditioning on low and were relieved that it made only a discreet hum. There would be no problems with recording the day's interrogation.

Herbie Kruger moved Louis Passau way back from the windows so that nobody could see them, and he began to talk as they sipped their second cup of coffee. Pucky played at being a dutiful hausfrau and cleared away the debris of breakfast.

Herbie pushed down the desire to spread last night's print out in front of Louis Passau and ask what it meant, but he knew that had to be saved for a moment when they were alone and nobody but Pucky could hear the answers. In any case, he still wanted to double-check with the Immigration and Naturalization Service (INS) mainframe. This was all very old history, and he was surprised, even a little amazed, at the efficiency of the State.

From outside, far away, came the sound of Elton John singing about somebody called Razor Face. Big Herbie ran a large hand across his jowls in a kind of Pavlovian reflex. "So you went through this great sense of loss, Lou? The grief began, yes?"

"What do you think? For over thirty years I had tried to get all of them into America. Letters—constantly writing, urging them. But they wouldn't come. I had even betrayed my country. Now it was too late. I was devastated with grief, and I carried guilt on my conscience like a shroud."

Herbie nodded. Somehow he did not believe in the shroud of guilt. Louis Passau was not one to allow such a small item like culpability to slow him down. Grief? Possibly.

Over the years, the old man most certainly had led another private life, a secret stream of consciousness running parallel to the real world, even parallel to his arcane world as an agent for the Nazis: a life recalled from long past, sometimes a daily retreat into how it had been. So he had nurtured a desire to bring his cousins over to America and relative safety, but the mind plays indescribable tricks.

"So, Lou, what then?"

He gave a small shrug. "Work." He said it firmly, as though his work, the music, the orchestra, had been salvation for him.

"You found consolation in work. Sure, why not? And your wife? Your child?"

"For a time, they were my sanity. My little girl was so wonderful. When I saw her it was like hearing a new, and outrageously beautiful, melody in my head. She danced me through the next few years, and Veronica was a pillar for me. Strength. Love. We all made music in our different ways." He gave a little, half-self-conscious chuckle. "You know, I believe that time was the only sustained period when I was never unfaithful to a wife."

"What, never?" Herbie gave a Gilbertian twinkle.

Passau shrugged, with a smile and a rolling of the eyes. "Well, hardly ever."

"Not Shakespeare," Herbie grunted. "Gilbert and Sullivan. *Pirates of Pen's Aunts.*"

"Penzance, Herb," Passau began, then snorted, realizing that Big Herbie had taken him for a ride. After a moment he spoke again—"That was the time when the orchestra just got better and better. We opened the Opera at the Center. Life was very full. You know how it is with orchestras and conductors. Rehearse, perform. Work more. Rehearse more. Up half the night and back in rehearsal at ten in the morning. Perform, perform, perform. The applause became music also—I will never deny that. Applause, acceptance, success is a heady business."

"So, Lou, what really? What really was next in the grand scheme of your life. You said it was good and bad. *Magnificat* and *De Profundis*."

"Sure."

"Well, tell me."

The familiar long silence followed, as though Passau were marshalling his memories, trying to find the starting point in the grand history's next turbulent chapter. Eventually, he spoke, very quietly. "Herb, this is the most difficult. This is my crown of thorns, and it is the worst thing in my entire life, actually. Forgive me if I go slow; if I stumble—even if I fall. Because this part of my life is the greatest disaster, and you have to hear it all."

The way he spoke, the tone of voice, and the manner in which he gave equal weight to each word, was a striking contrast to anything that had gone before. Never, from that first day in Virginia until the previous evening, when he had spun out the moving measure of his grief, had Louis Passau conveyed such a sense of doom.

"So tell me, Lou." His own voice altered to match the subject, laced with compassion, shot through with comprehension.

"Nineteen hundred forty-eight," Passau began. "September twenty-four is when it began. An exciting day. I found treasure any orchestra director would give his soul to discover. . . ."

Once every three months, the Passau Center gave auditions. Sometimes they were for a mixed and jumbled group—instrumentalists and singers. In 1948 Passau was looking mainly for singers. The Opera at the Center was starting to rival even the Met. He needed new, unknown, blood, and to get it he wrote, or personally contacted, practically every major music school in the world. He trawled both shallow and deep in the postwar traumatic shoals of Rome and Milan, Paris, the schools and colleges of his own country, even the Royal School of Music in London.

During that particular year, the auditions had netted him three sopranos whom he had put into the chorus of both orchestra and opera company, and one tenor, Luciano Peccatti, who was being watched and worked with, to determine whether he had that elusive quality that might eventually make him one of the operatic greats. The prognosis was not good, though Michael Dresden, the chorus master, had far from given up hope.

Now, on Friday, September 24, 1948, they were to hear four further hopefuls. A quartet of sopranos, all of whom came highly recommended: two from the Julliard—founded only two years earlier by an amalgamation of the Institute of Musical Art and the Julliard Graduate School; one all the way from the chorus of the Royal Opera House, in London, England; and a twenty-two-year-old who came highly praised, from the

Cincinnati College Conservatory. The latter had not arrived by the time the auditions were due to start.

In designing the Opera House, Louis had instructed the architects to follow the spirit of the great houses of Europe, but on a smaller scale. This they had done, and the interior was a miniature of La Scala, with touches of Covent Garden and Paris: gilt, red plush, marble, sweeping staircases, rich velvets and golden tassels.

They were mounting, and rehearsing, a production of *Aida* that fall, so during the days when there was no performance, two rows of the orchestra center seats were removed to make way for a director's table and all the paraphernalia associated with onstage rehearsals. There was also a ramp linking the stage with the auditorium.

Just before ten thirty that morning, Passau came down to join his Stage Director, Don Birch; the Assistant Musical Director, Adrian Helpenmann; Chorus Master, Michael Dresden; and the Center's Manager, Peter de Souza. To one side, sat Kerry Arlow—all six foot three of him. Arlow, the distinguished theater director, was doing *Aida* for them, and Passau had come to trust both the experience and intuition of this polished and brilliant giant of the theater.

The stage was bare but for the piano, a couple of stand chairs, and Helen Comfort, one of their three rehearsal pianists. Two solitary bare light bulbs dangled from the gantry, while one small shaded lamp burned on the director's desk. The shadows were stark, angular, in some ways sinister. The opulence of velvets and gold had dissolved into darkness.

"So are we ready?" Passau asked loudly as the Assistant Chorus Master, Freddie Edwards, came bustling onto the stage. He was a short, pugnacious, somewhat aggressive man. One of his legs was a fraction shorter than the other, a small deformity which had kept him from active service during the war. For this he had never forgiven either God or man.

"No, Maestro, we are *not* ready! I'm sorry, only three of them are here, and they've all chosen '*Un bel dì vedremo*' as their party piece. Why do these would-be divas always want to give us *Butterfly*?" Each applicant had been told to prepare two arias which they would have to sing, in character.

(In the present, Passau said, "'*Un bel dì vedremo.*' *Madama Butterfly.* 'One Fine Day.'"

"Sure, I know it's 'One Fine Day,' Maestro. English Summer."

"What?"

"One Fine Day. English Summer. Bad English joke."

"So what's funny about it?"

"Live in England for a year and you might smile.")

Back in September 1948 Passau sounded edgy. "So what're you doing about it?"

"They're drawing straws to see who gets to sing *Butterfly*. The losers will choose something else. I'm sorry, Maestro. Not out of the chorus yet, and already they've got monster egos."

"Okay, Freddie. Get them moving. We haven't all day. Kerry has a call at three."

"I'm doing what I can, Maestro, but you always say treat them with kid gloves in case one has potential."

"Get them moving with the kid gloves then, Freddie."

It was an almost disastrous morning. The two sopranos from the Julliard lost out on "One Fine Day," so the first girl did *"Tu, tu, piccolo Iddio,"* from the same opera—Butterfly's death. What should have been moving, revealing Butterfly's true self, became banal in this young woman. The voice was reasonable, but not a hundred percent accurate. Nor did she have the imagination it takes to breathe life into the character during her last moments in the opera. Passau did not even ask for exercises afterwards. Usually, if the voice was not half bad, he would at least give the singer scales, then particular notes to hit, his ear cocked to see if he or she had anything near perfect pitch.

The second Julliard girl did a pedestrian *"Cara nome,"* and Passau felt sickened by her. He still remembered the wonder of hearing Galli-Curci singing that aria, as he accompanied her at the party given for the great diva by Al Capone. As this girl sang, his mind slid back, almost slyly, to a time which seemed a million years ago; a life that he would now rather forget.

The girl from London fared better. She had drawn the long straw, so was the one who sang *"Un bel dì vedremo."* She had a sweet, clear voice and a definite grasp of character. Passau sat up and took notice. Listened. Asked her to do some scales. Took her through her paces. Gave her notes and passages to sing again. Then, for almost an hour, he gave what amounted to a breathtaking master class, coaxing her through *"Un bel dì vendremo,"* line by line, almost note by note, teaching her tricks here and there. Finally getting her to sing the aria again, from the beginning.

The others sat, silent and enthralled. Later Kerry Arlow maintained it was the greatest piece of direction he had ever seen. Thereafter, when he told the story of that morning—and there was certainly a story to tell— he always referred to it as the Day of the Singing Lesson which, in view of what was to occur, had a double edge to it. The girl's name was oddly foreign for a young woman from Surrey, England. Miranda Candelaria. Passau engaged her immediately for the chorus. Later she was to become one of the backbone leading sopranos of the Passau Center.

"So, we haven't completely wasted the entire morning." He beamed at his companions and, at that moment, Freddie Edwards appeared on the stage again, walking down the ramp, and into the orchestra.

Passau was aware of his presence, but chose to ignore him as he discussed a fine point about the aria which he had just gone through with such care and devotion. At last he turned, giving Edwards a curt nod, indicating that if he had something to say, he should say it now or forget about it.

"Miss Traccia, Maestro . . ."

"Who in hell is Miss Traccia?"

"The girl from Cincinatti, Maestro. The one who didn't turn up."

"Well, that's her loss, not ours."

"Maestro, she has telephoned. Her train was delayed. Two and a half hours. She called from the train station. It wasn't her fault, and she's coming now. By taxi."

Passau gave an enormous sigh. "Well, she's too late for us. If some half-trained soprano can't get here on time."

Edwards did the unthinkable and interrupted. "Maestro, she is coming with very high credentials. Already, at twenty-two, she's a B.M. and a M.M. Her teacher is Maestro . . ."

"Oh, yes." As though he had suddenly remembered, Passau spoke the name of the music teacher who had recommended her. He was a man held in great awe by many leading figures in music. He looked at his watch. "How long?"

"She should be here any minute, Maestro."

"Then we can wait for five, maybe ten, minutes. No longer."

"Thank you, Maestro. I'm sorry I'm late." The voice was clear, confident, and even in speech contained a quality and strength which made Passau quickly turn his head.

She stood near the top of the ramp, shrugging herself out of her street coat. Slender, heartbreakingly young, with shoulder-length dark hair that brushed her shoulders. Her face oval, a clear complexion, slightly flared nostrils, a thickness in the lips of what novelists, who should know better, would call "a generous mouth." Her eyes seemed huge, glittering, a deep brown under long lashes and, as she moved, so everyone's eyes were drawn to her.

In spite of her height—she was around five-eight—Miss Traccia carried herself with a composure and grace which was remarkable. She wore a dark maxidress, belted and with large pockets slanted forward on either side of her hips. As she walked, so the skirt swung enticingly. Dior had brought out the style during the previous year: the "New Look" as it was then called, a reaction to the former shortage of cloth, and as sexually inviting as the knee-length skirts of wartime utilitarian design.

She spoke to Helen Comfort, leaning over, talking rapidly to the pianist, throwing her coat over a chair, and coming forward again. "Thank you, Maestro—gentlemen. My name is Constance Traccia." A pause, then she quickly corrected herself. "Constanza Traccia. *Traviata,* '*Sempre libera*.'"

This was a good choice for a soprano's audition: Violetta's aria, "Ever free shall I hasten madly on from pleasure to pleasure." It requires range and certainly shows if the voice can sustain the top notes.

She began to sing, and Passau suddenly went very still. "She was so true, Herb. So complete and controlled. So clear. You ever been in a dry cold climate, where there's a lot of static? You ever tried to kiss another person in that kind of climate?"

Herbie nodded, a memory filling his mind for a second. Years ago. Finland. A hotel in some small town right up in the Arctic Circle. They had run a complex operation: brought someone in from the old U.S.S.R., and it had gone well. Standing by a bank of elevators, with one of the girls who had worked on the op, he leaned forward to kiss her in a moment of happiness. A spark had crackled through the air between their lips, stinging the soft flesh with a sharp shock.

"If you know," Passau said, "then you know what it was like in that theater. She had such range, such color to her voice. True, unforced, no strain. It was glorious to hear, and we all knew we had found something rare. When she finished, I could hardly speak."

But he had spoken. One word only. "More," he said in the past.

"Of course, Maestro Passau." A moment's thought, then a word to the pianist. "*Carmen*," she said. "The 'Habanera.'" A pace back, followed by a subtle movement of her body inside her dress.

"And this was amazing." Passau was looking through Herbie, not at him. "Carmen is for a mezzo. She was showing off an incredible range. Rare, moving, like being inside a crystal."

Again, there was absolute silence from those sitting around the director's table, as though they sensed something unusual. In the one movement of her body, Miss Traccia had performed the first part of that magical spell unique to great actors. In street clothes she had suddenly become the Flamenco cigarette girl of Bizet's opera. Helen Comfort began, and, for the first time, Louis Passau heard the sweep, fall, control and power of the extraordinary voice that was to become internationally famous within a few months.

To everyone there, in the early afternoon of September 24, 1948, Constanza Traccia became Carmen, a seductress displaying her sensuality for the doomed Don José. On that day, many of those present could have sworn she was reaching and touching Louis Passau as he sat, immobile, entranced at voice and assumed personality.

The AMD, Adrian Helpenmann, would later say that he could hear a full orchestra. "She had bewitched us, like some composers enchant by sheer genius: Rachmaninov's *Vespers*, for instance. You could swear it has an accompaniment, yet it is all a capella. This was almost unbelievable."

Of that moment, Michael Dresden was to write, "She seemed to do nothing, yet everything. Later I could not make up my mind whether it was all voice or a combination of great vocal and dramatic power."

Don Birch, the Chorus Master, said he could not take his eyes off her eyes. "My head was full of the music, but her eyes seemed to flash and glow, just as the part demands. She had me quite hypnotized."

It was not Passau's favorite opera. In the present, on that morning so many decades later, sitting in the apartment with Kruger, he admitted that his heart sank when she announced the "Habanera."

"Yet, when she began, Herb, you should have heard it, and seen it. Her voice seemed to glow with sexuality. She hardly moved, yet her body was alive to the rhythms. At one moment, I believe she tapped the three middle fingers of her right hand against the palm of the left, like a Flamenco. Her feet also rapped the stage, and that wonderful, clear, powerful voice had an undertow of smoke and sweat. When she finished, there was just a tiny pause, the fraction of a second, and we were all on our feet. I knew there was little I could ever teach her. She was one of those strange, incomprehensible artistes who are born. . . ."

"Like yourself, Lou?"

"Maybe. Yes, maybe. But she was there, she had arrived at her true birth, on that bare stage, in September 1948." Tears were close to the surface. He opened his mouth, then, as if he had thought better of it, he closed up again. His body gave one huge shudder, as though he was trying to hold back some flood of emotion, and his voice cracked as he said, "She . . . she was . . . my epiphany. . . ."

He raised his head, and Herbie found himself looking into a ruin, a face that had collapsed in almost mortal pain and agony. "God help me, Herb." He reached out and gripped his inquisitor's knee as though Herbie had the priestly right to shrive him. "She was my beginning and my end; my epiphany and my destruction. Constanza Traccia laid waste my soul, and when it was over—God help me—it was like the melodrama of Don José's last words in that small opera—'Carmen, my beloved Carmen.' In her I was razed to the ground."

"I been there, Lou. I know. I been there." Big Herbie Kruger, being the person he was, wanted to weep with the old man, for the passion, horror and depth of despair.

14

"THERE IS A STORY, LOU." Herbie tried to sound casual. "A story that you signed her straight off and then put her in the chorus. This story goes that she had a massive tantrum. There and then. Almost on the spot. That she expected to sing the leading roles immediately. Instant diva. True or false?"

The Maestro gave a sad little smile, fond and foolish at the same time. "Mostly true," he nodded.

It had taken almost an hour before Passau was able to talk again, and Kruger wanted to seize the moment: drag him back to that day in 1948 when something magical had happened on the half-empty stage in the Passau Center. This, he thought, is the great turning point. There is catastrophe here, and I shall be the first to hear of it. Also, this drama—whatever it was—impinges on his life as a Soviet agent, if that is what he truly was. Herbie was certain of it. Certain sure, as he would have said. He went to the kitchen and made coffee, taking some through to Pucky, then back to collect his, and Passau's, cups.

He stood looking at the percolator for several minutes, thinking of dates and times, and of the great eternal question mark that hung over the whole business. Why? Why bother with a ninety-year-old genius who just might have betrayed his country—twice?

The Nazi thing had obviously been low-key. Kruger had thought that from the start. Passau's confession, which had all the hallmarks of truth, bore that out. Blackmail which did not result in any serious intelligence calamity. Was Passau—had he ever been—a threat to national security, both here, in America, and across the ocean in Europe? Could be, he supposed. "Yet, what kind of ratings we got here?" he asked himself, almost aloud, part of it whispered.

Louis Passau's long-standing affair with Constanza Traccia, had lasted from 1949 until the mid-fifties, when its abrupt end led to his disappearance, his five years in the wilderness, and the writing of his one symphony. Yet there was more. Herbie thought of the days before he had traveled to New York, at the start of it all. Art Railton, Young Worboys and others briefing him on what they knew and did not know. Words floated back into his head.

"Erik the Red, 'Brightwater,' maintains the Sovs bought Passau—'bought him and paid for him,' were the words—in fifty-nine or sixty." Art Railton speaking.

"1960 would be about right," Worboys said. "It more or less coincides with his reappearance after the self-imposed exile. Get to the heart of that as fast as you can." At the time, Art had no idea of the restrictions that would be placed on Passau's interrogation.

Standing in the kitchen, Herb clenched both of his big fists and shook them in the air, whispering, "Push! Push! Push!" Then he went back to the Maestro, let him take a sip of coffee, and fired the question at him, its trajectory aimed exactly at putting the old man into his time machine, sending him back to 1948.

"Tell me about it, Lou. Tell me about the tantrum."

Louis had been all over her. Indeed, his colleagues had followed him up onto the stage congratulating her, as she stood there, smiling but unsurprised. They all told her she had a wonderful and bright career ahead. In turn, she seemed to acknowledge the fact with a smile and a short nod. With a voice, presence and dramatic talent like that, Constanza Traccia could not fail. Passau took her up to his office. On the way, he told Peter de Souza to draw up a contract.

Michael Dresden, the Chorus Master, walked ahead with the girl, talking earnestly. He was an intense man, who moved with arms locked behind his back, his head bent, looking at the ground so that he had no distractions, like some Oxford don. Dresden always appeared much older than his forty-six years. She was obviously incredibly knowledgeable about the voice as an instrument. The conversation floated back as they climbed the stairs to the executive offices. She talked technique, like a woman who had been at the heart of operatic life for twenty years or more, and that was just not possible, even though she had secured her bachelor's and master's degrees with stratospheric marks.

Passau was impressed. ("Impressed is not the real word for it, Herb. I couldn't believe what I was hearing. I didn't take it in.")

Quietly he whispered to de Souza that he wanted a standard exclusive contract. Ten years. Complete control. "Get hold of Martin Spinebrucker," he said. "No loopholes. Make it set in stone. No, make it set in steel."

He did not really know what he had got in Constanza Traccia. The family name seemed vaguely familiar, and the Carmen "Habanera" was obviously a very well-rehearsed party piece. Something she did effortlessly, like a conjuring trick or some routine learned in childhood. Experience told him she would need a great deal of work. There were few real divas who did not come directly from the Italian tradition and, while her name showed obvious Italian origins, she spoke clearly with an American accent. No hint of being a first-generation American: no Italian, or any other European, inflection. This girl had grown up in the United States and, though she had trained in Cincinatti, there had to be much for her to learn. Already, Passau was ticking off a mental list of teachers. His first thought would be to get the very best, put the teacher under an exclusive and make Traccia work night and day.

Once alone with the young woman, Louis Passau discovered it was not that simple.

"I want to put you under contract to my organization," he began.

She smiled, giving a little nod, part thanks, part triumph.

"There will be much to do," he continued. "I feel that, like most gifted sopranos who come to us, you should work for two years or so in the chorus. . . ."

The first explosion was minor. Her eyes glittered with irritation more than anger. "The chorus?" she asked, and her tone of voice should have alerted Passau. She repeated it, "The chorus?" as though she had not heard him correctly.

"I can give you extensive training. You're obviously a very gifted lady. If things go well, you'll progress quickly to understudying the leading soprano roles. After that, there's . . ."

"Understudying?" This time it was anger. Her mouth curled, the eyes flashed danger. "Maestro, I didn't come to you in order to understudy. I think I'd better go to the Met. I have friends there. . . ."

449

"But, Miss Traccia, *nobody* can expect to walk straight into the leading roles. You've graduated with spectacular success. Now, we must build on that. It takes years to learn the repertoire. . . ."

The softness of her voice, as she cut in on him, signaled a huge and consuming ego. "Maestro. I already *know* the repertoire. I've studied the repertoire since age ten." The way she said it, revealed something more than simple youthful assurance. It was as though she truly believed she had achieved, in her early twenties, a pinnacle which demanded instantaneous recognition.

"Since . . . ?"

"Since the age of ten. My father was Alberto Traccia. . . ."

Passau suddenly grasped why her name had seemed familiar. Alberto Traccia had been one of the great voice coaches at the Met. A man who had died suddenly, and young, some five years before. Alberto *had* come from the long apostolic succession of Italian opera. He opened his mouth, but only said, "Ah!" Then—"I knew your father. Once he came to dinner at my place near Rhinebeck. Your mother was ill and he came alone. But I knew him. A fine man. A kind of genius."

She stood glaring at him, and he again said, "Ah!"

"Ah, indeed, Maestro! My father was not a man who accepted second best. He began my training at age ten. Even before that I was exposed to music. From the cradle almost. Maybe before that. In the womb. I've worked for the day when I could put to use all those grueling hours of labor. I knew the bulk of the repertoire by heart, exact, before I reached my sixteenth birthday." Her voice had risen to the level of a cold and bitter storm. "If you're not going to give me my birthright, then there are others who will, and to hell with you, Maestro Passau. To hell with your organization!" She was on her feet, heading towards the door. With one hand on the knob, she turned her head and spat out one of the worst Italian oaths. "*Porco bastardo!!*"

In the present, Passau gave an enormous shrug. "You see, Herb, it was impossible. Impossible for any young woman of her age to have learned the repertoire. In America the great operatic tradition had been handed to us from Europe, but there were few opera companies to sustain it. Visiting companies came from Europe, and great operatic singers, but they were mainly transients in our country. A season here, a season there. Sure, they left their mark, but opera did not fully take root until after the war. It was there, but . . . well, you must know . . ."

"'Course I know, Lou. But this is a good story. What next, Lou?"

"I called her back."

She was spitting fire. Oaths in Italian that shocked Passau. She was out of control, shouting, shrieking at him like a toddler deprived of some treat.

"Miss Traccia, please. Please come back. Sit down. We'll work out something."

She stood in the doorway, enveloped in this storm of abuse. Passau could see Dresden and Adrian Helpenmann outside, their faces white with shock, for Constanza Traccia turned this kind of anger into an art form.

Helpenmann looked at Dresden. "It's a hurricane. A tornado." He gave a nervous little laugh. "La Tempesta," he said. He did not know that he had just given her a baptismal name for, in the time that followed, she was to become known all over the world as La Tempesta.

Then Passau shouted back. He was angry now. The great Louis Passau was not used to this kind of behavior, even from temperamental artists. It happened from time to time, but he could always give as much as he took—and more.

"Traccia!" he yelled: a command, as a drill sergeant will call a squad to attention. "Constanza Traccia! Come back and sit down. If you can sing, and if you do know the repertoire as you claim, then you will sing leading roles. This is my life, here. You can be part of it. So come and sit down. Now!"

It was obvious that she was unaccustomed to people talking back to her. She tossed her head, and her long hair rose and fell, like some exotic headdress, a dark halo. Quietly she closed the door in Dresden's and Helpenmann's faces. The anger was gone as she meekly resumed her seat, only traces of violence remained in the air, invisible between them.

"I'll tell you what I'll do, Miss Traccia." Passau, in a few seconds, had made up his mind. "I didn't know you until an hour ago. I knew *of* you only because I was told you were a brilliant student. How am I to know that you are completely familiar with the repertoire? I am not a mind reader, nor a soothsayer. Can we work together?"

She nodded, head still cocked high and arrogant.

"Might I presume to hear your competence for myself?"

"Whatever you wish, Maestro."

He gave her a big nod. A nod and a smile, then he slowly walked to the piano. "Come. Come and we will go over a couple of things."

On Captiva Island, Herbie saw the tears start in the old man's eyes again, the terrible emotion begin to crack the dam of his features.

"This was incredible, Herb," he said, his voice shot through with what could only be described as awe. "Look, I thought it would be a disaster. I had a very great talent with me, but thought she would still need much work. I imagined it was impossible for her to know what she claimed." A small, rusty laugh. "Because I was some kind of prodigy, I didn't expect another prodigy. Yet that's what I got."

Big Herbie nodded him on.

"I started on her, easy. Gave her Butterfly. 'Un bel dì vendremo,' like I had already heard that morning. Faultless. Extraordinary. But I thought, well, yes, of course. Yes, she would know that. I went through everything, each time getting harder and harder: *Tosca*, *Bohème*, Amelia in *Un Ballo in Maschera*, the really difficult—the gallows scene. God, I had known well-established sopranos who were utterly unconvincing: the great recitative and the aria. That scene calls for, *demands*, huge scale. Amelia is hysterical towards the end, leading to that top C. Incredibly hard. Yet, Herb, there was no strain at all. Sure, she wasn't competing with an orchestra and a full audience, but she was totally believable, absolutely convincing. And the voice. Jesus Christ, she just seemed to get better. Gave you the feeling she didn't even have to try. It was always like that with her."

"And that clinched it?"

"No. I gave her more. Oh, yes, my eyes, and my ears, were opened. I just wanted to hear more. I even recall exactly what we did: Senta, from *Holländer*." He meant *The Flying Dutchman*. Wagner. "And also Donna Elvira from *Don Giovanni*; then the music lesson from *Barbiere di Siviglia*; others—I remember *Manon Lescaut*, *Traviata*. More. No, I forget. In the next few years she was to sing practically everything, anyway. The impact, though—yes, I know I gave her *Aida*—the impact of that day. Sometimes I dream of it, or I should say sometimes I have nightmares."

"I know. I have dreams that seem peaceful, yet they are also nightmares, Maestro."

Passau grunted. "I doubt you've had a nightmare like mine." It was almost the old Louis. Anything you can do, I can do better.

In the short silence that followed, Herbie said, "So the rest is history, eh?"

"More or less. The start of the wild period of my life."

"Lou, it hadn't been exactly quiet up till then."

He nodded. "Sure, but I'm talking really wild."

"She sang in Kerry Arlow's *Aida*, three weeks later, right?"

"Yes. Three weeks, almost to the day."

"I saw it when you came to London. Was it fifty-two, or fifty-three? Never heard an *Aida* like it. . . ." Passau continued as though he had not even heard Kruger. "We had contracted a very great soprano. It caused a certain amount of havoc, but you got used to that when you were around Stanza." He was off, in the distance again. His mind had gone a-roving. "It's what I always called her. Stanza. Most other people had joke names for her—I mean other singers and directors. She thought it funny that she was called La Tempesta. But you know, Herb, the greatest thing about her was the joy she gave. In those days a lot of the great sopranos took themselves very seriously—and rightly so—but they believed in their position. Stars. Opera stars. Stanza was somehow different."

"How different?"

"She gave joy and she loved the joy. The joy of music, the fun of music, the emotion of music. When she stood on a stage she really gave herself—*all* of herself—to the audience. To every single person there. And in rehearsal, or when we recorded, she had the ability to joke when things went wrong: when she wasn't up to it, or when she made terrible errors. She would be very funny about herself."

"Even when she caused havoc?"

A small puff of laughter, "Umph! Yes, even then. Okay, *yes* she was La Tempesta. God, she could be a storm, but not always in the temperamental way. Sometimes it was almost delicate; and she worked. Shit, how she worked. Sometimes it was as though a devil drove her, as if she would run out of time." He went quiet, and Herbie, out of some misplaced respect, let him stay silent with his dreams and memories.

"It was incredible," he said, eventually. "Overnight, with the *Aida*, she became the most famous opera star in the world. Within less than twenty-four hours we had offers for her from all over—and I mean *everywhere*. La Scala wanted her, Covent Garden wanted her. Everywhere, for operas and also for concerts. She said no. She came to my office and said, "Maestro, I want to stay here, with the company. I want to work with you."

"And she did." Herbie looking Passau straight in the eyes. "She worked with you, and only you. Right?"

"Turned my life inside out, yes. Within one year everything had changed."

"The Passau Orchestra of America, Opera at the Center, your wife. All altered out of recognition."

"Sure. I even thought I believed in God for a time there. She turned me around: Constanza Traccia."

For that first year, for all of 1949, Constanza Traccia was at the vortex of a storm she alone created by her talent and her dedication. She appeared in no less that five operas: *Aida, Turandot, Lucia di Lammermoor,* Nedda in *Pagliacci* with Gigli in the title role.

Lastly, that season, there was a stunningly visual *Barbiere di Siviglia*, in which the sets gave such a depth of perspective, and looked so real, that audiences imagined they were looking at a strange new three-dimensional photography. Every production was sold out for its entire run.

In the meantime, Traccia also worked with Passau. In concerts, she sang in the Verdi and Brahms Requiems; in Passau's first public performance of the Mahler Second Symphony, and in a whole series of informal Sunday night appearances, works by Schubert, Schumann and the like. Louis Passau was her accompanist. One Sunday they had the whole orchestra in. She performed Mahler's *Kindertotenlieder—Songs on the Deaths of Children*. Gloomy, yet wonderful, uplifting, soaring towards hope. Pucky had found her recording of it. The CD was lying in the grip near the little CD player.

"She had another extraordinary talent, Herb. She was able to transcend language. You know how people are sometimes put off by opera, or choral works, even song recitals, because they don't understand the language?"

"Sure, many people . . ."

"With Constanza it was not like that. She seemed to be able to translate through her voice. Make people understand the song by the way she sang it. This was truly a remarkable gift."

It was as though with the advent of La Tempesta the whole of Passau's venture with the Center suddenly assumed even greater proportions. The New York critics, never anxious to praise, seemed to throw away their acid. Neither the orchestra nor the opera company could do wrong in their eyes, and the public followed them. It was a heady success, and Passau, the conscientious director and tireless worker, appeared to now play as hard as he worked.

As his reputation grew, so did his predilection for danger. He could be seen driving fast cars; he learned to fly and bought his own aircraft, a small four-seat Cessna. He spent nights on the town, in clubs and restaurants. Always, Constanza Traccia was at his side. They were greeted by name everywhere. People were known to have been moved from their tables because the Maestro and La Tempesta arrived unexpectedly.

In July 1949, Veronica Passau sued for divorce, citing La Tempesta. The case went uncontested, but the press sought out the couple and they were constant headline news.

"You never married her, Lou," Herbie said now, in the present. "I always thought that was odd. I mean you were famous for women, yet you never married her."

Passau gave a smile and a small shrug of the shoulders. "Perhaps that's why I never did it. Perhaps she didn't want to take the risk, Herb. Honestly, I forget now. Sudden memory loss. I swear it. Can't remember."

"I say, we will have no more marriages." Herbie gave his daft grin, and added, "Hamlet, Prince of Denmark." He pronounced it "Dane-Mark" just to be difficult.

Passau did not rise to *that* bait. "End of the summer that year," he said, "we found Corfu. In those days the islands around Greece were still fairly primitive. The annual trek to the sun by the package holiday firms had not yet started. Corfu was beautiful."

They had spent a month sailing off the Greek coast: courtesy of one of the Passau Center's wealthy patrons—between rehearsals and concerts. "We used to close down completely for all of August, so then it was feasible. Nobody knew where we were, because it was easier to give the press the slip at that time. They didn't even know we were on the yacht. I'll never forget it. One evening, just as the sun began to drop towards the horizon, we were on deck, approaching the island from the east. Corfu looked incredible. The light was so amazing, bright with golds and reds. There was rock, sand and lush greenery. I said something about it being like a romantic Victorian painting. You know, dust on the leaves, hanging in the air, crags rising from the sea. It could have been Prospero's island. You ever been to Corfu, Herb?"

Kruger shook his head, then quoted—

"The music crept by me upon the waters,
    Allaying both their fury, and my passion,
    With its sweet air."

"What, Herb?"

"You said it could've been Prospero's island. Shakespeare, Lou. *The Tempest*. La Tempesta."

"Oh, yeah. Sure. We went ashore the next day. Nobody knew who we were. It was wonderful; they just treated us like ordinary people. You know, the British gave Corfu two things: ginger beer and cricket. That's true, Herb. To this day. Ginger beer and cricket. God gave it a wonderful beauty. Mostly gone now. They built ugly beehive hotels, and gave all the visitors motor scooters. Terrible now.

"I bought the little villa a couple of days later. Bought it in the name of Martin Spinebrucker. We got local people to do the place up, and we'd go back there whenever we had a free week—which was not often—but it was worth the long journey and the jet-lag even for just five days. We had a very complicated routine to throw off the press when we went to Corfu. Worked every time, and nobody knew I even owned the villa. *Nobody*, Herb. Nobody but me and Stanza. Our hiding place. . . until . . ." He let it drift away.

"The villa was perched high up on a rocky cliff. Five rooms, nothing lavish. It became our trysting place. The next year we had steps cut in the rockface so we could walk down to the beach and bathe. It was truly idyllic. On the Paleokastritsa side of the island. Pity you've never been there, Herb. It was truly incredible to be there with Stanza." He stopped, though his mind had run on ahead of him, or backwards, depending on where he decided to be at that moment, and *who* he decided to be: the man who loved Constanza Traccia before the horror, or the man he became afterwards.

He saw the agile Constanza Traccia, long legs pumping, breasts hardly moving as she ran towards him along the golden sand, and he called to her, "Stanza! Stanza!" Never in all his lusts and desires had he loved a woman like her. Never had he loved.

Quietly, Herbie rose, going softly out to the kitchen to get lunch, leaving the old Maestro to his memories, so strong and redolent of pure happiness that Herbie could almost smell them in the silence.

A few minutes later, he heard Passau moving, digging into the CDs. Constanza Traccia's clean and clear, pure voice filled the apartment. Mahler. *Kindertotenlieder*. It was like a sad and beautiful chime, tolling for all who died before their time—

> *"Nun will die Sonn' so hell aufgehen,*
> Now the sun will rise as brightly
> as if no misfortune had befallen in the night.
> This misfortune happened to me alone,
> the sun shines for everyone."

Herbie stood still and thought his heart would break at the beauty and the unknown crucifixion he thought Passau must be undergoing.

15

BIG HERBIE MADE his famous omelettes aux fines herbes in the kitchen, while Constanza Traccia, with the Passau Symphony Orchestra of America, sang the winding, soaring, melancholy *Songs on the Deaths of Children*. The Maestro had been right. You did not have to understand German to know the emotion, horror and turmoil of which she sang. Her artistry, combined with Mahler's settings, told vividly of loss, heartache and grief which borders on madness. The instrument which was her voice etched in the tears and the agony of minds unable to accept the frightful loss of a small, deeply loved soul.

For some reason, for he was no expert on things Biblical, Herbie thought of the Lamentations of the Prophet Jeremiah—"Is it nothing to you, all ye that pass by? Behold, and see if there be any sorrow like unto my sorrow." What *was* Lou Passau's sorrow? Why had he been afflicted by this woman with her huge and wondrous talent?

In the main room, Louis Passau leaned back, his eyes closed, listening to the voice of his adored one. The only woman who had, for a brief period, made such a difference to his life. With dreadful clarity he summoned the ghosts of times long gone, so that their pictures haunted his mind, just as they so often frequented his dreams.

The pictures were powerful, flashing bright and all too real in his head: Stanza, at this very recording: he could even recall what she wore: very casual, a white silk shirt, black skirt, flared and swinging as her body swayed to the notes.

Singing in the relative privacy of a studio, she would move in a way never seen by audiences when she was onstage. Reaching effortlessly for a high note she would raise an arm, almost languidly, above her head, or at other times motion with her palm, as though flattening a sound, pushing it down so that it seemed to disappear into the air, a long diminution, leaving a shiver in its wake.

He saw her laughing across a dinner table, always full of mischief, her face endlessly mobile, a quick wit. He heard her speak now, the tremble of a smile in her tone, and the bubble as she added some telling line to a countless store of tales: never malicious, always amusing, overflowing with mirth.

Though he tried to expunge the scenes from his mind, Louis Passau also saw her naked, brimming with energy as they lay together on the huge bed in the Corfu villa: her long limbs stretching, arching her whole body to his. Skin as smooth as the silk she so often wore at these times. No blemish. They became one as he had never experienced it before. They reached the ultimate for lovers, that secret still-turning world that was theirs alone. Nobody could intrude and they were all relationships to each other. It seemed to surpass time and space, as though they had lived and loved time and again from the beginning to the end. Alpha and Omega.

"Play me again," she would whisper. "Oh, Lou, play me again. I love you."

He heard his own voice respond, and the shadow of their constant love-making fell across his heart, wrenching at some deep horror. Nights in strange hotels, sleepless and joyful. Mornings, dawn, waking and looking out of windows at views neither of them would ever forget: a sailboat far out across water, a seemingly endless forest somewhere on the Swiss border, the trees peeking up through a light mist, and the physical burn and ache, a constant reminder of the pleasure of the night. The music of the night. The memories were not self-indulgence. They were as real as the room in which he now sat. They were perfect in every detail.

"Oh, God," he wept. "Oh, God Almighty, save me."

She came back to him, onstage, in scene after scene, as immensely pleasing to the audience as she was to him when they were alone. She was so young, alive, loving, even when she became temper-tossed—La Tempesta—or when she became defensive because she knew what she was doing to an aria, or if a scene was wrong, even off by an infinitesimal amount. There only had to be one small thing not quite right and she would rage like a volcano, just as in their love for one another she was everything: fire and ice, wind, rain, turbulence and the softness of spring. She would weep at the first sign of snowdrops, just as *he* still wept when he saw those tiny flowers, for the memory was almost unbearable.

He saw them together, like an out-of-body experience: wrapped around each other as they walked in fair and fine weather—Paris, London, Rome, Berlin, Salzberg, Vienna, Venice. He stopped for a second, remembering her face one evening as she looked out across the Grand Canal, tears starting to her eyes because the view was so incredible; then the scene shifted to sunset at Key West, eyes reflecting the blood of the sinking sun as the great shaft of crimson flashed across the sea.

Always she was moved by the beauty of a view, a moment, a sight never to be captured again: the Jungfrau seen from some grassy vantage point at Interlaken, Switzerland; the House of Commons and Big Ben almost lost in a great swirl of snow late one afternoon in London; standing on a bridge in the grounds of Blenheim Palace, in Oxfordshire, catching her breath as a spear of light hit the water for a second, then was gone; her wonder, walking into the Place de l'Opéra in Paris, seeing it for the first time; even the New York skyline, lit by a raging electrical storm, seen from the windows of the apartment. She wanted to go out in it, feel the lightning, brave the danger, dare the electricity to strike her down. But Paris, that was a moment. . . .

With Paris there, in his head, he thought of an afternoon at the Louvre—again her first visit—when they quarreled for a minute, over something silly. How she had disappeared and he had been distraught, looking for her, only to find that she had bought a small Egyptian figurine, a kneeling slave. She presented it to him gravely, then her mouth puckered and she was full of laughter again. Her voice was always with him, though sometimes he could not capture her face because of the very nature of its mobility.

Their physical moments burst in him once more. The unexpected times, when they could not wait to get to the bedroom in Corfu, or the games they would play—a question and answer interrogation on music. The winner would choose how they would perform the act, for there were countless, amusing variations of that. Things which kept their most private moments sweet—she, the whore, he, the client; he, the innocent, she, the predator; the honeymoon couple—she had a way of unveiling something new every time they played *that* game.

Yet Stanza was an innocent when they first came together, locked, and unlocked, winding the spring and slowly easing it down until exhaustion. Just as her voice and talent onstage was natural, so she had come to him virtuous yet crammed full of the instincts of a woman's love. For a second he had a picture of her long hair tumbled over a pillow; then, again, hanging over her face, the tresses sweeping his belly. So, together, they found the elusive fount of youth and happiness.

It was a time that seemed endless. He thought they really believed nothing could change, that this thing they had was unquenchable, would stretch with them into eternity, for she had wrought a miracle in him. His work became better, his insight sharper, because of her. Sometimes they seemed to have exchanged minds. He had known entire days with her when neither spoke a word except the endearments of love, yet they knew what each was thinking.

A thousand moments spent with her—public and private—raced through his mind, like time-lapse photography. They had it. Then, suddenly, it was gone, leaving dust and ashes in his mouth, squeezing his heart until it cracked.

The last notes of the final song of *Kindertotenlieder* faded—

"In this weather, in this storm,
in this tumult,
they are resting, as if in their mother's house,
not frightened by any tempest
sheltered by God's hand,
they are resting, as if in their mother's house.
Sie ruhn wie in der Mutter Haus."

Big Herbie had taken an omelette to Pucky, who lay on the bed, grave and silent, listening to the voice that had launched and, possibly, sunk a thousand of Passau's ships. She looked up at him, reaching for him so that he had to put the tray down and take her in his arms. She whispered, "Whatever it is, Herb, it's not going to happen to us. Tell me it's not going to happen to us." So he told her, and held her body to him, as fragile as a small animal.

"Is not going to happen to us," he said quietly and left as the last notes faded and dissolved into the air. He thought again of *The Tempest*—

"Are melted into air, into thin air," he said aloud, then made Passau's omelette, took up his tray and with a deep breath, lumbered out to him, playing the idiot.

"There you are going, Maestro Passau. Three-egg omelette, with all the herbs I can find. 'Erbs as you Americans say. That gets on my wick, this pronunciation—'erbs.'"

Passau shrugged and looked emotionally drained.

"Hey, Lou, why don't I get us a nice glass of wine? Cheer us up, eh?"

"As you like."

"Okay, I like. Get my omelette and nice glasses of wine for the both, okay?"

He nodded and began to fork his omelette. When Herbie came back a few minutes later, with his own omelette and two large glasses of Zinfandel, Passau was being a shade more energetic about the food. "I had to teach Stanza about cooking from the beginning," he said. "Teach her even to boil an egg. She knew nothing."

"Not even spaghetti?"

"Especially not even spaghetti."

"But she was from an Italian American background, yes?"

"Of course, but her mama did everything for her. Taught her nothing. Her singing came first according to her father, so the mama didn't teach her squat."

"Shame on her mama. What was her family name?"

"Jacobi. Helluva name. Don't know where it came from." He went silent again.

"So, you taught her good, Maestro."

"I taught her excellent, but she was still a very literal woman. One day she decided she would keep house—we still got the Park Avenue apartment. Veronica got to keep Woodstoke Hall—the place outside Rhinebeck—and a large cash settlement. I kept Park Avenue. . . ."

"And the place on Lexington, Lou. Where you did the slap and ticklings on the side."

"When I was with Stanza there was no need for the place on Lexington," he snapped, and Herbie realized that, so far, Passau had not uttered a crude word about Constanza Traccia. Dear God, he thought, this is a first. With all the others he could not wait to describe his sexual athletics. This time he did not even attempt to brag. There was none of the street-talk language, none of the bounce. Constanza was the real one. Could it be, the only one?

"You still kept Lexington, Lou. I know it."

"Then if you know it . . ." He twirled his fork and shrugged. "When you know something, Herbie, don't bug me with it. How d'you know it?"

Herbie jumped in. "Because we have a mutual friend, Lou. But, as you would say, that comes later. Tell me about life and love with Constanza Traccia."

Passau paused in his eating, took a sip of wine. "A mutual . . . ?"

"That comes later. Stick with the chronology. She decided to keep house, you were saying."

"Oh, that. Yes."

"So, what was it like with La Tempesta, Lou?" Seeing if he would crack and talk of her as he talked of other women: almost malicious, giving away their secret physical selves.

Maestro Passau took another sip of wine, deeper this time. A nod, then— "The most productive period of my professional life; the most creative; the happiest. Check the record, Herb. From 1948, when I first met her, until 1955, I did more traveling than at any other time in my career up to then. Sure, I've traveled a lot since. Concerts everywhere, but the big foreign concerts started around forty-nine. The last was in the summer and early fall of fifty-five."

"Where did you go on that last one. The last tour with Miss Traccia?"

"We did London, Vienna, Paris and Venice. Seven weeks. Arduous."

"Okay, but what're your greatest memories of her?"

Slowly, Passau shook his head. "The memories are for me, Herb. Those I don't share. . . ."

"Confession time, Lou. You not telling me everything?"

"Only what matters. What is germane to my life."

"Okay, in a nutshell, tell me what it was like."

"Roller coaster; storm at sea; earthquake; doing aerobatics—I did aerobatics in a small plane. Learned them from an expert. There's nothing like stretching the envelope, Herb. Doing things that might make you stop living suddenly."

"Like rock climbing?"

"Better than climbing. You strap yourself in, climb into the air: high, where it seems clean and the earth is a long ways off below you. Then the precision. Like conducting, there has to be precision—rolls, loops, roll off the top, hesitation rolls, falling leaf, hammerheads, spins. Very precise. You got no time to throw up. Bet I could still do it. Want to try sometime?"

"No, Lou. I prefer feet on the ground."

"Pity. Nothing like it."

"Except living with Constanza Traccia?"

"Sometimes. Sure." He left Herbie for a moment, forking up the last morsel of the food, pushing the tray to one side, taking another sip of wine, his mind faraway, over the horizon of his memories.

"Difficult?" Herb asked, and Passau shook his head.

"Opera singers belong in a different cage to other people. Sure, Stanza belonged in a different cage. But, God, it was more an Aladdin's cave than a cage. With her it was wonderful and terrible at the same time. Beautiful. With her even the difficult times were shot with beauty."

"That good?"

Passau gave a mirthless laugh. "Sure, that good. But, like aerobatics, you had to know what you were doing. You had to know how she flew."

The long pause made Herbie think he was with Passau in a timeless, soundproof bubble. Faraway, out across the sand and water that was Captiva Island, he thought he heard singing. Passau's head came up, cocked. He also heard it. Timeless, clear, girls' voices in harmony from some launch offshore. You couldn't tell what they were singing.

Suddenly Passau said, "In Venice, the last time we were there, late one afternoon, early evening, we rode down the Grand Canal. Not much traffic on the water. Then we saw a large gondola—there's a name for them, I forget. Some of the kids from the chorus were singing. Would you believe it was the 'Barcarole' from *Tales of Hoffmann*? To hear it, low across the water, bouncing off the houses, was something wonderful. She joined in—we were a long way apart, but the voices met, swayed, like the gondolas." A count of twenty seconds or so. "There's a memory." Then, "You know poor Offenbach died during rehearsals of *Hoffmann*. Never got to hear the thing performed. Ironic."

"That was your last time in Venice with her?"

"Yes."

"You finished the tour in Venice, then back to Corfu. The place was a secret. How you manage that, Lou?"

"What you'd call tradecraft. The Germans taught me something, you see."

"And the Russians?"

He shook his head. Herbie thought there was a ghost of a smile on his lips. "In those days it was BT."

"BT?"

"Before Terrorists. You could book tickets in another name and nobody would really be any the wiser. From New York we would both shoot off in different directions. Tiny would drop me at La Guardia, PanAm Terminal; Stanza would get her driver to take her to what was then Idlewild—New York International. Then we'd both hop cabs. She'd go to La Guardia, I'd go to Idlewild. We'd fly different airlines to Athens. Mainly turbo-props in those days. Took forever. Usually an entire day. Sometimes we'd have to fly to other places, then change flights. We met up in a tiny hotel, out-of-the-way place, in Athens. I kept a small plane there—Martin Spinebrucker's name, like the villa. We'd fly to Corfu. Sleep one day afterwards, then enjoy what time was left."

"Nobody could get in touch?"

"Of course they could get in touch, but you got to remember, Herb, this was the fifties. Very little direct overseas dialing. Calls from London to New York took about an hour. You booked the call and they got through about an hour later. In France it was longer. In Italy it could take a day. On Corfu, sometimes two days—three even. People had a number for me in the States. Message service. I'd call in, collect the messages, but the orchestra and the company were in good hands. There was never any panic. Not until the last time." Again he was faraway. The look in his old eyes spoke danger; one hand started to tremble.

"But the last time you went from Venice?"

"From Venice, yes. That was easy. You know how travel works best, Herb? Best when you don't want anyone to know?"

"Hide in plain sight?"

"Just do it. Nobody thinks you just hop a plane. If they're looking for you, they approach the whole thing as though you'd be sneaky. Intrigue. We could only do that when we were in Europe. The press never got on to Corfu—well, not until 1960, and that was an accident."

"You said just now that nobody knew until the last time, Lou. You mean that? When the press found you?"

"No. I mean the last time I was there with Stanza." Mouth closed. A shutter coming down over the eyes. "We stop now, Herb?"

"No. No, we go on."

"Maybe I don't want to tell it."

"Confession, Lou. You said it would be everything. You have to know yourself, and to do that, you have to share."

"Sure. Like Tolstoy said, 'I am always with myself, and it is I who am my tormentor.' Melodramatic, huh?"

"Tell me, Lou. I'm your friend. Tell me."

He did not speak for almost a minute. "Don't know if I can tell you, Herb. Don't know if I've got the balls. Some things in life are so fucking awful that you hide them. Bury them deep and never dig them up."

"Dig this one up, Lou. You never told anyone about this before. Why? How? Do it, and do it now, Lou. Make you feel better. Sharing it."

For five minutes or so, the old man sat still, eyes not seeing, hands trembling. It was the trembling that was the worst thing. From his hands it seemed to progress through his entire body. His body did not shake physically, but Herbie could feel it.

At last, he said, "Okay. Let me take my time. This is very difficult for me. Okay?"

"We do it at your pace, Maestro. Just tell it all. Tell it how it happened."

He took a deep breath and nodded. "We flew direct. Venice-Athens. A beautiful morning. We took off from Athens, in my little plane, after lunch. No clouds. We had six entire days before being due back in New York. Couldn't have been happier. Got to the villa around five o'clock. Sun shining. Not a care in the world. . . ."

IT WAS LATE SUMMER. A warm evening, and the villa smelled of lemons. Stanza's favorite scent. She had soap brought over especially from France because she loved the smell.

They checked the villa, opened windows, unpacked. Even though they were tired, she suggested they should walk down to the taverna and eat out. Showering together, she was in a playful mood and began to soap him down. One thing led to another, so afterwards, they showered again, and he had to call her in from the little balcony that ran along one side of the upper story because she was standing there, dressed only in her underwear. Passau playfully berated her. "You want to get the whole village here? I'm going to have to fight them off. They'll be standing in line."

"And you'll be first, so I won't let any of them come in, my darling. Only you. So don't be such a prude."

"I'm not a prude. Just it's not seemly for . . ."

Her eyes opened wide. "You were going to say for a married woman, Louis. I saw the word forming on your lips. You were . . ."

"I was going to say, for a woman of your international importance, and reputation."

"They don't know that, here. They don't know who we are, but it won't last forever. They've started building new hotels near the town. Near Corfu itself. On our last visit, Nikko said that, eventually, they'll have hundreds of people here every summer—and, Lou, you *were* going to say 'married woman.'" She looked at his reflection in the mirror. His face was set and grave, brow wrinkled. "Admit it."

"Okay, I admit it."

"You want to be married, Lou? I thought we'd been through all that. I thought you said all marriages ended up as eventual failures. You weren't going to make a mistake again."

"This time it wouldn't be a mistake, Stanza. I've been thinking about it. Why don't we? Why don't we get married? Do it here. On the island. I'm tired of taking planes without you. I don't really care if the press know about this." He waved his hand, to indicate the whole villa.

"Maestro and Diva discovered in Greek love nest." She swirled up from the little dressing table and flung her arms around his neck. "I couldn't be more happy, Louis. Yes! Yes! Yes! Marriage. I'll even go through a Jewish wedding with you. Under the canopy, the breaking of the glass, everything."

Again, one thing led to another. When it finished she said, "I feel married already; who needs the piece of paper?"

He rolled away from her, his hands caressing her bare shoulders, eyes locked into her eyes. For Louis Passau, you could drown in her eyes. "We need the piece of paper, and the ceremony, Stanza. I don't care if it's Jewish or Catholic, but we need it."

She kissed him lightly. "Okay, so *we* need it. Let's do both. 'L'chayim' first, then 'Kyrie Eleison.'" Sliding from the bed, she began to get dressed again. "I'm not going to wash you off. I want you with me through dinner and later," giving him a wicked look, eyes flashing like a Gypsy. He thought of the first audition, and her Carmen.

Louis lay on the bed, his whole being swollen with happiness. This time, with Stanza, it would last forever.

The light was fading as they walked down towards the road, the moon already up and high. Constanza sang snatches of 'Porgi amor,' from *Figaro*—

> "*Porgi, amor, qualche ristoro*—
> Grant, love, that relief
> to my sorrow, to my sighing.
> Give me back my treasure,
> or at least let me die.

"You've been granted relief," Louis chuckled, clinging to her. "And nobody can return your treasure. It's gone forever and it's mine."

She laughed, wrapped her arms around him, "Grant, love, that relief. . . ."

She snuggled into his shoulder. "Please grant me relief, Lou, darling. More relief."

"I love you," he said.

"More than any other woman you've loved?"

"There were no women until you. What of your men?"

"You know all about that. Truly, were there no other women until me?"

"You know. I've told you. Yes, women, but they've gone. No memories even."

The trees loomed up on either side of the chalky road, the summer dust in the air, and the only sound to be heard was their own feet scuffing the dry surface. The air smelled of the day's dead sunlight. Ahead were the lights of the taverna, where Nikko greeted them with mock reverence, yet happy to see them. The waiters at the taverna knew them only as "The Lovers." They were not interested in names or greatness in the world, but they could recognize lovers, and warmed to them.

They ate fresh lobster, caught that afternoon and cooked by Nikko himself. First, a little taramasalata, with a glass of ouzo. Then lobster, a salad redolent of feta and olives. They chewed pita and drank retsina. It was as though they had never left the island. Always this was like coming home.

Then out came the bouzouki and the dancing began. They joined the waiters and three other guests and danced. The slow line of figures, pacing each other, then faster until, with flushed faces, they swayed and slapped their calves and stamped.

Constanza and Louis did not get back to the villa until one in the morning. Both of them glowed from the food, wine, dancing and their love for one another.

("Life there, Herb. It was so simple. The villa was furnished with simple things. Pine chairs and a table. Another table for work. We slept in a bed made of pine—a box with a mattress on it and sheets thrown over it. There we always slept with the windows wide open. In the second year we had mesh put up or the whole place would fill with insects, some of them huge green things like locusts. Stanza was frightened by them. The only things of any value in the villa were the piano and an old icon which we hung in the main room. Large, with mother-of-pearl and gold inlay. A mother and child.")

Louis decided to call the answering service in New York. "They won't get a line until the morning." He was already undressing Constanza. She loved being undressed. Found it very erotic to have each garment pulled away until she was naked. They began to make love again. Louis was not surprised that this would make the third time since they arrived. It was always like this when they came to Corfu. The air, sense of freedom and relaxation gave both of them fresh appetites.

Just as they were drifting into sleep, entwined one with another, the telephone rang. Louis grunted, and Constanza laughed, for he had been so wrong about the length of time it would take to get a line to New York.

He wrote the messages on a pad by the telephone, tore off the sheet and came back, up the simple open wooden stairs to their loftlike bedroom.

"Can they not do without us?" she asked, humor in her voice.

"Someone can't. Will I ring a number in Rome. I don't recognize the number." He stretched out beside her again and she took the paper from him. "It's for me. That's my mother's number." She made a tiny irritated noise.

Constanza rarely spoke of her mother. They had quarreled hopelessly after her father's death. Money had played a part in the dispute. Money. The Will. Lawyers were brought in. Constanza moved out of the family apartment in New York. Eventually, things were patched up, but they remained apart. Signora Traccia had moved back to Italy. Constanza said she lived with her sister in a very fashionable area of Rome. "They both live like high-class whores," she had once told him. "It's embarrassing. I only visited once. Stayed two days, then sent myself a telegram saying I had to get back to Cincinatti. It was the only time I'd been out of the country before I met you."

Now, in the darkness, she said she would put in a call tomorrow. "She probably wants another loan. I give her all she needs from what was left to me, but she spends it. Only gets in touch when she needs more. They were together, at the end, because of me. They should've split up years ago. She's not a very nice person, but my father . . . well, he worshipped her. Then he died. So sudden, Lou. There one minute, gone the next . . . and . . . oh, well. Tomorrow." It was about the longest sustained speech she had ever made to him about her parents.

It was almost noon when she bothered to put the call through. They had stayed in bed half the morning, talking between small bouts of loving. Often, in Corfu, they could go on like this all day. Start a little lovemaking, not finish it. Talk. Laugh. Another sexual encounter, unfinished. Talk again. Laugh again. Then one of them would say, "How about the grande finale?" They would go for it—so hard that it seemed both were trying to lose themselves in each other's body. They always said that they were simply two parts of one whole.

Like the call to New York during the night, Constanza's line to Rome came through within the hour. Louis had gone outside, to sniff at the afternoon air. When he came in, she was talking in Italian, fast, almost exasperated. "She wants to see me." She covered the receiver with one hand. Louis could hear a tinny voice rattling on at the distant end. "She says it's very important. Life or death matter."

"Then we'll go to Rome, if we have to."

"One minute, Mama," she said, hand over the phone again. "Lou, darling, she's a drama queen. Worse than opera singers. This is a terrible thing, she says, but she won't tell me what it is, not over the telephone. She's crazy—paranoid."

She went back to talking to her mother, her voice rising, the Italian getting faster and faster, more shrill.

Once more the hand over the telephone. "Louis, I don't want to go to fucking Roma. It'll be terrible."

"Okay, ask her here. She can come to the wedding."

She dazzled him with her smile ("Seemed to light up her entire body, completely, Herb"), then talked into the telephone again. Controlled now. Calm. Speaking with an obvious tact, smoothing over the hysteria at the distant end.

Finally, the conversation ended. Constanza gave a long sigh. "She's going to call back in an hour—which means about four hours. Has to make reservations. Pack. Get to the bank. She's coming as quickly as she can get here. I don't think you realize what you're doing, Lou. She'll be hell. She'll also try to steal you from me, and where's she going to sleep? Not here. I forbid it."

"Nikko'll give her a room at the taverna. If she's into seduction, let her get Nikko into bed."

"I'm hungry," she pouted. "Hungry! And she won't call back for hours. Shit!"

But, half an hour later, the telephone rang. The Signora Traccia was flying into Athens that night. She had a connection that would get her to the airport in Corfu at eleven the next morning.

"And she's being strange, Lou. Says she doesn't want us to meet her at the airport. Asked me to have her picked up and brought here."

"Good." They were lengthening the runway at what had been a tiny airstrip: preparing for the hordes of tourists. Until a year or so before, there were few scheduled flights from Athens. It was a recent thing, and driving to the airport, with all the construction going on, was a time-consuming business. "Good," he repeated. "Let's go and eat."

Nikko had a room, and promised to take the greatest care of the mother. They ate until around five, then came back to the villa for love in the afternoon. It was late when they walked down to the taverna again for dinner, and later still when they got home. By then, Nikko had even arranged to drive to the airport and meet "The Mother" as he called her.

That night they made love until three in the morning, and it was very special, like a wedding night. They swallowed each other's tongues, and probed each other's bodies as though they were instruments. Not for nothing did Stanza whisper, "Play me again, my dearest, darling Lou. My husband, my bridegroom."

In spite of it all, they were awake early. They wrapped towels around themselves and went down the steps cut into the rock. Down to the sand, and into the water, splashing like children. There was nobody to see their nakedness, and they swam out, floated together, then made love again, buoyant on the water, as though they had the ability to conquer the elements. Their bodies floated together, and they moved with the gentle swell, feeling the sun rising hot above them. When they climaxed, it was with a great rushing wave of water, as they lost control and thrashed in the foam that was of their own making.

Back in the villa, they showered. Constanza had only just dressed when Nikko's motor horn beeped outside. Louis was only half dressed, so she dashed down, telling him to hurry—". . . and, darling, don't let her use our room, not even for a second, or she'll unpack and we'll have to move out. She's every operatic villainess that's ever been written. I promise."

"Then I'll frighten her away. *Il Diavolo!*" He clawed the air with splayed, crooked fingers, and her laugh floated back to him as she disappeared.

He finished dressing, then heard the sound of voices below. Constanza's tone pitched high, as though her mother had already said something upsetting or hurtful. He heard the other voice, low and insistent. Something familiar drifted back, but he could not grasp at it.

As he walked down the stairs, he saw the two of them standing, looking up at him. Stanza's face had drained of color, but the woman next to him seemed confident, even challenging, in the way she stood, the manner in which she moved slightly. All of it was familiar, though it did not strike him until she spoke, and he had to get within a few paces of her before he recognized Constanza's mother.

"Hallo, Louis. It seems I've only just arrived in time." Sophie Giarre took a step back, as though afraid of him. "Carlo sends his good wishes," she said with a terrible smile. Behind her, the icon of the mother and child seemed to lower over them all.

In the Captiva apartment, old Louis Passau broke down completely and uncontrollably.

17

It took Louis Passau several minutes before the full truth penetrated his brain. At first he refused to believe it was Sophie. Then, once his mind accepted *that* fact, he could not assimilate the horror.

"Sophie?" Questioning if it was really her.

"It's been a long time, Pianist."

"What's . . . ?" Constanza stood behind her mother. She looked vulnerable. He had never seen her like this before: like a child; a very young teenager getting her first taste of the real world and finding that it could be an awful place.

Passau knew he looked like a ghost. He had this strange feeling that both of the women could see right through him.

"You *know* each other?" Constanza's eyes opened wide, bewildered. "Mama, this is Louis Passau, the man I'm going to marry. Please, what did you say about my father? I don't understand."

"Louis Passau?" Sophie's hands were on her hips, and somehow she appeared to have distanced herself from her daughter. "Maestro Passau. Yes, Constanza, you've done very well landing yourself the great Maestro Passau. When I knew him he was plain Louis Packer. They used to call him 'The Pianist,' right, Lou?"

"A long time ago, Sophie. Different people. Different world."

"Different people, yes. Same world, Lou."

"What's . . . ? What's going on? I don't . . . ? Mama, you said Louis Passau would listen to me sing. You told me . . . I don't . . . ?" Constanza's voice had become small, frightened, as though she knew something truly terrible was about to happen.

Sophie's head moved, her eyes raking her daughter with a look of such complete contempt that the air between them could have frozen.

"I last saw Lou around eight months before you were born, baby. He had picked up some bug. Had to get straight home, that last time I saw him. We were a good team: him on the piano, me singing my heart out—you'd have been proud of us. He knew I wanted to talk with him that night, but he told me we could talk the next day. He was in one hell of a hurry to drop out of my life. Where did you go, Lou? On that last night? They said you went off to meet the Gennas and, together, you hijacked a convoy of booze trucks coming in. That true? You left me for money?"

He heard and saw the entire thing. The last night in Chicago. How he had made excuses. *"Gee, I think I picked up a bug, Sophie. You shouldn't come near me, not tonight. I feel wretched."*

The way she had clung. *"Let me come back to your place, Lou. I'll tuck you up. Make you all cozy."*

"We were playing the Hawthorne Smoke Stack, right, Lou?"

Still not wanting to believe her, he nodded.

"The night before that—the night before we did our last show together, do you remember that?"

"A long time ago, Sophie."

"Sure, a long time ago." Her head whipped round again towards Constanza. "I don't want to shock you too much, my darling daughter, but that last night before the final show we did, Louis and I fucked our brains out. Right, Lou?"

"Long time . . ." he began, but she raised her voice, cutting him off as surely as a bullet could cut off his life. "Yes. Yes, it was a long time ago. The next day, Constanza, the next morning, when we were getting dressed, he was in a great hurry. Had an important appointment, and so did I. And in the evening, the very last time I saw him, I wanted to tell him about my appointment, because mine was at the doctor's office. I can't tell you how much I wanted to talk to him. You see, I was pregnant. I was having his baby." She stopped to look at each of them in turn. "I was pregnant with you, Constanza Maria Traccia."

In the present, the old man began to sob again, his head moving from side to side, then backwards and forwards, like an autistic child.

His pain and despair reached out—an icy, dead hand, clawing at Big Herbie Kruger's heart, so that he got to his feet and lumbered over to the old Maestro, put his big arms around him, cradling him like a child.

"Long ago, Lou. It's okay now. You've told it. It wasn't your fault. Is okay now." Soothing him, hushing him as though he were a distressed infant.

Presently, the emotion subsided. "I get you cup of tea, Maestro." Herbie ran a big hand over the old man's shoulder, then ruffled his hair. "In England that's remedy for all things. If things go wrong—death in the family, letter from tax man—always they say, 'Let's have nice cuppa. Cuppa tea.' You like that?"

Passau nodded. Even nodding seemed painful. "I didn't know," he said, very quietly, almost inaudible. "No idea. I've thought back many times. Not a hint."

"Not your fault. Lou." He went through into the kitchen, put the kettle on, then looked into the bedroom. Pucky's face was a mask of desolation. "You can forgive him a lot," she said.

"A little, yes. Not a lot, Puck. But some of it you can forgive, like God."

"You were great with him, Herb. Man of the Year."

"Yea, I know. Like in the kindergarten: gold star and a green rabbit. I have to keep it gentle for a while now. I need more time. A lot more time, and Art isn't going to give it to me. Before we know it, Lou'll be banged up with Gus Keene in the guest suite at Warminster."

She shook her head. "It has to be you, Herb. We've got to make it plain to Art."

"Maybe it's not up to Art."

He took the tea through to Passau. "Hot, strong, sweet. You can stand your spoon up in it, Lou. Get the other side of that, you be okay."

"Thank you, Herbie." The tone had altered. Kruger thought he even detected a tincture of humility.

They sat in silence for a while, then Passau began to talk, unasked and without any prodding from Herbie.

"I still don't know what happened after she dropped the bombshell, but I did know that what she said was true. There is an awful truth, Herb, a terrible truth when something is fully revealed to a man—something like that anyway. I knew what I had loved about Stanza—and I *did* love her, Herb. Loved her like nobody before or since. Now, with the distance of time, that love is pure. Difficult for you to understand, I think. That incest could be pure."

"Wasn't incest, Lou. Not knowing incest. Sophie was quite a monster, if you're telling it right. She put her daughter up to it."

Passau nodded, almost imperceptibly. "They left," he said. "I can't remember how, but I guess Nikko drove them back to the airport. I remember none of that, apart from Sophie saying that Carlo would catch up with me. One day, she said. Some day. I would spend the rest of my life looking over my shoulder. Stanza was sobbing; weeping. I heard her crying in that villa for months afterwards, just like she had somehow recorded it into the wood and stone. I'd wake in the night and hear it. For many weeks I would reach out for her, to comfort her, stop the tears. But she wasn't there. Sophie didn't even let her stay so we could talk, figure out what to do."

"So you just stayed there? Five years. Until someone spotted you, made you come back to the real world. . . ."

"Oh, I was in the real world all the time, Herb. Those five years were probably the last time I was ever truly in the real world." He took a long sip of the tea. "It's good." He nodded at the cup.

"Great secret, making good tea." Herbie tried to lighten the dreadful sense of anguish that lay between them, filling the room. "You just stayed there, in the villa, Lou?"

"She wrote to me, about a month after, from Rome." Passau did not appear to be answering the question. "Wrote and said she had read the press release in the paper. Pleaded that I should go back to work. I didn't even reply, because I thought Sophie would see the letter. Didn't know that, by then, she had moved away from her mother. Gone to live in Switzerland—Stanza, I mean."

"You had no doubts?"

"Doubts about what?"

"You were *sure* she was your daughter?"

"Certain."

"But did you check it out, Lou? Get the birth certificate? Look at the paper trail?"

Slowly he shook his head. "I didn't need any birth certificate. I knew. Fathers know. When I thought about it later, I realized why I loved her. She was like me. I could see it, feel it, hear it. Two sides of a coin, Herb. Constanza *was* my daughter."

"Lou, you didn't follow it up. You might've been conned."

"I know who she was." Uncompromising. It was like holding a pistol to Herbie's head and telling him to shut up otherwise he would pull the trigger.

"Okay, Lou. So you just stayed put. Let the time drift by."

"No. Yes, for the first month. No, afterwards. I knew I had to do something. I took my airplane and flew to Athens. Talked from there to everyone who mattered. Dictated a press release for the Center in New York—'Owing to illness and personal problems, Maestro Louis Passau is to take a sabbatical. . . .' You probably read that."

"It's in the books. But no explanation."

"I knew I could leave everything in other people's hands. The orchestra, the opera, the whole business ran itself. Sometimes I talked direct, from the villa, when anything difficult came up. In Athens, that first time—I spent about a week there—I fixed things so nobody could trace me. Moved money to Switzerland, and then to Greece. Easy. The Swiss banks never gave me away, no paper trail. Nobody gave me away. I bought a phonograph, and a record collection. Manuscript paper. Bought a gun. Handgun. Still got it. Hidden in the place on Lexington. Then I flew the whole lot back to Corfu and battened down the hatches."

"Wrote your symphony. . . ."

"Not straightaway, no. I did that in the third year. Most of the time I was self-indulgent. Got drunk a lot. Listened to music. Took in the view. Nikko looked after me. Never asked questions, never talked to anyone. He knew something appalling had occurred but he never talked about it. I'd eat at his place. Let the days float by. I sort of levitated. Then, I thought, this is no good, Lou. You've got to work. So I started to study again. Flew to Athens. Bought more recordings. Wrote the symphony. Thought about going back to New York. Take up the reins again. Three times I got as far as Athens. But I turned back every time. I think I was letting things drift. Waiting for something to happen. I couldn't make up my mind."

"Sure, like Hamlet."

"Just like Hamlet. I think for three years, even when I was writing the symphony, I was crazy. I guess I was waiting for events to tell me what to do. The time, Herb, the time passed very quickly. You'd think it would drag, yes?"

"Maybe."

"Didn't drag. Went by like a flash."

"And then the reporter spotted you? Came and did an interview? Published it, so you came back?"

Passau gave a dry laugh, utterly barren of humor. "No." Another laugh. "No. That came later—spring 1960. Someone else found me before then."

Herbie thought, "Now it begins. Now he starts his new secret life." He said nothing aloud. Asked no questions. Just sat, like a Freudian psychiatrist, waiting for his silence to nudge words out of his patient.

"Spring—early summer really—1959. That's when I was found. That's when I was rescued, if that's the right word."

He had taken to going down to Nikko's taverna most evenings. Usually at dusk, after a swim. He swam morning and evening, knowing that, whatever else, he had to exercise. During the first years he had done nothing in the way of working out, and his body became flabby, poisoned by the ouzo and retsina. By 1959 he was in good condition again—physically, if not mentally. Then, on this particular evening he walked down to the taverna, ate, talked to Nikko. Even danced a little.

Then, as he was sitting, having a last drink before walking back up the road and climbing up to the villa, a man—a tourist—came over and sat down next to him.

("Never said a word in English until he sat down next to me and ordered another drink for us both.")

"No, not for me. I've had enough. Very kind, but I must be going home." Passau did not want to give the stranger the brush-off. He was courteous, but firm.

"I insist, Maestro Passau. Really, I have to talk with you." The accent was just short of being American. A sort of mid-Atlantic favored by so many businessmen who worked the transatlantic route by then.

Passau started at the sound of his name. It was the first time anyone had used the name on the island. At Nikko's they called him "Filakas"— the Caretaker, the Watchman—because he had said that he was now only the caretaker of the villa. Looking after it for the lady who would return and live there, as he had planned.

("For a long while I really imagined she would come back. Just be with me. Father and daughter; you understand that, Herb?")

"What did you call me?" he asked, back then in 1959 at Nikko's taverna.

"I used your name. Louis Passau."

"That who you think I am?"

"No, that's who I know you are."

"Really. I must be going."

Almost under his breath, the stranger sang Groucho Marx's song "Hello, I must be going." Then he placed his hand on Passau's shoulder: a firm grip, like a police officer about to make an arrest. "Truly, Maestro, if you leave, I shall follow. You cannot walk away from this. Not now."

They locked eyes as stags will lock horns. "Who are you?" Passau had half risen. Now he sat down again. Nikko brought the drinks.

"Just call me Gregory." The stranger smiled, his hands now in sight, flat on the table.

Louis did not know whether this was another piece of his past sliding in, clammily, to haunt him. For a second he wondered if this man had come from Carlo. Don Carlo Giarre. Sophie's parting shot had been, "Carlo will be in touch. He says there will be no more warnings." He thought of being found, in the villa, with a couple of small-caliber bullets through the back of his head.

"Okay, Gregory. What you want with me, huh?"

"We know what you did during the war." Flat, without accusation.

"If I am Passau, I gave many concerts. Conducted an orchestra. Worked the whole time during the war."

"You are mentioned, by name, Mr. Passau, in many documents brought out of Nazi Germany. You are mentioned in some papers which came directly from Kaltenbrunner's department." Ernst Kaltenbrunner had been the chain-smoking head of the Nazi Security Services from 1943. He had been tried at Nuremberg, found guilty and executed. Gregory added, "Most of the documents were old. Inherited by Kaltenbrunner. I don't think he had much control over you. But you're there all right, next to your funny name—Unternehmen. So we know, Mr. Passau. So really we think you should now work for us. Work for the good of mankind. Can we go back to your villa and talk about that?"

In the present, Louis Passau sighed with a great weariness. "Herbie, today has been too much for me. Please can we end there?"

"With Gregory walking back to the villa with you?"

"Yes, he came back. Please, it's enough for one day. Difficult. Very difficult for me."

There was no way that the Maestro was going to continue. Herbie leaned forward and touched him on the shoulder—a touch that said "Courage. It will be well in the end."

Aloud he said, "Just one more question, Lou. One, that's all. Not about Constanza and the island."

Passau shrugged.

"The night you took out the booze convoy with the Gennas," Herb said. Matter-of-fact, no trace of slyness. "You've told us all about that. . . ."

"Sure, I gave you chapter and verse."

"One tiny point, Lou. Something I've never been sure of. Who started the shooting?"

"I told you. I told you all of it." He did not sound tired now; he was more defensive.

"Time for telling *all* the truth, Lou. Just for me, for the record, who started the shooting?"

An uncannily long pause. Then—

"Who d'you think started it, Herb. I didn't want anyone in the convoy to be alive. Okay. Right, I fired the first shot, lying next to Tony Genna. That what you wanted to hear?"

"It's what I suspected. Thanks, Lou."

Pucky came out a few minutes later. The sun was going down and Passau looked spent. "Elizabethans had a good word for how he looks. Shakespeare used it: shent. Really means disgraced, but that's how he looks—shent," Kruger said as they worked together in the kitchen, preparing what Pucky called salmon fishcakes—potatoes boiled and mashed, then mixed with two tins of salmon, bound together with eggs. They were edible if you used a lot of ketchup and pickle.

"I must go out first thing and get more supplies," Pucky said.

"If we're going to be here long enough," Herb whispered. "I must plead for more time. We're just now getting to the nub." His English had improved beyond measure. He was past the point of playing games.

They ate in partial silence, though both Pucky and Kruger were more sympathetic and helpful with the old man than they had ever been before. They both felt that his agony lay across the table, and reached back, buried deep within his bones, so they showed small kindnesses. Pucky even kissed his smooth, babylike cheek at one point, and they thought he would weep at the gesture.

"You want to hear some music before you go to bed, Maestro?" Kruger asked as he cleared the dishes from the table.

"I think so, yes. Yes." So they gathered, and nobody was surprised when he chose the only recording of his one symphony—*The Demonic*.

They sat through it in silence, and Kruger realized that only now could he really begin to understand it. The timpani roll and the sudden huge burst of sound, the C major chords—all the strings, deep, resonant, rising and falling in the definitive phrase that Kruger knew was Passau's mother's laugh: four notes which passed quickly, then disappeared until the final moments of the last movement.

The opening theme, he also recognized anew, for what so often seemed to be a clash of differently coordinated sounds now emerged as a single melody. Hopeful, with an undertone of something distinctively Jewish, and with the trumpet a long way off behind the strings and woodwinds. The lone trumpet playing a bluesy counter melody that you had to strain to hear—the trumpet little Louis Packensteiner had heard on that first night in New York.

In the second movement there was joy and laughter, mixed in with the drum rattle which some critics had said sounded like demented machine guns, then a very modern version of the first theme again, turned back on itself, played again and again as a series of variations, almost as though the composer wanted it to sound like themes culled from the great music makers. There was a hint of Bach, Mozart, Beethoven, Haydn. Then a reenactment of the same theme with a piano in the foreground. It could have been, but was never quite, Chopin mixed jarringly with Rachmaninov. The times were out of joint, it said.

At last, the final movement: despair, ridicule, horror leading to the big, over-the-top, arrangement of the Dies Irae: the choir chanting, shouting the words, against the massed forces of the orchestra, augmented by extra brass and timpani. Then the three bars of silence and a repetition of that first striking C major chord, and the four rising and falling notes that were Gerda Packensteiner's laugh. Another silence and the inevitable throbbing drums, decreasing into oblivion.

They were all weeping by the time it was done. For had they not now all shared in the life of Louis Passau, and its shattering decline into the last events on the island of Corfu?

They sat in silence, then Louis said he would go to bed. He was tired.

Pucky asked if he needed any help. "No, dear lady. No. No help. I'm strong enough, though tired, after today."

At the door, he looked at Herbie and said, "Thank you, Herb. It's been a great help."

"I'm glad." Then, almost as an afterthought, yet, perhaps to prepare the way, he said—"Tomorrow we'll hear about your friend Gregory and his masters in KGB, yes?"

Passau paused, gave a tiny smile, cocked his head—almost the old, arrogant man. "I told you," he said. "Many times, I told you, don't make assumptions. Gregory wasn't KGB. Gregory was CIA."

18

HALF AN HOUR LATER, Art came in, dressed in a jogging suit, with a headband which made him look like some ageing rock star. He smelled of garlic and sweat, surrounded by a lake of Dunhill eau de cologne.

"You get all that, Art? Make you think? Make you realize how lucky you are to be in this kind of work?" Kruger sounded angry and aggressive.

Art Railton dropped into a chair and looked at Herbie and Pucky with tired eyes. "Quite dramatic." He sounded as though nothing could ever surprise him again.

"Art, you said I got three days." Kruger had plumped himself down in a chair next to Railton. Pucky hovered, asking if they wanted coffee, which they did not.

"Yea, I said three days." As the old song went, "He wouldn't say yes, and he wouldn't say no. He wouldn't say stop, and he wouldn't say go."

"That mean I got tomorrow, then pouf?"

"Pouf what, Herb?"

"Pouf, the Maestro disappears. Clock strikes midnight, we all turn into pumpernickel."

"What's your problem, Herbie?" Art sounded more weary than aggressive.

"You heard my problem, if you were listening in. The guy's old. Today took a lot out of him. Must have shaken up his bowels back then, as well. Now, at last, we're getting to real object of exercise, as they used to say in training—back in the ark. I'm not going to get far in one more day, *that's* my problem. You listen in, Art? You know what the poor old bugger went through?"

"I know he's good at exit lines."

"How long I got, Art?"

Railton sighed, and the sag of his shoulders spoke of fatigue. "You should've had one more day, but it's probable you'll get two, maybe even three. Maybe more than that. London hasn't got its act together. Very clear on the fact that the old geezer mustn't be handed over to the Agency or the FBI, but mushy about getting him to the U.K. The Navy is wary about pulling him out in a submarine—so's the Foreign Office. Fears American intervention and a diplomatic incident."

"That would blow over, Art—what the hell?"

"Doesn't make them easier of mind. There's another possibility that calls for all sorts of duplicity. An RAF aircraft leaving Dulles next week. Taking embassy staff and military personnel back. They do regular runs between Dulles and Lyneham. Have to pass him through like the invisible man. Don't see it myself."

Suddenly, Big Herbie was full of confidence. "Give me a week and I can get him out, clean. One week. I set it up. Maybe less than a week."

Art passed a hand over his eyes. "Wishful thinking, Herb. It would appear that he's in genuine danger. We've got ourselves an old man heavy with sin, and the sinned against are after his hide. Agency people, FBI and the Mob are all combing the country. Trying to work out where we've got him. Everyone's lying through their teeth, and I'm seventy percent sure they've started to sniff around here."

"Tell me something new." Then Big Herbie did one of his famous double-takes. "You're joking? You seen 'em sniffing around here?"

"Possibly. Intuition mainly, but things have been noted. Probably simply checking out all your old contacts, Herb. Marty Foreman lives not a hundred miles from here, so I think they're sweeping the area. Marty's very old CIA and you were pretty close in the old days. We've seen two guys who look like FBI talking to the management. One of my people says he recognized an old Agency officer hanging around the pool yesterday. They've got a whiff of something—or, maybe, nothing."

"So, London going to get cold feet in the end? Hand him over to the wolves?"

"I really don't know, Herb. What we've got is a big enigma."

"Complete with variations, Art."

"Yes. This talented ancient has got a lot of people wound up. Ninety years of great music and a large dollop of chicanery. Agency, FBI, the Mob. They're not folks who forgive and forget."

"I can still get him out." Kruger sounded confident as a cardsharp holding all the aces.

"Speak to me, Herb."

Herbie talked for fifteen minutes, interrupted constantly by "But, Herb . . ." and "You think they're . . . ?" In the end Kruger leaned back. "Just tell me if I can give it whirl?"

"If they catch you, they'll throw you out for good, take the subject, bury him and play merry hell with the rest of us."

"I been in merry hell already, Art. Makes no difference to me. I know London would deny me anyway. Maybe I do it without telling you."

"Herbie, I . . ."

"There's strings attached if I get him back."

"What kind of strings?"

"That nobody lets Gus Keene and the Warminster wild bunch go near him. I finish the job I started."

Art chewed his lip. "I haven't got the authority, and you know London. They wouldn't . . ."

"But I suspect that if I did it, they'd be happy as chickens in shit."

"Pigs, Herb."

"Chickens, pigs, what's the difference?"

"Bacon and eggs."

"If you do get a go-ahead to lift him out . . ." Herbie trailed off.

"You'll have a good twenty-four hours' notice. Look, I was sure it would be the day after tomorrow, but that was a couple of days ago. Two days can be an awfully long time in politics."

"Two days can be an awfully long time in ninety years of life."

Art Railton left without anybody knowing what was to be done. Big Herbie was disinclined to talk about the possibility of FBI or Agency people sniffing around, and he was certainly not even going to think about a possible Mob contract being out on Passau. Why should he get agitated about something he knew to be true anyway? He had been there when they last had a go, and according to the old musician that wasn't the first time—*Carlo will be in touch. He says there will be no more warnings.* If that was what had been said so long ago, Don Carlo had taken his time: a very old man stalking another very old man as he had done down through the years. What the hell.

He cocked his head towards the bedroom. Once inside they started hacking again, using the Macintosh LC and its modem to get into two mainframes in Maryland: two super data banks which fed a myriad work stations in Federal buildings in D.C. The first one was easy.

"Where'd you get all these numbers from, Herb?" Pucky asked.

"Object lesson, Puck. Never throw anything away. In this business you got to be like a jackdaw or a squirrel."

"Squirrel?" she asked. She could not pronounce the word properly, mushing the "squ" so that it came out as "swirrel."

"You always put the nuts away for safekeeping. Same with jackdaws, with all that glitters and is not gold—though sometimes they strike gold. So do you. Keep everything you learn in little compartments in your head. Every name, every crypto, telephone number, dodgy people who can do dirty work, special leverage points. You store it up for a rainy day. Now is bloody pouring. So you reach into the compartments. . . ."

Getting the first data was, as Kruger put it, "Like falling off a ledge."

"You're starting to repeat yourself, sweetheart," Pucky told him.

"I really your sweetheart, Puck?"

"No doubt about it."

"Good, 'cuz it looks like this one's going to take a lot of time." He had made contact with the mainframe but couldn't get the password. "Have to go in through the back door," he muttered cryptically. "Good job you got this IBM emulator. This not going to be easy, but the idiots always think they've got complete security with a password and some safe program up front. They forget the guys who maintain these things always make their own little trapdoors."

She asked what he meant and he explained, in simple terms, that security programs for data bases were all very well but, if they got a serious crash on the systems, the tapes or some massive hard drive, the very things that were there to make the data bases secure would stop them getting in, because the passwords become corrupted. "The whizz-kids put in little programs of their own, so they can bypass the security. See." He worked the keyboard. After fifteen minutes a screen came up giving him lines of programmed text. "Man Friday," he said, cryptically.

"What's Man Friday?"

"The maintenance man's code. Probably checks this thing out on a Friday, regular. Once a month. Something like that. First Friday or last Friday. Bingo." The screen cleared, giving him a menu. "We ask about the Giarre family tree first, then go to the Traccias if we don't get the right answer from Giarre."

"How did you learn all this, Herb? You left the Firm before they started running advanced computer courses. I haven't even done one."

"Self-taught, honey pie. See, nobody expects an old floozy like me to know the hidden secrets of computers."

"Don't you mean 'fogey'?"

Herb looked at her with a watermelon smile, and gave her a great big wink. "Sure. Old fogey."

"You're not old, Herb."

"But I'm a fogey, yes?"

"You're a demon lover."

"Good. Double bingo. Giarre, Sophia Maria. Start printing it out, Pucky. Sooner we get this done, the sooner we get all cozy, eh? Then I show you fogey-pogey."

She could only hazard an intelligent guess at what he meant.

An hour later they were in bed.

"Still a demon lover, Puck?"

"Better than demon, darling Herb. More like the beast himself, with all those horns."

"Do my best for you."

"Deft, that's what you are, Herb. A deft lover."

"I got all my marbles. Stupid, maybe, but not daft."

"Deft, Herb. As in dexterous, agile, nimble."

"Ah." Then, thirty seconds later, "Nimble I like."

They lay in contented silence, holding hands, until Pucky asked, "What's going to happen, you big sweet man?"

"Happen?"

"When this is over and we go back to the real world. This is the land where time stood still."

"The real world, Ms. Pucky Curtiss, is wherever you want to make it. Run away with me?"

"You mean it?"

"Wouldn't ask you else."

"What about your . . ."

"Martha? My wife?"

"Your wife, yes, and the other one. The one they've got at Warminster now."

"I sweet-talk the wife. Common sense. Martha knew it was for companionship. Not the greatest affair since Romeo and Juliet. We have a sitdown. Maybe she wants to go back to Germany, anyhow. There'll be a soap opera for a few weeks, but she's strong, self-reliant. How should I know?"

"And your long-lost traitor."

"I said I'd kill her, but I don't mean this. I don't think I mean it. Don't know. I fix her, though. Make her life a bloody misery."

"As long as you don't make my life a misery, Herb."

"Shakespeare said it, Pucky, my dream—

"Make me a willow cabin at your gate,
And call upon my soul within the house;
Write loyal cantons of contemned love
And sing them loud even in the dead of night. . . ."

"You do have a way with words, Mr. Kruger."

"I have a way with Shakespeare's words, Ms. Curtiss. Best damned word man in the business." He leaned over and kissed her. She responded, kissing him deeply until nothing mattered but the slaking of their thirst again.

In the afterglow, she said, "I love you, Herb. Don't get too swell-headed."

"You really mean that?"

"I mean it. Don't quite know why. I started out for a bit of fun. See if I could conquer the old master. Now it's backfired. I love you."

"Okay, you said it." He turned onto his side, looking her straight in the eyes. "And I love you, Pucky Curtiss."

"You do? Truly?"

"Listen to me. Beware of me also, because I never thought I'd feel like this again, and I can only express myself in certain ways. Art's father taught me, so I do it through Shakespeare and people like that. Listen. You know what Winston Churchill wrote at the start of World War Two? When they made him prime minister?"

"He had a way with words."

"Sure. England was on its knees. They made Churchill Prime Minister, and he wrote—'I felt as if I were walking with destiny, and that all my past life had been but a preparation for this hour and this trial.' Is what I feel, Puck. Everything, all the days of my life have been training for two things. First, Maestro Passau. I think he holds the key to one of the most diabolical betrayals of the old, Cold War. If he does, then there are people who should stand accountable."

"Second. All the women, the loves, of my life—which means really two—have been preparing me for you. A man doesn't learn much about women in one lifetime, because they always turn up little surprises. But a man does accumulate some knowledge.

"All my dealings with women were paving the way for you. And also I think before that I was being prepared. Maybe other lives, like that actress believes. We all lived before, you follow?"

A nod, her eyes scouring his face.

"So, I've waited for you. Now, here you are."

"And the other one. The one that betrayed you?"

"Prepared me. Made me stronger. Okay? Pucky, I love you."

"Tell me about her, this Ursula."

"I told already."

"Everything."

So, again he poured it out. This time without the gaps. "I give it to you full frontal," he said at one point, and, naturally, he ended up in tears, sobbing against her shoulder, muttering, "Not manly this blubbings. Sorry, but the bitch screwed me, sucked me dry then spat me out. I found what I wanted now. Don't you betray me, and I'll never be your personal traitor. I been mixed up in this outdated profession too long. You get paranoid. You see heretics behind every shadow."

"Oh, Herb."

She took him in her arms, tended to his emotional needs, then the other demands of love.

Again, hours later, in the darkness, he said—

"I might even try it on my own."

"What?" Pucky's voice rose to a high C.

"Getting the old bugger out. Obvious we got to get him out. Why don't I just do it?"

"Not tell Art?"

"Not tell anyone. Just us, Puck. Get him out and take him to Warminster or, better still, hole up in some god-awful seaside resort. Finish pumping him clean, then hand him over, complete with the debrief."

"You think we could?"

"Bet your balls."

"No way."

"Bet *my* balls then."

"They're already in hock, Herb."

"SO WHAT NEXT, LOU? You take this fellow Gregory up to the villa and he turns out to be good American eagle, not bad Russian bear?" said Big Herbie Kruger, at nine o'clock the next morning in the living room, well back from the windows again, for the sun was out and skies were clear. People cruised the beach, and sleek speedboats provided a life on the ocean waves. Seabirds skimmed across the water.

"Something like that."

Gregory was a tall, thin man with high cheekbones and fair hair which made him look like an undernourished Scandinavian. "There's actually Indian blood way back in my family. Crow, I believe," he told Passau.

("Age of this guy, Lou?" Herbie asked.

"Late twenties, but how should I know. Yes, late twenties, had to be. Over thirty years ago and he's still with the Agency.")

They sat outside, on the veranda. There were scented candles, set in upturned earth-colored plant pots, spread around them to act as bug lights. The flame and scent lured the insects, which preferred them to a tasty nip of human blood. Louis thought of Stanza's habit of just walking out onto this same veranda without clothes, or in just her underwear. He had caught her one day, leaning over the guard rail chatting to a pop-eyed young boy who could not get enough of the blue silk and lace against the marble skin.

"You're going to blackmail me then, Gregory?"

"I wouldn't use so strong a word. Persuade, possibly, but what good would blackmail do? Some idiot judge might eventually put you in jail, or have you deported to Germany. We'd rather see your immeasurable talent flourish from the United States. You're one of a kind: the acclaimed master. You belong to the world, Maestro, and we would rather see you conquer the world from an American power base."

"Who's we?"

It was only then that he learned the stickman who called himself Gregory was with the Central Intelligence Agency.

"So, while I go and slave my guts out conducting, teaching, directing, you also want me to make friends and influence people?"

"Something like that. Actually it's a little more ingenious than simply making friends, using your undoubted influence. You're very big in your field, and we can make you even bigger."

"The Temptation of Maestro Passau, huh? You're going to show me the world and all its riches, then tell me I can have the entire bundle if I sell you my soul."

"That's about it, if you boil it down to plain facts. Yes."

"Don't bother to wrap it, I'll take it just as it is."

"I wonder if you will?"

"I did it for the Nazis, and they threw shit in my face. . . ."

"They threw shit in everyone's faces. . . ."

"So why shouldn't I do it for my own country?"

"Why indeed, but we have to be sure of you."

"That's not possible. You can't be one hundred percent sure of anyone."

Gregory smiled. He would have made a good understudy for Yorick— the jester whose skull Hamlet finds in Ophelia's half-dug grave. "Actually we *do* have ways of being ninety percent sure. What we'll be asking of you is something so under-the-table that you have to keep it hidden even from your own thoughts and certainly your own eyes."

"I cover myself with my cloak and cut my throat with my own dagger?"

"That would be one way of doing it."

The cicadas were active early that year. Now they raised their chirping sounds so that the whole night seemed to be impregnated with them.

"You can't give me a hint? What you want? What you want me to do?"

In the darkness, Gregory shook his head. "If you say no, or we decide you're not, after all, the right player for this team, nobody's even going to believe I talked to you. Actually, there are six men who, at this moment, will swear they're having dinner with me in Berlin. I'm nowhere near Corfu. You have to come to us blind."

"And if I tell you to go fuck a frog?"

"Oh, you'll find it very difficult to get back into the United States, Mr. Passau. Even before we ask you to play, before you accept, we own you. I promise you that. Lock, stock and proverbial barrel."

("Chilled my blood, Herb. Just sitting there, chatting casually. I believed him. They owned me. I had no doubts.")

Below, faraway—probably from Nikko's taverna—came the sound of the bouzouki, and voices raised in song.

"So how do we find out if I'm your man?"

"We flutter you. It's a kind of technical term, 'flutter.'" He gave a short laugh which sounded full of fun. "The old polygraph. The lie detector. Not one hundred percent accurate, but it's a good indicator."

"So, go ahead, polygraph me. When you want to do it?"

"No time like the present. This way we get you fresh and uncomplicated. I use your telephone?"

He made a call: quick, professional, one sentence.

"Takes two to flutter," he smiled. "I have a technician with me. He's bringing the box of tricks here. Ten minutes."

"How long've you been watching me?"

"Ask no secrets, Maestro Passau, and you'll hear no lies."

The technician turned out to be a little older than Gregory. He had the distinct feeling that the man who arrived with a black indestructible-looking custom case, was not in the technical league, but rather higher up the scale. Possibly senior to Gregory, who introduced him as Matthew.

On Captiva Island, Herbie's head whipped up. "This Matthew. A little older? How much?"

"A few years. *He's* also still about. Retired now, but stays in touch."

"Describe him."

"Short, thickset, muscular—in those days. Looked like a street fighter, and was uncouth in his language."

"And you were couth, Lou?"

"Compared to Matthew, I was angelic."

Herbie's head began to spin dreams. Matthew had been a favorite alias of Marty Foreman, who had entered the Agency via the old OSS—the wartime Office of Special Services, the organization begun by the legendary "Wild Bill" Donovan to fight the Nazis in secret. When the CIA came into being, under Allen Dulles, a number of old OSS hands had been its nucleus. The description of Matthew was that of Marty Foreman who had risen to great heights within that massive, high-budget organization which had fought in secret through the Cold War, Korea and Vietnam. Big Herbie had worked with him more times than he could remember. Now, he heard the tremor in his voice as he asked, "You ever get his family name?"

"Never. Never with any of them. Later, I knew this Matthew was the most senior. I tell you how things worked out?"

"Yes, Lou. What next?"

They went about their business with a cold, almost frighteningly calculated professionalism: selecting a chair and placing it close to the windows inside the main room of the villa, then drawing the curtains, so that Passau had no view to distract him.

When they had put on the blood pressure cuff, the pneumograph across the chest, and the electrodes on his fingers, they told him to settle down, and the more senior man began to ask the questions.

"You're Louis Isaak Passau?"

"Yes."

"You are an orchestra conductor?"

"You know I am."

"Ever been a member of the Nazi Party?"

"No."

"But you worked for the Nazis? Against your country? All through the war?"

"Yes. I was blackmailed into doing it."

"Just answer yes or no."

"Yes."

"You feel any remorse about betraying the United States?"

"I feel betrayed. Yes. Remorse, I suppose you'd call it."

"Okay. Any affiliation with the Communist Party?"

"'Course not. No."

"Then what *are* your politics?"

"None. I'm an artist. Music is all that counts."

"You're saying you have no politics?"

"I'm apolitical."

"But not asexual?"

In the here and now, Passau said he could not recall all the questions. "Long while ago, Herbie. But I had this done to me at regular intervals."

"Sure, Lou. Agency's famous for it."

"Asked all the usual stuff. Homosexual? Racist? Current status in affairs of the prick? You know what they ask."

"Sure, I've been asked also. This guy, Matthew?"

"Yes."

"He have an accent?"

"Broad. Tough. Brooklyn."

That was the clincher. Herbie was very familiar with what they called his handwriting. Marty was obsessed with fluttering people. Next to the automatic pistol, the polygraph was his favorite weapon. He had bludgeoned his way to the top of the agency with his fighting skills and a polygraph. He also said "toin" instead of "turn," and "rehoise" instead of "rehearse."

In his head he saw Marty watching the needles flick on the rolling paper of the polygraph. Knowing what the readouts meant, there in the Corfu villa so long ago. The needles flicked and made their marks, blood pressure and pulse tracings, tension, the galvanic reflexes. Marty could read the signals as an accountant might read a balance sheet. Passau, as he was then, would have been a sitting duck. If they did not own him before the polygraph, he certainly became their personal property once the test was over.

"So, next, Lou? They tell you what the deal was? Spell it out for you?"

"Slowly, they did. Took most of the night."

Back in 1959, the man called Matthew told Passau that it seemed to him the Maestro was prime cut. "You have the contacts, the ability to travel. You are famous; politically beyond reproach; a man who crosses frontiers because of his talent. Also, you're a very good liar, just what we need. Want to serve your country, Mr. Passau? Want to make up for the mistakes you made with the Nazis? Straight yes or no. If it's no, we'll try somewhere else." The offer on the table. "You think you're successful now—that you'll be greeted with cheers and applause if you return to the United States? Yes, you would. But all that can be magnified ten thousand times if you do as we ask. You'll be able to choose your concerts, operas, stars—even women. Anything and anyone can be yours. So how about it?"

They had gauged their victim well; played him with speed and dexterity. "Tell me more," Passau said.

"And they told you more?" asked Herbie in the present.

"Some."

"How much?"

"That this was something so secret, so sensitive, to United States' security, that only four people in the world would know about it, apart from me."

"Four. Only four people? They give you the names?"

"I knew them, all the time, under first names—obviously funny names: Matthew, Gregory, Duncan and Victor. Met them all over the years. It was contained. Four only. Matthew's out now, retired, but I'm still in contact with him. The others I suspect have very senior positions. In their early sixties now, all of them, heading for retirement."

"When did you last see any member of this little cabal?—Is good word, cabal?"

"I met with Gregory and Duncan after the last concert tour. After Budapest, Berlin, Sofia, Prague and Warsaw. This spring. Before the summer coup."

Herbie nodded. "Sure, Lou. Budapest, Berlin, Sofia, Prague, Warsaw *and* Tel Aviv. I know about that. You saw them after?"

"Six hours. Playing games like they always did. Doing the runaround. All big secret stuff."

"So what was the deal? The deal in 1959?"

"Do you know what an unwitting agent is, Mr. Passau?" Matthew asked him back on Corfu.

"Tell me."

"He's a guy you have under control, but he don't know nothing about it."

("Matthew talked like that, Herb."

"I know it.")

"Explain please?" Passau asked Matthew.

Gregory answered. "He is a subject to whom we—the CIA—can feed ideas. He doesn't know he's being used, but there's someone he trusts that we own. We feed him an idea, and he acts on it. Thinks it's his own idea really. A very subtle exercise in control."

"And you have someone like that?"

"Uh-huh. Yes."

"A Senator? Someone in government?"

"Oh, someone in government, Mr. Passau, but not our government. This unwitting agent is Russian. Part of the Soviet administration. We can give him ideas."

"So where do I come in?"

"We're going to give him an idea about you, Maestro. We're going to point out to him that you would make a very good Soviet spy. A Russian agent. If he then recruits you, we can pass anything we want through you to them, them being our main enemy. We can mislead them, misdirect them, give them a mass of disinformation."

On Captiva Island the telephone rang and Herbie Kruger jumped, being hauled from Passau's past to the present.

It was Art. "Got to meet you, Herb. This is very urgent. Ultra serious."

19

THEY MET IN THE apartment below—the one Pucky had rented so that they could control the entire building. Big Herbie had checked out the place every night, regularly. Art arrived with a solemn, dedicated-looking young man who wore slacks, a turtleneck and a shiny electric blue nylon windbreaker. "Fart and it turns green," Art said, trying to lighten the load. He sat down, gave a sigh, and ran his hands over his face. The young man walked around the apartment testing the doors and windows, looking in cupboards. Between doing these robotic chores he gave long, sideways looks at Herbie, who had pulled up a stand chair and settled his bulk onto it. A lot of Herbie projected over the sides, but he sat up straight, at attention.

"You do understand what we're getting into, Herb?" Art finally asked. "You *are* reading the signals?"

"Started reading them before you, Art."

"Recognize anybody?"

"Marty."

"Okay. Right. Marty Foreman, wizard of the Soviet Office at Langley for longer than any of us care to remember. How many times have you heard him call himself Matthew?"

"Four thousand and two, but who's counting? Old Marty used Matthew as his given name all the time when he didn't want people to know him, so I don't see why he'd change the pattern for Passau."

"Right. Gregory is another matter. Mike Alfoot, Marty's deputy for years; now the boss. Looking after agency people locked inside the crumbling empire. He's the only senior man with any Native American blood in him. I nearly went through the roof when Passau brought him out of the past. The fool bragged about it thirty years ago in Corfu. You think he goes around D.C. fighting for Native American rights now?"

"Very much doubt it. You recognize the other names? Duncan? Vincent?"

"Vincent just might be Tony de Paul—short guy, with a big schnoz and an execrable taste in ties. Try that on for size with the Maestro. In the sixties they hadn't really learned that to connect cryptos with their real names was not the wisest thing in the world. Like setting a lock with your date of birth."

Kruger looked puzzled.

Art thought he saw the problem. "Execrable, Herb. Means . . ."

"I know what execrable means. Why Tony de Paul?"

"Vincent de Paul. Saint. Martyr, I think."

"Oh, sure. Book of Comic Prayer; Missal. . .

"Yea, I know Tony de Paul. Also Soviet Office. Ran a couple of people over the Curtain, if I got the right one."

"Ran a lot of people, Herb. Duncan, I don't know, but you can bet your boots he was also Sov Office. What d'you make of the secret four scenario?"

"So secret only four people would know, apart from old Passau. Like a sore thumb, Art, sticks out. Sucks also."

"We have to assume . . ."

"Assume nothing, Art."

"This we *can* assume. Four of the Company's inner sanctum have been running an agent who's been recruited by KGB, and *nobody's* supposed to know but them. Passau, gifted as he is, was probably too naive to understand what was happening. You get the feeling he enjoyed it all?"

"Had a whale of a time, I should think. He's got a mind runs straight as an arrow where music's concerned, but he enjoys intrigue. That's how I read him."

"And I wonder who this unwitting agent was? One of the bigwigs in East Germany, or higher up the chain, Moscow Center brass?"

"Why East Germany, Art?"

"Ursula. *Your* Ursula held his hand, ran his intelligence from eighty onwards. Just thought . . ."

"Don't. She was Russian, Art, remember?"

"But worked out of Karlshorst. East Berlin."

"Forget it."

"We have her. I can set up a new line of enquiry via Gus."

"Tell him to use the branding irons, the boot and the rack while you're at it. This thing smells." Kruger's voice sounded like a dangerous buzz saw. He sighed, weary of everything. Art Railton gave him the kind of look usually reserved for people who stated the obvious. "Poor, maligned Jim Angleton," he said. "Spent his life trying to find a mole in the agency. Went paranoid, near crazy, yet maybe, just maybe, he had a whole operation going on right under his nose." James Jesus Angleton had been the CIA's head mole-hunter for decades: a man obsessed with the idea that the agency had been penetrated by the Russian service. He died, fired from the agency and paranoid about the past.

Very quietly, Herbie quoted T. S. Eliot—

"These with a thousand small deliberations
Protract the profit of their chilled delirium,
Excite the membrane, when the sense has cooled,
With pungent sauces, multiply variety
In a wilderness of mirrors. . . ."

"Perfect," Art continued, as though he had not heard. "The Sov Office would tell everyone hands off, we have a long-term operation running here. If anyone from outside decided to take a look-see, they'd find the old guy doing antisurveillance for some Soviet debriefer one day. The next he'd be in a debrief, cozy at an agency safe house. 'Our source,' they'd say. 'Keep off the grass, the Sovs think he's theirs. Leave him be.' Marty's so far up the chain they might believe him."

"Which means we should also believe him?"

Art made a tipping motion with his hand, palm down, fingers together. His eyes as restless as those of the young man.

"You still got a watch on this place twenty-four hours? Still looking after me?" Herbie as casual as jeans, sneakers and a T-shirt.

Art cut his eyes away. "Manpower's stretched thin. People aren't getting enough rest; not enough sleep. I have them there for most of the day. We're checking always after midnight, for a couple of hours. Last two nights there's been nobody watching between two to four in the morning. You noticed?"

"What you think?" He was not actually lying.

"You shouldn't have noticed, Herb. These guys are good. You shouldn't have seen them at all, but I suppose tired watchers aren't reliable. Can you cope between, say, two until four in the morning?"

"Sure, no problem. Pucky and I'll take care of it." He shot a quick look at the young man who was standing by the door trying to pretend he was not hearing any of this. "Tell you what, Art. Do the thing with Ursula. Tell Gus to probe. Ask who ran him from Moscow Center. Whose boy they thought he was. She might not know because he'd been active for twenty years by the time she came on the scene but, what the hell, they might just have let her peep at the file. Stranger things happen. Who was head boy at Moscow Center in sixty?"

"In sixty, Shelepin, but in sixty-one it was his buddy, Semichasny. The pair of them pulled the silent coup. Searched the files, incriminated Khrushchev. Tapped his phones, then asked him to step aside, make room for Brezhnev."

"KGB had its hands full at home. But they were cunning as cartload of monkeys. Sure, Art. Get old Gus to soften up Ursula. I'll get on with the old guy now. Push him fast. Only thirty years to go."

As he reached the door, the young man leaped to open it for him. "Mr. Kruger, sir?" He sounded almost reverential.

"That's me, last time I looked."

"Just wanted to say it's an honor to be working with you, Mr. Kruger."

"So what am I? A rock star?"

"No, sir. An inspiration, Mr. Kruger."

Herbie shook his head, puzzled, and went back upstairs, muttering, "Inspiration . . . inspiration . . . oh for a muse of fire."

Pucky had the percolator on, and he sat down again with Passau, observing that they could do another hour before lunch.

"Whatever," Passau smiled. The signs of strain had passed. Maybe, Herbie thought, he's got over the hump. Then, silently, in his head, he said, "Have I got news for him!"

"LOU, THE GUY you knew as Vincent? Was he short, with a big hooter?"

"Sorry, what is a hooter?"

"Schnoz; facial protuberance; proboscis; nose, like in German *Schnauze*, snout. A hooter is English slang, sorry."

"Now you come to mention it, yea. Yea, Vincent had a big conkola."

"Also wore ties of many colors?"

Passau gave a little shrug. The movement spoke of laughter. "Rainbows. Nudie girls on sky-blue-pink. If he'd ever worn a bow tie, it'd have lit up and spun around."

"And what of Duncan? Scottish descent? Duncan of Lochayle? Wore kilts? What?"

"Duncan?" The old man was somehow questioning himself. Searching the great barrier reef that was his memory of other days and other times. "Duncan?" he questioned again. "Duncan was, how can I put it? Duncan was a silent partner."

"You didn't see him? You didn't speak with him?"

"Sure, I saw him, talked with him, but I got the impression that Duncan was an observer."

"Physical description, Lou."

"Tallish, thinnish—gaunt is a good word: you know from gaunt?"

"Sure. Gaunt. Hollow cheeks, bones protruding."

"Duncan, he had long hair for most of the time—during the sixties certainly; later he had it trimmed. Last time I saw him it looked quite respectable . . . Ah!" As though he had found the Holy Grail. "Best description was he didn't fit. When the others wore suits, he had jeans and a leather jacket. When they came casual, he wore a suit. A cheap suit. Also he had rings on his fingers."

"And bells on his toes, Lou?"

"Never saw his toes. But he had about six hundred rings on his fingers—I exaggerate, Herb, but they were brassy, showy, cheap, like a hippie. As he got older, some of the rings disappeared and he became a yuppie. Suits made to measure, better haircut, washed more often."

Herbie nodded. In his head he said to himself, "Got him." Bains. Urquart Bains. Soviet Desk's fieldman elite. Seven languages, including Yiddish. German, Russian, Serbo-Croat and the rest. Given armfuls of jock-strap medals. Serviced agents from Poland to Minsk. Jesus, he thought, Urquart Bains was the CIA's Soviet Office's big time singleton. In and out, behind the Curtain, over the Wall, through the barbed wire. Go anywhere. Scarlet Pimpernel. Man of a thousand faces. Bains was involved in *this*? Art would be changing his shorts at this very moment if he had put a name to the description.

"You didn't see Duncan as often as the other three?" he asked, hoping his voice sounded free of the shakes.

"You're right, Herb. You're not wrong. Duncan I saw about once, maybe twice a year, if that. Some years I never saw him."

"So, Lou, what next? You came back to America and they treated you like the prodigal son."

"Sure. Downhill all the way now. It's all in the books. Concerts, operas, ballets, guest conducting, traveling the world. The Maestro of Maestros. You know it all."

"That was surface stuff."

"It was my life. My life's work. The part that really mattered. Success. Great reviews. King of the hill."

Herbie put on his patient voice. "Okay, Lou. We take that for granted. You are indisputably the greatest orchestra conductor of our time, bar none. You did it, and you did it your way, if you'll excuse the language."

"I did it, and it was hard work. Yet it was satisfying."

"I need the stuff under the surface. The CIA made a pass at you. I know this as a fact. You said okay. I also know this as a fact."

Passau was still off on his own. "You know I remained unmarried until 1981 also. An old man, yet Angela didn't care about age. She was a willing victim. She was also worth it."

"We'll get to that. Tell me about the operational techniques. These four CIA people, they train you at all? Send you to the Farm?"

Passau chuckled. It was surprising what one night of rest had done. The old man was now as spry as he had been during their first days in Virginia. There was even a twinkle in his eye. "You're being Tricky Dicky with me, Herbie. Think I don't know where the Farm is? What it is?"

"Not a trick question, Louis. Did they give you any training?"

"Sure, all the fun of the fair. Odd days, sometimes weekends, when I wasn't working or rehearsing or traveling. Sure, they taught me all that crazy spook stuff. I passed summa cum laude. Top of the form. M.S.A."

"M.S.A?"

"Master of Spook Arts."

"And where did they do this training?"

"Wherever I happened to be. Mostly in New York. Keep cultivating friends at the top, they would tell me. Get in with the people who matter. If you meet a general, do him a favor; Senators were also good; Navy people, Pentagon, State, White House. Didn't really worry them in the long run, because they always provided the stuff—the four of them. Herbie, for me it was a game. I knew the footwork, but it was like a hobby. I was never a bloody spy. They were the spies, shoveling what they called disinformation through me to the Russians. That's why this whole thing was a farce. I only really became involved with what you might call intrigue right at the end. Sure, the thing during the war was on my conscience, but never this. It was playing games." He took a deep breath. "Until the end, when some of the stuff didn't match up; when I smelled spoiled fish and the Stretchfield guy—the writer—was going to go public about the Nazi thing. Then I began to wonder, but it was too late. In the end I make my confession to you. What I got left? Maybe a year or two if I'm lucky."

"By 'stuff' you mean the intelligence you handed over to the Russians?"

"Sure. That was the deal. I was working hard, also serving my country, being a superagent. Everyone loved me. We handed over chicken feed."

"Good times, Herb. Gone now. They've changed the goalposts, and the days of spying are coming into the twilight. Like you said when we were in Virginia, we're dodos. Kaput. What was it all about, eh?" Pause. Count to ten. Big smile for the paying customers.

"Tell me about the training, Lou."

"Training? Everything. We did codes and ciphers; surveillance—how to spot and how to throw. I learned all that tradecraft shit, sneaking around, looking in plate-glass windows, dead drops, brush passes, sign language, body language, things to say on the telephone. All the stuff that's in the spy books, though they get a lot of that shit wrong, the writers of the spy books. I'm a connoisseur, Herb. Done it. Know it. Backwards and up my ass, okay?"

"I love you when you talk dirty, Lou. Okay. So how did the Russians get in touch? Letter, casual telephone call? Or did Matthew, Mark, Luke and John bless the bed that you got on?"

"Yes."

"Yes, what?"

"Yes. Matthew and, I think it was Vincent . . . though it may have been Gregory, I forget. They told me what would happen exactly."

"Exactly?"

"To the minute. Place, time, what the guy would look like."

"And what did he look like?"

"Like a fucking stockbroker. Party at the Waldorf Astoria. End of six-ty-one, November or December. I had done a guest spot. New York Phil at Carnegie Hall. Some benefit thing. Everyone there, Lenny, the whole bunch. Copeland was there, because I did *Appalachian Spring* that night. Also did the Shostakovich Second Piano Concerto. I'd forgotten that; Lenny was the soloist. Great night. Plenty of glitz. Party afterwards at a thousand bucks a throw—except for people like me, Aaron and Lenny. Everybody. This guy comes over: fat, dressed to kill, fancy tux, gold drip-ping from his wristwatch, cheeks smooth as a baby's tush, full lips, maybe a bit too red."

"Maestro, thank you for all the pleasure you've given us. This has been a real treat. Haven't enjoyed a concert so much since I don't know when. You conduct a lot of Shostakovich? Like him?"

Passau felt his stomach turn over. They had told him that whoever made contact would ask if he conducted much Shostakovich, and if he liked the composer.

"Never met him," Passau laughed. They had told him to say that. "Seriously, I think he's one of the greatest living composers. Too bad he's Russian." They had told him to say that as well, and the contact would tell him that he really preferred the old romantics. He would mention Tchaikovsky.

"Personally, I prefer the old romantics," the fat, tux-clad man smiled. "I'm very fond of Tchaikovsky."

"So what have you to tell me?"

"Could we, perhaps, meet one evening? I have a few ideas I'd like to discuss."

Passau told him certainly. They could meet tomorrow. Seven thirty at the place on Lexington. "Gave him the telephone number. Everything."

"And the next night?"

"We went out to dinner. Forget where. Didn't get his name. 'Just call me Alex,' you know?"

Herbie said he knew only too well.

Alex had talked at length. Passau said it was like some kind of psycho-logical interview. "He seemed to know almost everything about me. How much I smoked and drank. Places I liked. People I saw. As though they'd built up some dossier on me."

"They probably had. Way the Soviet service recruited. They had long questionnaires. Built up a profile of a possible recruit. Very detailed. Knew what you were thinking almost. What next?"

"Telephone call from Alex. Three weeks later. Wants a meeting. I have to be outside Saks Fifth Avenue. Two thirty on one of three dates. Says he'll pick me up."

"And you went?"

"On the last day. Last possible date."

"And he turns up."

"No, someone else comes. Called himself Simon. Heavy accent. Comes up behind me and says, 'What a beautiful dress.' It's in the window, the dress. On a dummy. I say, 'I'd prefer it in blue for my woman,' and he says, 'you could be right.' That's a match; what Alex told me would be the recognition. Simon's only in town for two days, then back to Moscow. Told me straight out. We walked together. Went into St. Pat's. Sat down and talked quietly. Made no secret of where he was coming from. Asked if I wanted to dance with them."

"Dance with . . . ?"

"Herb," Passau held up a hand. "He was being poetic, or something. Said that he heard I was a sympathizer with the Communist Party International. Did I want to serve the Party? I told him, yes. He said how I could be of value."

"Which was?"

"Almost the same as the fucking Nazis had briefed me. Stuff from Army, Navy, Air Force, politicos. The usual. He said they'd be very generous and I told him I didn't need the money. He just laughed. Gave me dead drops, telephone codes, numbers to memorize. There was one number I had to call once I had something for them, which wasn't for three months. Early sixty-one."

"And what happened, early sixty-one?"

"Gregory gives me a call and uses the mystic passwords. They tell me to go through the Russian routine with this telephone number. Do whatever I'm told, and give them a plastic bag—it was from F.A.O. Schwarz, Fifth Ave, the toy shop, which seemed appropriate. Gregory brought it round. In the bag there were a couple of rolls of film and some papers in a cardboard folder. Big deal, Gregory says. They think I'm letting them have the crown jewels. Okay? I say, 'Fine Greg,' and he tells me I should get a little package from them. Goes through the rules of the game.

"I make the call, they set up a meet. Outside. Central Park. Very specific. I can still show you the exact spot today. The contact'll be carrying a copy of the *New York Times* and *Wall Street Journal*. Under his left arm it's safe. Under right arm, piss off and go to a fallback, two hours. He went through all the jargon. Gave me a buzz, Herb. It was fun."

"And the man you met?"

"Pavel. Told me to call him Paul. Said he was my case officer, handler, and he was, for about ten years. Every three months or so. Regular. Nice guy. Would only meet outside. He also carried a Schwarz bag that first time. Exchanged bags as we walked. Very friendly. Really nice."

"So you went for a walk?"

"Gave me more numbers, one-liners for the telephones, and a couple of dead drops we might use. Did use them as well. New York Public Library and the lobby of the old Barclay Hotel—Intercontinental now."

"Know it well."

"He said good-bye. Gregory had told me I should walk up to the Plaza. Wait out front. Limo comes cruising in, dark windows, can't see inside. Driver leaps out, 'Mr. Passau, sir. Your car.' Opens the door. I get in. Matthew's sitting in back with a big smile. We drive off. He takes the bag from me and says, 'Well, Maestro, you are launched.' Talked like I was a fucking ship. We got food here, Herb?"

It was not quite midday, but Kruger wanted words with Pucky. She had gone out earlier to get provisions, but there was a job that had to be done that afternoon. In the kitchen he talked to her as they fried bacon.

"Hell on the old guy's cholesterol," she said.

"At ninety, he should worry. Listen, Puck, we got a lot to do," and he eased her into the bedroom, then gave her orders, in precise one-liners as she looked at him, eyes wide and unbelieving.

"You mean it?"

"'Course I bloody mean it. We go tonight, if you fix it. Dead of night. Around two thirty in the morning, so you'd better get it right. Need a Polaroid and some film as well. Got to doctor a passport."

"Yes, sir. Certainly, sir. Three bags full, sir."

"We'll only be taking three bags." Kruger was not in the amusing vein today.

He went back to tending the bacon, and thought about what Passau had said. *"The days of spying are coming into the twilight."* Twilight comes before the night, he considered. They had already been through years of night. Fighting the unseen in total darkness. Blind men with knives in a coal cellar. Or were they knives? It was over, but was it over? The whole thing, he decided, was too profound for him, so he started to listen, in his head, to the Mahler Ninth. It was apt because its music spoke of the great conundrum that was death: the composer preparing himself for his own mortality. Kruger, who knew all of Mahler by heart, had so often used this device, listening to the music in his head, without a score, without a recording. Hearing it, loving it. When he chose the Ninth he was usually in a mood to deal with his own ageing process, his personal secret meeting with the angel who was his final case officer: death. Halfway through the second movement, Passau, in the other room, began to play a recording of Strauss: *Death and Transfiguration*.

At least they were both thinking along the same lines.

IN ENGLAND, it was just after five in the evening, and Ursula Zunder was drinking tea in the guest suite when Gus and Carole Keene came in unannounced.

"We've got some questions, Ursula." Gus cradled his unlit pipe, and Carole merely looked friendly. They sat down, all cozy, chums sharing the good old British afternoon tea with little sandwiches and cakes.

"More questions?"

"Yes. Special questions. I want you to think very hard, Ursula, because this could be a matter of life or death. Kingfisher?"

"What about Kingfisher?"

"Before you became his case officer, did you ever get sight of his dossier? I don't mean gems from it, I mean the whole thing."

Ursula Zunder frowned. "Of course," she said. "Naturally. He was a big fish. I insisted that I know everything about him before I work with him. When you're going to service an agent in the field, you really have to get a good look at his profile."

"How much do you remember?"

Once more the frown. "All of it, naturally. I was a professional."

Gus Keene breathed a little sigh of relief. Art's cable had been most specific. "Tell us about it, love, would you?" He smiled at her and half understood the bleakness in her eyes.

20

"CAN WE SCHMOOZE a little this afternoon, Lou?"

Outside, rainclouds had started to gather. In the distance thunder rumbled, while the air had become like a Turkish bath. The Maestro gave him a little smile. "Schmooze all you want," he said. "What d'ya want to schmooze about?"

"Oh, this, that, the other. Maybe thirty years of operational techniques. What you call all the fun of the fair. Later we get down to closer details. This guy, Paul. You say he worked with you for ten years?"

"Thick and thin, all the way during the sixties, sure. Everything changed, didn't it, Herb? During the sixties? Stand-off in Cuba, JFK's assassination, Vietnam, the pop culture, drugs, protests. Bad time—good time. Two sides of the picture. Change of values. The youth revolution."

"And through it all, you met regularly with Paul, gave him stuff, took in the washing." Herbie wanted to press on. He kept hearing Art's voice, "Everyone's lying in their teeth, and I'm seventy percent sure they've started to sniff around here." Who was sniffing? FBI, CIA, Mob, or what was left of the four senior officers who had suborned Passau? Again he said, "And through it all, you met with the Russian guy, Paul."

"Him, and a couple of dead drops in New York. Once a drop in Finland—Helsinki. Once in London."

"Tell me about London."

"Did two concerts, Royal Festival Hall, then two weeks at Covent Garden, with the Passau Center's production of *Tosca*. Sixty-six . . ."

"All the sixes," Kruger mumbled. "In 1966 you met Paul in London?"

"No. Did a DLB."

"Professional, Lou. Talking DLBs. Not your common dead letter box, but a fabled DLB. Where?"

"Complicated. Can't remember it all now, but there were signals. Chalk marks to say it had been filled or emptied. Blue chalk, I remember, on a lamppost in South Audley Street, London. Later, back in New York, Paul asked if I'd gotten the joke. I hadn't. How would I know that the lamppost was almost directly outside a producer's office? Movies. Guy made famous spy thrillers. They thought that was very funny."

"And the DLB was?"

"Truly I forget. This was a long while ago. A church, I think. No, churchyard. Statue of Saint Francis talking with the birds. Base of the statue, yes."

"How did you get the instructions—in London, I mean?"

"Usual. I was told to telephone. They called me from D.C. Then I call. One-liners. 'Harry, this is Bill.' 'Don't know Bill from a hole in the head.' That kind of thing. 'Gray goose is flying tonight.'"

"But, Lou, you said the secret squirrels, the fabulous four, your quiet quartet, always gave you stuff to pass. You said 'stuff' meant chicken feed. The disinformation in which you were dealing."

"Oh, that." Almost a toss of the head. "Sure, one of the boys comes to my hotel room. Savoy. Great hotel. One of them comes in and gives me stuff. Says I got to call. Did it that night. Did the DLB next day. Remember it well. Pouring rain, like the Flood. Like what it's going to do here any minute." He glanced towards the windows. Lightning flickered like an artillery barrage, and the first drops banged against the glass—fall-out, shrapnel. Herbie hoped Pucky was being careful. He did not like driving in this kind of weather. If it set in, tonight would be murder. It would also be perfect. Can't have it both ways, Kruger. Take all the animals you can find; two by two into the Ark and sail to England.

"Which one?" he asked, detached, almost levitating he was so laid back.

"Which one what?"

"Which of your four? Your quartet, so secret you couldn't let left hand know what right hand was up to. Which one brought you the stuff?"

"I don't know. Wait. Yes. Duncan. It was Duncan. Came to the Savoy all long hair and dirty jeans. I was very embarrassed. A small packet. Film maybe."

"And the DLB in Helsinki?"

"Ha!" He threw back his head. "This was good, Helsinki. We did two concerts—Sibelius, who else? The orchestra was brilliant. I forget what else, but the DLB was really great. You know Helsinki?"

"Nodding acquaintance."

"You know the park they have with the statue of Sibelius, Finland's great composer? Just the head. The great domed head. Like looking at a woman's tit on a big movie screen; talk about over the top. They took me out to be photographed with this damned great piece of sculpture. I did the DLB at the same time. Dropped my camera. Filled the DLB as I picked up. Little hole round in back of Sibelius' neck. Package in, package out."

"And who gave you the stuff that time?"

"Funny. I been thinking. Again it was Duncan. 1967. I said to him, 'You get around. Always on the move; you take tablets for it?' Not very funny, I know, but he didn't even smile. Told me to do the job; just get on with it. That was it, so I asked him what he knew about Sibelius and he looked at me as though I were an idiot. Strange, Herb, the things that come back."

"Very." Herbie was lost for a moment in thoughts of the CIA's Soviet Office's heaviest field man being the one to feed Passau in London and Helsinki. "All in all it was a good ten years, yes?"

"Great. I nearly got myself into trouble a few times in the sixties, though, Herb. I got to tell you this because in a way it's kind of funny. Work was my real life. Being what I was. The rest? Game playing, maybe, but you know my besetting sin, Herb?"

"Sure, Lou. The ladies."

"Funny." He gave a smile and the old face lit up, making him seem young again.

"Funny ha-ha, or the other kind?"

"Bit of both, Herb. Bit of one and the other," and off he went, talking of conquests, fumbles in the dark, rejections, days of glory, nights of splendor.

"There was this harpist. Thirty years old and wanted to marry me," he told Herbie at one point. "I was a fool. Led her on. Thought, well, maybe, why not? Then changed my mind. She made my life a misery. You know the old saying, the screwing you get ain't worth the screwing you get."

"You had a harpist who made your life a misery? Not miserable enough to stop you being top of the classical pops, though, Lou."

"That's the truth. The orchestra, music, interpretation always came first—before women. Women, and what I was doing in this game. Secret game. Both came second to music. Music always finished a good four lengths ahead. Fast cars, some flying, good food, clothes, nice surroundings and the little secret game to keep the adrenaline flowing. They were all sidelines, hobbies."

"You were a bit of a bastard, Lou. No doubt about it."

"Eighteen-karat bastard. My path to hell. Bastards know they're bastards. Hey, you heard of this Chinese pianist, Lien Yao?"

"Beautiful girl, Lou. Still lovely though she ain't as young as she used to be."

"Twenty-two years of age when she came to my Center in New York. Huge talent for music. That would be 1969. Had a figure like no girl should be allowed."

"Still not bad, Lou. The recording companies these days, you got any comment on how they market female instrumentalists?"

"Sexist." Passau sounded almost prim and proper.

"The people who did the first album covers for that Lien Yao should've known better, Lou. In fact they're still doing it—taking the pictures, I mean. You seen her picture on the new album she's done? The concert in Moscow? How in hell do you make a girl with a piano look sexy?"

"I tell you, Herb. When she first came to me, she had been training since age five. Some smart-assed agent had taken charge of her. She arrives at my Center one morning with this smooth son of a bitch, and she has a portfolio with her—pictures they've just done. To my eyes they were almost pornographic."

"No?" Herbie had begun to camp it up, because he had read the story—or some of it-in the dossier at Warminster. "Pornographic?"

"Well, almost. You know, she was lying across the piano in this tight, white dress, showing all she had nearly. There was another of her reaching forward to start playing. Amazing, looked like she was about to rape the thing. Never figured out how they did it. Had her tongue touching her lips, and her bubbies thrust forward. Never figured it properly. Maybe the look in her eyes, or the way she was sitting. Maybe it was just her. She was what they'd call a turn-on those days. Legs right up to her neck; tits just right—melt in your mouth and not in your hand, know what I'm talking about?"

"I remember all that. I can call it to mind."

"What d'you mean, *remember*? You and the cute blonde here. Don't tell me you're not getting a slice?"

"Enough!" Kruger's palm slapped against his thigh, voice cracking like a piece of dry wood. He even surprised himself, then realized that he was losing his temper. Would not have a dirty word said against Pucky. What is this thing called love?

"Talk dirty about your women, Lou, but be careful what you say of others."

"Okay. Sorry."

"The Chinese girl? Tell me about Lien Yao."

"Sure. Really weird. She's a real prodigy, but you know that, you've heard her play. Very great young pianist. I give her concerts. Did the Rachmaninov Paganini Rhapsody; Shostakovich First Concerto; a great performance of Aaron's Piano Concerto; lots of things. So she's now a big hit. Fly to the moon if she wants. Just recorded the Busoni—strange piece that concerto, but she makes it alive, gives it depth. Fly anywhere that Lien Yao."

"Still flying from what I can make out."

"Why not? Great artiste. Nothing but respect for her. . . ." He wanted to add something but could not quite get it out.

"But, what, Lou?"

"Had a ring-a-ding with her."

"Serious?"

"She just set me on fire. I was well alight. I used to look at myself sometimes, in the buff, you know, when I was with her. I used to think I was never that big. She brought out the best in me, and don't you believe all that crap about Chinese women having short tongues . . ."

"So it was great sex?"

"We got close to Olympic standard. Then, somehow work got in the way. I was much in demand. Herbie, you know standing up there on the box isn't just a wham-bam thing. Some conductors just stroll through it. They have good coordination, and great charisma, but they don't work hard. Don't think enough. You have to study, get immersed. Then you have to pass that immersion on to the orchestra. It all takes time. My little Chinese firefucker knew that, but it didn't stop her from refusing to understand. Wanted to be with me all the time; got jealous—impossible. Then there were my four silent partners."

"What of them?"

"Matthew comes to me. Says I've got to cut myself free of her; stand back. See, it had got in the papers: gossip columnists, those kinda people. I argued with him, Matthew. As I see it, my relationships're none of his business. He says they are. Tells me some stuff. Lien Yao is a subversive. FBI on her tail. Connections with the Communist Party. Maybe damage what we've got going."

"So you drop her?"

"It was as good a time as any. She'd become a pain."

"You're a ruthless old bastard, Lou."

"No, I'm a pragmatist. A realist. I didn't believe that crap about her being a subversive."

"What if I told you it was, to some extent, true?"

"How would you know?"

"I'm in the business, Maestro. Read the files. I can tell you, in the eyes of some people, she was a subversive. When did you drop her?"

"Seventy-two, maybe seventy-three."

"So your case officer, Paul, was out of the picture?"

"By then, yes. But what about the lovely Chinese beauty being a subversive? Tell me about that."

"As you would say, Lou, that comes later. Lots of things I tell you about later. Straws in the wind. Who came after Paul? Someone took over early seventies. Who?"

Passau scratched his head, he looked like a Norman Rockwell character, an old guy looking puzzled, nonplussed. "Funny that. For the next ten years they changed a lot, like they had problems keeping me with one guy."

"Maybe they did. Case officers come and go, you know that, or you should."

He nodded, solemn, as though he understood the whole mystery of life. "Several, over ten years. Rubin, another guy who asked me to call him Aristotle—ever heard anything like that?—Denny; a girl, Sybil."

"Everything went on just the same. Regular?"

"Not really. No. Not when I come to think back. In the seventies it slowed down a lot, as though they didn't need me so much, or they weren't happy with me. Meetings didn't happen all that often."

"They give you a funny name also, Lou?"

He gave a puffing little laugh. "You want to know what they called me? 'Kingfisher.' How about that. I was Kingfisher. King of the fishermen, trawling secrets."

"You ever wonder about those secrets?"

"Didn't think about it. I was serving my country, that was all." His voice had suddenly become flat and, for the first time, Kruger suspected he was lying.

"So you didn't, at any time, take a peek at what they gave you?"

"Too busy." Too fast.

"And you didn't get concerned about the fact you always had to bring something back to your four flying friends?"

"Why should I?"

"Thought you might have wondered why. You were the one who was handing them intelligence, on a plate. Why would they send anything back?"

"Why not? They told me the Soviets wanted it to look like two-way traffic, only the Agency—CIA—was giving them the dog food. Simple. What was there to understand?"

"What about ideologies?"

"You mean politics?"

"Faith. Politics. Your place in the system. Which way should the world go: power to a few, or power to the people?"

"Same thing, ain't it? People who get power misuse it. Every time. Law of nature. Give anyone power and they'll misuse it."

"You had power. Power of music. You misuse it?"

"Different, Herbie my friend. Very different. I only have power to interpret. Power to make people feel happy or sad. Not real power. Nothing life or death. No power to drain the poor and enrich the rich; couldn't soak the rich and give it to the poor. All political systems suck. No time for them."

"But you had time to help the American intelligence service fight against communism?"

"Minute business. Tiny. Dust mote in time. We get philosophical and I want to throw up, Herb. If we talk, I have to tell it like it happened to me. Through my eyes. Through my viewpoint, and I don't have any view-point when it comes to politics or religion."

Kruger shifted in his chair, glancing outside. The rain was bucketing down, streaming in a sheet across the windows. "They ever get back on track? Give you one case officer instead of a football team?"

"Oh, sure. Seventy-nine, eighty. A doozy. Female of the species. Therese." He put the first finger and thumb of his right hand together, touched his lips with them and blew the kiss towards Herbie. "Handled me all possible ways. We stopped the walks in the park and meetings out-side public buildings. It was very comfortable. She came to me, the Lexington Avenue place. Always came with a little electronic gizmo. Said she had to sweep the place for bugs every time. Not allowed even to say hello until she did the search."

"Ever find anything?"

"Never. But she was thorough. Oh my goodness, she was thorough. Said she was there to comfort me with apples. Biblical."

"I know." Big Herbie Kruger felt the tears well up inside him. Knew his eyes were hard and cold. She had said the same to him, but in German—

"Oh, darling Herbie. Stay me with flagons, comfort me with apples: for I am sick of love." Her dark hair untidy on the pillow and her lips bruised with kisses. He could taste her now, just as he could hear her voice—"Rise up, my love, my fair one, and come away." She had loved the Song of Solomon, or so she said. Was it all part of the training, he wondered? Did they teach them the words? Learn these poems by heart, for these are the phrases that will press this target's buttons: the words that will finally drive the target insane.

"Hey, Herb, where'd you go?"

"To Therese. I knew her also, Lou, but that's a different story."

"You knew . . . ?"

"Different story, Maestro. Another place. Another time. I get some tea, eh?"

Passau shrugged.

In the kitchen, Herbie waited for the kettle to boil. He thought of the great emerging conundrum. The facts he had seen in black and white back at Warminster. The odd little hiccup back in the early seventies when suspicious minds had pressed the Chinese pianist to report back to FBI Counter-Intelligence. Was her boyfriend, Louis Passau, being used by some other government agency, or was he Mr. Clean? The FBI had some kind of hold over the girl, but the file did not specify, anymore than it determined the source of their original suspicions. A terse note was appended to the file—"Closed: No corroboration." He thought of what Louis had just told him.

"Matthew comes to me. Says I've got to cut myself free of her. Stand back . . . tells me some stuff. Lien Yao is a subversive. . . . Maybe damage what we've got going."

So who was lying? Who was game playing? *Closed: No corroboration.*

He had just made the tea when he heard Pucky's key in the door. She flashed him a smile, gave him a thumbs up—all set, everything fixed—as she turned in the small lobby, shaking herself and pulling back the hood on her raincoat, sopping. He nodded, then took Passau his tea.

"Tired, Lou?"

"Getting to me some."

"You were perky earlier. Spry."

"Catches up with you when you get older, Herb. You wait till you're my age."

Herbie said that he should try to get an early night. "Have some rest. Still a long way to go. Pucky's come in with more food. You fancy some liver? Liver and tomatoes. Liver does wonders for your blood count."

"Fuck the blood count. I'll have it with bacon."

Passau turned away, chose a CD and listened to music, sipping his tea and looking out at the teeming rain. Bach, the Goldberg Variations. Soothing. An antidote to insomnia.

In the bedroom, Herbie consulted with Pucky, who told him the details and slipped him the items he needed. He worried about the weather, for she said the driving conditions were almost impossible. "If we don't leave until two thirty, perhaps it'll have eased up."

He loaded the Polaroid camera, putting it out of sight under the bedcovers, then they packed what was needed before cooking the liver and bacon. It was only six thirty when they finished eating.

"I want you to listen, Lou," Herbie began, raising his voice for the benefit of the listeners.

"Sure. Don't I always listen to you?"

"Art tells me they got some security problems. So, to help out, we're going to sleep in the apartment downstairs tonight. Just for tonight. Puck'll come through and see what you're going to need. We should all get some rest, okay?"

It brought Art over on the double. He was there, dripping all over the carpet almost before Passau had meekly followed Pucky into his bedroom.

"What the hell're you up to, Herbie?" His voice was raised a tenth higher than normal, which for Art was serious.

21

"TRYING TO HELP, Art. What you think I'm doing? Contorting with the enemy?"

"Consorting, Herb." Railton had slipped out of his plastic rainslicker, tossing it into a corner of the small vestibule. His eyes were wary. When he spoke it was in a series of barks, and his face showed the strain. Sitting in a holiday apartment on the Gulf Coast, listening to Kruger interrogating the old man, waiting for coded telephone calls, watching for strange faces. All that had started to take its toll.

"What you think?" Herbie snapped again. He had a glass of Budweiser in his hand, and he saw Art's eyes flick towards it. "Don't like the local customs. Don't like drinking it from a can." He grinned. "Want some beer?"

"No. Thank you, no. What do *I* think, Herbie? I don't know what to think, that's why I'm here. What's going on? You almost doze away the afternoon, going around in lazy circles like a buzzard. What're we getting here? Selected gems from three decades of deception? Taking your time, playing nice to that evil old sod."

"Who's he talking to, Art? Who's making the running? Who's doing the interrogation?"

"I said we had to push him along. Fast."

"Sure. Art, all we're going to get is highlights. He probably doesn't even remember most of it. You heard him—and I believe him. This was a hobby, a sideline, something that gave him an extra fix of adrenaline. He really played a game—at least most of the time. Some things are still there, important things. He'll regurgitate them, given time and the following wind. That's right isn't it? Following wind?"

"Fine, okay, but I still want the highlights fast."

"You ain't going to get them fast, Art. Nobody's going to clean him out quickly. You notice how the detail has gone? All the early stuff, the time in Chicago; the horrors—Rita Crest; the terrible Traccia years—he has those times etched out, clear; even remembers conversations. Now, the last three decades are blurred: except what he *wants* to remember. I understand that." He stopped, staring at Art as a thought struck him. "We got orders to move? London finally coming up roses?"

Art shook his head: an angry movement, eyes down, then up, glaring. "Sounded like you'd lost heart. If that was pushing . . ."

"Hey, Mr. Railton, sir. I cut my teeth on technique with your devoted daddy. Don't tell me how to do it. Think, Art, just fucking think. I got an old man here. A very old man. Went through hell and gone yesterday. Brought the debris of his life out of the dark. Screwing his daughter all that time. In sodding *love* with his daughter. I sat with him, like some doctor in the intensive care unit. Louis Passau and his self-respect have parted company. So today he's almost untouchable. You say I was doing gems from thirty years. Sure I was, but did you catch the gems, or aren't you listening proper?"

"Properly, Herb."

"Shut the fuck up, Art. You're not hearing it as it is. We got two major things from him today, right?"

Art opened his mouth to answer, but Herbie's huge banana hand shot forward, landing very gently across Art's lips as though he was pushing the words back into the man's larynx. "Two very major items for the files. We got the identity of Duncan. That thin snake Urquart sodding Bains. Best singleton the Agency ever had. You forgotten that? You forgotten that guy. Slid around Europe, over the Wall, behind the Curtain, even into Moscow itself. Like a ghost. For years he worked under the eyes of the Sovs. Christ, I remember the old days, when the Cold War was giving people bloody hypothermia. I remember your father, Art. Your father and the old Chief. They used to get worried about Urquart fucking Bains."

For a second, no more, Big Herbie's mind engulfed a huge piece of his past. He heard the long-dead old Chief of the British Secret Intelligence Service talking to Naldo Railton. "The American, Bains, Naldo. He worries the hell out of me. It's as if he's fireproof. Comes and goes just as though he has an arrangement with the Ks." The Ks being how they spoke of KGB.

In the same second, Herbie saw other things that did not quite go with the words he heard. His last, illegal, trip into East Berlin. The time they had taken the great and visible Herbie Kruger, with the help of their long-term honeytrap, Ursula Zunder. There had been a point when he came back to consciousness, for a brief time, minutes, seconds maybe. He lay in what seemed to be a hospital bed. Now it was as if his own subconscious had allowed things to float to the surface. In those few seconds, years ago, he had glimpsed someone among the KGB team. Over the years the face had come back to him in nightmares, but had stayed hidden because Big Herbie Kruger was immersed in the personal way he had been betrayed. Since that time he had remained obsessed by the lovely Ursula Zunder whose laugh, sense of history, and devotion, together with her velvet thighs, had kept Herbie in thrall. Still kept him, trapped in that terrible past. Now he was nine-tenths sure who the face had belonged to. Urquart Bains.

The flash of insight calmed him, so that he now looked at Art in a different light. Big Herb was the one with an experience young Railton could never touch. Not anymore. "Art," his voice almost full of tenderness. "Art, we got Urquart Bains. Got him bang to rights. Duncan. Nail him to the wall now. Nail all of them—Marty Foreman, who I thought was my friend; Tony de Paul, who I hardly knew; Alfoot who was too high and mighty for me to be buddies with. We almost got them all. Matthew, Gregory, Vincent and Duncan."

"You think the Agency knows?" Art had come down from the speeding paranoia which had enveloped his body.

"If they do, then it's doubtful if the old man was going to live to be interrogated. Times've changed, Art. It's the Year of the Cuddly Bear. The Year of the Friendly Eagle, and the Nice Playful Brit Bulldog. Either they know and want to keep it very quiet, avoid scandal at all costs, or the old Soviet Office people think they're untouchable. Wouldn't put it past friends Gregory, Vincent and Duncan to be on the interrogation team. A fast pill in Passau's coffee and his heart would give out. They'd be home and dry. Christ, Art, Moscow's about to give up a lot of its secrets; the Krauts're putting people on trial for being part of the old evil empire. We all know the Agency has to be purged, reorganized. Same with us. If those four Americans floated to the surface, they'd stand trial. In a changing world there have to be sacrifices. So the Cold War's over, but what about the Cold War traitors? They'll hang them out to dry."

"And the old man? Is he an innocent babe? Did he know? Was he part of it?"

"Did he fall or was he pushed?" Herbie regarded Art Railton with cheerful eyes. Grinned. Made a little laughing, puffing sound with his lips. "That's what I'm here to find out. Long-term—very long-term—deception, treachery, betrayal. Does it matter? Probably not. Not as far as old Passau's concerned, but America the beautiful will probably want to render up its traitors. If they don't, there's no justice, so we got to point the way. So let me find out."

"Sorry, Herb. Yes. Yes, of course. Yes, you have to do it your way." He patted the side of his slacks with an open palm. "You touched on the Chinese girl as well."

"Sure I did. Give the man a lollipop. She's in our Passau File, and we still don't know who she was working for. We don't know shit about that, Arthur Railton. Who tipped the G-Men, if they *were* tipped at all? Who asked her to take a look-see? We don't know. But we do know that Matthew—friend Marty Foreman—was frightened as hell. Told old Louis to knock it off with Lien Yao, which he did. Not a nice man, basically, your Maestro Passau. You notice how, for the best part of ten years, the whole thing was scaled down?"

Art nodded. "You're right, of course, Herb. Sorry." Then the old snake of suspicion moved deep in his eyes. "What's this about moving downstairs? Why that little game?"

Herbie gave the greatest performance of his life, consisting of a small shrug, and a lifting of his forearms, hands palm upwards, fingers splayed, as though tossing his entire inner self at Art. It was over in a second, but the movement was a piece of business that the late Lord Olivier would have picked up and used without hesitation. "Art," it said. "Art, you know me. I am beyond suspicion. There's a job to be done and I've come back to do it. Art, for God's sake, trust me and don't try to sell me short. Believe in me. I'm yours. I obey orders." All that in the shrug and the movement of forearms and hands.

Aloud, he said, "You've got problems. Tired watchers, Art. I'm trying to help. You tell me you think the G-men're nosing around. You say an old Agency hand gets spotted by the pool. So who knows what's going on? One thing for sure. There's risk we got to minimalize. . . ."

("Minimize, Herb." Only he did not say it.)

"Your people got to have rest. I got to have safety. If they're sniffing they probably know where we are. So we move downstairs to sleep. Pucky and I take turns watching. We leave some lights on here. Got me?"

On cue, Pucky Curtiss came out of Passau's room. "Shit!" she said, loudly. "Oh, sorry, Art. Herb, I forgot the water. We only have half a bottle left. I'll drive up and get some. Sorry."

"Is okay, Puck. Plenty of time." Then, cocking a thumb at Passau's door, "He okay?"

"Out on his feet. Drained. Said I'd wake him later. Later, when we go downstairs." Her eyes shifted to Art. "You okay?" The smile was full of friendship. Done to a turn.

"Tired, Pucky, but that comes with the territory."

"Are we going to London?"

"Nothing yet. I've told Herbie I'll give him plenty of warning."

"I'll go get the water." Another smile, right up to the eyes, and she was putting on her raincoat: the belted one with the hood. Almost a trench coat. Dressing the part of a lady spy right out of central casting.

Herbie gave her a nod. "Drive careful, Puck." Nobody would even suspect she was off to pay the bill and tell reception they'd be leaving early in the morning. Calculated risk, Herb had said.

As the front door closed, so Art reached down for his rainslicker. "Sorry if I got shirty, Herb. You sure you can keep watch for a couple of hours? My people're really weary."

"Tell them to take the night off. We'll be downstairs. I told you. Pucky and I'll take it in turns. You got a number in case of a panic?"

Railton nodded, gave him the telephone number of the apartment they were using. "Just call if you need help. If anything—I mean anything—happens out of the ordinary. I'll call London again."

"Give 'em ultimatum. Tell 'em we're running out of time. If it's any help, I really think we are. I got to get through little old Louis' last defenses. Lay it out fair and square. Take him up to date. He should live that long." As he spoke, Big Herbie realized he meant every word. The thirty-six hours ahead of them could very easily push Passau into terminal fatigue. After all, he had got the big sin off his chest—or thought he had. He could die happy.

For a second, Kruger thought Art was going to embrace him, but the younger man drew back. Trust was all. Herb prayed to heaven that the true bond of trust had been forged anew; prayed that Art would really call off the dogs.

As it turned out, he did, though there were other phantom blood-hounds out there in the rain.

THEY LEFT JUST after two thirty in the morning. The rain had stopped, but only on a temporary basis, and even in the small hours there was enough heat to generate a foggy steam from the roads.

In the downstairs apartment, Kruger had strutted his stuff.

They sat Passau in a chair and took the Polaroid pix. The old man seemed to have recovered his perkiness and did not flinch when they went through the plan with him.

"It's going to be arduous, Lou," Herbie told him. "Sitting around waiting. Boring jet flights."

"I'm used to it. Sleep on a clothesline. I'll sleep on the flights."

The apartment, Herbie was certain, was unbugged. They could talk with ease. He went over the rooms before bringing Louis, Pucky and the luggage down. He knew Art's handwriting well enough to check the places he would have inserted the tiny grain-of-wheat-sized radio bugs. "Clean as the proverbial pig and whistle," he told Pucky.

After taking the pix, Herb retired to the main room with his traveling workshop, the little black plastic box containing scissors, punch, ruler—a portable office, the ads said, and he had bought it a couple of years ago in Bond Street, together with a leather holdall the size of a paperback book for other essentials.

You can never go completely private—as the argot called retirement from the intelligence service. When you go, you are still not free. Before and after leaving, Herbie had gathered a number of useful artifacts against the time he really did not think would ever come. The past cannot be completely sloughed off like a snake's skin. He knew that, so had made a private store, just for that rainy day they had told him about. Now that day was here.

He looked at the pictures of Passau, chose the one that would serve his purpose best, and cut it to passport size. Inserted it into the correct place. Filled in the spaces to fit. Used the tiny forger's seal, made of plastic and carried in the lining of his one piece of luggage. Passau was now also a Brit. Herbert Harold King. Retired. Real as hell itself, the passport battered and bent where he had carried it around for odd days, thumbed through it regularly.

During his last year of active service with the Firm, Herbie had given the blank passport some life, quietly adding an almost genuine American visa, and entry stamps for Portugal, Spain, the United States and France while waiting for a little piece of fake I.D. to be done in Maida Vale by one of the famed Printers' Devils—who did what they called "paper" for the service.

He turned the King passport over, smiling a little. Then he pushed it to one side and got rid of the other Polaroid shots, and the trimmings. Back at the table, he slit open a large manila envelope containing his final, long-hidden identity. These were papers he had never used. They were not in his own name. Not the Buckerbee I.D. he had shown at JFK. Neither the Professor Spinne nor the joke Gordon Lonsdale, but a virgin set. Helmut Auld. Naturalized British citizen since 1948. Credit cards kept up to date since retirement. Used occasionally. Pocket litter quietly renewed every six months because old habits die hard, and when the chips are down you trust nobody, not even your own people.

He took the Helmut Auld passport, placed it next to that of H. H. King, a.k.a. Louis Passau, and worked on a couple of I-94 blanks, those cards U.S. Immigration staples inside the passports of visitors, to be removed before leaving the country. Their system was not foolproof but it worked after a fashion. The hundreds of I-94s taken from visitors' passports each day were eventually checked against a central computer—eventually being the operative word. Sometimes it took a week, other times, months.

Herbie went into the bedroom and changed into a suit, crumpled, hanging like an old sack on his large frame. He took every other I.D. belonging to himself and burned it—except for his real passport and cards—Eberhardt Lucas Kruger: the passport which still had the "Foreign Service Retired" stamp. This, and his real credit cards, driver's license and the like, he put into the leather wallet and rammed it down into the almost, but not quite, hidden pocket in his case. He filled the pockets of his suit with the Auld litter, a battered wallet with the Auld credit cards and the stuff you needed to move around in the U.K.

Back in the main room, he made a little pile for H. H. King—passport, a couple of letters, one credit card, address book with next of kin in it. Then he began to deal with Pucky.

From her identities, he chose Patricia Anne Carmichael because it had her down as a Social Worker, which covered a multitude of sins. It did not take long for him to manufacture an I-94 for her. He had half a dozen I-94 blanks left so he burned them and flushed the ashes away in the bathroom. You could pick up I-94s anywhere.

So it was done. The papers were prepared, the briefings over. Now all they had to do was get out, pray, buy time—a couple of days, maybe three. Put old Louis on the rack again, then call in for an ambulance to Warminster.

"No doubt they're looking for us," he had told Pucky when the plan had formulated in his head. "No doubt at all. What you got to remember is they're blinkered. They'll be on the watch for three people, not two and one, but three. Also, they'll be watching direct exits to Europe from main airports. That's where they expect us to go. It's where we came from, so they figure we'll go back there. The trick is to make all the check-ins last minute and not disguise yourself. No wigs, no cute fake beards for the Maestro and myself. Just simple things. Buy the dress, Pucky, with the eye of a watcher."

Among the purchases of that afternoon, she had done as she was told. The dress was severe, blue, button-down, belted, little pockets, a white collar and epaulettes. With the raincoat she would be taken for some kind of nurse, especially if she was in charge of a wheelchair—Passau wrapped in blankets and both of them generating a lot of panic by last-minute arrivals.

"Making yourself totally visible is sometimes better than skulking," Herbie said. "Only thing to worry about is if either of our flights get in too early or, worse, too late. The timings look okay." He told her this as he divided up the tickets.

The three bags went into the trunk of the car at two twenty-five in the morning. Pucky carried the bag filled with bottled water and sandwiches as she followed Passau down the stairs. Herbie had already checked the outside of the hexagonal holiday apartment. The Lincoln faced outwards, its snout a couple of feet back from the road.

They made Passau comfortable in the back and Pucky drove, Kruger sitting next to her. No headlights until they reached the main buildings of South Seas Plantation. After that, it was simply concentration. Almost a four-hour slog.

Herbie was dropped off at Tampa International. "Don' forget what I told you." He leaned into the window. "Just drive around, find a motel.

Keep up the nurse-patient bit. Rest. Make sure the old man's comfortable. Also be certain you park with the license plates out of sight." He hefted his suitcase from the trunk. "See you tonight. If I don't make it, you know where to go." He looked her in the eyes, took a deep breath. "Love you, Pucky Curtiss. Take care." Then he was gone, walking with a slight limp, one shoulder higher than the other, into the departures area, heading towards the Avis counter where, as Helmut Auld, he rented a Cutlass, got some maps and drove away. It was six fifteen in the morning.

It took him all day, driving fast but with care. Never exceeding the speed limit, as he crossed the wide thumb of Florida, heading for Miami. To eke out the time he made diversions: doubling back on three occasions. He stopped four times. Gas, a pee and coffee. Once a tuna sandwich. The views were often bleak and deserted. Miles between the little farms and homesteads, hamlets and villages. Florida lives mainly on its coast. Other large towns or cities were easily bypassed.

He retuned the radio twelve times during the long drive. Flipping through the bands until he found a station playing classical music, wincing when he heard the sounds of country and western, or rock and roll.

"You're a musical snob, Herb. This is also music. Enjoy." He heard old Louis Passau's voice from the time they had done the long drive from Virginia to the Gulf Coast. Aloud, he said, "Okay, so I'm a snob."

It rained, on and off, the entire day. Twice, Herbie had to get off the road, for the downpour was so great that he could not even see the end of the hood; but mostly it was just a steady drizzle. Sometimes, in the far distance, he caught sight of lightning, and huge thunderheads building on the skyline.

He put it down to paranoia but was convinced, on at least seven occasions, that someone was on his tail. First a battered gray Dodge pickup with two oversized aerials. The Dodge was with him for miles, staying back a long way, eventually disappearing.

Then there was the Range Rover, equipped with extra lights, spots, two long whiplash aerials and three shorter ones sprouting from the roof. The Range Rover came and went in his mirror and only disappeared on the outskirts of Miami.

He made it to the international airport barely in time. Parking in the long-term area, sticking his gun in the glove compartment and throwing the keys into a drain as he raced down, running, puffing and panting, just making the check-in and the gate. "Y'all very lucky. I was about to close the door." The cheeky little flight attendant winked at him as he bent and clambered clumsily into the little Saab SF340. The turbo-prop whined into the air right on schedule, five forty-five in the stormy late afternoon. They landed five minutes late: six fifty p.m. Nassau International. BA264 was already boarding. Tighter than he would have wished, but there, just by the gate, was the tiny red circle stuck to the wall—the sticker he had given to Pucky. "Only if you can do it naturally," he had told her. "With luck, they'll get you on first, with the wheelchair. Just if you can. Put it somewhere near the gate. Where I can see it."

If things had gone as planned, Pucky and Passau would have spent the day resting in a motel near Tampa International, then gone to the airport, stashing the Lincoln away so it would not be found for a couple of days, making a flight out to the Bahamas at the last moment, then waiting for the final dash.

They were on and safe, so he stood, trying to look smaller, hunched, a bit stupid and nervous, in the line of people heading for the jetway. A few seconds before seven twenty-five the British Airways Tristar pointed its nose skyward, retracted its gear and climbed to its designated altitude. They would be at Heathrow around ten thirty local in the morning.

Herbie would not have known the young man sitting eight rows behind him. He had boarded the flight after Kruger and looked like any other tourist. There was absolutely nothing noteworthy about him. He appeared hot and tired, wore slacks and a sports coat that could have done with a visit to the cleaners. He knew Herbie, though. He also saw, as he glanced back while stowing a small case in the overhead bin, the nurse with the elderly patient who closed his eyes and went to sleep before they even began to push back.

"Drink, sir?" A severe-looking flight attendant stood by Kruger's seat, giving him a look that said, hurry up, I haven't got all day.

"Sure," Herbie gave her the benefit of the doubt and his extraspecial king-sized, I'm harmless, grin. "I could murder a good strong cup of tea."

She smiled. "Coming up, sir. Won't be long."

Big Herbie Kruger settled back. He knew the others were on board, so he had no problems until they reached Heathrow. If there was to be any trouble, Heathrow was the place to find it. He prayed that Art Railton had not blown his top and that the big guns back home would not overreact.

BOOK 3

(UNITED KINGDOM. AUTUMN 1991)

1

THE BUCKINGHAM HOTEL lies a few miles inland, in the sprawl which makes up the outer fringes of Torquay. Once the jewel of British West Country seaside resorts, Torquay in the early nineties has gone to seed. The Buckingham, formerly the site of great golfing tournaments and a monied clientele, has almost followed the town on its downward slide, though not quite.

People still go there to play golf. Companies hold their small sales conferences in the annex. Tour groups of Japanese ride in, stay for two nights, and are bused around the West Country. Couples check in on Friday evenings for weekend specials; in the season, families come for a week, have cream teas, do the sights of Devon, glorious Devon, and go home refreshed yet feeling that, somehow, they have not exactly got their money's worth.

The public rooms, and some of the private suites, still have traces of a more elegant time. The staff does its best, which is really not quite good enough. Like so many British seaside hotels marked with four stars by the Automobile Association, the Buckingham clings to the slippery surface of an England from which the thick patina of excellence has been almost removed by the vicissitudes of politicians and the tired erosion of a country at war with its morally bankrupt self.

From the Buckingham, a drive to the seafront takes about fifteen minutes, and in the holiday season you probably want to remove yourself from the delights of the Promenade, and the gaudy Pier, in less time than it takes to get there. In the summer, there is a constantly changing community, the pervading aroma of fish and chips, paper and empty cans litter the gutters, together with the uncertain feeling that violence could occur at any time of the day or night by way of hordes of yobbos with their yobbettes—noisy, looking for kicks. Overall, the vibrations are the same as anywhere else in the United Kingdom—a sense of dissatisfaction combined with a knowledge that you are looking towards the terminal moments of a dying glory.

Big Herbie Kruger, Pucky Curtiss and Louis Passau checked into the Buckingham Hotel at seven forty-five in the evening. In all they had been on the move for well over twenty-four hours.

Heathrow had been incredibly easy. Too easy, Herbie thought. The MI5 watcher, standing back from the passport control officer, did not register anything. In fact, he seemed to be looking the other way. To Herb, this meant they were letting him in, together with Pucky and the Maestro. Probably letting all three of them in and slamming the door closed behind them.

He rented a VW Passat from Hertz, did not hang around while they were processing the paperwork, saying he would return in half an hour. He went off, drank coffee, ate a bacon roll, cashed a very large amount of traveler's checks, and felt pleased he had shaved and spruced up on the aircraft.

Nobody appeared to be in the least bit interested in him. He picked up the car and drove the mile and a half to the Post House Hotel where he picked up the waiting Pucky with her charge.

They talked the next stage as Pucky did the driving. Passau slept in the back. "He's done little else but sleep and try to cop the occasional feel," she said. "A dirty old man of ninety." She saw Herbie's raised eyebrow and added, ". . . or whatever."

Kruger stepped from the car as they stopped at traffic lights just south of Windsor. He said, "See you, sweetheart," and was gone, lumbering away along the street, Windsor Castle rising in the distance above him.

Twenty minutes later, making certain nobody was on his back, he found a garage, where he paid cash for a dubious 1989 Peugeot with two hundred thousand on the clock. The test drive revealed nothing drastically wrong with the engine and the color was right—a brown. Dry dog shit covered with dust, Herb thought. The garage owner saw the crisp notes and did not bother to ask Mr. Fyfield for any I.D. Unless there was a phantom on his back, Kruger was away and clear.

Before leaving Windsor he used a public telephone to call the Shop. In the strange double-talk used by his chosen profession, he quickly told the duty officer that all three of them were okay, that he would be on again as soon as he had completed the job he had set out to do, and Art Railton should not get anxious. The line was open for less than ninety seconds. The equipment at the Shop took at least two and a half minutes to trace an incoming.

He drove to Basingstoke, known as "Doughnut City" because of its incredible number of roundabouts. People said of Basingstoke that the Ministry of Transport used it as a test bed for roundabouts and traffic flow.

In the main multistory garage, above the pedestrian precinct, he located the Passat, drove upwards through the lines of cars, then around the roof parking. There was no suspicion of a watcher van or car, so he took the Peugeot down, parking it in an empty slot four spaces from the Passat.

Pucky sat at the wheel and Passau snored loudly in the back. "Clean, I think," she said with a nervous little smile. Herb nodded and they all transferred to the Peugeot. Passau was awake for six minutes, looking completely disoriented. He snuffled a bit, cursed, then went back to sleep. Herbie took the wheel and headed west, through countryside tilled and prepared for winter. The autumn seemed almost over in England and the trees were mainly skeletal. A fine, misty rain was blown like gunsmoke by a fresh, cold breeze. Whatever dead leaves were left blew wet and ruined over the roads, clogging the gutters. As they drove further to the west, so the color returned to the trees. Not as wonderful as it would be in Virginia, but all the reds, golds and browns backlit the landscape. The fine rain remained, but the breeze lost some of its harshness.

At around two thirty they pulled up by a Little Chef. Kruger had not stopped the engine before Louis Passau woke, full of spirit. "Where the fuck are we, Herb? This looks like a piss-awful place. Also I'm cold. I think my balls're going to drop off, and what's this shitty chef joint? Not thinking of eating here are you? Get the runs for a week."

"Is what I like about you, Lou." Herbie moved his considerable bulk so that he could look at the Maestro sprawled in the back. "What I really like about you is your sophistication, and your incredible vocabulary. The greatest musical director of our age. You got a mouth on you like a fishwife."

"So Delius died of syph."

Herbie could not make that connection though he thought about it for a long time.

Once inside the Little Chef, Passau wanted to eat everything on the menu. In the end he settled for fried eggs, bacon, sausage, a slice of fried bread, tomatoes, mushrooms and coffee. "Lost your appetite?" Herbie asked as Lou grabbed the ketchup bottle.

When he had demolished the meal, Passau asked for a double apple pie. With cream. "You must forgive my father," Herbie told the amazed waitress. "He's been staying with my brother whose wife is very stringy with the food."

"Stingy, Herb." Pucky did not meet his eyes.

"Fuck that," Passau breathed, and Herbie apologized again. "My brother's wife also uses terrible language."

In the back of the car, the old Maestro fell asleep almost before they hit the road. It seemed the longest drive in Christendom. Herbie admitted that the slog across Florida had been a Sunday afternoon outing compared to the journey west.

When they arrived, Passau regarded the Buckingham Hotel with grave suspicion, but cheered up when they were shown the best suite. Four rooms costing a king's ransom. Herbie nodded and left him with Pucky, going down to negotiate a week's stay. He managed to cut the rate by one third and everyone seemed happy.

"There's an entertainment quiz on Friday nights," the girl at reception told him, as though she was offering him her body. "Your grandfather would probably enjoy that, sir. A lot of the older people enjoy our quizzes. Dancing on Saturdays. You and Mrs. Fyfield might like that. It's not for the very young. They play old-fashioned, classical music, like waltzes and foxtrots."

"My grandfather might like it also." Herb gave her his best "I'm a raver" smirk. "Loves the classics. Very hot on Xavier Cugat."

"That a group?" she asked.

"You'd better believe it." He gave her a roguish wink and headed for the unsteady elevator.

Back in the suite, Passau was in bed. "He's ordered a plate of tongue and salad, chocolate mousse and a bottle of wine." Pucky looked ruffled. "I've told him that *we're* going down to eat in the dining room." This last delivered as a kind of ultimatum.

"Sure you don't mind Pucky and I going down for a meal?" Herbie stood at the foot of the bed. Passau had taken the single-bedded room and was propped up with pillows, looking more than comfortable.

Already he had fixed up his portable CD player and the speakers. There was a telephone next to the bed and he seemed very calm.

"I'll be okay." He gave a long sigh. "If I don't feel too good, I'll have you paged. You're not going out of the building, are you?"

"Just going down for dinner."

"Well, don't worry about me. I'll be okay. I need the rest. Just let them know I might call down. At my age you can never tell. I need the rest though."

"Of course you do, Maestro. You know we've . . ." He was cut short by the arrival of room service—a reasonably tuned-in waiter who seemed to know what he was doing. Passau balanced the tray on his bed, looked over the mound of food and grinned. "This is the life," he said. "Love tongue. Can't get enough of it."

"I had heard. Maestro, tomorrow we go on talking. You understand that, don't you?"

"Tell you what I can. Got to finish my confession. Why we here, Herb? Someone after us?"

"Just thought you might like the change. Very bracing, the West Country." Big Herbie grinned and went through to wash, brush up and lead the gorgeous Ms. Curtiss down to dinner. She had put on a white pants suit with a lavender blouse, and her hair looked freshly washed. It smelled of summer hay, and Kruger thought how good it would be to roll in a field with her. He said as much and she laughed.

There were a dozen couples spread out at tables, far apart, in the big dining room, and every man eyed Pucky with the inevitable look of lechery. A tall maître d', with a manner just short of patronizing, showed them to a table set in a window recess. Burgundy velvet blotted out the damp night. On a small dais, a bearded man played the piano—a selection from Lloyd-Webber, Stephen Sondheim, Lerner and Loewe, all of whom he embellished with trills and runs.

"Must remember not to bring the old man down here for dinner." Herbie looked across the table at Pucky who suddenly seemed incredibly happy. "He'd be up there giving the guy a master class."

"This is the first time we've eaten away from him." She stretched a hand across the thick white linen and laid it over Herbie's big artisan's paw. "Things really going to be okay?"

"Things meaning Louis, or things meaning us?"

"Both."

Kruger made a long bobbing motion with his head. "I might get the whole goods from him in a couple of days. Three maybe. Gems from his golden years. After that it may be possible to tie up the loose ends. Art, and the Warminster people, can take over. I finish. I go private again. Funny, I'll miss that revolting old man. He's bloody genius, but genius can get on your wick."

"Us?" she queried, looking like a child pleading for candy.

"Is what you really want, Puck? Truly? Not just a shipboard romance?" She did not pause. "It's what I would like. Wanting is something else."

"Then, okay. I fix it. One thing at a time, eh?"

A tall, friendly waitress with the name Annie on a small plastic strip clipped to her uniform came over and asked if they were ready to order. She was gray, motherly, late fifties and looked as though she worked out regularly.

They ordered the asparagus soup, sole in fennel sauce, and the blanquette de veau. "Veal in a blanket," Herbie said, and the waitress laughed and moved away, her place taken by the snooty maître d' who was doubling as sommelier. Herbie crushed the man unmercifully, quizzing him on the quality of the wines, shooting educated questions at him, and finally settling for a dry white with an excellent pedigree. The maître d' left, eyebrows raised.

"Tell me about the secret four. Give me a full picture," Pucky said.

"What's to tell?"

"You seem to know them. I don't. Draw it for me, Herb."

He nodded and began talking about Marty Foreman. "Little guy, like steel, not couth, would've become a jailbird if it hadn't been for the war—second world variety. Brooklyn street fighter. A number of minor strikes against him when the Office of Special Services picked him up and shipped him to London, so that he could channel his aggression into something positive. A lot of those guys came from near-hoodlum backgrounds. That's what the OSS wanted—tough guys; people who wouldn't get squeamish.

"Marty came over to Europe with some of the others. Came on the old *Queen Mary*, which was being used as a troop ship. There's a story about him—could be apocryphal—that's right, apocryphal?"

She nodded.

"Well, some of the civilian stewards had been left on board the old *Queen*. These OSS guys found out that the stewards were creaming it off the top from the GI Joes going to give their lives for God and freedom. Story is that Marty, with a couple of others, decided to make an example to discourage the rip-offs. They tossed one of the senior stewards over the side. Mid-Atlantic. Who knew?"

"Jesus."

He shrugged. "If it's true. Marty never denied it. Never confirmed. They were thugs, but had their hearts in the right place."

The soup arrived, and was good. Between crumbling Melba toast and drinking his soup, Herbie continued.

"Marty became very good. Intelligent, loved the business. Full of intrigue. Thrived. Lived for it. They kept him on when OSS was dumped. He ended up in Covert Ops with the newborn CIA. Rose through the ranks. Agency was full of Ivy League types. Money, good backgrounds. Only a very few like Marty were allowed to stay. I worked with the guy during my early days. He always toted a gun, sometimes two. Real cowboy. Got things done. Great on extortion, burning people. Highly valued. Worked with the best, even under Jim Angleton for a time. Then he went to the Soviet Office, got promotion regular like clockwork. Became head of the department. Got a big office out at Langley. Picture of the President on the wall, good furniture, P.A., everything the American Dream demanded."

The maître d' brought the wine. "Let it do some deep breathing exercises for a while," Herb told him.

"Tell me about the Soviet Office."

"What's to tell? Proper title was Soviet Bloc Division in the end. Went through a lot of different names. Marty got to the top in no time flat. Like a shot. They ran agents behind the Curtain. Pulled in raw intelligence which other experts analyzed. Ended up with Mike Alfoot and Tony de Paul as his left and right hands. On their own, they worked directly for the DCI—Director Central Intelligence. I think they were basically figureheads, but they did have power, even though the DCI's office certainly supervised all agent running, and covert ops, on Soviet territory. In the end, Marty was very big wheel stuff, though."

"But he's out now?"

"Retired four, five, years ago. Getting on, I guess, but who isn't getting on, Puck?"

"And the others? Alfoot, de Paul . . . ?"

"Top drawer material. I knew them, but they regarded me as a German mercenary. I got the feeling I was never trusted. Didn't know them well enough. Last I heard, Mike Alfoot is Soviet Affairs. Top banana, with Tony de Paul as his Lord High Chancellor."

"Were they capable of . . . ?"

"Doing what we think? Probably. Whether we ever prove it is different matter."

The soup went and the fish arrived. Tasty, nicely presented.

"And the one called Duncan—what? Bains?"

"Urquart Bains, sure. Singleton as they call them. Worked on his own, more or less. Probably for Marty, then more recently for Alfoot. Real flyer. In and out behind the Curtain. Very good. Don't underestimate. Smooth, could have doubled Stalin—that was old joke about him."

"So, you think our friend Louis was innocent? Unwitting?"

"Nobody's totally innocent, Puck. I'm not, you're not. Wilderness of mirrors, Jim Angelton called our dying profession, and he was right. Problem with the Agency is its very structure. Too big, unwieldy. Targeted on the past. Like the French and British generals at beginning of Second World War. They saw conflict in terms of trenches—the Somme, Ypres, Passchendaele: thought they were going to fight First World War all over again. Same as the Agency, and our little Firm now. Both have similar problems, but the Firm's rooted in being part of the Foreign Service. Makes our people civil servants, and that's not the way you should run a railway. Always twenty-five years behind the times." He forked in the last mouthful of fish, signaled for the maître d' and told him to pour.

The veal came, with dishes of vegetables which made the table look pretty. The silver sparkled, and the white starched linen blazed like virgin snow. The pianist played "Memory" as though he were doing justice to Chopin.

"Talk about us, Puck?"

She shook her head, a little frown tracing furrows over her pink forehead, below the soft light hair. Herbie thought she looked edible and wanted her immediately. He had not felt this way since the bad old days when Ursula Zunder, honeytrap extraordinary, had been pulling his chain.

"If you're right, Herb, the last thirty years have been wasted time, money down the drain. Makes nonsense out of the Cold War."

"Nonsense anyway, like all wars. Could've just sat back, not bothered. Let history take charge. But what do I know? Maybe it isn't over, and maybe we didn't win. Forget it. Everyone's wasted their lives. Talk about us."

She seemed to be zoned out, looking at him though not seeing him. Faraway like Passau taking one of his trips into the past. A little shudder ran through her, barely visible to the eye: minus point five on the Richter scale.

"What's up, Puck? Touch of the Graham Greenes? *End of the Affair?* Or someone walk over your grave?"

She gave a little sigh. "Not serious. I'm just discovering what a really horrible, dirty, manipulative game this is."

"Got to have your eye on the ball and a strong stomach, lovely lady."

It was as though she had not heard him. "You sit in London, behind a desk. You go into meetings. Listen to policy decisions. Means nothing. Then you walk out into the world and find out it's cheating, lies, gambling, whoring . . . ."

"You're not whoring, Pucky. . . ."

"No. No, I didn't mean that, Herb. A couple of weeks or so in the field and I feel filthy. Unclean. Playing with other people's dirty laundry." She took a sip of wine, and the maître d' came over to ask if everything was all right, looking nervously at their plates, the food hardly touched.

"Everything's fine." Herbie gave him a chilling glance. "Fine and randy."

Pucky smiled, "You mean dandy, Herb."

"No, I mean what I say. Fine and randy." He lowered his voice. "Go away," he whispered to the maître d'. "I'm trying to seduce a young lady here."

The maître d' departed in confusion.

"So, you want go private like me, Puck? Get out while you're still a virgin?"

"Probably."

"Some things you can't walk away from. You can go hire a car, get on a train, sprout wings and fly, but you can't really leave. They'll pull on your leash. When the going gets tough . . ."

"I know, the tough go shopping."

"Wrong. The tough see it through before they get going. They put the house in order, finish the masterpiece, settle their bills. Only then can you think of going, Pucky, because even when you've gone, they have the power to haul you back in. So it's best to settle everything before you leave." He gave a sad smile and extended his hands. "Look at me. Case in point. I leave unfinished business when I went private. Now it's back haunting me. I got to finish. Stay and see it through, then we'll both leave. What you want? Cottage? Roses round the door? Baby Krugers running around practicing tradecraft in the bathroom?"

She seemed to gather warmth from somewhere: the bleak look was burned from her face. "I want whatever'll make you happy, sweet Herbie. God help me, I love you."

For the second time in the past days, Herbie whispered, "My mistress with a monster is in love." Then he took in a deep breath, swilled down his glass of wine, refilled it and gave her a quizzical look. "Good. Then let's get all this bloody stupidity finished. Let's win what's left of the Cold War, and then hand in our badges. When the next one breaks out, I'd rather be missing."

It sounded pretty reasonable, he thought, but the pianist had stopped and he wondered why he could hear the first bars of Mahler's Second Symphony—*The Resurrection*—pounding in his head. Quite unexpectedly he wanted to weep.

WHILE HERBIE and Pucky talked in the main dining room of the Buckingham Hotel, Torquay, the young man who had boarded the flight in Nassau after Herbie dialed a number in Vienna. The young man lay on the bed of a hotel room near Marble Arch, London.

A voice at the distant end spoke in German. "Yes?"

"Lost them," the young man said, his voice indicating neither apology nor concern.

"How?"

"They split. I followed the wrong one—the big one."

"Where?"

"Windsor. Then I lost him again."

"Okay, you know where to look next. They have to make some kind of contact. People have to join them. I think I'll come into London."

"Trouble? You think . . . ?"

"Nothing we can't handle. Just watch the airports. Get in touch with the secretarial pool. Have them send a couple of people out to Gatwick. Just do it. I'll be in touch. Where are you?"

The young man told him, then cradled the phone. He thought of going out. Living it up on expenses. Then decided to stay put. It had been a long and weary journey, but he was sure it was almost over. After that he could go home to his wife and children.

2

"So what next, Lou?"

Outside the big bow windows of the suite, looking down across a terrace, towards the golf course, bracketed by trees, it was still damp. Soggy. No rain or drizzle to speak of, but nobody was about to go sunbathing. The dampness hung in the air like the dry ice used in horror movies.

They had braved the dining room, taking Passau with them. "Nobody's going to recognize him here," Herbie said, his fingers crossed behind his back. The old man had made such a song and dance about going down to breakfast that it was the only way to keep him sweet. He wore tailored check trousers and a navy cardigan, complete with pockets and pearl buttons, hanging slack over a royal blue silk shirt. He looked shaved, polished and in his right mind. "Fancy a walk today, Herb. Long walk. Maybe by the sea," he said as they held their breath in the elevator.

"This is the only walk you're going to get, Bubbie. No walkies until we finish the story. Okay? And even this is not one hundred percent certain."

"What'd I say? What'd I do?"

"And watch the language, Lou," from Pucky. "They have nice people here. Good people."

"You're wearing a garter belt." Passau looked up at her with a brilliantly contented smile.

She slapped his wrist away. "You monstrous old man. Keep your hands to yourself."

"Lou," said Herbie. "You want to live another day?"

"You want the whole story? Then you gotta have me." He grinned at Kruger before adding, "Bubbie."

In fact he behaved very well. Annie, the waitress, took to him. Made a fuss. Giggled as he whispered something to her. Said, "Oh, you're awful,"

544

and blushed. He drank juice, ate a large bowl of a revolting-looking cereal—nuts, raisins and dried banana mixed in with the flakes. "This stuff," he began, motioning at it with his spoon. "This stuff keeps . . ."

"Don't you dare say it, Lou. It's not worth dying for."

He grinned and nodded, looking dapper, pink-cheeked, respectable and rich.

Annie brought his kippers. "Haven't had real kippers in a coon's age," he announced and began to sort the flesh from the bones.

So there was silence. Only the occasional murmured comment as Annie and a friendly young waiter brought toast, more coffee, and even more coffee. They fussed around Passau as though he were some prince.

As they were leaving, the young waiter sidled up to Herbie and muttered, "Your father, sir? Or is he your grandfather? Has he stayed with us before? I know his face from somewhere."

"Probably saw it on a wanted poster," Kruger snapped, then followed in the wake of Pucky trying to lead the old man towards the exit.

The suite had been cleaned, the beds made up. Herbie and the Maestro sat in comfortable chairs, well back from the windows. Passau wanted to sit and look at the view, but Herbie told him they were not yet safe. "I think that waiter recognized you." He looked grave as a tombstone. "Not a good idea to take you down again."

"Okay," the lascivious grin once more. "Okay, Herb, I stay up here with the chambermaids."

"Christ." Herbie clenched and unclenched his large hands. Then—

"So what next, Lou?"

"Forget where we got to. Been joyriding on all those airplanes. Flashing around in cars. You should've seen me when I used to drive regularly, Herb. You don't know what speed is. Where we got to?"

"The erotic eighties, and you were being erotic, regularly, with a little Russian swallow called Therese." Herbie felt the quick stab, the pain in the mind. He could not bear to think of his once-beloved Ursula ministering to Passau in the place on Lexington Avenue.

"Oh, yea. Now *there* was a girl."

"The ninth decade of this century. You were in your eighties, Lou, and still jumping on women?"

Passau gave him a neat little wink. "Therese knew how to look after a man. Patient, caring, gave me great pleasure."

"What else she give you?"

"Little packages. One of the guys would come to me—leave something. We'd exchange presents. That's what she called it. 'Lou, you got a little present for me?' I would say, 'Yes, of course. There you go.' 'I got one for you also,' she'd tell me. You know, Herb, I did buy her presents. Little things, frivolous things. She enjoyed our relationship."

"One of the guys would come in and pick up her present to you?"

"Always telephoned congratulations. 'You're doing a great job, Lou. One day the President himself's going to pin a medal on you.' I never saw them take the incoming gifts away."

"This part of the way it was fixed? The tradecraft?"

"Sure. Had it sewn up."

"And this went on? Right up to . . . when?"

"Almost to the end."

"And when was the end?"

"The last thing I did for them was this spring. Nothing since."

It was tempting. Big Herbie wanted to rush him, jump the ten years or so and bring him into this year. To the tour behind the old Curtain, when he had made the side trips. Sitdown meetings with the old guard of the former Eastern Bloc countries. He resisted it, and asked instead—

"Who did what? Your four friends—which of them did what?"

"I used to meet with Matthew and Gregory from time to time."

"They bring the stuff, as you like to call it?"

"No. They came to hold my hand. Once every couple of months or so they set up a little meeting. We'd drink some vodka; talk. They'd ask me how I was bearing up. Once they brought a doctor to give me a checkup—I think that was eighty-five, maybe eighty-six. Told them I didn't need a checkup. Had my own doctor."

Herbie nodded. They had given up all pretense of taping the conversations in secret. Pucky sat, silent, out of Passau's sight line, turning or changing the tapes. Herbie asked about Matthew and Gregory—"They never brought packages?"

"No, usually Vincent came breezing in with them. Vincent, the guy with the big schnozola and the noisy ties."

"And Therese? She came, how often, during those ten, twelve, years?"

"I can't recall exactly, Herb. Didn't keep count. I had work to do."

"Give me a guesstimate."

"Every couple of months. Sometimes once in three months. It varied."

"And how did you know she was coming?"

"Usual. Same as we did in the sixties, and not so often in the seventies. One of the guys'd call me. Give me a word. Confusing. Used to give me times that I had to add or subtract, to get the real time they wanted to see me. In the end—late eighties—they just told me the right time. I said if I could do it. If it was okay, I'd go to the Lexington Avenue apartment. Vincent would come in, we'd put the package in a hiding place. . . ."

"What kind of a . . ."

"Book. They gave me this book that was really a safe. Proper lock on it. Combination lock. Secret number to open it. Book as heavy as hell. Steel. Fireproof. Thick. Looked like a beautiful leather-bound copy. Title in gold leaf. *Kobe's Complete Opera Book*."

"What next, Lou? After the package was brought?"

"Next day, sometimes a couple of days later, I'd make my call. Same old dance around the gooseberry bush. Special number, like always. I'd call and say I had a couple of things to talk about. Then Therese would call to say she was coming. Had some great lines: 'Diamonds are a girl's best friend'; 'Wind in the willows'; 'Comfort ye my people'; Stuff like that."

"Those are real? Real signals?"

"Sure. Her favorite was, 'Is that the Man of Sorrows?' Pile of phrases. I was supposed to remember them. They needed me to be there. To be seen by her. Give her the stuff. Physically I had to be there. This was necessary to them, like I was the one doing all the work."

"So you went to the apartment. Exchanged presents. Then you left."

"Not straightaway. Therese was a nice girl. Made sure I was happy. Sometimes we talked. Sometimes she'd do striptease for me. Sometimes other things. Kept me sweet. Would've made someone a good wife. But you'd know that. Said you knew her."

"Leave it at that, Lou, okay? One of the boys would come in and take her present away? The one she brought?"

"I guess so. They all had keys to the place. Let themselves in. Worked the book. Took out the present she left."

"Okay, Lou. Ten, eleven, twelve years. 1980 to this year. Give me your really sharp memories of that time. I know you can't give a blow-by-blow account. Just fill in the things that really stick in your mind."

Louis Passau made a little grimace, then started to talk. Incidents, reminiscences, anecdotes flowed from him. For the first time he spoke of the men and women of his orchestra and organization and, also for the first time, Herbie saw him as a man who genuinely loved his fellow musicians. It was like suddenly getting a peep at the inner soul of someone who, until then, had appeared merely self-centered and autocratic. He told of his Concertmaster, Robin Cross, who had been with the orchestra for the past fifteen years, and had, according to Passau, "as much talent in one hand as the great Pinkie Perlman has in his entire body—and that isn't a put-down as far as Pinkie's concerned."

There were timpanists who had given up weeks without extra pay to work on special projects; oboe players whose fathers he had known; flautists who had slogged their hard way up from school bands, worked long hours, starved and studied to be what they had become—valued members of the Passau Symphony Orchestra of America. He talked of trumpeters who turned out in the night to help copy scores because someone had become sick. He held forth eloquently, for an hour or more, about these people, *his* orchestra, human beings with joys and sorrows. He loved them all, and loved them deeply. Pucky had the distinct impression that this foul-mouthed, unprincipled old man would have died for any and every one of his musicians.

He recalled performances which had moved him—a splendid rendition of the Verdi Requiem; a recording of the Rakhmaninov Second Symphony, of which he was particularly proud; an open-air Mozart festival in Virginia; the first performance of his suites based on the film scores for *Blood of a Nation* and *Nights of Lightning*—the ones written for Rita Crest and Stefan Greif all those years before.

There were productions of operas; his ballet company's premiere. "They did Copeland's *Appalachian Spring*—he wrote it for Martha Graham so it was well-known. And a wonderful *Slaughter on Tenth Avenue*. Also a specially choreographed *Medea's Dance of Vengeance*— Sam Barber's piece, part of the ballet *he* did for Martha Graham. All-American evening. Terrific."

He continued. Spoke of a Beethoven night at the Passau Center, remembered with great joy and tenderness. "I never hear the 'Ode to Joy' without thinking of old Aaron Hamovitch. Sometimes brings tears to my eyes: I was only a little boy then yet I remember everything."

"Don't go maudlin on me, Lou. Brings tears to my eyes."

There were other fragments, the recording of the complete Bruckner symphonies, and his great Mahler cycle, all done through the eighties.

He also spoke of a famous production at Glyndebourne. Benjamin Britten's A *Midsummer Night's Dream*. "There is true magic at the end of that opera. I wept at its beauty as I conducted. Glyndebourne was wonderful."

"That was when, Lou?"

"Glyndebourne? Eighty-three. I spent nearly all summer and fall in England. Got married there. Eighty-three."

"Tell me about it?"

"My getting married?"

"Why not?"

"Nothing to tell. Fell in love. Got married."

"At eighty-three years of age? To a woman of thirtysomething?"

"Why not? It's what she wanted. Not bad really for an old Jewish shoe-maker's son: the Honorable Angela Barnscome."

"Tell me about it, Lou."

He gave a little shrug, remained silent for a while, then muttered, "Okay," and told it from his viewpoint.

"Angela was a huge music-lover—*is* a huge music-lover. Yet she has a couple of problems. An inability to learn an instrument. It's like some kind of dyslexia. Just cannot learn. Broke her heart because she wanted to be a concert pianist, or some such. Just couldn't do it."

"What's the other problem?"

"Other? That's more complicated. Lord and Lady Barnscome had Angela when they were pretty old. In fact, I think Lady Barnscome's in *The Guinness Book of Records* for it. Gave birth at some ridiculous age, like sixty-one. Aberration, of course. Can never happen according to doctors. But it did. By the time Angela was in her teens she spent all her time looking after the old folk. After her birth they both aged quickly. When she was only eighteen Angela was caring for her mother, who had Alzheimers, and her father, who was recovering from a stroke. That way she got fixated on old people. That way she fell in love with me."

"This really true, Lou?"

"Would I lie to you, Herb?"

"Yes. Come on, I don't believe the bit about Lady Barnscome."

He gave a little grin, showing his teeth. "That was the story. In fact, and nobody'll tell you this but me, the old man—Lord Barnscome—put one of the young female grooms in the family way. They adopted Angela.

Title went to her uncle, so she remained only an Hon. Funny, the English and their titles."

"I heard some story where the Barnscomes tried to stop the wedding."

He gave a little laugh, contemptuous and amused. "The family, yes. Couple or three relatives. Much younger brother on the father's side, and a pair of cousins. Tried hard to stop it. Had Angela go see a shrink, who got up and told them she wasn't a nut. Poor old Angela, she was really cut up about it—I mean the attitude, not the shrink. He was on her side. Very cut up, Angela."

"She would be. What was in it for you, Lou?"

"I told you. Fell in love with her."

"Still love her?"

"'Course I still love her. What's a wife for? You love her. You cherish her. Name of the game."

"Bet the wedding night was a smash."

"A sell-out, Herb. Paying customers sitting in the aisles. Got a standing ovation, but that's none of your business."

"You've told us just about everything else. I don't see why this should be any different."

"She has her particular little foibles." He shut his mouth, closing teeth and lips like a trap. "That's all. Talk about something else."

"You still saw the lovely Therese, even though you had this great marriage."

"Sure I saw her."

"That summer and autumn in England? You saw her then?"

"Why not? Terms of the contract. Saw her twice."

"Where?"

"Dorchester Hotel. Angela and I had a suite at the Savoy. I met with Therese twice. Dorchester Hotel."

"And who serviced you?"

"She did. Once a striptease, second time a blow job. Did it well."

"I mean which of the boys gave you the goods and took her present away with them?"

"Oh, that. Sure. Duncan. Duncan did all the business. Abroad it was always Duncan. Come to think of it, you saw me abroad, or so you said. Heard the orchestra in Vienna. 1980, you said. See what a memory I've got when I put my mind to it. Heard my Mahler Second, right?"

Herbie nodded.

"Yes. Saw Therese in Vienna also. Duncan comes in one day. I do the calls and she follows up. Duncan enters, stage left, the day after. Three-day gig. All for God and country."

The old man had talked for almost three hours, backwards and forwards. It would have made a great interview for some classical music magazine. Herbie let him relax, chatting on about the music he had made in the eighties. Pucky went down and got sandwiches, coffee, a beer for Herbie. They ate in silence. Passau did not even want music, and Herbie sensed they were getting close to the Maestro's other dark night of the soul. What he really knew. What he suspected. What he had done.

They started again at ten past two in the afternoon, with a weak sun struggling to push through outside; golfers stalking little white balls over the course.

"In the eighties, Lou, you really got on well with the White House."

"I always got on well with the White House."

"Yes." Herbie moved his head, and his right hand, as though indicating that things were different in the eighties. "Yes, but you seemed to have a special relationship with the Presidents of that time. Little private dinners, lunches. Cozy chats. That's what I heard."

"Okay, so that's what you heard."

"Any truth in it?"

"Sure. I was on good terms with President Reagan. I *am* on good terms with President Bush."

"Ronnie and George?"

Passau sat up, as though bitten by a snake. "Never!" He was angry. "Never! Always Mr. President. We had—have—good rapport. After I married Angela, President and Mrs. Reagan asked specially to meet her. I was on the private list. Still am. President and Mrs. Bush ask us a couple, maybe three, times a year. We go there alone. Have a good meal. Good wine. Good talk."

"They ever say anything to you off the record?"

"You're joking. Why would they do that? Seems they admire my work. We just chat. Nothing deep."

"Any of the boys ask about your talks at the White House?"

"They ask about everything. Ask when I take a crap."

"What kind of things do they ask?"

"How I perceive the President? How's he bearing up? They ask if he makes any remarks, comments, on the current world situation—at any given time, that is."

"And you told them?"

"You think I'm stupid? Neither of the Presidents I've known well has indicated anything to me. I can't read them."

"So what did you tell your friends? The secret foursome?"

"The truth. No, nothing said out of the ordinary."

"If they'd have got you to Quantico, the night of your ninetieth birthday concert, the people there would have asked you. It was on the agenda. Did you learn anything untoward during your visits to the White House?"

"They'd have got a straight no. What do they think those guys are in the White House? They think they're going to blabber their inside feelings to an old fella who stands in front of an orchestra waving a stick?"

"You do more than that. You told me so, Lou. You said it's not like Tommy Beecham said—easy, just standing there waggling a stick."

"Herbie," spoken with a long exhalation. "Herbie, you know that. I know that. But for a lot of people that's what I do. Waggle a stick, and maybe that's how the President—both of them—saw me. I don't know."

"Which of the boys quizzed you about the lunches and dinners at the White House?"

"Does it matter?"

"It might."

"Okay. Gregory a couple of times. Vincent a couple of times. That do you?"

"For the moment, yes. Matthew never asked you?"

"Not that I recall."

There was a long silence. Kruger stuck to it. Use the psychologist's trick, he thought. Now seemed about the right time.

Eventually, Passau broke. "I also remember, in particular, an incredible concert we did in Washington. Two years back. Kennedy Center. Did Strauss, *Don Quixote* and Elgar's Cello Concerto. Special night. Benefit for something or other. Spectacular. Went back to New York and recorded both the following week."

"You trying to tell me something, Lou?"

"I'm telling you we did a stupendous *Quixote* and the Elgar Cello. What would I want to tell you apart from that?"

"The soloist, Lou. It would be Khavenin, right? Yevgeny Khavenin?"

"Right. Greatest living cellist. Why not?"

"Tell me about Yevgeny, Lou. Just tell me about him."

"What's to tell? Made a dash for it. Political asylum. We were the winners. Like the Cold War. We won that also."

"Did we, Lou? Did anybody win?"

"Don't know what you're talking about."

"Okay. When did you first hear about Khavenin?"

"Same as most people. Late seventies. Recordings coming out of Russia. Word of mouth. Lot of good press. Did a concert in London. Jesus, Herb, I flew over just to hear him. Two days on a fucking airplane, with a concert in between. Incredible. Better than Casals, better even than poor Jacqueline du Pré. What a tragedy that was. Yevgeny was, is, the indisputable maestro of the cello for this century."

"So when did you really hear about him, Lou? About him wanting asylum?"

A long, long, dragging pause, as though Passau was holding an orchestra in silence, taut, lips to instruments, bows drawn back, waiting while he held them for effect before bursting out again. There was a point in one of the Sibelius symphonies when he would do just that, but Kruger could not fasten upon it now. He waited. At last the music came—

"One of the boys. June 1987. There was to be a meeting. The place on Lexington. Gregory. Gregory came alone. He brought a package. Said I should make the usual call."

"And?"

He sat, lips pursed together. "She asked me a favor. Remember her exact words, because they had a special meaning for me. Maybe for you also." He paused, as though teasing the moment out. "It's why I was so glad to meet you, Herb."

"What did she say?"

"Louis," she said in the recent past. "Things are not getting easier in my country. One day I shall ask you to do a very big favor for me." She gave him a small, pouty glance. Movement in her eyes.

They were lying on the bed. Both of them naked, the old man and the now not so very young woman he knew as Therese. Naked and sated, for she had made love to him in a way she knew he enjoyed; a way from which he could still, at his age, get release, comfort and pleasure.

"Ask. If I can do it, I will."

"This is not yet for me, Louis. Not yet. But the time will come. If anything should happen to me. If I disappear. If you hear something strange about me, I want you to get in touch with a man in England. It will not be easy, Louis, my dear. The man works with the British. Secret people. The British organs, you know what I mean?"

"Sure, my little Bolshevik spy." He gave his big laugh which did not reveal the sudden butterflies in his stomach. This woman had played with his mind for a long time. Louis Passau had suffered sleepless nights worrying over his growing suspicions.

"But first I have to ask you small favor." She reached up and kissed the side of his mouth. "You know of Yevgeny Khavenin? Cellist? You know of him?"

"Of course I know. I know everything about him. Why?"

"He wants to come into the West. Wants asylum. Next month he is to be in New York. Big concert in Carnegie Hall. There will be people from the State Organs with him. You know who I mean?"

"You mean KGB. Sure." He began to strum against her, between her thighs, but she did not respond. "Listen, Louis. Please listen. You must arrange matters. You must go to the concert. Go round to see him afterwards. Take him to one side. Try to talk to him in private. Get him outside his dressing room and far away from KGB who look after him. Others will then see he gets to safety. Maybe they even use this apartment. You understand?"

"I've already got tickets, my dear. I'm going to be there in any case."

"Then do it for me, Louis. Do it for me."

"Of course. Yes. Of course I'll do it. But what about you? You said . . ."

She stopped his mouth with one hand. "This you must never reveal." She looked at him, her eyes tied within his eyes. Nothing on earth could have broken their gaze. "Never tell this. Never tell that I might soon want to leave also. This no one must know."

"Who's the man I must get in touch with if anything happens?"

"Louis, once I did this man a great wrong. But, if it is necessary, I will rely on him."

"His name?"

"It is a German name, though he is British national. Kruger. Eberhardt Lukas Kruger."

In the present, Herbie stifled a tiny sob, almost inaudible except to Pucky. Again the great silence descended on the room. Pucky could hear Big Herbie breathing, near to hyperventilating. After what seemed a very long time, he said, "You helped, of course? You helped to get Khavenin away from KGB hoods?"

"Sure. Matthew was there. Matthew, with people I had never seen before. KGB were angry. Not a nice scene. But they got him away, and later he came and thanked me. He played with the Passau Symphony Orchestra of America."

"What then, Lou?" Big Herbie's voice was a croaking whisper.

"What you mean, Herb?"

"I said, what next? What did you *think* next. You changed your thoughts after that conversation with Urs . . . Therese. Your entire view altered. What fucking next, Lou?"

"I saw the truth. Don't know why. But I saw through them."

"You went on working with them?"

"What else could I do? Pop song, Herb—'I can see clearly now, the rain has gone.' I could see what they had been doing, and what I had been doing."

"And you did nothing about it, Lou. You got spineless. Could have saved a lot of grief."

Passau seemed to hang his head. "I'm an old man, Herbie. I . . ."

"Not old enough, Lou. You were young enough to screw around; get married, record, conduct concerts. If you were young enough for that, you were young enough to go to someone. Tell them what had been going on."

"No guts, Herb."

"Right. No guts. They give you an emergency number? Like a fire alarm, police? Like in England 999, in U.S. 911? They give you one of those?"

"Of course."

"And if you call it, what happens?"

"They come running. One, maybe two of them. I don't know. I never tried it."

"Anywhere in the world, they come to you?"

"Within twenty-four hours, yes."

"Good." A big hand lifted, fingers splayed, raking through his short graying hair. To her dismay, Pucky saw that big, lovely, Herbie Kruger was wild-eyed, distraught.

"Class fucking dismissed for today. Right?" he shouted.

"Okay, Herb."

BIG HERBIE KRUGER went apart from them. Walked into the bedroom and sat, head in hands, looking out of the window at the golfers coming in after a long day on the links.

Pucky could not get to him, for he seemed to have withdrawn into a shell of his own manufacture. He stayed like that until nearly seven in the evening when he came out, looking his old self, but shaken.

She had called room service and shared a cream tea with Passau. The debris sat on a tray: scones, strawberry jam, thick clotted cream and a large teapot.

"These cream teas I like, Herbie." Passau sounded like a child trying to make up with his father after some terrible row. "Real good."

"You get to bed, Lou. Maybe we do more work later."

"I don't want to go to bed. I . . ."

"You do as you're fucking told, Maestro, otherwise I tear you limb from limb. Get the fuck to bed. Tell Puck what you want from room service. For dinner. We go down and eat, like last night, Puck. Okay?"

"Okay, Herbie." The air around them felt dangerous, full of electricity, in spite of the damp weather. A massive charge seemed to have built up around Kruger.

An hour later they went down, leaving Passau with soup and a great platter of prawns and salad, bread rolls and tea. Herbie forbade wine. "I told you, Lou. We not yet finished for the day, right? More work later. Don't answer the phone. Don't answer the door. Anyone tries the door, call reception. Call us."

"Sure, Herb. Anything, Herb."

Pucky felt Kruger smoldering as they walked to the elevator. As they went down, she took his hand and he looked at her, his eyes a desert, his face a wasteland. "Not your fault, Puck," he whispered, then squeezed her hand and bent, kissing her on the cheek.

He was not friendly with either the maître d' or Annie the waitress. There was no banter. No jokes. He just ordered, asked Pucky if she wanted wine. She inquired if he was drinking and he shook his head. "Two bottles Perrier water," he ordered, clipped and ungracious.

"We don't stock . . ." The maître d' looked bewildered. "Malvern or Ashdown water perhaps, sir?"

"Whatever. Okay?"

Halfway through the main course, Annie came over to ask if everything was all right. "The young waiter . . . ?" Herbie began.

"Dennis?"

"Young. He was on this morning."

"Yes, he's not here tonight, Dennis. Off until tomorrow night."

"Good." Another nod, ordering her away.

"Herb?" Pucky reached over and covered his hand with hers. "Herb, when do we hit him with the age thing? Which of the boys he was?"

"Maybe tonight, if we're all still alive."

"And there's the Traccia business. All the stuff we filched from the computers."

"Maybe tonight. Puck, I'm sorry. Rattled. Concerned." He waved Annie over again. "This Dennis? Where would I find him?"

"Tonight, sir?"

"Sure. Tonight."

"I know where he'll be. It's his night for rehearsal. Oratorio Society. Dennis is very in to classical music. Sings with the Oratorio . . ."

Herbie cut her off, eyes blazing towards Pucky. "Got to make a call." He pushed back the table and strode off through the dining room. The way he walked worried Pucky. The whole of his body seemed stiff, as though it was wrapped in concern and some dreadful anguish.

"Is your husband all right?" Annie looked puzzled.

Pucky shook her head. "Been working too hard." She apologized, stood, and followed Herbie out of the room.

EARLIER, AT SIX THIRTY that evening, Dennis Snooke, who had worked at the Buckingham since he was a teenager, entered the Cross Keys public house in Torquay. He usually went to the Cross Keys before rehearsal with the Oratorio Society. "Regular, like clockwork," as Herbie would have said. A pint before rehearsal and two pints, with the other tenors, afterwards.

Tonight, he found his old friend, Wayne Murphy, propping up the bar. He had been at school with him. Back then nobody would have thought that Wayne would join the police force, but join it he did. Now he was with CID. Plainclothes.

"Not keeping the villains in check tonight?" Dennis really did not take Wayne seriously.

"On in half an hour. What you having?"

"Usual. Pint of Real Ale. They keeping you busy?"

"Very. Bloody hooligans mostly. Could do with something more juicy. Never seem to get a good murder; they're always bloody cut and dried. My guv'nor says it's not like it used to be. Says he had to work at a case in the old days. Be a detective. Nowadays its paperwork and following rules of evidence. Mostly we collar the villains in a few days." He ordered the two pints of Real Ale. "What about you then, Den?" taking a great swallow. Wayne could chugalug with the best of them.

"Oh, the usual. Not many in at the moment. Bucks up weekends, when the adulterers come down . . ." He stopped short. "Bloody 'ell!" he said.

"What's up with you, then?"

"I just realized who the old geezer is."

"What old geezer?"

"Might be up your street an' all, Wayne."

"What?"

"Party comes down for breakfast this morning. Got in last night. Husband and wife. Husband talks with an accent. Foreign. Kraut, I'd say. They have his father, or grandfather, with them. Nice old geezer. Bit cheeky. Asked Annie if she wore a garter belt—suspender belt to you; this old fellow's got a funny sort of accent."

"So where's this going, Den?"

"I just realized who he is. Know him anywhere. He's the conductor. Bloody American conductor. I got some of his CDs. Wonderful. Better than von Karajan . . . bloody marvelous . . ."

"Oh, God, Den, get on with it. You and your classical bloody music. Why can't you be like the rest of us? Just enjoy rock and roll? Elton? Daltry? Mick?"

"No. Listen. I read something. Couple of weeks—maybe three weeks ago. The old guy was missing. Name of Louis Passau. Very famous, Wayne. Very. Went missing in New York. Some pitched battle. Gangs, that kind of thing. They're looking for the old gentleman."

"Spell it." Detective Constable Murphy had some vague recollection of hearing the name, or seeing it somewhere.

Dennis spelled it out. "Sure it's him. Dead bloody certain. Have to get his autograph. He's a wonder. Ninety years old and still conducting. There was a big piece on him in last month's *Gramophone*."

D.C. Murphy worried at the name as he sipped his beer. He would mention it to his guv'nor, the DCS, when he got into the nick. Perhaps it would mean something to him.

3

ART RAILTON AND HIS crew had only just flown in. The British Airways 747 from Miami was late; they were all tired and angry. Art himself felt betrayed. During the flight, he remembered something Big Herbie Kruger had said to him when they had talked of acts of treachery on Captiva Island.

"Art, you'll never know how it feels until you been through it." Herbie's eyes had changed—hardened with a dark distrust deep in the irises. "Always it gets personal. Makes you want to go in the shower, scrub yourself with lye, carbolic even. When you're close to any form of perfidy, it hits you like a bullet. Makes you never trust again. Sickens you. I know. Been a victim. Now we have to be buddies with the Ks. Like being close friends with Nazi SS from death camps."

Art even smiled, because Herbie had added, "Perfidy? Is right, perfidy, Art?" But his smile carried no conviction. He felt Kruger had betrayed him. It *was* personal.

At Heathrow, Art Railton told the others to go straight home while he went into the Shop and faced the music. He arrived on the fifth floor just after Big Herbie had spoken to Young Worboys.

Herbie had gone out. Walked up the road until he found a telephone booth. He left Pucky in charge, and had pulled Louis Passau from his bed, shaking him as a terrier would shake a rodent, then threw him back onto the bed. "Get your clothes on," he said, then told Pucky to keep the door locked. "When I knock, you ask who's there, okay? If I say Herbie, it's okay. If I say Kruger, call the main desk and tell them to get the police faster than bloody Lone Ranger—speeding bullet. Got it?"

"Got it."

Herbie felt nude. No weapons but his hands. Felt bad about leaving

Pucky up there alone with nothing in the way of defense. Poor cow, he thought. He had taken all the precautions, but Marty Foreman was very good in the old days, and there was no reason to think he had changed. His people, they said, were like truffle hounds. They could pick up a scent where no trace existed, then make themselves invisible. Once they had a sniff, Foreman's people would never let go.

From the telephone booth, he called the Shop on the safe number, shielded from all the other British Telecom lines. Untappable, unhearable with its scrambler at the distant end, and God knew how many other electronic devices. He told the Duty Operator, "Patch me through to the Prince. Now. Tell him it's breakfast time in condemned cell. I don't care where he is." The Prince was how they talked of Young Worboys, deputy to the Chief of the British Secret Intelligence Service.

The D.O. hesitated, "Who . . . ?" she began.

"Tell him it's Blue Boy, home from the hill. Fast, woman, Goddamnit!"

"Herb!" from Worboys. Desperation laced his voice, mixed with a double fury. "Where the . . . ?"

"Just listen. Shut up and listen, Tony." Kruger was one of the few people who remembered Worboys' given name.

The Deputy Chief went silent.

"I need a team. Lion tamers, drivers. Ambulance, van, cars. Faster than fast."

"Where are you?"

Herbie told him. "If you can get some uniforms here with cannons, it would help. Probably okay, but we need to come in. I think I just solved the riddle of the sphincter, son. So I need respect where we're going. Don't want half-arsed slap on the wrist. I have to go on talking to the old bugger. Don't want Gus coming the old acid."

"Room number?" Young Worboys steadied himself, holding the telephone with his chin, the right shoulder hunched, pencil in his hand, writing on the government-crested notepad. Herbie gave the details and hung up. Worboys turned around and saw Art Railton coming through the door looking like the wrath of God.

A mile or so away, the young man who had been on the Nassau flight, watching Kruger and the Maestro, was on the telephone again. "They came into Heathrow," he said quietly. "Now they've split up. I haven't got the manpower to eyeball all of them."

"Don't worry," the voice at the other end of the line sounded calm, untroubled. "If we've figured Kingfisher right, he'll be in touch. For years I've owned him body and soul. If there's a problem, he'll call for help. I should have come to Florida myself. Finished it there. Never mind, we'll see to it now." It was the same voice the young man had heard when calling Vienna. Now, its owner was here, in London.

BIG HERBIE KRUGER walked back to the hotel and waited in the foyer, anxious now that it was all unraveling. A terrible thought came to him. For two nights in a row they had left Passau alone, with a telephone. He leaned over the desk and hit the little call bell hard, causing a pink young woman to emerge from the office. She wore a pink skirt, pink angora sweater with a pink shirt. All were different shades of the color, and none of them matched her complexion.

He gave her the suite number, saying he wanted to check the bill.

"You're not leaving us so soon?" she asked with the fear of customer complaints in her voice.

"Don't know." Herbie tried the warmest of his daft smiles. "Maybe. Difficult with the old man."

She reappeared, pushing the printout over the counter. Herbie's eyes traveled quickly down the lines of figures. No outgoing calls, so he breathed again as the unmarked car hurtled noisily into the large porte cochere outside the main door. Two big men detached themselves from the vehicle, and the driver took off towards the parking facilities. The two men wore unbuttoned raincoats and stank of local law trying to make good. Herbie stopped them as they came into the foyer, muttering, "Kruger. You come to see me, yes?"

"Had a call, sir. You're Foreign Office, right?"

"Sure. I'm Foreign Office. Part of Whitehall also. Bit of the Cenotaph, I shouldn't wonder. . . ."

"Do what, sir?" The larger of the pair looked puzzled.

"What they tell you?"

"Said to make sure you were safe, sir. You, a young woman and an elderly gentleman. They issued firearms." He tapped his raincoat pocket. "You want us to take you down the nick—the police station?"

"No. We wait here for friends. Only want to make sure we're safe."

The younger man said that, within five minutes, they would own the hotel.

"Good. Needs to be under new management. Don't tamper with the dining room and kitchens. Food is good."

"I don't think . . ." the senior officer began.

"Is joke." Herbie flashed them his intelligent look and gave them the suite number. "Just stay outside the door for me. How long did they say . . . ?"

"Four, possibly five hours, sir."

"Okay. Don't both go for a pee the same time. Could be dangerous." He led them up to the suite, positioned them outside, knocked and said the magic word, "Herbie."

Pucky opened up. She looked alert, but pale and anxious. "We need to talk," she said as he closed the door behind him, snapping on the chain and safety lock.

"Okay, so we talk."

Passau sat, very quietly, in the seat he had occupied during the day's interrogation. "Hi, Herb," he said. It was almost a tentative greeting. "I got dressed like you said. We going round the world again?"

"Just a short ride, but there's plenty of time for us to talk. Don't move. Stay just as lovely as you are, Lou."

In the bedroom, Pucky put a hand on his sleeve. "It's her, isn't it?" she said, as though confronting Herbie with some infidelity.

"Sure. Is him also," cocking his head in the direction of the sitting room.

"You've told me everything, I know. But you're not over her yet, are you?"

"Not a question of being over. That old bastard gave me a signal. Told me a fairy tale. Ursula—the one he knew as Therese—would never ask for me. Not in a thousand years. Might ask *after* me, but not *for* me. I thought I had it figured, but maybe the old fraud's simply trying to dissociate himself from the past. Playing the innocent. Don't know, Puck, there's something not quite right. The fabulous four could be knocking on the door, so I got the local cops out. The Shop's sending a team in. We go to Warminster, but it'll be a while. Time to take him apart. Find out where he stands. See if he's being straight."

She nodded, reached up and kissed his cheek, patted the same cheek, let the tips of her long fingers slide down to his chin. "I love you, Herb."

She looked at him, her eyes searching his face as though trying to get some clue which would lead her to his most secret thoughts.

"Sure. Later. We talk of love, life, pursuit of happiness later. Let's go and unhinge him now." The smile this time was brutal.

"OKAY, LOU . . ." Herbie began.

"Don't say it, Herb. What's next? Right? Old refrain."

They sat where they had talked all through the day, where Maestro Louis Passau had finally shown them his good side: the tenderness and caring for the individuals who made up his orchestra; where he had finally revealed his doubts and, in revealing them, caused a sudden geyser of anxiety to rise in Kruger's mind.

"No," Herbie said quietly. "No, not what's next? Go back a couple of clicks, Lou. Back to your sweet Therese and the coming of Yevgeny Khavenin. You did as you were asked? You distracted his minders, got him out of his dressing room, put him in the hands of Matthew and Company?"

"I told you. The minders were angry. Quite a scene. Telephone calls to Soviet Delegation at the U.N. One of Matthew's people got me away."

"Lou, tell me, when you helped with this, what did you think you were doing?"

"Don't follow you, Herb. Don't understand your line of questioning."

"Okay, I make it easy. Child of five could answer. Therese asked you to help with bringing Khavenin into the fold. Also said that she might need your help in the future. You were over eighty years old then. You'd seen life. You'd lived. You're an intuitive man, Lou. Comes with your profession. You decipher all those notes on the page. Turn them into glory through the orchestra. How did you decipher Khavenin? What did you think he was?"

"Age is relative, Herbie. State of mind. Think young, I always say."

"Answer the question. What did you think Yevgeny Khavenin was?"

"Brilliant cellist."

"Okay, brilliant cellist. That's what you *knew* he was. . . ."

"That's what he proved he was. Worked with him a lot after that."

"Played music with him, yes. Gave him great assistance, provided a platform for his genius. I take that for granted, Lou, but did you work with him in any other way?"

"Don't understand, Herb. *What* other way?"

"Same thing you did with Matthew, Gregory, Vincent and Duncan. Same thing you were doing with Therese. Did you think he was more than a cellist? You told me, yourself, that you realized what was going on after Therese asked you to help with Khavenin, and signaled she also might need help. Christ, Lou, she spelled it out for you. She told you nobody must ever know that she might want to take a leap over the Curtain. You put two and two together. Made it come out right. I'm asking if you thought your cellist was an iffy Soviet."

"We're talking spies?"

"'Course we're talking spies."

"Then the answer is no. I have a mind, Herb. Intelligence. No, what would be the point of someone coming in to play music? What tricks could he run? What kind of important secrets could he tell anybody? Going to send back the plans for a nuclear violin? An interballistic French horn? A laser-guided oboe? Me? I was different. Knew people, went places. Me they could pass off as their spy. Agent XYZ, their source among the powerful."

"I want you to tell me. You saw through them, you said. So what did you think Khavenin was?"

"I told you. Genuine. A cellist who got disenchanted with the Communist Party, with the Soviets. Wanted to come over and play in freedom."

"So, how did you figure Therese?"

The old man raised his head, gave Herbie a quick look of contempt, then turned away. "The moment she told me I shouldn't mention her own dilemma, I realized what was going on. Like some missing piece of a puzzle. I knew what they had been doing. I could only guess, Herb, and I know I guessed right. Khavenin was straight, but Therese wanted to help him. I was her only contact. . . . Well, maybe *we* were her only contacts—Matthew, Gregory, Vincent, Duncan and I, the Kingfisher. Yevgeny wanted out and she helped him. I don't know what she told Matthew and the boys. Maybe she passed him off as some important link in the chain. Therese, I knew then, was trusted by my four friends. She didn't want them to know that she was thinking of walking out on the

Soviets, that she was also disillusioned. Wanted to come later. Defect. But Yevgeny, I thought he was genuine. From the start, genuine. Solid gold."

"And you would be right," Herbie said quietly. "I've seen the file, Lou. They watched Khavenin, listened to him, for over a year. They do that with anyone who comes in like he did. They weighed him in the balance. Found him kosher."

"So what's the fuss?"

"The fuss, Maestro, is *you*. How you saw the light. Got yourself converted, then didn't do a fucking thing about it. Why didn't you run straight to FBI, or some Senator, even your buddy the President? Why didn't you go and say, 'Look, I been taken for a sucker for years. You got four guys out at Langley who've been stealing you blind over thirty years.'? Why didn't you do that, Lou?"

Pucky, sitting way off in the corner, still out of the reach of Passau's eyes, thought she could hear the silence: knew what the old music master meant by pauses between bars and phrases. Silences in music, she considered for the first time, are often as poignant as the music itself. The listener is waiting, poised on the cusp of his or her senses: waiting for the next notes, the tremor of beauty, the iron fist of drama, or the shimmering draining of sadness. In the silence, the listener hears what has gone before, and almost assimilates what is to come. The music past fused with the music future—together in the great void of silence.

Finally, Passau said. "Herb, can you understand? This had nothing to do with fear. Not really. Sure, I didn't have the guts to come out of that closet. It was a game, like kids playing cops and robbers. My life had been long. Full of experiences. Joy and sorrow—great joy and greater sorrow. For thirty-odd years I played cops and robbers in my spare time then, suddenly, I found I'd been running with the robbers not the cops. I didn't have the strength to change sides. It was done. Over. I was hooked like a junky; couldn't leave the other woman even when I loved my wife; couldn't break the habit. What mattered was my work. This . . . this game . . . this extramural affair . . . this was my secret . . . a hobby that went wrong. You ever listen to Sam Barber's music, Herb?"

"Not all that good with American composers, Lou. Know the Adagio for Strings. Who doesn't since they used it for that movie—what was it? *Platoon?*"

Passau nodded. "You don't know *Knoxville: Summer of 1915?*"

"Can't say I do."

"Barber set some words to music. Soprano and orchestra. Quite lovely. The words written by James Agee—prose and poetry, both. Soprano sings like she is talking, idly reminiscing. Top of the manuscript is written, 'We are talking now of summer evenings in Knoxville, Tennessee, in the time that I lived there so successfully disguised to myself as a child.' When I first heard *Knoxville*, I realized that all my life I had successfully disguised myself as a child. Never put away childish things. I grew, I had a talent, but I *was* like a child, though my personal childhood had been almost nonexistent. A village, cousins long gone from me. Love won and lost in terrible agony. All my life I had so successfully disguised myself as a child, and I didn't want anything to change. Not even then, when I knew they had manipulated me."

The silence again. Both Herbie and Pucky waited for past and future to come together, bring forth a new melody, or some dreadful cacophony. When Passau spoke, they realized he was quoting from the words set to music by a beloved American composer: *Knoxville: Summer of 1915*—

> "On the rough wet grass of the back yard my father and mother have
> spread quilts. We all lie there, my mother, my father, my uncle, my
> aunt, and I too am lying there. . . . They are not talking much. . . .
> After a little I am taken in and put to bed. Sleep, soft smiling, draws
> me unto her; and those receive me, who quietly treat me, as one fa-
> miliar and well-beloved in that home; but will not, oh, will not, not
> now, not ever; but will not ever tell me who I am."

After several bars rest, again, it was Herbie who provided the new melody. "And who are you, Lou? Are you Saul Isaak Packensteiner, or Abraham Jacob Packensteiner?"

Passau lifted his head. His eyes glistened, moist, the tears not flowing yet. "Clever bugger, Herbie. Where'd you get that from?"

"In many ways, Lou, the United States is like the old Soviet Union. They don't realize it, but they have the ultimate propaganda machine. They feed people, from birth to death, tell them they're greatest people in the world, tell them they're lucky to be Americans, born liberated in the land of the free, the greatest country on earth. Yet the files, the information about individuals, are also there. You can tap into computers these days and find when your uncle Izzy first came over from Germany or Russia, or your grandfather Declan came into Ellis Island from County Cork. We tapped. We found. Which one are you, Lou? The elder brother or the younger?"

"The younger, of course. Abraham Joseph."

"So you're how old now, Lou? Not ninety. Almost, but not quite for a few years."

"Eighty-four, Herbie."

"So you never actually knew your wonderful cousins. You didn't play with them in the village."

"It felt like I knew them. I grew up listening to my elder brother. He was obsessed by our cousins. So were my father and mother. It's all I heard as a toddler in New York, New York, that wonderful town."

"And everything else, Lou?"

"Everything else is true. Six years difference in age and you got it."

"And your brother?"

"Saul? Never amounted to anything. Left home at seventeen. Like me, didn't care to be working with leather. Hated the shoe business. Unlike me, he parted amicably with our parents. Went West to make his fortune. Died in an accident aged twenty-one."

"You fudged all the figures, Lou? Why you do that?"

"You'd rather Capone's thugs, his heirs and successors, would catch up with me? We came to New York in 1908. . . ."

"I know, you made it sound later."

"Sure. I was twelve months old. By the time I was sixteen my father had the business going. All the stuff about my Uncle Chaim and the guy he'd tied my father to. . . ."

"Chorat?"

"Yea, Chorat. All happened before my time. I was a small child then. Family history."

"But everything else, Lou—Hamovitch . . ."

"When I was six years old, I had the fight with the kids and met dear Aaron Hamovitch. . . ."

"And the store? Your father's store? The money? Carlo Giarre?"

"All happened. I bugged out, went to Chicago at the age of seventeen."

"Randy little devil, Lou. So you left when . . . ? twenty-five? twenty-six?"

"Sure."

"Sure what, Lou?"

"Did the booze heist in 1927, twenty years old and I was a killer, a gangster with great music in my blood. Laid up. Changed my name. Added to my age. Should've known you were on to me. Nobody else ever queried. No journalists, nobody. I told them I was six years older, that was it. People don't do the sums in their heads. They accept what you say. I played around with dates, times, ages ever since. . . ."

Herbie stopped him, tried to do the sums, inched him back and forward trying on the dates and years. For over an hour he tried to make sense of old Passau's tangled chronology. In the end it was obvious that even Louis had only a glimmer of his true time scale when it was put next to the history of the past three or four decades. On several occasions he said, "Herb, music is my history. The politics of life don't interest me." Kruger decided that the old man had successfully warped his view of age and progress.

Then they got back to the moment of change, when he met Stephan Greif and Rita Crest. "Changed my name, Herb," he mused. "Strange, and that's another thing: nobody even said where'd the Louis come from, it's not a German name? Now they all say he looks wonderful for his age. . . ."

"You do, Lou. Even at eighty-four years, you look good. What about the bullshit, though?"

"Which particular bullshit?"

"The cousins? The letters? Your grief?"

Passau gave a sad little smile, his eyes still full and glittering. "I didn't have to meet them to love them. When my father cut me off . . . said he had no son called Abraham Joseph, which is what he did say. When he sent back the money torn in half. Then I knew they were the only family I had. A man needs a family. Particularly a Jewish man like me. Not a good Jewish man, but . . ."

"Talented Jewish man, Lou. Glad we cleared all that up. Puck and I spent a lot of hours trying to make your age, and the dates work out." Herbie swiveled in his chair to wink at Pucky. For the first time since he had returned to the room, she felt he was almost his old self and a pinpoint of hope returned to her.

"There's one other point, Lou."

"Okay."

Herbie paused again. Count of ten—maybe fifteen. "No. No, let's move on. Plenty of time to fill in that particular gap. Let's move. What next, Lou?"

"Whatever you want to hear."

"Not what I want to hear. What happened is what I need to hear. Your eyes were opened, but you went on, like before."

Passau nodded. "Same routine. Next important thing brings us almost up to date. That bastard historian. Stretchfield."

"Wrote *Hitler's Unknown Spies*, yes. See, I even get the title right now."

"A charlatan. Out for the quick buck."

"He got you against the wall though, Lou. Said so yourself. He got the dirt on you. Gave you a whole chapter to yourself. Blew fuses."

"I could've saved all the trouble it caused. He came to me—when? Last year? Beginning of last year. Called, very polite. Asked for a private appointment. Didn't know what to expect. Certainly didn't get what I expected."

"A little blackmail?"

"That's what the man is—a blackmailer. Now that all the spies are falling apart, I guess he'll be well into the extortion business, because he knows where some bodies are buried. Comes in. Says he has something interesting to show me. Puts all his proof on the table. Copies of old files with my name all over them. Says he won't publish if I'm cooperative."

"And you said?"

"What you think I said? I'm an old man. What can they do to me, put me in jail for life plus ninety-nine years? Anyway, people did know about that piece of my unhappy past. Matthew and Gregory knew, and they were obviously well connected. They'd take care of me, so why worry? In the end, Stretchfield leaves the first draft chapter with me. Says I should read it and think about it."

"And what did he want?"

"One million pictures of dead presidents. He calls. I tell him to fuck off. Anyway, I've got other worries."

"You tell any of this to Matthew, or one of the others?"

He shook his head. "Why should I? They knew. Nothing was going to happen to me. Because they knew, I was fireproof."

"You talk with your wife? With Angela?"

"Sure. Gave her a little history lesson. She understood. One in a million. Said she'd stand by me. So, as I say, I told Stretchfield to get lost."

"Did the right thing, Lou. You want to jump forward? Tell me about spring of this year. The little visit to the East? Budapest, Berlin, Sofia, Prague and Warsaw? Want to tell me what that was about?"

"I went to give joy. Take music. Make people happy."

"Of course you did. I know that, Lou. The FBI and the Agency knows that. So does the British SIS. We all know it. But the Brits—the folks I work for—are aware that you saw people while you were there."

"Who'd I see, Herb?"

"Come on, Lou. Don't be coy. You know exactly who you saw. Some of them are in pokey now. Arrested, or under house arrest. Others still missing. You saw all the old intelligence and security chiefs—Hungary, the former D.D.R., Bulgaria, Czecho, Poland. You saw all the hard-line old communist bastards who'd been put out of work by the reforms. You saw people longing to grasp at straws. Wanting to get back, get back, get back to where you once belonged—Elton John, yes? Out of Lennon and McCartney?"

"I wouldn't know. Thought you didn't like rock and roll, Herbie."

"I have *some* secrets left, Maestro. So have you. Now you must give them up. You went to see these men, yesterday's men. You take them a message? You take them a word of hope from the four just men? From Matthew, Gregory, Duncan and Vinnie, with the big hooter and rainbow ties?"

The nod was barely perceptible.

"What did you tell them, Lou? What was the word? Get this last one off your chest, then we take you somewhere really safe."

Louis Passau talked for a long time. Herbie hardly interrupted him, only the occasional nudge or question to clarify a point.

Pucky realized that Kruger had not even hinted at Tel Aviv. She heard him speaking in the past, in what seemed months ago now, in the lovely house in Virginia. ". . . all good agents give up stuff a piece at a time, until it's all out in the open," he had said. "Yet they all do the same thing. Like criminals they keep one vital piece of information: hold it back; keep it for the insurance. When we get to it, I shall have to extract the last piece. Mark me well."

Now she was marking him well.

When Passau finished, Big Herbie Kruger let out a long sigh, like a man who has been told good news, seen light at the end of a tunnel, or learned that he is suffering from indigestion, not cancer after all.

A couple of minutes later there was a tap on the door, and a voice called out. "Your people're here, Mr. Kruger."

Herbie lumbered towards the door. "Get one of them to identify himself."

Then, Young Worboys, loud and clear, "Herb, we've got the transport. I've come with a team. Art wants your guts for garters, so I've kept him away."

"Got a lot to tell you, Tony. Got things'll make your hair curl." For the first time in hours, Big Herbie started to laugh. He sounded much too cheerful.

4

THE PLACE EVERYONE in the British Intelligence Service speaks of as "Warminster" lies a little to the southeast of the old garrison town of that name, and ten miles or so from Stonehenge in Wiltshire.

It is a large, sprawling Georgian house, enclosed by thick hedges, stone walls and screens of trees, standing in more than a hundred acres of garden, meadow and woodland. Within its walls several generations of men and women have been trained to fight the secret wars—in particular, the now-dormant Cold War.

There are other buildings spread around what was once the parkland of some minor squire, including the fine underground, so-called, guest quarters. These are beautifully maintained and were built during the era of a high secret vote, when the Firm was rich and nothing was too good for the intelligence community. Countless defectors have felt the first flush of western democracy in the guest quarters, and many people have, as the jargon says, come in from the cold, to the warmth of those same little suites under the good Wiltshire earth.

From outside the house, the complex can only be identified by a large oblong mound of grass, on top of which stands a small building, housing the air-conditioning and heating plants. Access to it is via the cellars of the old main house: a wide and high tunnel leading into a kind of reception hall, from which flow several corridors. At first the guest quarters appear to have the ambiance of a private hospital. There are clean white walls and soft carpets, over which people move soundlessly. The decoration throughout is peaceful, designed to embrace its visitors in a loving warmth, and so put them at ease. The few paintings which adorn the walls are of calm and welcoming subjects: mainly watercolors—seascapes, quaint villages sitting on rocky headlands, landscapes of

573

rolling downland, or plowed fields; views of childhood when there was more time to suck in and retain a picture of the beauties of rural England.

There are four luxury suites within the complex, each with bedrooms, sitting room and kitchen; well-furnished, with a kind of taste seldom associated with the secret world. Each of these suites contains television, VCR, radio and stereo systems. The TVs and radios are switchable, controlled by the guardians of this debriefing center, so that the occupants do not necessarily have direct access to current BBC or ITV channels. There are times when those who stay within the guest quarters are better off not knowing anything about events in the real world.

As a further security, all four suites can be blocked off from one another, so that the temporary residents cannot fraternize, or even see one another. There are also three interrogation rooms: one hard, one soft and another for what the Russian Intelligence Service used to call "chemicals." The hard room is bare, but for a table and two chairs, bolted firmly to the floor. The soft room has the same soothing paintings visible in the rest of the bunker; easy chairs, a large glass-topped table, and speakers through which music can be piped. The third room is sterile—white tiles, large overhead lights—an operating theater. People who have worked there say their first impression is that of an abortion clinic, which is not far from the mark.

The convoy arrived at dawn and as they walked, or were shepherded, into the main house, most of them unconsciously caught the smells of autumn—woodsmoke hanging in the air and the afterscent of summer clashing with a hint of the hard winter to come.

Two of the four guest quarters were already occupied. Erik the Red still flatly refused to be eased back into the world, not believing most of what he was told about the way the old Soviet Union was splitting and being dragged into a new, uncertain era.

Ursula Zunder also remained there, for her debriefing would take several more months. In spite of communism having been declared D.O.A., the men and women of the British SIS were inclined to continue their research into the past, for who knew what was really happening to that great behemoth, the KGB? It was still possible that, in spite of assurances, the once black heart of the evil empire had simply changed its name and not its old function. As Louis Passau would have said, "Who knew?"

The old man, now creased with fatigue, showed signs of anxiety when they arrived, insisting that Herbie stay with him, as he was led through the tunnel to his new home. Yet once there he asked for Pucky to come in and help him to bed, a chore she performed reluctantly, for she had suffered enough of the Maestro's dexterous hands. When he had settled in, however, he seemed more quiescent: calm and less nervous about his future.

They brought in one of the service doctors who gave the old man a thorough going over, pronouncing him amazingly fit for his age, with a mental ability uneroded by the years. Herbie muttered something about being able to have told them that without recourse to doctors. In the end, the old man drifted off to sleep, his room monitored by a nurse—who was more than a nurse—sitting at a bank of television screens.

The guest quarters at Warminster, the old hands said, were the last state-of-the-secret-art buildings in the United Kingdom. Others would agree, for the true center of Warminster—the big old Georgian house—presented a different face: the smell of old schoolrooms, peeling paint-work, patches of rising damp, creaking floorboards, scuffed and utilitarian furniture. These were the outward and visible signs of decay reflecting the inward and spiritual decline of the espionage business.

By eight thirty, the protagonists were seated in the big, drafty old dining room where so many classes of trainees had breakfasted before them. They ate scrambled eggs, drank thick black coffee, chewed on toast and marmalade, the weariness taking its toll and giving most of them a sense of distance from reality akin to an out-of-body experience.

Young Worboys disappeared, only to return at nine o'clock to banish all but Herbie and Pucky, together with Gus Keene and his wife, Carole—the master inquisitors. The tapes were handed over to Carole, who bore them away, almost salivating, safe in the knowledge that two trained transcribers were already on their way from London.

At nine fifteen, Art Railton arrived, glaring at Herbie as he entered the room.

"You don't know what damage you did," he snapped at Kruger.

Herbie simply projected his daft smile and muttered, "Nobody knows the trouble I've seen."

"Could've got us all killed, Herb. Bloody stupid. Why'd you do it?"

"Had a feeling. Intuition. Thought they were close."

Art looked away, his anger subsiding, a telltale flush creeping up his cheeks. "How'd you do it, Herb?"

Kruger told him, in half a dozen precise sentences.

"What time did you get out?"

"Two thirty. Maybe five minutes either way. I did right, Art? Yes?"

Reluctantly Arthur Railton nodded, then gave his old friend a sheepish smile. "They got to the apartment at about four in the morning."

Big Herbie gave one of his "I-told-you-so" sighs. "See, Art. If I'd talked about it, you'd have had a gunfight at the K.O. Corral. . ."

"Okay, Herb."

"Sure. What happened?"

"We realized you'd gone. Around three thirty one of the boys went over because the listeners got anxious. When I was sure, we began to get ourselves together. Going to try and pick up your trail. Then they came. Two of them."

"You identify them?"

"No. Not worth it. Not worth the hassle. They picked the locks, went in, and found the birds had flown."

"You tape their conversation?"

"Only heard them moving about. They didn't speak inside four walls. Knew what they were doing."

Herbie gave a knowing nod. It was typical Russian tradecraft. They loathed to even whisper anything compromising within a safe house. He had been surprised that Ursula—Passau's Therese—had been allowed to talk openly in the Lexington Avenue apartment, though even she did a routine with an electronic bug detector every time she went in.

"Then they left. Quickly and very quietly," Art continued. "If you'd stayed, we might have nabbed them," trying to talk himself into a grudge once more.

"Art, is better the way it happened."

Young Worboys coughed, catching their attention, suggesting they should go into one of the more comfortable rooms. "The Chief's out of the country," he told them, kneading his hands together uncomfortably. "I spoke with him a little while ago. He can't get back for a week—Brussels. Economic Community talks on intelligence requirements."

They waited, looking at him, their eyes wary and mocking. "So, I'm in charge," he said finally. "There's a signal from him back at the Shop. I insisted he put it in writing. I am to use my discretion. Take the initiative."

"He doesn't want to know," Art half whispered, and Gus Keene nodded. There would be a general election at some point in the next twelve months. The Labour Party, the now-watered-down Socialists, had made a vow to bring the SIS to heel should they be elected to government. British Intelligence would find itself muzzled, hemmed in by Whitehall watchdogs, its fangs drawn, and its cash flow reduced to a trickle. The Chief wanted nothing to come back to haunt him should that happen.

"Covering his arse," Herbie said, getting up and stretching.

They all went into one of the smaller anterooms. There were old, fraying armchairs and a settee, a scratched table, circa 1949, covered with periodicals. Two framed posters hung on the wall, remnants of 1939–45. "Careless Talk Costs Lives"; "Be Like Dad! Keep Mum!"

They spread themselves out, Herbie taking over the old settee, stretching himself on it, draping his big legs over one end. From this relatively comfortable position he took charge. Nobody stopped him, neither Art Railton nor Young Worboys even attempting to regain control. Kruger, on that morning, demonstrated that he was the one person there who knew the score, had the experience, and was willing to take the ball and run, as their American relatives would have said.

He talked for an hour, giving them a brilliant précis of the life and times of Louis Passau. He left nothing out, and added little asides which constituted his reading of the situation. Occasionally Pucky or Art would throw out a fast one-liner, encouraging or bearing out Kruger's final analysis.

When he came to an end, stopping short of the other facts he had learned in the faded splendor of the Buckingham Hotel, Gus Keene began to chuckle, while Worboys could not resist an almost conspiratorial smile. It was Worboys who first broke the silence.

"Serve them right," he said with some vigor. "Serve them bloody right. They've spent years being toffee-nosed with us; telling us that we could never share their entire product; that we were like a bloody Swiss cheese, riddled with holes. Now it turns out they've spent the past thirty years with their Soviet Office leaking all over the Kremlin's carpets."

"Marty always was a clever bugger," from Art, leaning forward in his chair, reaching for the umpteenth cigarette. "They really showed incredible taste, choosing a man like Passau to be their messenger boy. Who was ever going to suspect a great musician like Passau?"

"They got some help," Herbie turned, looked Art in the eye. "They had help when they came across his indiscretions during the war. The Nazi tie-in. When we take Louis back down that road, which is something that has to be done, I think we'll find he gave the Germans very little. He does have a conscience, after all, though we'll need to search for it. I don't think he ever intended, or had the means, to sell out anything really juicy."

"You truly think he was an innocent from the sixties onward?" Gus Keene fiddled with his pipe. "You think he believed what Marty, Alfoot, de Paul and Bains fed him?"

"For a long time, sure. Sure, I think he did." Big Herbie frowned. When he frowned it was more like a scowl and the corners of his mouth seemed to be attached, by hidden wires, running to his forehead. "For a very long time—I guess until the early eighties—he imagined he was doing the United States a favor, helping to send disinformation into the Kremlin and acting as a channel for genuine intelligence coming all the way from Moscow. When he finally caught on, it was too late for him to back down. Louis also has a remarkable sense of survival. Luck and the devil play only a small part. He probably began by suspecting, then, later, knew with no doubt that he was being used. Is what he seems to be saying."

At long last, Gus Keene lit his pipe, his head surrounded by a cloud of smoke so that when he spoke it was almost a disembodied voice. "Ursula maintains that she definitely wanted out by 1987 or eighty-eight."

Kruger gave a grunt—irritated and heavy with disbelief. "Then why didn't she come over? Little Ursula could have done a walk-in any time she wanted, yet she waits until now."

"She appears to have had her reasons." Gus waved at the smoke, dispersing it.

"She say anything about the standard of the intelligence received via Passau?" Art asked.

Keene nodded. "High quality. Patchy, she tells me, but in the main high quality intelligence. Mainly microfilm, some copied docs, reports, briefings, in-depth studies, state of readiness, order of battle. NATO and the U.S., both."

"And what was she bringing in return?" Worboys this time.

"She says shopping lists plus watered-down intelligence. Moscow Center were very protective of the source. It seems they believed a lot of the information came directly from Passau: only hinted that he was possibly in cahoots with one other person at Langley."

"So," Kruger took the floor again. "So what was in it for Marty? Any ideas?"

Worboys shook his head. Gus Keene answered, "Marty, and three other highly placed CIA officers. If I read it correctly, he had a right to hire and fire by the early sixties. Marty handpicked the top brass for the Soviet Office, which means he selected people like Tony de Paul, Mike Alfoot, who is now in charge, and their tame roving reporter, Urquart Bains."

"Why didn't they just do it all through Bains?" Art stubbed out his cigarette, playing devil's advocate. "Simple. Keep it in the family."

"Too dangerous, Art." Herbie opened his eyes wide, as though waking from a doze. "Much too dangerous. Sure, Bains slid in and out of countries like a specter. Original invisible man. But to carry film, documents even, on a regular basis would have been very compromising. Marty wanted to play safe. He made certain they used the most unlikely person in the entire United States. Could've used a Texas oilman, sure; anybody he could have scammed, but he chose the best man for the job.

"Point was that they needed a name, a go-between. Both sides required it. If anyone pinned Marty down and said 'who's the lucky guy?' he could've told them—'I'm using a source who doesn't know what's going on. I've a deep source in the Kremlin. Hands over the stuff to an old friend of mine: Louis Passau, great conductor. It's him that does the business.' They probably had a funny name for him, like the Soviets called him 'Kingfisher.' The Sovs had to believe it was this man Kingfisher who had nothing to do with the CIA. Marty knew damned well that he did not dare let the Ks know the information was coming straight out of Langley.

"One thing about Louis is that he's a tiny bit of a snob. Deep down among all the foul language, and his womanizing, there's a sense of wanting to alter history, to help his country—as long as it doesn't interfere with his music. Also there was his guilt, and they played on that. Who in heaven would've fingered Maestro Louis Passau as a Soviet agent? Who would even have suspected he was having regular meetings with a courier from Dzerzhinsky Square? He was ideal, and handed to Marty on a plate." He stopped and looked belligerently at Keene. "Didn't finish answering my last question, Gus. What's in it for Marty?"

Gus lifted an eyebrow. "I think you know that, Herb. Same as was in it for Philby, Maclean, the rest of them. Marty came from the streets, from a brick-poor Brooklyn family. We've all met him, some of you've worked with him. You know what he was like. Always defensive about his background. Used that streetwise talk rather as the old Maestro uses it. They must have connected exceptionally well. Marty's very aware of his roots, maybe uncomfortable about them. As time went by he could well have started believing the United States was going the wrong way. Could've got religion—of the communist variety. Only one step from there—a seed in the mind—to doing something about it. Then, as a true believer, he would go out and proselytize the world. What better place to begin than Langley, and from what better power base to operate than the Soviet Office? We'll have to ask him."

Herbie's large head nodded, like the head of one of those stupid dogs people put in the back of their cars. "So, we going to ask him?" His gaze fell on Young Worboys. "Tony, you have the final say about that."

Worboys looked discomforted. "Well," he began. "How . . . ?" Then Art cut across him—

"One more thing. More than one actually. Herbie, we haven't yet heard what Louis Passau did this spring. What he talked about. What he said to those undesirables in the former Soviet Bloc."

"Ah, sixty-five-thousand-dollar question. Sure. Why not? Why don't I tell them about that, Pucky?"

Pucky gave a small sleepy twitch of the lips. "Knock their socks off, Herb."

So Kruger told them. First, he enumerated the people Passau had actually met, covertly, in the old Eastern Bloc: in Bulgaria the head of the former notorious Department 6, Ministry of the Interior. "You all know about him anyway," Herbie all businesslike. "He's still there, moved to the National Security Service. Rose by any other name, all that jazz, eh?"

In Czecho, he had talked to the former head of the defunct secret service, the StB, together with a number of other outlawed officers of that organization.

In Hungary, Passau went to meet discredited members of a group of renegade secret service officers, outlawed in 1990, by the new democratically elected government.

In Poland, he carried the word to the Office for Defense of the State, which operates from the same building in Warsaw as the one that housed the old secret service. This "new" organization still employs over a hundred-thousand members of the supposedly discredited communist service.

"And we all know whom he met in Berlin." He grinned at them. "Five members of the very old guard who'd give their all for the return of the good old days."

"So what did they talk about, Herbie?" Quietly spoken from Gus Keene.

"As he tells it," Kruger paused, to indicate that he believed every word Passau had said during that long wait at the Torquay hotel, when Worboys was dashing down with the Fifth Cavalry. "As he tells it, he gave them messages of greetings from their friends and colleagues in the CIA. That's what he was told to say. I checked it most thoroughly, asked him time and again, cross-questioned, once, twice, three times, ask Puck. By then he knew what he was doing. Nobody was pretending anymore. They—Marty and Company—didn't even wrap it up in chauvinistic terms. They told him to use the words, quote 'colleagues in the CIA' end quote."

"Just greetings, Herb?" Art paused as he lit another cigarette.

"Greetings and a message. It is the message that's really interesting. He told them to be ready for a new dawn. He told them the new dawn would come sometime in the summer, July or August. He told them that elements of the American CIA would back a return to the old order, and they should take their cue from Moscow. Now isn't *that* interesting? Marty, and his people, already knew about the coming August coup. They knew and supported it. They were all for turning back the clock. Sure, we now hear Langley had been warning Gorby, but . . ."

There was a long, uncomfortable silence. Faraway, as though counter-pointing the news, the wail of an ambulance, or police siren, floated from the distance.

Gus chuckled. "Could be argued," he said, with laughter in his voice, "could be argued they were trying to hang on to their jobs."

There were general subdued laughs, but the mirth was uneasy, uncon-vincing. Nobody in the intelligence communities of the West needed to look after their jobs. When one enemy dies, another takes its place. They were all only too aware of the dangers that lurked out there, in Europe, the Middle East, within the uneasy, unsettled borders of the former Soviet Union itself. Were they not conversant with the way some Third World countries were racing ahead towards a nuclear goal? Did they close their eyes to the dangers of financial ruin brought ruthlessly to Europe and the U.S.A. from Japan, and other countries? Were their ears blocked to the firm communist line taken by China? The illegal arms sales? The drug wars? The terrorist conflict? Everyone in the room became nervous when the Western powers talked of military cuts and the scaling down of bases the world over. What was happening within the fragmented old order of the Soviet Union, and what still went on in the rest of the world, posed a greater threat than the stable balance of superpowers which had existed throughout the Cold War. They trembled, and knew, to their extreme concern, that politicians and generals alike always tend to resist the advice of intelligence services, particularly when the man in the street wanted to hear the words peace and prosperity. Their biggest test was yet to come. A military, in Europe and the United States, with little bark and less bite, was something to lose sleep over.

"And Tel Aviv?" Art asked. "What did he tell them in Tel Aviv?"

Herbie gave a large shrug. "Didn't get around to asking him about Tel Aviv." The daft smile told all who knew him that Herbie Kruger had not got around to asking Passau the question, not because time had been short. He had not asked it because he wanted to put it to Maestro Passau at the right moment, and the right moment had yet to arrive.

"So, we going to ask Marty?" He looked at Worboys again.

"How can we? He's out. Private. Retired to Florida. Living off his pension. Watching the pelicans, dabbling in the surf."

"His lieutenants are still around." This was Art, already ahead of Worboys. "And I suspect where his lieutenants are, Marty isn't far behind. What's on your mind, Herb?"

"What we got left in safe houses, Tony?"

"What . . . ?"

"They all sold, even on a depressed market? The old Firm swapped them for a pot of message, or whatever the term is? The Firm bankrupt, or have we a nice, lonely place left on the books?"

"Such as?" Worboys tried to stare him down and failed badly.

"Such as the Charlton house, Tony. That still on our books?"

Young Worboys knew exactly where the Charlton house was located; knew the where and the why. He even knew the reason Herbie asked about it now, for the so-called Charlton house had played a large part in the operation they all thought of as Herbie Kruger's Passion and Resurrection. So many years ago, yet so near now with Ursula Zunder close confined in the guest quarters.

"Yes." He locked eyes with Herbie, saw the stubborn glitter, the hint of blood, in his eyes and looked away again. "Yes, it's still on the books. Just in time, Herb. It's down to go on the market next year. We're shedding a whole heap of flats and houses now the Ks aren't active. Kept them on because of the Gulf War. The Ks sent people in with intelligence about the Iraqis. We took it down in safe houses, in shorthand and on tape to pass on to Langley and the Pentagon. Now, it's either close down eighty percent of the flats and houses, or lose this place. And it's unthinkable to close Warminster."

"You open it up for me, Tony?"

"Let's hear the story first."

"Okay, simple. The old man has an emergency number. Worldwide. Fire, police, ambulance, emergency squad. Marty told him he only had to call, and they'd be there—or someone would be there—to take him out. Told him, within twenty-four hours. Bet Marty himself would come running if the Maestro gave it a whirl. We never shared Charlton with Langley, did we, Young Worboys?"

"Not to my knowledge. No."

"Then let's share it with them now."

"You really think Marty'd compromise himself. . . ?"

"He'd compromise the whole shooting match if he thought he could take Passau out of the picture. Wouldn't be surprised if they all came running."

"You believe it, Herb? One hundred percent?"

"Sure. Tethered pig routine."

"Goat, Herb," said an excited Art Railton from the comfort of his chair.

"Whatever. You're the boss, Tony Worboys. Chief gave it to you. Win a medal. Worboys victorious. New head of the school, what old sheep."

"Yes." Nobody could tell if Worboys was agreeing or just ruminating.

"Let's go then," Gus Keene winked broadly at Herbie. "Let's plug the Langley leak once and for all."

"Thirty years too late, but better than nothing." Pucky Curtiss rose, walked over to Herbie and kissed him firmly on the forehead.

"Sure. In D.C. they've been living it up, saying the Cold War is over. We won." Worboys had the bit between his teeth.

"You disappoint me, Tony." Herbie sounded gloomy. "Nobody won. Nobody lost. And I'm not all that sure it'll ever really be over. It's just that people want it over, and they're not yet counting the cost, or the danger, of the peace."

5

THE VILLAGE OF CHARLTON lies almost on the Oxfordshire and Berkshire borders, about ten miles from the Atomic Research Establishment at Harwell, and easily accessible by road from both London and Oxford. The Berkshire Downs are only a twenty-minute car ride away, and the setting is delightful, if modest.

The house of which Big Herbie Kruger had spoken is situated a mile or so out of the village, standing back from the road, screened by trees and a weathered red brick wall dotted with electronic eyes.

From the outside, the place looked unassuming but pleasant: the same red brick as the wall, but with well-established Virginia creeper crawling around the windows of its facade: the leaves were just fading from the burning red of autumn, so the building glowed with color.

Inside was a different story for, over the years, the service had made structural changes. There was what people spoke of as a "grannie flat"— three rooms, including a small kitchen tacked onto the side, with its own entrance. The grannie flat was there for one of the Shop's caretakers, usually someone who had retired from the trade, put out to pasture with a pension and a roof.

In the main house there were four bedrooms, two bathrooms, a large, sunny kitchen and two further good-sized rooms—living and dining rooms—with windows that gave clear views through the trees. The main room had a pair of French windows leading out to the lawn, flower beds and bushes: its furniture was heavy, good-quality, though not quite antique.

Big Herbie Kruger wandered around the place, touching things, reminding himself of the past. He knew the house by heart, every brick, though it seemed longer than eleven years since he had been there. In the early eighties, Herbie had conducted a fast and brutal interrogation in this place and on the Berkshire Downs. He recalled every last memory of that time as he roamed through the rooms, like a ghost returning to haunt a place of sadness, while Young Worboys and the technician checked the hidden mikes and the tape machines.

Herbie remembered Passau telling him of Ursula's one-line identification telephone codes. "A Man of Sorrows" had been one of them. Kruger felt like a man of sorrows for it was from this unlikely house that he had gone forth to cross the now-demolished Berlin Wall for the last time— the journey that had taken him to his own personal betrayal.

He needed to cauterize the wound, burn it completely from his mind. Martha, his wife, knew all about his dreams and nightmares; knew that she would not be with him for a lifetime.

Before they left Warminster, Pucky had begged to come, but they could not take the chance. Who knew if Marty would arrive mob-handed, as the term had it? There could well be foolishness, and Herb had suffered enough foolishness to last him a lifetime.

"You'll come back with the slate clean?" Pucky asked as they stood together alone in one of the smaller Warminster rooms, looking out onto the gravel of the turning circle and the cars that waited patiently. It was early afternoon and they had awakened Passau, telling him of one final trip. She put her arms around Herbie's big body. Hugged him and felt the hard butt of the automatic pistol lying against the small of his back.

She remembered a love poem from a different time and place. Did not know where it came from, but the words popped into her head like something she had not wanted to think about in years.

> For the Chinese, this is the Year of the Monkey.
> But, for me it will always be the Year of the Small of Your Back.

"Sure. Sure," Herbie whispered. "Sure, I'll come home clean, Puck. Then we'll do the right thing." He did not say what the right thing was, and she did not ask him, frightened now that their feelings for one another had been a mirage, a dream, or maybe a nightmare. All Pucky knew was that a great sadness overtook her as she watched him climb into the car.

The technician drove, with Worboys in the front, while Herbie and Art flanked the old Maestro in the back, a tight squeeze. "Maestro sandwich," Kruger muttered. He closed the door and the smoked glass of the windows blotted him from sight. The trail car, replete with thugs, followed them out of the driveway.

"You okay, Pucky?" Gus Keene had come into the room, silently. Identified first by the strong aroma of his pipe tobacco, then his voice.

"I'll live, Gus. What's going to happen?"

"Haven't the foggiest. Herb says the old boy has this emergency number. He's convinced Marty will come by himself, talk and therefore spill the beans. Young Worboys is concerned, and so he should be. It'll mean netting an American citizen, holding him against his will. Eventually we'll have to tell the Yanks, and there'll be all hell to pay. Langley can really do without the scandal."

"Like we could have done without the scandal of Kim Philby all that time ago?"

"That was our sister service, but it had repercussions. Yes, there were those who wanted it buried, those who wanted to give him the benefit of the doubt. Made it worse in the long run. As for Marty, I personally favor simply handing over the tapes. Let Langley clean up its own mess."

"There's no danger though, is there?"

"Puck, there's always danger."

On the road to the Charlton house, Herbie Kruger talked to the Maestro about danger.

"The ride we took out of New York, Lou. That was dangerous."

"All life is dangerous, Herbie. I want to go to sleep. At my age this shouldn't be happening."

"But New York was particularly dangerous. They shot at you outside Lincoln Center, and again in the tunnel."

"And you shot back, Herb. Killed a couple of guys. Did well. Won a silver trophy and a framed certificate."

"Who were *they*, Lou? Giarre's men, like you said? Or was it someone else?"

"'Course it was Carlo. Been trying for years."

"When did he try, before the New York business?"

Passau sighed, deeply, as though he had really heard enough questions and answers. "Once in Rome, mid-seventies. On the street. Ride-by shooting. Motorcycle, like the Arabs do it."

"Did it make the papers?"

The old man shook his head.

"Where else, Lou?"

"Oh, London, early eighties. Car bomb. The cops thought it was the IRA. Terrorists. I didn't disillusion them."

"Any other time?"

"Sure, again in the eighties, can't recall the time. Late summer. Few years ago. They broke into the Fifth Avenue apartment. Angela came home, realized something was wrong and didn't go in. Called the cops."

"You've been very lucky then, Lou."

"Sure."

"You certain it was Carlo?"

"'Course I'm fucking certain. What is it with the questions? Carlo wants revenge, preferably before he dies."

"Just for the booze heist?"

"The booze heist and . . . Constanza."

Now, Herbie shook his head. "Couldn't have been Constanza, Lou. Puck and I, we did some checking. Pulled Sophie's file. Used the magic computer. Hacked into the Federal mainframes. You did the booze heist in 1927, right?"

"I told you all about that."

"1927, right?"

"Yes. Sure, twenty-seven."

"And you first met Constanza Traccia when she auditioned for you. That was forty-eight?"

"I told you."

"And she told you her age. Age twenty-two, right?"

Passau gave a one-note laugh: dry, scoffing. "I never believed that. Like me she was also a prodigy. My daughter. Twenty when I met her again. Twenty years old and sang with the assurance of a fully fledged diva. Incredible."

"Would you believe nineteen, Lou?"

"Why?" Sullen, a hint of anger.

"Because that was her age. Infant prodigy, yes. Nineteen-year-old prodigy."

"How? Sophie and I . . . can't be. You've got your dates mixed up, Herb. Forget it."

Herbie grunted. "Let me give you the facts, Lou. Sure, sure Sophie could've been pregnant when you did the booze heist and ran out on her. All quite possible. But she must've lost the baby. Maybe your going was a shock to her, and she lost the child."

"Constanza was . . ."

"The record can't be altered, Lou. Go with it. In January of nineteen twenty-*nine*, Sophie got herself married to Alberto Traccia. A fine and loving musician. There were no children before that, or in tow. They married January twenty-nine. I seen the documents. Already she was pregnant, and that couldn't have been you. Constanza was born, August 1929. Unless Sophie had a two-year pregnancy." He stopped, silent, eyebrow cocked, half smile on his face. "She belong to Sophie and Alberto Traccia, Lou."

"Can't be." A half sob. "Impossible."

"No, Lou. Sophie wanted to hurt you, I've no doubt. Sophie wanted to scald you with the past. Probably went on loving you all those years. I guess Constanza also had reasons for lying about her age. You wouldn't take her seriously if she told you she was only nineteen. . . ."

"Of course I'd have taken her seriously. Who couldn't have? She was rare, Herbie. Rare and wonderful."

"And *not* your daughter, Lou. Puck and I got the proofs."

The old man was silent for almost twenty minutes. Herbie looked at him from the corner of his eyes. Passau just sat there, allowing his body to sway with the motion of the car, pushing first against Art and then against Kruger. Tears flowed freely down the smooth cheeks. Finally he rummaged around and pulled out a handkerchief. Blew his nose, mopped up his face. "All that agony," he whispered. "All the pain and anguish. And for a *shiksa*."

Herbie felt a needle prick of warning, but it really meant nothing to him. "Thought shiksas were no problem for you, Lou. No faith. You were a Jew in name only, you said. So why should a shiksa worry you?"

"Doesn't *worry* me, Herb. Jewish men have ties to their faith, whatever they believe in their hearts. Us Jews are special. So she was a shiksa. Couldn't be helped." He took a deep breath. "Sometimes I think all life can't be helped. All life means nothing. You work, love, sweat and die. A waste of time, and only half a wink of time in the eye of God—should He exist."

A little later Herbie asked again about the other times when Don Carlo Giarre had tried to have him assassinated. "Why were you so lucky, Lou? The kind of people Carlo had on his payroll wouldn't have gone on making mistakes."

"I had plenty of warning. Always there was good warning."

"From your friends at Langley? They would have ties into the FBI. FBI Mafia intelligence . . . the four boys at Langley tipped you off?"

"Something like that." Passau folded his arms, laid his head back, and pretended to sleep.

"You get any warnings about the attempt in New York, Lou? Lincoln Center? Then on the way to the airport?"

"Someone must've slipped up. Didn't tip me off."

"Or were those attempts the work of other people, Lou? Not Carlo?"

"What others?"

"You were being taken to Quantico. We all had lots of questions to ask you. Your friends, the fearless four, would have been nervous. Could they have tried to get you taken out?"

"No way. What're we talking about this for?"

"Because you're going to dial their emergency number. Matthew promised to get you out if you dialed the number. I need to know if he's coming to wipe you out rather than get you out."

Passau shrugged. "Who knows?"

Ten minutes from the Charlton house, Herbie said, "I know Matthew quite well, Lou. Worked with him a long time ago."

"So? You said you knew Therese as well."

"I know Therese. She's back where we came from. Living in one of those little suites you seemed to like so much. She's talking a lot. I suppose we need it for the history books."

"I wish Pucky was here, Herb. I miss Pucky."

"You think I don't?"

Now, as he paced around the house, Herbie worried away at what might happen when they came in answer to Passau's call. How long would they have to wait? How violent would Marty be if he knew his life was blown to hell? How cunning?

Young Worboys came down with the technician. They talked for ten minutes, then he went out to the trail car, got in and drove away. They had all told Worboys he should not be there when the trap went down.

"Benny's staying," Worboys told him. "He's a good all-rounder. He'll be added firepower if it comes to that."

"Who knows what it'll come to." Big Herbie shook his hand. "I really don't see Marty walking in on us cold. He's too streetwise; too experienced. A very careful man, Marty."

"Even careful men take risks when the chips are down, Herb. And his chips are well and truly down."

"Sure, he's got to be like the song. Got to accentuate the positive, eliminate the negative. Louis is the negative, right?"

"Wouldn't be surprised. Hope it isn't too messy, Herb."

"Give my love to Pucky, Tony. Tell her I'll be back."

"Sure you'll be back, Herb. You're going to be in the Warminster sweat box for a few months. It has to be that way. Full debrief, right?"

"Right. I know it. Hours of boredom. Telling the story for damage control."

He watched Worboys drive away, then went slowly upstairs. From the bedroom where they had put Passau, the sad, elegiac strains of Barber's *Adagio for Strings*, made the house seem even more desolate. Herbie thought he must get a recording of that, but he also wanted to hear the other piece Louis Passau had mentioned: *Knoxville: Summer of 1915.*

Carefully, he quizzed Passau about the emergency number. "You got an identifier, like 'Kingfisher'?"

"An identifier, sure. I say, 'This is Absalom.'"

"As in, 'Absalom, my son, my son Absalom! Would God I had died for thee. O Absalom, my son, my son.'?"

"You got it, Herbie. Thought you didn't know the Bible. Thought Shakespeare was your big thing."

"I know bits and pieces, Lou. Sometimes I think my entire life is merely bits and pieces."

"Join the club."

"So you call the number, do the Absalom bit, then what?"

"Give them a fix on my exact location. Also the situation. If there's danger. Whatever."

"And they come running?"

"That's what they told me. Call and we'll come for you. Get you out. Anywhere in the world."

"And you believe that?"

"Totally. I call. They come. No doubts."

"They give you a time scale?"

"Twenty-four hours at the outside. Within twenty-four hours of the call."

"A person picks up, yes?"

"Maybe. Maybe not. Maybe it's a tape." Pause for effect—that is what

Herbie felt. A studied pause, before, "I don't think you should listen in, Herb. They could have some kind of detection stuff at the other end. Give them the telephone number I'm calling from, and possibly identify how many sets are on the line. Also no tapes, right? Safer to have no tapes."

"Whatever you say, Louis. Now, let me tell you exactly where you are, and what you must say."

Herbie gave him the location of the house in some detail; told him the best way in—"You should say the French windows will be open, tell them you'll see to it, that there are no guards, only a couple of women looking after you. If you want to make it good, you should also say you've been hiding out with me. That I got you here, that nobody's put you to the question yet."

They went through it five or six times, to be certain that Passau was word perfect. He lay, propped up with pillows, the little CD player at hand, a pile of CDs within reach. Herbie brought the telephone over to the bed, and Passau took it, turning, shielding the touch pad with his shoulder so that Herbie could not see the number he was dialing. Kruger moved away and tried to keep the pattern of tones in his head—the beep-beep-boop-bip-boop. At least from that he knew Passau was dialing an overseas number.

Louis listened, then spoke. Calmly and with precision. The lesson learned and spoken word for word.

"It was a tape," he said when it was over.

"Lou, you're a star. You're a legend."

"'Course I'm a legend. You think I don't know that I'm a legend? Wait till you see all my clippings. Angela brought them up to date. Big leather-bound books. Make good reading in the September of my years, Herb."

"Where are you now?"

Passau make a small cackling noise. "About late August. Going to live forever. Well, got to make my hundred. When can I call Angela, Herb? She's a good girl. Tends to my needs. My every whim."

"When this is over you can call her. Maybe we'll bring her in to keep you company."

"You mean I'm not going home yet?"

"Lot of questions still to be asked, Lou. We'll make you comfortable, with Angela. She already knows you're safe. We had someone go and tell her. In person. No calls. Better that way."

"Okay, Herb. You been a good friend."

"Sure." Then his own therapeutic waiting pause. The psychiatrist's trick, before—"How long do you reckon, Lou? How long before someone comes?"

"Twenty-four hours minimum. Don't see how they could do it quicker."

"Listen to something happy. Merry." He looked at the CDs, making a gesture.

Passau cocked his head on one side, "Jaunty-jolly?"

"You got it."

As he went downstairs, Herbie heard Rossini. Overtures, bright and sparkling, full of life, fun and happiness.

In LONDON, the young man who had followed Herbie, Passau and Pucky on the flight from Nassau picked up the telephone on the second ring.

"He's called in," the voice at the not-so-distant end said quietly. "I've been monitoring the answering machine every hour. He called at five thirty this afternoon." It was the voice he had heard speaking from Vienna, and again close by.

The young man knew about the answering machine, had helped set it up. You could dial in from anywhere in the world, tap out a code and the messages would be relayed to you. Three thousand miles would not be a problem. By tapping codes you could run the message tape backwards and forwards. The young man thought they lived in an incredible world in which machines now gave instant progress reports. "Where is he?" he asked.

"Not far. Would you like to drive me down? It's time I took care of everything."

"I'll be at the usual place in an hour."

"I'll be ready. Getting near the end of the road. I shan't be sorry."

Somehow, the young man thought he detected a twinge of emotion in his superior's voice.

BENNY, THE TECHNICIAN, had gone outside, patrolling the grounds. They had told him to stay away from the line of trees where the alarms had been turned off, and to be certain he could not be seen from that area of the lawn over which they expected Marty to come.

Inside, Herbie had made one of his excellent omelettes. Spanish this time, heavy with diced vegetables. Passau got through his as though he had not eaten for a week. He washed it down with a Chablis, asking for another glass. Herbie poured for him, then took the tray down to the kitchen. From above he now heard more music. The Verdi Requiem. "Pray God, no," he said to himself, then set about doing the omelettes for Art and himself.

"You'd make someone a great wife," Art told him as they sat opposite each other, across the table in the dining room. "How d'you want to do it, Herb? Take turns? Three hours on and three off?"

"Make it four. Benny can do the threes. It won't be tonight."

"But we're taking no chances?"

"When did I take chances, Art?"

"Practically ever since I've known you. I'll do the first shift. Who knows how long it'll take? If I were Marty I wouldn't come within a hundred miles of this place."

"But you're not Marty, Arthur. Marty can be reckless. Comes from that deprived childhood. Look what he's done. Leaked from the Agency for thirty years and nobody ever suspected. Langley thought Jim Angleton was paranoid, not sleeping nights because he thought the Agency was shot through with moles. He was right, but nobody looked in the proper places. They're going to be well pissed when we tell them the truth."

They both stayed up until eleven o'clock, then Herbie took himself off to bed, peeking in on Passau, who was huddled in a fetal position, sound asleep, his breathing regular.

He came down again at three in the morning, and Art yawned. "All quiet on the Western Front," he said as he left the room.

Big Herbie sat on the stand chair just vacated by Art. Sat straight, alert, the pistol on his lap, eyes gradually adjusting to the pitch darkness so that, within ten minutes, he could pick out the furniture, the French windows with their curtains pulled halfway across. His ears picked up the night sounds. The sudden twitter and screech of an owl. He thought, bad luck, death. It was an old English country superstition, hear an owl screech in a built-up area and it signaled death. He could not count this as a built-up area. Or could he?

He thought about times past and times present. In his mind saw

Marty Foreman: the pugnacious face, shaved cannonball head, thick arms covered by a mat of hair, hard hands clutching at a pistol, aiming, firing, so many years ago, when they had cornered a long-hunted war criminal. Marty laughing, drinking, smiling as a good, tough friend. Marty with his arm slung up, grasping around Herbie's shoulders, standing on tiptoe to make it. Comrades in arms.

He hardly heard the tiny scrape of the foot, close to the house, outside the window. Heard it but did not register until the sound came again, then he was totally in the present: body ramrod straight in the chair, hardly breathing, the safety off the pistol, a quick glance at the luminous dial of his watch. Ten minutes to four on a chill morning and all is not well. The scrape again, then the movement at the curtain. The pistol up and the words spoken quietly.

"Come in, Marty, but come in with your hands on your head. Blow you to eternity if you try anything. We have watchers behind you." Lying, his heart in his mouth, finger too tight on the trigger as the curtains parted and he saw the figure—too tall—with hands raised, palms flat on the head.

He snapped the light on, and it was not Marty.

"It's not Marty," the man sad. "My name is Mark." He was tall, dark, slim. Handsome, carrying himself like a professional, walking with ease. "My name is Mark. You must be Mr. Kruger, I'm honored. Is the old man safe?"

6

BENNY HAD NOT BEEN doing the three on and three off. He came through the windows behind the tall stranger, putting a pistol close to the man's head. "Just very quiet, sir. Very still."

"I'm not here to cause problems." The man who called himself Mark was dressed in gray slacks, a double-breasted blazer, white shirt, regimental tie—though Herbie could not identify the regiment. On his feet were soft leather shoes. Probably Gucci. His face showed that he was a man of the sun, the tan smooth, darkening the already olive complexion, and his clear black eyes had that look of one who has spent years gazing over rocks and sand. Looking into the distance, towards mountains—if only in his mind. A man of the Promised Land, Herbie thought.

Benny was quietly patting him down, removing a small automatic pistol, papers, a wallet, an Israeli passport.

"Mark Ephron, Mr. Kruger, sir," Benny almost whispered with a kind of reverence. They were all taught that the Israeli Service was the best in the world. The best, and the most ruthless.

"It's an alias anyway." Ephron smiled, his eyes lighting up. Calm, unruffled, as though he had come in answer to a cocktail invitation.

Herbie nodded and asked the man to sit down. "It's okay, Benny."

"No," the Israeli turned his head slightly. "I have another young man out there. He's in the trees, where Louis told me to come through. His name is Peter, but he's only watching. He's there in case you have other visitors. I pledge he will do you no harm. This is true."

"I believe you." Kruger nodded him into a chair, realizing without looking that Art had come down, trousers and a jacket thrown on hastily. "He still asleep, Art?" Herbie asked, not turning his head.

"Sound as a baby."

"Good." Then to the man who called himself Mark, "Your transport?"

"Mile, mile and a half, down the road. We've driven around the area. There are no signs of any other strangers. Peter went into the local pub just before closing time. Asked pertinent questions. Nobody new. Only us, and we're here to talk. To tell you things you might like to know. Things you should know. To make certain that Louis Passau is safe."

Only then did he sit down. Benny faded away, through the curtains, like a magician's illusion. Herbie moved to one of the more comfortable armchairs, and Art came over to sit at his feet.

"I presume you're Mossad." Kruger still held the pistol, and did not put the safety back on.

"Naturally." Again a winning smile, warm, comfortable. The smile that said all is well. I come as a friend.

"One of the few field agents?"

"I have that honor. We're so lucky, Mr. Kruger. Just over a dozen field agents in the entire world. Amazing for such an intelligence service."

"The figures sound good, Mark, but they're not quite truthful. You have thousands of agents, and you know it."

Mark gave a small inclination of the head. "But we're lucky. The Diaspora—the Jews living . . ."

"Outside Israel. Sure, Mr. Ephron. I know what the Diaspora is."

"We have many to call upon."

"And you wanted to talk to me about Maestro Passau?"

"Yes. Yes, I do. Since he went missing with you, I have been expecting the call. Again, the Diaspora. We traced you more quickly than the FBI, the CIA, or even the Giarre family. The poor man has so many enemies. Peter managed to keep up with you when you broke out of the South Seas Plantation, on Captiva Island. He was on the aircraft from Nassau. Even though we expected Louis to call for us, we wanted to keep a watching brief."

"You were very good. I didn't make you." He thought of the Range Rover, the extra aerials and spotlights, glimpsed in his mirror as he crossed Florida in the rain. Realized that he *had* made them.

"Not me. I had business in Vienna. Peter did all the watching, with a little help from our brothers and sisters."

"So, what did you want to say about Maestro Passau?"

"I want to tell you a story. So that you will understand. We of Mossad—all Israelis I suppose—are not the most-loved people in the world, but we're not always difficult. We do try to be fair, to help when we can. Sometimes we even help in secret. But you know this, Mr. Kruger."

"I know it. The story?"

"It began a long time ago when a little boy found out that he understood music."

"Go on."

"The boy was Jewish. He became a legend. A man of talent, wealth, great charm, passion, sophisticated tastes. Also, as with so many who are cursed with genius, he was willful. Liked to take risks—on the podium when conducting, and in his life also. He was an American citizen, a musician first always, and a man second. Quite late in life he realized that, apart from all other things, he was also a Jew. He had responsibilities to his race, to Israel, and to the religion of his fathers."

"When did he realize this?"

"Oh, the fifties, I think. Maybe earlier, though he did not really make his peace until the mid to late 1960s. I don't know exactly, but there came a point in his life when he sought us out. Yes, I mean Mossad. He searched for us and, naturally, he found us.

"We knew of him, of course. We were proud of him. He had shown great reverence, great dignity, regarding the Holocaust. . . ."

"The concert? Belsen?"

"Yes, and there were other things also, but I don't suppose he talks of them. Then, finally, there was the ultimate act of faith. He came to senior members of Mossad. There was a meeting. In the King David Hotel, Jerusalem. Then, a few days later, in Tel Aviv. He made a confession. He told them that, during the time of the Holocaust, he had betrayed his people. This is a truth which is very hard for a Jew to face. He wanted to make an act of reparation. He wanted forgiveness. He had given information to the Nazis. Total betrayal.

"But those who ordered Mossad, at that time, understood him. They had also known pain and deception: necessary treachery. They saw the pressures he had been under. They gave him no penance. They did not want any sacrificial acts. Yet they did say he might be of use to them at some future time. After all, he was a figure of tremendous international importance. I think, sometimes, even he does not realize the joy and wonder he has brought to people. He is a man with what the Americans would call little self-esteem. Has he told you any of this?"

"Some, but certainly nothing about seeking out his people—your people."

"No. No, he would not tell that. I am here to put records straight. To take a burden from him. Maybe even to free him from what he probably imagines is a yoke he must bear, even to death.

"A few weeks after the confession in Tel Aviv, he got hold of our people again. He had been given various telephone numbers to use if he came across anything that might interest us."

"Like the telephone number he dialed this afternoon?"

Ephron's eyes twinkled. "Exactly. That was his emergency number. He was to call us if he was in trouble, danger, or if he just wished to be removed from a particular situation."

Big Herbie was very still, as though listening with his entire body. Art Railton, at his feet, did not move a muscle. "I understand," Herbie said.

"As I say, he got in touch again. Very quickly. Said he had not told everything. He still had matters on his conscience. He was very afraid.

"I have only been his case officer for the past ten years, so my knowledge of that time comes only from the files. He told my people that he was concerned. Worried. So a trained agent went to New York. They sat down and talked. I think you know what he told us."

"That he had been recruited by a senior officer of the Central Intelligence Agency?"

Ephron gave a little nod. "Indeed. He was right to be frightened. He thought that, somehow, they were lying to him. He thought he was being used as a channel, a line, between deep penetration agents within the CIA, and the KGB at Moscow Center. He did not fully understand what was happening. He did not know the words, the jargon. His language is music. International language. Music knows no barriers, unless it is repressed, like the music of Mendelssohn and Mahler during the years of the Nazis."

"And your people discovered he *was* being used?"

"We put a trained team into New York; had someone move very close to him, yes. It only took a couple of months for our people to discover the truth."

"That four officers of the CIA *had* made a pact with the Devil? Providing the KGB with highly classified intelligence, taking small amounts of intelligence in return—chicken feed, with the occasional out-of-date gold nugget?"

Ephron nodded again. "Any professional intelligence officer could have figured it out very quickly. The beauty of it was that nobody could possibly suspect a man of Mr. Passau's talent, or with his obsession with music, and his blatant apolitical position. No counterespionage team would give him a second look. Yet, these men, who were among the most trusted in the United States intelligence community, had linked themselves neatly to KGB in Moscow Center. They carried out their treachery at arm's length. Louis Passau was the channel, the conduit, through which huge amounts of classified information flowed into the Kremlin, and a waste product flowed back in the other direction.

"It was almost foolproof. Passau was made to think he was serving his country, by passing to the Soviets what was explained to him as disinformation. He was also led to believe that he was receiving good, high-octane, intelligence in return. He was a hero, they told him. One day the President would pin a medal on him for what he was doing. But Maestro Passau is no fool. He suspected, and my people told him exactly how he was being manipulated."

"I bet that made him happy."

"Delirious, Mr. Kruger. He was outraged. He wanted to blow the whistle on these people—you know the names?"

"Marty Foreman, Mike Alfoot, Tony de Paul and Urquart Bains? All of them top people in the Soviet Office, CIA, Langley, Virginia. Right?"

"Correct. If Maestro Passau had been given his head, all four of them would have been standing trial within a month. Scandal in Washington, and that would have been a great weight for the American people to bear. There were enough problems at that time, so we persuaded him to take his dish of revenge cold, and over a long period." Later, Art Railton said he detected a slightly sheepish look pass between Ephron and Kruger.

For the first time since Ephron's arrival, Big Herbie smiled. "You cooked the books," he said. "Cunning bastards, you cooked the books."

"In a way, yes. As I've said, we'd already put a team in, so that team set about training others. Specialists, people with time on their hands, ordinary Jewish men and women. We required only one full-time intelligence officer on the spot. The matter was totally contained, and there was always a link between him and our Tel Aviv headquarters."

"Spell out the logistics to me, Mr. Ephron. It sounds right up my street."

"It was really very simple, and you must understand that sometimes it didn't work, because things had to be done so quickly."

Herbie's big head bobbed. "Just tell me." He sounded like a man who was having trouble controlling his temper.

"One of the people we came to speak of as the 'Horsemen'—the Four Horsemen of the Apocalypse, you understand—would drop off a package to Maestro Passau. Our team would move in, take the package, and look at what the Horsemen were giving away. Then, our people would doctor it. Sometimes this was a very sophisticated operation; on other occasions, when time was short, we could only substitute minor alterations. By the eighties though, with new and instant technology, we became very adept. That was when I took over control. I can give you chapter and verse on it. Rolls of film were completely changed. Documents were doctored in a matter of hours. We bought an apartment in the same building. . . ."

"On Lexington Avenue?"

"As you say. After that, all through the last decade no nuggets went to Moscow Center. Only tiny truths." He gave a deep laugh. "Mostly we gave them what they wanted to hear. The kind of hearts and minds intelligence which Passau could have passed on—maybe even stuff straight out of the White House. What the country's leaders and politicians were really thinking, doing, saying in private. Minute things . . ."

"And you became heavy with secrets. America's secrets." There was no mistaking the accusation in Kruger's voice.

Ephron made a very Jewish movement of hands and head. "In the long run it helped all of us. Would I come to you with this information now, if we felt in any way embarrassed by it?" The charming, disarming, smile.

"Such chutzpah." Herbie's face split into the widest of smiles. "You want me to congratulate you? Only Mossad could come forward and tell us, now, when it is almost over, that they cut through a treacherous operation between Moscow Center moles at Langley and intelligence-gatherers in Dzerzhinsky Square. You slid the million-dollar bills from the wallets, kept them and substituted forgeries. Such chutzpah," he repeated. "Such elegance also. You want me to pat you on the head? Give you a stick of candy?"

"No, we merely want you to understand. Mossad blocked the flow of highly secret information spilling out to the old Soviet Union, and we substituted garbage. . . ."

"You were both the recipients and the donors."

"Something like that. But this is the foolish nature of all intelligence operations, Mr. Kruger. You know that. It's proven time and again. A secret war is a war between people trapped in a maze of trick mirrors. Everyone sees distortions. We contained the loss of many great secrets from the West to the East."

Kruger began to chuckle. "The old bastard." He punched Art almost playfully on the arm. "I hope we have the tapes running. I'd hate to try and explain this at Warminster without some backup material."

"The tapes are running, Herb. It's okay." Art hardly moved.

"And I will give you a complete and honest statement," Ephron continued. "I have been cleared to talk with your interrogation teams."

Kruger batted a big hand in front of his face. "The march of secret folly, eh, Mark Ephron?"

"Precisely. Simplicity is part of the elegance, I think."

"What Mark says is true, *Maestro* Kruger." Passau's voice, shaky, almost quavering, came from above them. He stood at the top of the stairs. Shaved, dressed, but looking older than Kruger had ever seen him.

Art went up to him, two stairs at a time, leaping, and then putting an arm around the old man, helping him down to the room.

Passau embraced Mark Ephron. "Shalom, my friend." There was the quiver of emotion in his voice and body. Ephron put his arms around the old man. The gesture was one of great affection. It was like a lovers' meeting.

When they had Passau seated, Big Herbie leaned forward, towards him. "Why didn't you tell me all this, Lou?"

Passau gave him an almost truculent look. "You didn't ask, Herb. It was your job to find out. You did the interrogating. It's an art. I gave you clues."

"You said you would tell me everything. Your last confession, you said."

Passau gave a weak grin. "Even last confessions often leave something to be desired."

Kruger remembered what he had said to Pucky Curtiss a few weeks ago. Remembered that he had told her the old Maestro would hold back at the end. Not give him everything. All agents do it. For the insurance. He looked at Ephron. "Didn't you . . . ? Didn't your organization look at the question of morality here?"

Ephron gave a smooth, humorless laugh. "What is morality in our business, Mr. Kruger? Our battle knows no morality. Comes with the territory, as the Americans would say."

Big Herbie shrugged, then nodded. Smiled. Nodded, then smiled again. "Let's have breakfast," he said. "Turn the tapes off, Art. Turn them off forever. It's over. We Cold Warriors should go out to pasture or stud: that would be even better. It's time for a new generation to deal with the idiocies of secrets. Anyway, the world's too dangerous a place for me now. You can't uninvent the nuclear deterrent, and it isn't a deterrent anymore. Any little dictator, any country with enough money, can buy nuclear from old stock. This is the way the world ends, and fools talk of a new age. A new age of peace. Boom!"

They brought Ephron's other man, Peter, into the house. Relaxed, made breakfast. Benny helped in the kitchen while Herbie went off to telephone Warminster. "You got a big surprise coming," he told Young Worboys. "Better send a lot of high-class muscle." He gave Ephron's name, and suggested they should seek out his bona fides.

Over the meal he pondered the imponderable, then put it into words. "What of Foreman and his gang?" he asked Ephron, but it was Peter, the other Mossad man, who replied. "They'll be defecating bricks I should think, but the last we heard, the man Alfoot was still in place at Langley. Also Tony de Paul is there."

"And Marty Foreman?"

"He's gone to earth. Also Urquart Bains is missing."

"You think they can find him—Passau? Whatever, if I know Marty, he'll want him dead and gone." Herbie's head bobbed in the direction of the Maestro.

"They can find your place at Warminster. They must know it well enough."

"But not here." Herbie sounded uncertain. "Marty doesn't know this place."

"Then you're probably safe enough." Ephron appeared unconcerned. "If I was running this, I'd certainly lay on heavy security at Warminster."

The telephone rang, and Herbie went off to talk with Young Worboys again. The Israelis were being cooperative, the Deputy Chief said. Ephron had been given clearance to talk with his British opposite numbers, as had the other officer—Peter Brack.

Herbie asked about security at Warminster, and demanded a very close guard for the journey back.

When he returned to the breakfast table, Passau was becoming restless. "I need air, Herb. I haven't been for a good walk in a hundred years."

Benny went out and made a sweep around the garden, poking in trees, taking a slow walk around the block. It was all clear. Nobody had turned up on their doorstep. With Ephron on one side and Herbie on the other, Passau strolled through the garden. Benny and Art moved around them, eyes everywhere. For half an hour, they walked and talked under a weak sun, a stiff breeze blowing dark clouds above them.

When they returned to the house, Passau seemed to have regained his old vitality. His cheeks were flushed and he talked with his old mixture of foul language and innuendo.

The telephone rang again. The small convoy was only twenty minutes away. They had to be ready. Young Worboys wanted everyone in and out in seconds. Ephron asked if his colleague could get their car. "I don't mind having some of your heavies with us, to make sure we don't run away," he said.

They let Peter Brack go off for the car. Already, Benny had removed all weapons that had been carried by the two Israelis.

While Art and Benny were tidying up, and the man from Mossad was washing the fatigue from his face, Herbie sat down with Passau.

"Why did you tell me about Stanza, Herb?" Old Passau seemed on the brink of weeping again.

"You wanted all the facts, Lou. You held out on me. Did you really believe she was your daughter? Did you not have any second thoughts?"

"Never." He gulped, and the tears began to flow. "Sophie broke me," he sobbed. "On the rack. Forever I shall feel guilty. You think Stanza knows? This was the great disaster of my life. The greatest love story ever, and the biggest calamity."

"I know." Herbie could not give him comfort. Passau had gone through a huge torment because of his love for Constanza Traccia. Like all things in life, what was done was done. Nothing could be changed. All of Louis Passau's life was a distortion.

"Perhaps," he took the Maestro's hands in his. "Perhaps, Lou, in a way she *was* your daughter. Perhaps that was what you were meant to believe. Maybe you should go on believing it."

"Perhaps." Passau's eyes fixed again at a point behind Herbie's shoulder, finding his gateway to the past once more.

Peter Brack brought Ephron's car to the front of the house just after the convoy arrived. Ten minutes later, Passau was taken out, surrounded by a phalanx of men who had lived through the worst days of the Cold War. They got him back to Warminster without incident, and Big Herbie Kruger gave a long sigh of triumph and relief, even though he knew it was going to be a hard winter.

He did not know just how hard it would be.

7

AT WARMINSTER THEY had a full house. The guest quarters were occupied to the hilt, and Gus Keene was forced to open up two of the secure rooms in the main house. It took three days, for they had been closed for years, since the underground guest quarters had been built.

There were also diplomatic incidents. The Chief returned from Brussels, looking as though he had been in conference with God who had found him guilty of every sin in the book.

Hard-faced, no frills men from Washington and Langley came and went: listened to tapes; talked with the two men from Mossad; spent time with Louis Passau, whose wife Angela had been jetted in, courtesy of the Royal Air Force. They poured over documents, flung angry questions at Big Herbie, and left with briefcases bulging, only to return again with frowns and more tough talk.

After a couple of weeks the news filtered back that Mike Alfoot and Tony de Paul had been removed from their positions of trust at Langley, and were holed up at the CIA's Farm at Camp Peary.

"They'll never come to trial," Young Worboys told Kruger. "The Americans need to sweep this under the carpet. Election next year. It's all too heavy for them to bear—the thought that, for thirty years, they had a massive leak is something they can't face."

"Shredding and burning going on like the last days in Saigon," Herbie said without glee. "Poor buggers. They'll have to pull the entire Agency apart and rebuild it."

"We're all going to do that, Herb." Worboys gave him a look which somehow spoke of pity.

Out in the real world, the face of the old Soviet Union was going through its own decomposition. Nobody knew where it would end. In the meantime, Marty Foreman and Urquart Bains were still missing. Men and women from Langley were searching the cities of America and Europe, combing the highways and byways, seeking clues. They found none as far as Warminster was concerned.

"They'll find them. Got to find them," Herbie said to Tony Worboys, though he did not sound confident.

"Not worried are you, Herb?"

"Marty always worried me. He used to say that he was really only a step away from being on the wrong side of the law. Also used to say he would always extract vengeance, even if it killed him."

"Figure of speech." Worboys' voice clouded with doubt.

"Marty never used figures of speech. I heard him say it many times. Once even saw him extract vengeance. As for Urquart Bains . . . well, he was always pretty crazy. They were both great risk takers in the old days." He paused, his thick fingers raking his hair. "Sure, Young Worboys. Sure I'm concerned. Will be until they find Urquart and Marty. Never know what they'd do."

Meanwhile, the debriefings continued. Grueling days of question and answer stuff. Nothing heavy; no signs of the rack or thumbscrews, but word had gone out that it had to be thorough. When the final history was written, all things must tally.

Louis Passau insisted that Herbie be with them during every session. In the end it became arduous. With Angela now present, the Passau' suite smelled of lemons, and Herbie remembered Constanza. He also realized, with a flash, that the old aristocratic English family, the Barnscomes, had come down through the ages from a Jewish line. Angela herself was Jewish. He now knew who the Mossad had put close to Passau.

Peter Brack was allowed to fly back to Tel Aviv, returning a few days later with more stacks of printouts and pages of dates and times.

The guards were tense. Security tight, and the hard-eyed men from D.C. came and went as though they held the power of life and death over everyone.

Herbie made several telephone calls to his wife, Martha. Their marriage had been one of complete openness, and she was always telling him that the time would eventually come when he would wish to walk away quietly. She knew that moment had arrived. Slowly she disentangled herself, so that the final call was almost lighthearted.

They spoke in German.

"It's time for decisions . . ." Herbie began.

"You've already made your decision. This time you're not coming home?"

"Probably, *Liebling*. Almost certainly not. I think it's time for you to visit your sister in Frankfurt."

There was a long, though not unhappy, silence.

"It's brutal, I know," Herbie said softly.

"I wasn't worried by the brutality. I was thinking what I should wear. I knew it was about to happen. Now it's come, I'm quite relieved, Eberhardt. Might I take the piano with me?"

"We don't have a piano, Martha."

"Then to hell with it. You will know where I am if you need me."

So, it was done. Completed.

In the evenings, Pucky and Herbie planned their future. They were like a pair of young lovers, discovering life. Herbie almost felt newborn. The joy showed on their faces; their friends and colleagues rejoiced for them. When the work was done, they would be married and take a year off. Pucky wanted to be in Venice for the Carnival. "I've always longed to be there for Carnival," she told him, as they lay close in their big double bed, courtesy of Gus Keene who had wooed and won his own wife in this same place, between long probing sessions of interrogating.

"We got the greatest love affair since the world began," Herbie said to her.

"Since Louis and Constanza," she replied, and was immediately ashamed, wanting to bite her tongue.

Herbie still had occasional dreams. The red wineglasses and the Dürer drawing came back, unwanted, when he least expected it. He put it down to the proximity of Ursula Zunder.

The people who handled security were careful to keep the various protagonists apart, but one morning, when Herbie took a shortcut, coming up onto the lawn from the bunker emergency exit, he walked straight into Ursula, who was being given her hour of outdoor exercise, two minders in tow.

They stopped, facing each other; the years now shrunk to a matter of a few feet.

"Herbie," she said with a little start of shock. "Oh, Herbie. You've forgiven me, yes?"

He looked at the woman, saw the changes, and also saw the original beneath. Hundreds of days and nights raced through his head. The happiness, joy, hardship, and final treachery, cut a great bleeding gash in his memory.

"No," he said coldly. "Some things nobody should ever forgive. Not just you. I can never forgive the Nazis. Be with me until I die, Ursula. That also goes for the bad old days of your lot. We cannot forgive, because that means forgetting also. If we forget, then we're doomed, because the past will creep back to poison our future. If I forgive—if we all forgive—then maybe we won't notice when the things we once hated return to bring chaos again." He gave her a quick, unfriendly nod and set off towards the house.

Pucky was coming towards him, her long legs striding out and the beautiful hair riding her head as though she were swimming through the air.

The true horror came in that time between Christmas and the New Year. Later, people said the security was relaxed because of the festivities. People had been brighter, more friendly. Gifts were exchanged. On Christmas Eve all of them, even Passau, Angela and the Mossad men, came into the big house and sang carols, the four Jews putting aside their own way of life to join hands with their Christian brothers. It meant nothing to them.

The days were bright, with no hint of fog or snow, and there was a sense of accomplishment among all of them. Soon they could go back into the world.

Two days after Christmas, Herbie and Pucky joined Louis and Angela Passau, together with three of the security men for a walk. A slow tramp around the estate. As they were leaving, Mark and Peter, from Israel, asked if they could also come.

They walked the entire perimeter, heading right around the house, back to the little woods and spinneys far from the road. Herbie told them of night exercises he had done along the edge of these wooded areas, long ago when he was learning about border crossings. "In those days," he said, "we had a huge staff here. An entire platoon of men who acted as KGB frontier guards. It was rough, tough and tumbling dangerous."

They were laughing, happy, only a few feet from the edge of a dense clump of trees, and it all happened very quickly. Later, when he thought of it—when the nightmares would not let go—Herbie saw it all in slow motion—

First, a sudden shout from one of the minders. He saw two of them draw their weapons, and his eyes came up, following the pistol barrels; saw the cannonball shaved head of Marty Foreman, and the tall, skinny, aged hippielike Urquart Bains, as they leaped, suicidally, from the bushes where they had laid up for two days (or so it was decided later).

Herbie went for his own pistol, shouted for them to get down, saw Pucky, in an act of complete and automatic folly, throw herself in front of old Maestro Passau, shielding him from the flying bullets.

Herbie's anguished cry, like an unearthly animal trapped in dreadful pain—"Noooooooooahhh!"

Foreman and Bains went down in seconds. The minders had riddled them with bullets in the time it took to draw breath, but the slugs from Marty's and Bains' weapons, aimed squarely at Passau, had torn into Pucky's chest. Terrible bullets. Glaser slugs that entered the body and exploded, sending dozens of number 12 shot to rape her flesh.

Herbie saw that Foreman and Bains were dead. He hurled himself onto Pucky, who lay in the little trench her flying body had dug into the soft grass. Her chest was one great gaping wound, but he held her to him, his own clothes soaked in her blood; tried to give her CPR; kept feeling for a pulse long gone. So suddenly had the terror struck that he thought it was another of the nightmares; could not believe the truth, even when they gently pulled him away, and he heard Mark and Peter, the Israelis, making their own act of respect, by saying Kaddish over the ravished body.

> "Yit'gadal v'yit kadash sh'me' raba. Amen.
> B'al'ma di v'ra chir'ute. Amen."
> "Magnified and sanctified be His great name. Amen.
> Throughout the world which He has created according to His will.
> Amen."

Somewhere, from faraway in his head, Herbie heard the sound of Pucky's golden laughter. Or was it, he wondered afterwards, the sound of weeping?

On the day after they buried her, he drove up onto the Berkshire Downs, to one of his favorite spots. A place where he had gone many times before to find peace. There, alone and far from other humans, he howled like King Lear. Then he looked across the swell of the earth, saw the smoke from far-off chimneys, and wept his heart out.

For Big Herbie Kruger it was all over. He had fought his war. Won it, lost it, won it again, then lost it irrevocably. He had faced bleak times on many occasions in the past, so he knew the strength would return, and the madness pass.

Now, he sought sanctuary in his old companion, the composer, Gustav Mahler. In his head, as he gazed out across the beauty of the landscape, he heard words from the *Songs on the Deaths of Children*:

> You must not enfold night within you,
> you must let it drown in everlasting light,
> A small lamp has gone out in my dwelling,
> hail to the joyous light of the world.

He sucked in air, ran a hand over his face, then lumbered back to the car, his uncoordinated walk almost that of a spastic child. In his head the music rose and fell. He thought of Louis Passau and his agony which, in the end, had never been an agony at all. He tried to draw hope from that: tried to draw some kind of faith; saw the old Maestro shrug, and heard him say, "Who knew, Herb? Who knew?"

He drove back to Warminster and dialed a number in Frankfurt, swallowing all pride, for he knew it was dangerous for him to go out into the world alone.